DISCOVERIES

S0-AQL-357

Foot Notes
7/22 s.m.

DISCOVERIES

Fifty Stories of the Quest

SECOND EDITION

HAROLD SCHECHTER
Queens College
The City University of New York

JONNA GORMELY SEMEIKS
Long Island University
C. W. Post Campus

New York   Oxford
OXFORD UNIVERSITY PRESS
1992

Oxford University Press

Oxford   New York   Toronto
Delhi   Bombay   Calcutta   Madras   Karachi
Kuala Lumpur   Singapore   Hong Kong   Tokyo
Nairobi   Dar es Salaam   Cape Town
Melbourne   Auckland

and associated companies in
Berlin   Ibadan

Copyright © 1992 by Oxford University Press, Inc.
Copyright © 1983 by Harold Schechter and Jonna Gormely Semeiks

Published by Oxford University Press, Inc.
198 Madison Avenue, New York, New York 10016-4314

Oxford is a registered trademark of Oxford University Press

All rights reserved. No part of this publication may be reproduced,
stored in a retrieval system, or transmitted, in any form or by any means,
electronic, mechanical, photocopying, recording, or otherwise,
without the prior permission of Oxford University Press.

Library of Congress Cataloging-in-Publication Data
Discoveries : fifty stories of the quest /
[compiled by] Harold Schechter, Jonna Gormely Semeiks.—2nd ed.
p.   cm.   ISBN 0-19-506850-5
1. Short stories.   I. Schechter, Harold.
II. Semeiks, Jonna Gormely.   II. Title: Quest.
PN6120.2.D56   1992   808.83'1—dc20   91-37400

6 8 9 7

Printed in the United States of America
on acid-free paper

Preface

Although this second edition of *Discoveries* retains much of the material that constituted the first, it offers several significant improvements. First, we have made substitutions amounting to roughly one-quarter of the contents—a dozen new stories in all. In making these changes, we have been mindful of the growing stress within academia on multicultural studies. Thus—though the first edition offered a healthy representation of writers from diverse cultural backgrounds—this revision goes even further in that direction by adding stories by writers like Amy Tan, Bharati Mukherjee, and R. K. Narayan. In the years since *Discoveries* was first published, the literary world has also witnessed a remarkable revitalization of the short story form. This new edition reflects that phenomenon by including works by a new generation of writers—not only Tan and Mukherjee but also Stephen Milhauser, Ellen Gilchrist, and Patrick McGrath.

Our alterations reflect another cultural phenomenon as well. In the decade since we first conceived of creating a short story anthology organized around the quest pattern as delineated by Joseph Campbell in *Hero with a Thousand Faces*, interest in Campbell's work has grown in ways we couldn't have foreseen. Thanks largely to his televised interviews with Bill Moyers (broadcast in 1988 as a six-part series, "Joseph Campbell and the Power of Myth"), Campbell has undergone a posthumous transformation from a beloved but relatively obscure scholar into an intellectual celebrity, whose writings and teachings have reached—and deeply touched—millions of Americans. The introductory apparatus to the original edition of *Discoveries* offered a summary and explication of Campbell's influential analysis of the quest myth. To this material we have now added a section on Campbell's life and work, which appears as part of the general introduction.

Finally, we have appended a section of concise, biographical entries on each of the fifty authors.

This second edition of *Discoveries* would not exist without the support and encouragement of our editor and friend, Phillip Leininger, to whom we owe a larger debt of gratitude than we can ever hope to repay.

New York   H. S.
November 1991   J. G. S.

Preface to the First Edition

Discoveries is an anthology that uses the traditional theme of the hero's quest as a way of organizing a wide-ranging selection of fifty short stories. In offering such a volume, we do not mean to suggest that there is only one way of approaching this material or that these stories are primarily interesting because they embody the same ancient narrative pattern. Our first consideration in making our choices was the quality of the fiction rather than its conformity to a particular organizational scheme. The works reprinted in *Discoveries* would constitute a rich and varied collection no matter how they were arranged. But we have found in our own classes that talking about stories in terms of the quest is an effective way of introducing students with limited experience in literary analysis to the close reading of fiction.

Before the unpracticed reader is ready to talk comfortably about point of view, symbolism, characterization, and the other important elements of fiction (definitions of which are provided in a separate introductory section and in the glossary at the end of this book), he or she can say what *happens* in a story: where the heroes are going; where they are coming from; what they seem to be seeking; what combination of circumstances has launched them on their adventures. Besides giving students immediate access to the literature, the use of the quest as an organizing theme serves another important function: it forces them to ground their perceptions and opinions in the concrete facts of the narrative. Seeing—and being able to say—precisely what occurs in a story is a precondition to being able to say *why* it happens and how the author uses the literary tools at his or her disposal to *make* it happen.

Moreover, looking at fiction in light of the quest gives greater coherence to the study of a very diverse body of writing. The universal presence of this pattern in literature makes it possible for *Discoveries* to include an unusually wide assortment of international authors (Gustave Flaubert, Alberto Moravia, Isaac Babel, Doris Lessing, Julio Cortázar, Gabriel García Márquez), nineteenth-century American writers (Edgar Allan Poe, Nathaniel Hawthorne, Mary E. Wilkins Freeman, Stephen Crane, Willa Cather), twentieth-century modernists (D. H. Lawrence, James Joyce), contemporary masters of the form (Eudora Welty, John Updike, Philip Roth), important new talents (Toni Cade Bambara, Ann Beattie, Max Apple), and many others. At the same time, our approach is not meant to minimize the substantial differences among these authors or to reduce all of world literature to the endless restatement of a handful of major themes. On the contrary, it is designed to do the very opposite by illuminating the inexhaustible variety of ways in which our best writers have responded to the crucial experiences all human beings encounter on their journeys through life. Seeing the variations James Joyce works on the traditional theme of the treasure-quest ("Araby"), Edgar Allan Poe on the motif of the double ("William Wilson"), or John Barth on the myth of the heroic odyssey ("Night-Sea Journey") reveals a great deal not only about the distinctive literary style of each of these authors but also about his characteristic concerns and unique artistic vision.

In the questions following each selection, we ask readers to view the stories in the context of the quest in all its many forms. We also stress those elements of more traditional interest to teachers of fiction: point of view, plot, character, setting, theme, imagery, metaphor, symbolism, and tone. These and other terms are defined in the "Glossary of Critical Terms." A primary purpose of most introductory fiction courses is to teach students how to explicate a text. Therefore, to familiarize students with the fundamentals of the short story form and provide them with a basic critical vocabulary, *Discoveries* includes "The Elements of Fiction," a discussion of fictional devices and techniques. In this way, we hope to encourage the people who use this book to consider its contents both as representations of a timeless, universally appealing narrative pattern and as outstanding examples of the short story writer's art.

We would like to thank the people who made important contributions to this book: our editors, James Smith and Diana Francoeur; James Kirkland, Miller Williams, and Betty Rizzo, who made valuable suggestions for improving the manuscript; and Abraham Schechter, who helped us read hundreds of stories. We are grateful to them all.

Contents

Contents by Alternate Themes

Contents by Technical Elements

DISCOVERIES

Introduction: The Quest

The fifty works of fiction collected in this anthology, whatever their considerable differences, are variations of a story that is as old as story-telling itself. Tales of the quest—of men and women heroes travelling a difficult road toward a goal that promises to transform their lives—are found throughout history, in all ages and cultures, and in a wide range of forms, from primitive myth to modern poetry, from simple folk tales to the most complex literary classics. As children, we listen with fascination to such famous quest stories as "Jack and the Beanstalk" and "Sleeping Beauty"; as adults, we encounter the quest in many of the greatest books our civilization has produced: *The Odyssey, The Divine Comedy, The Canterbury Tales, The Faerie Queene, The Pilgrim's Progress, Heart of Darkness, Moby-Dick.*

Obviously, a story we never tire of hearing has meaningful things to tell us about ourselves. Quest narratives "speak" to us because they portray, in straightforward or symbolic terms, very basic human experiences and reflect a common perception of life as a journey composed of separate stages, each with its own problems to be overcome and its own potential rewards. The emergence of the youth into full maturity, the triumph of the individual over forces in himself or herself that are limiting or even crippling, the courageous rejection of a safe but sterile existence for the struggle toward a more demanding but more fulfilling life, the final departure into the unknown realm of death—these are only a few of the fundamental experiences represented by the quest and depicted in the stories in this collection.

Joseph Campbell and the Quest Myth

Etymologically, our word "myth" derives from the Greek *mythos*, a story. Of all the mythic stories known to humankind, perhaps the most popular is that of the heroic quest. No one can say when this story first came into being. Like other common myths—tales of the creation of the world, for example, or of the origin of death—it has been told throughout the ages. Rooted in the very make-up of the human imagination, it may well be as old as the species itself.

It wasn't until the late nineteenth century, however, that scholars and psychologists began to recognize the importance of the quest myth to human culture. Since then, various efforts have been made to analyze its structure and meaning. The man who did most to enlarge our understanding of its significance is the noted mythologist, Joseph Campbell, whose writings and teachings have sparked a new, widespread interest not only in the hero's quest but in myth in general.

Born in New York City in 1904, Campbell was six years old when his anthropological interests were first aroused by a visit to Buffalo Bill's Wild West Show at Madison Square Garden, where he was riveted by the sight of the Indian warriors. Subsequent trips to the American Museum of Natural History in Manhattan, which houses a spectacular collection of totem poles and other artifacts, reinforced his fascination with Indian culture. Soon, Campbell was devouring every book he could find on the myths and legends of the North American tribes.

During his student years at the Canterbury prep school in Connecticut, Campbell continued to study myths, though biology had become his favorite academic subject. Under the guidance of the school's headmaster, he also cultivated his natural gifts as a writer. After a brief stint at Dartmouth College, Campbell transferred to Columbia University in 1922, where his academic focus shifted from biology to the humanities. A talented athlete and musician, Campbell set a half-mile record as a member of the college track team and picked up extra money playing jazz saxophone at fraternity dances.

In the summer of 1924, the year before his graduation, Campbell accompanied his family on a boat trip to Europe. During the homebound voyage, he was introduced to a fellow passenger, the Indian spiritual leader, Jiddu Krishnamurti. This meeting—and Campbell's subsequent reading of a book on Buddhism, Edward Arnold's *The Light of Asia*—kindled what was to become a lifelong interest in Eastern philosophy and religion.

Graduating from Columbia in 1925, Campbell stayed on for another year to compete with the track team and complete a Master's thesis on Arthurian romance. Awarded a travelling fellowship to Europe, he spent the next several years in Paris and Munich, studying medieval philology, Old French, Sanskrit, and mythology. At the same time, he found himself exhilarated by the revolutionary inno-vations of modern art, whose greatest literary masterpieces, from James Joyce's *Ulysses* to Thomas Mann's *The Magic Mountain,* are informed by mythic themes.

As Campbell delved more deeply into the realm of myth and sym-bol, he came to see that the same basic motifs—virgin birth, death and resurrection, the expulsion from paradise, and so on—were common to cultures all over the world. His growing awareness of the underlying connections among widely scattered mythologies drew him to the theories of Carl Jung, the Swiss psychologist who postu-lated the existence of a "collective unconscious"—a fundamental level of the human psyche that is identical in everyone and produces uni-versal symbols (or "archetypes") that are the basis for all the world's mythologies.

By the time he returned to America, just two weeks before the Wall Street Crash of 1929, Campbell had already decided that the standard academic path was too narrow for him. Abandoning work on his Ph.D., he retired to a cabin in the upstate New York town of Woodstock, where—subsisting on savings from his jazz-playing days—he spent the next several years following the bent of his own schol-arly interests.

In 1932, he accepted a temporary position at his alma mater, the Canterbury School. Two years later, he was invited to join the fac-ulty of the newly founded Sarah Lawrence College. Campbell's skills as a storyteller, combined with his vast erudition, made him a spell-binding lecturer. For the next thirty-eight years, until his retire-ment in 1972, he remained at Sarah Lawrence, teaching an enor-mously popular course in comparative mythology.

Campbell's first major book, written in collaboration with Henry Morton Robinson, was *A Skeleton Key to Finnegan's Wake.* Pub-lished in 1944, it remains a standard work in the field of James Joyce scholarship.

In the mid-1940s, Campbell began to write a book on mythology based on his classroom lectures. The result was his most famous and influential work, *The Hero with a Thousand Faces,* a comparative study of quest myths from around the world. Drawing together a wealth of examples, from Eskimo fairy tales to Buddhist parables, Campbell demonstrates that, while every culture creates its own im-age of the hero, all quest narratives follow the same fundamental plot or pattern. Jason's pursuit of the Golden Fleece, Jonah's de-scent into the belly of the whale, Jack's climb up the magical bean-stalk, Gilgamesh's search for the plant of immortality—these and the countless other quest adventures that have been told throughout the ages are versions of the same "shape-shifting but marvelously constant story." Campbell calls this universal quest pattern "the monomyth."

Campbell was a rarity among academics—a scholar who could write ravishing prose. He was also extremely prolific. Following the publication of *The Hero with a Thousand Faces* in 1949, he went on to produce other major books, including *The Masks of God* (1959–68), a monumental, four-volume study of world mythology; *The Mythic Image (1974)*, an examination of mythic themes as they are embodied in visual art; and the first half of his final multivolume opus, *The Historical Atlas of World Mythology*, left uncompleted at the time of his death in 1987.

The Hero with a Thousand Faces, however, remained his most widely read book. During the 1960s, it became a countercultural bible to millions of young Americans, who saw their own quest for higher experience—for a transcendent reality beyond the material realm—reflected in its pages. Campbell began to be revered as a guru.

Following his retirement from Sarah Lawrence in 1972, Campbell went out on the lecture circuit. His renown as the world's foremost authority on myth continued to spread. One thousand admirers attended his eightieth birthday celebration at the Palace of Fine Arts in San Francisco in 1984. The following year, at a dinner held in his honor by the National Arts Club of New York, George Lucas, the creator of the *Star Wars* movies, gratefully acknowledged Campbell as a major influence on his work. Other popular artists, such as Richard Adams (author of the bestselling fantasy novel, *Watership Down*) and filmmaker George Miller (director of *The Road Warrior*), also cited *The Hero with a Thousand Faces* as a source of inspiration. In 1986, Campbell shared the stage with members of The Grateful Dead at a symposium called "From Ritual to Rapture."

In February 1987, a documentary about Campbell's life and work, *The Hero's Journey: The World of Joseph Campbell*, premiered at the Museum of Modern Art in New York City. Eight months later, on October 31, 1987, Campbell died at his home in Honolulu, Hawaii, at the age of 83.

Campbell's greatest fame, however, was still to come. During the spring of 1988, PBS aired a six-part series on his work called "The Power of Myth," condensed from twenty-three hours of conversations which journalist Bill Moyers had taped with Campbell over the course of several years, mostly at George Lucas' Skywalker Ranch. The series was an extraordinary success, attracting a record number of viewers, turning Campbell's books into enormous bestsellers, and making the man himself a posthumous pop phenomenon.

Campbell's charismatic abilities as a storyteller had something to do with his mass appeal. But even more important was his conception of myth, which clearly touched a deep and responsive chord in millions of Americans hungry for spiritual teaching.

Campbell taught that myths are not lies or fabrications. They are not pre-scientific explanations of natural processes invented by primitive people too unenlightened to know the truth. On the contrary, myths convey the most profound and enduring truths. Arising, like dreams, from the depths of the psyche, they symbolize the human soul's everlasting experience of the wonders, terrors, and mysteries of existence. "Myths are clues," Campbell explained, "to the spiritual potentialities of . . . life." Seen in this light, the quest myth can be read as the story not of an actual, physical adventure but of an inner one—the journey of self-discovery that enlarges our sense of our own, and of life's, possibilities.

The Quest Pattern

The stories in *Discoveries* are divided into six chapters:

The Call
The Other
The Journey
Helpers and Guides
The Treasure
Transformation

These categories correspond to the main stages of the quest, based on the model established by Joseph Campbell in his classic study of world mythology, *The Hero with a Thousand Faces*. The following is a brief summary of these stages; more detailed definitions will be found at the beginning of each chapter. Throughout this anthology, we are indebted to the insights set forth in Campbell's book, which we recommend to any reader interested in a comprehensive account of the hero's quest as it appears in folklore, religion, and myth.

The stories in "The Call" portray heroes on the brink of a great change. Some of these characters are desperately unhappy and experience their lives as a lethal trap. Others inhabit a more comfortable but no less stultifying world, one which, in its very orderliness and familiarity, comes to seem sterile and confining: a kind of wasteland. In either case, the hero is kept from changing, from growing—in short, from *living*.

It is possible for heroes to blunder into the quest, to make some sort of mistake and find themselves quite suddenly embarked on a difficult journey. Generally, though, they are called to this adventure. The summons can come from any source: a friend, a relative, a stranger, an alluring object, or an impulse within the characters themselves. If the protagonist possesses the necessary courage and resolve, she or he is off on the quest, however fearful or arduous it may seem.

"The Other" focuses on a figure, male or female, who may be the protagonist's most intimate friend or, conversely, a mysterious, if oddly familiar, stranger. Whether friend or stranger, this figure possesses a personality that is, in every crucial respect, the exact opposite of the hero's. The hero and the Other stand in the same relation as a photographic portrait and the negative from which it is printed: wherever the first appears white, the second is black, and vice versa, though a close examination reveals that the two figures are one and the same. The Other, then, embodies the hidden side of the hero's public personality, the unseen character traits that lie behind the face the protagonist presents to the world—all the latent tendencies, drives, and unfulfilled desires the hero keeps concealed from society and, often, from her or his own conscious awareness. Thus, meeting the Other—a crucial event on the hero's journey toward the ultimate goal—always signifies the possibility, at least, of increased self-awareness for the protagonists of these stories, for it means that they have come face to face for the first time in their lives with a side of themselves that they have never confronted, have never been ready or willing to confront, before.

The third chapter, "The Journey," contains stories that demonstrate how difficult and how *variously* difficult the hero's quest is. In some cases, the central characters are tried most by forces within themselves: forces that tempt them to give up, to seek safety, to rest, to settle for less, to go back to the old life or the old ways of perceiving and experiencing things. In other stories, the protagonists face external enemies, agents of conservatism or conformity that must be overcome. In still other instances, the protagonists must fight against nature: they may have a dangerous mountain range to cross or a rough sea to navigate. Although the trials these heroes undergo are extremely varied, they all stand for the same thing: the difficulties involved in achieving any goal worth having.

The stories in "Helpers and Guides" feature figures who assist the protagonist along the difficult road. The assistance may be either material or spiritual; it may seem, at first glance, insignificant or mundane. But through this unforeseen support, the main characters learn; they move on; they come closer to their goals.

The heroes in the stories in Chapter Five, "The Treasure," may be after a literal treasure, an actual object of great monetary value. At other times, the treasure is material, but its value is largely sentimental or symbolic: to anyone other than the hero its possession is relatively meaningless. Or the treasure might have chiefly an aesthetic or spiritual significance. In still other stories, the treasure is not a tangible object at all. It might be knowledge—of the world or of the self—or the solution to a mystery. The prize the protagonist seeks, in short, may assume as many different outward forms as the trials required to achieve it. In essence, however, the goal of the quest is always a priceless *psychological gain:* an expanded consciousness, a saving insight, or the release of long-suppressed creative powers.

The stories in "Transformation" feature characters who are transfigured by the quest they have undertaken and completed. The lives of these characters may be radically different from what they were before, or the protagonists may see everything differently: though the outward circumstances of their lives may seem the same, nothing they look at will be untouched by what they have been through. The ideal outcome of the hero's quest is a profound experience of rebirth and inner liberation—a renewed sense of life's limitless possibilities.

This is a much abbreviated summary of a very ancient theme that still maintains a powerful hold on the human imagination, as the selections in *Discoveries* make clear. In longer quest narratives— epic poems, novels, and even movies (*Stagecoach, The Wizard of Oz,* and the *Star Wars* cycle are only three examples)—this pattern usually appears in its entirety. As you will see when you read the fiction in this book, however, this is generally not the case with the short story. The short story's compact nature, strictly limited action, and circumscribed setting usually do not allow the writer to unfold and develop the complete narrative pattern we have been discussing. Thus, the works here typically focus on a single stage of the quest, though other stages are often present as well. Willa Cather's story "Paul's Case," for example, is primarily concerned with the call, and is therefore included in that section, although the title character actually embarks on his adventure and even manages, however briefly, to hold the treasure in his hands.

Moreover, while the majority of the stories in the collection are faithful to the standard pattern of the quest, others deviate from it or deal with it in a deliberately ironic way. For instance, F. Scott Fitzgerald's "Babylon Revisited" ends, not with the hero's triumph, but on a note of defeated expectation that is characteristic of the author. Certain stories in "The Call" portray heroes who refuse to heed or never hear the summons when it comes; the spiritual guide of the young protagonist in Philip Roth's "The Conversion of the Jews" is exposed as a narrow-minded dogmatist. Indeed, not every main character in these stories can even be considered a hero in the strict sense of the term: some are anti-heroes, and others, like the protagonist of Poe's "William Wilson," are actually criminals. We have included these atypical or ironic versions of the quest because they contrast in interesting and illuminating ways with the other works. They also demonstrate how vital and versatile this age-old story remains. As you see how each of the authors in this collection creates her or his own traditional or untraditional version of the quest, you become aware of the immense skill and resourcefulness of our best literary artists—of their ability, while working within the tight boundaries of the short story form, to convey so many true and important things about the central experiences of our lives.

The Elements
of Fiction

Story-telling is one of the most fundamental of human activities, and short fictional narratives of various kinds—myths, folk tales, fables, parables, and more—have existed throughout history. It was not until the nineteenth century, however, that what we call the *short story*, a distinct literary genre with special characteristics and possibilities, was created by a handful of American authors. Edgar Allan Poe, along with Washington Irving and Nathaniel Hawthorne, was one of the originators of the form. Poe first defined the short story in a review of Hawthorne's collection *Twice-Told Tales:*

> A skillful literary artist has constructed a tale. He has not fashioned his thoughts to accommodate his incidents, but having deliberately conceived a certain *single effect* to be wrought, he then invents such incidents, he then combines such events, and discusses them in such tone as may best serve him in establishing this preconceived effect. If the very first sentence tend not to the outbringing of this effect, then in his very first step has he committed a blunder. In the whole composition there should be no word written of which the tendency, direct or indirect, is not to the one pre-established design.

The important insight contained in this famous passage is that the short story is not simply an entertaining or edifying anecdote that the writer relates in the most interesting possible way. The short story is not the written equivalent of a campfire tale, and the author is not primarily a raconteur trying to spin an absorbing yarn. If anything, Poe suggests, the writer of a short story is more like a poet, an artist working with the medium of language. The writer meticulously arranges words into a tightly organized linguistic structure, not to tell us an interesting sequence of events or to teach us a lesson, but to produce what Poe describes as a single, intense *effect*.

11

In the case of Poe's own fiction, the effect he often strove for and, in his best stories, achieved was one of preternatural horror, and he produced that result by the careful, highly self-conscious combination of the fictional elements that are the raw materials of the short story writer's art. Though the events in "William Wilson," for example, are certainly unsettling, the tale's special power, its intensely nightmarish quality, derives not from the storyline *per se* but from Poe's masterful orchestration of a variety of factors: tone, atmosphere, imagery, point of view, and the very sound and rhythm of his sentences.

What Poe recognized was that the short story, like every other form of art—a painting, a sculpture, or a musical composition—is a *made object*. Further, the ultimate "meaning" of a short story is not what happens in it and certainly not a moral that can be abstracted from it but something conveyed to the reader through the interaction of its particular fictional ingredients. The meaning of any short story, in other words, derives from the way it has been put together. This is true even for those recent works of experimental short fiction (sometimes called *anti-stories*) whose "meaning" depends on the deliberate violation of all the conventions that characterize the traditional "well-made" story as first defined by Poe. An interpretation of a short story, therefore, requires a close analysis of its constituent parts, and this in turn requires a familiarity with those basic elements of fiction out of which the writer constructs his or her work.

Theme

No true work of art can be reduced to a simple statement of meaning. This is as true for a good short story as it is for an oil painting by Picasso or a Bach sonata. Poe acknowledged this fact in his critical writing, vigorously attacking what he called "the heresy of the Didactic," the notion that it is the purpose of literature to "inculcate a moral." Nevertheless, as Poe also recognized, one of the legitimate aims of the serious short story is the communication of a significant theme—an insight into the human condition that is embodied by the work. The theme is not a message flatly stated by the author or by one of the characters. Indeed, a definitive statement of the theme may be impossible, because the "truth" or generalization about life the story is meant to reveal may be so subtle, complex, and richly suggestive that it cannot be summed up in a few sentences. The theme of the story is conveyed by the work as a whole, each part of which must serve to reinforce the idea, perception, or sense of life that the writer is attempting to express. In Hawthorne's "My Kinsman, Major Molineux," for example, everything in the story—its characters, action, setting, atmosphere, and symbolism—relates to the theme of an innocent young man's discovery of ambiguity and evil, of his initiation into the dark complexities of the human soul. A primary task of the critical reader, therefore, is to engage in a process of literary "dissection" in order to discern the writer's intent and see how the various elements of the story function thematically.

Plot

It is not unusual for a short story writer to base a work on actual events. Stephen Crane's "The Open Boat," for example, is a fictionalized account of a shipwreck he lived through and first wrote about in a newspaper article headlined "Stephen Crane's Own Story" (*New York Press*, January 7, 1897). This piece of journalism is a straightforward sequential narrative, with no other purpose than to report an out-of-the-ordinary episode the writer had experienced firsthand. "The Open Boat," however, has an additional purpose—a larger meaning, a theme—which makes it something more than a simple narrative account. It deals with one individual's tragic realization of humanity's insignificant place in a vast, indifferent universe.

In order to convey this theme, this vision of human existence, Crane had to take the random, chaotic occurrences of actual life, select the ones that best suited his purpose, and combine them into a meaningful shape. Among other things, this involved ordering the events of his narrative in the most effective manner, in a way that would both draw the reader into the story and contribute to the meaning Crane was trying to express. At other times, an author might arrange the episodes of a story in a particular way, not to reinforce a theme, but to elicit an emotional response from the reader: suspense, horror, surprise. It is this deliberate, artful selection and arrangement of a story's events for the purpose of achieving a specific artistic goal that we mean when we speak of *plot*. Therefore, when, as critical readers, we examine the plot of a story, we do not simply look at what happens in it; we look at its construction, at the way the author has put together the story's incidents and at the effect produced by this organization.

In his book *Aspects of the Novel*, E.M. Forster offers a useful definition of plot. "The king died and then the queen died," says

Forster, is merely a sequence of events. "The king died and then the queen died of grief," however, is a plot: a narrative in which the events do not simply follow each other but are related in a way that gives the story shape and meaning. Forster's third example makes this concept even clearer: "The queen died, no one knew why, until it was discovered that it was through grief at the death of the king." In this case, the author has shaped the identical events into a kind of mystery story. Like every other element of the short story, the plot—the manipulated sequence of events in the narrative—is determined by the author's intention, by what Poe calls the "pre-established design."

Character

While it is true that literary analysis requires us to dismantle a short story into its constituent parts in order to see what makes it work, there is something arbitrary, even misleading, about this process. A successful short story represents a seamless and complete fusion of fictional elements; we can never say absolutely where one element ends and another begins. This is particularly true of plot and character, since the actions in a story are obviously inseparable from the people who perform them. As Henry James remarks in *The Art of Fiction,* "What is character but the determination of incident? What is incident but the illustration of character?" Nevertheless, there are certain aspects of literary characterization that the critical reader must be aware of in attempting to understand the artistic intention, the "pre-established design," that lies behind a fictional work.

Writers use two basic methods to present their characters: the *expository* and the *dramatic.* With the expository method, the author *tells* us about a person in the story. In "The Horse Dealer's Daughter," for example, D.H. Lawrence directly describes his protagonist, Mabel Pervin:

> She had suffered badly during the period of poverty. Nothing, however, could shake the curious, sullen, animal pride that dominated each member of the family. Still she would not cast about her. She would follow her own way just the same. She would always hold the keys of her own situation. Mindless and persistent, she endured from day to day.

Later on in the story, when Mable passionately embraces the doctor's thighs and murmurs, "You love me. I know you love me," her personality is illuminated in a different way: through her actions and speech. This is an example of the dramatic method of characterization, in which the people in a story reveal themselves indirectly, through their behavior, language, and thoughts.

The protagonist of Lawrence's story impresses us as a relatively complex individual, driven by powerful, at times contradictory, impulses. Such a fictional character, whose personality seems as rich and distinctive as an actual human being's, is known as *round* or *three-dimensional*. Often, however, an author deliberately creates a *two-dimensional* or *flat* character, one whose personality seems to consist of a single trait. The figure known as "The Master of the Perfect Word," for example, in Hermann Hesse's "The Poet"—a story meant to have the suggestive simplicity of a folk tale—is the personification of higher wisdom. Similarly, the characters in Stephen Crane's "The Open Boat" are, for the most part, rather flat. As we have seen, Crane's story was based on an actual experience, one he shared with three other survivors of the shipwreck. His purpose in writing the story, however, was not to describe the incident but to embody a perception about the human condition. As a result, the characters in his story are not fully fleshed out or particularized. They are portrayed as representative human types, not as the unique individuals their real-life counterparts obviously were. The cook is a *typical* cook, fat, "stove-like," always dreaming of food; the captain is a *typical* captain, stalwart, brave, devastated by the loss of his ship; and so on. Like the butcher, the baker, and the candlestick-maker of the nursery rhyme, they are not (with one exception) even referred to by name—a deliberate strategy that clearly conforms to Crane's larger purpose.

It is also central to Crane's purpose that his main character, the correspondent, has learned an important, if cheerless, lesson by the end of the story. Such a character, who changes in a significant way over the course of a story, is known as *dynamic*. By contrast, a character who remains untouched by experience, who stays the same throughout (such as the narrator of James Alan MacPherson's "The Story of a Dead Man"), is referred to as *static*.

Point of View

In constructing a short story, the author must choose the point of view: who will narrate the work and from what "vantage point." There are two main choices available to the writer. The story can be narrated by somebody within the work itself, a character speaking as "I." This is known as *first-person* narration. Or the story can be narrated by somebody "outside" the work, whose voice we generally assume is the author's own. This point of view, in which all the characters are referred to as "he," "she," "they," and by their names, is *third-person* narration.

In first-person narration, the point of view is necessarily *limited* and highly *subjective:* we, as readers, experience the action entirely from the perspective of the character who is telling us about it. All we can know is what the narrator knows, sees, hear, thinks, understands, and reveals.

Third-person narration can also be limited to the thoughts, feelings, and perceptions of a single character. In Kate Chopin's "The Story of an Hour," for example, we are taken into the mind of a single character, Mrs. Mallard.

At the other extreme is the third-person *omniscient* point of view, in which the author moves freely from place to place, across time, and among the various characters, showing us the action through the eyes of each. The third-person point of view can also be completely *objective:* we are not given access to the thoughts of any of the characters; instead, we view the action "from a distance," as though watching the story unfold before us on a movie screen.

The author, of course, selects the point of view that best suits his or her purpose. Hawthorne's use of a third-person limited point of view in "My Kinsman, Major Molineux," for instance—in which the author relates the night's events as they are experienced by the young hero—allows him to comment ironically on his protagonist's naiveté while sustaining the mystery of Molineux's whereabouts until the climax of the tale. Hawthorne could not have maintained this mystery if he had made us privy to the thoughts of any of the other characters.

Setting

The locale of a story, the place where the action occurs, is known technically as the setting. In certain kinds of novels and films, such as the sweeping, romantic-adventure variety, setting serves mainly as an exotic or picturesque backdrop to the dramatic doings of the heroes and villains. However, the setting of a short story is always an important functional element, designed to support the central theme or overall effect of the work.

In creating the setting for a story, the writer must make certain fundamental decisions. The first and most obvious of these, of course, is the choice of the location itself—*where* to set the work. Sometimes, a writer depicts a particular locale because a primary purpose of the story is to explore the way life is lived in such surroundings. This is true, for example, of the writings of both John Updike, whose typical fictional territory is middle-class suburbia, and Mary E. Wilkins Freeman, one of America's finest "local color" writers. *Local color* is a term used to describe the work of various nineteenth-century American authors who strove to portray, with as much accuracy as possible, the customs and folkways of different regions of the country (New England in Freeman's case). At other times, a writer invents a setting to reinforce meaning or illuminate character. The rooms that serve as the main settings of Kate Chopin's "The Story of an Hour" and Jean Stafford's "The Liberation" give the reader important information about the lives, personalities, and emotional predicaments of the protagonists.

The second decision an author makes in regard to setting is the way the location is described: how much or how little we are told about it, what features of the setting are emphasized and what details are downplayed or omitted altogether. Again, this choice depends on the writer's intent. Hawthorne's deliberate vagueness in identifying the location of "My Kinsman, Major Molineux"—the fact that we are never told precisely where the action takes place—adds to our sense that the protagonist is lost, not in any ordinary city, but in the kind of place we sometimes find ourselves wandering through in a bad dream. Hawthorne's intention, in short, is to endow a real place (presumably eighteenth-century Boston) with an air of unreality by describing it in shadowy terms. Ursula K. Le Guin's handling of setting in "Semley's Necklace," on the other hand, has the opposite aim: to make an imaginary world seem totally real by describing it in rich, concrete detail.

Symbol

Our lives are filled with symbols. For example, what makes a wedding ring different from any other piece of jewelry is its symbolic quality. To the individual wearing one, a wedding ring is never merely a circle of gold, because of the various meanings, many of them deep, inexpressible, and emotionally charged, that cluster around it. One person, confronted by a robber's gun, will readily hand over belongings worth a great deal of money before relinquishing a plain gold band that costs relatively little. Another, removing a wedding ring for the first time after long years of an unhappy marriage, will experience a profound sense of liberation. In each case, the ring possesses a value that is neither intrinsic nor "sentimental"—in the way that a memento of the past might be—but powerfully symbolic, filled with significance.

A literary symbol is something in a story—an object, a detail of the setting, or an action—that suggests a "larger meaning" beyond itself. Because it is a function of art to communicate larger meanings, to illuminate life in significant ways, the short story writer frequently relies on symbols. Symbolism is not (as inexperienced readers sometimes assume) a technique authors use to obscure their meanings or to endow their work with a sort of spurious complexity. Rather, a symbol is a necessary device which artists, at times, *must* use because the perception, insight, or intuition they are trying to convey cannot be expressed in any other or better way (just as the particular cluster of meanings embodied by a wedding ring cannot be expressed in any other way).

Certain symbols are *universal;* that is, they seem to suggest meanings in themselves, apart from whatever work they are found in. The journey, the ocean, forests and caves, the seasons of the year are a few of these inherently significant symbols that appear in myths, folk tales, and works of art throughout the world. A second, opposite type of symbol is referred to as *private* or *created,* because its significance derives from the way it is employed by a particular artist in a specific work. Ralph Ellison, in his story "Flying Home," manages to make two concrete objects with no "naturally" symbolic overtones—an airplane and a buzzard—resonate with rich suggestions of meaning.

A category of writing related to but distinct from symbolic literature is *allegory.* An allegory is a narrative in which every character, event, and detail of the setting stands for something else: an abstract idea, a social, philosophical, or religious concept, a psychological state, an historical figure, etc. Thus, like a symbol, an allegorical sign refers to a meaning beyond itself. But, whereas the meaning of a symbol is so complex and elusive that it can never be fully expressed in other terms, the "something else" an allegorical sign represents can, indeed *must,* be precisely identified if we are to understand the work. It is impossible to appreciate John Bunyan's famous religious allegory *The Pilgrim's Progress,* for example, unless we perceive that its hero, Christian, is a personification of the Christian soul and that the events that befall him on his journey to the Celestial City represent stages in a spiritual process. Similarly, Kay Boyle's allegorical story "Astronomer's Wife" becomes clear only when we recognize that her two male characters are meant to be embodiments of opposing aspects of manhood.

The short story, then, is a literary form that demands an especially high degree of technical skill, since there is no leeway for laxity or digression in the composition of a story: everything in it must be there for a reason, must relate directly to its central purpose. To appreciate just how much craftsmanship and care is involved in this type of writing, the reader might begin by examining Robert Penn Warren's "Blackberry Winter," the first selection in this book. At a glance, the story seems to be primarily a nostalgic recollection of the narrator's boyhood life, of the people and places that were important to him. A closer look, however, reveals that the story has been meticulously constructed so that each of its characters, episodes, and images serves an important thematic purpose.

The story is told from the point of view of an older man, recalling a day out of his childhood past, a day that clearly holds a special significance for him. The singular quality of the day is indicated immediately: unlike every other June morning in the young boy's memory, this one is so cold that he is forbidden to go outside without shoes. "It's June," his mother says, "but it's blackberry winter." Cold and winter—along with death, with which they are archetypically associated—are motifs that run throughout the story, recurring in significant ways in virtually all of its episodes. Another, related motif, that of the passage of time, is also introduced right away, in a long, memorable passage that powerfully evokes a child's experience of time as something changeless and eternal.

The arrival of the cold spell coincides with the appearance of the unsavory tramp, who represents the sudden intrusion of a sinister, alien element into the boy's benign and timeless world. Though it is possible to see this figure as the personification of pure evil—the serpent in the garden—the story is not an allegory, and the tramp's significance cannot be reduced to a single abstraction. Rather, he embodies a host of harsh realities, a dark dimension of existence to which the boy has never been exposed within his safe and sheltered world.

With the tramp's arrival, the boy sets off on a brief but eventful quest, at every point of which—at the creek, at Jebb and Dellie's house, and finally back at his own home—he confronts a new and disturbing sight, learning something important about the cruelty and unpleasantness life contains and about the painful alterations that time inevitably inflicts. By the end of the story, the golden world of his boyhood has been devastated by change and death. Only Jebb, whom Warren's imagery associates with the earth itself, remains the same. And yet, the last line of the story (which makes sense only when interpreted figuratively) tells us that the narrator has achieved the kind of mature acceptance of life's inevitable vicissitudes which a person must have to function successfully in the world and not remain fixated to the past. The narrator now realizes the malevolent tramp played an important part in his life, the part of the "herald," summoning him across a critical threshold. Though the boy could not have known it at the time, the coming of the tramp signalled the end of the narrator's childhood—of his carefree, enclosed, blissfully innocent state—and the starting point of that journey that carries all of us into a world where we must confront and learn to deal with certain hard, inescapable realities: transience, adversity, mortality. Thus, "Blackberry Winter" is not simply a vivid evocation of a particular time and place, but, even more important, it is also a powerful expression of a theme with universal significance.

CHAPTER ONE

The Call

As the stories in this anthology show, anyone can undertake a quest. Young or old, female or male, married or single, black or white: these accidents of time and circumstance are unimportant. However, people must possess certain qualities, notably insight, courage, and endurance, before they can attempt such a venture. They need insight to perceive the limitations of their lives, particularly when, as is often the case, the rest of the world regards those lives as enviable. They need courage and endurance to fight against the fate others succumb to, against social convention and the expectations of family and friends, or even against the stable but unsatisfying conditions their own secret fears and long-established habits urge them to settle for.

The heroes of the stories in this chapter are of various ages and circumstances. The unhappily married astronomer's wife of Kay Boyle's story lives in a primitive villa in some unnamed country. The unmarried, equally downtrodden young woman of Jean Stafford's "The Liberation" is a member of an old Colorado family. The setting of "Blackberry Winter" is rural Tennessee, where the nine-year-old protagonist resides in absolute security with his mother and father, whom he both loves and respects. Paul, the adolescent hero of Willa Cather's story, finds his home in industrial Pittsburgh ugly, depressing, and indifferent to spiritual needs.

Whatever the conditions of their lives, the heroes of these stories share certain characteristics and perceptions. Each is on the brink of a decisive change—some *feel* themselves to be standing unsteadily on that brink—and each comes to see his or her life, however attractive it might appear to someone else, as safe but emotionally unprofitable: as a trap. Some of these traps are more comfortable than others. The title character of "Astronomer's Wife" lives with her husband in a beautiful locale. Their relationship is so intensely unhappy, however, that she is nearly effaced by it; she has forgotten that she is "youngish," and the light has gone out of her eyes. The protagonist of the Kate Chopin story, on the other hand, does not even realize how imprisoning her conventionally successful marriage has become. It is not until a tragic accident occurs that she is awakened to her own dissatisfactions. The boy in "Blackberry Winter" inhabits a kind of paradise, but it is essentially the paradise of every happy childhood. As is always the case, it must be left behind if the child is to grow and learn, if he is to become an adult. The worlds depicted in these stories, though they may once have seemed or even been completely fulfilling, have begun to close in on the main characters.

In order for these individuals to undertake a quest, it is essential that they consciously or unconsciously perceive the danger of remaining where they are. We spoke above of the hero's need for insight. To leave the security and familiarity of the known world for the unknown, as the quest demands, may seem more dangerous than staying put. But it is not. The quest motif in myth and literature symbolizes the absolute necessity of radical, defiant, creative change in the individual's life—and, we might add, in the life of any culture. Like all other forms of biological life, people must alter and grow. In the case of human beings, this includes psychic or spiritual development; to arrest this development is to invite stagnation. The hero learns to accept the difficult truth that all is in flux, that all must change, that one's life is an unending cycle of deaths and rebirths, a discarding of the things that were meaningful to us yesterday for those that assume new significance as the future unfolds. The hero's willingness to undertake the quest is the sign that she or he understands and accepts these exacting conditions of human life.

The hero's quest begins with, in Joseph Campbell's terminology, a "call to adventure." A "herald" appears and issues this call. The herald is often someone or something external, though there are many instances when the call arises from inside the hero in the form of a powerful impulse or sudden craving. Herman Melville's nineteenth-century quest novel *Moby-Dick* is a good example. Its narrator, Ishmael, is suffering from a near-suicidal depression, which impels him to leave his safe but confining life on land for the mystery and excitement of a whaling voyage.

More often, though, the call comes from a source outside the hero. For example, in James Dickey's novel *Deliverance*, the main character, Ed Gentry, an out-of-shape suburbanite passing through what is popularly known as a "mid-life crisis," starts out on a wilderness journey at the prompting of his sportsman friend, Lewis Medlock. At other times, the call comes from a nonhuman creature. Myths and fairy tales are full of such heralds: giants, dwarves, or enchanted beasts bearing challenges or messages that set the story in motion. Animals occasionally play the part of heralds in modern literature, too, as in two novellas, William Faulkner's *The Bear* and D. H. Lawrence's *St. Mawr*, in which, respectively, a bear and a horse launch the central characters on profoundly disturbing and enriching adventures.

Frequently, the herald is an extraordinary event or an intriguing object that makes a sudden, dramatic appearance, disrupting the day-to-day existence of the hero. The accidental discovery of a supernatural ring leads to the perilous quest chronicled in J. R. R. Tolkien's fantasy trilogy *The Lord of the Rings*. In L. Frank Baum's children's classic *The Wizard of Oz*, the herald that sets Dorothy off on her adventure is a tornado, which spirits the girl away from the gray dreariness of her aunt and uncle's Kansas farm to the bright, magical land of Oz. At the beginning of *Star Wars*, Luke Skywalker, the hero of the movie, lives on an equally dreary "moisture farm" with *his* aunt and uncle. His exploits begin with another herald that literally appears from "out of the blue": a strange little robot rocketing down from the sky on an urgent mission. Whether the call comes from outside the heroes or within, however, it always signifies that their present situations have become stale, sterile, and unrewarding and that they are ripe for a change, that they are ready, if not necessarily willing or able, to leave their old, familiar lives behind and move on to something new.

The stories in this chapter portray a variety of calls. As in many detective books and movies, where the hero's quest begins in response to an actual telephone call or Western Union message, the herald in Kate Chopin's story takes the form of a telegram containing shocking news. In Willa Cather's "Paul's Case" the call appears as an unexpected opportunity: a bank book placed in the title character's hands launches him on a doomed quest after beauty, art, and material splendor. In Kay Boyle's story, a plumber summons the unhappily married protagonist into an unexplored subterranean realm, which, in its fecundity and earthiness, is a metaphor for the radically different kind of love he offers her. A mysterious stranger plays the part of the herald in Robert Penn Warren's "Blackberry Winter," in which a menacing tramp makes it possible for the young hero to escape the limitations of a child's innocent vision and begin to see the world through the eyes of an adult, which is to say, to begin to see its tragedies, cruelties, and baffling injustices. In Sherwood Anderson's "Adventure," the call is the long-awaited summons from the heroine's departed lover, Ned Currie.

In the end—despite Alice Hindman's stubborn faith that Ned will one day return—that summons never arrives. What happens when a person lives in perpetual expectation of a call that never comes or, as in the case of Chopin's protagonist, Mrs. Mallard, is denied the chance to follow through when it finally does? It is significant that, at the end of their respective stories, Mrs. Mallard is dead of a heart attack and Alice Hindman is bolted into the darkness of her cold, lonely room. Similarly, Cather's young hero, Paul, whose quest is aborted almost as soon as it starts, ends up a suicide. What the selections in this chapter show us, then, is that there are times in our lives when our very survival—spiritual, psychological, even physical—depends on our ability to grow, to answer the inner challenge that urges us to change our lives. At such time, to stay where we are, out of fear or habit or conventional morality, is to condemn ourselves to a kind of living death.

Blackberry Winter

ROBERT PENN WARREN

It was getting into June and past eight o'clock in the morning, but there was a fire—even if it wasn't a big fire, just a fire of chunks—on the hearth of the big stone fireplace in the living room. I was standing on the hearth, almost into the chimney, hunched over the fire, working my bare toes slowly on the warm stone. I relished the heat which made the skin of my bare legs warp and creep and tingle, even as I called to my mother, who was somewhere back in the dining room or kitchen, and said: "But it's June, I don't have to put them on!"

"You put them on if you are going out," she called.

I tried to assess the degree of authority and conviction in the tone, but at that distance it was hard to decide. I tried to analyze the tone, and then I thought what a fool I had been to start out the back door and let her see that I was barefoot. If I had gone out the front door or the side door she would never have known, not till dinner time anyway, and by then the day would have been half gone and I would have been all over the farm to see what the storm had done and down to the creek to see the flood. But it had never crossed my mind that they would try to stop you from going barefoot in June, no matter if there had been a gully-washer and a cold spell.

Nobody had ever tried to stop me in June as long as I could remember, and when you are nine years old, what you remember seems forever; for you remember everything and everything is important and stands big and full and fills up Time and is so solid that you can walk around and around it like a tree and look at it. You are aware that time passes, that there is a movement in time, but that is not what Time is. Time is not a movement, a flowing, a wind then, but is, rather, a kind of climate in which things are, and when a thing happens it begins to live and keeps on living and stands solid in Time like the tree that you can walk around. And if there is a movement, the movement is not Time itself, any more than a breeze is climate, and all the breeze does is to shake a little the leaves on the tree which is alive and solid. When you are nine, you know that there are things that you don't know, but you know that when you know something you know it. You know how a thing has been and you know that you can go barefoot in June. You do not understand that voice from back in the kitchen which says that you cannot go barefoot outdoors and run to see what has happened and rub your feet over the wet shivery grass and make the perfect mark of your foot in the smooth, creamy, red mud and then muse upon it as though you had suddenly come upon that single mark on the glistening auroral beach of the world. You have never seen a beach, but you have read the book and how the footprint was there.

The voice had said what it had said, and I looked savagely at the black stockings and the strong, scuffed brown shoes which I had brought from my closet as far as the hearth rug. I called once more, "But it's June," and waited.

"It's June," the voice replied from far away, "but it's blackberry winter."

I had lifted my head to reply to that, to make one more test of what was in that tone, when I happened to see the man.

The fireplace in the living room was at the end; for the stone chimney was built, as in so many of the farmhouses in Tennessee, at the end of a gable, and there was a window on each side of the chimney. Out of the window on the north side of the fireplace I could see the man. When I saw the man I did not call out what I had intended, but, engrossed by the strangeness of the sight, watched him, still far off, come along the path by the edge of the woods.

What was strange was that there should be a man there at all. That path went along the yard fence, between the fence and the woods which came right down to the yard, and then on back past the chicken runs and on by the woods until it was lost to sight where the woods bulged out and cut off the back field. There the path disappeared into the woods. It led on back, I knew, through the woods and to the swamp, skirted the swamp where the big trees gave way to sycamores and water oaks and willows and tangled cane, and then led on to the river. Nobody ever went back there except people who wanted to gig frogs in the swamp or to fish in the river or to hunt in the woods, and those people, if they didn't have a standing permission from my father, always stopped to ask permission to cross the farm. But the man whom I now saw wasn't, I could tell even at that distance, a sportsman. And what would a sportsman have been doing down there after a storm? Besides, he was coming from the river, and nobody had gone down there that morning. I knew that for a fact, because if anybody had passed, certainly if a stranger had passed, the dogs would have made a racket and would have been out on him. But this man was coming up from the river and had come up through the woods. I suddenly had a vision of him moving up the grassy path in the woods, in the green twilight under the big trees, not making any sound on the path, while now and then, like drops off the eaves, a big drop of water would fall from a leaf or bough and strike a stiff oak leaf lower down with a small, hollow sound like a drop of water hitting tin. That sound, in the silence of the woods, would be very significant.

When you are a boy and stand in the stillness of woods, which can be so still that your heart almost stops beating and makes you want to stand there in the green twilight until you feel your very feet sinking into and clutching the earth like roots and your body breathing slow through its pores like the leaves—when you stand there and wait for the next drop to drop with its small, flat sound to a lower leaf, that sound seems to measure out something, to put an end to something, to begin something, and you cannot wait for it to happen and are afraid it will not happen, and then when it has happened, you are waiting again, almost afraid.

But the man whom I saw coming through the woods in my mind's eye did not pause and wait, growing into the ground and breathing with the enormous, soundless breathing of the leaves. Instead, I saw him moving in the green twilight inside my head as he was moving at that very moment along the path by the edge of the woods, coming toward the house. He was moving steadily, but not fast, with his shoulders hunched a little and his head thrust forward, like a man who has come a long way and has a long way to go. I shut my eyes for a couple of seconds, thinking that when I opened them he would not be there at all. There was no place for him to have come from, and there was no reason for him to come where he was coming, toward our house. But I opened my eyes, and there he was, and he was coming steadily along the side of the woods. He was not yet even with the back chicken yard.

"Mama," I called.

"You put them on," the voice said.

"There's a man coming," I called, "out back."

She did not reply to that, and I guessed that she had gone to the kitchen window to look. She would be looking at the man and wondering who he was and what he wanted, the way you always do in the country, and if I went back there now she would not notice right off whether or not I was barefoot. So I went back to the kitchen.

She was standing by the window. "I don't recognize him," she said, not looking around at me.

"Where could he be coming from?" I asked.

"I don't know," she said.

"What would he be doing down at the river? At night? In the storm?"

She studied the figure out the window, then said, "Oh, I reckon maybe he cut across from the Dunbar place."

That was, I realized, a perfectly rational explanation. He had not been down at the river in the storm, at night. He had come over this morning. You could cut across from the Dunbar place if you didn't mind breaking through a lot of elder and sassafras and blackberry bushes which had about taken over the old cross path, which nobody ever used any more. That satisfied me for a moment, but only for a moment. "Mama," I asked, "what would he be doing over at the Dunbar place last night?"

Then she looked at me, and I knew I had made a mistake, for she was looking at my bare feet. "You haven't got your shoes on," she said.

But I was saved by the dogs. That instant there was a bark which I recognized as Sam, the collie, and then a heavier, churning kind of bark which was Bully, and I saw a streak of white as Bully tore round the corner of the back porch and headed out for the man. Bully was a big, bone-white bull dog, the kind of dog that they used to call a farm bull dog but that you don't see any more, heavy chested and heavy headed, but with pretty long legs. He could take a fence as light as a hound. He had just cleared the white paling fence toward the woods when my mother ran out to the back porch and began calling, "Here you, Bully! Here you!"

Bully stopped in the path, waiting for the man, but he gave a few more of those deep, gargling, savage barks that reminded you of something down a stone-lined well. The red clay mud, I saw, was splashed up over his white chest and looked exciting, like blood.

The man, however, had not stopped walking even when Bully took the fence and started at him. He had kept right on coming. All he had done was to switch a little paper parcel which he carried from the right hand to the left, and then reach into his pants pocket to get something. Then I saw the glitter and knew that he had a knife in his hand, probably the kind of mean knife just made for devilment and nothing else, with a blade as long as the blade of a frog-sticker, which will snap out ready when you press a button in the handle. That knife must have had a button in the handle, or else how could he have had the blade out glittering so quick and with just one hand?

Pulling his knife against the dogs was a funny thing to do, for Bully was a big, powerful brute and fast, and Sam was all right. If those dogs had meant business, they might have knocked him down and ripped him before he got a stroke in. He ought to have picked up a heavy stick, something to take a swipe at them with and something which they could see and respect when they came at him. But he apparently did not know much about dogs. He just held the knife blade close against the right leg, low down, and kept on moving down the path.

Then my mother had called, and Bully had stopped. So the man let the blade of the knife snap back into the handle, and dropped it into his pocket, and kept on coming. Many women would have been afraid with the strange man who they knew had that knife in his pocket. That is, if they were alone in the house with nobody but a nine-year-old boy. And my mother was alone, for my father had gone off, and Dellie, the cook, was down at her cabin because she wasn't feeling well. But my mother wasn't afraid. She wasn't a big woman, but she was clear and brisk about everything she did and looked everybody and everything right in the eye from her own blue eyes in her tanned face. She had been the first woman in the county to ride a horse astride (that was back when she was a girl and long before I was born), and I have seen her snatch up a pump gun and go out and knock a chicken hawk out of the air like a busted skeet when he came over her chicken yard. She was a steady and self-reliant woman, and when I think of her now after all the years she has been dead, I think of her brown hands, not big, but somewhat square for a woman's hands, with square-cut nails. They looked, as a matter of fact, more like a young boy's hands than a grown woman's. But back then it never crossed my mind that she would ever be dead.

She stood on the back porch and watched the man enter the back gate, where the dogs (Bully had leaped back into the yard) were dancing and muttering and giving sidelong glances back to my mother to see if she meant what she had said. The man walked right by the dogs, almost brushing them, and didn't pay them any attention. I could see now that he wore old khaki pants, and a dark wool coat with stripes in it, and a gray felt hat. He had on a gray shirt with blue stripes in it, and no tie. But I could see a tie, blue and reddish, sticking in his side coat-pocket. Everything was wrong about what he wore. He ought to have been wearing blue jeans or overalls, and a straw hat or an old black felt hat, and the coat, granting that he might have been wearing a wool coat and not a jumper, ought not to have had those stripes. Those clothes, despite the fact that they were old enough and dirty enough for any tramp, didn't belong there in our back yard, coming down the path, in Middle Tennessee, miles away from any big town, and even a mile off the pike.

When he got almost to the steps, without having said anything, my mother, very matter-of-factly, said, "Good morning."

"Good morning," he said, and stopped and looked her over. He did not take off his hat, and under the brim you could see the perfectly unmemorable face, which wasn't old and wasn't young, or thick or thin. It was grayish and covered with about three days of stubble. The eyes were a kind of nondescript, muddy hazel, or something like that, rather bloodshot. His teeth, when he opened his mouth, showed yellow and uneven. A couple of them had been knocked out. You knew that they had been knocked out, because there was a scar, not very old, there on the lower lip just beneath the gap.

"Are you hunting work?" my mother asked him.

"Yes," he said—not "yes, mam"—and still did not take off his hat.

"I don't know about my husband, for he isn't here," she said, and didn't mind a bit telling the tramp, or whoever he was, with the mean knife in his pocket, that no man was around, "but I can give you a few things to do. The storm has drowned a lot of my chicks. Three coops of them. You can gather them up and bury them. Bury them deep so the dogs won't get at them. In the woods. And fix the coops the wind blew over. And down yonder beyond that pen by the edge of the woods are some drowned poults. They got out and I couldn't get them in. Even after it started to rain hard. Poults haven't got any sense."

"What are them things—poults?" he demanded, and spat on the brick walk. He rubbed his foot over the spot, and I saw that he wore a black, pointed-toe low shoe, all cracked and broken. It was a crazy kind of shoe to be wearing in the country.

"Oh, they're young turkeys," my mother was saying. "And they haven't got any sense. I oughtn't to try to raise them around here with so many chickens anyway. They don't thrive near chickens, even in separate pens. And I won't give up my chickens." Then she stopped herself and resumed briskly on the note of business. "When you finish that, you can fix my flower beds. A lot of trash and mud and gravel has washed down. Maybe you can save some of my flowers if you are careful."

"Flowers," the man said, in a low, impersonal voice which seemed to have a wealth of meaning, but a meaning which I could not fathom. As I think back on it, it probably was not pure contempt. Rather, it was a kind of impersonal and distant marveling that he should be on the verge of grubbing in a flower bed. He said the word, and then looked off across the yard.

"Yes, flowers," my mother replied with some asperity, as though she would have nothing said or implied against flowers. "And they were very fine this year." Then she stopped and looked at the man. "Are you hungry?" she demanded.

"Yeah," he said.

"I'll fix you something," she said, "before you get started." She turned to me, "Show him where he can wash up," she commanded, and went into the house.

I took the man to the end of the porch where a pump was and where a couple of wash pans sat on a low shelf for people to use before they went into the house. I stood there while he laid down his little parcel wrapped in newspaper and took off his hat and looked around for a nail to hang it on. He poured the water and plunged his hands into it. They were big hands, and strong looking, but they did not have the creases and the earth-color of the hands of men who work outdoors. But they were dirty, with black dirt ground into the skin and under the nails. After he had washed his hands, he poured another basin of water and washed his face. He dried his face, and with the towel still dangling in his grasp, stepped over to the mirror on the house wall. He rubbed one hand over the stubble on his face. Then he carefully inspected his face, turning first one side and then the other, and stepped back and settled his striped coat down on his shoulders. He had the movements of a man who has just dressed up to go to church or a party—the way he settled his coat and smoothed it and scanned himself in the mirror.

Then he caught my glance on him. He glared at me for an instant out of the bloodshot eyes, then demanded in a low, harsh voice, "What you looking at?"

"Nothing," I managed to say, and stepped back a step from him.

He flung the towel down, crumpled, on the shelf, and went toward the kitchen door and entered without knocking.

My mother said something to him which I could not catch. I started to go in again, then thought about my bare feet, and decided to go back of the chicken yard, where the man would have to come to pick up the dead chicks. I hung around behind the chicken house until he came out.

He moved across the chicken yard with a fastidious, not quite finicking motion, looking down at the curdled mud flecked with bits of chicken-droppings. The mud curled up over the soles of his black shoes. I stood back from him some six feet and watched him pick up the first of the drowned chicks. He held it up by one foot and inspected it.

There is nothing deader looking than a drowned chick. The feet curl in that feeble, empty way which back when I was a boy, even if I was a country boy who did not mind hog-killing or frog-gigging, made me feel hollow in the stomach. Instead of looking plump and fluffy, the body is stringy and limp with the fluff plastered to it, and the neck is long and loose like a little string of rag. And the eyes have that bluish membrane over them which makes you think of a very old man who is sick about to die.

The man stood there and inspected the chick. Then he looked all around as though he didn't know what to do with it.

"There's a great big old basket in the shed," I said, and pointed to the shed attached to the chicken house.

He inspected me as though he had just discovered my presence, and moved toward the shed.

"There's a spade there, too," I added.

He got the basket and began to pick up the other chicks, picking each one up slowly by a foot and then flinging it into the basket with a nasty, snapping motion. Now and then he would look at me out of the blood-shot eyes. Every time he seemed on the verge of saying something, but he did not. Perhaps he was building up to say something to me, but I did not wait that long. His way of looking at me made me so uncomfortable that I left the chicken yard.

Besides, I had just remembered that the creek was in flood, over the bridge, and that people were down there watching it. So I cut across the farm toward the creek. When I got to the big tobacco field I saw that it had not suffered much. The land lay right and not many tobacco plants had washed out of the ground. But I knew that a lot of tobacco round the country had been washed right out. My father had said so at breakfast.

My father was down at the bridge. When I came out of the gap in the osage hedge into the road, I saw him sitting on his mare over the heads of the other men who were standing around, admiring the flood. The creek was big here, even in low water; for only a couple of miles away it ran into the river, and when a real flood came, the red water got over the pike where it dipped down to the bridge, which was an iron bridge, and high over the floor and even the side railings of the bridge. Only the upper iron work would show, with the water boiling and frothing red and white around it. That creek rose so fast and so heavy because a few miles back it came down out of the hills, where the gorges filled up with water in no time when a rain came. The creek ran in a deep bed with limestone bluffs along both sides until it got within three quarters of a mile of the bridge, and when it came out from between those bluffs in flood it was boiling and hissing and steaming like water from a fire hose.

Whenever there was a flood, people from half the county would come down to see the sight. After a gully-washer there would not be any work to do anyway. If it didn't ruin your crop, you couldn't plow and you felt like taking a holiday to celebrate. If it did ruin your crop, there wasn't anything to do except to try to take your mind off the mortgage, if you were rich enough to have a mortgage, and if you couldn't afford a mortgage you needed something to take your mind off how hungry you would be by Christmas. So people would come down to the bridge and look at the flood. It made something different from the run of days.

There would not be much talking after the first few minutes of trying to guess how high the water was this time. The men and kids just stood around, or sat their horses or mules, as the case might be, or stood up in the wagon beds. They looked at the strangeness of the flood for an hour or two, and then somebody would say that he had better be getting on home to dinner and would start walking down the gray, puddled limestone pike, or would touch heel to his mount and start off. Everybody always knew what it would be like when he got down to the bridge, but people always came. It was like church or a funeral. They always came, that is, if it was summer and the flood unexpected. Nobody ever came down in winter to see high water.

When I came out of the gap in the bodock hedge, I saw the crowd, perhaps fifteen or twenty men and a lot of kids, and saw my father sitting his mare, Nellie Gray. He was a tall, limber man and carried himself well. I was always proud to see him sit a horse, he was so quiet and straight, and when I stepped through the gap of the hedge that morning, the first thing that happened was, I remember, the warm feeling I always had when I saw him up on a horse, just sitting. I did not go toward him, but skirted the crowd on the far side, to get a look at the creek. For one thing, I was not sure what he would say about the fact that I was barefoot. But the first thing I knew, I heard his voice calling, "Seth!"

I went toward him, moving apologetically past the men, who bent their large, red or thin, sallow faces above me. I knew some of the men, and knew their names, but because those I knew were there in a crowd, mixed with the strange faces, they seemed foreign to me, and not friendly. I did not look up at my father until I was almost within touching distance of his heel. Then I looked up and tried to read his face, to see if he was angry about my being barefoot. Before I could decide anything from that impassive, high-boned face, he had leaned over and reached a hand to me. "Grab on," he commanded.

I grabbed on and gave a little jump, and he said, "Up-see-daisy!" and whisked me, light as a feather, up to the pommel of his McClellan saddle.

"You can see better up here," he said, slid back on the cantle a little to make me more comfortable, and then, looking over my head at the swollen, tumbling water, seemed to forget all about me. But his right hand was laid on my side, just above my thigh, to steady me.

I was sitting there as quiet as I could, feeling the faint stir of my father's chest against my shoulders as it rose and fell with his breath, when I saw the cow. At first, looking up the creek, I thought it was just another big piece of driftwood steaming down the creek in the ruck of water, but all at once a pretty good-size boy who had climbed part way up a telephone pole by the pike so that he could see better yelled out, "Golly-damn, look at that-air cow!"

Everybody looked. It was a cow all right, but it might just as well have been driftwood; for it was dead as a chunk, rolling and rolling down the creek, appearing and disappearing, feet up or head up, it didn't matter which.

The cow started up the talk again. Somebody wondered whether it would hit one of the clear places under the top girder of the bridge and get through or whether it would get tangled in the drift and trash that had piled against the upright girders and braces. Somebody remembered how about ten years before so much driftwood had piled up on the bridge that it was knocked off its foundations. Then the cow hit. It hit the edge of the drift against one of the girders, and hung there. For a few seconds it seemed as though it might tear loose, but then we saw that it was really caught. It bobbed and heaved on its side there in a slow, grinding, uneasy fashion. It had a yoke around its neck, the kind made out of a forked limb to keep a jumper behind fence.

"She shore jumped one fence," one of the men said.

And another: "Well, she done jumped her last one, fer a fack."

Then they began to wonder about whose cow it might be. They decided it must belong to Milt Alley. They said that he had a cow that was a jumper, and kept her in a fenced-in piece of ground up the creek. I had never seen Milt Alley, but I knew who he was. He was a squatter and lived up the hills a way, on a shirt-tail patch of set-on-edge land, in a cabin. He was pore white trash. He had lots of children. I had seen the children at school, when they came. They were thin-faced, with straight, sticky-looking, dough-colored hair, and they smelled something like old sour buttermilk, not because they drank so much buttermilk but because that is the sort of smell which children out of those cabins tend to have. The big Alley boy drew dirty pictures and showed them to the little boys at school.

That was Milt Alley's cow. It looked like the kind of cow he would have, a scrawny, old, sway-backed cow, with a yoke around her neck. I wondered if Milt Alley had another cow.

"Poppa," I said, "do you think Milt Alley has got another cow?"

"You say 'Mr. Alley,' " my father said quietly.

"Do you think he has?"

"No telling," my father said.

Then a big gangly boy, about fifteen, who was sitting on a scraggly little old mule with a piece of croker sack thrown across the saw-tooth spine, and who had been staring at the cow, suddenly said to nobody in particular, "Reckin anybody ever et drownt cow?"

He was the kind of boy who might just as well as not have been the son of Milt Alley, with his faded and patched overalls ragged at the bottom of the pants and the mud-stiff brogans hanging off his skinny, bare ankles at the level of the mule's belly. He had said what he did, and then looked embarrassed and sullen when all the eyes swung at him. He hadn't meant to say it, I am pretty sure now. He would have been too proud to say it, just as Milt Alley would have been too proud. He had just been thinking out loud, and the words had popped out.

There was an old man standing there on the pike, an old man with a white beard. "Son," he said to the embarrassed and sullen boy on the mule, "you live long enough and you'll find a man will eat anything when the time comes."

"Time gonna come fer some folks this year," another man said.

"Son," the old man said, "in my time I et things a man don't like to think on. I was a sojer and I rode with Gin'l Forrest, and them things we et when the time come. I tell you. I et meat what got up and run when you taken out yore knife to cut a slice to put on the fire. You had to knock it down with a carbeen butt, it was so active. That-air meat would jump like a bullfrog, it was so full of skippers."

But nobody was listening to the old man. The boy on the mule turned his sullen sharp face from him, dug a heel into the side of the mule and went off up the pike with a motion which made you think that any second you would hear mule bones clashing inside that lank and scrofulous hide.

"Cy Dundee's boy," a man said, and nodded toward the figure going up the pike on the mule.

"Reckin Cy Dundee's young-uns seen times they'd settle fer drownt cow," another man said.

The old man with the beard peered at them both from his weak, slow eyes, first at one and then at the other. "Live long enough," he said, "and a man will settle fer what he kin git."

Then there was silence again, with the people looking at the red, foam-flecked water.

My father lifted the bridle rein in his left hand, and the mare turned and walked around the group and up the pike. We rode on up to our big gate, where my father dismounted to open it and let me myself ride Nellie Gray through. When he got to the lane that led off from the drive about two hundred yards from our house, my father said, "Grab on." I grabbed on, and he let me down to the ground. "I'm going to ride down and look at my corn," he said. "You go on." He took the lane, and I stood there on the drive and watched him ride off. He was wearing cowhide boots and an old hunting coat, and I thought that that made him look very military, like a picture. That and the way he rode.

I did not go to the house. Instead, I went by the vegetable garden and crossed behind the stables, and headed down for Dellie's cabin. I wanted to go down and play with Jebb, who was Dellie's little boy about two years older than I was. Besides, I was cold. I shivered as I walked, and I had gooseflesh. The mud which crawled up between my toes with every step I took was like ice. Dellie would have a fire, but she wouldn't make me put on shoes and stockings.

Dellie's cabin was of logs, with one side, because it was on a slope, set on limestone chunks, with a little porch attached to it, and had a little white-washed fence around it and a gate with plow-points on a wire to clink when somebody came in, and had two big white oaks in the yard and some flowers and a nice privy in the back with some honeysuckle growing over it. Dellie and Old Jebb, who was Jebb's father and who lived with Dellie and had lived with her for twenty-five years even if they never had got married, were careful to keep everything nice around their cabin. They had the name all over the community for being clean and clever Negroes. Dellie and Jebb were what they used to call "white-folks' niggers." There was a big difference between their cabin and the other two cabins farther down where the other tenants lived. My father kept the other cabins waterproof, but he couldn't undertake to go down and pick up after the litter they strewed. They didn't take the trouble to have a vegetable patch like Dellie and Jebb or to make preserves from wild plum, and jelly from crab apple the way Dellie did. They were shiftless, and my father was always threatening to get shed of them. But he never did. When they finally left, they just up and left on their own, for no reason, to go and be shiftless somewhere else. Then some more came. But meanwhile they lived down there, Matt Rawson and his family, and Sid Turner and his, and I played with their children all over the farm when they weren't working. But when I wasn't around they were mean sometimes to Little Jebb. That was because the other tenants down there were jealous of Dellie and Jebb.

I was so cold that I ran the last fifty yards to Dellie's gate. As soon as I had entered the yard, I saw that the storm had been hard on Dellie's flowers. The yard was, as I have said, on a slight slope, and the water running across had gutted the flower beds and washed out all the good black woods-earth which Dellie had brought in. What little grass there was in the yard was plastered sparsely down on the ground, the way the drainage water had left it. It reminded me of the way the fluff was plastered down on the skin of the drowned chicks that the strange man had been picking up, up in my mother's chicken yard.

I took a few steps up the path to the cabin, and then I saw that the drainage water had washed a lot of trash and filth out from under Dellie's house. Up toward the porch, the ground was not clean any more. Old pieces of rag, two or three rusted cans, pieces of rotten rope, some hunks of old dog dung, broken glass, old paper, and all sorts of things like that had washed out from under Dellie's house to foul her clean yard. It looked just as bad as the yards of the other cabins, or worse. It was worse, as a matter of fact, because it was a surprise. I had never thought of all that filth being under Dellie's house. It was not anything against Dellie that the stuff had been under the cabin. Trash will get under any house. But I did not think of that when I saw the foulness which had washed out on the ground which Dellie sometimes used to sweep with a twig broom to make nice and clean.

I picked my way past the filth, being careful not to get my bare feet on it, and mounted to Dellie's door. When I knocked, I heard her voice telling me to come in.

It was dark inside the cabin, after the daylight, but I could make out Dellie piled up in bed under a quilt, and Little Jebb crouched by the hearth, where a low fire simmered. "Howdy," I said to Dellie, "how you feeling?"

Her big eyes, the whites surprising and glaring in the black face, fixed on me as I stood there, but she did not reply. It did not look like Dellie, or act like Dellie, who would grumble and bustle around our kitchen, talking to herself, scolding me or Little Jebb, clanking pans, making all sorts of unnecessary noises and mutterings like an old-fashioned black steam thrasher engine when it has got up an extra head of steam and keeps popping the governor and rumbling and shaking on its wheels. But now Dellie just lay up there on the bed, under the patch-work quilt, and turned the black face, which I scarcely recognized, and the glaring white eyes to me.

"How you feeling?" I repeated.

"I'se sick," the voice said croakingly out of the strange black face which was not attached to Dellie's big, squat body, but stuck out from under a pile of tangled bedclothes. Then the voice added: "Mighty sick."

"I'm sorry," I managed to say.

The eyes remained fixed on me for a moment, then they left me and the head rolled back on the pillow. "Sorry," the voice said, in a flat way which wasn't question or statement of anything. It was just the empty word put into the air with no meaning or expression, to float off like a feather or a puff of smoke, while the big eyes, with the whites like the peeled white of hard-boiled eggs, stared at the ceiling.

"Dellie," I said after a minute, "there's a tramp up at the house. He's got a knife."

She was not listening. She closed her eyes.

I tiptoed over to the hearth where Jebb was and crouched beside him. We began to talk in low voices. I was asking him to get out his train and play train. Old Jebb had put spool wheels on three cigar boxes and put wire links between the boxes to make a train for Jebb. The box that was the locomotive had the top closed and a length of broom stick for a smoke stack. Jebb didn't want to get the train out, but I told him I would go home if he didn't. So he got the train, and the colored rocks, and fossils of crinoid stems, and other junk he used for the load, and we began to push it around, talking the way we thought trainmen talked, making a chuck-chucking sound under the breath for the noise of the locomotive and now and then uttering low, cautious toots for the whistle. We got so interested in playing train that the toots got louder. Then, before he thought, Jebb gave a good, loud *toot-toot*, blowing for a crossing.

"Come here," the voice said from the bed.

Jebb got up slow from his hands and knees, giving me a sudden, naked, inimical look.

"Come here!" the voice said.

Jebb went to the bed. Dellie propped herself weakly up on one arm, muttering, "Come closer."

Jebb stood closer.

"Last thing I do, I'm gonna do it," Dellie said. "Done tole you to be quiet."

Then she slapped him. It was an awful slap, more awful for the kind of weakness which it came from and brought to focus. I had seen her slap Jebb before, but the slapping had always been the kind of easy slap you would expect from a good-natured, grumbling Negro woman like Dellie. But this was different. It was awful. It was so awful that Jebb didn't make a sound. The tears just popped out and ran down his face, and his breath came sharp, like gasps.

Dellie fell back. "Cain't even be sick," she said to the ceiling. "Git sick and they won't even let you lay. They tromp all over you. Cain't even be sick." Then she closed her eyes.

I went out of the room. I almost ran getting to the door, and I did run across the porch and down the steps and across the yard, not caring whether or not I stepped on the filth which had washed out from under the cabin. I ran almost all the way home. Then I thought about my mother catching me with the bare feet. So I went down to the stables.

I heard a noise in the crib, and opened the door. There was Big Jebb, sitting on an old nail keg, shelling corn into a bushel basket. I went in, pulling the door shut behind me, and crouched on the floor near him. I crouched there for a couple of minutes before either of us spoke, and watched him shelling the corn.

He had very big hands, knotted and grayish at the joints, with calloused palms which seemed to be streaked with rust with the rust coming up between the fingers to show from the back. His hands were so strong and tough that he could take a big ear of corn and rip the grains right off the cob with the palm of his hand, all in one motion, like a machine. "Work long as me," he would say, "and the good Lawd'll give you a hand lak cassion won't nuthin' hurt." And his hands did look like cast iron, old cast iron streaked with rust.

He was an old man, up in his seventies, thirty years or more older than Dellie, but he was strong as a bull. He was a squat sort of man, heavy in the shoulders, with remarkably long arms, the kind of build they say the river natives have on the Congo from paddling so much in their boats. He had a round bullet-head, set on powerful shoulders. His skin was very black, and the thin hair on his head was now grizzled like tufts of old cotton batting. He had small eyes and a flat nose, not big, and the kindest and wisest old face in the world, the blunt, sad, wise face of an old animal peering tolerantly out on the goings-on of the merely human creatures before him. He was a good man, and I loved him next to my mother and father. I crouched there on the floor of the crib and watched him shell corn with the rusty cast-iron hands, while he looked down at me out of the little eyes set in the blunt face.

"Dellie says she's might sick," I said.

"Yeah," he said.

"What's she sick from?"

"Woman-mizry," he said.

"What's woman-mizry?"

"Hit comes on 'em," he said. "Hit just comes on 'em when the time comes."

"What is it?"

"Hit is the change," he said. "Hit is the change of life and time."

"What changes?"

"You too young to know."

"Tell me."

"Time come and you find out everthing."

I knew that there was no use in asking him any more. When I asked him things and he said that, I always knew that he would not tell me. So I continued to crouch there and watch him. Now that I had sat there a little while, I was cold again.

"What you shiver fer?" he asked me.

"I'm cold. I'm cold because it's blackberry winter," I said.

"Maybe 'tis and maybe 'tain't," he said.

"My mother says it is."

"Ain't sayen Miss Sallie doan know and ain't sayen she do. But folks doan know everthing."

"Why isn't it blackberry winter."

"Too late fer blackberry winter. Blackberries done bloomed."

"She said it was."

"Blackberry winter just a leetle cold spell. Hit come and then hit go away, and hit is growed summer of a sudden lak a gunshot. Ain't no tellen hit will go way this time."

"It's June," I said.

"June," he replied with great contempt. "That what folks say. What June mean? Maybe hit is come cold to stay."

"Why?"

"Cause this-here old yearth is tahrd. Hit is tahrd and ain't gonna perduce. Lawd let hit come rain one time forty days and forty nights, 'cause He wus tahrd of sinful folks. Maybe this-here old yearth say to the Lawd, Lawd, I done plum tahrd, Lawd, lemme rest. And Lawd say, Yearth, you done yore best, you give 'em cawn and you give 'em taters, and all they think on is they gut, and, Yearth, you kin take a rest."

"What will happen?"

"Folks will eat up everthing. The yearth won't perduce no more. Folks cut down all the trees and burn 'em cause they cold, and the yearth won't grow no more. I been tellen 'em. I been tellen folks. Sayen, maybe this year, hit is the time. But they doan listen to me, how the yearth is tahrd. Maybe this year they find out."

"Will everything die?"

"Everthing and everbody, hit will be so."

"This year?"

"Ain't no tellen. Maybe this year."

"My mother said it is blackberry winter," I said confidently, and got up.

"Ain't sayen nuthin' agin Miss Sallie," he said.

I went to the door of the crib. I was really cold now. Running, I had got up a sweat and now I was worse.

I hung on the door, looking at Jebb, who was shelling corn again.

"There's a tramp came to the house," I said. I had almost forgotten the tramp.

"Yeah."

"He came by the back way. What was he doing down there in the storm?"

"They comes and they goes," he said, "and ain't no tellen."

"He had a mean knife."

"The good ones and the bad ones, they comes and they goes. Storm or sun, light or dark. They is folks and they comes and they goes lak folks."

I hung on the door, shivering.

He studied me a moment, then said, "You git on to the house. You ketch yore death. Then what yore mammy say?"

I hesitated.

"You git," he said.

When I came to the back yard, I saw that my father was standing by the back porch and the tramp was walking toward him. They began talking before I reached them, but I got there just as my father was saying, "I'm sorry, but I haven't got any work. I got all the hands on the place I need now. I won't need any extra until wheat thrashing."

The stranger made no reply, just looked at my father.

My father took out his leather coin purse, and got out a half-dollar. He held it toward the man. "This is for half a day," he said.

The man looked at the coin, and then at my father, making no motion to take the money. But that was the right amount. A dollar a day was what you paid them back in 1910. And the man hadn't even worked half a day.

Then the man reached out and took the coin. He dropped it into the right side pocket of his coat. Then he said, very slowly and without feeling: "I didn't want to work on your—farm."

He used the word which they would have frailed me to death for using.

I looked at my father's face and it was streaked white under the sunburn. Then he said, "Get off this place. Get off this place or I won't be responsible."

The man dropped his right hand into his pants pocket. It was the pocket where he kept the knife. I was just about to yell to my father about the knife when the hand came back out with nothing in it. The man gave a kind of twisted grin, showing where the teeth had been knocked out above

the new scar. I thought that instant how maybe he had tried before to pull
a knife on somebody else and had got his teeth knocked out.

So now he just gave that twisted, sickish grin out of the unmemorable,
grayish face, and then spat on the brick path. The glob landed just about
six inches from the toe of my father's right boot. My father looked down at
it, and so did I. I thought that if the glob had hit my father's boot something would have happened. I looked down and saw the bright glob, and
on one side of it my father's strong cowhide boots, with the brass eyelets
and the leather thongs, heavy boots splashed with good red mud and set
solid on the bricks, and on the other side the pointed-toe, broken, black
shoes, on which the mud looked so sad and out of place. Then I saw one
of the black shoes move a little, just a twitch first, then a real step backward.

The man moved in a quarter circle to the end of the porch, with my
father's steady gaze upon him all the while. At the end of the porch, the
man reached up to the shelf where the wash pans were to get his little
newspaper-wrapped parcel. Then he disappeared around the corner of the
house and my father mounted the porch and went into the kitchen without
a word.

I followed around the house to see what the man would do. I wasn't
afraid of him now, no matter if he did have that knife. When I got around
in front, I saw him going out the yard gate and starting up the drive toward
the pike. So I ran to catch up with him. He was sixty yards or so up the
drive before I caught up.

I did not walk right up even with him at first, but trailed him, the way
a kid will, about seven or eight feet behind, now and then running two or
three steps in order to hold my place against his longer stride. When I first
came up behind him, he turned to give me a look, just a meaningless look,
and then fixed his eyes up the drive and kept on walking.

When we had got around the bend in the drive which cut the house
from sight, and were going along by the edge of the woods, I decided to
come up even with him. I ran a few steps, and was by his side, or almost,
but some feet off to the right. I walked along in this position for a while,
and he never noticed me. I walked along until we got within sight of the
big gate that let on the pike.

Then I said: "Where did you come from?"

He looked at me then with a look which seemed almost surprised that I
was there. Then he said, "It ain't none of yore business."

We went on another fifty feet.

Then I said, "Where are you going?"

He stopped, studied me dispassionately for a moment, then suddenly
took a step toward me and leaned his face down at me. The lips jerked
back, but not in any grin, to show where the teeth were knocked out and
to make the scar on the lower lip come white with the tension.

He said: "Stop following me. You don't stop following me and I cut yore
throat, you little son-of-a-bitch."

Then he went on to the gate, and up the pike.

That was thirty-five years ago. Since that time my father and mother have died. I was still a boy, but a big boy, when my father got cut on the blade of a mowing machine and died of lockjaw. My mother sold the place and went to town to live with her sister. But she never took hold after my father's death, and she died within three years, right in middle life. My aunt always said, "Sallie just died of a broken heart, she was so devoted." Dellie is dead, too, but she died, I heard, quite a long time after we sold the farm.

As for Little Jebb, he grew up to be a mean and ficey Negro. He killed another Negro in a fight and got sent to the penitentiary, where he is yet, the last I heard tell. He probably grew up to be mean and ficey from just being picked on so much by the children of the other tenants, who were jealous of Jebb and Dellie for being thrifty and clever and being white-folks' niggers.

Old Jebb lived forever. I saw him ten years ago and he was about a hundred then, and not looking much different. He was living in town then, on relief—that was back in the Depression—when I went to see him. He said to me: "Too strong to die. When I was a young feller just comen on and seen how things wuz, I prayed the Lawd. I said, Oh, Lawd, gimme strength and meke me strong fer to do and to in-dure. The Lawd heark-ened to my prayer. He give me strength. I was in-duren proud fer being strong and me much man. The Lawd give me my prayer and my strength. But now He done gone off and fergot me and left me alone with my strength. A man doan know what to pray fer, and him mortal."

Jebb is probably living yet, as far as I know.

That is what has happened since the morning when the tramp leaned his face down at me and showed his teeth and said: "Stop following me. You don't stop following me and I cut yore throat, you little son-of-a-bitch." That was what he said, for me not to follow him. But I did follow him, all the years.

QUESTIONS

"Blackberry Winter"

1. What is the point of view in this story?

2. How is the June day on which the story takes place different from any other June day young Seth has known? Why can't he go barefoot? What is "blackberry winter"?

3. Take a close look at the narrator's long discussion of time near the start of the story. How does he describe his childhood perception of time? Where else in the story do other characters describe time and change? How do these passages relate to the story's theme?

4. Describe the tramp. What incongruities does Seth notice in regard to the tramp's dress and behavior? What do his clothes, his facial features, and his tone of voice reveal about him? What is so sinister and alien about the tramp?

5. How does the narrator describe the drowned chicks? What other images of and references to death can you find in the story? What do these references have to do with the story's theme?

6. Describe Seth's parents and the quality of his life with them. What physical details does Warren emphasize in his description of Seth's mother and father? In what sense can Seth's childhood world be seen as a kind of paradise?

7. "Blackberry Winter" has an episodic structure: the story consists of a string of events, in each of which young Seth witnesses something depressing or unsavory he has never been exposed to before. Describe each of these episodes and explain how it contributes to the story's meaning. In what sense does this string of events constitute a quest—a difficult, painful, but ultimately essential journey—for the young hero?

8. How does the narrator's life change forever on this particular day? In what ways does the tramp serve as the "herald" who issues the call to change? In what way does Seth undergo a fall from innocence to experience, from an eternal, sheltered, carefree world into the world of time, history, transience, and death?

9. Look at the language Warren uses in the paragraphs that describe old Jebb. How does Warren make highly skillful use of imagery to portray Jebb as somehow more than ordinarily human? What is Jebb's function in the story?

10. Explain the last line of the story. In what sense does Seth follow the tramp?

Paul's Case

WILLA CATHER

It was Paul's afternoon to appear before the faculty of the Pittsburgh High School to account for his various misdemeanours. He had been suspended a week ago, and his father had called at the Principal's office and confessed his perplexity about his son. Paul entered the faculty room suave and smiling. His clothes were a trifle outgrown, and the tan velvet on the collar of his open overcoat was frayed and worn; but for all that there was something of the dandy about him, and he wore an opal pin in his neatly knotted black four-in-hand, and a red carnation in his buttonhole. This latter adornment the faculty somehow felt was not properly significant of the contrite spirit befitting a boy under the ban of suspension.

Paul was tall for his age and very thin, with high, cramped shoulders and a narrow chest. His eyes were remarkable for a certain hysterical brilliancy, and he continually used them in a conscious, theatrical sort of way, peculiarly offensive in a boy. The pupils were abnormally large, as though he were addicted to belladonna, but there was a glassy glitter about them which that drug does not produce.

When questioned by the Principal as to why he was there, Paul stated, politely enough, that he wanted to come back to school. This was a lie, but Paul was quite accustomed to lying; found it, indeed, indispensable for overcoming friction. His teachers were asked to state their respective charges against him, which they did with such a rancour and aggrievedness as evinced that this was not a usual case. Disorder and impertinence were among the offences named, yet each of his instructors felt that it was scarcely possible to put into words the real cause of the trouble, which lay in a sort of hysterically defiant manner of the boy's; in the contempt which they all knew he felt for them, and which he seemingly made not the least effort to conceal. Once, when he had been making a synopsis of a paragraph at the blackboard, his English teacher had stepped to his side and attempted to guide his hand. Paul had started back with a shudder and thrust his hands violently behind him. The astonished woman could scarcely have been more hurt and embarrassed had he struck at her. The insult was so involuntary and definitely personal as to be unforgettable. In one way and another, he had made all his teachers, men and women alike, conscious of the same feeling of physical aversion. In one class he habitually sat with his hand shading his eyes; in another he always looked out of the window during the recitation; in another he made a running commentary on the lecture, with humorous intent.

His teachers felt this afternoon that his whole attitude was symbolized by his shrug and his flippantly red carnation flower, and they fell upon him without mercy, his English teacher leading the pack. He stood through it smiling, his pale lips parted over his white teeth. (His lips were continually twitching, and he had a habit of raising his eyebrows that was contemptuous and irritating to the last degree.) Older boys than Paul had broken down and shed tears under that ordeal, but his set smile did not once desert him, and his only sign of discomfort was the nervous trembling of the fingers that toyed with the buttons of his overcoat, and an occasional jerking of the other hand which held his hat. Paul was always smiling, always glancing about him, seeming to feel that people might be watching him and trying to detect something. This conscious expression, since it was as far as possible from boyish mirthfulness, was usually attributed to insolence or "smartness."

As the inquisition proceeded, one of his instructors repeated an impertinent remark of the boy's, and the Principal asked him whether he thought that a courteous speech to make to a woman. Paul shrugged his shoulders slightly and his eyebrows twitched.

"I don't know," he replied. "I didn't mean to be polite or impolite, either. I guess it's a sort of way I have, of saying things regardless."

The Principal asked him whether he didn't think that a way it would be well to get rid of. Paul grinned and said he guessed so. When he was told that he could go, he bowed gracefully and went out. His bow was like a repetition of the scandalous red carnation.

His teachers were in despair, and his drawing-master voiced the feeling of them all when he declared there was something about the boy which none of them understood. He added: "I don't really believe that smile of his comes altogether from insolence; there's something sort of haunted about it. The boy is not strong, for one thing. There is something wrong about the fellow."

The drawing-master had come to realize that, in looking at Paul, one saw only his white teeth and the forced animation of his eyes. One warm afternoon the boy had gone to sleep at his drawing-board, and his master had noted with amazement what a white, blue-veined face it was; drawn and wrinkled like an old man's about the eyes, the lips twitching even in his sleep.

His teachers left the building dissatisfied and unhappy; humiliated to have felt so vindictive toward a mere boy, to have uttered this feeling in cutting terms, and to have set each other on, as it were, in the gruesome game of intemperate reproach. One of them remembered having seen a miserable street cat set at bay by a ring of tormentors.

As for Paul, he ran down the hill whistling the Soldiers' Chorus from

"Faust," looking wildly behind him now and then to see whether some of his teachers were not there to witness his light-heartedness. As it was now late in the afternoon and Paul was on duty that evening as usher at Carnegie Hall, he decided that he would not go home to supper.

When he reached the concert hall, the doors were not yet open. It was chilly outside, and he decided to go up into the picture gallery—always deserted at this hour—where there were some of Raffelli's gay studies of Paris streets and an airy blue Venetian scene or two that always exhilarated him. He was delighted to find no one in the gallery but the old guard, who sat in the corner, a newspaper on his knee, a black patch over one eye and the other closed. Paul possessed himself of the place and walked confidently up and down, whistling under his breath. After a while he sat down before a blue Rico and lost himself. When he bethought him to look at his watch, it was after seven o'clock, and he rose with a start and ran downstairs, making a face at Augustus Caesar, peering out from the cast-room, and an evil gesture at the Venus of Milo as he passed her on the stairway.

When Paul reached the ushers' dressing-room, half-a-dozen boys were there already, and he began excitedly to tumble into his uniform. It was one of the few that at all approached fitting, and Paul thought it very becoming—though he knew the tight, straight coat accentuated his narrow chest, about which he was exceedingly sensitive. He was always excited while he dressed, twanging all over to the tuning of the strings and the preliminary flourishes of the horns in the music-room; but tonight he seemed quite beside himself, and he teased and plagued the boys until, telling him that he was crazy, they put him down on the floor and sat on him.

Somewhat calmed by his suppression, Paul dashed out to the front of the house to seat the early comers. He was a model usher. Gracious and smiling he ran up and down the aisles. Nothing was too much trouble for him; he carried messages and brought programmes as though it were his greatest pleasure in life, and all the people in his section thought him a charming boy, feeling that he remembered and admired them. As the house filled, he grew more and more vivacious and animated, and the colour came to his cheeks and lips. It was very much as though this were a great reception and Paul were the host. Just as the musicians came out to take their places, his English teacher arrived with cheques for the seats which a prominent manufacturer had taken for the season. She betrayed some embarrassment when she handed Paul the tickets, and a hauteur which subsequently made her feel very foolish. Paul was startled for a moment, and had the feeling of wanting to put her out; what business had she here among all these fine people and gay colours? He looked her over and decided that she was not appropriately dressed and must be a fool to sit downstairs in such togs. The tickets had probably been sent her out of kindness, he reflected, as he put down a seat for her, and she had about as much right to sit there as he had.

When the symphony began, Paul sank into one of the rear seats with a long sigh of relief, and lost himself as he had done before the Rico. It was not that symphonies, as such, meant anything in particular to Paul, but the first sight of the instruments seemed to free some hilarious spirit within him; something that struggled there like the Genius in the bottle found by the Arab fisherman. He felt a sudden zest of life; the lights danced before his eyes and the concert hall blazed into unimaginable splendour. When the soprano soloist came on, Paul forgot even the nastiness of his teacher's being there, and gave himself up to the peculiar intoxication such personages always had for him. The soloist chanced to be a German woman, by no means in her first youth, and the mother of many children; but she wore a satin gown and a tiara, and she had that indefinable air of achievement that world-shine upon her, which always blinded Paul to any possible defects.

After a concert was over, Paul was often irritable and wretched until he got to sleep—and to-night he was even more than usually restless. He had the feeling of not being able to let down; of its being impossible to give up this delicious excitement which was the only thing that could be called living at all. During the last number he withdrew and, after hastily changing his clothes in the dressing-room, slipped out to the side door where the singer's carriage stood. Here he began pacing rapidly up and down the walk, waiting to see her come out.

Over yonder the Schenley, in its vacant stretch, loomed big and square through the fine rain, the windows of its twelve stories glowing like those of a lighted cardboard house under a Christmas tree. All the actors and singers of any importance stayed there when they were in the city, and a number of the big manufacturers of the place lived there in the winter. Paul had often hung about the hotel, watching the people go in and out, longing to enter and leave schoolmasters and dull care behind him forever.

At last the singer came out, accompanied by the conductor, who helped her into her carriage and closed the door with a cordial *auf wiedersehen*—which set Paul to wondering whether she were not an old sweetheart of his. Paul followed the carriage over to the hotel, walking so rapidly as not to be far from the entrance when the singer alighted and disappeared behind the swinging glass doors which were opened by a Negro in a tall hat and a long coat. In the moment that the door was ajar, it seemed to Paul that he, too, entered. He seemed to feel himself go after her up the steps, into the warm, lighted building, into an exotic, a tropical world of shiny, glistening surfaces and basking ease. He reflected upon the mysterious dishes that were brought into the dining-room, the green bottles in buckets of ice, as he had seen them in the supper-party pictures of the Sunday supplement. A quick gust of wind brought the rain down with sudden vehemence, and Paul was startled to find that he was still outside in the slush of the gravel driveway; that his boots were letting in the water and his scanty overcoat was clinging wet about him; that the lights in front of the concert hall were out, and that the rain was driving in sheets between him and the orange glow of the windows above him. There it was, what he wanted—tangibly before him, like the fairy world of a Christmas pantomime; as the rain beat in his face. Paul wondered whether he were destined always to shiver in the black night outside, looking up at it.

He turned and walked reluctantly toward the car tracks. The end had to come sometime; his father in his night-clothes at the top of the stairs, explanations that did not explain, hastily improvised fictions that were forever tripping him up, his upstairs room and its horrible yellow wallpaper, the creaking bureau with the greasy plush collar-box, and over his painted wooden bed the pictures of George Washington and John Calvin, and the framed motto, 'Feed my Lambs,' which had been worked in red worsted by his mother, whom Paul could not remember.

Half an hour later, Paul alighted from the Negley Avenue car and went slowly down one of the side streets off the main thoroughfare. It was a highly respectable street, where all the houses were exactly alike, and where businessmen of moderate means begot and reared large families of children, all of whom went to Sabbath-School and learned the shorter catechism, and were interested in arithmetic; all of whom were as exactly alike as their homes, and of a piece with the monotony in which they lived. Paul never went up Cordelia Street without a shudder of loathing. His home was next the house of the Cumberland minister. He approached it to-night with the nerveless sense of defeat, the hopeless feeling of sinking back forever into ugliness and commonness that he had always had when he came home. The moment he turned into Cordelia Street he felt the waters close above his head. After each of these orgies of living, he experienced all the physical depression which follows a debauch; the loathing of respectable beds, of common food, of a house permeated by kitchen odours; a shuddering repulsion for the flavourless, colourless mass of every-day existence; a morbid desire for cool things and soft lights and fresh flowers.

The nearer he approached the house, the more absolutely unequal Paul felt to the sight of it all: his ugly sleeping chamber; the cold bathroom with the grimy zinc tub, the cracked mirror, the dripping spigots; his father, at the top of the stairs, his hairy legs sticking out from his nightshirt, his feet thrust into carpet slippers. He was so much later than usual that there would certainly be enquiries and reproaches. Paul stopped short before the door. He felt that he could not be accosted by his father to-night; that he could not toss again on that miserable bed. He would not go in. He would tell his father that he had no car-fare, and it was raining so hard he had gone home with one of the boys and stayed all night.

Meanwhile, he was wet and cold. He went around to the back of the house and tried one of the basement windows, found it open, raised it cautiously, and scrambled down the cellar wall to the floor. There he stood, holding his breath, terrified by the noise he had made; but the floor above him was silent, and there was no creak on the stairs. He found a soapbox, and carried it over to the soft ring of light that streamed from the furnace door, and sat down. He was horribly afraid of rats, so he did not try to sleep, but sat looking distrustfully at the dark, still terrified lest he might have awakened his father.

In such reactions, after one of the experiences which made days and nights out of the dreary blanks of the calendar, when his senses were deadened, Paul's head was always singularly clear. Suppose his father had heard him getting in at the window and had come down and shot him for a burglar? Then, again, suppose his father had come down, pistol in hand, and he had cried out in time to save himself, and his father had been horrified to think how nearly he had killed him? Then, again, suppose a day should come when his father would remember that night, and wish there had been no warning cry to stay his hand? With this last supposition Paul entertained himself until daybreak.

The following Sunday was fine; the sodden November chill was broken by the last flash of autumnal summer. In the morning Paul had to go to church and Sabbath-School, as always. On seasonable Sunday afternoons the burghers of Cordelia Street usually sat out on their front "stoops," and talked to their neighbours on the next stoop, or called to those across the street in neighbourly fashion. The men sat placidly on gay cushions placed upon the steps that led down to the sidewalk, while the women, in their Sunday "waists," sat in rockers on the cramped porches, pretending to be greatly at their ease. The children played in the streets; there were so many of them that the place resembled the recreation grounds of a kindergarten. The men on the steps, all in their shirtsleeves, their vests unbuttoned, sat with their legs well apart, their stomachs comfortably protruding, and talked of the prices of things, or told anecdotes of the sagacity of their various chiefs and overlords. They occasionally looked over the multitude of squabbling children, listened affectionately to their high-pitched, nasal voices, smiling to see their own proclivities reproduced in their offspring, and interspersed their legends of the iron kings with remarks about their sons' progress at school, their grades in arithmetic, and the amounts they had saved in their toy banks.

On this last Sunday of November, Paul sat all the afternoon on the lowest step of his "stoop," staring into the street, while his sisters, in their rockers, were talking to the minister's daughters next door about how many shirtwaists they had made in the last week, and how many waffles someone had eaten at the last church supper. When the weather was warm, and his father was in a particularly jovial frame of mind, the girls made lemonade, which was always brought out in a red-glass pitcher, ornamented with forget-me-nots in blue enamel. This the girls thought very fine, and the neighbours joked about the suspicious colour of the pitcher.

Today Paul's father, on the top step, was talking to a young man who shifted a restless baby from knee to knee. He happened to be the young man who was daily held up to Paul as a model, and after whom it was his father's dearest hope that he would pattern. This young man was of a ruddy complexion, with a compressed, red mouth, and faded, nearsighted eyes, over which he wore thick spectacles, with gold bows that curved about his ears. He was clerk to one of the magnates of a great steel corporation and was looked upon in Cordelia Street as a young man with a future. There was a story that, some five years ago—he was now barely twenty-six—he had been a trifle "dissipated," but in order to curb his appetites and save the loss of time and strength that a sowing of wild oats might have entailed, he had taken his chief's advice, oft reiterated to his employees, and at twenty-one had married the first woman whom he could persuade to share his fortunes. She happened to be an angular schoolmistress, much older than he, who also wore thick glasses, and who had now borne him four children, all nearsighted like herself.

The young man was relating how his chief, now cruising in the Mediterranean, kept in touch with all the details of the business, arranging his office hours on his yacht just as though he were at home, and "knocking off work enough to keep two stenographers busy." His father told, in turn, the plan his corporation was considering, of putting in an electric railway plant at Cairo. Paul snapped his teeth; he had an awful apprehension that they might spoil it all before he got there. yet he rather liked to hear these legends of the iron kings, that were told and retold on Sundays and holidays; these stories of palaces in Venice, yachts on the Mediterranean, and high play at Monte Carlo appealed to his fancy, and he was interested in the triumphs of cash-boys who had become famous, though he had no mind for the cash-boy stage.

After supper was over, and he had helped to dry the dishes, Paul nervously asked his father whether he could go to George's to get some help in his geometry, and still more nervously asked for car-fare. This latter request he had to repeat, as his father, on principle, did not like to hear requests for money, whether much or little. He asked Paul whether he could not go to some boy who lived nearer, and told him that he ought not to leave his school work until Sunday; but he gave him the dime. He was not a poor man, but he had a worthy ambition to come up in the world. His only reason for allowing Paul to usher was that he thought a boy ought to be earning a little.

Paul bounded upstairs, scrubbed the greasy odour of dishwater from his hands with the ill-smelling soap he hated, and then shook over his fingers a few drops of violet water from the bottle he kept hidden in his drawer. He left the house with his geometry conspicuously under his arm, and the moment he got out of Cordelia Street and boarded a downtown car, he shook off the lethargy of two deadening days, and began to live again.

The leading juvenile of the permanent stock company which played at one of the downtown theatres was an acquaintance of Paul's, and the boy had been invited to drop in at the Sunday-night rehearsals whenever he could. For more than a year Paul had spent every available moment loitering about Charley Edwards's dressing-room. He had won a place among Edwards's following, not only because the young actor, who could not afford to employ a dresser, often found him useful, but because he recognized in Paul something akin to what churchmen term "vocation."

It was at the theatre and at Carnegie Hall that Paul really lived; the rest was but a sleep and a forgetting. This was Paul's fairy tale, and it had for him all the allurement of a secret love. The moment he inhaled the gassy, painty, dusty odour behind the scenes, he breathed like a prisoner set free, and felt within him the possibility of doing or saying splendid, brilliant things. The moment the cracked orchestra beat out the overture from "Martha," or jerked at the serenade from "Rigoletto," all stupid and ugly things slid from him, and his senses were deliciously, yet delicately fired.

Perhaps it was because, in Paul's world, the natural nearly always wore the guise of ugliness, that a certain element of artificiality seemed to him necessary in beauty. Perhaps it was because his experience of life elsewhere was so full of Sabbath-School picnics, petty economies, wholesome advice as to how to succeed in life, and the unescapable odours of cooking, that he found this existence so alluring, these smartly-clad men and women so attractive, that he was so moved by these starry apple orchards that bloomed perennially under the limelight. It would be difficult to put it strongly enough how convincingly the stage entrance of that theatre was for Paul the actual portal of Romance. Certainly none of the company ever suspected it, least of all Charley Edwards. It was very like the old stories that used to float about London of fabulously rich Jews, who had subterranean halls, with palms, and fountains, and soft lamps and richly apparelled women who never saw the disenchanting light of London day. So, in the midst of that smoke-palled city, enamoured of figures and grimy toil, Paul had his secret temple, his wishing-carpet, his bit of blue-and-white Mediterranean shore bathed in perpetual sunshine.

Several of Paul's teachers had a theory that his imagination had been perverted by garish fiction; but the truth was he scarcely ever read at all. The books at home were not such as would either tempt or corrupt a youthful mind, and as for reading the novels that some of his friends urged upon him—well, he got what he wanted much more quickly from music; any sort of music, from an orchestra to a barrel-organ. He needed only the spark, the indescribable thrill that made his imagination master of his senses, and he could make plots and pictures enough of his own. It was equally true that he was not stage-struck—not, at any rate, in the usual acceptation of that expression. He had no desire to become an actor, any more than he had to become a musician. He felt no necessity to do any of these things; what he wanted was to see, to be in the atmosphere, float on the wave of it, to be carried out, blue league after league, away from everything.

After a night behind the scenes, Paul found the schoolroom more than ever repulsive; the bare floors and naked walls; the prosy men who never wore frock coats, or violets in their buttonholes; the women with their dull gowns, shrill voices, and pitiful seriousness about prepositions that govern the dative. He could not bear to have the other pupils think, for a moment, that he took these people seriously; he must convey to them that he considered it all trivial, and was there only by way of a joke, anyway. He had autographed pictures of all the members of the stock company which he showed his classmates, telling them the most incredible stories of his familiarity with these people, of his acquaintance with the soloists who came to Carnegie Hall, his suppers with them and the flowers he sent them. When these stories lost their effect, and his audience grew listless, he would bid all the boys goodbye, announcing that he was going to travel for a while, going to Naples, to California, to Egypt. Then, next Monday, he would slip back, conscious and nervously smiling; his sister was ill, and he would have to defer his voyage until spring.

Matters went steadily worse with Paul at school. In the itch to let his instructors know how heartily he despised them, and how thoroughly he was appreciated elsewhere, he mentioned once or twice that he had no time to fool with theorems; adding—with a twitch of the eyebrows and a touch of that nervous bravado which so perplexed them—that he was help-ing the people down at the stock company; they were old friends of his.

The upshot of the matter was that the Principal went to Paul's father, and Paul was taken out of school and put to work. The manager at Carnegie Hall was told to get another usher in his stead; the doorkeeper at the the-atre was warned not to admit him to the house; and Charley Edwards remorsefully promised the boy's father not to see him again.

The members of the stock company were vastly amused when some of Paul's stories reached them—especially the women. They were hard-working women, most of them supporting indolent husbands or brothers, and they laughed rather bitterly at having stirred the boy to such fervid and florid inventions. They agreed with the faculty and with his father, that Paul's was a bad case.

The east-bound train was ploughing through a January snowstorm; the dull dawn was beginning to show grey when the engine whistled a mile out of Newark. Paul started up from the seat where he had lain curled in uneasy slumber, rubbed the breath-misted window-glass with his hand, and peered out. The snow was whirling in curling eddies above the white bottom lands, and the drifts lay already deep in the fields and along the fences, while here and there the long dead grass and dried weed stalks protruded black above it. Lights shone from the scattered houses, and a gang of labourers who stood beside the track waved their lanterns.

Paul had slept very little, and he felt grimy and uncomfortable. He had made the all-night journey in a day coach because he was afraid if he took a Pullman he might be seen by some Pittsburgh business man who had noticed him in Denny & Carson's office. When the whistle woke him, he clutched quickly at his breast pocket, glancing about him with an uncertain smile. But the little, clay-bespattered Italians were still sleeping, the slat-ternly women across the aisle were in open-mouthed oblivion and even the crumby, crying babies were for the nonce stilled. Paul settled back to struggle with his impatience as best he could.

When he arrived at the Jersey City station, he hurried through his breakfast, manifestly ill at east and keeping a sharp eye about him. After he reached the Twenty-Third Street station, he consulted a cabman, and had himself driven to a men's furnishing establishment which was just opening for the day. He spent upward of two hours there, buying with endless reconsidering and great care. His new street suit he put on in the fitting-room; the frock coat and dress clothes he had bundled into the cab with his new shirts. Then he drove to a hatter's and a shoe house. His next errand was at Tiffany's, where he selected silver-mounted brushes and a scarf-pin. He would not wait to have his silver marked, he said. Lastly, he stopped at a trunk shop on Broadway, and had his purchases packed into various travelling-bags.

It was a little after one o'clock when he drove up to the Waldorf, and, after settling with the cabman, went into the office. He registered from Washington; said his mother and father had been abroad, and that he had come down to await the arrival of their steamer. He told his story plausibly and had no trouble, since he offered to pay for them in advance, in engaging his rooms; a sleeping-room, sitting-room, and bath.

Not once, but a hundred times Paul had planned this entry into New York. He had gone over every detail of it with Charley Edwards, and in his scrapbook at home there were pages of description about New York hotels, cut from the Sunday papers.

When he was shown to his sitting-room on the eighth floor, he saw at a glance that everything was as it should be; there was but one detail in his mental picture that the place did not realize, so he rang for the bell-boy and sent him down for flowers. He moved about nervously until the boy returned, putting away his new linen and fingering it delightedly as he did so. When the flowers came, he put them hastily into water, and then tumbled into a hot bath. Presently he came out of his white bathroom, resplendent in his new silk underwear, and playing with the tassels of his red robe. The snow was whirling so fiercely outside his windows that he could scarcely see across the street; but within, the air was deliciously soft and fragrant. He put the violets and jonquils on the tabouret beside the couch, and threw himself down with a long sigh, covering himself with a Roman blanket. He was thoroughly tired; he had been in such haste, he had stood up to such a strain, covered so much ground in the last twenty-four hours, that he wanted to think how it had all come about. Lulled by the sound of the wind, the warm air, and the cool fragrance of the flowers, he sank into deep, drowsy retrospection.

It had been wonderfully simple; when they had shut him out of the theatre and concert hall, when they had taken away his bone, the whole thing was virtually determined. The rest was a mere matter of opportunity. The only thing that at all surprised him was his own courage—for he realized well enough that he had always been tormented by fear, a sort of apprehensive dread that, of late years, as the meshes of the lies he had told closed about him, had been pulling the muscles of his body tighter and tighter. Until now, he could not remember a time when he had not been dreading something. Even when he was a little boy, it was always there—behind him, or before, or on either side. There had always been the shadowed corner, the dark place into which he dared not look, but from which something seemed always to be watching him—and Paul had done things that were not pretty to watch, he knew.

But now he had a curious sense of relief, as though he had at last thrown down the gauntlet to the thing in the corner.

Yet it was but a day since he had been sulking in the traces; but yesterday afternoon that he had been sent to the bank with Denny & Carson's deposit, as usual—but this time he was instructed to leave the book to be balanced. There was above two thousand dollars in cheques, and nearly a thousand in the banknotes which he had taken from the book and quietly transferred to his pocket. At the bank he had made out a new deposit slip. His nerves had been steady enough to permit of his returning to the office, where he had finished his work and asked for a full day's holiday to-morrow, Saturday, giving a perfectly reasonable pretext. The bank book he knew, would not be returned before Monday or Tuesday, and his father would be out of town for the next week. From the time he slipped the banknotes into his pocket until he boarded the night train for New York, he had not known a moment's hesitation.

How astonishingly easy it had all been; for here he was, the thing done; and this time there would be no awakening, no figure at the top of the stairs. He watched the snowflakes whirling by his window until he fell asleep.

When he awoke, it was four o'clock in the afternoon. He bounded up with a start; one of his precious days gone already! He spent nearly an hour in dressing, watching every stage of his toilet carefully in the mirror. Everything was quite perfect; he was exactly the kind of boy he had always wanted to be.

When he went downstairs, Paul took a carriage and drove up Fifth Avenue toward the Park. The snow had somewhat abated; carriages and tradesmen's wagons were hurrying soundlessly to and fro in the winter twilight; boys in woollen mufflers were shovelling off the doorsteps; the Avenue stages made fine spots of colour against the white street. Here and there on the corners whole flower gardens blooming behind glass windows, against which the snowflakes stuck and melted; violets, roses, carnations, lilies-of-the-valley—somehow vastly more lovely and alluring that they blossomed thus unnaturally in the snow. The Park itself was a wonderful stage winter-piece.

When he returned, the pause of the twilight had ceased, and the tune of the streets had changed. The snow was falling faster, lights streamed from the hotels that reared their many stories fearlessly up into the storm, defying the raging Atlantic winds. A long, black stream of carriages poured down the Avenue, intersected here and there by other streams, tending horizontally. There were a score of cabs about the entrance of his hotel, and his driver had to wait. Boys in livery were running in and out of the awning stretched across the sidewalk, up and down the red velvet carpet laid from the door to the street. Above, about, within it all, was the rumble and roar, the hurry and toss of thousands of human beings as hot for pleasure as himself, and on every side of him towered the glaring affirmation of the omnipotence of wealth.

The boy set his teeth and drew his shoulders together in a spasm of realization; the plot of all dramas, the text of all romances, the nerve-stuff of all sensations was whirling about him like the snowflakes. He burnt like a faggot in a tempest.

When Paul came down to dinner, the music of the orchestra floated up the elevator shaft to greet him. As he stepped into the thronged corridor, he sank back into one of the chairs against the wall to get his breath. The lights, the chatter, the perfumes, the bewildering medley of colour—he had, for a moment, the feeling of not being able to stand it. But only for a moment; these were his own people, he told himself. He went slowly about the corridors, through the waiting-rooms, smoking-rooms, reception-rooms, as though he were exploring the chambers of an enchanted palace, built and peopled for him alone.

When he reached the dining-room he sat down at a table near a window. The flowers, the white linen, the many-coloured wine-glasses, the gay toilettes of the women, the low popping of corks, the undulating repetitions of the "Blue Danube" from the orchestra, all flooded Paul's dream with bewildering radiance. When the roseate tinge of his champagne was added— that cold, precious, bubbling stuff that creamed and foamed in his glass— Paul wondered that there were honest men in the world at all. This was what all the world was fighting for, he reflected; this was what all the struggle was about. He doubted the reality of his past. Had he ever known a place called Cordelia Street, a place where fagged-looking business men boarded the early car? Mere rivets in a machine they seemed to Paul— sickening men, with combings of children's hair always hanging to their coats, and the smell of cooking in their clothes. Cordelia Street—Ah, that belonged to another time and country! Had he not always been thus, had he not sat here night after night, from as far back as he could remember, looking pensively over just such shimmering textures, and slowly twirling the stem of a glass like this one between his thumb and middle finger? He rather thought he had.

He was not in the least abashed or lonely. He had no especial desire to meet or to know any of these people; all he demanded was the right to look on and conjecture, to watch the pageant. The mere stage properties were all he contended for. Nor was he lonely later in the evening, in his loge at the Opera. He was entirely rid of his nervous misgivings, of his forced aggressiveness, of the imperative desire to show himself different from his surroundings. He felt now that his surroundings explained him. Nobody questioned the purple; he had only to wear it passively. He had only to glance down at his dress coat to reassure himself that here it would be impossible for anyone to humiliate him.

He found it hard to leave his beautiful sitting-room to go to bed that night, and sat long watching the raging storm from his turret window. When he went to sleep, it was with the lights turned on in his bedroom; partly because of his old timidity, and partly so that, if he should wake in the night, there would be no wretched moment of doubt, no horrible suspicion of yellow wallpaper, or of Washington and Calvin above his bed.

On Sunday morning the city was practically snowbound. Paul breakfasted late, and in the afternoon he fell in with a wild San Francisco boy, a freshman at Yale, who said he had run down for a "little flyer" over Sunday. The young man offered to show Paul the night side of the town, and the two boys went off together after dinner, not returning to the hotel until seven o'clock the next morning. They had started out in the confiding warmth of a champagne friendship, but their parting in the elevator was singularly cool. The freshman pulled himself together to make his train, and Paul went to bed. He awoke at two o'clock in the afternoon, very thirsty and dizzy, and rang for ice-water, coffee, and the Pittsburgh papers.

On the part of the hotel management, Paul excited no suspicion. There was this to be said for him, that he wore his spoils with dignity and in no way made himself conspicuous. His chief greediness lay in his ears and eyes, and his excesses were not offensive ones. His dearest pleasures were the grey winter twilights in his sitting-room; his quiet enjoyment of his flowers, his clothes, his wide divan, his cigarette, and his sense of power. He could not remember a time when he had felt so at peace with himself. The mere release from the necessity of petty lying, lying every day and every day, restored his self-respect. He had never lied for pleasure, even at school; but to make himself noticed and admired, to assert his difference from other Cordelia Street boys; and he felt a good deal more manly, more honest, even now that he had no need for boastful pretensions, now that he could, as his actor friends used to say, "dress the part." It was characteristic that remorse did not occur to him. His golden days went by without a shadow, and he made each as perfect as he could.

On the eighth day after his arrival in New York, he found the whole affair exploited in the Pittsburgh papers, exploited with a wealth of detail which indicated that local news of a sensational nature was at a low ebb. The firm of Denny & Carson announced that the boy's father had refunded the full amount of his theft, and that they had no intention of prosecuting. The Cumberland minister had been interviewed, and expressed his hope of yet reclaiming the motherless lad, and Paul's Sabbath-School teacher declared that she would spare no effort to that end. The rumour had reached Pittsburgh that the boy had been seen in a New York hotel, and his father had gone East to find him and bring him home.

Paul had just come in to dress for dinner; he sank into a chair, weak in the knees, and clasped his head in his hands. It was to be worse than jail, even; the tepid waters of Cordelia Street were to close over him finally and forever. The grey monotony stretched before him in hopeless, unrelieved years;—Sabbath-School, Young People's Meeting, the yellow-papered room, the damp dishtowels; it all rushed back upon him with sickening vividness. He had the old feeling that the orchestra had suddenly stopped, the sinking sensation that the play was over. The sweat broke out on his face, and he sprang to his feet, looked about him with his white, conscious smile, and winked at himself in the mirror. With something of the childish belief in miracles with which he had so often gone to class, all his lessons unlearned, Paul dressed and dashed whistling down the corridor to the elevator.

He had no sooner entered the dining-room and caught the measure of the music than his remembrance was lightened by his old elastic power of claiming the moment, mounting with it, and finding it all-sufficient. The glare and glitter about him, the mere scenic accessories had again, and for the last time, their old potency. He would show himself that he was game, he would finish the thing splendidly. He doubted, more than ever, the existence of Cordelia Street, and for the first time he drank his wine recklessly. Was he not, after all, one of these fortunate beings? Was he not still himself, and in his own place? He drummed a nervous accompaniment to the music and looked about him, telling himself over and over that it had paid.

He reflected drowsily, to the swell of the violin and the chill sweetness of his wine, that he might have done it more wisely. He might have caught an outbound steamer and been well out of their clutches before now. But the other side of the world had seemed too far away and too uncertain then; he could not have waited for it; his need had been too sharp. If he had to choose over again, he would do the same thing to-morrow. He looked affectionately about the dining-room, now gilded with a soft mist. Ah, it had paid indeed!

Paul was awakened next morning by a painful throbbing in his head and feet. He had thrown himself across the bed without undressing, and had slept with his shoes on. His limbs and hands were lead-heavy and his tongue and throat were parched. There came upon him one of those fateful attacks of clear-headedness that never occurred except when he was physically exhausted and his nerves hung loose. He lay still and closed his eyes and let the tide of realities wash over him.

His father was in New York; "stopping at some joint or other," he told himself. The memory of successive summers on the front stoop fell upon him like a weight of black water. He had not a hundred dollars left; and he knew now, more than ever, that money was everything, the wall that stood between all he loathed and all he wanted. The thing was winding itself up; he had thought of that on his first glorious day in New York, and had even provided a way to snap the thread. It lay on his dressing-table now; he had got it out last night when he came blindly up from dinner— but the shiny metal hurt his eyes, and he disliked the look of it, anyway.

He rose and moved about with a painful effort, succumbing now and again to attacks of nausea. It was the old depression exaggerated; all the world had become Cordelia Street. Yet somehow he was not afraid of anything, was absolutely calm; perhaps because he had looked into the dark corner at last, and knew. It was bad enough, what he saw there; but somehow not so bad as his long fear of it had been. He saw everything clearly now. He had a feeling that he had made the best of it, that he had lived the sort of life he was meant to live, and for half an hour he sat staring at the revolver. But he told himself that was not the way, so he went downstairs and took a cab to the ferry.

When Paul arrived at Newark, he got off the train and took another cab, directing the driver to follow the Pennsylvania tracks out of the town. The snow lay heavy on the roadways and had drifted deep in the open fields. Only here and there the dead grass or dried weed stalks projected, singularly black, above it.

Once well into the country, Paul dismissed the carriage and walked, floundering along the tracks, his mind a medley of irrelevant things. He seemed to hold in his brain an actual picture of everything he had seen that morning. He remembered every feature of both his drivers, the toothless old woman from whom he had bought the red flowers in his coat, the agent from whom he had got his ticket, and all of his fellow-passengers on the ferry. His mind, unable to cope with vital matters near at hand, worked feverishly and deftly at sorting and grouping these images. They made for him a part of the ugliness of the world, of the ache in his head, and the bitter burning on his tongue. He stooped and put a handful of snow into his mouth as he walked, but that, too, seemed hot. When he reached a little hillside, where the tracks ran through a cut some twenty feet below him, he stopped and sat down.

The carnations in his coat were drooping with the cold, he noticed; all their red glory over. It occurred to him that all the flowers he had seen in the show windows that first night must have gone the same way, long before this. It was only one splendid breath they had, in spite of their brave mockery at the winter outside the glass. It was a losing game in the end, it seemed, this revolt against the homilies by which the world is run. Paul took one of the blossoms carefully from his coat and scooped a little hole in the snow, where he covered it up. Then he dozed awhile, from his weak condition, seeming insensible to the cold.

The sound of an approaching train woke him and he started to his feet, remembering only his resolution, and afraid lest he should be too late. He stood watching the approaching locomotive, his teeth chattering, his lips drawn away from them in a frightened smile; once or twice he glanced nervously sidewise, as though he were being watched. When the right moment came, he jumped. As he fell, the folly of his haste occurred to him with merciless clearness, the vastness of what he had left undone. There flashed through his brain, clearer than ever before, the blue of Adriatic water, the yellow of Algerian sands.

He felt something strike his chest—his body was being thrown swiftly through the air, on and on immeasurably far and fast, while his limbs gently relaxed. Then, because the picture-making mechanism was crushed, the disturbing visions flashed into black, and Paul dropped back into the immense design of things.

QUESTIONS

"Paul's Case"

1. Describe Paul. What makes him different from the other people in the story: his teachers, his father, "the young man who was daily held up to Paul as a model"?

2. Compare and contrast life on Cordelia Street to the life Paul dreams of for himself. How does Paul's loathing of the former affect both your understanding of him and your reaction to him?

3. What recurrent metaphor does Cather use to convey Paul's feelings about Cordelia Street?

4. In what sense is Paul's home a wasteland from which he must escape in order to be fully alive? Why do the things his father wishes for Paul amount to a kind of death in the boy's eyes? What is, for Paul, "the only thing that could be called living at all"?

5. Can you pinpoint a specific moment in this story when Paul receives his "call to adventure," when destiny seems to summon him and he is launched on his adventure? What does Paul quest for when he reaches New York? How does his life in New York affect your understanding of him?

6. How do you regard Paul's suicide: as an act of integrity and courage or of cowardice, rashness, and despair? How does he feel about his act in the instant before he dies?

7. It is possible to read this story as an attack on American materialism and especially on commercialism, which glorifies businessmen, like the up-and-coming clerk of the steel corporation magnate, but regards artistic, sensitive spirits like Paul as aberrant personalities. The latter attitude is summed up by Paul's drawing master, who concludes that "there is something wrong about the fellow." Discuss this story as a commentary on American society, an examination of the conflict between the practical, hard-headed, material world and the realm of imagination and spirit. Are there other ways of reading Cather's story? What is the significance of the fact that Paul himself comes to feel that "money was everything"?

8. How does Cather use flowers as symbols in this story? What are they symbolic of?

9. Explain the last line of the story.

Astronomer's Wife

KAY BOYLE

There is an evil moment on awakening when all things seem to pause. But for women, they only falter and may be set in action by a single move: a lifted hand and the pendulum will swing, or the voice raised and through every room the pulse takes up its beating. The astronomer's wife felt the interval gaping and at once filled it to the brim. She fetched up her gentle voice and sent it warily down the stairs for coffee, swung her feet out upon the oval mat, and hailed the morning with her bare arms' quivering flesh drawn taut in rhythmic exercise: left, left, left my wife and fourteen children, right, right, right in the middle of the dusty road.

The day would proceed from this, beat by beat, without reflection, like every other day. The astronomer was still asleep, or feigning it, and she, once out of bed, had come into her own possession. Although scarcely ever out of sight of the impenetrable silence of his brow, she would be absent from him all the day in being clean, busy, kind. He was a man of other things, a dreamer. At times he lay still for hours, at others he sat upon the roof behind his telescope, or wandered down the pathway to the road and out across the mountains. This day, like any other, would go on from the removal of the spot left there from dinner on the astronomer's vest to the severe thrashing of the mayonnaise for lunch. That man might be each time the new arching wave, and woman the undertow that sucked him back, were things she had been told by his silence were so.

In spite of the earliness of the hour, the girl had heard her mistress's voice and was coming up the stairs. At the threshold of the bedroom she paused, and said: "Madame, the plumber is here."

The astronomer's wife put on her white and scarlet smock very quickly and buttoned it at the neck. Then she stepped carefully around the motionless spread of water in the hall.

"Tell him to come right up," she said. She laid her hands on the bannisters and stood looking down the wooden stairway. "Ah, I am Mrs. Ames," she said softly as she saw him mounting. "I am Mrs. Ames," she said softly, softly down the flight of stairs. "I am Mrs. Ames," spoken soft as a willow weeping. "The professor is still sleeping. Just step this way."

The plumber himself looked up and saw Mrs. Ames with her voice hushed, speaking to him. She was a youngish woman, but this she had forgotten. The mystery and silence of her husband's mind lay like a chiding finger on her lips. Her eyes were gray, for the light had been extinguished in them. The strange dim halo of her yellow hair was still uncombed and sideways on her head.

For all of his heavy boots, the plumber quieted the sound of his feet, and together they went down the hall, picking their way around the still lake of water that spread as far as the landing and lay docile there. The plumber was a tough, hardy man; but he took off his hat when he spoke to her and looked her fully, almost insolently in the eye.

"Does it come from the wash-basin," he said, "or from the other . . . ?"

"Oh, from the other," said Mrs. Ames without hesitation.

In this place the villas were scattered out few and primitive, and although beauty lay without there was no reflection of her face within. Here all was awkward and unfit; a sense of wrestling with uncouth forces gave everything an austere countenance. Even the plumber, dealing as does a woman with matters under hand, was grave and stately. The mountains round about seemed to have cast them into the shadow of great dignity.

Mrs. Ames began speaking of their arrival that summer in the little villa, mourning each event as it followed on the other.

"Then, just before going to bed last night," she said, "I noticed something was unusual."

The plumber cast down a folded square of sack-cloth on the brimming floor and laid his leather apron on it. Then he stepped boldly onto the heart of the island it shaped and looked long into the overflowing bowl.

"The water should be stopped from the meter in the garden," he said at last.

"Oh, I did that," said Mrs. Ames, "the very first thing last night. I turned it off at once, in my nightgown, as soon as I saw what was happening. But all this had already run in."

The plumber looked for a moment at her red kid slippers. She was standing just at the edge of the clear, pure-seeming tide.

"It's no doubt the soil lines," he said severely. "It may be that something has stopped them, but my opinion is that the water seals aren't working. That's the trouble often enough in such cases. If you had a valve you wouldn't be caught like this."

Mrs. Ames did not know how to meet this rebuke. She stood, swaying a little, looking into the plumber's blue relentless eye.

"I'm sorry—I'm sorry that my husband," she said, "is still—resting and cannot go into this with you. I'm sure it must be very interesting. . ."

"You'll probably have to have the traps sealed," said the plumber grimly, and at the sound of this Mrs. Ames' hand flew in dismay to the side of her face. The plumber made no move, but the set of his mouth as he looked at her seemed to soften. "Anyway, I'll have a look from the garden end," he said.

"Oh, do," said the astronomer's wife in relief. Here was a man who spoke of action and object as simply as women did! But however hushed her voice had been, it carried clearly to Professor Ames who lay, dreaming and solitary, upon his bed. He heard their footsteps come down the hall, pause, and skip across the pool of overflow.

"Katherine!" said the astronomer in a ringing tone. "There's a problem worthy of your mettle!"

Mrs. Ames did not turn her head, but led the plumber swiftly down the stairs. When the sun in the garden struck her face, he saw there was a wave of color in it, but this may have been anything but shame.

"You see how it is," said the plumber, as if leading her mind away. "The drains run from these houses right down the hill, big enough for a man to stand upright in them, and clean as a whistle too." There they stood in the garden with the vegetation flowering in disorder all about. The plumber looked at the astronomer's wife. "They come out at the torrent on the other side of the forest beyond there," he said.

But the words the astronomer had spoken still sounded in her in despair. The mind of man, she knew, made steep and sprightly flights, pursued illusion, took foothold in the nameless things that cannot pass between the thumb and finger. But whenever the astronomer gave voice to the thoughts that soared within him, she returned in gratitude to the long expanses of his silence. Desert-like they stretched behind and before the articulation of his scorn.

Life, life is an open sea, she sought to explain it in sorrow, and to survive women cling to the floating debris on the tide. But the plumber had suddenly fallen upon his knees in the grass and had crooked his fingers through the ring of the drains' trap-door. When she looked down she saw that he was looking up into her face, and she saw too that his hair was as light as gold.

"Perhaps Mr. Ames," he said rather bitterly, "would like to come down with me and have a look around?"

"Down?" said Mrs. Ames in wonder.

"Into the drains," said the plumber brutally. "They're a study for a man who likes to know what's what."

"Oh, Mr. Ames," said Mrs. Ames in confusion. "He's still—still in bed, you see."

The plumber lifted his strong, weathered face and looked curiously at her. Surely it seemed to him strange for a man to linger in bed, with the sun pouring yellow as wine all over the place. The astronomer's wife saw his lean cheeks, his high, rugged bones, and the deep seams in his brow. His flesh was as firm and clean as wood, stained richly tan with the climate's rigor. His fingers were blunt, but comprehensible to her, gripped in the ring and holding the iron door wide. The backs of his hands were bound round and round with ripe blue veins of blood.

"At any rate," said the astronomer's wife, and the thought of it moved her lips to smile a little, "Mr. Ames would never go down there alive. He likes going up," she said. And she, in her turn, pointed, but impudently, towards the heavens. "On the roof. Or on the mountains. He's been up on the tops of them many times."

"It's a matter of habit," said the plumber, and suddenly he went down the trap. Mrs. Ames saw a bright little piece of his hair still shining, like a star, long after the rest of him had gone. Out of the depths, his voice, hollow and dark with foreboding, returned to her. "I think something has stopped the elbow," was what he said.

This was speech that touched her flesh and bone and made her wonder. When her husband spoke of height, having no sense of it, she could not picture it nor hear. Depth or magic passed her by unless a name were given. But madness in a daily shape, as elbow stopped, she saw clearly and well. She sat down on the grasses, bewildered that it should be a man who had spoken to her so.

She saw the weeds springing up, and she did not move to tear them up from life. She sat powerless, her senses veiled, with no action taking shape beneath her hands. In this way some men sat for hours on end, she knew, tracking a single thought back to its origin. The mind of man could balance and divide, weed out, destroy. She sat on the full, burdened grasses, seeking to think, and dimly waiting for the plumber to return.

Whereas her husband had always gone up, as the dead go, she knew now that there were others who went down, like the corporeal being of the dead. That men were then divided into two bodies now seemed clear to Mrs. Ames. This knowledge stunned her with its simplicity and took the uneasy motion from her limbs. She could not stir, but sat facing the mountains' rocky flanks, and harking in silence to lucidity. Her husband was the mind, this other man the meat, of all mankind.

After a little, the plumber emerged from the earth: first the light top of his head, then the burnt brow, and then the blue eyes fringed with whitest lash. He braced his thick hands flat on the pavings of the garden-path and swung himself completely from the pit.

"It's the soil lines," he said pleasantly. "The gases," he said as he looked down upon her lifted face, "are backing up the drains."

"What in the world are we going to do?" said the astronomer's wife softly. There was a young and strange delight in putting questions to which true answers would be given. Everything the astronomer had ever said to her was a continuous query to which there could be no response.

"Ah, come, now," said the plumber, looking down and smiling. "There's a remedy for every ill, you know. Sometimes it may be that," he said as if speaking to a child, "or sometimes the other thing. But there's always a help for everything amiss."

Things come out of herbs and make you young again, he might have been saying to her; or the first good rain will quench any drought; or time of itself will put a broken bone together.

"I'm going to follow the ground pipe out right to the torrent," the plumber was saying. "The trouble's between here and there and I'll find it on the way. There's nothing at all that can't be done over for the caring," he was saying, and his eyes were fastened on her face in insolence, or gentleness, or love.

The astronomer's wife stood up, fixed a pin in her hair, and turned around towards the kitchen. Even while she was calling the servant's name, the plumber began speaking again.

"I once had a cow that lost her cud," the plumber was saying. The girl came out on the kitchen-step and Mrs. Ames stood smiling at her in the sun.

"The trouble is very serious, very serious," she said across the garden. "When Mr. Ames gets up, please tell him I've gone down."

She pointed briefly to the open door in the pathway, and the plumber hoisted his kit on his arm and put out his hand to help her down.

"But I made her another in no time," he was saying, "out of flowers and things and what-not."

"Oh," said the astronomer's wife in wonder as she stepped into the heart of the earth. She took his arm, knowing that what he said was true.

QUESTIONS

"Astronomer's Wife"

1. What is your impression of Mrs. Ames? How does Boyle convey this impression—what details of dress, speech, and behavior does she provide in her portrayal of Mrs. Ames? What sort of woman and wife does the protagonist seem to be? What do her days consist of?

2. What opinion of men has Mrs. Ames formed as a result of living with her husband?

3. How has her marriage affected Mrs. Ames? What has it done to her?

4. Why does Boyle offer no physical description of the astronomer? How, in spite of this lack of concrete description, does she convey a strong sense of his character? What kind of man does he seem to be? What kind of relationship does he have with his wife? What does he think of women and their place in life?

5. How does the astronomer spend his days? Compare his pursuits to his wife's.

6. Compare the plumber to the astronomer. What contrasts does Boyle draw between the two men? What different realm does each inhabit? What is the significance of their respective professions? Look closely at the language Boyle uses when she talks about each character. What physical details does she emphasize in her description of the plumber?

7. Why does Mrs. Ames follow the plumber at the end of the story—heed his "call"? Where does he lead her? What kind of life does he represent? What kind of life is she leaving behind?

8. Can Mrs. Ames be regarded as a true hero? Why or why not?

9. How would you describe the author's tone in this story, her attitude toward Mrs. Ames, the astronomer, and the plumber?

10. Does "Astronomer's Wife" seem strictly realistic, or does it have the quality of an allegory? What, for example, is the significance of Mrs. Ames's realization that "Her husband was the mind, this other man the meat, of all mankind"?

The Island at Noon

JULIO CORTÁZAR

The first time he saw the island, Marini was politely leaning over the seats on the left, adjusting a plastic table before setting a lunch tray down. The passenger had looked at him several times as he came and went with magazines or glasses of whisky; Marini lingered while he adjusted the table, wondering, bored, if it was worth responding to the passenger's insistent look, one American woman out of many, when in the blue oval of the window appeared the coast of the island, the golden strip of the beach, the hills that rose toward the desolate plateau. Correcting the faulty position of the glass of beer, Marini smiled to the passenger. "The Greek islands," he said. "Oh, yes, Greece," the American woman answered with false interest. A bell rang briefly, and the steward straightened up, without removing the professional smile from his thin lips. He began attending to a Syrian couple, who ordered tomato juice, but in the tail of the plane he gave himself a few seconds to look down again; the island was small and solitary, and the Aegean Sea surrounded it with an intense blue that exalted the curl of a dazzling and kind of petrified white, which down below would be foam breaking against reefs and coves. Marini saw that the deserted beaches ran north and west; the rest was the mountain which fell straight into the sea. A rocky and deserted island, although the lead-gray spot near the northern beach could be a house, perhaps a group of primitive houses. He started opening the can of juice, and when he had straightened up the island had vanished from the window; only the sea was left, an endless green horizon. He looked at his wrist-watch without knowing why; it was exactly noon.

Marini liked being assigned to the Rome-Teheran line. The flight was less gloomy than on the northern lines, and the girls seemed happy to go to the Orient or to get to know Italy. Four days later, while he was helping a little boy who had lost his spoon and was pointing downheartedly at his dessert plate, he again discovered the edge of the island. There was a difference of eight minutes, but when he leaned over to a window in the tail he had no doubts; the island had an unmistakable shape, like a turtle whose paws were barely out of the water. He looked at it until they called for him, this time sure that the lead-gray spot was a group of houses; he man-

65

aged to make out the lines of some cultivated fields that extended to the
beach. During the stop at Beirut he looked at the stewardess's atlas and
wondered if the island wasn't Horos. The radio operator, an indifferent
Frenchman, was surprised at his interest. "All those islands look alike. I've
been doing this route for two years, and I don't care a fig about them. Yes,
show it to me next time." It wasn't Horos but Xiros, one of the many
islands on the fringe of the tourist circuits. "It won't last five years," the
stewardess said to him while they had a drink in Rome. "Hurry up if you're
thinking of going, the hordes will be there any moment now. Genghis Cook
is watching." But Marini kept thinking about the island, looking at it when
he remembered or if there was a window near, almost always shrugging
his shoulders in the end. None of it made any sense—flying three times a
week at noon over Xiros was as unreal as dreaming three times a week that
he was flying over Xiros. Everything was falsified in the futile and recurrent vision; except, perhaps, the desire to repeat it, the consulting of the
wrist-watch before noon, the brief, pricking contact with the dazzling white
band at the edge of an almost black blue, and the houses where the fishermen would barely lift their eyes to follow the passage of that other unreality.

Eight or nine weeks later, when they offered him the New York run,
with all its advantages, Marini thought it was the chance to end that innocent and annoying obsession. In his pocket he had a guide book in which
an imprecise geographer with a Levantine name gave more details about
Xiros than was usual. He answered no, hearing himself as from a distance,
and, avoiding the shocked surprise of a boss and two secretaries, he went
to have a bite in the company's canteen, where Carla was waiting for him.
Carla's bewildered disappointment did not disturb him; the southern coast
of Xiros was uninhabitable, but toward the west remained traces of a Lyd-
ian or perhaps Creto-Mycenaean colony, and Professor Goldmann had found
two stones carved with hieroglyphics that the fishermen used as piles for
the small dock. Carla's head ached, and she left almost immediately; octopus was the principal resource for the handful of inhabitants, every five
days a boat arrived to load the fish and leave some provisions and materials. In the travel agency they told him he would have to charter a special
boat from Rynos, or perhaps it would be possible to go in the small boat
that picked up the octopuses, but Marini could find out about this only in
Rynos, where the agency didn't have an agent. At any rate, the idea of
spending a few days on the island was just a plan for his June vacation; in
the weeks that followed he had to replace White on the Tunis run, and
then there was a strike, and Carla went back to her sisters' house in Pa-
lermo. Marini went to live in a hotel near the Piazza Navona, where there
were secondhand bookstores; he amused himself not very enthusiastically
by looking for books on Greece, and from time to time he leafed through
a conversation manual. The word *kalimera* pleased him, and he tried it out
on a redhead in a cabaret; he went to bed with her, learned about her
grandfather in Odos and about certain unaccountable sore throats. In Rome

it rained, in Beirut Tania was always waiting for him; there were other stories, always relatives or sore throats; one day it was again the Teheran run, the island at noon. Marini stayed glued to the window so long that the new stewardess considered him a poor partner and let him know how many trays she had served. That night Marini invited the stewardess for dinner at the Firouz, and it wasn't difficult to make her forgive him for the morning's distraction. Lucia advised him to have his hair cut American-style; he talked to her about Xiros for a while, but later he realized she preferred the vodka-lime of the Hilton. Time passed in things like that, in infinite trays of food, each one with the smile to which the passenger had the right. On the return trips the plane flew over Xiros at eight in the morning; the sun glared against the larboard windows, and you could scarcely see the golden turtle; Marini preferred to wait for the noons of the trip going, knowing that then he could stay a long minute against the window, while Lucia (and then Felisa) somewhat ironically took care of things. Once he took a picture of Xiros, but it came out blurred; he already knew some things about the island, he had underlined the rare mentions in a couple of books. Felisa told him that the pilots called him the madman of the island, but that didn't bother him. Carla had just written that she had decided not to have the baby, and Marini sent her two weeks' wages and thought that the rest would not be enough for his vacation. Carla accepted the money and let him know through a friend that she'd probably marry the dentist from Treviso. Everything had such little importance at noon, on Mondays and Thursdays and Saturdays (twice a month on Sundays).

As time went on, he began to realize that Felisa was the only one who understood him a little; there was a tacit agreement that she would take care of the flight at noon, as soon as he stationed himself by the tail window. The island was visible for a few minutes, but the air was always so clean, and it was outlined by the sea with such a minute cruelty that the smallest details were implacably adjusted to the memory of the preceding flight: the green spot of the headland to the north, the lead-gray houses, the nets drying on the sand. When the nets weren't there, Marini felt as if he had been robbed, insulted. He thought of filming the passage over the island, to repeat the image in the hotel, but he preferred to save the money on the camera since there was less than a month left for vacation. He didn't keep a very strict account of the days; sometimes it was Tania in Beirut, sometimes Felisa in Teheran, almost always his younger brother in Rome, all a bit blurred, amiably easy and cordial and as if replacing something else, filling the hours before or after the flight, and during the flight, everything, too, was blurred and easy and stupid until it was time to lean toward that ail window, to feel the cold crystal like the boundary of an aquarium, where the golden turtle slowly moved in the thick blue.

That day, the nets were clearly sketched on the sand, and Marini could have sworn that the black dot on the left, at the edge of the sea, was a fisherman who must have been looking at the plane. *"Kalimera,"* he absurdly thought. It no longer made any sense to wait. Mario Merolis would lend him the money he needed for the trip, and in less than three days he would be in Xiros. With his lips against the window, he smiled, thinking that he would climb to the green spot, that he would enter the sea of the northern coves naked, that he would fish octopuses with the men, communicating through signs and laughter. Nothing was difficult once decided—a night train, the first boat, another old and dirty boat, the night on the bridge, close to the stars, the taste of *anis* and mutton, daybreak among the islands. He landed with the first lights, and the captain introduced him to an old man, probably the elder. Klaios took his left hand and spoke slowly, looking him in the eyes. Two boys came, and Marini found out that they were Klaios' sons. The captain of the small boat exhausted his English: Twenty inhabitants, octopus, fish, five houses, Italian visitor would pay lodging Klaios. The boys laughed when Klaios discussed drachmas; Marini, too, already friends with the younger boys, watching the sun come up over a sea not as dark as from the air, a poor, clean room, a pitcher of water, smell of sage and tanned hides.

They left him alone to go load the small boat, and after tearing off his traveling clothes and putting on bathing trunks and sandals, he set out for a walk on the island. You still couldn't see anybody; the sun slowly but surely rose, and from the thickets grew a subtle smell, slightly acidic, mixing with the iodine of the wind. It must have been ten when he reached the northern headland and recognized the largest of the coves. He preferred being alone, although he would have liked to bathe at the sand beach even better; the island impregnated him, and he enjoyed it with such intimacy that he was incapable of thinking or choosing. His skin burned from sun and wind when he undressed to thrust himself into the sea from a rock; the water was cold and did him good. He let a sly current carry him to the entrance of a grotto, he returned to the open sea, rolled over on his back, accepted it all in a single act of conciliation that was also a name for the future. He knew without the slightest doubt that he would not leave the island, that somehow he would stay forever on the island. He managed to imagine his brother, Felisa, their faces when they found out he had stayed to live off fishing on a large solitary rock. He had already forgotten them when he turned over to swim toward the shore.

The sun dried him immmediately, and he went down toward the house, where two astonished women looked at him before running inside and closing their doors. He waved a greeting in the void and walked down toward the nets. One of Klaios' sons was waiting for him on the beach, and Marini pointed to the sea, inviting him. The boy hesitated, pointing to his cloth pants and red shirt. Then he ran toward one of the houses and came back almost naked; they dived together into an already lukewarm sea, dazzling under the eleven o'clock sun.

Drying himself in the sand, Ionas began to name things. *"Kalimera,"* Marini said, and the boy doubled over with laughter. Then Marini repeated the new sentences, teaching Ionas Italian words. Almost on the horizon the small boat grew smaller and smaller; Marini felt that now he was really alone on the island with Klaios and his people. He would let some days pass, he would pay for his room and learn to fish; some afternoon, when they were well acquainted, he would talk to them about staying and working with them. Getting up, he held out his hand to Ionas and started walking slowly toward the hill. The slope was steep, and he savored each pause, turning around time and again to look at the nets on the beach, the figures of the women speaking gaily to Ionas and Klaios and looking at him askance, laughing. When he reached the green spot he entered a world where the smell of thyme and sage were one with the fire of the sun and the sea breeze. Marini looked at his wrist-watch and then, with an impatient gesture, put it in the pocket of his bathing trunks. It wouldn't be easy to kill the former man, but there up high, tense with sun and space, he felt the enterprise was possible. He was in Xiros, he was there where he had so often doubted he could reach. He let himself fall back among the hot stones, he endured their edges and inflamed ridges and looked vertically at the sky; far away he could hear the hum of an engine.

Closing his eyes, he told himself he wouldn't look at the plane; he wouldn't let himself be contaminated by the worst of him that once more was going to pass over the island. But in the shadows of his eyelids he imagined Felisa with the trays, in that very moment distributing the trays, and his replacement, perhaps Giorgio or someone new from another line, someone who would also be smiling as he served the wine or the coffee. Unable to fight against all that past he opened his eyes and sat up, and in the same moment saw the right wing of the plane, almost over his head, tilt unaccountably, the changed sound of the jet engines, the almost vertical drop into the sea. He rushed down the hill, knocking against rocks and lacerating his arm among thorns. The island hid the place of the fall from him, but he turned before reaching the beach and through a predictable short-cut he passed the first ridge of the hill and came out onto the smaller beach. The plane's tail was sinking some 100 yards away, in total silence. Marini ran and dived into the water, still waiting for the plane to come up to float; but all you could see was the soft line of the waves, a cardboard box bobbing absurdly near the place of the fall, and almost at the end, when it no longer made sense to keep swimming, a hand out of the water, just for a second, enough time for Marini to change direction and dive under to catch by his hair the man who struggled to hold onto him and hoarsely swallowed air that Marini let him breathe without getting too close. Towing him little by little he got him to the shore, took the body dressed in white in his arms, and laying him on the sand he looked at the face full of foam where death had already settled, bleeding through an enormous gash in his throat. What good was artificial respiration if, with each convulsion, the gash seemed to open a little more and was like a repugnant mouth that called to Marini, tore him from his little happiness of such few hours on the island, shouted to him between torrents something he was no longer able to hear. Klaios' sons came running and behind them the women. When Klaios arrived, the boys gathered around the body lying on the sand,

unable to understand how he had had the strength to swim to shore and
drag himself there bleeding. "Close his eyes," one of the women begged
crying. Klaios looked toward the sea, searching for other survivors. But, as
always, they were alone on the island, and the open-eyed corpse was all
that was new between them and the sea.

QUESTIONS

"The Island at Noon"

1. The call in "The Island at Noon" differs from the ones portrayed in the
other selections in this chapter. How? What is the summons that Marini responds to? Where does it lead him?

2. From what point of view is this story told? How much do we learn about
Marini—about his appearance, his personality, his thoughts?

3. Describe the kind of life Marini leads as an airline steward. Does his life
seem full? Empty? How does he seem to feel about his work?

4. Describe Marini's relationships with the other people we see in the first
part of the story: the passengers and the various women in his life.

5. Who is Carla? Why is she upset when Marini turns down the "New York
run"? Why does he do it?

6. What details of this story suggest that Marini is psychologically ready to
be called to a quest?

7. Why does the island of Xiros hold so much fascination for Marini? What
does he see in it? What do his fellow workers see in it? How do they react to
Marini's obsession?

8. Describe Xiros and its inhabitants. What is life like on the island? Does
it seem an attractive place to you? How does the island differ from the kind of
world Marini has always known?

9. In what sense can this story be said to have a surprise ending? How
does the story end? Who is the "open-eyed corpse" lying on the sand?

10. Late in the story, Marini takes off his wrist watch and then reflects, "It
wouldn't be easy to kill the former man. . . ." In what sense do all questing
heroes and heroines have to "kill" their former selves? How is the end of the
story an ironic comment on Marini's reflection and the act that precedes it?

The Liberation

JEAN STAFFORD

On the day Polly Bay decided to tell her Uncle Francis and his sister, her Aunt Jane, that in a week's time she was leaving their house and was going East to be married and to live in Boston, she walked very slowly home from Nevilles College, where she taught, dreading the startled look in their eyes and the woe and the indignation with which they would take her news. Hating any derangement of the status quo, her uncle, once a judge, was bound to cross-examine her intensively, and Aunt Jane, his perfect complement, would bolster him and baffle her. It was going to be an emotional and argumentative scene; her hands, which now were damp, would presently be dripping. She shivered with apprehension, fearing her aunt's asthma and her uncle's polemic, and she shook with rebellion, knowing how they would succeed in making her feel a traitor to her family, to the town, and to Colorado, and obscurely, to her country.

Uncle Francis and Aunt Jane, like their dead kinsmen, Polly's father and her grandfather and her great-grandmother, had a vehement family and regional pride, and they counted it virtue in themselves that they had never been east of the Mississippi. They had looked on the departures of Polly's sisters and her cousins as acts of betrayal and even of disobedience. They had been distressed particularly by removals to the East, which were, they felt, iconoclastic and, worse, rude; how, they marveled, could this new generation be so ungrateful to those intrepid early Bays who in the forties had toiled in such peril and with such fortitude across the plains in a covered wagon and who with such perseverance had put down the roots for their traditions in this town that they had virtually made? Uncle Francis and Aunt Jane had done all in their power—through threats and sudden illnesses and cries of "Shame!"—to prevent these desertions, but, nevertheless, one by one, the members of the scapegrace generation had managed to fly, cut off without a penny, scolded to death, and spoken of thereafter as if they were unredeemed, treasonous, and debauched. Polly was the last, and her position, therefore, was the most uncomfortable of all; she and her aunt and uncle were the only Bays left in Adams, and she knew that because she was nearly thirty they had long ago stopped fearing that she, too, might go. As they frequently told her, in their candid way, they

71

felt she had reached "a sensible age"—it was a struggle for them not to use the word "spinster" when they paid her this devious and crushing compliment. She knew perfectly well, because this, too, they spoke of, that they imagined she would still be teaching *Immensee* in German I years after they were dead, and would return each evening to the big, drafty house where they were born, and from which they expected to be carried in coffins ordered for them by Polly from Leonard Harper, the undertaker, whose mealy mouth and shifty eye they often talked about with detestation as they rocked and rocked through their long afternoons.

Polly had been engaged to Robert Fair for five months now and had kept his pretty ring in the desk in her office at college; she had not breathed a word to a soul. If she had spoken out when she came back from the Christmas holidays in her sister's Boston house, her uncle and aunt, with a margin of so much time for their forensic pleas before the college year was over, might have driven her to desperate measures; she might have had to flee, without baggage, in the middle of the night on a bus. Not wanting to begin her new life so haphazardly, she had guarded her secret, and had felt a hypocrite.

But she could not keep silent any longer; she had to tell them and start to pack her bags. She did not know how to present her announcement— whether to disarm them with joy or to stun them with a voice of adamant intention. Resenting the predicament, which so occupied her that her love was brusquely pushed aside, and feeling years younger than she was—an irritable adolescent, nerve-racked by growing pains—she now snatched leaves from the springtime bushes and tore them into shreds. It was late May and the purple lilacs were densely in blossom, offering their virtuous fragrance on the wind; the sun was tender on the yellow willow trees; the mountain range was blue and fair and free of haze. But Polly's senses were not at liberty today to take in these demure delights; she could not respond today at all to the flattering fortune that was to make her a June bride; she could not remember of her fiancé anything beyond his name, and, a little ruefully and a little cynically, she wondered if it was love of him or boredom with freshmen and with her aunt and uncle that had caused her to get engaged to him.

Although she loitered like a school child, she had at last to confront the house behind whose drawn blinds her aunt and uncle awaited her return, innocent of the scare they were presently to get and anticipating the modest academic news she brought each day to serve them with their tea. She was so unwilling that when she came in sight of the house she sat down on a bench at a trolley stop, under the dragging branches of a spruce tree, and opened the book her uncle had asked her to bring from the library. It was *The Heart of Midlothian*. She read with distate; her uncle's pleasures were different from her own.

Neither the book, though, nor the green needles could hide from her interior eye that house where she had lived for seven years, since her father had died; her mother had been dead for many years and her sisters had long been gone—Fanny to Washington and Mary to Boston—but she had stayed on, quiet and unquestioning. Polly was an undemanding girl and she liked to teach and she had not been inspired to escape; she had had, until now, no reason to go elsewhere although, to be sure, these years had not been exclusively agreeable. For a short time, she had lived happily in an apartment by herself, waking each morning to the charming novelty of being her own mistress. But Uncle Francis and Aunt Jane, both widowed and both bereft of their heartless children, had cajoled her and played tricks upon her will until she had consented to go and live with them. It was not so much because she was weak as it was because they were so extremely strong that she had at last capitulated out of fatigue and had brought her things in a van to unpack them, sighing, in two wallpapered rooms at the top of the stout brown house. This odious house, her grandfather's, was covered with broad, unkempt shingles; it had a turret, and two bow windows within which begonia and heliotrope fed on the powerful mountain sun. Its rooms were huge, but since they were gorged with furniture and with garnishments and clumps and hoards of artifacts of Bays, you had no sense of space in them and, on the contrary, felt cornered and nudged and threatened by hanging lamps with dangerous dependencies and by the dark, bucolic pictures of Polly's forebears that leaned forward from the walls in their insculptured brassy frames.

The house stood at the corner of Oxford Street and Pine, and at the opposite end of the block, at the corner of Pine and Plato (the college had sponsored the brainy place names), there was another one exactly like it. It had been built as a wedding present for Uncle Francis by Polly's grandfather, and here Uncle Francis and his wife, Aunt Lacy, had reared an unnatural daughter and two unnatural sons, who had flown the coop, as he crossly said, the moment they legally could; there was in his tone the implication that if they had gone before they had come of age, he would have haled them back, calling on the police if they offered to resist. Uncle Francis had been born litigious; he had been predestined to arraign and complain, to sue and sentence.

Aunt Jane and Uncle Richard had lived in Grandpa's house, and their two cowed, effeminate sons had likewise vanished when they reached the age of franchise. When both Uncle Richard and Aunt Lacy had been sealed into the Bay plot, Uncle Francis had moved down the street to be with his sister for the sake of economy and company, taking with him his legal library, which, to this day, was still in boxes in the back hall, in spite of the protests of Mildred, their truculent housekeeper. Uncle Francis had then, at little cost, converted his own house into four inconvenient apartments, from which he derived a shockingly high income. A sign over the front door read, "The Bay Arms."

Polly's parents' red brick house, across the street from Uncle Francis's— not built but bought for them, also as a wedding present—had been torn down. And behind the trolley bench on which she sat there was the biggest

and oldest family house of all, the original Bay residence, a vast grotes-
querie of native stone, and in it, in the beginning of Polly's life, Great-
grandmother had imperiously lived, with huge, sharp diamonds on her fi-
chus and her velvet, talking without pause of red Indians and storms on
the plains, because she could remember nothing else. The house was now
a historical museum; it was called, not surprisingly, the Bay. Polly never
looked at it without immediately remembering the intricate smell of the
parlor, which had in it moss, must, belladonna, dry leaves, wet dust, oil of
peppermint, and something that bound them all together—a smell of tribal
history, perhaps, or the smell of a house where lived a half-cracked and
haughty old woman who had come to the end of the line.

In those early days, there had been no other houses in this block, and
the Bay children had had no playmates except each other. Four generations sat down to Sunday midday dinner every week at Great-grandmother's
enormous table; the Presbyterian grace was half as long as a sermon; the
fried rabbit was dry. On Christmas Eve, beneath a towering tree in Grandpa's house, sheepish Uncle Richard, as Santa Claus, handed round the presents while Grandpa sat in a central chair like a king on a throne and
stroked his proud goatee. They ate turkey on Thanksgiving with Uncle
Francis and Aunt Lacy, shot rockets and pinwheels off on the Fourth of
July in Polly's family's back yard. Even now, though one of the houses was
gone and another was given over to the display of minerals and wagon
wheels, and though pressed-brick bungalows had sprung up all along the
block, Polly never entered the street without the feeling that she came
into a zone restricted for the use of her blood kin, for there lingered in it
some energy, some air, some admonition that this was the territory of Bays
and that Bays and ghosts of Bays were, and forever would be, in residence.
It was easy for her to vest the wind in the spruce tree with her great-
grandmother's voice and to hear it say, "Not a one of you knows the sensation of having red Indian arrow whiz by your sunbonnet with wind enough
to make the ribbons wave." On reflection, she understood the claustropho-
bia that had sent her sisters and cousins all but screaming out of town;
horrified, she felt that her own life had been like a dream of smothering.

She was only pretending to read Walter Scott and the sun was setting
and she was growing cold. She could not postpone any longer the discharge
of the thunderbolt, and at last she weakly rose and crossed the street,
feeling a convulsion of panic grind in her throat like a hard sob. Besides
the panic, there was a heavy depression, an ebbing away of self-respect, a
regret for the waste of so many years. Generations should not be mingled
for daily fare, she thought; they are really contemptuous of one another,
and the strong individuals, whether they belong to the older or the younger,
impose on the meek their creeds and opinions, and, if they are strong
enough, brook no dissent. Nothing can more totally subdue the passions
than familial piety. Now Polly saw, appalled and miserably ashamed of herself, that she had never once insisted on her own identity in this house.

She had dishonestly, supinely (thinking, however, that she was only being polite), allowed her uncle and aunt to believe that she was contented in their house, in sympathy with them, and keenly interested in the minutiae that preoccupied them: their ossifying arteries and their weakening eyes, their dizzy spells and migrant pains, their thrice-daily eucharist of pills and drops, the twinges in their old, uncovered bones. She had never disagreed with them, so how could they know that she did not, as they did, hate the weather? They assumed that she was as scandalized as they by Uncle Francis's tenants' dogs and children. They had no way of knowing that she was bored nearly to frenzy by their vicious quarrels with Mildred over the way she cooked their food.

In the tenebrous hall lined with closed doors, she took off her gloves and coat, and, squinting through the shadows, saw in the mirror that her wretchedness was plain in her drooping lips and frowning forehead; certainly there was no sign at all upon her face that she was in love. She fixed her mouth into a bogus smile of courage, she straightened out her brow; with the faintest heart in the world she entered the dark front parlor, where the windows were always closed and the shades drawn nearly to the sill. A coal fire on this mild May day burned hot and blue in the grate.

They sat opposite each other at a round, splayfooted table under a dim lamp with a beaded fringe. On the table, amid the tea things, there was a little mahogany casket containing the props with which, each day, they documented their reminiscences of murders, fires, marriages, bankruptcies, and of the triumphs and the rewards of the departed Bays. It was open, showing cracked photographs, letters sallow-inked with age, flaccid and furry newspaper clippings, souvenir spoons flecked with venomous green, little white boxes holding petrified morsels of wedding cake. As Polly came into the room, Aunt Jane reached out her hand and, as if she were pulling a chance from a hat, she picked a newspaper clipping out of the box and said, "I don't think you have ever told Polly the story of the time you were in that train accident in the Royal Gorge. It's such a yarn."

Her uncle heard Polly then and chivalrously half rose from his chair; tall and white-haired, he was distinguished, in a dour way, and dapper in his stiff collar and his waistcoat piped with white. He said, "At last our strayed lamb is back in the fold." The figure made Polly shiver.

"How late you are!" cried Aunt Jane, thrilled at this small deviation from routine. "A department meeting?" If there had been a department meeting, the wreck in the Royal Gorge might be saved for another day.

But they did not wait for her answer. They were impelled, egocentrically and at length, to tell their own news, to explain why it was that they had not waited for her but had begun their tea. Uncle Francis had been hungry, not having felt quite himself earlier in the day and having, therefore, eaten next to nothing at lunch, although the soufflé that Mildred had made was far more edible than customary. He had several new symptoms and was going to the doctor tomorrow; he spoke with infinite peace of mind. Painstakingly then, between themselves, they discussed the advisability of

Aunt Jane's making an appointment at the beauty parlor for the same hour
Uncle Francis was seeing Dr. Wilder; they could in this way share a taxi.
And what was the name of that fellow who drove the Town Taxi whom
they both found so cautious and well-mannered? Bradley, was it? They
might have him drive them up a little way into the mountains for the view;
but, no, Francis might have got a bad report and Jane might be tired after
her baking under the dryer. It would be better if they came straight home.
Sometimes they went on in this way for hours.

Polly poured herself a cup of tea, and Aunt Jane said, as she had said
probably three thousand times in the past seven years, "You may say what
you like, there is simply nothing to take the place of a cup of tea at the
end of the day."

Uncle Francis reached across the table and took the newspaper clipping
from under his sister's hand. He adjusted his glasses and glanced at the
headlines, smiling. "There was a great deal of comedy in that tragedy," he
said.

"Tell Polly about it," said Aunt Jane. Polly knew the details of this story
by heart—the number of the locomotive and the name of the engineer and
the passengers' injuries, particularly her uncle's, which, though minor, had
been multitudinous.

Amazing herself, Polly said, "Don't!" And, amazed by her, they stared.

"Why, Polly, what an odd thing to say!" exclaimed Aunt Jane. "My dear,
is something wrong?"

She decided to take them aback without preamble—it was the only way—
and so she said, "Nothing's wrong. Everything's right at last. I am going to
be married ten days from today to a teacher at Harvard and I am going to
Boston to live."

They behaved like people on a stage; Aunt Jane put her teacup down,
rattling her spoon, and began to wring her hands; Uncle Francis, holding
his butter knife as it were a gavel, glared.

"What are you talking about, darling?" he cried. "Married? What do you
mean?"

Aunt Jane wheezed, signaling her useful asthma, which, however, did
not oblige her. "Boston!" she gasped. "What ever for?"

Polly returned her uncle's magisterial look, but she did so obliquely, and
she spoke to her cuffs when she said, "I mean 'married,' the way you were
married to Aunt Lacy and the way Aunt Jane was married to Uncle Richard. I am in love with a man named Robert Fair and *he* is with me and
we're going to be married."

"How lovely," said Aunt Jane, who, sight unseen, hated Robert Fair.

"Lovely perhaps," said Uncle Francis the magistrate, "and perhaps not.
You might, if you please, do us the honor of enlightening us as to the
qualifications of Mr. Fair to marry and export you. To the best of my
knowledge I have never heard of him."

"I'm quite sure we don't know him," said Aunt Jane; she coughed exper-
imentally, but her asthma was still in hiding.

"No, you don't know him," Polly said. "He has never been in the West."
She wished she could serenely drink her tea while she talked, but she did
not trust her hand. Fixing her eyes on a maidenhair fern in a brass jardi-
niere on the floor, she told them how she had first met Robert Fair at her
sister Mary's cottage in Edgartown the summer before.

"You never told us," said Uncle Francis reprovingly. "I thought you said
the summer had been a mistake. Too expensive. Too hot. I thought you
agreed with Jane and me that summer in the East was hard on the constitution." (She had; out of habit she had let them deprecate the East, which
she had loved at first sight, had allowed them to tell her that she had had
a poor time when, in truth, she had never been so happy.)

Shocked by her duplicity, Aunt Jane said, "We ought to have suspected
something when you went back to Boston for Christmas with Mary instead
of resting here beside your own hearth fire."

Ignoring this sanctimonious accusation, Polly continued, and told them
as much of Robert Fair as she thought they deserved to know, eliding some
of his history—for there was a divorce in it—but as she spoke, she could
not conjure his voice or his face, and he remained as hypothetical to her
as to them, a circumstance that alarmed her and one that her astute uncle
sensed.

"You don't seem head over heels about this Boston fellow," he said.

"I'm nearly thirty," replied his niece. "I'm not sixteen. Wouldn't it be
unbecoming at my age if I *were* lovesick?" She was by no means convinced
of her argument, for her uncle had that effect on her; he could make her
doubt anything—the testimony of her own eyes, the judgments of her own
intellect. Again, and in vain, she called on Robert Fair to materialize in
this room that was so hostile to him and, through his affection, bring a
persuasive color to her cheeks. She did not question the power of love nor
did she question, specifically, the steadfastness of her own love, but she
did observe, with some dismay, that, far from conquering all, love lazily
sidestepped practical problems; it was no help in this interview; it seemed
not to cease but to be temporarily at a standstill.

Her uncle said, "Sixteen, thirty, sixty, it makes no difference. It's true I
wouldn't like it if you were wearing your heart on your sleeve, but, my
Lord, dear, I don't see the semblance of a light in your eye. You look quite
sad. Doesn't Polly strike you as looking downright blue, Jane? If Mr. Fair
makes you so doleful, it seems to me you're better off with us."

"It's not a laughing matter," snapped Aunt Jane, for Uncle Francis, mad-
deningly, had chuckled. It was a way he had in disputation; it was intended
to enrage and thereby rattle his adversary. He kept his smile, but for a
moment he held his tongue while his sister tried a different tack. "What I
don't see is why you have to go to Boston, Polly," she said. "Couldn't he
teach Italian at Nevilles just as well as at Harvard?"

Their chauvinism was really staggering. When Roddy, Uncle Francis's
son, went off to take a glittering job in Brazil, Aunt Jane and his father had
nearly reduced this stalwart boy to kicks and tears by reiterating that if

there had been anything of worth or virtue in South America, the grandparent Bays would have settled there instead of in the Rocky Mountains.

"I don't think Robert would like it here," said Polly.

"What wouldn't he like about it?" Aunt Jane bridled. "I thought our
college had a distinguished reputation. Your great-grandfather, one of the
leading founders of it, was a man of culture, and unless I am sadly misin-
formed, his humanistic spirit is still felt on the campus. Did you know that
his critical study of Isocrates is *highly* esteemed among classical scholars?"

"I mean I don't think he would like the West," said Polly, rash in her
frustration.

She could have bitten her tongue out for the indiscretion, because her
jingoistic uncle reddened instantly and menacingly and he banged on the
table and shouted, "How does he know he doesn't like the West? You've
just told us he's never been farther west than Ohio. How does he dare to
presume to damn what he doesn't know?"

"I didn't say he damned the West. I didn't even say he didn't like it. I
said *I* thought he wouldn't."

"Then *you* are presuming," he scolded. "I am impatient with Easterners
who look down their noses at the West and call us crude and barbaric. But
Westerners who renounce and denounce and derogate their native ground
are worse."

"Far worse," agreed Aunt Jane. "What can have come over you to turn
the man you intend to marry against the land of your forebears?"

Polly had heard it all before. She wanted to clutch her head in her hands
and groan with helplessness; even more, she wished that this were the
middle of next week.

"We three are the last left of the Bays in Adams," pursued Aunt Jane,
insinuating a quaver into her firm, stern voice. "And Francis and I will not
last long. You'll only be burdened and bored with us a little while longer."

"We have meant to reward you liberally for your loyalty," said her uncle.
"The houses will be yours when we join our ancestors."

In the dark parlor, they leaned toward her over their cups of cold tea,
so tireless in their fusillade that she had no chance to deny them or to
defend herself. Was there to be, they mourned, at last not one Bay left to
lend his name and presence to municipal celebrations, to the laying of
cornerstones and the opening of fairs? Polly thought they were probably
already fretting over who would see that the grass between the family graves
was mown.

Panicked, she tried to recall how other members of her family had extri-
cated themselves from these webs of casuistry. Now she wished that she
had more fully explained her circumstances to Robert Fair and had told
him to come and fetch her away, for he, uninvolved, could afford to pay
the ransom more easily than she. But she had wanted to spare him such a
scene as this; they would not have been any more reticent with him; they
would have, with this same arrogance—and this underhandedness—used

their advanced age and family honor to twist the argument away from its premise.

Darkness had shrunk the room to the small circle where they sat in the thin light of the lamp; it seemed to her that their reproaches and their jeremiads took hours before they recommenced the bargaining Aunt Jane had started.

Reasonably, in a judicious voice, Uncle Francis said, "There is no reason at all, if Mr. Fair's attainments are as you describe, that he can't be got an appointment to our Romance Language Department. What is the good of my being a trustee if I can't render such a service once in a way?"

As if this were a perfectly wonderful and perfectly surprising solution, Aunt Jane enthusiastically cried, "But of course you can! That would settle everything. Polly can eat her cake and have it, too. Wouldn't you give them your house, Francis?"

"I'd propose an even better arrangement. Alone here, Jane, you and I would rattle. Perhaps we would move into one of my apartments and the Robert Fairs could have this house. Would that suit you?"

"It would, indeed it would," said Aunt Jane. "I have been noticing the drafts here more and more."

"I don't ask you to agree today, Polly," said Uncle Francis. "But think it over. Write your boy a letter tonight and tell him what your aunt and I are willing to do for him. The gift of a house, as big a house as this, is not to be scoffed at by young people just starting out."

Her "boy," Robert, had a tall son who in the autumn would enter Harvard. "Robert has a house," said Polly, and she thought of its dark-green front door with the brilliant brass trimmings; on Brimmer Street, at the foot of Beacon Hill, its garden faced the Charles. Nothing made her feel more safe and more mature than the image of that old and handsome house.

"He could sell it," said her indomitable aunt.

"He could rent it," said her practical uncle. "That would give you additional revenue."

The air was close; it was like the dead of night in a sealed room and Polly wanted to cry for help. She had not hated the West till now, she had not hated her relatives till now; indeed, till now she had had no experience of hate at all. Surprising as the emotion was—for it came swiftly and authoritatively—it nevertheless cleared her mind and, outraged, she got up and flicked the master switch to light up the chandelier. Her aunt and uncle blinked. She did not sit down again but stood in the doorway to deliver her valediction. "I don't want Robert to come here because I don't want to live here any longer. I want to live my own life."

"Being married is hardly living one's own life," said Aunt Jane.

At the end of her tether now, Polly all but screamed at them, "We *won't* live here and that's that! You talk of my presuming, but how can *you* presume to boss not only me but a man you've never seen? I don't want your houses! I hate these houses! It's true—I hate, I despise, I abominate the West!"

So new to the articulation of anger, she did it badly and, ashamed to death, began to cry. Though they were hurt, they were forgiving, and both of them rose and came across the room, and Aunt Jane, taking her in a spidery embrace, said, "There. You go upstairs and have a bath and rest and we'll discuss it later. Couldn't we have some sherry, Francis? It seems to me that all our nerves are unstrung."

Polly's breath toiled against her sobs, but all the same she took her life in her hands and she said, "There's nothing further to discuss. I am leaving. I am not coming back."

Now, for the first time, the old brother and sister exchanged a look of real anxiety; they seemed, at last, to take her seriously; each waited for the other to speak. It was Aunt Jane who hit upon the new gambit. "I mean, dear, that we will discuss the wedding. You have given us very short notice but I daresay we can manage."

"There is to be no wedding," said Polly. "We are just going to be married at Mary's house. Fanny is coming up to Boston."

"Fanny has known all along?" Aunt Jane was insulted. "And all this time you've lived under our roof and sat at our table and never told *us* but told your sisters, who abandoned you?"

"Abandoned me? For God's sake, Aunt Jane, they had their lives to lead!"

"Don't use that sort of language in this house, young lady," said Uncle Francis.

"I apologize. I'm sorry. I am just so sick and tired of—"

"Of course you're sick and tired," said the adroit old woman. "You've had a heavy schedule this semester. No wonder you're all nerves and tears."

"Oh, it isn't that! Oh, leave me alone!"

And, unable to withstand a fresh onslaught of tears, she rushed to the door. When she had closed it upon them, she heard her aunt say, "I simply can't believe it. There must be some way out. Why, Francis, we would be left altogether *alone*," and there was real terror in her voice.

Polly locked the door to her bedroom and dried her eyes and bathed their lids with witch hazel, the odor of which made her think of her Aunt Lacy, who, poor simple creature, had had to die to escape this family. Polly remembered that every autumn Aunt Lacy had petitioned Uncle Francis to let her take her children home for a visit to her native Vermont, but she had never been allowed to go. Grandpa, roaring, thumping his stick, Uncle Francis bombarding her with rhetoric and using the word "duty" repeatedly, Polly's father scathing her with sarcasm, Aunt Jane slyly confusing her with red herrings had kept her an exhausted prisoner. Her children, as a result, had scorned their passive mother and had wounded her, and once they finally escaped, they had not come back—not for so much as a visit. Aunt Lacy had died not having seen any of her grandchildren; in the last years of her life she did nothing but cry. Polly's heart ached for the plight of that gentle, frightened woman. How lucky *she* was that the means of escape had come to her before it was too late! In her sister's Boston drawing room, in a snowy twilight, Robert Fair's proposal of marriage had seemed to release in her an inexhaustible wellspring of life; until that moment she had not known that she was dying, that she was being killed—by inches, but surely killed—by her aunt and uncle and by the green yearlings in her German classes and by the dogmatic monotony of the town's provincialism. She shuddered to think of her narrow escape from wasting away in these arid foothills, never knowing the cause or the name of her disease.

Quiet, herself again, Polly sat beside the window and looked out at the early stars and the crescent moon. Now that she had finally taken her stand, she was invulnerable, even though she knew that the brown sherry was being put ceremoniously on a tray, together with ancestral Waterford glasses, and though she knew that her aunt and uncle had not given up—that they had, on, the contrary, just begun. And though she knew that for the last seven days of her life in this house she would be bludgeoned with the most splenetic and most defacing of emotions, she knew that the worst was over; she knew that she would survive, as her sisters and her cousins had survived. In the end, her aunt and uncle only *seemed* to survive; dead on their feet for most of their lives, they had no personal history; their genesis had not been individual—it had only been a part of a dull and factual plan. And they had been too busy honoring their family to love it, too busy defending the West even to look at it. For all their pride in their surroundings, they had never contemplated them at all but had sat with the shades drawn, huddled under the steel engravings. They and her father had lived their whole lives on the laurels of their grandparents; their goal had already been reached long before their birth.

The mountains had never looked so superb to her. She imagined a time, after Uncle Francis and Aunt Jane were dead, when the young Bays and their wives and husbands might come back, free at last to admire the landscape, free to go swiftly through the town in the foothills without so much as a glance at the family memorials and to gain the high passes and the peaks and the glaciers. They would breathe in the thin, lovely air of summits, and in their mouths there would not be a trace of the dust of the prairies where, as on a treadmill, Great-grandfather Bay's oxen plodded on and on into eternity.

The next days were for Polly at once harrowing and delightful. She suffered at the twilight hour (the brown sherry had become a daily custom, and she wondered if her aunt and uncle naively considered getting her drunk and, in this condition, persuading her to sign an unconditional indenture) and all through dinner as, by turns self-pitying and contentious, they sought to make her change her mind. Or, as they put it, "come to her senses." At no time did they accept the fact that she was going. They wrangled over summer plans in which she was included; they plotted anniversary speeches in the Bay museum; one afternoon Aunt Jane even started making a list of miners' families among whom Polly was to distribute Christmas baskets.

But when they were out of her sight and their nagging voices were out of her hearing, they were out of her mind, and in it, instead, was Robert Fair, in his rightful place. She graded examination papers tolerantly, through a haze; she packed her new clothes into her new suitcases and emptied her writing desk completely. On these starry, handsome nights, her dreams were charming, although, to be sure, she sometimes woke from them to hear the shuffle of carpet slippers on the floor below her as her insomniac aunt or uncle paced. But before sadness or rue could overtake her, she burrowed into the memory of her late dream.

The strain of her euphoria and her aunt's and uncle's antipodean gloom began at last to make her edgy, and she commenced to mark the days off on her calendar and even to reckon the hours. On the day she met her classes for the last time and told her colleagues goodbye and quit the campus forever, she did not stop on the first floor of the house but went directly to her room, only pausing at the parlor door to tell Aunt Jane and Uncle Francis that she had a letter to get off. Fraudulently humble, sighing, they begged her to join them later on for sherry. "The days are growing longer," said Aunt Jane plaintively, "but they are growing fewer."

Polly had no letter to write. She had a letter from Robert Fair to read, and although she knew it by heart already, she read it again several times. He shared her impatience; his students bored him, too; he said he had tried to envision her uncle's house, so that he could imagine her in a specific place, but he had not been able to succeed, even with the help of her sister. He wrote, "The house your malicious sister Mary describes could not exist. Does Aunt Jane *really* read Ouida?"

She laughed aloud. She felt light and purged, as if she had finished a fever. She went to her dressing table and began to brush her hair and to gaze, comforted, upon her young and loving face. She was so lost in her relief that she was pretty, and that she was going to be married and was going away, that she heard neither the telephone nor Mildred's feet upon the stairs, and the housekeeper was in the room before Polly had turned from her pool.

"It's your sister calling you from Boston," said Mildred with ice-cold contempt; she mirrored her employers. "I heard those operators back East giving themselves *some* airs with their la-di-da way of talking."

Clumsy with surprise and confusion (Mary's calls to her were rare and never frivolous), and sorry that exigency and not calm plan took her downstairs again, she reeled into that smothering front hall where hat trees and cane stands stood like people. The door to the parlor was closed, but she knew that behind it Aunt Jane and Uncle Francis were listening.

When Mary's far-off, mourning voice broke to Polly the awful, the impossible, the unbelievable news that Robert Fair had died that morning of the heart disease from which he had intermittently suffered for some years,

Polly, wordless and dry-eyed, contracted into a nonsensical, contorted position and gripped the telephone as if this alone could keep her from drowning in the savage flood that had come from nowhere.

"Are you there, Polly? Can you hear me, darling?" Mary's anxious voice came louder and faster. "Do you want me to come out to you? Or can you come on here now?"

"I can't come now," said Polly. "There's nothing you can do for me." There had always been rapport between these sisters, and it had been deeper in the months since Robert Fair had appeared upon the scene to rescue and reward the younger woman. But it was shattered; the bearer of ill tidings is seldom thanked. "How can you help me?" Polly demanded, shocked and furious. "You can't bring him back to life."

"I can help bring you back to life," her sister said. "You must get out of *there*, Polly. It's more important now than ever."

"Do you think that was why I was going to marry him? Just to escape this house and this town?"

"No, no! Control yourself! We'd better not try to talk any more now— you call me when you can."

The parlor door opened, revealing Uncle Francis with a glass of sherry in his hand.

"Wait, Mary! Don't hang up!" Polly cried. There was a facetious air about her uncle; there was something smug. "I'll get the sleeper from Denver tonight," she said.

When she hung up, her uncle opened the door wider to welcome her to bad brown sherry; they had not turned on the lights, and Aunt Jane, in the twilight, sat in her accustomed place.

"Poor angel," said Uncle Francis.

"I am so sorry, so very sorry," said Aunt Jane.

When Polly said nothing but simply stared at their impassive faces, Uncle Francis said, "I think I'd better call up Wilder. You ought to have a sedative and go straight to bed."

"I'm going straight to Boston," said Polly.

"But why?" said Aunt Jane.

"Because he's there. I love him and he's there."

They tried to detain her; they tried to force the sherry down her throat; they told her she must be calm and they asked her to remember that at times like this one needed the love and the support of one's blood kin.

"I am going straight to Boston," she repeated, and turned and went quickly up the stairs. They stood at the bottom, calling to her: "You haven't settled your affairs. What about the bank?" "Polly, get hold of yourself! It's terrible, I'm heartbroken for you, but it's not the end of the world."

She packed nothing; she wanted nothing here—not even the new clothes she had bought in which to be a bride. She put on a coat and a hat and gloves and a scarf and put all the money she had in her purse and went downstairs again. Stricken but die-hard, they were beside the front door.

"Don't go!" implored Aunt Jane.

"You need us now more than ever!" her uncle cried.

"And we need you. Does that make no impression on you, Polly? Is your heart that cold?"

She paid no attention to them at all and pushed them aside and left the house. She ran to the station to get the last train to Denver, and once she had boarded it, she allowed her grief to overwhelm her. She felt chewed and mauled by the niggling hypochondriacs she had left behind, who had fussily tried to appropriate even her own tragedy. She felt sullied by their disrespect and greed.

How lonely I have been, she thought. And then, not fully knowing what she meant by it but believing in it faithfully, she said half aloud, "I am not lonely now."

QUESTIONS

"The Liberation"

1. What kind of people are Uncle Francis and Aunt Jane? What do their days consist of? Their conversations? How do they feel about being Western-ers? Why do you think that all of their children have "flown the coop"?

2. How does Stafford's description of Polly's behavior toward her aunt and uncle create a vivid sense of her character? What is your impression of Polly? What kind of life does she lead? Why has she kept her engagement a secret from her uncle and aunt?

3. Why does Polly feel as though "her own life had been like a dream of smothering"? How does Stafford make the reader share Polly's sense of claus-trophobia?

4. What details does Stafford use in describing the inside of Uncle Francis and Aunt Jane's house? What kind of atmosphere does the writer create? Look, for example, at the description of the "little mahogany casket" that sits on the front parlor table.

5. How do Polly's aunt and uncle respond to the news of her engagement? Why do they regard the East with such contempt? What tactics do they use in their efforts to prevent Polly from "abandoning" them?

6. Why does Polly have so much trouble recalling what her fiancé looks like? Do you have the impression that she is deeply in love with him?

7. This story is filled with images of death and decay. Find them and ex-plain what function they serve.

8. Polly feels as though she is being "killed . . . by her aunt and uncle." Is this feeling justified? Does the story make you share this feeling?

9. Why does Stafford "kill off" Robert Fair? How would the meaning of the story have been different if Polly had gone off to get married, as planned?

10. Compare the ending of this story to that of Kay Boyle's "Astronomer's Wife." Which protagonist do you find more admirable? Why? Do you see any similarities between Stafford's story and Kate Chopin's? Do they make similar statements about women and freedom?

11. What is the "call" in this story? Can Polly be considered a hero? Why or why not?

The Story of an Hour

KATE CHOPIN

Knowing that Mrs. Mallard was afflicted with a heart trouble, great care was taken to break to her as gently as possible the news of her husband's death.

It was her sister Josephine who told her, in broken sentences, veiled hints that revealed in half concealing. Her husband's friend Richards was there, too, near her. It was he who had been in the newspaper office when intelligence of the railroad disaster was received, with Brently Mallard's name leading the list of "killed." He had only taken the time to assure himself of its truth by a second telegram, and had hastened to forestall any less careful, less tender friend in bearing the sad message.

She did not hear the story as many women have heard the same, with a paralyzed inability to accept its significance. She wept at once, with sudden, wild abandonment, in her sister's arms. When the storm of grief had spent itself she went away to her room alone. She would have no one follow her.

There stood, facing the open window, a comfortable, roomy armchair. Into this she sank, pressed down by a physical exhaustion that haunted her body and seemed to reach into her soul.

She could see in the open square before her house the tops of trees that were all aquiver with the new spring life. The delicious breath of rain was in the air. In the street below a peddler was crying his wares. The notes of a distant song which some one was singing reached her faintly, and countless sparrows were twittering in the eaves.

There were patches of blue sky showing here and there through the clouds that had met and piled above the other in the west facing her window.

She sat with her head thrown back upon the cushion of the chair quite motionless, except when a sob came up into her throat and shook her, as a child who has cried itself to sleep continues to sob in its dreams.

She was young, with a fair, calm face, whose lines bespoke repression and even a certain strength. But now there was a dull stare in her eyes, whose gaze was fixed away off yonder on one of those patches of blue sky. It was not a glance of reflection, but rather indicated a suspension of intelligent thought.

There was something coming to her and she was waiting for it, fearfully. What was it? She did not know; it was too subtle and elusive to name. But she felt it, creeping out of the sky, reaching toward her through the sounds, the scents, the color that filled the air.

Now her bosom rose and fell tumultuously. She was beginning to recognize this thing that was approaching to possess her, and she was striving to beat it back with her will—as powerless as her two white slender hands would have been.

When she abandoned herself a little whispered word escaped her slightly parted lips. She said it over and over under her breath: "Free, free, free!" The vacant stare and the look of terror that had followed it went from her eyes. They stayed keen and bright. Her pulses beat fast, and the coursing blood warmed and relaxed every inch of her body.

She did not stop to ask if it were not a monstrous joy that held her. A clear and exalted perception enabled her to dismiss the suggestion as trivial.

She knew that she would weep again when she saw the kind, tender hands folded in death; the face that had never looked save with love upon her, fixed and gray and dead. But she saw beyond that bitter moment a long procession of years to come that would belong to her absolutely. And she opened and spread her arms out to them in welcome.

There would be no one to live for during those coming years; she would live for herself. There would be no powerful will bending her in that blind persistence with which men and women believe they have a right to impose a private will upon a fellow-creature. A kind intention or a cruel intention made the act seem no less a crime as she looked upon it in that brief moment of illumination.

And yet she had loved him—sometimes. Often she had not. What did it matter! What could love, the unsolved mystery, count for in face of this possession of self-assertion which she suddenly recognized as the strongest impulse of her being.

"Free! Body and soul free!" she kept whispering.

Josephine was kneeling before the closed door with her lips to the keyhole, imploring for admission. "Louise, open the door! I beg; open the door—you will make yourself ill. What are you doing, Louise? For heaven's sake open the door."

"Go away. I am not making myself ill." No; she was drinking in a very elixir of life through that open window.

Her fancy was running riot along those days ahead of her. Spring days, and summer days, and all sorts of days that would be her own. She breathed a quick prayer that life might be long. It was only yesterday she had thought with a shudder that life might be long.

She arose at length and opened the door to her sister's importunities. There was a feverish triumph in her eyes, and she carried herself unwittingly like a goddess of Victory. She clasped her sister's waist, and together they descended the stairs. Richards stood waiting for them at the bottom.

Some one was opening the front door with a latchkey. It was Brently Mallard who entered, a little travel-stained, composedly carrying his grip-sack and umbrella. He had been far from the scene of accident, and did not know there had been one. He stood amazed at Josephine's piercing cry; at Richards' quick motion to screen him from the view of his wife.

But Richards was too late.

When the doctors came they said she had died of heart disease—of joy that kills.

QUESTIONS

"The Story of an Hour"

1. Chopin does not describe her protagonist at length, but the few details she does provide are important. What do these details reveal about Mrs. Mallard?

2. What are Mrs. Mallard's feelings for her husband? How does she respond to the news of his death?

3. What type of husband has Brently Mallard been? Does his wife's reaction to the news of his death seem justified? Why or why not?

4. How important is setting here? Why does Chopin place her protagonist, for most of this very short story, seated before an open window in a closed room? Why is the description of the view through Mrs. Mallard's window significant?

5. In a very literal way, both Mr. Richards and Mrs. Mallard's sister Josephine can be seen as the heralds in this story, since they are the ones who deliver the shocking news that will bring about a dramatic change in the protagonist's life. But in what way can the "thing that was approaching to possess" Mrs. Mallard be regarded as a "herald"? What is this "subtle and elusive" thing, and what does it seem to offer?

6. What is the function of Mrs. Mallard's sister, Josephine, in the story? What sort of woman does she seem to be?

7. How would you describe Chopin's attitude toward marriage? Toward love between men and women?

8. Why does Mrs. Mallard fall dead at the sight of her husband?

9. Explain the last line of the story. Is there irony in it?

10. What is the significance of the title?

11. Discuss "The Story of an Hour" as an aborted quest.

Adventure

SHERWOOD ANDERSON

Alice Hindman, a woman of twenty-seven when George Willard was a mere boy, had lived in Winesburg all her life. She clerked in Winney's Dry Goods Store and lived with her mother, who had married a second husband.

Alice's step-father was a carriage painter, and given to drink. His story is an odd one. It will be worth telling some day.

At twenty-seven Alice was tall and somewhat slight. Her head was large and overshadowed her body. Her shoulders were a little stooped and her hair and eyes brown. She was very quiet but beneath a placid exterior a continual ferment went on.

When she was a girl of sixteen and before she began to work in the store, Alice had an affair with a young man. The young man, named Ned Currie, was older than Alice. He, like George Willard, was employed on the *Winesburg Eagle* and for a long time he went to see Alice almost every evening. Together the two walked under the trees through the streets of the town and talked of what they would do with their lives. Alice was then a very pretty girl and Ned Currie took her into his arms and kissed her. He became excited and said things he did not intend to say and Alice, betrayed by her desire to have something beautiful come into her rather narrow life, also grew excited. She also talked. The outer crust of her life, all of her natural diffidence and reserve, was torn away and she gave herself over to the emotions of love. When, late in the fall of her sixteenth year, Ned Currie went away to Cleveland where he hoped to get a place on a city newspaper and rise in the world, she wanted to go with him. With a trembling voice she told him what was in her mind. "I will work and you can work," she said. "I do not want to harness you to a needless expense that will prevent your making progress. Don't marry me now. We will get along without that and we can be together. Even though we live in the same house no one will say anything. In the city we will be unknown and people will pay no attention to us."

Ned Currie was puzzled by the determination and abandon of his sweetheart and was also deeply touched. He had wanted the girl to become his mistress but changed his mind. He wanted to protect and care for her.

"You don't know what you're talking about," he said sharply; "you may be sure I'll let you do no such thing. As soon as I get a good job I'll come back. For the present you'll have to stay here. It's the only thing we can do."

On the evening before he left Winesburg to take up his new life in the city, Ned Currie went to call on Alice. They walked about through the streets for an hour and then got a rig from Wesley Moyer's livery and went for a drive in the country. The moon came up and they found themselves unable to talk. In his sadness the young man forgot the resolutions he had made regarding his conduct with the girl.

They got out of the buggy at a place where a long meadow ran down to the bank of Wine Creek and there in the dim light became lovers. When at midnight they returned to town they were both glad. It did not seem to them that anything that could happen in the future could blot out the wonder and beauty of the thing that had happened. "Now we will have to stick to each other, whatever happens we will have to do that," Ned Currie said as he left the girl at her father's door.

The young newspaper man did not succeed in getting a place on a Cleveland paper and went west to Chicago. For a time he was lonely and wrote to Alice almost every day. Then he was caught up by the life of the city; he began to make friends and found new interests in life. In Chicago he boarded at a house where there were several women. One of them attracted his attention and he forgot Alice in Winesburg. At the end of a year he had stopped writing letters, and only once in a long time, when he was lonely or when he went into one of the city parks and saw the moon shining on the grass as it had shone that night on the meadow by Wine Creek, did he think of her at all.

In Winesburg the girl who had been loved grew to be a woman. When she was twenty-two years old her father, who owned a harness repair shop, died suddenly. The harness maker was an old soldier, and after a few months his wife received a widow's pension. She used the first money she got to buy a loom and became a weaver of carpets, and Alice got a place in Winney's store. For a number of years nothing could have induced her to believe that Ned Currie would not in the end return to her.

She was glad to be employed because the daily round of toil in the store made the time of waiting seem less long and uninteresting. She began to save money, thinking that when she had saved two or three hundred dollars she would follow her lover to the city and try if her presence would not win back his affection.

Alice did not blame Ned Currie for what had happened in the moonlight in the field, but felt that she could never marry another man. To her the thought of giving to another what she still felt could belong only to Ned seemed monstrous. When other young men tried to attract her attention she would have nothing to do with them. "I am his wife and shall remain his wife whether he comes back or not," she whispered to herself, and for all of her willingness to support herself could not have understood the growing modern idea of a woman's owning herself and giving and taking for her own ends in life.

Alice worked in the dry goods store from eight in the morning until six at night and on three evenings a week went back to the store to stay from seven until nine. As time passed and she became more and more lonely she began to practice the devices common to lonely people. When at night she went upstairs into her own room she knelt on the floor to pray and in her prayers whispered things she wanted to say to her lover. She became attached to inanimate objects, and because it was her own, could not bear to have anyone touch the furniture of her room. The trick of saving money, begun for a purpose, was carried on after the scheme of going to the city to find Ned Currie had been given up. It became a fixed habit, and when she needed new clothes she did not get them. Sometimes on rainy afternoons in the store she got out her bank book and, letting it lie open before her, spent hours dreaming impossible dreams of saving money enough so that the interest would support both herself and her future husband.

"Ned always liked to travel about," she thought. "I'll give him the chance. Some day when we are married and I can save both his money and my own, we will be rich. Then we can travel together all over the world."

In the dry goods store weeks ran into months and months into years as Alice waited and dreamed of her lover's return. Her employer, a grey old man with false teeth and a thin grey mustache that drooped down over his mouth, was not given to conversation, and sometimes, on rainy days and in the winter when a storm raged in Main Street, long hours passed when no customers came in. Alice arranged and rearranged the stock. She stood near the front window where she could look down the deserted street and thought of the evenings when she had walked with Ned Currie and of what he had said. "We will have to stick to each other now." The words echoed and re-echoed through the mind of the maturing woman. Tears came into her eyes. Sometimes when her employer had gone out and she was alone in the store she put her head on the counter and wept. "Oh, Ned, I am waiting," she whispered over and over, and all the time the creeping fear that he would never come back grew stronger within her.

In the spring when the rains have passed and before the long hot days of summer have come, the country about Winesburg is delightful. The town lies in the midst of open fields, but beyond the fields are pleasant patches of woodlands. In the wooded places are many little cloistered nooks, quiet places where lovers go to sit on Sunday afternoons. Through the trees they look out across the fields and see farmers at work about the barns or people driving up and down on the roads. In the town bells ring and occasionally a train passes, looking like a toy thing in the distance.

For several years after Ned Currie went away Alice did not go into the wood with other young people on Sunday, but one day after he had been gone for two or three years and when her loneliness seemed unbearable, she put on her best dress and set out. Finding a little sheltered place from which she could see the town and a long stretch of the fields, she sat down.

Fear of age and ineffectuality took possession of her. She could not sit still, and arose. As she stood looking out over the land something, perhaps the thought of never ceasing life as it expresses itself in the flow of the seasons, fixed her mind on the passing years. With a shiver of dread, she realized that for her the beauty and freshness of youth had passed. For the first time she felt that she had been cheated. She did not blame Ned Currie and did not know what to blame. Sadness swept over her. Dropping to her knees, she tried to pray, but instead of prayers words of protest came to her lips. "It is not going to come to me. I will never find happiness. Why do I tell myself lies?" she cried, and an odd sense of relief came with this, her first bold attempt to face the fear that had become a part of her every-day life.

In the year when Alice Hindman became twenty-five two things happened to disturb the dull uneventfulness of her days. Her mother married Bush Milton, the carriage painter of Winesburg, and she herself became a member of the Winesburg Methodist Church. Alice joined the church because she had become frightened by the loneliness of her position in life. Her mother's second marriage had emphasized her isolation. "I am becoming old and queer. If Ned comes he will not want me. In the city where he is living men are perpetually young. There is so much going on that they do not have time to grow old," she told herself with a grim little smile, and went resolutely about the business of becoming acquainted with people. Every Thursday evening when the store had closed she went to a prayer meeting in the basement of the church and on Sunday evening attended a meeting of an organization called The Epworth League.

When Will Hurley, a middle-aged man who clerked in a drug store and who also belonged to the church, offered to walk home with her she did not protest. "Of course I will not let him make a practice of being with me, but if he comes to see me once in a long time there can be no harm in that," she told herself, still determined in her loyalty to Ned Currie.

Without realizing what was happening, Alice was trying feebly at first, but with growing determination, to get a new hold upon life. Beside the drug clerk she walked in silence, but sometimes in the darkness as they went stolidly along she put out her hand and touched softly the folds of his coat. When he left her at the gate before her mother's house she did not go indoors, but stood for a moment by the door. She wanted to call to the drug clerk, to ask him to sit with her in the darkness on the porch before the house, but was afraid he would not understand. "It is not him that I want," she told herself; "I want to avoid being so much alone. If I am not careful I will grow unaccustomed to being with people."

During the early fall of her twenty-seventh year a passionate restlessness took possession of Alice. She could not bear to be in the company of the drug clerk, and when, in the evening, he came to walk with her she sent him away. Her mind became intensely active and when, weary from the long hours of standing behind the counter in the store, she went home and crawled into bed, she could not sleep. With staring eyes she looked into the darkness. Her imagination, like a child awakened from long sleep, played about the room. Deep within her there was something that would not be cheated by phantasies and that demanded some definite answer from life.

Alice took a pillow into her arms and held it tightly against her breasts. Getting out of bed, she arranged a blanket so that in the darkness it looked like a form lying between the sheets and, kneeling beside the bed, she caressed it, whispering words over and over, like a refrain. "Why doesn't something happen? Why am I left here alone?" she muttered. Although she sometimes thought of Ned Currie, she no longer depended on him. Her desire had grown vague. She did not want Ned Currie or any other man. She wanted to be loved, to have something answer the call that was growing louder and louder within her.

And then one night when it rained Alice had an adventure. It frightened and confused her. She had come home from the store at nine and found the house empty. Bush Milton had gone off to town and her mother to the house of a neighbor. Alice went upstairs to her room and undressed in the darkness. For a moment she stood by the window hearing the rain beat against the glass and then a strange desire took possession of her. Without stopping to think of what she intended to do, she ran downstairs through the dark house and out into the rain. As she stood on the little grass plot before the house and felt the cold rain on her body a mad desire to run naked through the streets took possession of her.

She thought that the rain would have some creative and wonderful effect on her body. Not for years had she felt so full of youth and courage. She wanted to leap and run, to cry out, to find some other lonely human and embrace him. On the brick sidewalk before the house a man stumbled homeward. Alice started to run. A wild, desperate mood took possession of her. "What do I care who it is. He is alone, and I will go to him," she thought; and then without stopping to consider the possible result of her madness, called softly. "Wait!" she cried. "Don't go away. Whoever you are, you must wait."

The man on the sidewalk stopped and stood listening. He was an old man and somewhat deaf. Putting his hand to his mouth, he shouted. "What? What say?" he called.

Alice dropped to the ground and lay trembling. She was so frightened at the thought of what she had done that when the man had gone on his way she did not dare get to her feet, but crawled on hands and knees through the grass to the house. When she got to her own room she bolted the door and drew her dressing table across the doorway. Her body shook as with a chill and her hands trembled so that she had difficulty getting into her nightdress. When she got into bed she buried her face in the pillow and wept brokenheartedly. "What is the matter with me? I will do something dreadful if I am not careful," she thought, and turning her face to the wall, began trying to force herself to face bravely the fact that many people must live and die alone, even in Winesburg.

QUESTIONS

"Adventure"

1. What was Alice Hindman like at sixteen? Why does she fall in love with Ned Currie? How deep is his devotion to her?

2. After Ned leaves Winesburg, what is Alice's life like? What does her determination to remain faithful to him, even when he has been gone for six years, reveal about her? Anderson writes that she is not like a modern woman. What does he mean by this?

3. At various points in Anderson's story, the protagonist is depicted in a natural setting—out in the woods and meadows and on lawns. What function do these natural settings have in the story? How does the protagonist respond to nature?

4. Why does her mother's remarriage frighten Alice? Explain why her remarriage causes Alice to join the Methodist church. What does Alice gain by it?

5. Why doesn't Alice respond to Will Hurvey's romantic overtures? Would she be likely at this point to welcome any man's attentions? She believes she is striving "to get a new hold on life." Do you agree?

6. What do you think the experience Alice has on the rainy night means? What is its significance to her? What is she seeking in this adventure? What does she discover? Notice her actions once she returns to her house: she moves her dressing table in front of her bedroom door. What is the meaning of this gesture?

7. What, in your opinion, is ultimately responsible for Alice's sterile, dismal existence? Does she lack certain qualities that would allow her to respond to life, to the risks, challenges and rewards it offers? Or is the force of circumstance—being a female in a small, provincial turn-of-the-century town—so crushing that it must be held responsible? It would be instructive to compare Alice Hindman with the protagonist of Jean Stafford's story "The Liberation" and with Mable Pervin of D. H. Lawrence's "The Horse-Dealer's Daughter," both reprinted in this volume.

CHAPTER TWO

The Other

The Other, also known as the double or the alter ego, frequently appears in stories of the quest and is a common character in literature of all kinds. Like a shadow, which is a dark, distorted, but ultimately recognizable image of the person who casts it, the Other may at first glance bear little resemblance to the hero. In fact, the two characters often look and behave in diametrically opposite ways. A close examination, however, reveals that they are intimately related—indeed, inseparable. Sometimes, this relationship is quite literal: the Other may be the hero's sibling or best friend. However, this is not always the case: the Other may be a complete stranger, even if oddly familiar. Seeing the Other for the first time, the hero may feel that they have met someplace before, though she or he cannot remember where or when. As they get to know each other better, surprising similarities may come to light, beginning with the stranger's name, which sometimes may even be the same as the hero's own.

The stranger who is uncannily familiar, the enemy who looks so much like the hero that they might be twins, the "black sheep of the family," the close friend to whom the central character is tied despite their totally contrasting personalities—each of these possible identities testifies to the Other's special nature, to the powerful bond between the protagonists of these stories and the inescapable figures who follow them. Though the protagonist may try to break or deny this bond, to disavow any connection to the Other, or even to run away, the reader gradually becomes aware that, in some sense, the two characters cannot exist without each other. Like Neil Simon's "Odd Couple," they are not mismatched but complementary, each possessing precisely those traits that his or her opposite number lacks. So perfectly do the two members of the pair mesh, in fact, that they sometimes seem less like distinct individuals than like two halves of a single human being.

Symbolically, the Other represents precisely that dark, unlived, and generally unacknowledged part of the central character's personality, kept hidden away from the eyes of the world and often from the protagonist's own awareness. For this reason, Robert Louis Stevenson gives the name "Mr. Hyde" to the character who embodies the violent and lustful impulses, the bestial underside, of the seemingly spotless hero, Dr. Jekyll. Often, doubles are rejected or despised because, like Mr. Hyde, they are actively evil or immoral: personifications of primitive energies and desires, the untamed urges society trains us to repress. Thus, the Other is frequently portrayed as an outright criminal, like Flannery O'Connor's mass murderer, The Misfit, or the homicidal maniac of Alberto Moravia's "He and I," both of whom represent the barbaric drives that lurk beneath and occasionally burst through the orderly and rational surface of our day-to-day lives.

In many instances, the Other represents a more personal form of the unacceptable. As Billy Joel's song "The Stranger" reminds us, "we all have a face that we hide away forever." Doubles frequently are shunned, feared, or despised because they are embodiments not of behavior condemned by society at large but rather of fantasies and drives that seem hateful or unsavory to particular individuals. These urges may be incompatible with the kind of human beings they imagine themselves to be, with their idealized self-images. The adoring father, for example, who slaves at a soul-crushing job for years, sacrificing his own happiness to give his children a better life, may repress a part of himself that longs to be free of his family, of the restraints and responsibilities they impose on him. The loving daughter who spends her young adulthood taking care of her invalid father may experience rage and hatred that she cannot possibly acknowledge. In stories about the Other, ordinary people often come face to face with figures who possess the very characteristics the protagonists have refused to recognize in themselves or from which they have cut themselves off. The title character of Leslie Silko's "Yellow Woman" encounters a dangerously seductive figure who embodies (among other things) all the passionate impulses missing from her humdrum marriage. The stuffy, pretentious narrator of James Alan McPherson's "The Story of a Dead Man," yearning for conformity and middle-class respectability, is dogged by his rough, thoroughly disreputable cousin, Billy Renfro, who represents an aspect of the protagonist's own background and experience, his identity, which he is ashamed of and is desperately trying to flee.

The name of McPherson's story is significant, because it invites the reader to wonder exactly who the title character, the "dead man," is: Billy Renfro or the narrator. The latter, it is clear, has achieved his coveted middle-class status at the cost of something vital and authentic in himself. Billy may be uncouth, even criminal, but he is alive, whereas the narrator, we come to feel, is a hollow man. The point is that when individuals are unable or unwilling to admit that the character traits embodied by the Other are actually a rejected or despised part of themselves, they suffer. On the other hand, coming to know and accept the double is always beneficial. Some stories emphasize the positive qualities of the Other. In Joseph Conrad's classic, frequently anthologized short story "The Secret Sharer," for example, the hero, a young ship's captain, somewhat lacking in confidence and uncomfortable with his new authority, meets a bold, intrepid double who puts the protagonist in touch with his own untapped powers. In Edgar Allen Poe's "William Wilson," it is the protagonist who is depraved and his mysterious alter ego who represents all the good qualities, the benevolent impulses latent in the narrator's character.

But even when the Other is portrayed as repulsive or base, it is important for the hero to come to terms with this figure. Meeting the Other is a crucial event in the hero's journey toward the ultimate goal. Indeed, it is often the first significant stage of the quest after the departure, since the hero cannot proceed along the dangerous path unless she or he is armed with the self-awareness that acceptance of the Other brings. Such acceptance, however, is difficult to achieve; by definition, the Other represents precisely those things people have the most trouble facing up to in themselves. Only true heroes can look unflinchingly at their Others—who embody everything they find most frightening or repellent in themselves— and admit that what they see is their own mirror images.

Thus, not every story depicts a successful encounter between a protagonist and a double. (Though this is rare, in some stories the protagonist *is* the double; that is, these stories are told from the point of view of the Other.) Frequently, the main characters steadfastly refuse to recognize their own features in the Other's face, insist to themselves that this distasteful figure has nothing to offer them, deny that the mysterious bond between them exists. Such individuals remain psychologically stunted, trapped, by their fear of what they might discover about themselves, within the narrow confines of a rigid self-definition. Such people are also likely to become their own worse enemies. Because they are incapable of accepting the dark sides of their personalities, people like the crazed narrator of Alberto Moravia's "He and I" and the title character of Isaac Bashevis Singer's "Getzel the Monkey" fall victim to the Other, become possessed by it. We see this happen in our own lives when our inability to admit to an unpleasant emotion—anger, for example—causes it not to disappear but to sink to a level of our minds where it remains hidden, even from our own awareness, where it grows stronger and stronger until it unexpectedly bursts forth in an inappropriate or destructive way. When this occurs, one is likely to say, "I don't know what came over me," or "I wasn't myself," and, at such moments, the stranger inside is temporarily in control. When it is rejected, the Other can easily turn from a potential helper, a figure who holds out the promise of increased self-knowledge and a fuller life, into an adversary. As Singer reminds us at the very end of his tale, the Other that we persistently spurn and despise "is an enemy. When it has the chance, it takes revenge."

William Wilson

EDGAR ALLAN POE

What say of it? what say CONSCIENCE *grim, That spectre in my path?*

CHAMBERLAIN's Pharronida

Let me call myself, for the present, William Wilson. The fair page now lying before me need not be sullied with my real appellation. This has been already too much an object for the scorn—for the horror—for the detestation of my race. To the uttermost regions of the globe have not the indignant winds bruited its unparalleled infamy? Oh, outcast of all outcasts most abandoned!—to the earth art thou not for ever dead? to its honors, to its flowers, to its golden aspirations?—and a cloud, dense, dismal, and limitless, does it not hang eternally between thy hopes and heaven?

I would not, if I could, here or to-day, embody a record of my later years of unspeakable misery, and unpardonable crime. This epoch—these later years—took unto themselves a sudden elevation in turpitude, whose origin alone it is my present purpose to assign. Men usually grow base by degrees. From me, in an instant, all virtue dropped bodily as a mantle. From comparatively trivial wickedness I passed, with the stride of a giant, into more than the enormities of an Elah-Gabalus. What chance—what one event brought this evil thing to pass, bear with me while I relate. Death approaches; and the shadow which foreruns him has thrown a softening influence over my spirit. I long, in passing through the dim valley, for the sympathy—I had nearly said for the pity—of my fellow men. I would fain have them believe that I have been, in some measure, the slave of circumstances beyond human control. I would wish them to seek out for me, in the details I am about to give, some little oasis of *fatality* amid a wilderness of error. I would have them allow—what they cannot refrain from allowing—that, although temptation may have erewhile existed as great, man was never *thus*, at least, tempted before—certainly, never *thus* fell. And is it therefore that he had never thus suffered? Have I not indeed been living in a dream? And am I not now dying a victim to the horror and the mystery of the wildest of all sublunary visions?

I am the descendant of a race whose imaginative and easily excitable temperament has at all times rendered them remarkable; and, in my earliest infancy, I gave evidence of having fully inherited the family character. As I advanced in years it was more strongly developed; becoming, for many reasons, a cause of serious disquietude to my friends, and of positive injury to myself. I grew self-willed, addicted to the wildest caprices, and a prey to the most ungovernable passions. Weak-minded, and beset with constitutional infirmities akin to my own, my parents could do but little to check the evil propensities which distinguished me. Some feeble and ill-directed efforts resulted in complete failure on their part, and, of course, in total triumph on mine. Thenceforward my voice was a household law; and at an age when few children have abandoned their leading-strings, I was left to the guidance of my own will, and became, in all but name, the master of my own actions.

My earliest recollections of a school-life are connected with a large, rambling, Elizabethan house, in a misty-looking village of England, where were a vast number of gigantic and gnarled trees, and where all the houses were excessively ancient. In truth, it was a dream-like and spirit-soothing place, that venerable old town. At this moment, in fancy, I feel the refreshing chilliness of its deeply-shadowed avenues, inhale the fragrance of its thousand shrubberies, and thrill anew with undefinable delight, at the deep hollow note of the church-bell, breaking, each hour, with sullen and sudden roar, upon the stillness of the dusky atmosphere in which the fretted Gothic steeple lay imbedded and asleep.

It gives me, perhaps, as much of pleasure as I can now in any manner experience, to dwell upon minute recollections of the school and its concerns. Steeped in misery as I am—misery, alas! only too real—I shall be pardoned for seeking relief, however slight and temporary, in the weakness of a few rambling details. These, moreover, utterly trivial, and even ridiculous in themselves, assume, to my fancy, adventitious importance, as connected with a period and a locality when and where I recognize the first ambiguous monitions of the destiny which afterward so fully overshadowed me. Let me then remember.

The house, I have said, was old and irregular. The grounds were extensive, and a high and solid brick wall, topped with a bed of mortar and broken glass, encompassed the whole. This prison-like rampart formed the limit of our domain; beyond it we saw but thrice a week—once every Saturday afternoon, when, attended by two ushers, we were permitted to take brief walks in a body through some of the neighboring fields—and twice during Sunday, when we were paraded in the same formal manner to the morning and evening service in the one church of the village. Of this church the principal of our school was pastor. With how deep a spirit of wonder and perplexity was I wont to regard him from our remote pew in the gallery, as, with step solemn and slow, he ascended the pulpit! This reverend man, with countenance so demurely benign, with robes so glossy and so clerically flowing, with wig so minutely powdered, so rigid, and so vast— could this be he who, of late, with sour visage, and in snuffy habiliments, administered, ferule in hand, the Draconian Laws of the academy? Oh, gigantic paradox, too utterly monstrous for solution!

At an angle of the ponderous wall frowned a more ponderous gate. It was riveted and studded with iron bolts, and surmounted with jagged iron spikes. What impressions of deep awe did it inspire! It was never opened save for the three periodical egressions and ingressions already mentioned; then, in every creak of its mighty hinges, we found a plenitude of mystery—a world of matter for solemn remark, or for more solemn meditation.

The extensive enclosure was irregular in form, having many capacious recesses. Of these, three or four of the largest constituted the play-ground. It was level, and covered with fine hard gravel. I well remember it had no trees, nor benches, nor anything similar within it. Of course it was in the rear of the house. In front lay a small parterre, planted with box and other shrubs, but through this sacred division we passed only upon rare occasions indeed—such as a first advent to school or final departure thence, or perhaps, when a parent or friend having called for us, we joyfully took our way home for the Christmas or Midsummer holidays.

But the house!—how quaint an old building was this!—to me how veritably a palace of enchantment! There was really no end to its windings— to its incomprehensible subdivisions. It was difficult, at any given time, to say with certainty upon which of its two stories one happened to be. From each room to every other there were sure to be found three or four steps either in ascent or descent. Then the lateral branches were innumerable— inconceivable—and so returning in upon themselves, that our most exact ideas in regard to the whole mansion were not very far different from those with which we pondered upon infinity. During the five years of my residence here, I was never able to ascertain with precision, in what remote locality lay the little sleeping apartment assigned to myself and some eighteen or twenty other scholars.

The school-room was the largest in the house—I could not help thinking, in the world. It was very long, narrow, and dismally low, with pointed Gothic windows and a ceiling of oak. In a remote and terror-inspiring angle was a square enclosure of eight or ten feet, comprising the *sanctum*, "during hours," of our principal, the Reverend Dr. Bransby. It was a solid structure, with massy door, sooner than open which in the absence of the "Dominie," we would all have willingly perished by the *peine forte et dure*. In other angles were two other similar boxes, far less reverenced, indeed, but still greatly matters of awe. One of these was the pulpit of the "classical" usher, one of the "English and mathematical." Interspersed about the room, crossing and recrossing in endless irregularity, were innumerable benches and desks, black, ancient, and time-worn, piled desperately with much bethumbed books, and so beseamed with initial letters, names at full length, grotesque figures, and other multiplied efforts of the knife, as to have entirely lost what little of original form might have been their portion in days long departed. A huge bucket with water stood at one extremity of the room, and a clock of stupendous dimensions at the other.

Encompassed by the massy walls of this venerable academy, I passed, yet not in tedium or disgust, the years of the third lustrum of my life. The teeming brain of childhood requires no external world of incident to occupy or amuse it; and the apparently dismal monotony of a school was replete with more intense excitement than my riper youth has derived from luxury, or my full manhood from crime. Yet I must believe that my first mental development had in it much of the uncommon—even much of the *outré*. Upon mankind at large the events of very early existence rarely leave in mature age any definite impression. All is gray shadow—a weak and irregular remembrance—an indistinct regathering of feeble pleasures and phantasmagoric pains. With me this is not so. In childhood I must have felt with the energy of a man what I now find stamped upon memory in lines as vivid, as deep, and as durable as the *exergues* of the Carthaginian medals.

Yet in fact—in the fact of the world's view—how little was there to remember! The morning's awakening, the nightly summons to bed; the connings, the recitations; the periodical half-holidays, and perambulations; the play-ground, with its broils, its pastimes, its intrigues—these, by a mental sorcery long forgotten, were made to involve a wilderness of sensation, a world of rich incident, an universe of varied emotion, of excitement the most passionate and spirit-stirring. *"Oh, le bon temps, que ce siècle de fer!"*

In truth, the ardor, the enthusiasm, and the imperiousness of my disposition, soon rendered me a marked character among my schoolmates, and by slow, but natural gradations, gave me an ascendancy over all not greatly older than myself—over all with a single exception. This exception was found in the person of a scholar, who, although no relation, bore the same Christian and surname as myself—a circumstance, in fact, little remarkable; for, notwithstanding a noble descent, mine was one of those everyday appellations which seem, by prescriptive right, to have been, time out of mind, the common property of the mob. In this narrative, I have therefore designated myself as William Wilson—a fictitious title not very dissimilar to the real. My namesake alone, of those who in school phraseology constituted "our set," presumed to compete with me in the studies of the class—in the sports and broils of the play-ground—to refuse implicit belief in my assertions, and submission to my will—indeed, to interfere with my arbitrary dictation in any respect whatsoever. If there is on earth a supreme and unqualified despotism, it is the despotism of a mastermind in boyhood over the less energetic spirits of its companions.

Wilson's rebellion was to me a source of the greatest embarrassment; the more so as, in spite of the bravado with which in public I made a point of treating him and his pretensions, I secretly felt that I feared him, and could not help thinking the equality which he maintained so easily with myself, a proof of his true superiority; since not to be overcome, cost me a perpet-

ual struggle. Yet this superiority—even this equality—was in truth acknowledged by no one but myself; our associates, by some unaccountable
blindness, seemed not even to suspect it. Indeed, his competition, his resistance, and especially his impertinent and dogged interference with my
purposes, were not more pointed than private. He appeared to be destitute
alike of the ambition which urged, and of the passionate energy of mind
which enabled me to excel. In his rivalry he might have been supposed
actuated solely by a whimsical desire to thwart, astonish, or mortify myself;
although there were times when I could not help observing, with a feeling
made up of wonder, abasement, and pique, that he mingled with his injuries, his insults, or his contradictions, a certain most inappropriate, and
assuredly most unwelcome *affectionateness* of manner. I could only con-
ceive this singular behavior to arise from a consummate self-conceit assuming the vulgar airs of patronage and protection.

Perhaps it was this latter trait in Wilson's conduct, conjoined with our
identity of name, and the mere accident of our having entered the school
upon the same day, which set afloat the notion that we were brothers,
among the senior classes in the academy. These do not usually inquire with
much strictness into the affairs of their juniors. I have before said, or should
have said, that Wilson was not, in a most remote degree, connected with
my family. But assuredly if we *had* been brothers we must have been twins;
for, after leaving Dr. Bransby's, I casually learned that my namesake was
born on the nineteenth of January, 1813—and this is a somewhat remarkable coincidence; for the day is precisely that of my own nativity.

It may seem strange that in spite of the continual anxiety occasioned me
by the rivalry of Wilson, and his intolerable spirit of contradiction, I could
not bring myself to hate him altogether. We had, to be sure, nearly every
day a quarrel in which, yielding me publicly the palm of victory, he, in
some manner, contrived to make me feel that it was he who had deserved
it; yet a sense of pride on my part, and a veritable dignity on his own, kept
us always upon what are called "speaking terms," while there were many
points of strong congeniality in our tempers, operating to awake in me a
sentiment which our position alone, perhaps, prevented from ripening into
friendship. It is difficult, indeed, to define, or even to describe, my real
feelings toward him. They formed a motley and heterogeneous admix-
ture—some petulant animosity, which was not yet hatred, some esteem,
more respect, much fear, with a world of uneasy curiosity. To the moralist
it will be unnecessary to say, in addition, that Wilson and myself were the
most inseparable of companions.

It was no doubt the anomalous state of existing affairs between us, which
turned all my attacks upon him (and there were many, either open or co-
vert) into the channel of banter or practical joke (giving pain while assuming the aspect of mere fun) rather than into a more serious and determined
hostility. But my endeavors on this head were by no means uniformly successful, even when my plans were the most wittily concocted; for my
namesake had much about him, in character, of that unassuming and quiet

austerity which, while enjoying the poignancy of its own jokes, has no heel of Achilles in itself, and absolutely refuses to be laughed at. I could find, indeed, but one vulnerable point, and that, lying in a personal peculiarity, arising, perhaps, from constitutional disease, would have been spared by any antagonist less at his wit's end than myself—my rival had a weakness in the facial or gutteral organs, which precluded him from arising his voice at any time *above a very low whisper*. Of this defect I did not fail to take what poor advantage lay in my power.

Wilson's retaliations in kind were many; and there was one form of his practical wit that disturbed me beyond measure. How his sagacity first discovered at all that so petty a thing would vex me, is a question I never could solve; but having discovered, he habitually practised the annoyance. I had always felt aversion to my uncourtly patronymic, and its very common, if not plebeian praenomen. The words were venom in my ears; and when, upon the day of my arrival, a second William Wilson came also to the academy, I felt angry with him for bearing the name, and doubly disgusted with the name because a stranger bore it, who would be the cause of its twofold repetition, who would be constantly in my presence, and whose concerns, in the ordinary routine of the school business, must inevitably, on account of the detestable coincidence, be often confounded with my own.

The feeling of vexation thus engendered grew stronger with every circumstance tending to show resemblance, moral or physical, between my rival and myself. I had not then discovered the remarkable fact that we were of the same age; but I saw that we were of the same height, and I perceived that we were even singularly alike in general contour of person and outline of feature. I was galled, too, by the rumor touching a relationship, which had grown current in the upper forms. In a word, nothing could more seriously disturb me (although I scrupulously concealed such disturbance) than any allusion to a similarity of mind, person, or condition existing between us. But, in truth, I had no reason to believe that (with the exception of relationship, and in the case of Wilson himself) this similarity had ever been made a subject of comment, or even observed at all by our schoolfellows. That *he* observed it in all its bearings, and as fixedly as I, was apparent; but that he could discover in such circumstances so fruitful a field of annoyance, can only be attributed, as I said before, to his more than ordinary penetration.

His cue, which was to perfect an imitation of myself, lay both in words and in actions; and most admirably did he play his part. My dress it was an easy matter to copy; my gait and general manner were without difficulty, appropriated; in spite of his constitutional defect, even my voice did not escape him. My louder tones were, of course, unattempted, but then the key—it was identical; *and his singular whisper, it grew the very echo of my own.*

How greatly this most exquisite portraiture harassed me (for it could not justly be termed a caricature), I will not now venture to describe. I had but one consolation—in the fact that the imitation, apparently, was noticed by myself alone, and that I had to endure only the knowing and strangely sarcastic smiles of my namesake himself. Satisfied with having produced in my bosom the intended effect, he seemed to chuckle in secret over the sting he had inflicted, and was characteristically disregardful of the public applause which the success of his witty endeavors might have so easily elicited. That the school, indeed, did not feel his design, perceive its accomplishment, and participate in his sneer, was, for many anxious months, a riddle I could not resolve. Perhaps the *graduation* of his copy rendered it not readily perceptible; or, more possibly, I owed my security to the masterly air of the copyist, who, disdaining the letter (which in a painting is all the obtuse can see), gave but the full spirit of his original for my individual contemplation and chagrin.

I have already more than once spoken of the disgusting air of patronage which he assumed toward me, and of his frequent officious interference with my will. This interference often took the ungracious character of advice; advice not openly given, but hinted or insinuated. I received it with repugnance which gained strength as I grew in years. Yet, at this distant day, let me do him the simple justice to acknowledge that I can recall no occasion when the suggestions of my rival were on the side of those errors or follies so usual to his immature age and seeming inexperience; that his moral sense, at least, if not his general talents and worldly wisdom, was far keener than my own; and that I might, to-day, have been a better and thus a happier man, had I less frequently rejected the counsels embodied in those meaning whispers which I then but too cordially hated and too bitterly despised.

As it was I at length grew restive in the extreme under his distasteful supervision, and daily resented more and more openly, what I considered his intolerable arrogance. I have said that, in the first years of our connection as schoolmates, my feelings in regard to him might have been easily ripened into friendship; but, in the latter months of my residence at the academy, although the intrusion of his ordinary manner had, beyond doubt, in some measure, abated, my sentiments, in nearly similar proportion, partook very much of positive hatred. Upon one occasion he saw this, I think, and afterward avoided, or made a show of avoiding me.

It was about the same period, if I remember aright, that, in an altercation of violence with him, in which he was more than usually thrown off his guard, and spoke and acted with an openness of demeanor rather foreign to his nature, I discovered, or fancied I discovered, in his accent, in his air, and general appearance, a something which first startled, and then deeply interested me, by bringing to mind dim visions of my earliest infancy—wild, confused, and thronging memories of a time when memory herself was yet unborn. I cannot better describe the sensation which oppressed me, than by saying that I could with difficulty shake off the belief of my having been acquainted with the being who stood before me, at some epoch very long ago—some point of the past even infinitely remote.

The delusion, however, faded rapidly as it came; and I mention it at all but to define the day of the last conversation I there held with my singular namesake.

The huge old house, with its countless subdivisions, had several large chambers communicating with each other, where slept the greater number of the students. There were, however (as must necessarily happen in a building so awkwardly planned), many little nooks or recesses, the odds and ends of the structure; and these the economic ingenuity of Dr. Bransby had also fitted up as dormitories; although, being the merest closets, they were capable of accommodating but a single individual. One of these small apartments was occupied by Wilson.

One night, about the close of my fifth year at the school, and immediately after the altercation just mentioned, finding everyone wrapped in sleep, I arose from bed, and, lamp in hand, stole through a wilderness of narrow passages, from my own bedroom to that of my rival. I had long been plotting one of those ill-natured pieces of practical wit at his expense in which I had hitherto been so uniformly unsuccessful. It was my intention, now, to put my scheme in operation and I resolved to make him feel the whole extent of the malice with which I was imbued. Having reached his closet, I noiselessly entered, leaving the lamp, with a shade over it, on the outside. I advanced a step and listened to the sound of his tranquil breathing. Assured by his being asleep, I returned, took the light, and with it again approached the bed. Close curtains were around it, which in the prosecution of my plan, I slowly and quietly withdrew, when the bright rays fell vividly upon the sleeper, and my eyes at the same moment, upon his countenance. I looked—and a numbness, an iciness of feeling instantly pervaded my frame. My breast heaved, my knees tottered, my whole spirit became possessed with an objectless yet intolerable horror. Gasping for breath, I lowered the lamp in still nearer proximity to the face. Were these—*these* the lineaments of William Wilson? I saw, indeed, that they were his, but I shook as if with a fit of the ague, in fancying they were not. What *was* there about them to confound me in this manner? I gazed—while my brain reeled with a multitude of incoherent thoughts. Not thus he appeared—assuredly not *thus*—in the vivacity of his waking hours. The same name! the same contour of person! the same day of arrival at the academy! And then his dogged and meaningless imitation of my gait, my voice, my habits, and my manner! Was it, in truth, within the bounds of human possibility, that *what I now saw* was the result, merely, of the habitual practice of this sarcastic imitation? Awe-stricken, and with a creeping shudder, I extinguished the lamp, passed silently from the chamber, and left, at once, the halls of that old academy, never to enter them again.

After a lapse of some months, spent at home in mere idleness, I found myself a student at Eton. The brief interval had been sufficient to enfeeble my remembrance of the events at Dr. Bransby's, or at least to effect a material change in the nature of the feelings with which I remembered them.

The truth—the tragedy—of the drama was no more. I could now find room to doubt the evidence of my senses; and seldom called up the subject at all but with wonder at the extent of human credulity, and a smile at the vivid force of the imagination which I hereditarily possessed. Neither was this species of skepticism likely to be diminished by the character of the life I led at Eton. The vortex of thoughtless folly into which I there so immediately and so recklessly plunged, washed away all but the froth of my past hours, engulfed at once every solid or serious impression, and left to memory only the veriest levities of a former existence.

I do not wish, however, to trace the course of my miserable profligacy here—a profligacy which set at defiance the laws, while it eluded the vigilance of the institution. Three years of folly, passed without profit, had but given me rooted habits of vice, and added, in a somewhat unusual degree, to my bodily stature, when, after a week of soulless dissipation, I invited a small party of the most dissolute students to a secret carousal in my chambers. We met at a late hour of the night; for our debaucheries were to be faithfully protracted until morning. The wine flowed freely, and there were not wanting other and perhaps more dangerous seductions; so that the gray dawn had already faintly appeared in the east while our delirious extravagance was at its height. Madly flushed with cards and intoxication, I was in the act of insisting upon a toast of more than wonted profanity, when my attention was suddenly diverted by the violent, although partial, unclosing of the door of the apartment, and by the eager voice of a servant from without. He said that some person, apparently in great haste, demanded to speak with me in the hall.

Wildly excited with wine, the unexpected interruption rather delighted than surprised me. I staggered forward at once, and a few steps brought me to the vestibule of the building. In this low and small room there hung no lamp; and now no light at all was admitted, save that of the exceedingly feeble dawn which made its way through the semi-circular window. As I put my foot over the threshold, I became aware of the figure of a youth about my own height, and habited in a white kerseymere morning frock, cut in the novel fashion of the one I myself wore at the moment. This the faint light enabled me to perceive; but the feature of his face I could not distinguish. Upon my entering, he strode hurriedly up to me, and, seizing me by the arm with a gesture of petulant impatience, whispered the words "William Wilson" in my ear.

I grew perfectly sober in an instant.

There was that in the manner of the stranger, and in the tremulous shake of his uplifted finger, as he held it between my eyes and the light, which filled me with unqualified amazement; but it was not this which had so violently moved me. It was the pregnancy of solemn admonition in the singular, low, hissing utterance; and, above all, it was the character, the tone, *the key,* of those few, simple, and familiar, yet *whispered* syllables, which came with a thousand thronging memories of bygone days, and struck upon my soul with the shock of a galvanic battery. Ere I could recover the use of my senses he was gone.

Although this event failed not of a vivid effect upon my disordered imagination, yet was it evanescent as vivid. For some weeks, indeed, I busied myself in earnest enquiry, or was wrapped in a cloud of morbid speculation. I did not pretend to disguise from my perception the identity of the singular individual who thus perseveringly interfered with my affairs, and harassed me with his insinuated counsel. But who and what was this Wilson?—and whence came he?—and what were his purposes? Upon neither of these points could I be satisfied—merely ascertaining, in regard to him, that a sudden accident in his family had caused his removal from Dr. Bransby's academy on the afternoon of the day in which I myself had eloped. But in a brief period I ceased to think upon the subject, my attention being all absorbed in a contemplated departure for Oxford. Thither I soon went, the uncalculating vanity of my parents furnishing me with an outfit and annual establishment, which would enable me to indulge at will in the luxury already so dear to my heart—to vie in profuseness of expenditure with the haughtiest heirs of the wealthiest earldoms in Great Britain.

Excited by such appliances to vice, my constitutional temperament broke forth with redoubled ardor, and I spurned even the common restraints of decency in the mad infatuation of my revels. But it were absurd to pause in the detail of my extravagance. Let it suffice, that among spendthrifts I out-Heroded Herod, and that, giving name to a multitude of novel follies, I added no brief appendix to the long catalogue of vices then usual in the most dissolute university of Europe.

It could hardly be credited, however, that I had, even here, so utterly fallen from the gentlemenly estate, as to seek acquaintance with the vilest arts of the gambler by profession, and, having become an adept in his despicable science, to practice it habitually as a means of increasing my already enormous income at the expense of the weak-minded among my fellow-collegians. Such, nevertheless, was the fact. And the very enormity of this offence against all manly and honorable sentiment proved, beyond doubt, the main if not the sole reason of the impunity with which it was committed. Who, indeed, among my most abandoned associates, would not rather have disputed the clearest evidence of his senses, than have suspected of such courses, the gay, the frank, the generous William Wilson—the noblest and most liberal commoner at Oxford—him whose follies (said his parasites) were but the follies of youth and unbridled fancy—whose errors but inimitable whim—whose darkest vice but a careless and dashing extravagance?

I had been now two years successfully busied in this way, when there came to the university a young *parvenu* nobleman, Glendinning—rich, said report, as Herodes Atticus—his riches, too, as easily acquired. I soon found him of weak intellect, and, of course, marked him as a fitting subject for my skill. I frequently engaged him in play, and contrived, with the gambler's usual art, to let him win considerable sums, the more effectually to entangle him in my snares. At length, my schemes being ripe, I met him (with the full intention that this meeting should be final and decisive) at the chambers of a fellow-commoner (Mr. Preston), equally intimate with both, but who, to do him justice, entertained not even a remote suspicion of my design. To give to this a better coloring, I had contrived to have assembled a party of some eight or ten, and was solicitously careful that the introduction of cards should appear accidental, and originate in the proposal of my contemplated dupe himself. To be brief upon a vile topic, none of the low finesse was omitted, so customary upon similar occasions, that it is a just matter for wonder how any are still found so besotted as to fall its victim.

We had protracted our sitting far into the night, and I had at length effected the manoeuvre of getting Glendinning as my sole antagonist. The game, too, was my favorite *écarté*. The rest of the company, interested in the extent of our play, had abandoned their own cards, and were standing around us as spectators. The *parvenu*, who had been induced by my artifices in the early part of the evening, to drink deeply, now shuffled, dealt, or played, with a wild nervousness of manner for which his intoxication, I thought, might partially, but could not altogether account. In a very short period he had become my debtor to a large amount, when, having taken a long draught of port, he did precisely what I had been coolly anticipating—he proposed to double our already extravangant stakes. With a well-feigned show of reluctance, and not until after my repeated refusal had seduced him into some angry words which gave a color of *pique* to my compliance, did I finally comply. The result, of course, did but prove how entirely the prey was in my toils: in less than an hour he had quadrupled his debt. For some time his countenance had been losing the florid tingle lent it by the wine; but now, to my astonishment, I perceived that it had grown to a pallor truly fearful. I say, to my astonishment. Glendinning had been represented to my eager inquiries as immeasurably wealthy; and the sums which he had as yet lost, although in themselves vast, could not, I supposed, very seriously annoy, much less so violently affect him. That he was overcome by the wine just swallowed, was the idea which most readily presented itself; and, rather with a view to the preservation of my own character in the eyes of my associates, than from any less interested motive, I was about to insist, peremptorily, upon the discontinuance of the play, when some expressions at my elbow from among the company, and an ejaculation evincing utter despair on the part of Glendinning, gave me to understand that I had effected his total ruin under circumstances which, rendering him an object for the pity of all, should have protected him from the ill offices even of a fiend.

What now might have been my conduct it is difficult to say. The pitiable condition of my dupe had thrown an air of embarrassed gloom over all; and, for some moments, a profound silence was maintained, during which I could not help feeling my cheeks tingle with the many burning glances of scorn or reproach cast upon me by the less abandoned of the party. I will even own that an intolerable weight of anxiety was for a brief instant lifted from my bosom by the sudden and extraordinary interruption which ensued. The wide, heavy folding doors of the apartment were all at once thrown open, to their full extent, with a vigorous and rushing impetuosity that extinguished, as if by magic, every candle in the room. Their light, in dying, enabled us just to perceive that a stranger had entered, about my own height, and closely muffled in a cloak. The darkness, however, was not total; and we could only *feel* that he was standing in our midst. Before any one of us could recover from the extreme astonishment into which this rudeness had thrown all, we heard the voice of the intruder.

"Gentlemen," he said, in a low, distinct, and never-to-be-forgotton *whisper* which thrilled to the very marrow of my bones, "Gentlemen, I make an apology for this behavior, because in thus behaving, I am fulfilling a duty. You are, beyond doubt, uninformed of the true character of the person who has tonight won at *écarté* a large sum of money from Lord Glendinning. I will therefore put you upon an expeditious and decisive plan of obtaining this very necessary information. Please to examine, at your leisure, the inner linings of the cuff of his left sleeve, and the several little packages which may be found in the somewhat capacious pockets of his embroidered morning wrapper."

While he spoke, so profound was the stillness that one might have heard a pin drop upon the floor. In ceasing, he departed at once, and as abruptly as he had entered. Can I—shall I describe my sensations? Must I say that I felt all the horrors of the damned? Most assuredly I had little time for reflection. Many hands roughly seized me upon the spot, and lights were immediately reprocured. A scarch ensued. In the lining of my sleeve were found all the court cards essential in *écarté*, and, in the pockets of my wrapper, a number of packs, fac-similes of those used at our sittings, with the single exception that mine were of the species called, technically, *arrondees;* the honors being slightly convex at the ends, the lower cards slightly convex on the sides. In this disposition, the dupe who cuts, as customary, at the length of the pack, will invariably find that he cuts his antagonist an honor; while the gambler, cutting at the breadth, will, as certainly, cut nothing for his victim which may count in the records of the game.

Any burst of indignation upon this discovery would have affected me less than the silent contempt, or the sarcastic composure, with which it was received.

"Mr. Wilson," said our host, stooping to remove from beneath his feet an exceedingly luxurious cloak of rare furs, "Mr. Wilson, this is your property." (The weather was cold; and, upon quitting my own room, I had thrown a cloak over my dressing wrapper, putting it off upon reaching the scene of the play.) "I presume it is supererogatory to seek here" (eyeing the folds of the garment with a bitter smile) "for any farther evidence of your skill. Indeed, we have had enough. You will see the necessity, I hope, of quitting Oxford—at all events, of quitting instantly my chambers."

Abased, humbled to the dust as I then was, it is probable that I should have resented this galling language by immediate personal violence, had not my whole attention been at the moment arrested by a fact of the most startling character. The cloak which I had worn was of a rare description of fur; how rare, how extravagantly costly, I shall not venture to say. Its fashion, too, was of my own fantastic invention; for I was fastidious to an absurd degree of coxcombry, in matters of this frivolous nature. When, therefore, Mr. Preston reached me that which he had picked up upon the floor, and near the folding-doors of the apartment, it was with an astonishment nearly bordering upon terror, that I perceived my own already hanging on my arm (where I had no doubt unwittingly placed it), and that the one presented me was but its exact counterpart in every, in even the minutest possible particular. The singular being who had so disastrously exposed me, had been muffled, I remembered, in a cloak; and none had been worn at all by any of the members of our party, with the exception of myself. Retaining some presence of mind, I took the one offered me by Preston; placed it, unnoticed, over my own; left the apartment with a resolute scowl of defiance; and, next morning ere dawn of day, commenced a hurried journey from Oxford to the continent, in a perfect agony of horror and of shame.

I fled in vain. My evil destiny pursued me as if in exultation, and proved, indeed, that the exercise of its mysterious dominion had as yet only begun. Scarcely had I set foot in Paris, ere I had fresh evidence of the detestable interest taken by this Wilson in my concerns. Years flew, while I experienced no relief. Villain!—at Rome, with how untimely, yet with how spectral an officiousness, stepped he in between me and my ambition! at Vienna, too—at Berlin—and at Moscow! Where, in truth, had I *not* bitter cause to curse him within my heart? From his inscrutable tyranny did I at length flee, panic-stricken, as from a pestilence; and to the very ends of the earth *I fled in vain.*

And again, and again, in secret communion with my own spirit, would I demand the questions "Who is he?—whence came he?—and what are his objects?" But no answer was there found. And now I scrutinized, with a minute scrutiny, the forms, and the methods, and the leading traits of his impertinent supervision. But even here there was very little upon which to base a conjecture. It was noticeable, indeed, that, in no one of the multiplied instances in which he had of late crossed my path, had he so crossed it except to frustrate those schemes, or to disturb those actions, which, if fully carried out, might have resulted in bitter mischief. Poor justification this, in truth, for an authority so imperiously assumed! Poor indemnity for natural rights of self-agency so pertinaciously, so insultingly denied!

I had also been forced to notice that my tormentor, for a very long period of time (while scrupulously and with miraculous dexterity maintaining his whim of an identity of apparel with myself) had so contrived it, in the execution of his varied interference with my will, that I saw not, at any moment, the features of his face. Be Wilson what he might, *this* at least, was but the veriest of affectation, or of folly. Could he, for an instant, have supposed that, in my admonisher at Eton—in the destroyer of my honor at Oxford—in him who thwarted my ambition at Rome, my revenge at Paris, my passionate love at Naples, or what he falsely termed my avarice

in Egypt—that in this, my arch-enemy and evil genius, I could fail to recognize the William Wilson of my school-boy days—the namesake, the companion, the rival—the hated and dreaded rival at Dr. Bransby's? Impossible!—but let me hasten to the last eventful scene of the drama.

Thus far I had succumbed supinely to this imperious domination. The
sentiment of deep awe with which I habitually regarded the elevated character, the majestic wisdom, the apparent omnipresence and omnipotence
of Wilson, added to a feeling of even terror, with which certain other traits
in his nature and assumptions inspired me, had operated hitherto, to impress me with an idea of my own utter weakness and helplessness, and to
suggest an implicit, although bitterly reluctant submission to his arbitrary
will. But, of late days, I had given myself up entirely to wine; and its
maddening influence upon my hereditary temper rendered me more and
more impatient of control. I began to murmur—to hesitate—to resist. And
was it only fancy which induced me to believe that, with the increase of
my own firmness, that of my tormentor underwent a proportional diminu-
tion? Be this as it may, I now began to feel the inspiration of a burning
hope, and at length nurtured in my secret thoughts a stern and desperate
resolution that I would submit no longer to be enslaved.

It was at Rome, during the Carnival of 18–, that I attended a masquerade
in the palazzo of the Neapolitan Duke Di Broglio. I had indulged more
freely than usual in the excesses of the wine-table; and now the suffocating
atmosphere of the crowded rooms irritated me beyond endurance. The
difficulty, too, of forcing my way through the mazes of the company contributed not a little to the ruffling of my temper; for I was anxiously seeking
(let me not say with what unworthy motive) the young, the gay, the beautiful wife of the aged and doting Di Broglio. With a too unscrupulous confidence she had previously communicated to me the secret of the costume
in which she would be habited, and now, having caught a glimpse of her
person, I was hurrying to make my way into her presence. At this moment
I felt a light hand placed upon my shoulder, and that ever-remembered,
low, damnable *whisper* within my ear.

In an absolute frenzy of wrath, I turned at once upon him who had thus
interrupted me, and seized him violently by the collar. He was attired, as
I had expected, in a costume altogether similar to my own; wearing a Spanish cloak of blue velvet, begirt about the waist with a crimson belt sustaining a rapier. A mask of black silk entirely covered his face.

"Scoundrel!" I said, in a voice husky with rage, while every syllable I
uttered seemed as new fuel to my fury; "scoundrel! imposter! accursed
villain! you shall not—you *shall not* dog me unto death! Follow me, or I
stab you where you stand!"—and I broke my way from the ballroom into a
small antechamber adjoining, dragging him unresistingly with me as I went.

Upon entering, I thrust him furiously from me. He staggered against the
wall, while I closed the door with an oath, and commanded him to draw.
He hesitated but for an instant; then, with a slight sigh, drew in silence,
and put himself upon his defence.

The contest was brief indeed. I was frantic with every species of wild excitement, and felt within my single arm the energy and power of a multitude. In a few seconds I forced him by sheer strength against the wainscotting, and thus, getting him at mercy, plunged my sword, with brute ferocity, repeatedly through and through his bosom.

At that instant some person tried the latch of the door. I hastened to prevent an intrusion, and then immediately returned to my dying antagonist. But what human language can adequately portray *that* astonishment, *that* horror which possessed me at the spectacle then presented to view? The brief moment in which I averted my eyes had been sufficient to produce, apparently, a material change in the arrangements at the upper or farther end of the room. A large mirror—so at first it seemed to me in my confusion—now stood where none had been perceptible before; and as I stepped up to it in extremity of terror, mine own image, but with features all pale and dabbled in blood, advanced to meet me with a feeble and tottering gait.

Thus it appeared, I say, but was not. It was my antagonist—it was Wilson, who then stood before me in the agonies of his dissolution. His mask and cloak lay, where he had thrown them, upon the floor. Not a thread in all his raiment—not a line in all the marked and singular lineaments of his face which was not, even in the most absolute identity, *mine own!*

It was Wilson; but he spoke no longer in a whisper, and I could have fancied that I myself was speaking while he said:

"*You have conquered, and I yield. Yet henceforth art thou also dead— dead to the World, to Heaven, and to Hope! In me didst thou exist—and, in my death, see by this image, which is thine own, how utterly thou hast murdered thyself.*"

QUESTIONS

"William Wilson"

1. What is the significance of the epigraph at the start of the story?

2. How much does Poe's style contribute to the effect of the story? How does the language of the opening section create a sense of barely controlled hysteria, of a mind tottering on the brink of madness? Does this feverish tone remain consistent throughout the story?

3. The narrator believes himself to "have been, in some measure, the slave of circumstances beyond human control." Do you agree with this feeling? Why or why not?

4. Describe the school, the "venerable academy," the narrator attends as a

boy. Why does Poe describe it in so much detail? Does this lengthy description add anything to the story? Explain.

5. How does the narrator account for the peculiar circumstance that his rival has "the same Christian and surname" as himself? What other, similar coincidences appear in the story?

6. What is the narrator's position in respect to his schoolmates? How do they feel about him? Treat him? What is the nature of the "resistance" the narrator feels his namesake constantly directs at him? What kind of relationship do the two William Wilsons have? How do you explain their being "the most inseparable of companions"?

7. What is the "personal peculiarity that afflicts the speaker's double? What is its significance? Why does Poe endow the character with this particular trait?

8. Certain things about the second William Wilson, such as his "intolerable spirit of contradiction" and his perfect mimicry of the protagonist, are especially galling to the latter. How do you account for the strange fact that nobody else is aware of these things, that the other students are totally oblivious of the behavior the narrator finds so intolerable in his double? How does the narrator explain it?

9. What form does the second William Wilson's "interference" take?

10. What does the narrator see on the night he sneaks into his sleeping rival's bedroom and looks at his namesake's face in the lamplight? Why is the narrator so "awestricken" and terrified?

11. On what kinds of occasions does the narrator's mysterious double appear after the two leave school? Why does the narrator come to regard his namesake as a "tormentor" and a tyrant?

12. Explain what happens at the end of the story. In what sense is the double's last sentence true?

13. Repeatedly in the story, the narrator is tormented by the question of his "arch-enemy's" identity: ". . . who and what was this Wilson?—and whence came he?—and what were his purposes?" Poe, however, makes the answers to these questions clear to the reader. What are the answers?

The Lost Explorer

PATRICK MCGRATH

One fresh and gusty day in the damp autumn of her twelfth year Evelyn found a lost explorer in the garden of her parents' London home. He was lying in a small tent beneath a mosquito net so torn and gaping as to be quite inadequate, were there any mosquitoes for it to protect him from. His clothes were stained with sweat and blood, and a grizzled beard stubbled his emaciated face. On the folding stool beside the camp bed stood a flask, empty, a revolver, unloaded, two bullets, three matches, a small oil lamp, and a dirty, creased map of the upper reaches of the Congo. He was delirious with fever and occasionally gibbered about the pygmies. Evelyn thought he was wonderful.

And he thought she was wonderful, too. When the delirium had passed and he lay, pale, spent, and shivering, she loomed out of the fog that was his consciousness like a bright ministering angel.

"Agatha," he whispered. "I want a drink of water." The angel vanished, and the explorer lay panting feebly in his tiny tent. In the deep, still place at the center of his frenzied mind a flame of hope was lit, for Agatha was here. What had happened was this: the explorer had mistaken Evelyn for the nanny who'd nursed him through a childhood illness!

Evelyn returned to the tent with a cup of water. She folded back the ragged netting and helped the explorer onto an elbow. Much of the water spilled onto his bush jacket, but at length his parched lips smacked up their fill and he lay back, exhausted. Evelyn gazed down at him with benevolent compassion."

"Agatha," he whispered, "give me your hand." She knelt on the ground beside the camp bed and took the explorer's clammy palm in her fingers. A ghost of a smile hovered at the cracked edges of the man's lips. "Agatha," he sighed; but then, seized suddenly with a fresh wave of panic, he started up from his bed. "The pygmies, Agatha!" he shouted. "I hear the pygmies!"

Evelyn remained calm. She laid her cool hand upon his fevered temples. The traffic of London murmured in the thoroughfares beyond. "They're miles away," she whispered. "They don't know you're here."

"They're coming!" he shouted, his head jerking from side to side and his red-rimmed eyes abulge. "They're coming to eat us!"

"Nonsense," breathed Evelyn, stroking that troubled brow. "No one's going to eat us."

The panic passed; a moment later the tension was visibly draining from the explorer's body. He sank back onto the camp bed. "Agatha," he said weakly, his hand still clutching hers. "You're good."

"Rest," murmured Evelyn. "Sleep. You're safe now. Sleep."

When she was sure the explorer was sound asleep, Evelyn skipped up the garden to the house. A washing line was strung from a post at the top of the steps to a tree by the wall at the side of the house. To this line were pegged three white sheets, all flapping wildly in the wind. Dead leaves spun about the girl as she pattered gracefully up the steps from the garden. She opened the back door. Her mother and Mrs. Guppy were bent over the oven with their backsides to her.

"Are you quite sure it's done, Mrs. Guppy?" her mother was saying.

"It's had twenty-five minutes, Mrs. Piker-Smith. It must be done."

"Oh, I do hope so. Gerald is so fussy about his chop. Ah, there you are, Evelyn. Run and wash your hands, dear, and we'll eat."

Mrs. Piker-Smith was a plump, tweedy woman, and she was commonly in the throes of mild anxiety. Ten minutes later she sat at the dining-room table gazing at her husband, Gerald, the eminent surgeon. He in turn was gazing at his chop. Evelyn had already started to eat, and paid no attention to either of them.

"Is it all right, dear?" said Mrs. Piker-Smith. "We gave it almost half-an-hour." Her own knife and fork were poised at a shallow angle above her plate. A sudden gust rattled the windowpane. The surgeon tentatively sliced a small section of meat and raised the fork to his lips. He chewed the meat thoughtfully, his eyes wandering about the ceiling and upper walls as he did so. Finally he swallowed and, laying down his cutlery, dabbed at his lips with a starched white napkin. "It's quite thoroughly cooked, Denise," he said, his eyes suddenly settling upon his wife's troubled face. "You need not worry so."

"Oh, good," said Mrs. Piker-Smith, brightening, and with some gusto cut a potato in two. "What have you been doing all morning, Evelyn?" she said, turning to her daughter.

"Oh, nothing."

"Nothing?" said her father, eating.

"Just playing in the garden, Daddy."

"What ever does the child get up to?" he murmured, as he transferred a spot of English mustard from the side of his plate to a neat rectangle of chop.

"Daddy."

"Yes, Evelyn?"

"Are there still pygmies in the Congo?"

A frown briefly ruffled the calm surface of the surgeon's fine-domed brow, like a breeze whispering across a lake. "I believe so. Why do you ask?"

"Oh, school."

"Are you doing Africa, darling?" said Mrs. Piker-Smith.

"Sort of."

"It's not called the Congo anymore," said Daddy. "It became Zaïre when the Belgians left."

"When was that, Daddy?"

"Nineteen-sixty, I think."

After lunch Evelyn always had to go to her room and read on her bed for an hour. Today she stood at the bedroom window, gazing into the garden and thinking about her explorer. White clouds fled like driven rags across the blustering blue sky, and the branches of the great elm at the bottom of the garden flailed about like the arms of drowning men. The Piker-Smiths' was one of those long narrow gardens enclosed by an old wall whose crumbling red bricks were overgrown with ivy. The path ran from the foot of the back-door steps between two flowerbeds and then twisted over a stretch of lawn before arriving at a small round goldfish pond, the surface of which was half-hidden by clusters of green-fronded water lilies. Beyond the pond a gardening shed, its windows misted with dust and cobwebs and its door secured by a huge rusting padlock, clung in ramshackle fashion to the corner formed by the east wall and the end wall. The rest of the garden beyond the pond was a tangled and overgrown mass of rhododendron bushes, into whose labyrinthine depths, since the death of the old gardener, only Evelyn now ventured. It was in that tangled thicket of evergreens that the explorer's tent was pitched, and there that the man himself lay struggling with a furious malaria. The three white sheets billowed in the wind, and for an instant Evelyn imagined the house and the garden as a great ship shouldering on to the tropics. Absently she picked up a jar containing a pickled thumb that Daddy had given her. She swirled it round in its liquid and willed the time to pass.

When her hour was up, Evelyn came downstairs to find Daddy in the hall just leaving for the hospital. He was telling Mummy something about dinner: the Cleghorns were coming and there was no sherry in the house. Then Daddy said goodbye and left.

"Now, darling," said Mrs. Piker-Smith, "I'm off to my bridge. You'll be all right till Mrs. Guppy gets back?"

"Yes, Mummy."

Then Mrs. Piker-Smith left too. Evelyn was alone. She was down the back-door steps in a flash, under the billowing sheets, across the lawn and into the bushes. The explorer was still fast asleep. Evelyn knelt beside him and watched his face with intense concentration for some minutes. Then her gaze drifted to the objects on his camp stool, and settled on the black revolver. She had never touched a gun before, and it fascinated her. She reached out hesitantly, and clasped it by the grip. How cold and slippery it was! And how heavy! She lifted it and pressed the barrel to her cheek.

It smelled metallic and oily. She touched it once with her tongue, and recoiled with a small shock as she tasted its steely sweetness. Ugh! She cradled it in her palms, in her lap, and stared at it solemnly. How would you put bullets into it? She could turn the cylinder, but she could not release it. Perhaps this little catch . . .

Evelyn screamed: a large, scarred hand, dark brown, very dirty, with hair on the back and cracked fingernails, had clamped onto her own slim fingers and held them fast. It was the explorer's hand. He was up on one elbow, staring at her, and his harrowed face was clenched and twitching with anger. She gazed at him with wide, shocked eyes. He took the revolver from her. "And the bullet," he growled, picking it from her open palm. He took the other bullet from the camp stool and then, his eyes darting from the girl to the revolver, he loaded two chambers.

"One for you, Agatha," he said hoarsely, "one for me." He nodded several times. "This way: quick—sure—painless. Better death, foil the pygmies, what." He subsided onto his back, suddenly exhausted. His fingers twitched upon the sweat-stained canvas of the cot, and a sudden access of perspiration left him pale and dripping. His eyes bulged, then fixed upon a point on the roof of the tent. His whole body shivered, and a limp hand fluttered from the canvas like an injured bird. "Agatha," he moaned; and Evelyn, dropping to her knees, took his hand.

All afternoon the fever raged, and the explorer mumbled incoherently throughout. On several occasions he was convulsed with terror, and rose up shouting that the pygmies were hard by; but each time Evelyn calmed and soothed the troubled man, mopped his brow and gave him water; and in his few moments of lucidity he gazed at her with weak, shining eyes and murmured the name Agatha. For in the turmoil of his disordered mind he lay in a child's bedroom, in a child's bed, with a stuffed golliwog beside him, and a kindly woman in a sort of ruffled white cap and a starched white apron briskly ministering to his child's disease; and thus did Evelyn appear to him.

When the light began at last to thicken, and the dusk of that autumnal day crept into the explorer's tent and pooled itself in clots of shadow in the corners of the tent, a voice came calling, "Evelyn! Evelyn!" The man stirred in his uneasy doze, muttering, and Evelyn leaned close to him. "I have to go," she whispered. "Sleep now, and I'll come back. . . ."

He seemed about to rise from the camp bed and cry out; his eyes opened wide for an instant; but then the netherworld of shadows and confusion reclaimed him, and he sank once more into sleep of a sort. Evelyn spread upon his twitching limbs the blanket she had brought out from the house; and then she padded silently away, through the bushes, and onto the path back to the house.

The Cleghorns were old friends of the family, so Evelyn was permitted to eat with the grown-ups. Mrs. Cleghorn—Auntie Vera—was a large dark woman with good teeth. She wore heavy lipstick and was married to an anesthetist called Frank—Uncle Frank—a colleague of Gerald's. Mummy and Auntie Vera often played bridge together, and it was about bridge that they were talking when Evelyn entered the drawing room, just before dinner. Everybody was drinking a rather nice South African sherry, and Evelyn was invited to have a juice. Then Mrs. Piker-Smith went to see Mrs. Guppy in the kitchen, and as the two men drew aside to talk shop for a moment Auntie Vera's great black eyes swiveled round on Evelyn like a pair of undimmed headlights.

"Evelyn," she cried, plumping a cushion with a large white hand. "Come here and sit next to me. How is school?" Evelyn liked Auntie Vera, but she was rather in awe of her. She sat down on the sofa, pressing her slender legs together and clasping her hands in her lap. "We're on half-term," she said, looking at the carpet.

"Half-term!" cried Auntie Vera. "How marvelous!"

"Yes," said Evelyn with great seriousness. "Do you know anything about Africa, Auntie Vera?" A coal fire crackled in the grate; above the mantelpiece hung a mirror, and invitations to social functions, mostly connected to the hospital, were tucked into the inside edge of the frame.

"Frank took me to Cairo for our honeymoon," said Auntie Vera, taking Evelyn's hand. "He pretended I was Cleopatra!" Evelyn turned toward her and found the great black headlamps shining with delight and the tip of Auntie Vera's tongue resting on her top lip.

Conversation at the dinner table ranged widely from the price of sherry to the price of beef. Gerald mentioned a rather interesting colostomy he'd performed after lunch, and Uncle Frank made some quips which might, in a nonmedical household, have been taken in rather bad taste. Only once did Evelyn pay any attention, and that was during the main course, when Auntie Vera turned to her husband and said, "Frank, Evelyn is interested in Africa."

Is she?" said Frank Cleghorn.

"Not all Africa, Uncle Frank," said Evelyn. "Just the Congo."

"Ah, the Congo!" said Uncle Frank flatly, and began to tell the story of Henry Morton Stanley, digressing rather amusingly to mention the tragic shooting death of John Hanning Speke mere hours before the eagerly awaited debate with Richard Burton on the source of the Nile; that was in 1864. Evelyn was sitting opposite Uncle Frank, who had his back to the door of the dining room, which was half-open; as Evelyn half-listened to his affable drone, she suddenly saw, over his shoulder, pausing in the doorway as he shuffled toward the stairs, the explorer. He turned his head and stared at her. Fortunately, she did not cry out; Auntie Vera was deep in animated bridge talk with Mummy, and Daddy was concentrating on a delicate incision he was about to make in a slice of reddish beef. Uncle Frank warbled on, and in the doorway behind his back stood the haggard, feverish man, and oh, how ill he looked! His head hung weakly on sagging shoulders; his eyes burned with a low, sickly gleam out of sunken sockets in an unshaven face deeply etched with gullies of suffering. His clothes looked extraordinarily ragged and filthy against the beige flowered wallpaper of the hallway, and his scarred, grimy hands still twitched convulsively where they dangled at his sides. Evelyn stared at him wide-eyed, and Uncle Frank was flattered at the raptness of her attention. It was only after some moments that he realized her eyes were focused not upon his own but beyond them; and he began, even as his discourse flowed forward, to turn in his seat. But at precisely the same instant the explorer shuffled off down the hallway out of sight; so that Uncle Frank, seeing nothing, turned back and talked on. Daddy, having completed his incision, lifted his fork and his eyes and turned to the anesthetist as his teeth closed upon the meat; and Auntie Vera lifted her wineglass while Mummy peered anxiously into the gravy boat.

When at last Evelyn was able to get away, she dashed upstairs; and as she had half-feared, and half-hoped, the explorer was in her bedroom. Not only was he in her bedroom, he was in her *bed*, fully clothed, the sheets up to his chin. His teeth were chattering loudly and his whole body shivered beneath the bedclothes.

"Cold," he grunted as Evelyn closed the door behind her and ran to the bed. "Cold, Agatha," he said more clearly, and she reached under the bedclothes for his hand. It was frigid. Something else was down there too—she felt the hard metallic bulge of the revolver, stuffed into the explorer's waistband. "Let me have the gun," she whispered.

A tremor passed across the pathetic features of the dying man. "Need will," he muttered. "Need will to do it. Pygmies . . ." Here he paused, and his chest heaved painfully with the effort to talk, the effort to think. Oh, how he wanted simply to slip away, let go, sink into peace and rest and silence and darkness!—but he could not let go, not yet. "Pygmies," he said, more loudly, and Evelyn with terror clapped her hand upon his parched and cracking lips. The wild eyes darted to her bedroom door. He knew they were near. "Pygmies," he whispered, when she lifted her palm from his mouth. "Coming to eat us. One for you, Agatha, one for me . . ."

"Don't talk," said Evelyn, her finger to her lips. "We won't be eaten. Sleep. I'll give you a drink."

Evelyn fetched a drink of water, and the explorer's eyes, as she supported his shoulders and held the cup to his lips, rested on her face with an expression of such profound pain, and gratitude, and spirit that it tested the girl's mettle pretty sternly. But she did not flinch nor falter, and when he had drunk she eased his head back onto her pillow and stroked his chilly brow.

"Agatha," he murmured, "Agatha," and his grip on her fingers loosened very slightly.

The rest of that evening was nerve-racking for Evelyn. She went downstairs to say good night to Uncle Frank and Auntie Vera, and to Mummy and Daddy, and then darted back up to her bedroom. She could only hope that Mummy wouldn't come to tuck her in tonight; it was something she did occasionally, by no means invariably. Evelyn made up a bed for herself on the carpet, and turned off the light. The explorer seemed to be sleeping soundly. She listened in the darkness for Mummy and Daddy coming up to bed. Daddy was first; she heard him brushing his teeth in the bathroom. Then Mummy came up, and stopped at the top of the stairs. Evelyn's heart was beating fit to burst; hot chemicals discharged and flooded in turmoil about her viscera; go to bed, Mummy, a voice in her brain screamed silently, *go to bed, Mummy!* Steps across the landing, and then—*a hand on Evelyn's door handle!*

The tension, in the few moments that followed, was, to Evelyn, lying there in the darkness, her eyes wide and her stomach awash with adrenaline, almost unendurable. Frightful scenarios unfolded at lightning speed in her febrile imagination. How could Mummy and Daddy be expected to understand about the explorer? And the gun! What if—

"Denise!"

Even as the handle turned, her father's voice called from the bathroom.

"What is it, Gerald?" replied her mother in hushed tones.

"Have we any dental floss?"

"On the shelf, dear." The door handle was still depressed; Evelyn desperately wanted to go to the bathroom herself.

"No, I don't see it."

"Oh, Gerald," murmured Mrs. Piker-Smith; and, wifely duty superseding maternal solicitude in the ethical hierarchy of that good woman, she tiptoed to the bathroom and located the dental floss. A short conversation about the beef ensued; and then Mrs. Piker-Smith went into the bedroom, closely followed by her husband, and their door; to Evelyn's immense relief, closed behind them. But it was another excruciating hour before she dared get up and creep to the bathroom.

The next morning the explorer was dead. Silently, and, one hopes, peacefully, in the middle of the night, he had passed away. Evelyn awoke at six and realized it immediately. He was stiff and staring, and when she laid her hand upon his face, his skin was even colder than it had been last night. She closed his eyes; and then she lay on the bed beside him, on top of the blankets, and she wept quietly for ten minutes. She wept into her blankets as the fact of the loss of that long-suffering man rose up starkly in her heart, and she wept too for herself, for she was desolate. Her sorrow was keen, but it would not fester; and when she rose from her bed, wet-eyed and gulping back the hot taste of grief in her throat, she tried to think clearly what was best. But first she must air the room, and the bed, and change the sheets, for the stink of a man too long in the jungle hung heavy in Evelyn's bedroom.

Fever had weakened him, diminished him, and the body was light. Evelyn, though skinny, was strong from hockey, and she dragged him from the bed to the closet quite easily. She sat him in the darkest corner, covered him up with a pair of old school raincoats, and pushed all her clothes to that end of the rail. Then she opened wide the windows, stuffed the sheets into her laundry basket, and climbed under the blankets, where she lay in a state of rising anxiety till Mummy should come to wake her.

"Darling, you'll catch your death!" cried Mrs. Piker-Smith when she came in at half past eight. The windows were wide open and the day was very blustery indeed. The curtains flapped wildly and the air was chill. Even so, there were traces. "What's that funny smell, darling?" said Mummy, standing by the closet door and wrinkling her nose. Evelyn, simulating a slow awakening, mumbled incomprehensibly from the bed. Mrs. Piker-Smith stood frowning a moment more. "It must be your hockey things," she decided. "Give them to Mrs. Guppy, darling, and they'll be clean for school."

Mumble.

"It's eight-thirty, darling"—and she went downstairs.

Evelyn stood panting in the tent. All morning the explorer had remained in her closet, and those hours had not been easy for the girl. But after lunch Daddy had gone back to the hospital, Mummy had gone to her bridge, and Mrs. Guppy had gone shopping. Evelyn breathed a prayer of thanks that all their lives were subject to such seemingly immutable routine. She'd hauled him out of the closet then and dragged him downstairs. She'd moved slowly, backwards, clutching him by the armpits. His head lolled about on his chest and his feet bumped limply on the stairs. In death he seemed so small, so light, that Evelyn was again unhappy, and her eyes brimmed with tears as she dragged him across the linoleum of the kitchen floor. She laid him down for a moment and went for a glass of water. Over the sink was the kitchen window, and it looked down on the garden. Mrs. Guppy had brought in the three white sheets; her own sheets had not yet replaced them; instead, the line was alive in the wind with her parents' underwear. The elm at the bottom of the garden was once more whipping its limbs about. A large Persian cat paused upon the wall by the gardener's old shed, then stalked off with dignity, picking a path along the top of the wall with its tail stiffly aloft. Evelyn had drunk her water and then manhandled the explorer down the steps, between the flowerbeds, across the lawn and round the goldfish pond, into the bushes and so to the tent. And now she would bury him.

Evelyn had long since broken open the old padlock on the shed door, and it hung there now only to hold the door. She slipped it out of the eye and the door swung open. A damp, fetid smell, dusty, earthy, filled the shed. The light with difficulty penetrated the place; a large heap of sacks moldered gently in the corner, and the old plank floor was suspiciously damp thereabouts. Evelyn had once poked about in that corner, but now she tended to avoid it, for the floor was rotten beneath the sacks, and the three substances, sacking, wood, and the earth beneath the rotten wood, had begun to coalesce, as if attempting, in their nostalgia for some primeval state of slime, to abandon structure and identity, all that could distinguish or separate them. Other signs of regression and breakdown were manifest in that dusty old shed; upon the windowsill, beneath the vast network of cobwebs, lay the stiff little corpses, some partially digested, of flies and other small winged insects, many with their tiny legs curled pathetically over them as if in a final and futile gesture of self-closure. An old cardboard box, moist with decay, was damply merging with the wall, and in it a heap of parts from some long-forgotten automobile engine congealed blackly rigid, petrifying like coal as the work of time and damp smudged them with rust and rendered their decadent inutility ever more irrevocable. Photographs had once been pinned to the wall of the shed; these now curled at the edges like the legs of the flies, and as regards their degenerated content barely a trace could now be detected of the humans who had stood, once, before the camera, vital, one presumes, and alive. It was as though they had died in the bad air, the malaria, of that neglected little corner of the garden, the thin dusty air of the old shed, within which everything must devolve to a fused state of formless unity. . . .

But Evelyn had no time to relish regression today. She stepped across the floor and seized up a spade, its blade spotted orange with rust but its handle as yet sturdy and whole. This she took from the shed and, closing the rickety door behind her and replacing the great padlock, ran back through the windy sunshine of that October afternoon and again entered the bushes.

And now she worked briskly and methodically. She collapsed the filthy tent, noticing as she did so the multitudes of tiny equatorial insects clustering in the seams and corners. She dropped it in the corner of the clearing, and then laid the explorer upon it, and his bed beside him, and then the camp stool with its few pitiful possessions—remnants of the explorer's last wild dash from the Congo, pursued by anthropophagous pygmies who had once existed either in the reality of that far jungle or in the fevered mind of her strange and needy visitor, Evelyn could not know which. And then she dug. For two hours she dug; her young limbs strong from hockey, she tore a steadily widening, steadily deepening hole out of the earth in the center of the clearing in the midst of the rhododendron bushes at the bottom of the garden. And when she was finished she lined the hole with the tent. And then she burned that old map of his, creased and sweat-stained; she set it afire with the odd vestas he had left on the folding stool, and the ashes fell into the pit. And then she tossed in the gun, having hauled it with a sob from the dead man's waistband; and then the flask and the oil lamp, and then the man himself, into his grave, but not unmourned, and maybe this is all that any of us can ask for.

She saw him, occasionally, in the months that followed, always from her bedroom window when the moon was up. He'd be standing at the goldfish pond, his face pale and gleaming in the moonlight and his hands twitching at his sides. He'd look up at her window and she'd slowly move her palm back and forth in greeting. And though the fever was still upon him, he seemed no longer in mortal fear of the pygmies—yes, a subtle theme of peace had entered the symphony of his diseased being, if being indeed he was. Perhaps, after all, he was nothing; Evelyn began to see him less and less frequently after that, and at around the time—she'd have been about fourteen-and-a-half then—the time she decided to become a doctor, he disappeared from her life completely, and she never saw him again.

QUESTIONS

"The Lost Explorer"

1. Look closely at the first sentence of the story. How does it establish the tone for the narrative that follows? Why is this tone (which seems to accept the utterly marvelous with absolute matter-of-factness) so apt, given the subject of the story?

2. What kind of girl is Evelyn? Does she strike you as a typical child? Why or why not? How does she differ from her parents? How would you describe her parents and their day-to-day existence? To what degree does Evelyn inhabit a dramatically different kind of world?

3. Characterize the tone of the following sentence: "Conversation at the dinner table ranged widely from the price of sherry to the price of beef." What comment is the author making about the interests and sensibilities of adults as compared to those of children?

4. Describe the lost explorer. Is he real or imaginary? Support your answer with specific references to the story.

5. In what sense can the explorer be seen as the Other—the personification of Evelyn's secret inner life? What aspects of that life does he embody?

6. Look at the extended description of the gardening shed. Why does the author depict its decaying interior in such detail? Is this passage simply an adroit bit of descriptive writing—a beautifully drawn but gratuitous picture of rot and "regression"? Or does it serve some larger, thematic purpose in the story? Explain.

7. What happens at the ends of the story? What gives the last line its poignancy? What does "becoming a doctor" seem to represent to the author? What does he appear to be saying about the process of growing up and its effect on the imagination?

Double Face

~~~~~~~~~~~~~~~~~~~~~~~

AMY TAN

My daughter wanted to go to China for her second honeymoon, but now she is afraid.

"What if I blend in so well they think I'm one of them?" Waverly asked me. "What if they don't let me come back to the United States?"

"When you go to China," I told her, "you don't even need to open your mouth. They already know you are an outsider."

"What are you talking about?" she asked. My daughter likes to speak back. She likes to question what I say.

"Aii-ya," I said. "Even if you put on their clothes, even if you take off your makeup and hide your fancy jewelry, they know. They know just watching the way you walk, the way you carry your face. They know you do not belong."

My daughter did not look pleased when I told her this, that she didn't look Chinese. She had a sour American look on her face. Oh, maybe ten years ago, she would have clapped her hands—hurray!—as if this were good news. But now she wants to be Chinese, it is so fashionable. And I know it is too late. All those years I tried to teach her! She followed my Chinese ways only until she learned how to walk out the door by herself and go to school. So now the only Chinese words she can say are *shsh, houche, chr fan,* and *gwan deng shweijyau.* How can she talk to people in China with these words? Pee-pee, choo-choo train, eat, close light sleep. How can she think she can blend in? Only her skin and her hair are Chinese. Inside—she is all American-made.

It's my fault she is this way. I wanted my children to have the best combination: American circumstances and Chinese character. How could I know these two things do not mix?

I taught her how American circumstances work. If you are born poor here, it's no lasting shame. You are first in line for a scholarship. If the roof crashes on your head, no need to cry over this bad luck. You can sue anybody, make the landlord fix it. You do not have to sit like a Buddha under a tree letting pigeons drop their dirty business on your head. You can buy an umbrella. Or go inside a Catholic church. In America, nobody says you have to keep the circumstances somebody else gives you.

She learned these things, but I couldn't teach her about Chinese character. How to obey parents and listen to your mother's mind. How not to show your own thoughts, to put your feelings behind your face so you can take advantage of hidden opportunities. Why easy things are not worth pursuing. How to know your own worth and polish it, never flashing it around like a cheap ring. Why Chinese thinking is best.

No, this kind of thinking didn't stick to her: She was too busy chewing gum, blowing bubbles bigger than her cheeks. Only that kind of thinking stuck.

"Finish your coffee," I told her yesterday. "Don't throw your blessings away."

"Don't be so old-fashioned, Ma," she told me, finishing her coffee down the sink. "I'm my own person."

And I think, How can she be her own person? When did I give her up?

My daughter is getting married a second time. So she asked me to go to her beauty parlor, her famous Mr. Rory. I know her meaning. She is ashamed of my looks. What will her husband's parents and his important lawyer friends think of this backward old Chinese woman?

"Auntie An-mei can cut me," I say.

"Rory is famous," says my daughter, as if she had no ears. "He does fabulous work."

So I sit in Mr. Rory's chair. He pumps me up and down until I am the right height. Then my daughter criticizes me as if I were not there. "See how it's flat on one side," she accuses my head. "She needs a cut and a perm. And this purple tint in her hair, she's been doing it at home. She's never had anything professionally done."

She is looking at Mr. Rory in the mirror. He is looking at me in the mirror. I have seen this professional look before. Americans don't really look at one another when talking. They talk to their reflections. They look at others or themselves only when they think nobody is watching. So they never see how they really look. They see themselves smiling without their mouth open, or turned to the side where they cannot see their faults.

"How does she want it?" asked Mr. Rory. He thinks I do not understand English. He is floating his fingers through my hair. He is showing how his magic can make my hair thicker and longer.

"Ma, how do you want it?" Why does my daughter think she is translating English for me? Before I can even speak, she explains my thoughts: "She wants a soft wave. We probably shouldn't cut it too short. Otherwise it'll be too tight for the wedding. She doesn't want it to look kinky or weird."

And now she says to me in a loud voice, as if I had lost my hearing, "Isn't that right, Ma? Not too tight?"

I smile. I use my American face. That's the face Americans think is Chinese, the one they cannot understand. But inside I am becoming ashamed. I am ashamed she is ashamed. Because she is my daughter and I am proud of her, and I am her mother but she is not proud of me.

Mr. Rory pats my hair more. He looks at me. He looks at my daughter. Then he says something to my daughter that really displeases her: "It's uncanny how much you two look alike!"

I smile, this time with my Chinese face. But my daughter's eyes and her smile become very narrow, the way a cat pulls itself small just before it bites. Now Mr. Rory goes away so we can think about this. I hear him snap his fingers, "Wash! Mrs. Jong is next!"

So my daughter and I are alone in this crowded beauty parlor. She is frowning at herself in the mirror. She sees me looking at her.

"The same cheeks," she says. She points to mine and then pokes her cheeks. She sucks them outside in to look like a starved person. She puts her face next to mine, side by side, and we look at each other in the mirror.

"You can see your character in your face," I say to my daughter without thinking, "You can see your future."

"What do you mean?" she says.

And now I have to fight back my feelings. These two faces, I think, so much the same! The same happiness, the same sadness, the same good fortune, the same faults.

I am seeing myself and my mother, back in China, when I was a young girl.

My mother—your grandmother—once told me my fortune, how my character could lead to good and bad circumstances. She was sitting at her table with the big mirror. I was standing behind her, my chin resting on her shoulder. The next day was the start of the new year. I would be ten years by my Chinese age, so it was an important birthday for me. For this reason maybe she did not criticize me too much. She was looking at my face.

She touched my ear. "You are lucky," she said. "You have my ears, a big thick lobe, lots of meat at the bottom, full of blessings. Some people are born so poor. Their ears are so thin, so close to their head, they can never hear luck calling to them. You have the right ears, but you must listen to your opportunities."

She ran her thin finger down my nose. "You have my nose. The hole is not too big, so your money will not be running out. The nose is straight and smooth, a good sign. A girl with a crooked nose is bound for misfortune. She is always following the wrong things, the wrong people, the worst luck."

She tapped my chin and then hers. "Not too short, not too long. Our longevity will be adequate, not cut off too soon, not so long we become a burden."

She pushed my hair away from my forehead. "We are the same," concluded my mother. "Perhaps your forehead is wider, so you will be even more clever. And your hair is thick, the hairline is low on your forehead. This means you will have some hardships in your early life. This happened to me. But look at my hairline now. High! Such a blessing for my old age. Later you will learn to worry and lose your hair, too."

She took my chin in her hand. She turned my face toward her, eyes facing eyes. She moved my face to one side, then the other. "The eyes are honest, eager," she said. "They follow me and show respect. They do not look down in shame. They do not resist and turn the opposite way. You will be a good wife, mother, and daughter-in-law."

When my mother told me these things, I was still so young. And even though she said we looked the same, I wanted to look more the same. If her eye went up and looked surprised, I wanted my eye to do the same. If her mouth fell down and was unhappy, I too wanted to feel unhappy.

I was so much like my mother. This was before our circumstances separated us: a flood that caused my family to leave me behind, my first marriage to a family that did not want me, a war from all sides, and later, an ocean that took me to a new country. She did not see how my face changed over the years. How my mouth began to droop. How I began to worry but still did not lose my hair. How my eyes began to follow the American way. She did not see that I twisted my nose bouncing forward on a crowded bus in San Francisco. Your father and I, we were on our way to church to give many thanks to God for all our blessings, but I had to subtract some for my nose.

It's hard to keep your Chinese face in America. At the beginning, before I even arrived, I had to hide my true self. I paid an American-raised Chinese girl in Peking to show me how.

"In America," she said, "you cannot say you want to live there forever. If you are Chinese, you must say you admire their schools, their ways of thinking. You must say you want to be a scholar and come back to teach Chinese people what you have learned."

"What should I say I want to learn?" I asked. "If they ask me questions, if I cannot answer . . ."

"Religion, you must say you want to study religion," said this smart girl. "Americans all have different ideas about religion, so there are no right and wrong answers. Say to them, I'm going for God's sake, and they will respect you."

For another sum of money, this girl gave me a form filled out with English words. I had to copy these words over and over again as if they were English words formed from my own head. Next to the word NAME, I wrote *Lindo Sun*. Next to the word BIRTHDATE, I wrote *May 11, 1918*, which this girl insisted was the same as three months after the Chinese lunar new year. Next to the word BIRTHPLACE, I put down *Taiyuan, China*. And next to the word OCCUPATION, I wrote *student of theology*.

I gave the girl even more money for a list of addresses in San Francisco, people with big connections. And finally, this girl gave me, free of charge, instructions for changing my circumstances. "First," she said, "you must find a husband. An American citizen is best."

She saw my surprise and quickly added, "Chinese! Of course, he must be Chinese. 'Citizen' does not mean Caucasian. But if he is not a citizen, you should immediately do number two. See here, you should have a baby. Boy or girl, it doesn't matter in the United States. Neither will take care of you in your old age, isn't that true?" And we both laughed.

"Be careful, though," she said. "The authorities there will ask if you have children now or if you are thinking of having some. You must say no. You should look sincere and say you are not married, you are religious, you know it is wrong to have a baby."

I must have looked puzzled, because she explained further: "Look here now, how can an unborn baby know what it is not supposed to do? And once it has arrived, it is an American citizen and can do anything it wants. It can ask its mother to stay. Isn't that true?"

But that is not the reason I was puzzled. I wondered why she said I should look sincere. How could I look any other way when telling the truth?

See how truthful my face still looks. Why didn't I give this look to you? Why do you always tell your friends that I arrived in the United States on a slow boat from China? This is not true. I was not that poor. I took a plane. I had saved the money my first husband's family gave me when they sent me away. And I had saved money from my twelve years' work as a telephone operator. But it is true I did not take the fastest plane. The plane took three weeks. It stopped everywhere: Hong Kong, Vietnam, the Philippines, Hawaii. So by the time I arrived, I did not look sincerely glad to be here.

Why do you always tell people that I met your father in the Cathay House, that I broke open a fortune cookie and it said I would marry a dark, handsome stranger, and that when I looked up, there he was, the waiter, your father. Why do you make this joke? This is not sincere. This was not true! Your father was not a waiter, I never ate in that restaurant. The Cathay House had a sign that said "Chinese Food," so only Americans went there before it was torn down. Now it is a McDonald's restaurant with a big Chinese sign that says *mai dong lou*—"wheat," "east," "building." All nonsense. Why are you attracted only to Chinese nonsense? You must understand my real circumstances, how I arrived, how I married, how I lost my Chinese face, why you are the way you are.

When I arrived, nobody asked me questions. The authorities looked at my papers and stamped me in. I decided to go first to a San Francisco address given to me by this girl in Peking. The bus put me down on a wide street with cable cars. This was California Street. I walked up this hill and then I saw a tall building. This was Old St. Mary's. Under the church sign, in handwritten Chinese characters, someone had added: "A Chinese Ceremony to Save Ghosts from Spiritual Unrest 7 A.M. and 8:30 A.M." I memorized this information in case the authorities asked me where I worshipped my religion. And then I saw another sign across the street. It was painted on the outside of a short building: "Save Today for Tomorrow, at Bank of America." And I thought to myself, This is where American people worship. See, even then I was not so dumb! Today that church is the same size, but where that short bank used to be, now there is a tall building, fifty stories high, where you and your husband-to-be work and look down on everybody.

My daughter laughed when I said this. Her mother can make a good joke.

So I kept walking up this hill. I saw two pagodas, one on each side of the street, as though they were the entrance to a great Buddha temple. But when I looked carefully, I saw the pagoda was really just a building topped with stacks of tile roofs, no walls, nothing else under its head. I was surprised how they tried to make everything look like an old imperial city or an emperor's tomb. But if you looked on either side of these pretend-pagodas, you could see the streets became narrow and crowded, dark, and dirty. I thought to myself, Why did they choose only the worst Chinese parts for the inside? Why didn't they build gardens and ponds instead? Oh, here and there was the look of a famous ancient cave or a Chinese opera. But inside it was always the same cheap stuff.

So by the time I found the address the girl in Peking gave me, I knew not to expect too much. The address was a large green building, so noisy, children running up and down the outside stairs and hallways. Inside number 402, I found an old woman who told me right away she had wasted her time waiting for me all week. She quickly wrote down some addresses and gave them to me, keeping her hand out after I took the paper. So I gave her an American dollar and she looked at it and said, "*Syaujye*"—Miss— "we are in America now. Even a beggar can starve on this dollar." So I gave her another dollar and she said, "Aii, you think it is so easy getting this information?" So I gave her another and she closed her hand and her mouth.

With the addresses this old woman gave me, I found a cheap apartment on Washington Street. It was like all the other places, sitting on top of a little store. And through the three-dollar list, I found a terrible job paying me seventy-five cents an hour. Oh, I tried to get a job as a salesgirl, but you had to know English for that. I tried for another job as a Chinese hostess, but they also wanted me to rub my hands up and down foreign men, and I knew right away this was as bad as fourth-class prostitutes in China! So I rubbed that address out with black ink. And some of the other jobs required you to have a special relationship. They were jobs held by families from Canton and Toishan and the Four Districts, southern people who had come many years ago to make their fortune and were still holding onto them with the hands of their great-grandchildren.

So my mother was right about my hardships. This job in the cookie factory was one of the worst. Big black machines worked all day and night pouring little pancakes onto moving round griddles. The other women and I sat on high stools, and as the little pancakes went by, we had to grab them off the hot griddle just as they turned golden. We would put a strip of paper in the center, then fold the cookie in half and bend its arms back just as it turned hard. If you grabbed the pancake too soon, you would burn your fingers on the hot, wet dough. But if you grabbed too late, the cookie would harden before you could even complete the first bend. And then you had to throw these mistakes in a barrel, which counted against you because the owner could sell those only as scraps.

After the first day, I suffered ten red fingers. This was not a job for a stupid person. You had to learn fast or your fingers would turn into fried sausages. So the next day only my eyes burned, from never taking them off the pancakes. And the day after that, my arms ached from holding them out ready to catch the pancakes at just the right moment. But by the end of my first week, it became mindless work and I could relax enough to notice who else was working on each side of me. One was an older woman who never smiled and spoke to herself in Cantonese when she was angry. She talked like a crazy person. On my other side was a woman around my age. Her barrel contained very few mistakes. But I suspected she ate them. She was quite plump.

"Eh, *Syaujye*," she called to me over the loud noise of the machines. I was grateful to hear her voice, to discover we both spoke Mandarin, although her dialect was coarse-sounding. "Did you ever think you would be so powerful you could determine someone else's fortune?" she asked.

I didn't understand what she meant. So she picked up one of the strips of paper and read it aloud, first in English: "Do not fight and air your dirty laundry in public. To the victor go the soils." Then she translated in Chinese: "You shouldn't fight and do your laundry at the same time. If you win, your clothes will get dirty."

I still did not know what she meant. So she picked up another one and read in English: "Money is the root of all evil. Look around you and dig deep." And then in Chinese: "Money is a bad influence. You become restless and rob graves."

"What is this nonsense?" I asked her, putting the strips of paper in my pocket, thinking I should study these classical American sayings.

"They are fortunes," she explained. "American people think Chinese people write these sayings."

"But we never say such things!" I said. "These things don't make sense. These are not fortunes, they are bad instructions."

"No Miss," she said, laughing, "it is our bad fortune to be here making these and somebody else's bad fortune to pay to get them."

So this is how I met An-mei Hsu. Yes, yes, Auntie An-mei, now so old-fashioned. An-mei and I still laugh over those bad fortunes and how they later become quite useful in helping me catch a husband.

"Eh, Lindo," An-mei said to me one day at our workplace. "Come to my church this Sunday. My husband has a friend who is looking for a good Chinese wife. He is not a citizen, but I'm sure he knows how to make one." So that is how I first heard about Tin Jong, your father. It was not like my first marriage, where everything was arranged. I had a choice. I could choose to marry your father, or I could choose not to marry him and go back to China.

I knew something was not right when I saw him: He was Cantonese! How could An-mei think I could marry such a person? But she just said: "We are not in China anymore. You don't have to marry the village boy. Here everybody is now from the same village even if they come from different parts of China." See how changed Auntie An-mei is from those old days.

So we were shy at first, your father and I, neither of us able to speak to each other in our Chinese dialects. We went to English class together, speaking to each other in those new words and sometimes taking out a piece of paper to write a Chinese character to show what we meant. At least we had that, a piece of paper to hold us together. But it's hard to tell someone's marriage intentions when you can't say things aloud. All those little signs—the teasing, the bossy, scolding words—that's how you know if it is serious. But we could talk only in the manner of our English teacher. I see cat. I see rat. I see hat.

But I saw soon enough how much your father liked me. He would pretend he was in a Chinese play to show me what he meant. He ran back and forth, jumped up and down, pulling his fingers through his hair, so I knew—*mangjile!*—what a busy, exciting place this Pacific Telephone was, this place where he worked. You didn't know this about your father—that he could be such a good actor? You didn't know your father had so much hair?

Oh, I found out later his job was not the way he described it. It was not so good. Even today, now that I can speak Cantonese to your father, I always ask him why he doesn't find a better situation. But he acts as if he were in those old days, when he couldn't understand anything I said.

Sometimes I wonder why I wanted to catch a marriage with your father. I think An-mei put the thought in my mind. She said, "In the movies, boys and girls are always passing notes in class. That's how they fall into trouble. You need to start trouble to get this man to realize his intentions. Otherwise, you will be an old lady before it comes to his mind."

That evening An-mei and I went to work and searched through strips of fortune cookie papers, trying to find the right instructions to give your father. An-mei read them aloud, putting aside ones that might work: "Diamonds are a girl's best friend. Don't ever settle for a pal." "If such thoughts are in your head, it's time to be wed." "Confucius say a woman is worth a thousand words. Tell your wife she's used up her total."

We laughed over those. But I knew the right one when I read it. It said: "A house is not home when a spouse is not at home." I did not laugh. I wrapped up this saying in a pancake, bending the cookie with all my heart.

After school the next afternoon, I put my hand in my purse and then made a look, as if a mouse had bitten my hand. "What's this?" I cried. Then I pulled out the cookie and handed it to your father. "Eh! So many cookies, just to see them makes me sick. You take this cookie."

I knew even then he had a nature that did not waste anything. He opened the cookie and he crunched it in his mouth, and then read the piece of paper.

"What does it say?" I asked. I tried to act as if it did not matter. And when he still did not speak, I said, "Translate, please."

We were walking in Portsmouth Square and already the fog had blown in and I was very cold in my thin coat. So I hoped your father would hurry and ask me to marry him. But instead, he kept his serious look and said, "I don't know this word 'spouse.' Tonight I will look in my dictionary. Then I can tell you the meaning tomorrow."

The next day he asked me in English, "Lindo, can you spouse me?" And I laughed at him and said he used that word incorrectly. So he came back and made a Confucius joke, that if the words were wrong, then his intentions must also be wrong. We scolded and joked with each other all day long like this, and that is how we decided to get married.

One month later we had a ceremony in the First Chinese Baptist Church, where we met. And nine months later your father and I had our proof of citizenship, a baby boy, your big brother Winston. I named him Winston because I liked the meaning of those two words "wins ton." I wanted to raise a son who would win many things, praise, money, a good life. Back then, I thought to myself, At last I have everything I wanted. I was so happy, I didn't see we were poor. I saw only what we had. How did I know Winston would die later in a car accident? So young! Only sixteen!

Two years after Winston was born, I had your other brother, Vincent. I named him Vincent, which sounds like "win cent," the sound of making money, because I was beginning to think we did not have enough. And then I bumped my nose riding on the bus. Soon after that you were born.

I don't know what caused me to change. Maybe it was my crooked nose that damaged my thinking. Maybe it was seeing you as a baby, how you looked so much like me, and this made me dissatisfied with my life. I wanted everything for you to be better. I wanted you to have the best circumstances, the best character. I didn't want you to regret anything. And that's why I named you Waverly. It was the name of the street we lived on. And I wanted you to think, This is where I belong. But I also knew if I named you after this street, soon you would grow up, leave this place, and take a piece of me with you.

Mr. Rory is brushing my hair. Everything is soft. Everything is black.

"You look great, Ma," says my daughter. "Everyone at the wedding will think you're my sister."

I look at my face in the beauty parlor mirror. I see my reflection. I cannot see my faults, but I know they are there. I gave my daughter these faults. The same eyes, the same cheeks, the same chin. Her character, it came from my circumstances. I look at my daughter and now it is the first time I have seen it.

"Ai-ya! What happened to your nose?"

She looks in the mirror. She sees nothing wrong. "What do you mean? Nothing happened," she says. "It's just the same nose."

"But how did you get it crooked?" I ask. One side of her nose is bending lower, dragging her cheek with it.

"What do you mean?" she asks. "It's your nose. You gave me this nose."

"How can that be? It's drooping. You must get plastic surgery and correct it."

But my daughter has no ears for my words. She puts her smiling face to my worried one. "Don't be silly. Our nose isn't so bad," she says. "It makes us look devious." She looks pleased.

"What is this word, 'devious,' " I ask.

"It means we're looking one way, while following another. We're for one side and also the other. We mean what we say, but our intentions are different."

"People can see this in our face?"

My daughter laughs. "Well, not everything that we're thinking. They just know we're two-faced."

"This is good?"

I think about our two faces. I think about my intentions. Which one is American? Which one is Chinese? Which one is better? If you show one, you must always sacrifice the other.

It is like what happened when I went back to China last year, after I had not been there for almost forty years. I had taken off my fancy jewelry. I did not wear loud colors. I spoke their language. I used their local money. But still, they knew. They knew my face was not one hundred percent Chinese. They still charged me high foreign prices.

So now I think, What did I lose? What did I get back in return? I will ask my daughter what she thinks.

QUESTIONS

"Double Face"

1. What is the history of the narrator of this story? Why did Lindo Sun want to come to America? Presumably she was still quite young when she emigrated from China. What qualities of character must a young woman possess to travel thousands of miles alone to a new home among strangers whose language she does not speak and whose culture is entirely foreign?

2. Explain the narrator's vision of America. In her eyes, what is distinctive or characteristic about America and the American people?

3. In contrast, what is the narrator's attitude toward China? Do you think that her attitude has changed as she has aged?

4. Describe the narrator's daughter, Waverly. What behavior of Waverly's does her mother find distressing or displeasing?

5. Why does Waverly become annoyed when told she looks like her mother? Lindo Sun smiles at this information and at Waverly's discomfiture. Why? How is Waverly's response in this scene contrasted with the narrator's attitude toward her own mother?

6. The narrator dislikes the extent to which her daughter has become an American and hence has lost her Chinese "self." How was Lindo Sun, however, partly responsible for this? Are there hints in the story that Waverly is more like her mother than the latter wants to admit—hints that Waverly is Lindo Sun's double or "other"? Explain.

7. According to the narrator's mother, a girl who possesses a crooked nose is "bound for misfortune. She is always following the wrong things, the wrong people, the worst luck." For what sort of misfortune do you think the narrator believes Waverly is headed? How did Lindo Sun's crooked nose influence her life? What is Waverly's interpretation of the meaning of her and her mother's crooked noses? How is her explanation related to the theme of the story?

8. What is your answer to the questions Lindo Sun asks in the last paragraph of the story? What do you think Waverly's answer would be?

Getzel the Monkey

ISAAC BASHEVIS SINGER

1

My dear friends, we all know what a mimic is. Once we had such a man living in our town, and he was given a fitting name. In that day they gave nicknames to everybody but the rich people. Still, Getzel was even richer than the one he tried to imitate, Todrus Broder. Todrus himself lived up to his fancy name. He was tall, broad-shouldered like a giant, with a black beard as straight as a squire's and a pair of dark eyes that burned through you when they looked at you. Now, I know what I'm talking about. I was still a girl then, and a good-looking one, too. When he stared at me with those fiery eyes, the marrow in my bones trembled. If an envious man were to have a look like that, he could, God preserve us, easily give you the evil eye. Todrus had no cause for envy, though. He was as healthy as an ox, and he had a beautiful wife and two graceful daughters, real princesses. He lived like a nobleman. He had a carriage with a coachman, and a hansom as well. He went driving to the villages and played around with the peasant women. When he threw coins to them, they cheered. Sometimes he would go horseback riding through the town, and he sat up in the saddle as straight as a Cossack.

His surname was Broder, but Todrus came from Great Poland, not from Brody. He was a great friend of all the nobles. Count Zamoysky used to come to his table on Friday nights to taste his gefilte fish. On Purim the count sent him a gift, and what do you imagine the gift turned out to be? Two peacocks, a male and a female!

Todrus spoke Polish like a Pole and Russian like a Russian. He knew German, too, and French as well. What didn't he know? He could even play the piano. He went hunting with Zamoysky and he shot a wolf. When the Tsar visited Zamosc and the finest people went to greet him, who do you think spoke to him? Todrus Broder. No sooner were the first three words out of his mouth than the Tsar burst out laughing. They say that later the two of them played a game of chess and Todrus won. I wasn't there, but it probably happened. Later Todrus received a gold medal from Petersburg.

His father-in-law, Falk Posner, was rich, and Falk's daughter Fogel was a real beauty. She had a dowry of twenty thousand rubles, and after her father's death she inherited his entire fortune. But don't think that Todrus married her for her money. It is said that she was traveling with her mother to the spas when suddenly Todrus entered the train. He was still a bachelor then, or perhaps a widower. He took one look at Fogel and then he told her mother that he wanted her daughter to be his wife. Imagine, this happened some fifty years ago. . . . Everyone said that it was love at first sight for Todrus, but later it turned out that love didn't mean a thing to him. I should have as many blessed years as the nights Fogel didn't sleep because of him! They joked saying that if you were to dress a shovel in a woman's skirts, he would chase after it. In those days, Jewish daughters didn't know about love affairs, so he had to run after Gentile girls and women.

Not far from Zamosc, Todrus had an estate where the greatest nobles came to admire his horses. But he was a terrible spendthrift, and over the years his debts grew. He devourd his father-in-law fortune, and that is the plain truth.

Now, Getzel the Monkey, whose name was really Getzel Bailes, decided to imitate everything about Todrus Broder. He was a rich man, and stingy to boot. His father had also been known as a miser. It was said that he had built up his fortune by starving himself. The son had a mill that poured out not flour but gold. Getzel had an old miller who was as devoted as a dog to him. In the fall, when there was a lot of grain to mill, this miller stayed awake nights. He didn't even have a room for himself; he slept with the mice in the hayloft. Getzel grew rich because of him. In those times people were used to serving. If they didn't serve God, they served the boss.

Getzel was a moneylender, too. Half the town's houses were mortgaged to him. He had one precious little daughter, Dishke, and a wife, Risha Leah, who was as sick as she was ugly. Getzel could as soon become Todrus as I the rabbi of Turisk. But a rumor spread through the town that Getzel was trying to become another Todrus. At the beginning it was only the talk of the peddlers and the seamstresses, and who pays attention to such gossip? But then Getzel went to Selig the tailor and he ordered a coat just like Todrus's, with a broad fox collar and a row of tails. Later he had the shoemaker fit him with a pair of boots exactly the same as Todrus's, with low uppers and shiny toes. Zamosc isn't Warsaw. Sooner or later everyone knows what everyone else is doing. So why mimic anyone? Still, when the rumors reached Todrus's ears he merely said, "I don't care. It shows that he has a high opinion of my taste." Todrus never spoke a bad word about anyone. If he was going down Lublin Street and a girl of twelve walked by, he would lift his hat to her just as though she were a lady. Had a fool done this, they would have made fun of him. But a clever person can afford to be foolish sometimes. At weddings Todrus got drunk and cracked such jokes that they thought he, not Berish Venngrover, was the jester. When he danced a kozotsky, the floor trembled.

Well, Getzel Bailes was determined to become a second Todrus. He was small and thick as a barrel, and a stammerer to boot. To hear him try to get a word out was enough to make you faint. The town had something to mock. He bought himself a carriage, but it was a tiny carriage and the horses were two old nags. Getzel rode from the marketplace to the mill and from the mill to the marketplace. He wanted to be gallant, and he tried to take his hat off to the druggist's wife. Before he could raise his hand, she had already disappeared. People were barely able to keep from laughing in his face, and the town rascals immediately gave him his nickname.

Getzel's wife, Risha Leah, was a shrew, but she had sense enough to see what was happening. They began to quarrel. There was no lack in Zamosc of curious people who listened at the cracks in the shutters and looked through the keyhole. Risha Leah said to him, "You can as much become Todrus as I can become a man! You are making a fool of yourself. Todrus is Todrus; you stay Getzel."

But who knows what goes on in another person's head? It seemed to be an obsession. Getzel began to pronounce his words like a person from Great Poland and to use German expressions: *mädchen, schmädchen, grädchen*. He found out what Todrus ate, what he drank, and, forgive me for the expression, what drawers he wore. He began to chase women, too. And, my dear friends, just as Todrus had succeeded in everything, so Getzel failed. He would crack a joke and get a box on the ear in return. Once, in the middle of a wedding celebration, he tried to seduce a woman, and her husband poured chicken soup down the front of his gaberdine. Dishke cried and implored him, "Daddy, they are making fun of you!" But it is written somewhere that any fancy can become a madness.

Getzel met Todrus in the street and said, "I want to see your furniture."

"With the greatest pleasure," said Todrus and took him into his living room. What harm would it do Todrus, after all, if Getzel copied him?

So Getzel kept on mimicking. He tried to imitate Todrus's voice. He tried to make friends with the squires and their wives. He had studied everything in detail. Getzel had never smoked, but suddenly he came out with cigars and the cigars were bigger than he was. He also started a subscription to a newspaper in Petersburg. Todrus's daughters went to a Gentile boarding school, and Getzel wanted to send Dishke there, even though she was already too old for that. Risha Leah raised an uproar and she was barely able to prevent him from doing it. If he had been a pauper, Getzel would have been excommunicated. But he was loaded with money. For a long time Todrus didn't pay any attention to all of this, but at last in the marketplace he walked over to Getzel and asked: "Do you want to see how

I make water?" He used plain language, and the town had something to
laugh about.

2

Now, listen to this. One day Risha Leah died. Of what did she die? Really,
I couldn't say. Nowadays people run to the doctor; in those times a person
got sick and it was soon finished. Perhaps it was Getzel's carryings on that
killed her. Anyway, she died and they buried her. Getzel didn't waste any
tears over it. He sat on the stool during the seven days of mourning and
cracked jokes like Todrus. His daughter Dishke was already engaged. After
the thirty days of bereavement the matchmakers showered him with offers,
but he wasn't in a hurry.

Two months hadn't passed when there was bedlam in the town. Todrus
Broder had gone bankrupt. He had borrowed money from widows and
orphans. Brides had invested their dowries with him, and he owed money
to nobles. One of the squires came over and tried to shoot him. Todrus's
wife wept and fainted, and the girls hid in the attic. It came out that
Todrus owed Getzel a large sum of money. A mortgage, or God knows
what. Getzel came to Todrus. He was carrying a cane with a silver tip
and an amber handle, just like Todrus's, and he pounded on the floor
with it. Todrus tried to laugh off the whole business, but you could tell
that he didn't feel very good about it. They wanted to auction off all his
possessions, tear him to pieces. The women called him a murderer,
a robber, and a swindler. The brides howled: "What did you do with our
dowries?" and wailed as if it were Yom Kippur. Todrus had a dog as big
as a lion, and Getzel had gotten one the image of it. He brought the dog
with him, and both animals tried to devour each other. Finally Getzel
whispered something to Todrus; they locked themselves in a room and
stayed there for three hours. During that time the creditors almost tore
the house down. When Todrus came out, he was as pale as death;
Getzel was perspiring. He called out to the men: "Don't make such a racket!
I'll pay all the debts. I have taken over the business from Todrus." They
didn't believe their own ears. Who puts a healthy head into a sickbed?
But Getzel took out his purse, long and deep, just like Todrus's. However,
Todrus's was empty, and this one was full of bank notes. Getzel began to
pay on the spot. To some he paid off the whole debt and to others an
advance, but they all knew that he was solvent. Todrus looked on silently.
Fogel, his wife, came to herself and smiled. The girls came out of their
hiding places. Even the dogs made peace; they began to sniff each other
and wag their tails. Where had Getzel put together so much cash? As a
rule, a merchant has all his money in his business. But Getzel kept on
paying. He had stopped stammering and he spoke now as if he really were
Todrus. Todrus had a bookkeeper whom they called the secretary, and he

brought out the ledgers. Meanwhile, Todrus had become his old self again. He told jokes, drank brandy, and offered a drink to Getzel. They toasted *l'chayim.*

To make a long story short, Getzel took over everything. Todrus Broder left for Lublin with his wife and daughters, and it seemed that he had moved out altogether. Even the maids went with him. But then why hadn't he taken his feather beds with him? By law, no creditor is allowed to take these. For three months there was no word of them. Getzel had already become the boss. He went here, he went there, he rode in Todrus's carriage with Todrus's coachman. After three months Fogel came back with her daughters. It was hard to recognize her. They asked her about her husband and she answered simply,

"I have no more husband." "Some misfortune, God forbid?" they asked, and she answered no, that they had been divorced.

There is a saying that the truth will come out like oil on water. And so it happened here. In the three hours that Getzel and Todrus had been locked up in the office, Todrus had transferred everything to Getzel—his house, his estate, all his possessions, and on top of it all, his wife. Yes, Fogel married Getzel. Getzel gave her a marriage contract for ten thousand rubles and wrote up a house—it was actually Todrus's—as estate. For the daughters he put away large dowries.

The turmoil in the town was something awful. If you weren't in Zamosc then, you have no idea how excited a town can become. A book could be written about it. Not one book, ten books! Even the Gentiles don't do such things. But that was Todrus. As long as he could, he acted like a king. He gambled, he lost, and then it was all over; he disappeared. It seems he had been about to go to jail. The squires might have murdered him. And in such a situation, what won't a man do to save his life? Some people thought that Getzel had known everything in advance and that he had plotted it all. He had managed a big loan for Todrus and had lured him into his snare. No one would have thought that Getzel was so clever. But how does the saying go? If God wills, a broom will shoot.

Todrus's girls soon got married. Dishke went to live with her in-laws in Lemberg. Fogel almost never showed her face outside. Todrus's grounds had a garden with a pavilion, and she sat there all summer. In the winter she hid inside the house. Todrus Broder had vanished like a stone in the water. Some held that he was in Krakow; others, that he had gone to Warsaw. Still others said that he had converted and had married a rich squiress. Who can understand such a man? If a Jew is capable of selling his wife in such a way, he is no longer a Jew. Fogel had loved him with a great love, and it was clear that she had consented to everything just to save him. In the years that followed, nobody could say a word against Todrus to her. On Rosh Hashanah and Yom Kippur she stood in her pew in the women's section at the grating and she didn't utter a single word to anybody. She remained proud.

Getzel took over Todrus's language and his manners. He even became

taller, or perhaps he put lifts on his boots. He became a bosom friend of
the squires. It was rumored that he drank forbidden wine with them. After
he had stopped stammering, he had begun to speak Polish like one of them.

Dishke never wrote a word to her father. About Todrus's daughters I
heard that they didn't have a good end. One died in childbirth. Another
was supposed to have hanged herself. But Getzel became Todrus and I saw
it happen with my own eyes, from beginning to end. Yes, mimicking is
forbidden. If you imitate a person, his fate is passed on to you. Even with
a shadow one is not allowed to play tricks. In Zamosc there was a young
man who used to play with his shadow. He would put his hands together
so that the shadow on the wall would look like a buck with horns, eating
and butting. One night the shadow jumped from the wall and gored the
young man as if with real horns. He got such a butt that he had two holes
in his forehead afterwards. And so it happened here.

Getzel did not need other people's money. He had enough. But suddenly he began to borrow from widows and orphans. Anywhere he could
find credit he did, and he paid high interest. He didn't have to renovate
his mill either. The flour was as white as snow. But he built a new mill
and put in new millstones. His old and devoted miller had died, and Getzel
hired a new miller who had long mustaches, a former bailiff. This one
swindled him right and left. Getzel also bought an estate from a nobleman
even though he already had an estate with a stable and horses. Before this
he had kept to his Jewishness, but now he began to dress like a fop. He
stopped coming to the synagogue except on High Holy Days. As if this
wasn't enough, Getzel started a brewery and he sowed hops for beer. He
didn't need any of this. Above all, it cost him a fortune. He imported
machines, God knows from where, and they made such a noise at night
that the neighbors couldn't sleep. Every few weeks he made a trip to Warsaw. Who can guess what really happened to him? Ten enemies don't do
as much harm to a man as he does to himself. One day the news spread
that Getzel was bankrupt. My dear friends, he didn't have to go bankrupt;
it was all an imitation of Todrus. He had taken over the other's bad luck.
People streamed from every street and broke up his windowpanes. Getzel
had no imitator. No one wanted his wife; Fogel was older than Getzel by
a good many years. He assured everyone that he wouldn't take anything
away from them. But they beat him up. A squire came and put his pistol
to Getzel's forehead in just the same way as the other had to Todrus.

To make a long story short, Getzel ran away in the middle of the night.
When he left, the creditors took over and it turned out that there was more
than enough for everybody. Getzel's fortune was worth God knows how
much. So why had he run away? And where had he gone? Some said that
the whole bankruptcy was nothing but a sham. There was supposed to have
been a woman involved, but what does an old man want with a woman? It
was all to be like Todrus. Had Todrus buried himself alive, Getzel would
have dug his own grave. The whole thing was the work of demons. What
are demons if not imitators? And what does a mirror do? This is why they

cover a mirror when there is a corpse in the house. It is dangerous to see the reflection of the body.

Every piece of property Getzel had owned was taken away. The creditors didn't leave as much as a scrap of bread for Fogel. She went to live in the poorhouse. When this happened I was no longer in Zamosc. But may my enemies have such an old age as they say Fogel had. She lay down on a straw mattress and she never got up again. It was said that before her death she asked to be inscribed on the tombstone not as the wife of Getzel but as the wife of Todrus. Nobody even bothered to put up a stone. Over the years the grave became overgrown and was finally lost.

What happened to Getzel? And what happened to Todrus? No one knew. Somebody thought they might have met somewhere, but for what purpose? Todrus must have died. Dishke tried to get a part of her father's estate, but nothing was left. A man should stay what he is. The troubles of the world come from mimicking. Today they call it fashion. A charlatan in Paris invents a dress with a train in front and everybody wears it. They are all apes, the whole lot of them.

I could also tell you a story about twins, but I wouldn't dare to talk about it at night. They had no choice. They were two bodies with one soul. Both sisters died within a single day, one in Zamosc and the other in Kovle. Who knows? Perhaps one sister was real and other was her shadow?

I am afraid of a shadow. A shadow is an enemy. When it has the chance, it takes revenge.

QUESTIONS

"Getzel the Monkey"

1. From whose point of view is this story told? How would you describe the speaker's voice? What sort of person does she seem to be? What kind of community does she live in?

2. Compare and contrast Todrus and Getzel. In what ways are they opposites?

3. Why does Getzel decide "to imitate everything about Todrus Broder"—to turn himself into Todrus's double? Does Singer provide us with a satisfactory explanation for Getzel's bizarre behavior? How do you account for it?

4. The story contains a good deal of "folk wisdom," much of it in the form of sayings and proverbs cited by the narrator. Find some of these sayings. What do they contribute to the story?

5. How does Todrus respond to Getzel's efforts to mimic him?

6. Why does Singer include the anecdote about the young man from Zamosc

"who used to play with his shadow"? How is it relevant to the story of Getzel? What other references to shadows do you find in the story?

7. What eventually happens to Getzel? Why does he come to such a bad end?

8. Does the narrator seem overly superstitious to you? What are some of the supernatural things she believes in? Do you think there is any validity to these beliefs—for example, her conviction that what happened to Getzel "was the work of demons"?

The Story of a Dead Man

JAMES ALAN MCPHERSON

It is not true that Billy Renfro was killed during that trouble in Houston. The man is an accomplished liar and likes to keep his enemies nervous. It was he who spread this madness. The truth of what happened, he told me in Chicago, was this: After tracking the debtor to a rented room, Billy Renfro's common sense was overwhelmed by the romantic aspects of the adventure. That was why he kicked open the door, charged boldly into the room and shouted, "Monroe Ellis, give *up* Mr. Floyd's Cadillac that you done miss nine payments on!" Unhappily for Billy, neither Monroe Ellis nor the woman with him was in the giving-up mood. The woman fired first, aiming from underneath Ellis on the bed. Contrary to most reports, that bullet only wounded Billy's arm. It was one of the subsequent blasts from Monroe's .38 that entered Billy's side. But this wound did not slow Billy's retreat from the room, the rooming house, or the city of Houston. He was alive and fully recovered when I saw him in Chicago, on his way back from Harvey after reclaiming a defaulted Chevy.

Neither is it true, as certain of his enemies have maintained, that Billy's left eye was lost during a rumble with that red-neck storekeep outside Limehouse, South Carolina. That eye, I now have reason to believe, was lost during domestic troubles. That is quite another story. But I have his full account of the Limehouse difficulty: Billy had stopped off there en route to Charleston to repossess another defaulting car for this same Mr. Floyd Dillingham. He entered the general store with the sole intention of buying a big orange soda. However, the owner of the joint, a die-hard white supremacist, refused to execute the transaction. Being naturally suspicious of governmental intervention, Billy fell back on his own resources: He reached for the .22 he carried under his shirt for just such dalliances. But the storekeep was too swift. While Billy's right hand was still moving cloth, the red-neck was caressing the trigger of his Springfield and looking joyous. "Private club, *Mr.* Nigger!" the red-neck sang. Though he is a liar and a madman, my cousin Billy Renfro is no fool. He allowed himself to be two-stepped and back-backed out of the place, the storekeep, of course, making all the leading moves. As Billy sped off, the redneck fired several rounds into the air and gave a hungry rebel yell. Billy did not respond.

On his return from Charleston, however, the defaulted car reclaimed,

he experienced an overpowering thirst for a big orange soda. This thirst
became obsessive as he neared Limehouse. It was a hot sleepy day, nearing sunset, and his arrival at the general store went unnoticed. Billy was
at the counter blowing gently on his .22 before the storekeep could resur-
face from the reveries he enjoyed, dozing in his wicker rocking chair. *"Two
big orange sodas and a dill pickle!"* my cousin ordered. Liar that he is, he
told me in Chicago that he belched nonchalantly before departing from the
store. I do not believe this, but I believe him when he said he shot off five
rounds and gave a swamp cry, when he was in his car and pointed toward
Atlanta. Ah, Billy! It is part of his style to add such touches.

I bother to refute these rumors because the man is my cousin, and I am
honor-bound to love him as I know he really is. He and I are one with the
same ancestors, and whatever fires rage in him I must look to find smol-
derings of within myself. Recognizing this obligation, I here attempt to
deflate mean rumors circulated by his enemies, cut through the fat of Billy's
own lies, and lay bare the muscle of his life. From youth onward, he has
possessed a warm heart and a certain tolerance of misfortune; and he is as
likely, for a friend, to strip the shirt from his own back as he is to murder.
That he contains such broad extremes speaks favorably of his eventual re-
form.

I myself have contributed considerable energy toward this goal. In Chicago, when we drank together in that dive on Halstead, I offered my best
advice for whatever it was worth to him. "We are no longer young men,"
I said. "The foam has settled down into the beer. I, myself, no longer chase
women, speak hotly, challenge opinions too far different from my own. I
have learned it is to my advantage to get along. Chelseia, the woman I
plan to marry, you will meet in a few hours. She is steady and refined, and
will bear me sturdy children. In short, Billy, in my manhood I have become aware of complexity. You owe it to the family, and to the memory of
your mother, to do the same."

Billy swished his Scotch and drank it down, then rapped the glass on the
table to alert the barmaid. When she looked, he pointed two fingers downward toward our glasses and kissed at her. Then, turning to focus his single, red-rimmed eye on my face, he said, "Bullshit!"

He was dressed in the black gabardine suit of an undertaker. Dried
purple-black blood streaked his coat sleeves, his black string tie, and the
collars of the dirty white shirt he wore.

"People change, Billy," I said.

"Bullshit!" Billy Renfro said.

I looked closely at him and saw a gangster. He was not the kind of man
I wanted to meet my family. I glanced at my watch and sipped my drink.
I listened to his stories.

Billy spun his usual lies.

This meeting in Chicago took place three years after he began work for
this Mr. Dillingham, seven years after his mother's death, and thirteen
years after Billy, at seventeen, went to prison for life. But I will speak here

of his life before he went to prison, for insights into what he might have become. His mother was my father's sister, and both gave their first-born males the same treasured family name. Both my cousin and I were named "William" after our paternal grandfather, Willie Joe Warner, a jackleg Baptist preacher. But because her child was somewhat older, Billy's mother claimed for him the more affectionate nickname "Billy." I will not speak here of the grandfather in whose shadow we both lived, but I have heard it mentioned in the family that he favored, in his old age, the name "William" over the more secular "Billy." I would not swear to this, however, because my father winked when he told it to me. And Billy's mother, whom we nicknamed "Mama Love," laughed loudly when I asked her confirmation. I accepted my name. Billy gloried in his, draining from it as much territory as the world would concede.

He outgrew me from the start, perhaps because his father succumbed to alcohol before Billy was ten. And his mother, soon afterward made invalid by a stroke, let her son roam freely. Evenings at his house, playing in his room, Billy taught me the dozens, chanted bawdy songs, drilled me on how to eyeball a girl with maximum style. I followed as much of his advice, given the stricter circumstances of my home, as was discreet. I loved him, but I loved his mother more. Billy loved only the streets. And since Mama Love could not contain his wanderings, she gave up finally and developed a defensive sense of humor. While Billy gallivanted, I would go and sit with her and listen to her spin raucous anecdotes about her wayward son. She loved him deeply. This was witnessed in the contrast between her merry, mysterious eyes and her unhappy face whenever she shook her head and sighed, and said, "Ah, Billy! He just won't *do!*"

I suffered with Mama Love when Billy, at sixteen, threw away his youth. Here, as I recall, is how it happened: Always one to embrace completely any adventure, Billy ran wild with a crowd of older boys whose imaginations lacked the brakes of self-restraint. Following their tottering lead, Billy was dared to test the first full wetness of his manhood in the arms of a much experienced girl. This girl, I have reason to believe, knew better than he how unerringly passion can boomerang, especially when heated by the trusting flame of innocence. I believe that Billy was unaware. At least this was his defense to the girl's father, and also to the female judge notorious in our city for curbing wayward boys, and protecting the coffers of the state, with one stiff dose of justice.

"You feed that baby," Judge Gladys Moon told him.

I was with him in court that day and heard Billy's plea. He said, "Judge, that baby don't even *look* like me."

Judge Moon sat stone-faced and sober. "You feed it anyway," she told Billy, "and it might look like you. Feed it for twenty-one years, and if it don't look like you after twenty-one years, you don't have to feed it no more."

While I completed school, he worked as the relay man on a garbage truck. While I attended church and learned social graces, he became more a loner, grew sullen, worked a tentative cynicism into his voice. The whites of his eyes reddened. He cultivated a process, dressed flashily, began socializing on a certain street corner sanctified by a tree that had once stood there. These developments cracked his mother's heart. She believed with Judge Gladys Moon that it was Billy's baby. He protested this violently, expressing bitterness that of all the boys who had known the girl, he alone had had to pay. And because Mama Love could not bear to fight him, she ordered him finally out of her home. Yet she still loved her son, and often sent messages and food to him by me. But during this time I began avoiding most social contacts with Billy, because I too believed that he was guilty. Besides, our vocabularies were growing rapidly apart. He moved into a rented room with his common-law wife and child, a room in a section of the city I dreaded to enter. The year I finished high school and won a church scholarship to college, Billy stabbed during a dice game a man who had questioned the honor of Billy's common-law wife. But to Billy's credit it must be said that he waited until the man, who was winning, had lost back to the others in the game as much as they had lost to him. The code required such graciousness, even before a deadly act. This man died, and Billy's life was finished.

As a favor to his mother, who could not go herself, I took off from college and went by bus to Harper's Farm, where, in those days, black men were stocked for the road gangs. I waited for Billy in the moist, chicken-wired reception room. Around me sat weeping mothers, sportily dressed sweethearts, somber wives. The pungent smells of overripe peaches, sweat, potato salad, toilet water and fried chicken assaulted my nose. Over in a corner, on a wooden bench, a sun-whipped trustee, with his eyes closed and his face turned upward toward the ceiling, was singing:

> They 'cuse me of mur-der,
> Never harm a man
> Never harm a man.
> I say, "Wake up, old Dead Man
> Help me ca'ry my load
> Help me ca'ry my load! . . ."

I did not want to be in such a place.

When Billy came out and took his seat, I studied him through the chicken wire. This was long before he lost the eye, and there was the beginning of a rough handsomeness about his face. His hair, processed heavily now in the style of Nat King Cole, was protected from the flies and red dust by a blue and yellow cloth bandanna. He wore prison-issue blues, the worn paleness of which contrasted favorably with his sun-glossed skin. He chewed gum rapidly. Behind him, coming in the door from the prison section, I could see gelded young men walking with legs jangling loosely. Caged, they seemed bent on proving, to watching wives and sweethearts, that their manhood was still intact.

"Billy," I said through the dirty wire, "why do you insist on breaking your mama's heart? She suffers because she cannot be here. Yet she would suffer even more if she could see you here in this death-infected place. Look around you at these wasted men," I urged him, "then look me in the eye and tell me you like the future you have set for yourself."

But he would not look me in the eye. Nor would he respond to my pleadings. Instead, he chewed arrogantly. Then he smiled. In that smile was a mysterious humor that I had not, before this meeting, observed in his manner. Billy looked past me, perhaps at the waiting women seated on the benches against the walls, perhaps at the humming trustee. He tossed his head and said, "Me, I'm a dead man."

I drew my chair up closer to the wire. "It does not have to end that way," I told him.

"What you doin' with you life?" he asked me.

"Making something of it," I answered.

"That's good," Billy said.

Over in the corner, the trustee stopped humming and sang:

> Well, the load so *hea-vy*
> I can *hardly* go
> I can *hardly* go . . .

I talked a while about college. Billy chewed in a relaxed way and listened. I tried my best to communicate to him some sense of the broader options available to the man in possession of salable knowledge. I mapped out my future in blocks of years, stepladders of subgoals, ending with an affirmation of my ultimate ambition to settle into the good life in Los Angeles.

Billy smiled and gave several agreeable nods. But when my conversation came to dwell on the wonders of Los Angeles, he interrupted suddenly. "Looka here," he said. "How 'bout runnin' cross the road and get me a hot sausage sandwich, heavy on the mustard, and a big orange soda."

I looked hard at him and wanted to weep. "Is that *all* you want?" I asked.

Billy chewed steadily. "No," he answered, looking out over the crowded room. "Bring me a side of fries, hold the salt."

Then he laughed, a strange, uncaring demon laughter. The sound bragged of his urge to self-destruct. Ah, Billy! He just would not *do!* He listened only to the beating of his own heart.

The last time I saw him, before we drank together in Chicago, was when he was furloughed from Harper's Farm to attend Mama Love's funeral. She died, I believe, from a broken heart and loneliness, although the doctor claimed it was the predictable second stroke. I returned home from college to gather with the family. And after the burial, while the others ate, Billy and I drank heavily together in the back room of his mother's rented house. All day he had smiled broadly at the grief and embarrassment of the family. Now he sat on his old bed, drinking with absolute detachment. I sat near him on a hard-back chair, talking aimlessly of college, of the admirable habits of girls met there, of my ambition to find, in a year or so, permanent employment in Los Angeles. Billy said nothing. But toward midnight, after the other members of the family had left and I grew tearful in recollecting the martyred life of Mama Love, Billy turned to face me. "What *you* cryin' for, *motherfucker?*" he said. "It's *my* mama!" Just then the prison guard, who had escorted him home, came in the room and touched Billy on the shoulder. My cousin rose slowly from the bed, and laughing with that same clucking sound in his chest, he sang:

> I'm Wild Nigger Bill
> From Red Pepper Hill;
> I never did die, and I never will . . .

He chanted this song with such complete absorption, and laughed so menacingly, that I shuddered, and covered my face, and knew with his mother that Billy was doomed.

Seven years later, following his parole, Billy Renfro began work for Mr. Floyd Dillingham of Atlanta's Dillingham Automotives, Inc. A liberal man, Mr. Dillingham had negotiated with the state for Billy's release. The job was to track down Negroes who had defaulted on their car payments. No white man would even consider such employment. I do believe that Dillingham wanted a Negro with a reputation for ruthlessness sufficient to strike fear into the hearts of the deadbeats. In the inevitable tug between desire and justice, some of Dillingham's clients had been known to kill. Paid agents do not grow old in such an enterprise. Had I seen Billy Renfro I would have advised him of this, but I did not see him after the funeral for almost ten years. However, word-of-mouth reports from members of the family, bits of gossip from home folk passing through, placed him now in New York, now in California, one month wounded in a Detroit hospital, another month married to a woman romanced during a repossession mission outside Baton Rouge.

In contrast to him, I moved westward, but only as far as Chicago, and settled in against this city's soul-killing winter winds. I purged from my speech all traces of the South and warmed myself by the fire of my thirty-year plan. Employment was available in the credit reference section of the Melrose Department Store, and there I established, though slowly, a reputation for efficiency and tact. Because I got along, I began moving up. In my second year in Chicago, I found and courted Chelseia Raymond, a fam-

ily-backed, efficiency-minded girl. She was the kind of woman I needed to
make my children safe. Her family loved me, and had the grace to overlook the fact that I had once been a poor migrant from the South. Third-
generation Chicagoans, they nonetheless opened their hearts and home to
me as if I had been native to their city. With their backing, I settled into
this rough-and-tumble city and learned to dodge all events detracting attention from the direction in which I had determined to move. From time
to time, trudging through the winter slush on Michigan, I would pause to
explore a reflection of myself in a store window. By my fifth year in Chicago, I became satisfied that no one could have mistaken me for a refugee
from the South.

This was my situation when Billy Renfro came to visit.

But it is certainly not true, as Billy has gossiped among the family, that
when he arrived I refused to see him at my office. I do not call the man a
liar, but I do say his imagination is sometimes a stranger to the truth. For
the sake of accuracy, here is the truth of what happened: It was not my
fault that Billy got only as far into our office as the receptionist's desk. It
may be he was not dressed properly for the occasion. I know that I received his card from Mrs. Mohr only *after* he had left the building, when
I was going out to lunch. She told me, with a nervousness I could not at
first understand, "The gentleman said he's related to you." On my honor
as a member of the family, I did not deny the bond. I accepted his card.
Its face was embossed in elegant script:

RED PEPPER COLLECTION AGENCY
"We Bring Back the Goods"
B. J. Renfro, Pres.

On the back of the card Billy had scribbled:" "Got me a turkee over in
Harvey. Call soon. Yours truly, Billy Joe."

We met, as I have said, in the late afternoon of the following day at a
bar over on Halstead. At first I did not recognize Billy. The years had
treated him so unkindly. A single red eye inspected me as I approached
the booth where he sat drinking. His left eye socket was hollow, no more
than a shriveled piece of flesh pressed grimly against skull. His outfit—the
black gabardine suit, the dirty white shirt, the black string tie—brought to
my mind the image of an undertaker. Dried blood and dirt smeared the
fabric of his sleeve, looking eerily green in the blue-smoked light. We shook
hands awkwardly, and I slid into the booth across from him. I looked closely
at his face and saw death walking.

Billy grinned foolishly.

"I have heard," I began with much politeness, "that at the point of death
your whole life passes in review before your eyes. Knowing this, I wonder
about the agony you will suffer with only one eye in service. Won't it take

twice as long, and prolong your pains, before your full life passes and goes away?"

Billy looked hurt. He insisted the eye had been lost during domestic troubles with a woman. I did not believe this, and he began embellishing the statement with extravagant lies. He drained his glass, leaned forward across the table, and said, "It was a hard-hearted woman down in Eufaula, Alabama, that done it, a widow-woman name of Miss Ruby Watson. I was laid up at her place, tired of runnin' the road for Mr. Floyd. She done root work, said she was gonna make me smart and set me up in business, if I done right by her. It didn't make no nevermind to me. I just laid on in the cut and took these white pills she give me. But I didn't feel no smarter. Mr. Floyd, he sent a telegram over there. He said, "Billy Joe, *son*, come on *home*, these niggers just *a-stealin*' my cars!" Billy laughed loudly, using the sound to catch the attention of the barmaid. When she looked, he held up two rough brown fingers. She brought the drinks over and Billy tried to feel her rump. The woman jostled playfully against his arm. He rinsed his mouth with the Scotch and continued.

"I said, '*Motherfuck a Mr. Floyd!* I'm livin' my life *right here!*' I kept takin' them pills, layin' steady in the cut, but I didn't feel no smarter. Then one day I seed her go out to the fields. I seed her pickin' up *jackrabbit* shit. I didn't say nothin'. I just snuck on back to the house and got in bed with my twenty-two. She come in and go to give me the stuff. I sit up and say, 'Miss Ruby, all this time I been wastin' round here, and all you been givin' me is jackrabbit shit!' She was a old widow-woman, Ruby, and I guess they just crafty that way. She just laugh at me and stood over the bed and say, '*Now* you gettin' *smart.*' Well, that's when I whip my twenty-two under her nose. But she just keep laughin' and say, 'Them bullets *dead* by now. Don't you know them bullets dead?' She had me. She knowed it. I knowed it. She sat down on the bed and commence to stroke my chest. She say, 'Now ain't *you* a sight? Don't even know whichaway is up. But you *my* sweetmeat now, and there ain't a damn thing you can do about it.' "

Billy looked calmly around the barroom, like a priest about to say Mass. And yet beneath his cool exterior I thought I sensed, in the broad sweep of his red eye, the hint of a certain rough pride. "When she said that," he went on, "I *knowed* what I had to do. I gived the gun to her. I made her point it at my head. I told Miss Ruby, 'Me, I'm just dumb enough to believe it ain't even loaded. And if it is, it won't be the first time I been dead.' Then I ram my fist in her jaw."

I waited. The clink of glasses and the noisy blend of barroom voices teased my anticipating ear. Billy was a master of suspense. Finally, I said, "So you called her bluff, got your eye shot out, but proved you were a man."

Billy laughed, his demon thumbing triumphantly in his chest. "Naw," he said. "She pulled the trigger and *killed* me. That's how come I'm back on the road for Mr. Floyd today."

Such were his lies that evening in that bar on Halstead.

While the purple and red jukebox belted accommodating rhythms, and while a couple slow-dragged, Billy spun yarns about his adventures. He told magnificent lies. He spoke of the chain gang, of buddies still anchored there, and hummed snatches of songs, remembered from that time, which still sustained him. He assessed his errors in the Houston incident, and as an aside contrasted the pungency of Mexican cuisine in joints as far apart as Brownsville, Oakland, Tempe, Arizona. Billy pantomimed, while standing, his one eye fixed on the barmaid, the body movements of black men in Savannah and San Francisco, and speculated how the spirit of a region informed the rhythms of a man's fucking. From this he moved to assessments of women in Buffalo, Cleveland, Hartford, Newark, and East Saint Louis, offering details about liaisons in these cities that convinced him, should he ever marry, that Southern women provide the safest, strongest havens. He spoke of Limehouse, South Carolina, but only in passing on his way to recollections of a Newark house-rent party, the highlights of a fish fry in Baltimore, the economics of picking beans in New Jersey if one is ever stranded there, in August, without cash. Billy recited his contributions to bus-depot graffiti inscribed on stalls in Memphis, Little Rock, Phoenix, and Los Angeles, and observed that practitioners of this art became more assertive, sexually and politically, the farther west one went. I heard his accounts of fights, poker games, epic bouts of wrestling, with recalcitrant claimers of defaulted cars. Billy conveyed the flow of his emotions while contracting an assignation, on a lonely highway driving southward from Denver, when he and the woman driver of a car licensed in Maine sped sexual brags for three hundred miles before ending, in silent completion, in a wet cornfield just west of Kansas City.

While he was still reciting, I went quickly to the telephone and called Chelseia.

It is certainly not true, though Billy maintains otherwise, that my in-laws and Chelseia ordered him out of their home. What happened that evening with the Raymonds is still fresh in my mind. They were civil to Billy, though a little bit wary about why he wore blue sunshades. I had advised him to take this precaution while at my apartment, where Billy had bathed and shaved and changed into one of my better suits. Before visiting the Raymonds he had been completely transformed. His muscles rippled in the close embrace of my gray pinstripe; his face, clean shaven now, was set off favorably by one of my sky blue shirts; my very best red and white polka-dot tie swept deftly into the V of my chest-hugging vest. Even Billy's scuffed shoes had been spit-polished and shone like hot tar. This outfit, together with my blue sunshades shielding his eyesocket from inspection, gave Billy the appearance of a publicity-shy banker.

Mr. and Mrs. Raymond were enormously impressed.

"What business are you in, Mr. Renfro?" Mrs. Raymond asked, while her husband passed around the cheese board.

Conforming to my warnings, Billy spoke briefly. "Automotives," he answered.

Chelseia, seated next to me on the sofa, said nothing. But she watched Billy very closely.

"Selling?" Mrs. Raymond asked. She was a round, self-possessed woman who called me "darling" and winked reassuringly whenever we drank more than two glasses of sherry. She had already given me the understanding that Chelseia was mine. "You have a dealership, then?" she asked Billy.

He sat on a purple settee, his legs crossed elegantly, a glass of sherry posed in his hand. He pretended he had not heard Mrs. Raymond.

I had not anticipated that Chelseia's parents would be at home. Usually on Thursday evenings they played canasta with a church group. But, being selfless people, they had canceled their engagement when they heard from Chelseia that my cousin was in town. Mr. Raymond himself had prepared the dinner. I wanted things to go smoothly. "Billy is more a traveling salesman," I answered for my cousin. "His business takes him around the country."

Mr. Raymond sighed and stroked the top of his head. He was completely bald. He said, "It does my heart good to see the younger generation getting a few breaks. Why, in my day, with two degrees, all I could get was being a redcap down at the Union Station."

"Of course you've been out to California?" Mrs. Raymond said quickly. Both she and her husband had worked very hard to achieve the good life, and she did not like to hear him reminisce.

"Yes, m'am," Billy answered.

"We've got relatives out in Culver City," Chelseia volunteered. She had sensed my tension, and had not asked why Billy was wearing a suit she had selected for me at Marshall Fields. But she stared long and hard at the blue-tinted sunshades, familiar to her from our long summer walks along the lakeshore.

"Is it true what they say about those movie stars?" Mr. Raymond asked Billy.

Such was the flow of conversation during dinner.

For well over an hour, Billy successfully maintained his cloud of mystery. And at such moments when it seemed about to break apart in the breeze of chitchat, I puffed it back into place with a swift retort. We were relaxed until after dinner, when Mr. Raymond, still rummaging in the storehouses of his youth, lit up a cigar and became expansive. He loosened his tie and began telling anecdotes about his escapades as a redcap. Chelseia, her eyes flitting nervously, kept saying, "Please, don't get naughty now, daddy." But her words were of no avail. Billy, puffing fiercely on a cigar, laughed and egged him on. Mrs. Raymond smiled painfully. Several times Chelseia knocked her knee against my leg beneath the table. Toward ten-thirty Mr. Raymond brought out a bottle of bourbon. He said, "How about a little snort, Mr. Renfro," and winked at Billy. My cousin willfully ignored the suggestion in my stare. "Call me Billy," he said to Mr. Raymond, draining his water glass.

In less than half an hour, drunk now, Billy was offering tales about his own exploits on the Coast. Mr. Raymond kept laughing, shaking his head wistfully, and saying, "I *knew* it was true what they say about them stars." And while Billy dived for more details on this point, Mr. Raymond regaled us with anecdotes drawn from his days as a bellhop at the Palmer House. When he mentioned the adventures of a hustling bellhop named "Swifty," Billy leaned forward, pounded the table, and shouted, "Damn if I don't *know* that nigger. He in *Dee*-troit now, still *just as crazy as a bedbug!*"

Mrs. Raymond coughed violently and left the room.

From this point onward the evening deteriorated. Chelseia sat with a cold and distant expression on her face. From time to time she kicked my foot beneath the table. I flashed signals to Billy, tried to head off his speech when I perceived where it was leading, suggested many times that we should go. But none of it was of any use. Billy seemed to have induced some unhealthy chemical reaction in Mr. Raymond. He and Billy seemed locked in some unholy union. He laughed, giggled, and hooted as he talked. Even when Mrs. Raymond returned to the room in a housecoat, her husband did not lower his voice. When Mr. Raymond, on his fourth bourbon, started to recite a salacious jingle, Billy jumped up and overruled it with a more earthy variant. But in the rush of excitement while reciting the punch line, he laughed lustily, screeched, and tore off his glasses. This one gesture destroyed all his mystery. His single eye, red-rimmed and watery, flashed horribly in the soft glow of the green and red Tiffany lamp.

Chelseia gasped.

"Why, Mr. Renfro," said Mrs. Raymond, the back of her hand drawn to her mouth, "whatever happened to your eye?"

"Nothing but a knife fight," Chelseia muttered.

"Let it go," called Mr. Raymond across the littered dining table. "It's not our business." He was drunk, but there was an extreme soberness in his voice. He said to all of us, "Let it go."

Mrs. Raymond acted on this cue. "When you get back South," she said to Billy, "tell the family that William is a very nice young man." She rounded the table with her right arm outstretched. She grasped and wagged Billy's limp right hand. "What did you say your business was?"

Billy looked confused. "Automotives, m'am," he told her.

"Washing or pumping gas?" Chelseia said. It was not a question, and the tone of her voice I had heard before in the chill of winter winds off Lake Michigan. When I looked at Chelseia I saw in her face a vengeful twist I had not before then, and have never since, seen in her store of expressions. Mrs. Raymond had this very same look.

Billy stiffened. He jerked his hand away from Mrs. Raymond. He looked enraged.

The rest of the evening has been clouded by his lies.

But it is certainly true that I tried hard to save the situation, although

Billy has maintained that I turned on him. The man is a notorious liar, and likes to keep the family jumpy. Here is the truth of what happened: I moved quickly to Billy's side. I put my hand on his shoulder. I faced the Raymonds for the two of us. I said, "Thank you for a splendid evening." But all my tact was introduced too late. With a purposeful shrug, Billy separated his shoulder from my hand. All our eyes were on him. Only Mr. Raymond, sitting drooped and still in his chair, seemed distracted by thoughts of other matters.

Someone had to take control. I took it as best I could. "A red-neck down in South Carolina shot out Billy's eye," I said. "Billy is too proud to speak of it."

"*Bull*shit!" Billy said.

By this one word, and through his subsequent actions, Billy himself completely severed what was left of our family bond.

He stripped off my coat, my vest, my polka-dot tie. These he flung on the purple settee. My sky blue shirt he let fall to the floor. Billy stood broad-shouldered and brown in a ragged, yellowed undershirt. He directed all our eyes to weltlike scars on his arms and neck. "These here come from runnin' round the country," he grinned. "And I'm *keep* runnin' till the pork chops get thicker and they give me two dollars more."

"Please, Billy," I pleaded. "Please, Billy, tell the truth now."

He laughed wickedly, his teeth clamped tight. His eyes darted from me, to Chelseia, to Mrs. Raymond standing by the table with her right hand clutching her chest.

But Billy did not tell the truth. His story to me in the bar on Halstead vanished like a summer cloud. He pointed to his empty eye socket and said, "I lost this over in Harvey several years ago. Mr. Floyd Dillingham, my boss, was the one that sent me up here. He had this here turkey that flew the coop with a fistful of notes due on his Impala. Nigger's name was Wilfred 'Inner City' Jones, and he had balls enough to cruise pass Mr. Floyd's lot and honk when he was leavin' town. People on the corner saw him frontin' off Mr. Floyd. It looked bad. Mr. Floyd called me in and gived me my runnin' orders. He say, '*Fuck* the *money*, Billy. What he done is bad for *business!* Now bring me back my *car* or that nigger's *ass!*'" He pounded the table twice, with great seriousness in his face, as if still hearing the beat of his boss's voice. Mrs. Raymond and Chelseia jumped each time he pounded. But Mr. Raymond remained seated in his chair, his head bowed, his eyes closed. Billy smiled slightly. "I put out word I was lookin' for Inner City. He put out word he was lookin' for me to come lookin' for him. Said I would find him waitin' for me over in Birmingham, if I came lookin' that far. But I knowed that Earline, his old lady, was up here in Harvey and he only felt safe with his head up under her dress. So I bought me a one-way bus ticket." Billy moved to the table, swished the last of the bourbon in his glass and drank it down. Then he set the glass on the white tablecloth and arranged soiled knives and forks around it, setting the scene. "He must have been layin' for me," he went on, "cause when I knock on the door people commence to scuffle round inside. Then Earline sing out, 'What you want?' I holler back, 'Them keys to that Impala park outside or a piece of Inner City's ass, it don't matter to me which one!" They was quiet for a minute, then Inner City holler, 'Come on in, *motherfucker*, and take your choice!' I went on in."

His single eye, though red-rimmed and watery, sparkled dimly with pride. I sensed that he was enjoying himself, though Mrs. Raymond was almost in a swoon. She was dabbing excitedly at her forehead with a dinner napkin. I saw Billy watching her. I saw him smile. I thought I saw him lick his lips. "Inner City was shootin' wild from behind the bed," he continued. "Though he is in bad with Mr. Floyd, I won't bad-talk his reputation by sayin' where them bullets hit. But I stood in the middle of the room and shout, 'Missed me, *sapsucker!*' Then I opened up with my thirty-eight, whistlin' whilst I worked. My habit is to aim high when ladies is present, cause a scared woman can talk quick sense to a hard-headed man. Pretty soon Inner City yell out, 'Hey Billy, let's be *gentlemens* and do this without no heat!' He slide his gun out from under the bed. I throwed mine on the sheets and wait. Then Earline yell, 'Hey Billy, what about that twenty-two you keeps strap to your spine?' They was quiet for a minute. Me, I didn't move. Then I heard Inner City pop Earline in the jaw. While she was still hollerin' he rise up from under the bed, limber as a bear. His eyes was steamin' and his jaws was tight. He wolf, 'I'ma *keep* that Impala, Billy, but first I'ma do me some business on your *ass!*' "

By now Billy had moved the gravy-stained knife closer to the glass. He leaned over the table like a magician about to pluck a pigeon from thin air. But suddenly his body relaxed. He straightened and reached one hand into his pocket. "Now I ain't sayin' it was *easy*," he said, looking directly at Chelseia, "but I *do* say I just ain't *use* to buyin' no bus ticket and ridin' with a sore ass and a bleedin' eye all the way home." He tossed a set of car keys onto the table. Tiny flecks of dried blood flew from the keys as they clinked against the glass. Then Billy laughed loud and confidently. It was an even, bass-filled laughter that sounded the image of a persistent demon pounding happily against a friendly door. "One of us knowed he had to die," he announced calmly. "Next time, it might be *me*."

"You common *street nigger!*" Chelseia shouted.

Billy held his naked arm toward me as if he were a ringmaster introducing an act. "And this here's my cousin William," he told Chelseia.

Mrs. Raymond shuddered and rushed from the room.

And then there came a burst of wild, almost hysterical laughter. But this was not Billy. I turned and saw Mr. Raymond. His bald head was bent almost into his empty plate. He seemed to be shedding tears.

"Billy!" I pleaded. "Tell the truth. Sometimes, Billy, please tell the *truth!*"

But he ignored me. Instead, he joined with Mr. Raymond in this wild, uncaring laughter.

"Gangster!" Chelseia shouted.

"God bless Mr. Floyd!" Billy yelled.

Someone had to keep order. I assumed that responsibility. I was the one who asked Billy out.

But it is not true, contrary to rumors circulating in my family, that Billy Renfro is unwelcome in my home. His own lying stories spread this madness, and both he and I know the truth of where I stand. As far as I am concerned, he is welcome here at any time. Chelseia is another matter, but even she has said she would not interfere if Billy chose to come again. She would even let me prepare dinner for him. Whenever I am confronted by members of the family with one of his lies, I say this in response. For whatever it is worth to them, or to Billy. The man is, after all, my cousin. It is a point of family pride. Chelseia agrees, and says our family unit will likely be the place where Billy finds ultimate reconstruction, once he has put aside his wanderings. I say it is just a matter of time. We are, after all, the same age. Yet I have already charted my course. I have settled into Chicago, against the winter whippings of this city's winds. He can do the same. But as things stand now, he is still someplace out there, with a single eye flickering over open roadways, in his careless search for an exciting death. Ah, *Billy!*

QUESTIONS

"The Story of a Dead Man"

1. Like the Raymond family, we can learn much about Billy Renfro by listening to the way he talks. The same is true of the narrator, William. What does their language reveal about these men?

2. The narrator's attitude toward his cousin is a complex one, composed of many contradictory feelings. Describe that attitude. Do you share William's assessment of Billy in all its particulars? Explain.

3. How does each of the five or six anecdotes the narrator tells us about Billy Renfro contribute to our understanding of him?

4. Why does Billy Renfro have the power to horrify Mrs. Raymond and her daughter Chelseia? Why does Mr. Raymond respond so warmly to him? Why does he react as he does when Billy removes his glasses, revealing that he has lost an eye?

5. From the time he was an adolescent, William has been pursuing one dream, one goal, with single-minded energy: middle-class respectability and conventionality, which have until recently been defined in America by whites. Describe his progress toward that goal. What has it cost him?

6. Look at the passage in which Billy strips off the clothes William has lent him and points out his scars. What purposes does this scene serve?

7. At first glance, the title of this story seems to point to Billy Renfro, particularly since there are references throughout the story to Billy's dying, to his being dead. However, does he seem like a "dead man"? If so, in what respects? Is it possible to read the title ironically?

8. In what sense is Billy Renfro the narrator's double, a personification of all those qualities William is trying to repudiate in himself?

9. Discuss McPherson's story in connection with Edgar Allan Poe's "William Wilson." What similarities can you find? How are your responses to the protagonist in "William Wilson" and to the double in McPherson's story different? How does Poe's work help you to understand the dramatic conflict in "The Story of a Dead Man"?

Yellow Woman

LESLIE MARMON SILKO

I

My thigh clung to his with dampness, and I watched the sun rising up through the tamaracks and willows. The small brown water birds came to the river and hopped across the mud, leaving brown scratches in the alkali-white crust. They bathed in the river silently. I could hear the water, almost at our feet where the narrow fast channel bubbled and washed green ragged moss and fern leaves. I looked at him beside me, rolled in the red blanket on the white river sand. I cleaned the sand out of the cracks between my toes, squinting because the sun was above the willow trees. I looked at him for the last time, sleeping on the white river sand.

I felt hungry and followed the river south the way we had come the afternoon before, following our footprints that were already blurred by lizard tracks and bug trails. The horses were still lying down, and the black one whinnied when he saw me but he did not get up—maybe it was because the corral was made out of thick cedar branches and the horses had not yet felt the sun like I had. I tried to look beyond the pale red mesas to the pueblo. I knew it was there, even if I could not see it, on the sandrock hill above the river, the same river that moved past me now and had reflected the moon last night.

The horse felt warm underneath me. He shook his head and pawed the sand. The bay whinnied and leaned against the gate trying to follow, and I remembered him asleep in the red blanket beside the river. I slid off the horse and tied him close to the other horse. I walked north with the river again, and the white sand broke loose in footprints over footprints.

"Wake up."

He moved in the blanket and turned his face to me with his eyes still closed. I knelt down to touch him.

"I'm leaving."

He smiled now, eyes still closed. "You are coming with me, remember?" He sat up now with his bare dark chest and belly in the sun.

"Where?"

"To my place."

"And will I come back?"

He pulled his pants on. I walked away from him, feeling him behind me and smelling the willows.

"Yellow Woman," he said.

I turned to face him. "Who are you?" I asked.

He laughed and knelt on the low, sandy bank, washing his face in the river. "Last night you guessed my name, and you knew why I had come."

I stared past him at the shallow moving water and tried to remember the night, but I could only see the moon in the water and remember his warmth around me.

"But I only said that you were him and that I was Yellow Woman—I'm not really her—I have my own name and I come from the pueblo on the other side of the mesa. Your name is Silva and you are a stranger I met by the river yesterday afternoon.

He laughed softly. "What happened yesterday has nothing to do with what you will do today, Yellow Woman."

"I know—that's what I'm saying—the old stories about the ka'tsina spirit and Yellow Woman can't mean us."

My old grandpa liked to tell those stories best. There is one about Badger and Coyote who went hunting and were gone all day, and when the sun was going down they found a house. There was a girl living there alone, and she had light hair and eyes and she told them that they could sleep with her. Coyote wanted to be with her all night so he sent Badger into a prairie-dog hole, telling him he thought he saw something in it. As soon as Badger crawled in, Coyote blocked up the entrance with rocks and hurried back to Yellow Woman.

"Come here," he said gently.

He touched my neck and I moved close to him to feel his breathing and to hear his heart. I was wondering if Yellow Woman had known who she was—if she knew that she would become part of the stories. Maybe she'd had another name that her husband and relatives called her so that only the ka'tsina from the north and the storytellers would know her as Yellow Woman. But I didn't go on; I felt him all around me, pushing me down into the white river sand.

Yellow Woman went away with the spirit from the north and lived with him and his relatives. She was gone for a long time, but then one day she came back and she brought twin boys.

"Do you know the story?"

"What story?" He smiled and pulled me close to him as he said this. I was afraid lying there on the red blanket. All I could know was the way he felt, warm, damp, his body beside me. This is the way it happens in the stories, I was thinking, with no thought beyond the moment she meets the ka'tsina spirit and they go.

"I don't have to go. What they tell in stories was real only then, back in time immemorial, like they say."

He stood up and pointed at my clothes tangled in the blanket. "Let's go," he said.

I walked beside him, breathing hard because he walked fast, his hand around my wrist. I had stopped trying to pull away from him, because his hand felt cool and the sun was high, drying the river bed into alkali. I will see someone, eventually I will see someone, and then I will be certain that he is only a man—some man from nearby—and I will be sure that I am not Yellow Woman. Because she is from out of time past and I live now and I've been to school and there are highways and pickup trucks that Yellow Woman never saw.

It was an easy ride north on horseback. I watched the change from the cottonwood trees along the river to the junipers that brushed past us in the foothills, and finally there were only piñons, and when I looked up at the rim of the mountain plateau I could see pine trees growing on the edge. Once I stopped to look down, but the pale sandstone had disappeared and the river was gone and the dark lava hills were all around. He touched my hand, not speaking, but always singing softly a mountain song and looking into my eyes.

I felt hungry and wondered what they were doing at home now—my mother, my grandmother, my husband, and the baby. Cooking breakfast, saying, "Where did she go?—maybe kidnaped," and Al going to the tribal police with the details: "She went walking along the river."

The house was made with black lava rock and red mud. It was high above the spreading miles of arroyos and long mesas. I smelled a mountain smell of pitch and buck brush. I stood there beside the black horse, looking down on the small, dim country we had passed, and I shivered.

"Yellow Woman, come inside where it's warm."

II

He lit a fire in the stove. It was an old stove with a round belly and an enamel coffeepot on top. There was only the stove, some faded Navajo blankets, and a bedroll and cardboard box. The floor was made of smooth adobe plaster, and there was one small window facing east. He pointed at the box.

"There's some potatoes and the frying pan." He sat on the floor with his arms around his knees pulling them close to his chest and he watched me fry the potatoes. I didn't mind him watching me because he was always watching me—he had been watching me since I came upon him sitting on the river bank trimming leaves from a willow twig with his knife. We ate from the pan and he wiped the grease from his fingers on his Levis.

"Have you brought women here before?" He smiled and kept chewing, so I said, "Do you always use the same tricks?"

"What tricks?" He looked at me like he didn't understand.

"The story about being a ka'tsina from the mountains. The story about Yellow Woman."

Silva was silent; his face was calm.

"I don't believe it. Those stories couldn't happen now," I said.

He shook his head and said softly, "But someday they will talk about us, and they will say, 'Those two lived long ago when things like that happened.'"

He stood up and went out. I ate the rest of the potatoes and thought about things—about the noise the stove was making and the sound of the mountain wind outside. I remembered yesterday and the day before, and then I went outside.

I walked past the corral to the edge where the narrow trail cut through the black rim rock. I was standing in the sky with nothing around me but the wind that came down from the blue mountain peak behind me. I could see faint mountain images in the distance, miles across the vast spread of mesas and valleys and plains. I wondered who was over there to feel the mountain wind on those sheer blue edges—who walks on the pine needles in those blue mountains.

"Can you see the pueblo?" Silva was standing behind me.

I shook my head. "We're too far away."

"From here I can see the world." He stepped out on the edge. "The Navajo reservation begins over there." He pointed to the east. "The Pueblo boundaries are over here." He looked below us to the south, where the narrow trail seemed to come from. "The Texans have their ranches over there, starting with that valley, the Concho Valley. The Mexicans run some cattle over there too."

"Do you ever work for them?"

"I steal from them," Silva answered. The sun was dropping behind us and shadows were filling the land below. I turned away from the edge that dropped forever into the valleys below.

"I'm cold," I said; "I'm going inside." I started wondering about this man who could speak the Pueblo language so well but who lived on a mountain and rustled cattle. I decided that this man Silva must be Navajo, because Pueblo men didn't do things like that.

"You must be a Navajo."

Silva shook his head gently. "Little Yellow Woman," he said, "you never give up, do you? I have told you who I am. The Navajo people know me, too." He knelt down and unrolled the bedroll and spread the extra blankets out on a piece of canvas. The sun was down, and the only light in the house came from outside—the dim orange light from sundown.

I stood there and waited for him to crawl under the blankets.

"What are you waiting for?" he said, and I lay down beside him. He undressed me slowly like the night before beside the river—kissing my face gently and running his hands up and down my belly and legs. He took off my pants and then he laughed.

"Why are you laughing?"

"You are breathing so hard."

I pulled away from him and turned my back to him.

He pulled me around and pinned me down with his arms and chest. "You don't understand, do you, little Yellow Woman? You will do what I want."

And again he was all around me with his skin slippery against mine, and I was afraid because I understood that his strength could hurt me. I lay underneath him and I knew that he could destroy me. But later, while he slept beside me, I touched his face and I had a feeling—the kind of feeling for him that overcame me that morning along the river. I kissed him on the forehead and he reached out for me.

When I woke up in the morning he was gone. It gave me a strange feeling because for a long time I sat there on the blankets and looked around the little house for some object of his—some proof that he had been there or maybe that he was coming back. Only the blankets and the cardboard box remained. The .30-30 that had been leaning in the corner was gone, and so was the knife I had used the night before. He was gone, and I had my chance to go now. But first I had to eat, because I knew it would be a long walk home.

I found some dried apricots in the cardboard box, and I sat down on a rock at the edge of the plateau rim. There was no wind and the sun warmed me. I was surrounded by silence. I drowsed with apricots in my mouth, and I didn't believe that there were highways or railroads or cattle to steal.

When I woke up, I stared down at my feet in the black mountain dirt. Little black ants were swarming over the pine needles around my foot. They must have smelled the apricots. I thought about my family far below me. They would be wondering about me, because this had never happened to me before. The tribal police would file a report. But if old Grandpa weren't dead he would tell them what happened—he would laugh and say, "Stolen by a ka'tsina, a mountain spirit. She'll come home—they usually do." There are enough of them to handle things. My mother and grandmother will raise the baby like they raised me. Al will find someone else, and they will go on like before, except that there will be a story about the day I disappeared while I was walking along the river. Silva had come for me; he said he had. I did not decide to go. I just went. Moonflowers blossom in the sand hills before dawn, just as I followed him. That's what I was thinking as I wandered along the trail through the pine trees.

It was noon when I got back. When I saw the stone house I remembered that I had meant to go home. But that didn't seem important any more, maybe because there were little blue flowers growing in the meadow behind the stone house and the gray squirrels were playing in the pines next to the house. The horses were standing in the corral, and there was a beef carcass hanging on the shady side of a big pine in front of the house. Flies buzzed around the clotted blood that hung from the carcass. Silva was washing his hands in a bucket full of water. He must have heard me coming because he spoke to me without turning to face me.

"I've been waiting for you."

"I went walking in the big pine trees."

I looked into the bucket full of bloody water with brown-and-white animal hairs floating in it. Silva stood there letting his hands drip, examining me intently.

"Are you coming with me?"

"Where?" I asked him.

"To sell the meat in Marquez."

"If you're sure it's O.K."

"I wouldn't ask you if it wasn't," he answered.

He sloshed the water around in the bucket before he dumped it out and set the bucket upside down near the door. I followed him to the corral and watched him saddle the horses. Even beside the horses he looked tall, and I asked him again if he wasn't Navajo. He didn't say anything; he just shook his head and kept cinching up the saddle.

"But Navajos are tall."

"Get on the horse," he said, "and let's go."

The last thing he did before we started down the steep trail was to grab the .30-30 from the corner. He slid the rifle into the scabbard that hung from his saddle.

"Do they ever try to catch you?" I asked.

"They don't know who I am."

"Then why did you bring the rifle?"

"Because we are going to Marquez where the Mexicans live."

III

The trail leveled out on a narrow ridge that was steep on both sides like an animal spine. On one side I could see where the trail went around the rocky gray hills and disappeared into the southeast where the pale sandrock mesas stood in the distance near my home. On the other side was a trail that went west, and as I looked far into the distance I thought I saw the little town. But Silva said no, that I was looking in the wrong place, that I just thought I saw houses. After that I quit looking off into the distance; it was hot and the wildflowers were closing up their deep-yellow petals. Only the waxy cactus flowers bloomed in the bright sun, and I saw every color that a cactus blossom can be; the white ones and the red ones were still buds, but the purple and the yellow were blossoms, upon full and the most beautiful of all.

Silva saw him before I did. The white man was riding a big gray horse, coming up the trail toward us. He was traveling fast and the gray horse's feet sent rocks rolling off the trail into the dry tumbleweeds. Silva motioned for me to stop and we watched the white man. He didn't see us right away, but finally his horse whinnied at our horses and he stopped. He looked at us briefly before he loped the gray horse across the three hundred yards that separated us. He stopped his horse in front of Silva, and his young fat face was shadowed by the brim of his hat. He didn't look mad, but his small, pale eyes moved from the blood-soaked gunny sacks hanging from my saddle to Silva's face and then back to my face.

"Where did you get the fresh meat?" the white man asked.

"I've been hunting," Silva said, and when he shifted his weight in the saddle the leather creaked.

"The hell you have, Indian. You've been rustling cattle. We've been looking for the thief for a long time."

The rancher was fat, and sweat began to soak through his white cowboy shirt and the wet cloth stuck to the thick rolls of belly fat. He almost seemed to be panting from the exertion of talking, and he smelled rancid, maybe because Silva scared him.

Silva turned to me and smiled. "Go back up the mountain, Yellow Woman."

The white man got angry when he heard Silva speak in a language he couldn't understand. "Don't try anything, Indian. Just keep riding to Marquez. We'll call the state police from there."

The rancher must have been unarmed because he was very frightened and if he had a gun he would have pulled it out then. I turned my horse around and the rancher yelled, "Stop!" I looked at Silva for an instant and there was something ancient and dark—something I could feel in my stomach—in his eyes, and when I glanced at his hand I saw his finger on the trigger of the .30-30 that was still in the saddle scabbard. I slapped my horse across the flank and the sacks of raw meat swung against my knees as the horse leaped up the trail. It was hard to keep my balance, and once I thought I felt the saddle slipping backward; it was because of this that I could not look back.

I didn't stop until I reached the ridge where the trail forked. The horse was breathing deep gasps and there was a dark film of sweat on its neck. I looked down in the direction I had come from, but I couldn't see the place. I waited. The wind came up and pushed warm air past me. I looked up at the sky, pale blue and full of thin clouds and fading vapor trails left by jets.

I think four shots were fired—I remember hearing four hollow explosions that reminded me of deer hunting. There could have been more shots after that, but I couldn't have heard them because my horse was running again and the loose rocks were making to much noise as they scattered around his feet.

Horses have a hard time running downhill, but I went that way instead of uphill to the mountain because I thought it was safer. I felt better with the horse running southeast past the round gray hills that were covered with cedar trees and black lava rock. When I got to the plain in the distance I could see the dark green patches of tamaracks that grew along the river; and beyond the river I could see the beginning of the pale sandrock mesas. I stopped the horse and looked back to see if anyone was coming; then I got off the horse and turned the horse around, wondering if it would go back to its corral under the pines on the mountain. It looked back at me for a moment and then plucked a mouthful of green tumbleweeds before it trotted back up the trail with its ears pointed forward, carrying its head daintily to one side to avoid stepping on the dragging reins. When the horse disappeared over the last hill, the gunny sacks full of meat were still swinging and bounding.

IV

I walked toward the river on a wood-hauler's road that I knew would eventually lead to the paved road. I was thinking about waiting beside the road for someone to drive by, but by the time I got to the pavement I had decided it wasn't very far to walk if I followed the river back the way Silva and I had come.

The river water tasted good, and I sat in the shade under a cluster of silvery willows. I thought about Silva, and I felt sad at leaving him; still, there was something strange about him, and I tried to figure it out all the way back home.

I came back to the place on the river bank where he had been sitting the first time I saw him. The green willow leaves that he had trimmed from the branch were still lying there, wilted in the sand. I saw the leaves and I wanted to go back to him—to kiss him and to touch him—but the mountains were too far away now. And I told myself, because I believe it, he will come back sometime and be waiting again by the river.

I followed the path up from the river into the village. The sun was getting low, and I could smell supper cooking when I got to the screen door of my house. I could hear their voices inside—my mother was telling my grandmother how to fix the Jell-O and my husband, Al, was playing with the baby. I decided to tell them that some Navajo had kidnapped me, but I was sorry that old Grandpa wasn't alive to hear my story because it was the Yellow Woman stories he liked to tell best.

QUESTIONS

"Yellow Woman"

1. From whose point of view is Silko's story told? What limitations does this perspective impose? What are the things we cannot know, because the narrator does not? Why did Silko choose a narrator with a limited point of view?

2. Who is the "Yellow Woman" of the title? What do we learn about her?

Why are the traditional stories about her so appealing to the narrator? Why don't we ever learn the narrator's "real" name?

3. Describe the man known as Silva, who claims to be a ka'tsina spirit. What buried aspects of the narrator does Silva represent?

4. Though we learn little about the narrator's husband, it is clear that he is different from Silva. In what ways are the two men dissimilar? How does the way of life symbolized by Silva differ from the life lived by the narrator and her family back at the pueblo?

5. At several points in the story, the narrator clearly has a chance to escape from her "kidnapper." Why doesn't she? Look at the passage in which she describes how her family will deal with her abandonment of them. How would you characterize her tone here? How close to Silva does she seem at this point and at the later point when she says she sees in Silva's eyes "something ancient and dark—something I could feel in my stomach"?

6. Why does the narrator finally leave Silva? Is she saying more than she is aware of when she says it is "safer" to run her horse downhill toward the pueblo than uphill toward Silva's house? What kind of safety is she concerned about?

7. What details of the story help to give it a dreamlike quality? Why is this dream mood appropriate to the story?

8. What is the symbolic value of the scene in which Silva, standing with the narrator on top of the mountain near his home, points out features of the landscape below?

A Good Man Is Hard to Find

FLANNERY O'CONNOR

The grandmother didn't want to go to Florida. She wanted to visit some of her connections in east Tennessee and she was seizing at every chance to change Bailey's mind. Bailey was the son she lived with, her only boy. He was sitting on the edge of his chair at the table, bent over the orange sports section of the *Journal*. "Now look here, Bailey," she said, "see here, read this," and she stood with one hand on her thin hip and the other rattling the newspaper at his bald head. "Here this fellow that calls himself The Misfit is aloose from the Federal Pen and headed toward Florida and you read here what it says he did to these people. Just you read it. I wouldn't take my children in any direction with a criminal like that aloose in it. I couldn't answer to my conscience if I did."

Bailey didn't look up from his reading so she wheeled around then and faced the children's mother; a young woman in slacks, whose face was as broad and innocent as a cabbage and was tied around with a green handkerchief that had two points on the top like rabbit's ears. She was sitting on the sofa, feeding the baby his apricots out of a jar. "The children have been to Florida before," the old lady said. "You all ought to take them somewhere else for a change so they would see different parts of the world and be broad. They never have been to east Tennessee."

The children's mother didn't seem to hear her, but the eight-year-old boy, John Wesley, a stocky child with glasses, said, "If you don't want to go to Florida, why dontcha stay at home?" He and the little girl, June Star, were reading the funny papers on the floor.

"She wouldn't stay at home to be queen for a day," June Star said without raising her yellow head.

"Yes, and what would you do if this fellow, The Misfit, caught you?" the grandmother asked.

"I'd smack his face," John Wesley said.

"She wouldn't stay at home for a million bucks," June Star said. "Afraid she'd miss something. She has to go everywhere we go."

"All right, Miss," the grandmother said. "Just remember that the next time you want me to curl your hair."

June Star said her hair was naturally curly.

The next morning the grandmother was the first one in the car, ready to go. She had her big black valise that looked like the head of a hippopotamus in one corner, and underneath it she was hiding a basket with Pitty Sing, the cat, in it. She didn't intend for the cat to be left alone in the house for three days because he would miss her too much and she was afraid he might brush against one of the gas burners and accidentally asphyxiate himself. Her son, Bailey, didn't like to arrive at a motel with a cat.

She sat in the middle of the back seat with John Wesley and June Star on either side of her. Bailey and the children's mother and the baby sat in the front and they left Atlanta at eight forty-five with the mileage on the car at 55890. The grandmother wrote this down because she thought it would be interesting to say how many miles they had been when they got back. It took them twenty minutes to reach the outskirts of the city.

The old lady settled herself comfortably, removing her white cotton gloves and putting them up with her purse on the shelf in front of the back window. The children's mother still had on slacks and still had her head tied up in a green kerchief, but the grandmother had on a navy blue straw sailor hat with a bunch of white violets on the brim and a navy blue dress with a small white dot in the print. Her collar and cuffs were white organdy trimmed with lace and at her neckline she had pinned a purple spray of cloth violets containing a sachet. In case of an accident, anyone seeing her dead on the highway would know at once that she was a lady.

She said she thought it was going to be a good day for driving, neither too hot nor too cold, and she cautioned Bailey that the speed limit was fifty-five miles an hour and that the patrolmen hid themselves behind billboards and small clumps of trees and sped out after you before you had a chance to slow down. She pointed out interesting details of the scenery: Stone Mountain; the blue granite that in some places came up to both sides of the highway; the brilliant red clay banks slightly streaked with purple; and the various crops that made rows of green lace-work on the ground. The trees were full of silver-white sunlight and the meanest of them sparkled. The children were reading comic magazines and their mother had gone back to sleep.

"Let's go through Georgia fast so we won't have to look at it much," John Welsey said.

"If I were a little boy," said the grandmother, "I wouldn't talk about my native state that way. Tennessee has the mountains and Georgia has the hills."

"Tennessee is just a hillbilly dumping ground," John Wesley said, "and Georgia is a lousy state too."

"You said it," June Star said.

"In my time," said the grandmother, folding her thin veined fingers, "children were more respectful of their native states and their parents and everything else. People did right then. Oh look at the cute little pickaninny!" she said and pointed to a Negro child standing in the door of a

shack. "Wouldn't that make a picture, now?" she asked and they all turned
and looked at the little Negro out of the back window. He waved.

"He didn't have any britches on," June Star said.

"He probably didn't have any," the grandmother explained. "Little niggers in the country don't have things like we do. If I could paint, I'd paint
that picture," she said.

The children exchanged comic books.

The grandmother offered to hold the baby and the children's mother
passed him over the front seat to her. She set him on her knee and bounced
him and told him about the things they were passing. She rolled her eyes
and screwed up her mouth and stuck her leathery thin face into his smooth
bland one. Occasionally he gave her a faraway smile. They passed a large
cotton field with five or six graves fenced in the middle of it, like a small
island. "Look at the graveyard!" the grandmother said, pointing it out. "That
was the old family burying ground. That belonged to the plantation."

"Where's the plantation?" John Wesley asked.

"Gone With the Wind," said the grandmother. "Ha. Ha."

When the children finished all the comic books they had brought, they
opened the lunch and ate it. The grandmother ate a peanut butter sandwich and an olive and would not let the children throw the box and the
paper napkins out the window. When there was nothing else to do they
played a game by choosing a cloud and making the other two guess what
shape it suggested. John Wesley took one the shape of a cow and June Star
guessed a cow and John Wesley said, no, an automobile, and June Star
said he didn't play fair, and they began to slap each other over the grandmother.

The grandmother said she would tell them a story if they would keep
quiet. When she told a story, she rolled her eyes and waved her head and
was very dramatic. She said once when she was a maiden lady she had
been courted by a Mr. Edgar Atkins Teagarden from Jasper, Georgia. She
said he was a very good-looking man and a gentleman and that he brought
her a watermelon every Saturday afternoon with his initials cut in it, E.A.T.
Well, one Saturday, she said, Mr. Teagarden brought the watermelon and
there was nobody at home and he left it on the front porch and returned
in his buggy to Jasper, but she never got the watermelon, she said, because
a nigger boy ate it when he saw the initials, E.A.T.! This story tickled John
Wesley's funny bone and he giggled and giggled but June Star didn't think
it was any good. She said she wouldn't marry a man that just brought her
a watermelon on Saturday. The grandmother said she would have done
well to marry Mr. Teagarden because he was a gentleman and had brought
Coca-Cola stock when it first came out and that he had died only a few
years ago, a very wealthy man.

They stopped at The Tower for barbecued sandwiches. The Tower was a
part-stucco and part-wood filling station and dance hall set in a clearing
outside of Timothy. A fat man named Red Sammy Butts ran it and there

were signs stuck here and there on the building and for miles up and down the highway saying, TRY RED SAMMY'S FAMOUS BARBECUE. NONE LIKE FAMOUS RED SAMMY'S! RED SAM! THE FAT BOY WITH THE HAPPY LAUGH, A VETERAN! RED SAMMY'S YOUR MAN!

Red Sammy was lying on the bare ground outside The Tower with his head under a truck while a gray monkey about a foot high, chained to a small chinaberry tree, chattered nearby. The monkey sprang back into the tree and got on the highest limb as soon as he saw the children jump out of the car and run toward him.

Inside, The Tower was a long dark room with a counter at one end and tables at the other and dancing space in the middle. They all sat down at a broad table next to the nickelodeon and Red Sam's wife, a tall burnt-brown woman with hair and eyes lighter than her skin, came and took their order. The children's mother put a dime in the machine and played "The Tennessee Waltz," and the grandmother said that tune always made her want to dance. She asked Bailey if he would like to dance but he only glared at her. He didn't have a naturally sunny disposition like she did and trips made him nervous. The grandmother's brown eyes were very bright. She swayed her head from side to side and pretended she was dancing in her chair. June Star said play something she could tap to so the children's mother put in another dime and played a fast number and June Star stepped out onto the dance floor and did her tap routine.

"Ain't she cute?" Red Sam's wife said, leaning over the counter. "Would you like to come be my little girl?"

"No, I certainly wouldn't," June Star said. "I wouldn't live in a broken-down place like this for a million bucks!" and she ran back to the table.

"Ain't she cute?" the woman repeated, stretching her mouth politely.

"Aren't you ashamed?" hissed the grandmother.

Red Sam came in and told his wife to quit lounging on the counter and hurry with these people's order. His khaki trousers reached just to his hip bones and his stomach hung over them like a sack of meal swaying under his shirt. He came over and sat down at a table nearby and let out a combination sigh and yodel. "You can't win," he said. "You can't win," and he wiped his sweating red face off with a gray handkerchief. "These days you don't know who to trust," he said. "Ain't that the truth?"

"People are certainly not nice like they used to be," said the grandmother.

"Two fellers come in here last week," Red Sammy said, "driving a Chrysler. It was a old beat-up car but it was a good one and these boys looked all right to me. Said they worked t the mill and you know I let them fellers charge the gas they bought? Now why did I do that?"

"Because you're a good man!" the grandmother said at once.

"Yes'm, I suppose so," Red Sam said as if he were struck with the answer.

His wife brought the orders, carrying the five plates all at once without a tray, two in each hand and one balanced on her arm. "It isn't a soul in this green world of God's that you can trust," she said. "And I don't count nobody out of that, not nobody," she repeated, looking at Red Sammy.

"Did you read about that criminal, The Misfit, that's escaped?" asked the grandmother.

"I wouldn't be a bit surprised if he didn't attack this place right here," said the woman. "If he hears about it being here, I wouldn't be none surprised to see him. If he hears it's two cent in the cash register, I wouldn't be a tall surprised if he. . . ."

"That'll do," Red Sam said. "Go bring these people their Co'-Colas," and the woman went off to get the rest of the order.

"A good man is hard to find," Red Sammy said. "Everything is getting terrible. I remember the day you could go off and leave your screen door unlatched. Not no more."

He and the grandmother discussed better times. The old lady said that in her opinion Europe was entirely to blame for the way things were now. She said the way Europe acted you would think we were made of money and Red Sam said it was no use talking about it, she was exactly right. The children ran outside into the white sunlight and looked at the monkey in the lacy chinaberry tree. He was busy catching fleas on himself and biting each one carefully between his teeth as it if were a delicacy.

They drove off again into the hot afternoon. The grandmother took cat naps and woke up every few minutes with her own snoring. Outside of Toombsboro she woke up and recalled an old plantation that she had visited in this neighborhood once when she was a young lady. She said the house had six white columns across the front and that there was an avenue of oaks leading up to it and two little wooden trellis arbors on either side in front where you sat down with your suitor after a stroll in the garden. She recalled exactly which road to turn off to get to it. She knew that Bailey would not be willing to lose any time looking at an old house, but the more she talked about it, the more she wanted to see it once again and find out if the little twin arbors were still standing. "There was a secret panel in this house," she said craftily, not telling the truth but wishing that she were, "and the story went that all the family silver was hidden in it when Sherman came through but it was never found. . . ."

"Hey!" John Wesley said. "Let's go see it! We'll find it! We'll poke all the wood work and find it! Who lives there? Where do you turn off at? Hey Pop, can't we turn off there?"

"We never have seen a house with a secret panel!" June Star shrieked. "Let's go to the house with the secret panel! Hey, Pop, can't we go see the house with the secret panel!"

"It's not far from here, I know," the grandmother said. "It wouldn't take over twenty minutes."

Bailey was looking straight ahead. His jaw was as rigid as a horseshoe. "No," he said.

The children began to yell and scream that they wanted to see the house with the secret panel. John Wesley kicked the back of the front seat and June Star hung over her mother's shoulder and whined desperately into her ear that they never had any fun even on their vacation, that THEY could never do what THEY wanted to do. The baby began to scream and John Wesley kicked the back of the seat so hard that his father could feel the blows in his kidney.

"All right!" he shouted and drew the car to a stop at the side of the road. "Will you all shut up? Will you all just shut up for one second? If you don't shut up, we won't go anywhere."

"It would be very educational for them," the grandmother murmured.

"All right," Bailey said, "but get this. This is the only time we're going to stop for anything like this. This is the one and only time."

"The dirt road that you have to turn down is about a mile back," the grandmother directed. "I marked it when we passed."

"A dirt road," Bailey groaned.

After they had turned around and were headed toward the dirt road, the grandmother recalled other points about the house, the beautiful glass over the front doorway and the candle lamp in the hall. John Wesley said that the secret panel was probably in the fireplace.

"You can't go inside this house," Bailey said. "You don't know who lives there."

"While you all talk to the people in front, I'll run around behind and get in a window," John Wesley suggested.

"We'll all stay in the car," his mother said.

They turned onto the dirt road and the car raced roughly along in a swirl of pink dust. The grandmother recalled the times when there were no paved roads and thirty miles was a day's journey. The dirt road was hilly and there were sudden washes in it and sharp curves on dangerous embankments. All at once they would be on a hill, looking down over the blue tops of trees for miles around, then the next minute, they would be in a red depression with the dust-coated trees looking down on them.

"This place had better turn up in a minute," Bailey said, "or I'm going to turn around."

The road looked as if no one had traveled on it in months.

"It's not much farther," the grandmother said and just as she said it, a horrible thought came to her. The thought was so embarrassing that she turned red in the face and her eyes dilated and her feet jumped up, upsetting her valise in the corner. The instant the valise moved, the newspaper top she had over the basket under it rose with a snarl and Pitty Sing, the cat, sprang onto Bailey's shoulder.

The children were thrown to the floor and their mother, clutching the baby, was thrown out the door onto the ground; the old lady was thrown into the front seat. The car turned over once and landed right-side-up in a gulch on the side of the road. Bailey remained in the driver's seat with the cat—gray-striped with a broad white face and an orange nose—clinging to his neck like a caterpillar.

As soon as the children saw they could move their arms and legs, they scrambled out of the car, shouting, "We've had an ACCIDENT!" The grandmother was curled up under the dashboard, hoping she was injured so that Bailey's wrath would not come down on her all at once. The horrible thought she had had before the accident was that the house she had remembered so vividly was not in Georgia but in Tennessee.

Bailey removed the cat from his neck with both hands and flung it out the window against the side of a pine tree. Then he got out of the car and started looking for the children's mother. She was sitting against the side of the red gutted ditch, holding the screaming baby, but she only had a cut down her face and a broken shoulder. "We've had an ACCIDENT!" the children screamed in a frenzy of delight.

"But nobody's killed," June Star said with disappointment as the grandmother limped out of the car, her hat still pinned to her head but the broken front brim standing up at a jaunty angle and the violet spray hanging off the side. They all sat down in the ditch, except the children, to recover from the shock. They were all shaking.

"Maybe a car will come along," said the children's mother hoarsely.

"I believe I have injured an organ," said the grandmother, pressing her side, but no one answered her. Bailey's teeth were clattering. He had on a yellow sport shirt with bright blue parrots designed in it and his face was as yellow as the shirt. The grandmother decided that she would not mention that the house was in Tennessee.

The road was about ten feet above and they could see only the tops of the trees on the other side of it. Behind the ditch they were sitting in there were more woods, tall and dark and deep. In a few minutes they saw a car some distance away on top of a hill, coming slowly as if the occupants were watching them. The grandmother stood up and waved both arms dramatically to attract their attention. The car continued to come on slowly, disappeared around a bend and appeared again, moving even slower, on top of the hill they had gone over. It was a big black battered hearselike automobile. There were three men in it.

It came to a stop just over them and for some minutes, the driver looked down with a steady expressionless gaze to where they were sitting, and didn't speak. Then he turned his head and muttered something to the other two and they got out. One was a fat boy in black trousers and a red sweat shirt with a silver stallion embossed on the front of it. He moved around on the right side of them and stood staring, his mouth partly open in a kind of loose grin. The other had on khaki pants and a blue striped coat and a gray hat pulled down very low, hiding most of his face. He came around slowly on the left side. Neither spoke.

The driver got out of the car and stood by the side of it, looking down at them. He was an older man than the other two. His hair was just beginning to gray and he wore silver-rimmed spectacles that gave him a scholarly look. He had a long creased face and didn't have on any shirt or undershirt. He had on blue jeans that were tight for him and was holding a black hat and a gun. The two boys also had guns.

"We've had an ACCIDENT!" the children screamed.

The grandmother had the peculiar feeling that the bespectacled man was someone she knew. His face was as familiar to her as if she had known him all her life but she could not recall who he was. He moved away from the car and began to come down the embankment, placing his feet carefully so that he wouldn't slip. He had on tan and white shoes and no socks, and his ankles were red and thin. "Good afternoon," he said. "I see you all had you a little spill."

"We turned over twice!" said the grandmother.

"Oncet," he corrected. "We seen it happen. Try their car and see will it run, Hiram," he said quietly to the boy with the gray hat.

"What you got that gun for?" John Wesley asked. "Whatcha gonna do with that gun?"

"Lady," the man said to the children's mother, "would you mind calling them children to sit down by you? Children make me nervous. I want all you all to sit down right together there where you're at."

"What are you telling us what to do for?" June Star asked.

Behind them the line of woods gaped like a dark open mouth. "Come here," said their mother.

"Look here now," Bailey began suddenly, "we're in a predicament! We're in. . ."

The grandmother shrieked. She scrambled to her feet and stood staring. "You're The Misfit!" she said. "I recognized you at once!"

"Yes'm," the man said, smiling slightly as if he were pleased in spite of himself to be known, "but it would have been better for all of you, lady, if you hadn't of reckernized me."

Bailey turned his head sharply and said something to his mother that shocked even the children. The old lady began to cry and The Misfit reddened.

"Lady," he said, "don't you get upset. Sometimes a man says things he don't mean. I don't reckon he meant to talk to you thataway."

"You wouldn't shoot a lady, would you?" the grandmother said and removed a clean handkerchief from her cuff and began to slap at her eyes with it.

The Misfit pointed the toe of his shoe into the ground and made a little hole and then covered it up again. "I would hate to have to," he said.

"Listen," the grandmother almost screamed, "I know you're a good man. You don't look a bit like you have common blood. I know you must come from nice people!"

"Yes mam," he said, "finest people in the world." When he smiled he showed a row of strong white teeth. "God never made a finer woman than my mother and my daddy's heart was pure gold," he said. The boy with the red sweat shirt had come around behind them and was standing with his gun at his hip. The Misfit squatted down on the ground. "Watch them children, Bobby Lee," he said. "You know they make me nervous." He looked at the six of them huddled together in front of him and he seemed to be embarrassed as if he couldn't think of anything to say. "Ain't a cloud in the sky," he remarked, looking up at it. "Don't see no sun but don't see no cloud neither."

"Yes, it's a beautiful day," said the grandmother. "Listen," she said, "you shouldn't call yourself The Misfit because I know you're a good man at heart. I can just look at you and tell."

"Hush!" Bailey yelled. "Hush! Everybody shut up and let me handle this!" He was squatting in the position of a runner about to sprint forward but he didn't move.

"I pre-chate that, lady," The Misfit said and drew a little circle in the ground with the butt of his gun.

"It'll take a half a hour to fix this here car," Hiram called, looking over the raised hood of it.

"Well, first you and Bobby Lee get him and that little boy to step over yonder with you," The Misfit said, pointing to Bailey and John Wesley. "The boys want to ask you something," he said to Bailey. "Would you mind stepping back in them woods there with them?"

"Listen," Bailey began, "we're in a terrible predicament! Nobody realizes what this is," and his voice cracked. His eyes were as blue and intense as the parrots in his shirt and he remained perfectly still.

The grandmother reached up to adjust her hat brim as if she were going to the woods with him but it came off in her hand. She stood staring at it and after a second she let it fall on the ground. Hiram pulled Bailey up by the arm as if he were assisting an old man. John Wesley caught hold of his father's hand and Bobby Lee followed. They went off toward the woods and just as they reached the dark edge, Bailey turned and supporting himself against a gray naked pine trunk, he shouted, "I'll be back in a minute, Mamma, wait on me!"

"Come back this instant!" his mother shrilled but they all disappeared into the woods.

"Bailey Boy!" the grandmother called in a tragic voice but she found she was looking at The Misfit squatting on the ground in front of her. "I just know you're a good man," she said desperately. "You're not a bit common!"

"Nome, I ain't a good man," The Misfit said after a second as if he had considered her statement carefully, "but I ain't the worst in the world neither. My daddy said I was a different breed of dog from my brothers and sisters. 'You know,' Daddy said, 'it's some that can live their whole life out without asking about it and it's others has to know why it is, and this boy is one of the latters. He's going to be into everything!'" He put on his black hat and looked up suddenly and then away deep into the woods as if he were embarrassed again. "I'm sorry I don't have on a shirt before you ladies," he said, hunching his shoulders slightly. "We buried our clothes that we had on when we escaped and we're just making do until we can get better. We borrowed these from some folks we met," he explained.

"That's perfectly all right," the grandmother said. "Maybe Bailey has an extra shirt in his suitcase."

"I'll look and see terrectly," The Misfit said.

"Where are they taking him?" the children's mother screamed.

"Daddy was a card himself," The Misfit said. "You couldn't put anything over on him. He never got in trouble with the Authorities though. Just had the knack of handling them."

"You could be honest too if you'd only try," said the grandmother. "Think how wonderful it would be to settle down and live a comfortable life and not have to think about somebody chasing you all the time."

The Misfit kept scratching in the ground with the but of his gun as if he were thinking about it. "Yes'm, somebody is always after you," he murmured.

The grandmother noticed how thin his shoulder blades were just behind his hat because she was standing up looking down on him. "Do you ever pray?" she asked.

He shook his head. All she saw was the black hat wiggle between his shoulder blades. "Nome," he said.

There was a pistol shot from the woods, followed closely by another. Then silence. The old lady's head jerked around. She could hear the wind move through the tree tops like a long satisfied insuck of breath. "Bailey Boy!" she called.

"I was a gospel singer for a while," The Misfit said. "I been most everything. Been in the arm service, both land and sea, at home and abroad, been twict married, been an undertaker, been with the railroads, plowed Mother Earth, been in a tornado, seen a man burnt alive oncet," and he looked up at the children's mother and the little girl who were sitting close together, their faces white and their eyes glassy; "I even seen a woman flogged," he said.

"Pray, pray," the grandmother began, "pray, pray . . ."

"I never was a bad boy that I remember of," The Misfit said in an almost dreamy voice, "but somewheres along the line I done something wrong and got sent to the penitentiary. I was buried alive," and he looked up and held her attention to him by a steady stare.

"That's when you should have started to pray," she said. "What did you do to get sent to the penitentiary that first time?"

"Turn to the right, it was a wall," The Misfit said, looking up again at the cloudless sky. "Turn to the left, it was a wall. Look up it was a ceiling, look down it was a floor. I forget what I done, lady. I set there and set there, trying to remember what it was I done and I ain't recalled it to this day. Oncet in a while, I would think it was coming to me, but it never come."

"Maybe they put you in by mistake," the old lady said vaguely.

"Nome," he said. "It wasn't no mistake. They had the papers on me."

"You must have stolen something," she said.

The Misfit sneered slightly. "Nobody had nothing I wanted," he said. "It was a head-doctor at the penitentiary said what I had done was kill my daddy but I know that for a lie. My daddy died in nineteen ought nineteen of the epidemic flu and I never had a thing to do with it. He was buried in the Mount Hopewell Baptist churchyard and you can go there and see for yourself."

"If you would pray," the old lady said, "Jesus would help you."

"That's right," The Misfit said.

"Well then, why don't you pray?" she asked trembling with delight suddenly.

"I don't want no hep," he said. "I'm doing all right by myself."

Bobby Lee and Hiram came ambling back from the woods. Bobby Lee was dragging a yellow shirt with bright blue parrots in it.

"Throw me that shirt, Bobby Lee," The Misfit said. The shirt came flying at him and landed on his shoulder and he put it on. The grandmother couldn't name what the shirt reminded her of. "No, lady," The Misfit said while he was buttoning it up, "I found out the crime don't matter. You can do one thing or you can do another, kill a man or take a tire off his car, because sooner or later you're going to forget what it was you done and just be punished for it."

The children's mother had begun to make heaving noises as if she couldn't get her breath. "Lady," he asked, "would you and that little girl like to step off yonder with Bobby Lee and Hiram and join your husband?"

"Yes, thank you," the mother said faintly. Her left arm dangled helplessly and she was holding the baby, who had gone to sleep, in the other. "Hep that lady up, Hiram," The Misfit said as she struggled to climb out of the ditch, "and Bobby Lee, you hold onto that little girl's hand."

"I don't want to hold hands with him," June Star said. "He reminds me of a pig."

The fat boy blushed and laughed and caught her by the arm and pulled her off into the woods after Hiram and her mother.

Alone with The Misfit, the grandmother found that she had lost her voice. There was not a cloud in the sky nor any sun. There was nothing around her but woods. She wanted to tell him that he must pray. She opened and closed her mouth several times before anything came out. Finally she found herself saying, "Jesus. Jesus," meaning, Jesus will help you, but the way she was saying it, it sounded as if she might be cursing.

"Yes'm," The Misfit said as if he agreed. "Jesus thrown everything off balance. It was the same case with Him as with me except He hadn't committed any crime and they could prove I had committed one because they had the papers on me. Of course," he said, "they never shown me my papers. That's why I sign myself now. I said long ago, you get you a signature and sign everything you do and keep a copy of it. Then you'll know what you done and you can hold up the crime to the punishment and see do they match and in the end you'll have something to prove you ain't been treated right. I call myself The Misfit," he said, "because I can't make what all I done wrong fit what all I gone through in punishment."

There was a piercing scream from the woods, followed closely by a pistol report. "Does it seem right to you, lady, that one is punished a heap and another ain't punished at all?"

"Jesus!" the old lady cried. "You've got good blood! I know you wouldn't shoot a lady! I know you come from nice people! Pray! Jesus, you ought not to shoot a lady. I'll give you all the money I've got!"

"Lady," The Misfit said, looking beyond her far into the woods, "there never was a body that give the undertaker a tip."

There were two more pistol reports and the grandmother raised her head like a parched old turkey hen crying for water and called, "Bailey Boy, Bailey Boy!" as if her heart would break.

"Jesus was the only One that ever raised the dead," The Misfit continued, "and He shouldn't have done it. He thrown everything off balance. If He did what He said, then it's nothing for you to do but throw away everything and follow Him, and if He didn't then it's nothing for you to do but enjoy the few minutes you got left the best way you can—by killing somebody or burning down his house or doing some other meanness to him. No pleasure but meanness," he said and his voice had become almost a snarl.

"Maybe He didn't raise the dead," the old lady mumbled, not knowing what she was saying and feeling so dizzy that she sank down in the ditch with her legs twisted under her.

"I wasn't there so I can't say He didn't," The Misfit said. "I wisht I had of been there," he said, hitting the ground with his fist. "It ain't right I wasn't there because if I had to been there I would of known. Listen lady," he said in a high voice, "if I had of been there I would of known and I wouldn't be like I am now." His voice seemed about to crack and the grandmother's head cleared for an instant. She saw the man's face twisted close to her own as if he were going to cry and she murmured, "Why, you're one of my babies. You're one of my own children!" She reached out and touched him on the shoulder. The Misfit sprang back as if a snake had bitten him and shot her three times through the chest. Then he put his gun down on the ground and took off his glasses and began to clean them.

Hiram and Bobby Lee returned from the woods and stood over the ditch, looking down at the grandmother who half sat and half lay in a puddle of blood with her legs crossed under her like a child's and her face smiling up at the cloudless sky.

Without his glasses, The Misfit's eyes were red-rimmed and pale and defenseless-looking. "Take her off and throw her where you thrown the others," he said, picking up the cat that was rubbing itself against his leg.

"She was a talker, wasn't she?" Bobby Lee said, sliding down the ditch with a yodel.

"She would of been a good woman," The Misfit said, "if it had been somebody there to shoot her every minute of her life."

"Some fun!" Bobby Lee said.

"Shut up, Bobby Lee," The Misfit said. "It's no real pleasure in life."

QUESTIONS

"A Good Man Is Hard to Find"

1. Characterize the different members of the family, taking into account what they say, how they act, and what the narrator tells us about them. In what sense are they typical characters: the grandmother a typical grandmother, Bailey a typical middle-aged son, his wife the typical "little woman," and so on? Why has O'Connor created such characters? What does this suggest about her intention in regard to the story's theme?

2. How does O'Connor create a sense of inevitability in this story? How does she make the reader feel right from the start that the family's encounter with The Misfit is somehow fated and inescapable?

3. Part of what makes "A Good Man Is Hard to Find" so disquieting is its sudden shift in tone from the humorous to the horrific. Point to some of its comical, almost burlesque elements. What effects does O'Connor achieve by including these humorous moments in the story? How do they contribute to and reinforce the story's theme?

4. How would you characterize O'Connor's style—the way she uses language? What makes it so effective, so vivid and alive? One critic has written that O'Connor's "most frequent stylistic device is the simile." Can you point to any particularly vivid similes in this story?

5. The Misfit obviously plays the role of the Other in this story, but what sort of Other is he? How does he embody the dark underside of the world represented by the grandmother and her family?

6. When the grandmother first sees The Misfit, his face seems "as familiar to her as if she had known him all her life." Why does the grandmother have this sense? How do you account for it? How does it relate to the theme of the Other?

7. What is it about The Misfit and his gang that makes them such profoundly disturbing characters? What details in the latter part of the story associate The Misfit with the figure of Death?

8. How does The Misfit feel about Jesus? Explain what he means in the speech that begins "Jesus was the only One that ever raised the dead. . . ." Why does he believe that Jesus threw "everything off balance"?

9. Explain the significance of the title. Is there irony in it?

He and I

ALBERTO MORAVIA

I started talking to myself a short time after my wife had left me because, so she said, she was tired of my silence. It is true, I was silent with her, as indeed with everyone else; but I was silent because I loved her. When you love someone there is no need of words, is there? All you want is to be near the person you love, to look at her, to feel that she's there. Having been silent with her, perhaps even too much so, I became talkative with myself, as I have said, as soon as she deserted me. I am a shoemaker, and a shoemaker's job, as we all know, demands concentration, if only because working in leather is fine work and it doesn't do to make mistakes: the human foot doesn't allow for mistakes. So, when I went home in the evening, my eyes dazzled, my head ringing with the sound of hammering, my lips hurting from all the nails I shove into my mouth to damp them before driving them into the leather soles, I should have liked to find—what shall I say?—a smile, a kind word, a kiss on the forehead, a bowl of hot soup. Instead of which—nothing at all. Merely, in the darkness, the dripping sound of the drinking-water tap in the kitchen. Now silence is a lovely thing when you are in the company of a person you love and when you know that you can speak to her if you want to; but it is a torment if it is imposed on you. And so, after my wife went back to her mother, while I got my supper ready, all alone, in the kitchen, and then, still alone, ate it very slowly, almost without knowing what I was doing, sitting at a corner of the table, I began thinking out loud.

At first the things I used to say were impersonal and were not really addressed either to myself or to anyone else. For instance, I would say: "How cold it is in this house, my goodness, how cold it is!"; or: "If it wasn't for the mice frolicking about between the ceiling and the roof, there wouldn't be a sound in this place except the tap dripping"; or again: "The bed's still unmade since this morning. Never mind, it's too late now, I'll make it to-morrow." I said these things aloud, sometimes very loudly, insignificant as they were; but it pleased me to hear my voice echoing round those three deserted rooms. Then, one day, when I was sitting as usual in the kitchen, I said: "Wine is good stuff, wine is comforting, you only need to drink a litre of wine and your troubles disappear"; and all of a sudden—

how it happened, I don't know—I heard myself answering, still in a loud voice: "Guglielmo, you're a miserable wretch and you know it. Yes, of course, wine is good stuff, but it isn't comforting. You might drink a whole demijohn but still you wouldn't forget your wife nor the fact that she's left you. Yes, wine is good, but the company of a woman who loves you is very much better." I was struck by the truth of these words, and I answered— that is, my first voice answered: "You're right. But, when all's said and done, what is there left for me now? I'm fifty, and my wife, who is twenty-five, has deserted me. Where can I find another woman who would adapt herself to living with me? There's nothing left to me now except wine— isn't that so?" Then the other voice said: "Now listen, and don't act the philosopher. You know perfectly well that you haven't given up all hope of your wife." "Who told you that?" I replied; "I *have* given up hope, I have indeed." "No, you haven't," he said; "if you had, you wouldn't burst into sobs at the sole thought of her, wherever you may happen to be, even in the lavatory or on the stairs." Well then, I now had two voices, one of which, so to speak, spoke for me, and another which spoke for someone else who was also me but at the same time wasn't. Thus it was that, without realizing it, I changed over from monologue to dialogue—that is, from talking to myself to having arguments with myself.

These arguments, moreover, were not always arguments. Sometimes we were in complete agreement, he and I. For example, in the evening, after I had drunk my litre and a half or even two litres, I would go into the bedroom and there, in front of the wardrobe mirror, would make faces, just to amuse myself. Then he would say: "Here we go again, you've been drinking. A good thing you're at home and not in the street. You've been drinking and you can't stand up straight. But aren't you ashamed, at your age?"; he would say this, however, not without a hint of complacency in his voice. We went on like this for perhaps a couple of months, more or less in agreement; until one night, when I had drunk more than usual, a whole big flask of wine, lo and behold, when I took up my position in front of the mirror and put out my tongue, I was dumbfounded to see that *he*, in the mirror, remained serious and composed, with his tongue not out and his mouth not open. Then, after looking at me lingeringly and with compassion, he said: "Guglielmo, I'm fed up with you." "Why?" I asked. "Because," he said, "instead of fighting and struggling, you're letting yourself go. You've resigned yourself to the loss of your wife, you've become a drunkard, you've even lost your love of your work." "Who says so, I should like to know?" "*I* say so. Everyone in the neighbourhood knows you drink. And people take their shoes to be re-soled elsewhere. D'you know what you are, now? Just a rag of humanity."

This made me uneasy, and I scratched my head; then I asked: "Well then, what ought I to do, according to you?" "You ought to fight and struggle and make a firm stand." "But what for?" "To get your wife home again. Seeing that, without her, your life has come to an end, try to get her back again. Aren't you the husband? Haven't you the right to have her with you?

Well then, bestir yourself, go ahead and take action." "But what ought I to do?" "What ought you to do, indeed! You know perfectly well what you ought to do." "No, honestly, I don't know." Then he stared straight at me and said: "You must contrive, by fair means or foul, to make her come home." He spoke these words in a particular tone of voice which, I confess, frightened me. "By fair means I've tried," I answered, and it was no use. By foul means I don't want even to attempt it. I don't want to do anything bad." It seemed to me I had spoken rightly, in a way that ought to convince him; but he shook his head and said threateningly: "Very well. We'll speak of this again." At the same time he vanished from the looking-glass and I was left alone.

I went to bed much worried. No sooner had I put out the light than, suddenly, his voice began speaking again in the darkness: "Now that you're calmer and no longer tipsy, I'll tell you what you must do to get your wife back again. But don't interrupt me, listen till I've finished what I have to say." I told him to continue, that I was listening; and he went on to tell me, in a joking sort of way, that I must go next morning to the shop, fetch my shoemaker's knife, then go and find my wife, hold the knife under her nose and give her this warning: "Either you come home at once or else— you see this? . . ." I replied immediately, in the darkness: "You're crazy, it's no use even talking about such a thing. I want to get my wife back, that's understood. But there's a great difference between that and threatening her with a knife. I don't in the least want to end up in prison." "No," he said, "of course you don't want to go to prison. And yet, just possibly, you might be better off in prison than you are here." "Whatever do you mean?" "I mean that in prison at least you wouldn't be alone. In fact, you have nothing to lose: either your wife comes away with you, in which case, so much the better; or else she doesn't come, you give her a touch of the knife and end up in prison, and then at any rate you'd have the company of the other prisoners." "You're mad." "I'm not mad, and you know it. You're so lonely, Guglielmo, that even the idea of prison makes your mouth water." At this point I couldn't bear it any longer and, sitting up in bed, I said with energy: "It's no use even talking about it. And now be quiet, shut that wicked mouth of yours and let me go to sleep." "I warn you that, if you don't do this, I shall do it." "I told you to let me sleep." "I shall do it no later than to-morrow morning." "Shut up!" "Then we're agreed." I hung out of the bed, snatched up a shoe from the floor and hurled it at him, just like that, in the dark. He must have dodged it, cunning devil that he was. I heard a crash of breaking china and realized I had hit the water-jug on the chest of drawers. Then I fell asleep.

Next morning, however, when I woke up, I was at once conscious that there was no time to lose. Of him there was no sign, in any of the three rooms. It was quite possible that, while I was lingering at home warming up some coffee, he would run off to the shop (unfortunately he had the key, I had given it to him myself), would snatch up the knife, and then— the fat would be in the fire. It made my flesh creep, on my word of honour it did, to think of what might happen. And so, without waiting for any coffee, without washing or shaving, unkempt and with hair unbrushed, I rushed out, slipping into my coat as I went downstairs. It was very early in the morning, with a heavy dew and the streets full of mist, and just a few people on their way to work, their breath hanging in little clouds in front of their mouths. My shop was in the Vicolo del Fiume, and I almost ran all the way along Via Ripetta; as I turned the corner, I saw him in the distance coming out of the shop, very stealthily, and then running off in the direction of the Tiber. "Now we're for it," I said to myself. "He's a man of his word, no doubt about it, he said he'd do it and he's doing it. And now I've got to stop him." I too hurried into the shop, I too snatched up a knife in case he should turn his fury against me, then I went into a bar close by where there was a telephone kiosk. "There's no coffee, the machine isn't working yet," called out the barman, who knew me. I shrugged my shoulders; "Never mind about the coffee," I said. To tell the truth, I was so agitated that my hands were fluttering as I turned the pages of the directory, looking for the number of the police station. At last I found it, dialed the number, a voice asked me what I wanted, I explained what had happened: "You must go there at once. He's armed with a shoemaker's knife. It's a matter of life and death." The voice at the other end of the line enquired: "What's the name of this man?" I thought for a moment and then replied: "Palombini; Guglielmo Palombini," which is my own name too—one of those odd coincidences. I was assured on the telephone that they would attend to the matter as quickly as possible; and then I flew off to Piazza del Popolo, to the taxi rank: it was always possible that the police might arrive too late, and the best plan was for me to go there too. I called out the address as I jumped into the taxi, adding: "And quickly, for God's sake; it's a matter of life and death." The driver, an old man with white hair, asked what was the matter, and I told him: "A chap called Palombini, a shoemaker, has armed himself with a knife and is on his way now, in a taxi, to his wife who has left him, and he intends to kill her. . . . He's got to be stopped." "Have you informed the Police?" "Of course I have." "But how did *you* come to know about it?" "Well, Palombini and I are friends, in a way. He told me himself." The taxi-driver reflected a moment and then said: "There are plenty of people who pretend to be tough and then, when the moment comes, they go soft." "You're wrong, this man's really serious; I know him." All this time we were moving quickly through the deserted streets towards Via Giulia, where my wife was living.

The taxi stopped, I got out and paid and the driver went off; then I turned to look down the street, empty as far as the eye could reach, and saw him, the murderous ruffian, entering, at that very moment, the door of my wife's house. I recollected that my mother-in-law, a pious old bigot, always went off to church at that hour of the day; so that my wife would be alone in the flat, and in bed, into the bargain, for she was lazy and liked to sleep late in the morning. "He's chosen the right moment," I thought;

"there's no denying it, he thinks of everything. . . . Now quickly, let's hurry; otherwise there's going to be bloodshed here." So I rushed in at the front door, ran upstairs four steps at a time and reached the landing just in time to see him knocking loudly at the closed door and shouting: "Gas meter, please!"—which is as good a way as any of getting a door opened to you. I drew back and, a moment later, was aware of the sound of shuffling slippers inside the flat; then the door was opened and I heard the sleepy, sing-song voice of my wife: "The meter's in the kitchen." He, as a matter of form, waited a moment, then slipped into the flat; I followed.

The corridor was in darkness; I recognized the warm, youthful smell of her body refreshed with sleep, and it made me feel faint for a moment. Walking on tiptoe, I went straight to the far end of the passage, where I knew her room to be, pushed open the door which she had left ajar when she went back to bed, and entered. The room was in darkness too, but not so much that I was unable to distinguish the double bed and, white and full beneath the black hair spread loose over the pillow, the bare shoulders of my wife as she lay on one side, having gone back to sleep again. In truth, when I saw those shoulders, I was stricken with such a painful longing for the time when I used to see them in my own home, as I left stealthily in the morning to go to work, that I immediately forgot him and his knife, threw myself down on my knees and, seizing her hand as it lay on the coverlet, said: "My love, my darling, come back with me. Without you I can't go on living." I am sure that my wife, in such circumstances, would on this occasion have let herself be persuaded, if that vile wretch had not suddenly risen up on the other side of the bed, his hand raised holding the knife, and, shaking her by the shoulder, commanded her in a voice of terror: "You're coming back with me now; otherwise—do you see this?"

I do not intend to describe what happened after that: how I struggled with him, trying to disarm him; how my wife, screaming and upsetting things right and left, rushed half-naked across the room; and how a number of policemen suddenly burst in and jumped on me. I was careful to shout out: "Arrest him! He's dangerous. And look out for the knife!!" But the policemen, possibly because I myself also had a knife in my hand, did not make such distinctions; they seized hold of me as well and hauled me bodily out of the flat and then down the stairs, while I struggled and kept repeating, with all the voice I had left: "It's *him* you must arrest, not me . . . you're making a mistake." In the street there was a great crowd. They forced me into the police van, and when I looked up, there he was, sitting handcuffed between two policemen, right opposite me, the sarcastic smile on his face seeming to say: "You see what I've done." I pointed at him and cried: "He's ruined me, that scoundrel over there . . . he's ruined me"; and then I fainted.

Now I'm in a padded cell, and they say they are keeping me under observation because they're afraid my mind has been affected by grief. I do not complain; but I feel so very alone. As for him, they took him off to

the Regina Coeli prison, and thus we have been separated, he in gaol and
I in an asylum. And so the only company I had has been taken away from
me, and I have no one now, and I shall have to stay silent for ever.

QUESTIONS

"He and I"

1. Who is the Other in this story?

2. "He and I" charts the narrator's gradual mental deterioration, his descent
into madness. Describe the successive stages in the breakdown of his sanity.
What causes this breakdown? Do you find the story a convincing depiction of
madness?

3. What kind of person is Guglielmo? How much do we learn about him?
Why does his wife leave him?

4. How important is point of view in this story? Would the story have worked
as a third-person narrative?

5. Why does Moravia rely so heavily on dialogue in constructing his story?
How effective is this technique?

6. How does Guglielmo feel about his double? Describe their relationship.

7. Why does the narrator call the police to warn them that a man named
Guglielmo Palombini is on his way to commit murder?

8. Compare this story to Poe's "William Wilson." How are the stories similar? How does the relationship between the two Guglielmo Palombinis differ
from that between the two William Wilsons? How do the two doubles differ
from each other? How do they function in opposite ways? Which story do you
think is more successful? Why?

CHAPTER THREE

The Journey

From *The Odyssey* to the legends of King Arthur and the Knights of the Round Table to such modern-day fairy tales as the fantasy books of J.R.R. Tolkien, the central action of all quest stories is the peril-filled journey the heroes must undertake to reach their goals. The preliminary parts of the quest, the call and the meeting with the Other, present their own problems and require courage and determination, but the hardships heroes must face do not fully begin until they have left their familiar surroundings and crossed into a mysterious world. In this new world, they must survive a series of ordeals, traveling a hard and dangerous path (sometimes called "the road of trials") to win the prize they seek.

The precise nature of this alien realm varies widely from one quest story to the next. In nonrealistic literature, such as myths, fairy tales, and folk stories, the heroes invariably journey into fantastic regions that exist nowhere in the actual world. The title character of "Jack and the Beanstalk" departs from his mother's cottage and climbs a magical plant to a giant's kingdom in the clouds. The child heroes of C. S. Lewis's "The Chronicles of Narnia" step through a wardrobe in an English country house and find themselves in a wonderland of witches and talking animals. Raven, a folk hero of the Bering Strait Eskimos, is swallowed by a whale and carried in the monster's belly on a voyage to the East (a motif known as "the night-sea journey"). Classic heroes such as Odysseus, Orpheus, and Heracles descend into the depths of Hades, the land of the dead.

In spite of their differences, each of these incredible locales is essentially the same: a visionary landscape, a dreamworld, equivalent to the dark, sometimes enchanting, often threatening places all of us enter nightly in our sleep. Even works that take place in "real," identifiable settings—the Boston of Nathaniel Hawthorne's "My

Kinsman, Major Molineux," the New York City of Bernard Malamud's "Idiots First" (both reprinted in this chapter), or the Los Angeles of Raymond Chandler's classic detective novel *The Big Sleep*—
often possess a distinctly dreamlike quality. Sometimes, as in two of
the other selections in this chapter, Stephen Crane's "The Open
Boat" and Richard Wright's "Big Boy Leaves Home," a sudden, horrible accident turns the hero's everyday world into a living nightmare.

What makes this stage of the quest a descent into nightmare or a
voyage to hell is not only the strange, inhospitable land itself but
also the kind of experiences he or she encounters there. In this
"kingdom of the dark," to use Joseph Campbell's phrase, the protagonists are subjected to a variety of ordeals that test their capacity for
heroic behavior. In more fantastic forms of quest literature, this part
of the narrative is generally the most entertaining. It portrays the
heroes in a succession of exciting situations: climbing the slopes of
an impossibly steep mountain; fighting their way through deadly
jungles or enchanted forests; doing battle with dragons, giants, and
other supernatural foes; crossing a bottomless chasm on a bridge as
narrow as the edge of a knife; and a limitless variety of similar obstacles and hazards. In realistic works of fiction, the ordeals are usually more mundane though no less demanding, since the protagonists themselves are ordinary individuals rather than heroes of mythic
stature or superhuman ability. Thus, in some of the stories contained in this chapter, we meet a young boy on a summer vacation
who struggles to swim through a narrow underwater passageway, a
group of shipwrecked men trying to make their way past the break-
ers into shore, a reformed alcoholic fighting the ghosts of his past,
and an ancient black woman who, on a journey through the woods,
must surmount seemingly minor obstacles that are as formidable to
her as any forest of thorns in a Grimm Brothers' fairy tale. Only in
John Barth's explicitly fantastic story "Night-Sea Journey" do we find
a protagonist who describes his adventures in terms of the traditional perils of the mythic hero's quest: "decimation by whirlpool,
poisoned cataract, sea-convulsion. . . ."

In all other respects, however, Barth's narrator is completely nontraditional, especially in his view of the quest as an utterly meaningless affair. For most of the protagonists in these selections, the journey does have a purpose: it is a process of discovery in which the
heroes learn essential truths about themselves, their society, and
the nature of human existence. The rigors of the journey, the trials
and even tortures the heroes must undergo, are a sign that these
truths are very difficult to face, not only because they are often pain-

ful in themselves, but also because accepting them requires that the
individuals rid themselves of their familiar, if outmoded, assumptions, values, and self-images. In short, they must "die" to their
former way of life before they can be born into a new one. In this
sense, then, most quest narratives are stories of initiation.

Indeed, the quest narrative reproduces the pattern of the so-called
"rites of passage" performed in many primitive societies, in which
youths are initiated into the privileges and obligations of adulthood
after being put through a series of extremely harsh ordeals, such as
beatings, lack of food and sleep, and even physical mutilation, all of
which are meant both to enact and to effect the initiates' death to
their childhood state. (Such archaic practices still survive in modern
society in the form of fraternity "hazing" and similar initiation rituals.) Similarly, the journeys portrayed in myth and literature may
feature episodes in which the hero undergoes a symbolic death or
"return to the womb." In this chapter, we see this motif in "Through
the Tunnel," "Big Boy Leaves Home," and in a very literal way
"Night-Sea Journey." The same motif can be found in other stories
in this anthology; D. H. Lawrence's "The Horse-Dealer's Daughter"
is one example.

The knowledge heroes gain through their experiences on the journey is always important, if not always pleasant or easy to accept.
They may be forced, for instance, to face a hard fact about their
place in a particular culture or in the world at large. The young title
character of Richard Wright's story learns a terrible lesson about the
precarious position of blacks in a racist society; the survivors of the
shipwreck in "The Open Boat," who want to believe, as many of us
do, that there is something in the universe concerned about or at
least aware of them, discover that the universe is, on the contrary,
utterly indifferent to their fate, indeed oblivious to their existence.
Even the bitter protagonist of Barth's story, who "abjures and rejects the night-sea journey," arrives at a major, if dismal, realization
about the nature and purpose of life. At other times, the protagonists gain insight into vital areas of their own natures, for the voyage
to the netherworld is sometimes representative of a psychological
journey, a descent into the dark, unexplored regions of the hero's
heart and soul, where the dragons and demons that must be faced
and overcome are the embodiments of his or her own personal
weaknesses, limitations, and fears.

In a larger sense, the "road of trials" *always* leads to an illumination of character. Though some protagonists may remain blind to the
reality of their natures even at the end of their stories, their responses to the perils and pitfalls of the quest tell the reader a great

deal about them. For this reason, the journey is the ultimate revelation or test of a character's heroic potential—a test some of the protagonists in these stories fail. For example, the central figure of F. Scott Fitzgerald's "Babylon Revisited" is finally defeated by certain psychological flaws he has not, in spite of his good intentions, fully come to terms with. On the other hand, precisely because the journey consists of unremitting hardship and the ever-present possibility of defeat, it also represents a rare opportunity for triumph, for proving to a despairing and cynical world that human beings are in fact capable of heroic behavior.

Ironically, such heroism is displayed most completely in the following selections by the two characters who at first glance seem least capable of it: Mendel, the dying Jewish father in Bernard Malamud's "Idiots First," and Phoenix, the equally decrepit black grandmother of Eudora Welty's "A Worn Path." Their infirmities cannot keep them from seeking help for the people they love. Compared to the supernatural terrors of the mythic hero's quest, the obstacles these characters must surmount seem almost laughably trivial—a venal pawnbroker, a callous nurse, a barbed-wire fence, a field of corn, a dog. Nevertheless, the poverty and physical weakness of Mendel and Phoenix make their journeys as difficult as any undertaken by a Jason or Odysseus. The courage, fortitude, and selflessness with which these frail and simple people face their trials not only raise them to the level of genuine heroes but also redeem the journey from meaninglessness, transform it from what it is in Barth's story—a series of senseless horrors, a metaphor for the terrible absurdity of life—into an affirmation of something undefeatable in the human spirit.

My Kinsman, Major Molineux

NATHANIEL HAWTHORNE

After the kings of Great Britain had assumed the right of appointing the colonial governors, the measures of the latter seldom met with the ready and general approbation which had been paid to those of their predecessors, under the original charters. The people looked with most jealous scrutiny to the exercise of power which did not emanate from themselves, and they usually rewarded their rulers with slender gratitude for the compliances by which, in softening their instructions from beyond the sea, they had incurred the reprehension of those who gave them. The annals of Massachusetts Bay will inform us, that of six governors in the space of about forty years from the surrender of the old charter, under James II, two were imprisoned by a popular insurrection; a third, as Hutchinson inclines to believe, was driven from the province by the whizzing of a musket-ball; a fourth, in the opinion of the same historian, was hastened to his grave by continual bickerings with the House of Representatives; and the remaining two, as well as their successors, till the Revolution, were favored with few and brief intervals of peaceful sway. The inferior members of the court party, in times of high political excitement, led scarcely a more desirable life. These remarks may serve as a preface to the following adventures, which chanced upon a summer night, not far from a hundred years ago. The reader, in order to avoid a long and dry detail of colonial affairs, is requested to dispense with an account of the train of circumstances that had caused much temporary inflammation of the popular mind.

It was near nine o'clock of a moonlight evening, when a boat crossed the ferry with a single passenger, who had obtained his conveyance at that unusual hour by the promise of an extra fare. While he stood on the landing-place, searching in either pocket for the means of fulfilling his agreement, the ferryman lifted a lantern, by the aid of which, and the newly risen moon, he took a very accurate survey of the stranger's figure. He was a youth of barely eighteen years, evidently country-bred, and now, as it should seem, upon his first visit to town. He was clad in a coarse gray coat, well worn, but in excellent repair; his under garments were durably constructed of leather, and fitted tight to a pair of serviceable and well-shaped limbs; his stockings of blue yarn were the incontrovertible work of a mother or a sister; and on his head was a three-cornered hat, which in its better days had perhaps sheltered the graver brow of the lad's father. Under his left arm was a heavy cudgel formed of an oak sapling, and retaining a part of the hardened root; and his equipment was completed by a wallet, not so abundantly stocked as to incommode the vigorous shoulders on which it hung. Brown, curly hair, well-shaped features, and bright, cheerful eyes were nature's gifts, and worth all that art could have done for his adornment.

The youth, one of whose names was Robin, finally drew from his pocket the half of a little province bill of five shillings, which, in the depreciation in that sort of currency, did but satisfy the ferryman's demand, with the surplus of a sexangular piece of parchment, valued at three pence. He then walked forward into the town, with as light a step as if his day's journey had not already exceeded thirty miles, and with as eager an eye as if he were entering London city, instead of the little metropolis of a New England colony. Before Robin had proceeded far, however, it occurred to him that he knew not whither to direct his steps; so he paused, and looked up and down the narrow street, scrutinizing the small and mean wooden buildings that were scattered on either side.

"This low hovel cannot be my kinsman's dwelling," thought he, "nor yonder old house, where the moonlight enters at the broken casement; and truly I see none hereabouts that might be worthy of him. It would have been wise to inquire my way of the ferryman, and doubtless he would have gone with me, and earned a shilling from the Major for his pains. But the next man I meet will do as well."

He resumed his walk, and was glad to perceive that the street now became wider, and the houses more respectable in their appearance. He soon discerned a figure moving on moderately in advance, and hastened his steps to overtake it. As Robin drew nigh, he saw that the passenger was a man in years, with a full periwig of gray hair, a wide-skirted coat of dark cloth, and silk stockings rolled above his knees. He carried a long and polished cane, which he struck down perpendicularly before him at every step; and at regular intervals he uttered two successive hems, of a peculiarly solemn and sepulchral intonation. Having made these observations, Robin laid hold of the skirt of the old man's coat, just when the light from the open door and windows of a barber's shop fell upon both their figures.

"Good evening to you, honored sir," said he, making a low bow, and still retaining his hold of the skirt. "I pray you tell me whereabouts is the dwelling of my kinsman, Major Molineux."

The youth's question was uttered very loudly; and one of the barbers, whose razor was descending on a well-soaped chin, and another who was dressing a Ramillies wig, left their occupations, and came to the door. The citizen, in the mean time, turned a long-favored countenance upon Robin, and answered him in a tone of excessive anger and annoyance. His two sepulchral hems, however, broke into the very centre of his rebuke, with most singular effect, like a thought of the cold grave obtruding among wrathful passions.

"Let go my garment, fellow! I tell you, I know not the man you speak of. What! I have authority, I have—hem, hem—authority; and if this be the respect you show for your betters, your feet shall be brought acquainted with the stocks by daylight, tomorrow morning!"

Robin released the old man's skirt, and hastened away, pursued by an ill-mannered roar of laughter from the barber's shop. He was at first considerably surprised by the result of his question, but, being a shrewd youth, soon thought himself able to account for the mystery.

"This is some country representative," was his conclusion, "who has never seen the inside of my kinsman's door, and lacks the breeding to answer a stranger civilly. The man is old, or verily—I might be tempted to turn back and smite him on the nose. Ah, Robin, Robin! even the barber's boys laugh at you for choosing such a guide! You will be wiser in time, friend Robin."

He now became entangled in a succession of crooked and narrow streets, which crossed each other, and meandered at no great distance from the water-side. The smell of tar was obvious to his nostrils, the masts of vessels pierced the moonlight above the tops of the buildings, and the numerous signs, which Robin paused to read, informed him that he was near the centre of business. But the streets were empty, the shops were closed, and lights were visible only in the second stories of a few dwelling-houses. At length, on the corner of a narrow lane, through which he was passing, he beheld the broad countenance of a British hero swinging before the door of an inn, whence proceeded the voices of many guests. The casement of one of the lower windows was thrown back, and a very thin curtain permitted Robin to distinguish a party at supper, round a well-furnished table. The fragrance of the good cheer steamed forth into the outer air, and the youth could not fail to recollect that the last remnant of his traveling stock of provision had yielded to his morning appetite, and that noon had found and left him dinnerless.

"Oh, that a parchment three-penny might give me a right to sit down at yonder table!" said Robin, with a sigh. "But the Major will make me welcome to the best of his victuals; so I will even step boldly in, and inquire my way to his dwelling."

He entered the tavern, and was guided by the murmur of voices and the fumes of tobacco to the public-room. It was a long and low apartment, with oaken walls, grown dark in the continual smoke, and a floor which was thickly sanded, but of no immaculate purity. A number of persons—the larger part of whom appeared to be mariners, or in some way connected with the sea—occupied the wooden benches, or leather-bottomed chairs, conversing on various matters, and occasionally lending their attention to some topic of general interest. Three or four little groups were draining as many bowls of punch, which the West India trade had long since made a familiar drink in the colony. Others, who had the appearance of men who lived by regular and laborious handicraft, preferred the insulated bliss of an unshared potation, and became more taciturn under its influence. Nearly all, in short, evinced a predilection for the Good Creature in some of its various shapes, for this is a vice to which, as Fast Day sermons of a hundred years ago will testify, we have a long hereditary claim. The only guests to whom Robin's sympathies inclined him were two or three sheepish countrymen, who were using the inn somewhat after the fashion of a Turkish caravansary; they had gotten themselves into the darkest corner of the room, and heedless of the Nicotian atmosphere, were supping on the bread of their own ovens, and the bacon cured in their own chimney-smoke. But though Robin felt a sort of brotherhood with these strangers, his eyes were attracted from them to a person who stood near the door, holding whispered conversation with a group of ill-dressed associates. His features were separately striking almost to grotesqueness, and the whole face left a deep impression on the memory. The forehead bulged out into a double prominence, with a vale between; the nose came boldly forth in an irregular curve, and its bridge was of more than a finger's breadth; the eyebrows were deep and shaggy, and the eyes glowed beneath them like fire in a cave.

While Robin deliberated of whom to inquire respecting his kinsman's dwelling, he was accosted by the innkeeper, a little man in a stained white apron, who had come to pay his professional welcome to the stranger. Being in the second generation from a French Protestant, he seemed to have inherited the courtesy of his parent nation; but no variety of circumstances was ever known to change his voice from the one shrill note in which he now addressed Robin.

"From the country, I presume, sir?" said he, with a profound bow. "Beg leave to congratulate you on your arrival, and trust you intend a long stay with us. Fine town here, sir, beautiful buildings, and much that may interest a stranger. May I hope for the honor of your commands in respect to supper?"

"The man sees a family likeness! the rogue has guessed that I am related to the Major!" thought Robin, who had hitherto experienced little superfluous civility.

All eyes were now turned on the country lad, standing at the door, in his worn three-cornered hat, gray coat, leather breeches, and blue yarn stockings, leaning on an oaken cudgel, and bearing a wallet on his back.

Robin replied to the courteous innkeeper, with such an assumption of confidence as befitted the Major's relative. "My honest friend," he said, "I shall make it a point to patronize your house on some occasion, when"—here he could not help lowering his voice—"when I may have more than a parchment three-pence in my pocket. My present business," continued he, speaking with lofty confidence, "is merely to inquire my way to the dwelling of my kinsman, Major Molineux."

There was a sudden and general movement in the room, which Robin interpreted as expressing the eagerness of each individual to become his guide. But the innkeeper turned his eyes to a written paper on the wall, which he read, or seemed to read, with occasional recurrences to the young man's figure.

"What have we here?" said he, breaking his speech into little dry fragments. " 'Left the house of the subscriber, bounden servant, Hezekia Mudge,—had on, when he went away, gray coat, leather breeches, master's third-best hat. One pound currency reward to whosoever shall lodge him in any jail of the province.' Better trudge, boy; better trudge!"

Robin had begun to draw his hand towards the lighter end of the oak cudgel, but a strange hostility in every countenance induced him to relinquish his purpose of breaking the courteous innkeeper's head. As he turned to leave the room, he encountered a sneering glance from the bold-featured personage whom he had before noticed; and no sooner was he beyond the door, than he heard a general laugh, in which the innkeeper's voice might be distinguished, like the dropping of small stones into a kettle.

"Now, is it not strange," thought Robin, with his usual shrewdness,—"is it not strange that the confession of an empty pocket should outweigh the name of my kinsman, Major Molineux? Oh, if I had one of those grinning rascals in the woods, where I and my oak sapling grew up together, I would teach him that my arm is heavy though my purse be light!"

On turning the corner of the narrow lane, Robin found himself in a spacious street, with an unbroken line of lofty houses on each side, and a steepled building at the upper end, whence the ringing of a bell announced the hour of nine. The light of the moon, and the lamps from the numerous shop-windows, discovered people promenading on the pavement, and amongst them Robin hoped to recognize his hitherto inscrutable relative. The result of his former inquiries made him unwilling to hazard another, in a scene of such publicity, and he determined to walk slowly and silently up the street, thrusting his face close to that of every elderly gentleman, in search of the Major's lineaments. In his progress, Robin encountered many gay and gallant figures. Embroidered garments of showy colors, enormous periwigs, goldlaced hats, and silver-hilted swords glided past him and dazzled his optics. Travelled youths, imitators of the European fine gentlemen of the period, trod jauntily along, half dancing to the fashionable tunes which they hummed, and making poor Robin ashamed of his quiet and natural gait. At length, after many pauses to examine the gorgeous display of goods in the shop-windows, and after suffering some rebukes for the impertinence of his scrutiny into people's faces, the Major's kinsman found himself near the steepled building, still unsuccessful in his search. As yet, however, he had seen only one side of the thronged street; so Robin crossed, and continued the same sort of inquisition down the opposite pavement, with stronger hopes than the philosopher seeking an honest man, but with no better fortune. He had arrived about midway towards the lower end, from which his course began, when he overheard the approach of some one who struck down a cane on the flag-stones at every step, uttering, at regular intervals, two sepulchral hems.

"Mercy on us!" quoth Robin, recognizing the sound.

Turning a corner, which chanced to be close at his right hand, he hastened to pursue his researches in some other part of the town. His patience now was wearing low, and he seemed to feel more fatigue from his rambles since he crossed the ferry, than from his journey of several days on the other side. Hunger also pleaded loudly within him, and Robin began to balance the propriety of demanding, violently, and with lifted cudgel, the necessary guidance from the first solitary passenger whom he should meet. While a resolution to this effect was gaining strength, he entered a street of mean appearance, on either side of which a row of ill-built houses was straggling towards the harbor. The moonlight fell upon no passenger along the whole extent, but in the third domicile which Robin passed there was a half-opened door, and his keen glance detected a woman's garment within.

"My luck may be better here," said he to himself.

Accordingly, he approached the door, and beheld it shut closer as he did so; yet an open space remained, sufficing for the fair occupant to observe the stranger, without a corresponding display on her part. All that Robin could discern was a strip of scarlet petticoat, and the occasional sparkle of an eye, as if the moonbeams were trembling on some bright thing.

"Pretty mistress," for I may call her so with a good conscience, thought the shrewd youth, since I know nothing to the contrary,—"my sweet pretty mistress, will you be kind enough to tell me whereabouts I must seek the dwelling of my kinsman Major Molineux?"

Robin's voice was plaintive and winning, and the female, seeing nothing to be shunned in the handsome country youth, thrust open the door, and came forth into the moonlight. She was a dainty little figure, with a white neck, round arms, and a slender waist, at the extremity of which her scarlet petticoat jutted out over a hoop, as if she were standing in a balloon. Moreover, her face was oval and pretty, her hair dark beneath the little cap, and her bright eyes possessed a sly freedom, which triumphed over those of Robin.

"Major Molineux dwells here," said this fair woman.

Now, her voice was the sweetest Robin had heard that night, the airy counterpart of a stream of melted silver; yet he could not help doubting whether that sweet voice spoke Gospel truth. He looked up and down the mean street, and then surveyed the house before which they stood. It was a small, dark edifice of two stories, the second of which projected over the lower floor, and the front apartment had the aspect of a shop for petty commodities.

"Now, truly, I am in luck," replied Robin, cunningly, "and so indeed is my kinsman, the Major, in having so pretty a housekeeper. But I prithee trouble him to step to the door; I will deliver him a message from his friends in the country, and then go back to my lodgings at the inn."

"Nay, the Major has been abed this hour or more," said the lady of the scarlet petticoat; "and it would be to little purpose to disturb him to-night, seeing his evening draught was of the strongest. But he is a kind-hearted man, and it would be as much as my life's worth to let a kinsman of his turn away from the door. You are the good old gentleman's very picture, and I could swear that was his rainy-weather hat. Also he has garments very much resembling those leather small-clothes. But come in, I pray, for I bid you hearty welcome in his name."

So saying, the fair and hospitable dame took our hero by the hand; and the touch was light, and the force was gentleness, and though Robin read in her eyes what he did not hear in her words, yet the slender-waisted woman in the scarlet petticoat proved stronger than the athletic country youth. She had drawn his half-willing footsteps nearly to the threshold, when the opening of a door in the neighborhood startled the Major's housekeeper, and, leaving the Major's kinsman, she vanished speedily into her own domicile. A heavy yawn preceded the appearance of a man, who, like the Moonshine of Pyramus and Thisbe, carried a lantern, needlessly aiding his sister luminary in the heavens. As he walked sleepily up the street, he turned his broad, dull face on Robin, and displayed a long staff, spiked at the end.

"Home, vagabond, home!" said the watchman, in accents that seemed to fall asleep as soon as they were uttered. "Home, or we'll set you in the stocks by peep of day!"

"This is the second hint of the kind," thought Robin. "I wish they would end my difficulties, by setting me there to-night."

Nevertheless, the youth felt an instinctive antipathy towards the guardian of midnight order, which at first prevented him from asking his usual question. But just when the man was about to vanish behind the corner, Robin resolved not to lose the opportunity, and shouted lustily after him,—

"I say, friend! will you guide me to the house of my kinsman, Major Molineux?"

The watchman made no reply, but turned the corner and was gone; yet Robin seemed to hear the sound of drowsy laughter stealing along the solitary street. At that moment, also, a pleasant titter saluted him from the open window above his head; he looked up, and caught the sparkle of a saucy eye; a round arm beckoned to him, and next he heard light footsteps descending the staircase within. But Robin, being of the household of a New England clergyman, was a good youth, as well as a shrewd one; so he resisted temptation, and fled away.

He now roamed desperately, and at random, through the town, almost ready to believe that a spell was on him, like that by which a wizard of his country had once kept three pursuers wandering, a whole winter night, within twenty paces of the cottage which they sought. The streets lay before him, strange and desolate, and the lights were extinguished in almost every house. Twice, however, little parties of men, among whom Robin distinguished individuals in outlandish attire, came hurrying along; but, though on both occasions they paused to address him, such intercourse did not at all enlighten his perplexity. They did but utter a few words in some language of which Robin knew nothing, and perceiving his inability to answer, bestowed a curse upon him in plain English and hastened away. Finally, the lad determined to knock at the door of every mansion that might appear worthy to be occupied by his kinsman, trusting that perseverance would overcome the fatality that had hitherto thwarted him. Firm in this resolve, he was passing beneath the walls of a church, which formed the corner of two streets, when, as he turned into the shade of its steeple, he encountered a bulky stranger, muffled in a cloak. The man was proceeding with the speed of earnest business, but Robin planted himself full before him, holding the oak cudgel with both hands across his body as a bar to further passage.

"Halt, honest man, and answer me a question," said he, very resolutely. "Tell me, this instant, whereabouts is the dwelling of my kinsman, Major Molineux!"

"Keep your tongue between your teeth, fool, and let me pass!" said a deep, gruff voice, which Robin partly remembered. "Let me pass, I say, or I'll strike you to the earth!"

"No, no, neighbor!" cried Robin, flourishing his cudgel, and then thrusting its larger end close to the man's muffled face. "No, no, I'm not the fool you take me for, nor do you pass till I have an answer to my question. Whereabouts is the dwelling of my kinsman, Major Molineux?"

The stranger, instead of attempting to force his passage, stepped back into the moonlight, unmuffled his face, and stared full into that of Robin.

"Watch here an hour, and Major Molineux will pass by," said he.

Robin gazed with dismay and astonishment on the unprecedented physiognomy of the speaker. The forehead with its double prominence, the broad hooked nose, the shaggy eyebrows, and fiery eyes were those which he had noticed at the inn, but the man's complexion had undergone a singular, or, more properly, a twofold change. One side of the face blazed an intense red, while the other was black as midnight, the division line being in the broad bridge of the nose; and a mouth which seemed to extend from ear to ear was black or red, in contrast to the color of the cheek. The effect was as if two individual devils, a fiend of fire and a fiend of darkness, had united themselves to form this infernal visage. The stranger grinned in Robin's face, muffled his parti-colored features, and was out of sight in a moment.

"Strange things we travellers see!" ejaculated Robin.

He seated himself, however, upon the steps of the church-door, resolving to wait the appointed time for his kinsman. A few moments were consumed in philosophical speculations upon the species of man who had just left him; but having settled this point shrewdly, rationally, and satisfactorily, he was compelled to look elsewhere for his amusement. And first he threw his eyes along the street. It was of more respectable appearance than most of those into which he had wandered, and the moon, creating, like

the imaginative power, a beautiful strangeness in familiar objects, gave
something of romance to a scene that might not have possessed it in the
light of day. The irregular and often quaint architecture of the houses,
some of whose roofs were broken into numerous little peaks, while others
ascended, steep and narrow, into a single point, and others again were
square; the pure snow-white of some of their complexions, the aged darkness of others, and the thousand sparklings, reflected from bright substances in the walls of many; these matters engaged Robin's attention for a
while, and then began to grow wearisome. directly in front of the church-
door, where he was stationed. It was a large, square mansion, distinguished from its neighbors by a balcony, which rested on tall pillars, and
by an elaborate Gothic window, communicating therewith."

"Perhaps this is the very house I have been seeking," thought Robin.

Then he strove to speed away the time, by listening to a murmur which
swept continually along the street, yet was scarcely audible, except to an
unaccustomed ear like his; it was a low, dull, dreamy sound, compounded
of many noises, each of which was at too great a distance to be separately
heard. Robin marvelled at this snore of a sleeping town, and marvelled
more whenever its continuity was broken by now and then a distant shout,
apparently loud where it originated. But altogether it was a sleep-inspiring
sound, and, to shake off its drowsy influence, Robin arose, and climbed a
window-frame, that he might view the interior of the church. There the
moonbeams came trembling in, and fell down upon the deserted pews, and
extended along the quiet aisles. A fainter yet more awful radiance was hov-
ering around the pulpit, and one solitary ray had dared to rest upon the
open page of the great Bible. Had nature, in that deep hour, become a
worshipper in the house which man had builded? Or was that heavenly
light the visible sanctity of the place,—visible because no earthly and im-
pure feet were within the walls? The scene made Robin's heart shiver with
a sensation of loneliness stronger than he had ever felt in the remotest
depths of his native woods; so he turned away and sat down again before
the door. There were graves around the church, and now an uneasy thought
obtruded into Robin's breast. What if the object of his search, which had
been so often and so strangely thwarted, were all the time mouldering in
his shroud? What if his kinsman should glide through yonder gate, and nod
and smile to him in dimly passing by?

"Oh that any breathing thing were here with me!" said Robin.

Recalling his thoughts from this uncomfortable track, he sent them over
forest, hill, and stream, and attempted to imagine how that evening of
ambiguity and weariness had been spent by his father's household. He
pictured them assembled at the door, beneath the tree, the great old tree,
which had been spared for its huge twisted trunk and venerable shade,
when a thousand leafy brethren fell. There, at the going down of the summer sun, it was his father's custom to perform domestic worship, that the
neighbors might come and join with him like brothers of the family, and
that the wayfaring man might pause to drink at that fountain, and keep his

heart pure by freshening the memory of home. Robin distinguished the seat of every individual of the little audience; he saw the good man in the midst, holding the Scriptures in the golden light that fell from the western clouds; he beheld him close the book and all rise up to pray. He heard the old thanksgivings for daily mercies, the old supplications for their continuance, to which he had so often listened in weariness, but which were now among his dear remembrances. He perceived the slight inequality of his father's voice when he came to speak of the absent one; he noted how his mother turned her face to the broad and knotted trunk; how his elder brother scorned, because the beard was rough upon his upper lip, to permit his features to be moved; how the younger sister drew down a low hanging branch before her eyes; and how the little one of all, whose sports had hitherto broken the decorum of the scene, understood the prayer for her playmate, and burst into clamorous grief. Then he saw them go in at the door; and when Robin would have entered also, the latch tinkled into its place, and he was excluded from his home.

"Am I here, or there?" cried Robin, starting; for all at once, when his thoughts had become visible and audible in a dream, the long wide, solitary street shone out before him.

He aroused himself, and endeavored to fix his attention steadily upon the large edifice which he had surveyed before. But still his mind kept vibrating between fancy and reality; by turns, the pillars of the balcony lengthened into the tall, bare stems of pines, dwindled down to human figures, settled again into their true shape and size, and then commenced a new succession of changes. For a single moment, when he deemed himself awake, he could have sworn that a visage—one which he seemed to remember, yet could not absolutely name as his kinsman's—was looking towards him from the Gothic window. A deeper sleep wrestled with and nearly overcame him, but fled at the sound of footsteps along the opposite pavement. Robin rubbed his eyes, discerned a man passing at the foot of the balcony, and addressed him in a loud, peevish, and lamentable cry.

"Hallo, friend! Must I wait here all night for my kinsman, Major Molineux?"

The sleeping echoes awoke, and answered the voice; and the passenger, barely able to discern a figure sitting in the oblique shade of the steeple, traversed the street to obtain a nearer view. He was himself a gentleman in his prime, of open, intelligent, cheerful, and altogether prepossessing countenence. Perceiving a country youth, apparently homeless and without friends, he accosted him in a tone of real kindness, which had become strange to Robin's ears.

"Well, my good lad, why are you sitting here?" inquired he. "Can I be of service to you in any way?"

"I am afraid not, sir," replied Robin, despondingly; "yet I shall take it kindly, if you'll answer me a single question. I've been searching, half the night, for one Major Molineux; now, sir, is there really such a person in these parts, or am I dreaming?"

"Major Molineux! The name is not altogether strange to me," said the gentleman, smiling. "Have you any objection to telling me the nature of your business with him?"

Then Robin briefly related that his father was a clergyman, settled on a small salary, at a long distance back in the country, and that he and Major Molineux were brothers' children. The Major, having inherited riches, and acquired civil and military rank, had visited his cousin, in great pomp, a year or two before; had manifested much interest in Robin and an elder brother, and being childless himself, had thrown out hints respecting the future establishment of one of them in life. The elder brother was destined to succeed to the farm which his father cultivated in the interval of sacred duties; it was therefore determined that Robin should profit by his kinsman's generous intentions, especially as he seemed to be rather the favorite, and was thought to possess other necessary endowments.

"For I have the name of being a shrewd youth," observed Robin, in this part of his story.

"I doubt not you deserve it," replied his new friend, good-naturedly; "but pray proceed."

"Well, sir, being nearly eighteen years old, and well grown, as you see," continued Robin, drawing himself up to his full height, "I thought it high time to begin the world. So my mother and sister put me in handsome trim, and my father gave me half the remnant of his last year's salary, and five days ago I started for this place, to pay the Major a visit. But, would you believe it, sir! I crossed the ferry a little after dark, and have yet found nobody that would show me the way to his dwelling; only, an hour or two since, I was told to wait here, and Major Molineux would pass by."

"Can you describe the man who told you this?" inquired the gentleman.

"Oh, he was a very ill-favored fellow, sir," replied Robin, "with two great bumps on his forehead, a hook nose, fiery eyes; and, what struck me as the strangest, his face was of two different colors. Do you happen to know such a man, sir?"

"Not intimately," answered the stranger, "but I chanced to meet him a little time previous to your stopping me. I believe you may trust his word, and that the Major will very shortly pass through this street. In the mean time, as I have a singular curiosity to witness your meeting, I will sit down here upon the steps and bear you company."

He seated himself accordingly, and soon engaged his companion in animated discourse. It was but of brief continuance, however, for a noise of shouting, which had long been remotely audible, drew so much nearer that Robin inquired its cause.

"What may be the meaning of this uproar?" asked he. "Truly, if your town be always as noisy, I shall find little sleep while I am an inhabitant."

"Why, indeed, friend Robin, there do appear to be three or four riotous fellows abroad to-night," replied the gentleman. "You must not expect all the stillness of your native woods here in our streets. But the watch will shortly be at the heels of these lads and"—

"Ay, and set them in the stocks by peep of day," interrupted Robin, recollecting his own encounter with the drowsy lantern-bearer. "But, dear sir, if I may trust my ears, an army of watchmen would never make head against such a multitude of rioters. There were at least a thousand voices went up to make that one shout."

"May not a man have several voices, Robin, as well as two complexions?" said his friend.

"Perhaps a man may; but Heaven forbid that a woman should!" responded the shrewd youth, thinking of the seductive tones of the Major's housekeeper.

The sounds of a trumpet in some neighboring street now became so evident and continual, that Robin's curiosity was strongly excited. In addition to the shouts, he heard frequent bursts from many instruments of discord, and a wild and confused laughter filled up the intervals. Robin rose from the steps, and looked wistfully towards a point whither people seemed to be hastening.

"Surely some prodigious merry-making is going on," exclaimed he. "I have laughed very little since I left home, sir, and should be sorry to lose an opportunity. Shall we step round the corner by that darkish house, and take our share of the fun?"

"Sit down again, sit down, good Robin," replied the gentleman, laying his hand on the skirt of the gray coat. "You forget that we must wait here for your kinsman; and there is reason to believe that he will pass by, in the course of a very few moments."

The near approach of the uproar had now disturbed the neighborhood; windows flew open on all sides; and many heads, in the attire of the pillow, and confused by sleep suddenly broken, were protruded to the gaze of whoever had leisure to observe them. Eager voices hailed each other from house to house, all demanding the explanation, which not a soul could give. Half-dressed men hurried towards the unknown commotion, stumbling as they went over the stone steps that thrust themselves into the narrow foot-walk. The shouts, the laughter, and the tuneless bray, the antipodes of music, came onwards with increasing din, till scattered individuals, and then denser bodies, began to appear round a corner at the distance of a hundred yards.

"Will you recognize your kinsman, if he passes in this crowd?" inquired the gentleman.

"Indeed, I can't warrant it, sir; but I'll take my stand here, and keep a bright lookout," answered Robin, descending to the outer edge of the pavement.

A mighty stream of people now emptied into the street, and came rolling slowly towards the church. A single horseman wheeled the corner in the midst of them, and close behind him came a band of fearful wind-instruments, sending forth a fresher discord now that no intervening buildings kept it from the ear. Then a redder light disturbed the moonbeams, and a dense multitude of torches shone along the street, concealing, by their glare, whatever object they illuminated. The single horseman, clad in a military dress, and bearing a drawn sword, rode onward as the leader, and, by his fierce and variegated countenance, appeared like war personified; the red of one cheek was an emblem of fire and sword; the blackness of the other betokened the mourning that attends them. In his train were wild figures in the Indian dress, and many fantastic shapes without a model, giving the whole march a visionary air, as if a dream had broken forth from some feverish brain, and were sweeping visibly through the midnight streets. A mass of people, inactive, except as applauding spectators, hemmed the procession in; and several women ran along the sidewalk, piercing the confusion of heavier sounds with their shrill voices of mirth or terror.

"The double-faced fellow has his eye upon me," muttered Robin, with an indefinite but an uncomfortable idea that he was himself to bear a part in the pageantry.

The leader turned himself in the saddle, and fixed his glance full upon the country youth, as the steed went slowly by. When Robin had freed his eyes from those fiery ones, the musicians were passing before him, and the torches were close at hand; but the unsteady brightness of the latter formed a veil which he could not penetrate. The rattling of wheels over the stones sometimes found its way to his ear, and confused traces of a human form appeared at intervals, and then melted into the vivid light. A moment more, and the leader thundered a command to halt: the trumpets vomited a horrid breath, and then held their peace; the shouts and laughter of the people died away, and there remained only a universal hum, allied to silence. Right before Robin's eyes was an uncovered cart. There the torches blazed the brightest, there the moon shone out like day, and there, in tar-and-feathery dignity, sat his kinsman Major Molineux!

He was an elderly man, of large and majestic person, and strong, square features, betokening a steady soul; but steady as it was, his enemies had found means to shake it. His face was pale as death, and far more ghastly; the broad forehead was contracted in his agony, so that his eyebrows formed one grizzled line; his eyes were red and wild, and the foam hung white upon his quivering lip. His whole frame was agitated by a quick and continual tremor, which his pride strove to quell, even in those circumstances of overwhelming humiliation. But perhaps the bitterest pang of all was when his eyes met those of Robin; for he evidently knew him on the instant, as the youth stood witnessing the foul disgrace of a head grown gray in honor. They stared at each other in silence, and Robin's knees shook, and his hair bristled, with a mixture of pity and terror. Soon, however, a bewildering excitement began to seize upon his mind; the preceding adventures of the night, the unexpected appearance of the crowd, the torches, the confused din and the hush that followed, the spectre of his kinsman reviled by that great multitude,—all this, and, more than all, a perception of tremendous ridicule in the whole scene, affected him with a sort of mental inebrity. At that moment a voice of sluggish merriment saluted Robin's ears; he turned instinctively, and just behind the corner of the church stood the lantern-bearer, rubbing his eyes, and drowsily enjoying the lad's amazement. Then he heard a peal of laughter like the ringing of silvery bells; a woman twitched his arm, a saucy eye met his, and he saw the lady of the scarlet petticoat. A sharp, dry cachinnation appealed to his memory, and, standing on tiptoe in the crowd, with his white apron over his head, he beheld the courteous little innkeeper. And lastly, there sailed over the heads of the multitude a great, broad laugh, broken in the midst by two sepulchral hems; thus, "Haw, haw, haw,—hem, hem,—haw, haw, haw, haw!"

The sound proceeded from the balcony of the opposite edifice, and thither Robin turned his eyes. In front of the Gothic window stood the old citizen, wrapped in a wide gown, his gray periwig exchanged for a nightcap, which was thrust back from his forehead, and his silk stockings hanging about his legs. He supported himself on his polished cane in a fit of convulsive merriment, which manifested itself on his solemn old features like a funny inscription on a tombstone. Then Robin seemed to hear the voices of the barbers, of the guests of the inn, and of all who had made sport of him that night. The contagion was spreading among the multitude, when all at once, it seized upon Robin, and he sent forth a shut of laughter that echoed through the street,—every man shook his sides, every man emptied his lungs, but Robin's shout was the loudest there. The cloud-spirits peeped from their silvery islands, as the congregated mirth went roaring up the sky! The Man in the Moon heard the far bellow. "Oho," quoth he, "the old earth is frolicsome tonight!"

When there was a momentary calm in that tempestuous sea of sound, the leader gave the sign, the procession resumed its march. On they went, like fiends that throng in mockery around some dead potentate, mighty no more, but majestic still in his agony. On they went, in counterfeited pomp, in senseless uproar, in frenzied merriment, trampling all on an old man's heart. On swept the tumult, and left a silent street behind.

"Well, Robin, are you dreaming?" inquired the gentleman, laying his hand on the youth's shoulder.

Robin started, and withdrew his arm from the stone post to which he had instinctively clung, as the living stream rolled by him. His cheek was somewhat pale, and his eye not quite as lively as in the earlier part of the evening.

"Will you be kind enough to show me the way to the ferry?" said he, after a moment's pause.

"You have, then, adopted a new subject of inquiry?" observed his companion, with a smile.

"Why, yes, sir," replied Robin, rather dryly. "Thanks to you, and to my other friends, I have at last met my kinsman, and he will scarce desire to see my face again. I begin to grow weary of a town life, sir. Will you show me the way to the ferry?"

"No, my good friend Robin,—not to-night, at least," said the gentleman.

"Some few days hence, if you wish it, I will speed you on your journey. Or, if you prefer to remain with us, perhaps, as you are a shrewd youth, you may rise in the world without the help of your kinsman, Major Molineux."

QUESTIONS

"My Kinsman, Major Molineux"

1. What is the purpose of the brief historical background Hawthorne provides in the introductory paragraph?

2. What kind of person is Robin? How old is he? What does he look like? What kind of clothes is he wearing? What do his clothes tell us about him? Is his name significant?

3. Why has Robin come to the city? Where has he come from?

4. Describe the various characters Robin meets on his journey through the city streets. How do they behave toward him? How does the young man deal with their mysterious behavior? What is the "road of trials" that Robin must travel to reach his goal?

5. What is Robin's opinion of himself? Does the narrator seem to share it, or is there irony in his treatment of the main character?

6. This story establishes an opposition between the country and the city. How is each described? What qualities and values are associated with each? How are they contrasted?

7. What is the significance of the oak cudgel Robin carries? How does it function symbolically?

8. What does the episode with the "lady of the scarlet petticoat" reveal about Robin?

9. Who is the sinister stranger Robin meets on several occasions in the story—the man with the "parti-colored features"?

10. Look closely at the passage in which Robin, at the lowest point in his quest, recalls the scene at his "father's household." How is that scene described? In what way is this moment a turning point in the story? Is Robin correct in feeling that he has been "excluded from his home"?

11. How is the procession at the climax of the story described? How does Hawthorne give this episode the quality of a nightmare?

12. Describe Major Molineux. Does the author make you feel that the old man deserves such horrible, humiliating treatment? Where do your sympathies lie?

13. Why does Robin join in the laughter at the end of the story? What does this response reveal about him? What does it reveal to him?

14. Look at the last line of the story. What does it mean? Would you say that the story ends on a positive or negative note?

15. Discuss "My Kinsman, Major Molineux" as an initiation story—the tale of a young man who passes or falls from a state of childlike innocence into one of knowledge and experience. What sort of knowledge does Robin acquire? Has he learned anything about himself? Has he changed? If so, has that change been for the better?

Babylon Revisited

F. SCOTT FITZGERALD

I

"And where's Mr. Campbell?" Charlie asked.

"Gone to Switzerland. Mr. Campbell's a pretty sick man, Mr. Wales."

"I'm sorry to hear that. And George Hardt?" Charlie inquired.

"Back in America, gone to work."

"And where is the Snow Bird?"

"He was in here last week. Anyway, his friend, Mr. Schaeffer, is in Paris."

Two familiar names from the long list of a year and a half ago. Charlie scribbled an address in his notebook and tore out the page.

"If you see Mr. Schaeffer, give him this," he said. "It's my brother-in-law's address. I haven't settled on a hotel yet."

He was not really disappointed to find Paris was so empty. But the stillness in the Ritz bar was strange and portentous. It was not an American bar any more—he felt polite in it, and not as if he owned it. It had gone back into France. He felt the stillness from the moment he got out of the taxi and saw the doorman, usually in a frenzy of activity at this hour, gossiping with a *chasseur* by the servants' entrance.

Passing through the corridor, he heard only a single, bored voice in the once-glamorous women's room. When he turned into the bar he travelled the twenty feet of green carpet with his eyes fixed straight ahead by old habit; and then, with his foot firmly on the rail, he turned and surveyed the room, encountering only a single pair of eyes that fluttered up from a newspaper in the corner. Charlie asked for the head barman, Paul, who in the latter days of the bull market had come to work in his own custom-built car—disembarking, however, with due nicety at the nearest corner. But Paul was at his country house today and Alix giving him information.

"No, no more," Charlie said, "I'm going slow these days."

Alix congratulated him: "You were going pretty strong a couple of years ago."

"I'll stick to it all right," Charlie assured him. "I've stuck to it for over a year and a half now."

"How do you find conditions in America?"

"I haven't been to America for months. I'm in business in Prague, representing a couple of concerns there. They don't know about me down there."

Alix smiled.

"Remember the night of George Hardt's bachelor dinner here?" said Charlie. "By the way, what's become of Claude Fessenden?"

Alix lowered his voice confidentially: "He's in Paris, but he doesn't come here any more. Paul doesn't allow it. He ran up a bill of thirty thousand francs, charging all his drinks and his lunches, and usually his dinner, for more than a year. And when Paul finally told him he had to pay, he gave him a bad check."

Alix shook his head sadly.

"I don't understand it, such a dandy fellow. Now he's all bloated up—" He made a plump apple of his hands.

Charlie watched a group of strident queens installing themselves in a corner.

"Nothing affects them," he thought. "Stocks rise and fall, people loaf or work, but they go on forever." The place oppressed him. He called for the dice and shook with Alix for the drink.

"Here for long, Mr. Wales?"

"I'm here for four or five days to see my little girl."

"Oh-h! You have a little girl?"

Outside, the fire-red, gas-blue, ghost-green signs shone smokily through the tranquil rain. It was late afternoon and the streets were in movement; the *bistros* gleamed. At the corner of the Boulevard des Capucines he took a taxi. The Place de la Concorde moved by in pink majesty; they crossed the logical Seine, and Charlie felt the sudden provincial quality of the Left Bank.

Charlie directed his taxi to the Avenue de l'Opéra, which was out of his way. But he wanted to see the blue hour spread over the magnificent facade, and imagine that the cab horns, playing endlessly the first few bars of *Le Plus que Lent*, were the trumpets of the Second Empire. They were closing the iron grill in front of Brentano's Book-store, and people were already at dinner behind the trim little bourgeois hedge of Duval's. He had never eaten at a really cheap restaurant in Paris. Five-course dinner, four francs fifty, eighteen cents, wine included. For some odd reason he wished that he had.

As they rolled on to the Left Bank and he felt its sudden provincialism, he thought, "I spoiled this city for myself. I didn't realize it, but the days came along one after another, and then two years were gone, and everything was gone, and I was gone."

He was thirty-five and good to look at. The Irish mobility of his face was sobered by a deep wrinkle between his eyes. As he rang his brother-in-law's bell in the Rue Palatine, the wrinkle deepened till it pulled down his brows; he felt a cramping sensation in his belly. From behind the maid who opened the door darted a lovely little girl of nine who shrieked "Daddy!"

and flew up, struggling like a fish, into his arms. She pulled his head around by one ear and set her cheek against his.

"My old pie," he said.

"Oh, daddy, daddy, daddy, daddy, dads, dads, dads!"

She drew him into the salon, where the family waited, a boy and girl his daughter's age, his sister-in-law and her husband. He greeted Marion with his voice pitched carefully to avoid either feigned enthusiasm or dislike, but her response was more frankly tepid, though she mimimized her expression of unalterable distrust by directing her regard toward his child. The two men clasped hands in a friendly way and Lincoln Peters rested his for a moment in Charlie's shoulder.

The room was warm and comfortably American. The three children moved intimately about, playing through the yellow oblongs that led to other rooms; the cheer of six o'clock spoke in the eager smacks of the fire and the sounds of French activity in the kitchen. But Charlie did not relax; his heart sat up rigidly in his body and he drew confidence from his daughter, who from time to time came close to him, holding in her arms the doll he had brought.

"Really extremely well," he declared in answer to Lincoln's question. "There's a lot of business there that isn't moving at all, but we're doing even better than ever. In fact, damn well. I'm bringing my sister over from America next month to keep house for me. My income last year was bigger than it was when I had money. You see, the Czechs—"

His boasting was for a specific purpose; but after a moment, seeing a faint restiveness in Lincoln's eye, he changed the subject:

"Those are fine children of yours, well brought up, good manners."

"We think Honoria's a great little girl too."

Marion Peters came back from the kitchen. She was a tall woman with worried eyes, who had once possessed a fresh American loveliness. Charlie had never been sensitive to it and was always surprised when people spoke of how pretty she had been. From the first there had been an instinctive antipathy between them.

"Well, how do you find Honoria?" she asked.

"Wonderful. I was astonished how much she's grown in ten months. All the children are looking well."

"We haven't had a doctor for a year. How do you like being back in Paris?"

"It seems very funny to see so few Americans around."

"I'm delighted," Marion said vehemently. "Now at least you can go into a store without their assuming you're a millionaire. We've suffered like everybody, but on the whole it's a good deal pleasanter."

"But it was nice while it lasted," Charlie said. "We were a sort of royalty, almost infallible, with a sort of magic around us. In the bar this afternoon"—he stumbled, seeing his mistake—"there wasn't a man I knew."

She looked at him keenly. "I should think you'd have had enough of bars."

"I only stayed a minute. I take one drink every afternoon, and no more."

"Don't you want a cocktail before dinner?" Lincoln asked.

"I take only one drink every afternoon, and I've had that."

"I hope you keep to it," said Marion.

Her dislike was evident in the coldness with which she spoke, but Charlie only smiled; he had larger plans. Her very aggressiveness gave him an advantage, and he knew enough to wait. He wanted them to initiate the discussion of what they knew had brought him to Paris.

At dinner he couldn't decide whether Honoria was most like him or her mother. Fortunate if she didn't combine the traits of both that had brought them to disaster. A great wave of protectiveness went over him. He thought he knew what to do for her. He believed in character; he wanted to jump back a whole generation and trust in character again as the eternally valuable element. Everything else wore out.

He left soon after dinner, but not to go home. He was curious to see Paris by night with clearer and more judicious eyes than those of other days. He bought a *strapontin* for the Casino and watched Josephine Baker go through her chocolate arabesques.

After an hour he left and strolled toward Montmartre, up the Rue Pigalle into the Place Blanche. The rain had stopped and there were a few people in evening clothes disembarking from taxis in front of cabarets, and *cocottes* prowling singly or in pairs, and many Negroes. He passed a lighted door from which issued music, and stopped with the sense of familiarity; it was Bricktop's, where he had parted with so many hours and so much money. A few doors farther on he found another ancient rendezvous and incautiously put his head inside. Immediately an eager orchestra burst into sound, a pair of professional dancers leaped to their feet and a maître d'hôtel swooped toward him, crying, "Crowd just arriving, sir!" But he withdrew quickly.

"You have to be damn drunk," he thought.

Zelli's was closed, the bleak and sinister cheap hotels surrounding it were dark; up in the Rue Blanche there was more light and a local, colloquial French crowd. The Poet's Cave had disappeared, but the two great mouths of the Café of Heaven and the Café of Hell still yawned—even devoured, as he watched, the meagre contents of a tourist bus—a German, a Japanese, and an American couple who glanced at him with frightened eyes.

So much for the effort and ingenuity of Montmartre. All the catering to vice and waste was on an utterly childish scale, and he suddenly realized the meaning of the word "dissipate"—to dissipate into thin air; to make nothing out of something. In the little hours of the night every move from place to place was an enormous human jump, an increase of paying for the privilege of slower and slower motion.

He remembered thousand-franc notes given to an orchestra for playing a single number, hundred-franc notes tossed to a doorman for calling a cab.

But it hadn't been given for nothing.

It had been given, even the most wildly squandered sum, as an offering to destiny that he might not remember the things most worth remembering, the things that now he would always remember—his child taken from his control, his wife escaped to a grave in Vermont.

In the glare of a *brasserie* a woman spoke to him. He bought her some eggs and coffee, and then, eluding her encouraging stare, gave her a twenty-franc note and took a taxi to his hotel.

II

He woke upon a fine fall day—football weather. The depression of yesterday was gone and he liked the people on the streets. At noon he sat opposite Honoria at Le Grand Vatel, the only restaurant he could think of not reminiscent of champagne dinners and long luncheons that began at two and ended in a blurred and vague twilight.

"Now, how about vegetables? Oughtn't you to have some vegetables?"

"Well, yes."

"Here's *épinards* and *chou-fleur* and carrots and *haricots*."

"I'd like *chou-fleur*."

"Wouldn't you like to have two vegetables?"

"I usually only have one at lunch."

The waiter was pretending to be inordinately fond of children. "*Qu'elle est mignonne la petite! Elle parle exactement comme une française.*"

"How about dessert? Shall we wait and see?"

The waiter disappeared. Honoria looked at her father expectantly.

"What are we going to do?"

"First we're going to that toy store in the Rue Saint-Honoré and buy you anything you like. And then we're going to the vaudeville at the Empire."

She hesitated. "I like it about the vaudevelle, but not the toy store."

"Why not?"

"Well, you brought me this doll." She had it with her. "And I've got lots of things. And we're not rich any more, are we?"

"We never were. But today you are to have anything you want."

"All right," she agreed resignedly.

When there had been her mother and a French nurse he had been inclined to be strict; now he extended himself, reached out for a new tolerance; he must be both parents to her and not shut any of her out of communication.

"I want to get to know you," he said gravely. "First let me introduce myself. My name is Charles J. Wales, of Prague."

"Oh, daddy!" her voice cracked with laughter.

"And who are you, please?" he persisted, and she accepted a rôle immediately: "Honoria Wales, Rue Palatine, Paris."

"Married or single?"

"No, not married. Single."

He indicated the doll. "But I see you have a child, madame."

Unwilling to disinherit it, she took it to her heart and thought quickly: "Yes, I've been married, but I'm not married now. My husband is dead."

He went on quickly, "And the child's name?"

"Simone. That's after my best friend at school."

"I'm very pleased that you're doing so well at school."

"I'm third this month," she boasted. "Elsie"—that was her cousin—"is only about eighteenth, and Richard is about at the bottom."

"You like Richard and Elsie, don't you?"

"Oh, yes, I like Richard quite well and I like her all right."

Cautiously and casually he asked: "And Aunt Marion and Uncle Lincoln—which do you like best?"

"Oh, Uncle Lincoln, I guess."

He was increasingly aware of her presence. As they came in, a murmur of ". . . adorable" followed them, and now the people at the next table bent all their silences upon her, staring as if she were something no more conscious than a flower.

"Why don't I live with you?" she asked suddenly. "Because mamma's dead?"

"You must stay here and learn more French. It would have been hard for daddy to take care of you so well."

"I don't really need much taking care of any more. I do everything for myself."

Going out of the restaurant, a man and a woman unexpectedly hailed him.

"Well, the old Wales!"

"Hello there, Lorraine. . . . Dunc."

Sudden ghosts out of the past: Duncan Schaeffer, a friend from college. Lorraine Quarrles, a lovely, pale blonde of thirty; one of a crowd who had helped them make months into days in the lavish times of three years ago.

"My husband couldn't come this year," she said, in answer to his question. "We're poor as hell. So he gave me two hundred a month and told me I could do my worst on that. . . . This your little girl?"

"What about coming back and sitting down?" Duncan asked.

"Can't do it." He was glad for an excuse. As always, he felt Lorraine's passionate, provocative attraction, but his own rhythm was different now.

"Well, how about dinner?" she asked.

"I'm not free. Give me your address and let me call you."

"Charlie, I believe you're sober," she said judicially. "I honestly believe he's sober, Dunc. Pinch him and see if he's sober."

Charlie indicated Honoria with his head. They both laughed.

"What's your address?" said Duncan sceptically.

He hesitated, unwilling to give the name of his hotel.

"I'm not settled yet. I'd better call you. We're going to see the vaudeville at the Empire."

"There! That's what I want to do," Lorraine said. "I want to see some clowns and acrobats and jugglers. That's just what we'll do, Dunc."

"We've got to do an errand first," said Charlie. "Perhaps we'll see you there."

"All right, you snob. . . . Good-by, beautiful little girl."

"Good-by."

Honoria bobbed politely.

Somehow, an unwelcome encounter. They liked him because he was functioning, because he was serious; they wanted to see him, because he was stronger than they were now, because they wanted to draw a certain sustenance from his strength.

At the Empire, Honoria proudly refused to sit upon her father's folded coat. She was already an individual with a code of her own, and Charlie was more and more absorbed by the desire of putting a little of himself into her before she crystalized utterly. It was hopeless to try to know her in so short a time.

Between the acts they came upon Duncan and Lorraine in the lobby where the band was playing.

"Have a drink?"

"All right, but not up at the bar. We'll take a table."

"The perfect father."

Listening abstractedly to Lorraine, Charlie watched Honoria's eyes leave their table, and he followed them wistfully about the room, wondering what they saw. He met her glance and she smiled.

"I liked that lemonade," she said.

What had she said? What had he expected? Going home in a taxi afterward, he pulled her over until her head rested against his chest.

"Darling, do you ever think about your mother?"

"Yes, sometimes," she answered vaguely.

"I don't want you to forget her. Have you got a picture of her?"

"Yes, I think so. Anyhow, Aunt Marion has. Why don't you want me to forget her?"

"She loved you very much."

"I loved her too."

They were silent for a moment.

Daddy, I want to come and live with you," she said suddenly.

His heart leaped; he had wanted it to come like this.

"Aren't you perfectly happy?"

"Yes, but I love you better than anybody. And you love me better than anybody, don't you, now that mummy's dead?"

"Of course I do. But you won't always like me best, honey. You'll grow up and meet somebody your own age and go marry him and forget you ever had a daddy."

"Yes, that's true," she agreed tranquilly.

He didn't go in. He was coming back at nine o'clock and he wanted to keep himself fresh and new for the thing he must say then.

"When you're safe inside, just show yourself in that window."

"All right. Good-by, dads, dads, dads, dads."

He waited in the dark street until she appeared all warm and glowing, in the window above and kissed her fingers out into the night.

III

They were waiting. Marion sat behind the coffee service in a dignified black dinner dress that just faintly suggested mourning. Lincoln was walking up and down with the animation of one who had already been talking. They were as anxious as he was to get into the question. He opened it almost immediately:

"I suppose you know what I want to see you about—why I really came to Paris."

Marion played with the black stars on her necklace and frowned.

"I'm awfully anxious to have a home," he continued. "And I'm awfully anxious to have Honoria in it. I appreciate your taking in Honoria for her mother's sake, but things have changed now"—he hesitated and then continued more forcibly—"changed radically with me, and I want to ask you to reconsider the matter. It would be silly for me to deny that about three years ago I was acting badly—"

Marion looked up at him with hard eyes.

"—but all that's over. As I told you, I haven't had more than a drink a day for over a year, and I take that drink deliberately, so that the idea of alcohol won't get too big in my imagination. You see the idea?"

"No," said Marion succinctly.

"It's a sort of stunt I set myself. It keeps the matter in proportion."

"I get you," said Lincoln. "You don't want to admit it's got any attraction for you."

"Something like that. Sometimes I forget and don't take it. But I try to take it. Anyhow, I couldn't afford to drink in my position. The people I represent are more than satisfied with what I've done, and I'm bringing my sister over from Burlington to keep house for me, and I want awfully to have Honoria too. You know that even when her mother and I weren't getting along well we never let anything that happened touch Honoria. I know she's fond of me and I know I'm able to take care of her and—well, there you are. How do you feel about it?"

He knew that now he would have to take a beating. It would last an hour or two hours, and it would be difficult, but if he modulated his inevitable resentment to the chastened attitude of the reformed sinner, he might win his point in the end.

Keep your temper, he told himself. You don't want to be justified. You want Honoria.

Lincoln spoke first: "We've been talking it over ever since we got your letter last month. We're happy to have Honoria here. She's a dear little thing, and we're glad to be able to help her, but of course that isn't the question—"

Marion interrupted suddenly. "How long are you going to stay sober, Charlie?" she asked.

"Permanently, I hope."

"How can anybody count on that?"

"You know I never did drink heavily until I gave up business and came over here with nothing to do. Then Helen and I began to run around with—"

"Please leave Helen out of it. I can't bear to hear you talk about her like that."

He stared at her grimly; he had never been certain how fond of each other the sisters were in life.

"My drinking only lasted about a year and a half—from the time we came over until I—collapsed."

"It was time enough."

"It was time enough," he agreed.

"My duty is entirely to Helen," she said. "I try to think what she would have wanted me to do. Frankly, from the night you did that terrible thing you haven't really existed for me. I can't help that. She was my sister."

"Yes."

"When she was dying she asked me to look out for Honoria. If you hadn't been in a sanitarium then, it might have helped matters."

He had no answer.

"I'll never in my life be able to forget the morning when Helen knocked at my door, soaked to the skin and shivering, and said you'd locked her out."

Charlie gripped the sides of the chair. This was more difficult than he expected; he wanted to launch out into a long expostulation and explanation, but he only said: "The night I locked her out—" and she interrupted, "I don't feel up to going over that again."

After a moment's silence Lincoln said: "We're getting off the subject. You want Marion to set aside her legal guardianship and give you Honoria. I think the main point for her is whether she has confidence in you or not."

"I don't blame Marion," Charlie said slowly, "but I think she can have entire confidence in me. I had a good record up to three years ago. Of course, it's within human possibilities I might go wrong any time. But if we wait much longer I'll lose Honoria's childhood and my chance for a home." He shook his head, "I'll simply lose her, don't you see?"

"Yes, I see," said Lincoln.

"Why didn't you think of all this before?" Marion asked.

"I suppose I did, from time to time, but Helen and I were getting along badly. When I consented to the guardianship, I was flat on my back in a sanitarium and the market had cleaned me out. I knew I'd acted badly, and I thought if it would bring any peace to Helen, I'd agree to anything. But now it's different. I'm functioning, I'm behaving damn well, so far as—"

"Please don't swear at me," Marion said.

He looked at her, startled. With each remark the force of her dislike became more and more apparent. She had built up all her fear of life into one wall and faced it toward him. This trivial reproof was possibly the result of some trouble with the cook several hours before. Charlie became increasingly alarmed at leaving Honoria in this atmosphere of hostility against himself; sooner or later it would come out, in a word here, a shake of the head there, and some of that distrust would be irrevocably implanted in Honoria. But he pulled his temper down out of his face and shut it up inside him; he had won a point, for Lincoln realized the absurdity of Marion's remark and asked her lightly since when she had objected to the word "damn."

"Another thing," Charlie said: "I'm able to give her certain advantages now. I'm going to take a French governess to Prague with me. I've got a lease on a new apartment—"

He stopped, realizing that he was blundering. They couldn't be expected to accept with equanimity the fact that his income was again twice as large as their own.

"I suppose you can give her more luxuries than we can," said Marion. "When you were throwing away money we were living along watching every ten francs. . . . I suppose you'll start doing it again."

"Oh, no," he said. "I've learned. I worked hard for ten years, you know— until I got lucky in the market, like so many people. Terribly lucky. It didn't seem any use working any more, so I quit. It won't happen again."

There was a long silence. All of them felt their nerves straining, and for the first time in a year Charlie wanted a drink. He was sure now that Lincoln Peters wanted him to have his child.

Marion shuddered suddenly; part of her saw that Charlie's feet were planted on the earth now, and her own maternal feeling recognized the naturalness of his desire; but she had lived for a long time with a prejudice—a prejudice founded on a curious disbelief in her sister's happiness, and which, in the shock of one terrible night, had turned to hatred for him. It had all happened at a point in her life where the discouragement of ill health and adverse circumstances made it necessary for her to believe in tangible villainy and a tangible villain.

"I can't help what I think!" she cried out suddenly. "How much you were responsible for Helen's death, I don't know. It's something you'll have to square with your own conscience."

An electric current of agony surged through him; for a moment he was almost on his feet, an unuttered sound echoing in his throat. He hung on to himself for a moment, another moment.

"Hold on there," said Lincoln uncomfortably. "I never thought you were responsible for that."

"Helen died of heart trouble," Charlie said dully.

"Yes, heart trouble." Marion spoke as if the phrase had another meaning for her.

Then in the flatness that followed her outburst, she saw him plainly and she knew he had somehow arrived at control over the situation. Glancing at her husband, she found no help from him, and as abruptly as if it were a matter of no importance, she threw up the sponge.

"Do what you like!" she cried, springing up from her chair. "She's your child. I'm not the person to stand in your way. I think if it were my child I'd rather see her—" She managed to check herself. "You two decide it. I can't stand this. I'm sick. I'm going to bed."

She hurried from the room; after a moment Lincoln said:

"This has been a hard day for her. You know how strongly she feels—" His voice was almost apologetic: "When a woman gets an idea in her head."

"Of course."

"It's going to be all right. I think she sees now that you—can provide for the child, and so we can't very well stand in your way or Honoria's way."

"Thank you, Lincoln."

"I'd better go along and see how she is."

"I'm going."

He was still trembling when he reached the street, but a walk down the Rue Bonaparte to the quais set him up, and as he crossed the Seine, fresh and new by the quai lamps, he felt exultant. But back in his room he couldn't sleep. The image of Helen haunted him. Helen whom he had loved so until they had senselessly begun to abuse each other's love, tear it into shreds. On that terrible February night that Marion remembered so vividly, a slow quarrel had gone on for hours. There was a scene at the Florida, and then he attempted to take her home, and then she kissed young Webb at a table; after that there was what she had hysterically said. When he arrived home alone he turned the key in the lock in wild anger. How could he know she would arrive an hour later alone, that there would be a snowstorm in which she wandered about in slippers, too confused to find a taxi? Then the aftermath, her escaping peneumonia by a miracle, and all the attendant horror. They were "reconciled," but that was the beginning of the end, and Marion, who had seen with her own eyes and who imagined it to be one of many scenes from her sister's martyrdom, never forgot.

Going over it again brought Helen nearer, and in the white, soft light that steals upon half sleep near morning he found himself talking to her again. She said that he was perfectly right about Honoria and that she wanted Honoria to be with him. She said she was glad he was being good and doing better. She said a lot of other things—very friendly things—but she was in a swing in a white dress, and swinging faster and faster all the time, so that at the end he could not hear clearly all that she said.

IV

He woke up feeling happy. The door of the world was open again. He made plans, vistas, futures for Honoria and himself, but suddenly he grew sad, remembering all the plans he and Helen had made. She had not planned to die.

The present was the thing—work to do and someone to love. But not to love too much, for he knew the injury that a father can do to a daughter or a mother to a son by attaching them too closely; afterward, out in the world, the child would seek in the marriage partner the same blind tenderness and, failing probably to find it, turn against love and life.

It was another bright, crisp day. He called Lincoln Peters at the bank where he worked and asked if he could count on taking Honoria when he left for Prague. Lincoln agreed that there was no reason for delay. One thing—the legal guardianship. Marion wanted to retain that a while longer. She was upset by the whole matter, and it would oil things if she felt that the situation was still in her control for another year. Charlie agreed, wanted only the tangible, visible child.

Then the question of a governess. Charlie sat in a gloomy agency and talked to a cross Béarnaise and to a buxom Breton peasant, neither of whom he could have endured. There were others whom he would see tomorrow.

He lunched with Lincoln Peters at Griffons, trying to keep down his exultation.

"There's nothing quite like your own child," Lincoln said. "But you understand how Marion feels too."

"She's forgotten how hard I worked for seven years there," Charlie said. "She just remembers one night."

"There's another thing." Lincoln hesitated. "While you and Helen were tearing around Europe throwing money away, we were just getting along. I didn't touch any of the prosperity because I never got ahead enough to carry anything but my insurance. I think Marion felt there was some kind of injustice in it—you not even working toward the end, and getting richer and richer."

"It went just quick as it came," said Charlie.

"Yes, a lot of it stayed in the hand of *chasseurs* and saxophone players and maîtres d'hôtel—well, the big party's over now. I just said that to explain Marion's feeling about those crazy years. If you drop in about six o'clock tonight before Marion's too tired, we'll settle the details on the spot."

Back at his hotel, Charlie found a *pneumatique* that had been redirected from the Ritz bar where Charlie had left his address for the purpose of finding a certain man.

Dear Charlie:
You were so strange when we saw you the other day that I wondered if I did something to offend you. If so, I'm not conscious of it. In fact, I have thought about you too much for the last year, and it's always been in the back of my mind that I might see you if I came over here. We *did* have such good times that crazy spring, like the night you and I stole the butcher's tricycle, and the time we tried to call on the president and you had the old derby rim and the wire cane. Everybody seems so old lately, but I don't feel old a bit. Couldn't we get together some time today for old time's sake? I've got a vile hangover for the moment, but will be feeling better this afternoon and will look for you about five in the sweat-shop at the Ritz.
                                                        Always devotedly,
                                                             Lorraine.

His first feeling was one of awe that he had actually, in his mature years, stolen a tricycle and pedalled Lorraine all over the Étoile between the small hours and dawn. In retrospect it was a nightmare. Locking out Helen didn't fit in with any other act of his life, but the tricycle incident did—it was one of many. How many weeks or months of dissipation to arrive at that condition of utter irresponsibility?

He tried to picture how Lorraine had appeared to him then—very attractive; Helen was unhappy about it, though she said nothing. Yesterday, in the restaurant, Lorraine had seemed trite, blurred, worn away. He emphatically did not want to see her, and he was glad Alix had not given away his hotel address. It was a relief to think, instead, of Honoria, to think of Sundays spent with her and of saying good morning to her and of knowing she was there in his house at night, drawing her breath in the darkness.

At five he took a taxi and bought presents for all the Peters—a piquant cloth doll, a box of Roman soldiers, flowers for Marion, big linen handkerchiefs for Lincoln.

He saw, when he arrived in the apartment, that Marion had accepted the inevitable. She greeted him now as though he were a recalcitrant member of the family, rather than a menacing outsider. Honoria had been told she was going; Charlie was glad to see that her tact made her conceal her excessive happiness. Only on his lap did she whisper her delight and the question "When?" before she slipped away with the other children.

He and Marion were alone for a minute in the room, and on an impulse he spoke out boldly:

"Family quarrels are bitter things. They don't go according to any rules. They're not like aches or wounds; they're more like splits in the skin that won't heal because there's not enough material. I wish you and I could be on better terms."

"Some things are hard to forget," she answered. "It's a question of confidence." There was no answer to this and presently she asked, "When do you propose to take her?"

"As soon as I can get a governess. I hoped the day after tomorrow."

"That's impossible. I've got to get her things in shape. Not before Saturday."

He yielded. Coming back into the room, Lincoln offered him a drink.

"I'll take my daily whisky," he said.

It was warm here, it was a home, people together by a fire. The children felt very safe and important; the mother and father were serious, watchful. They had things to do for the children more important than his visit here. A spoonful of medicine was, after all, more important than the strained relations between Marion and himself. They were not dull people, but they were very much in the grip of life and circumstances. He wondered if he couldn't do something to get Lincoln out of his rut at the bank.

A long peal at the door-bell; the *bonne toute faire* passed through and went down the corridor. The door opened upon another long ring; and then voices, and the three in the salon looked up expectantly; Richard moved to bring the corridor within his range of vision, and Marion rose. Then the maid came back along the corridor, closely followed by the voices, which developed under the light into Duncan Schaeffer and Lorraine Quarrles.

They were gay, they were hilarious, they were roaring with laughter. For a moment Charlie was astounded; unable to understand how they ferreted out the Peter's address.

"Ah-h-h!" Duncan wagged his finger roguishly at Charlie. "Ah-h-h!"

They both slid down another cascade of laughter. Anxious and at a loss, Charlie shook hands with them quickly and presented them to Lincoln and Marion. Marion nodded, scarcely speaking. She had drawn back a step toward the fire; her little girl stood beside her, and Marion put an arm about her shoulder.

With growing annoyance at the intrusion, Charlie waited for them to explain themselves. After some concentration Duncan said:

"We came to invite you out to dinner. Lorraine and I insist that all this shishi, cagey business 'bout your address got to stop."

Charlie came closer to them, as if to force them backward down the corridor.

"Sorry, but I can't. Tell me where you'll be and I'll phone you in half an hour."

This made no impression. Lorraine sat down suddenly on the side of a chair, and focussing her eyes on Richard, cried, "Oh, what a nice little boy! Come here, little boy." Richard glanced at his mother, but did not move. With a perceptible shrug of her shoulders, Lorraine turned back to Charlie:

"Come and dine. Sure your cousins won' mine. See you so sel'om. Or solemn."

"I can't," said Charlie sharply. "You two have dinner and I'll phone you."

Her voice became suddenly unpleasant. "All right, we'll go. But I remember once when you hammered on my door at four A.M. I was enough of a good sport to give you a drink. Come on, Dunc."

Still in slow motion, with blurred, angry faces, with uncertain feet, they retired along the corridor.

"Good night," Charlie said.

"Good night!" responded Lorraine emphatically.

When he went back into the salon Marion had not moved, only now her son was standing in the circle of her other arm. Lincoln was still swinging Honoria back and forth like a pendulum from side to side.

"What an outrage!" Charlie broke out. "What an absolute outrage!"

Neither of them answered. Charlie dropped into an armchair, picked up his drink, set it down again and said:

"People I haven't seen for two years having the colossal nerve—"

He broke off. Marion had made the sound "Oh!" in one swift furious breath, turned her body from him with a jerk and left the room.

Lincoln set down Honoria carefully.

"You children go in and start your soup," he said, and when they obeyed, he said to Charlie:

"Marion's not well and she can't stand shocks. That kind of people make her really physically sick."

"I didn't tell them to come here. They wormed your name out of somebody. They deliberately—"

"Well, it's too bad. It doesn't help matters. Excuse me a minute."

Left alone, Charlie sat tense in his chair. In the next room he could hear the children eating, talking in monosyllables, already oblivious to the scene between their elders. He heard a murmur of conservation from a farther room and then the ticking bell of a telephone receiver picked up, and in a panic he moved to the other side of the room and out of earshot.

In a minute Lincoln came back. "Look here, Charlie. I think we'd better call off dinner for tonight. Marion's in bad shape."

"Is she angry with me?"

"Sort of," he said, almost roughly. "She's not strong and—"

"You mean she's changed her mind about Honoria?"

"She's pretty bitter right now. I don't know. You phone me at the bank tomorrow."

"I wish you'd explain to her I never dreamed these people would come here. I'm just as sore as you are."

"I couldn't explain anything to her now."

Charlie got up. He took his coat and hat and started down the corridor. Then he opened the door of the dining room and said in a strange voice, "Good night, children."

Honoria rose and ran around the table to hug him.

"Good night, sweetheart," he said vaguely, and then trying to make his voice more tender, trying to conciliate something, "Good night, dear children."

V

Charlie went directly to the Ritz bar with the furious idea of finding Lorraine and Duncan, but they were not there, and he realized that in any case there was nothing he could do. He had not touched his drink at the Peters', and now he ordered a whisky-and-soda. Paul came over to say hello.

"It's a great change," he said sadly. "We do about half the business we did. So many fellows I hear about back in the States lost everything, maybe not in the first crash, but then in the second. Your friend George Hardt lost every cent, I hear. Are you back in the States?"

"No, I'm in business in Prague."

"I heard that you lost a lot in the crash."

"I did," and he added grimly, "but I lost everything I wanted in the boom."

"Selling short?"

"Something like that."

Again the memory of those days swept over him like a nightmare—the people they had met travelling; the people who couldn't add a row of figures or speak a coherent sentence. The little man Helen had consented to dance with at the ship's party, who had insulted her ten feet from the table; the women and girls carried screaming with drink or drugs out of public places—

—The men who locked their wives out in the snow, because the snow of twenty-nine wasn't real snow. If you didn't want it to be snow, you just paid some money.

He went to the phone and called the Peters' apartment; Lincoln answered.

"I called up because this thing is on my mind. Has Marion said anything definite?"

"Marion's sick," Lincoln answered shortly. "I know this thing isn't altogether your fault, but I can't have her go to pieces about it. I'm afraid we'll have to let it slide for six months; I can't take the chance of working her up to this state again."

"I see."

"I'm sorry, Charlie."

He went back to his table. His whisky glass was empty, but he shook his head when Alix looked at it questioningly. There wasn't much he could do now except send Honoria some things; he would send her a lot of things tomorrow. He thought rather angrily that this was just money—he had given so many people money. . . .

"No, no more," he said to another waiter. "What do I owe you?"

He would come back some day; they couldn't make him pay forever. But he wanted his child, and nothing was much good now, beside that fact. He wasn't young any more, with a lot of nice thoughts and dreams to have by himself. He was absolutely sure Helen wouldn't have wanted him to be so alone.

QUESTIONS

"Babylon Revisited"

1. Babylon was a large and ancient city, once the capital of the Chaldee empire, known for its luxury and corruption. References to it appear in the Bible several times. From 603–536 B.C., the Jews were exiled from their native land to Babylon and held captive there. Psalm 137 expresses the sense of loss

and alienation experienced by the exiles. In addition, we are told in Revelation that Babylon was eventually destroyed by God because of its sinful and materialistic inhabitants. Given these facts, why would Fitzgerald choose to call his story "Babylon Revisited"?

2. What is the object of Charles Wales's quest? What trials must be endure during his quest? What obstacles must be overcome?

3. How has Paris changed from the days when Charles and his wife lived there? How are these changes accounted for and how does Charles respond to them? What has happened to the Waleses' former drinking friends?

4. What was the Waleses' life in Paris like? In what sense was that life a wasteland? How does Charles feel about his past?

5. Why does Charles believe it is essential to take his daughter to Prague immediately?

6. At one point, the narrator says of Charles, "He believed in character; he wanted to jump back a whole generation and trust in character again as the eternally valuable element. Everything else wore out." Why does Charles place such emphasis on character? Does he have "character"? Does character wear out like "everything" else, or does it endure? How is character related to the hero's quest?

7. Why does Marion Peters dislike Charles Wales so intensely? Why does she begin to yield to his request to be allowed to take his daughter away? How much does her unalterable dislike of him affect her decision at the end of the story?

8. What is Charles Wales's attitude toward his sister-in-law and her husband? How does he feel about the home they have created for his daughter and her cousins?

9. This story was first published in the heart of the Depression, and financial failures are mentioned from time to time in it, along with other kinds of failures. What does Charles mean when he tells the Ritz's bartender that, although he lost a great deal of money in the stockmarket crash, he "lost everything [he] wanted in the boom"?

10. How does Fitzgerald manage to make Duncan Schaeffer and Lorraine Quarrles, in our brief glimpses of them, unpleasant, irresponsible, and alien to the quiet domestic scenes into which they intrude? Do you think Marion Peters's reaction to them is excessive?

11. After Lorraine and Duncan leave the Peters apartment, we see Lincoln holding Charles's daughter, "swinging Honoria back and forth like a pendulum from side to side." What does this image suggest to you?

12. In the first scene of the story, we see Charles leaving Lincoln Peters's address with a barman at the Ritz, to be delivered to Duncan Schaeffer. Why does he do this? How do you account for his astonishment when Duncan appears at the Peters apartment? What does his reaction indicate about the inter-

nal obstacles to his quest, obstacles Charles is apparently unaware of? Why is it a mistake to tell Marion that he hasn't seen Duncan and Lorraine in two years?

13. What is the prevailing mood of "Babylon Revisited"? How does the story's preoccupation with time and waste affect its mood?

A Worn Path

EUDORA WELTY

It was December—a bright frozen day in the early morning. Far out in the country there was an old Negro woman with her head tied in a red rag, coming along a path through the pinewoods. Her name was Phoenix Jackson. She was very old and small and she walked slowly in the dark pine shadows, moving a little from side to side in her steps, with the balanced heaviness and lightness of a pendulum in a grandfather clock. She carried a thin, small cane made from an umbrella, and with this she kept tapping the frozen earth in front of her. This made a grave and persistent noise in the still air, that seemed meditative like the chirping of a solitary little bird.

She wore a dark striped dress reaching down to her shoe tops, and an equally long apron of bleached sugar sacks, with a full pocket: all neat and tidy, but every time she took a step she might have fallen over her shoelaces, which dragged from her unlaced shoes. She looked straight ahead. Her eyes were blue with age. Her skin had a pattern all its own of numberless branching wrinkles and as though a whole little tree stood in the middle of her forehead, but a golden color ran underneath, and the two knobs of her cheeks were illumined by a yellow burning under the dark. Under the red rag her hair came down on her neck in the frailest of ringlets, still black, and with an odor like copper.

Now and then there was a quivering in the thicket. Old Phoenix said, "Out of my way, all you foxes, owls, beetles, jack rabbits, coons and wild animals! . . . Keep out from under these feet, little bob-whites. . . . Keep the big wild hogs out of my path. Don't let none of those come running my direction. I got a long way." Under her small black-freckled hand her cane, limber as a buggy whip, would switch at the brush as if to rouse up any hiding things.

On she went. The woods were deep and still. The sun made the pine needles almost too bright to look at, up where the wind rocked. The cones dropped as light as feathers. Down in the hollow was the mourning dove—it was not too late for him.

The path ran up a hill. "Seem like there is chains about my feet, time I get this far," she said, in the voice of argument old people keep to use with themselves. "Something always take a hold of me on this hill—pleads I should stay."

After she got to the top she turned and gave a full, severe look behind her where she had come. "Up through pines," she said at length. "Now down through oaks."

Her eyes opened their widest, and she started down gently. But before she got to the bottom of the hill a bush caught her dress.

Her fingers were busy and intent, but her skirts were full and long, so that before she could pull them free in one place they were caught in another. It was not possible to allow the dress to tear. "I in the thorny bush," she said. "Thorns, you doing your appointed work. Never want to let folks pass, no sir. Old eyes thought you was a pretty little *green* bush."

Finally, trembling all over, she stood free, and after a moment dared to stoop for her cane.

"Sun so high!" she cried, leaning back and looking, while the thick tears went over her eyes. "The time getting all gone here."

At the foot of this hill was a place where a log was laid across the creek.

"Now comes the trial," said Phoenix.

Putting her right foot out, she mounted the log and shut her eyes. Lifting her skirt, leveling her cane fiercely before her, like a festival figure in some parade, she began to march across. Then she opened her eyes and she was safe on the other side.

"I wasn't as old as I thought," she said.

But she sat down to rest. She spread her skirts on the bank around her and folded her hands over her knees. Up above her was a tree in a pearly cloud of mistletoe. She did not dare to close her eyes, and when a little boy brought her a plate with a slice of marble-cake on it she spoke to him. "That would be acceptable," she said. But when she went to take it there was just her own hand in the air.

So she left that tree, and had to go through a barbed-wire fence. There she had to creep and crawl, spreading her knees and stretching her fingers like a baby trying to climb the steps. But she talked loudly to herself: she could not let her dress be torn now, so late in the day, and she could not pay for having her arm or her leg sawed off if she got caught fast where she was.

At last she was safe through the fence and risen up out in the clearing. Big dead trees, like black men with one arm, were standing in the purple stalks of the withered cotton field. There sat a buzzard.

"Who you watching?"

In the furrow she made her way along.

"Glad this not the season for bulls," she said, looking sideways, "and the good Lord made his snakes to curl up and sleep in the winter. A pleasure I don't see no two-headed snake coming around that tree, where it come once. It took a while to get by him, back in the summer."

She passed through the old cotton and went into a field of dead corn. It whispered and shook and was taller than her head. "Through the maze now," she said, for there was no path.

Then there was something tall, black, and skinny there, moving before her.

At first she took it for a man. It could have been a man dancing in the field. But she stood still and listened, and it did not make a sound. It was as silent as a ghost.

"Ghost," she said sharply, "who be you the ghost of? For I have heard of nary death close by."

But there was no answer—only the ragged dancing in the wind.

She shut her eyes, reached out her hand, and touched a sleeve. She found a coat and inside that an emptiness, cold as ice.

"You scarecrow," she said. Her face lighted. "I ought to be shut up for good," she said with laughter. "My senses is gone. I too old. I the oldest people I ever know. Dance, old scarecrow," she said, "while I dancing with you."

She kicked her foot over the furrow, and with mouth drawn down, shook her head once or twice in a little strutting way. Some husks blew down and whirled in streamers about her skirts.

Then she went on, parting her way from side to side with the cane, through the whispering field. At last she came to the end, to a wagon track where the silver grass blew between the red ruts. The quail were walking around like pullets, seeming all dainty and unseen.

"Walk pretty," she said. "This the easy place. This the easy going."

She followed the track, swaying through the quiet bare fields, through the little strings of trees silver in their dead leaves, past cabins silver from weather, with the doors and windows boarded shut, all like old women under a spell sitting there. "I walking in their sleep," she said, nodding her head vigorously.

In a ravine she went where a spring was silently flowing through a hollow log. Old Phoenix bent and drank. "Sweet-gum makes the water sweet," she said, and drank more. "Nobody know who made this well, for it was here when I was born."

The track crossed a swampy part where the moss hung as white as lace from every limb. "Sleep on, alligators, and blow your bubbles." Then the track went into the road.

Deep, deep the road went down between the high green-colored banks. Overhead the live-oaks met, and it was as dark as a cave.

A black dog with a lolling tongue came up out of the weeds by the ditch. She was meditating, and not ready, and when he came at her she only hit him a little with her cane. Over she went in the ditch, like a little puff of milkweed.

Down there, her senses drifted away. A dream visited her, and she reached her hand up, but nothing reached down and gave her a pull. So she lay there and presently went to talking. "Old woman," she said to herself, "that black dog come up out of the weeds to stall you off and now there he sitting on his fine tail, smiling at you."

A white man finally came along and found her—a hunter, a young man, with his dog on a chain.

"Well, Granny!" he laughed. "What are you doing there?"

"Lying on my back like a June-bug waiting to be turned over, mister," she said, reaching up her hand.

He lifted her up, gave her a swing in the air, and set her down. "Anything broken, Granny?"

"No sir, them old dead weeds is springy enough," said Phoenix, when she had got her breath. "I thank you for your trouble."

"Where do you live, Granny?" he asked, while the two dogs were growling at each other.

"Away back yonder, sir, behind the ridge. You can't even see it from here."

"On your way home?"

"No, sir, I going to town."

"Why, that's too far! That's as far as I walk when I come out myself, and I get something for my trouble." He patted the stuffed bag he carried, and there hung down a little closed claw. It was one of the bob-whites, with its beak hooked bitterly to show it was dead. "Now you go on home, Granny!"

"I bound to go to town, mister," said Phoenix. "The time come around."

He gave another laugh, filling the whole landscape. "I know you old colored people! Wouldn't miss going to town to see Santa Claus!"

But something held old Phoenix very still. The deep lines in her face went into a fierce and different radiation. Without warning, she had seen with her own eyes a flashing nickel fall out of the man's pocket onto the ground.

"How old are you, Granny?" he was saying.

"There is no telling, mister," she said, "no telling."

Then she gave a little cry and clapped her hands and said, "Git on away from here dog! Look! Look at that dog!" She laughed as if in admiration. "He ain't scared of nobody. He a big black dog." She whispered, "Sic him!"

"Watch me get rid of that cur," said the man. "Sic him, Pete! Sic him!"

Phoenix heard the dogs fighting, and heard the man running and throwing sticks. She even heard a gunshot. But she was slowly bending forward by that time, further and further forward, the lids stretched down over her eyes, as if she was doing this in her sleep. Her chin was lowered almost to her knees. The yellow palm of her hand came out from the fold of her apron. Her fingers slid down and along the ground under the piece of money with the grace and care they would have in lifting an egg from under a setting hen. Then she slowly straightened up, she stood erect, and the nickel was in her apron pocket. A bird flew by. Her lips moved. "God watching me the whole time. I come to stealing."

The man came back, and his own dog panted about them. "Well, I scared him off that time," he said, and then he laughed and lifted his gun and pointed it at Phoenix.

She stood straight and faced him.

"Doesn't the gun scare you?" he said, still pointing it.

"No, sir, I seen plenty go off closer by, in my day, and for less than what I done," she said, holding utterly still.

He smiled, and shouldered the gun. "Well, Granny," he said "you must be a hundred years old, and scared of nothing. I'd give you a dime if I had any money with me. But you take my advice and stay home, and nothing will happen to you."

"I bound to go on my way, mister," said Phoenix. She inclined her head in the red rag. Then they went in different directions, but she could hear the gun shooting again and again over the hill.

She walked on. The shadows hung from the oak tree to the road like curtains. Then she smelled wood-smoke, and smelled the river, and she saw a steeple and the cabins on their steep steps. Dozens of little black children whirled around her. There ahead was Natchez shining. Bells were ringing. She walked on.

In the paved city it was Christmas time. There were red and green electric lights strung and crisscrossed everywhere, and all turned on in the daytime. Old Phoenix would have been lost if she had not distrusted her eyesight and depended on her feet to know where to take her.

She paused quietly on the sidewalk where people were passing by. A lady came along in the crowd, carrying an armful of red-, green- and silver-wrapped presents; she gave off perfume like the red roses in hot summer, and Phoenix stopped her.

"Please, missy, will you lace up my shoe?" She held up her foot.

"What do you want, Grandma?"

"See my shoe," said Phoenix. "Do all right for out in the country, but wouldn't look right to go in a big building."

"Stand still then, Grandma," said the lady. She put her packages down on the sidewalk beside her and laced and tied both shoes tightly.

"Can't lace 'em with a cane," said Phoenix. "Thank you, missy. I doesn't mind asking a nice lady to tie up my shoe, when I gets out on the street."

Moving slowly and from side to side, she went into the big building, and into a tower of steps, where she walked up and around and around until her feet knew to stop.

She entered a door, and there she saw nailed up on the wall the document that had been stamped with the gold seal and framed in the gold frame, which matched the dream that was hung up in her head.

"Here I be," she said. There was a fixed and ceremonial stiffness over her body.

"A charity case, I suppose," said an attendant who sat at the desk before her.

But Phoenix only looked above her head. There was sweat on her face, the wrinkles in her skin shone like a bright net.

"Speak up, Grandma," the woman said. "What's your name? We must have your history, you know. Have you been here before? What seems to be the trouble with you?"

Old Phoenix only gave a twitch to her face as if a fly were bothering her.

"Are you deaf?" cried the attendant.

But then the nurse came in.

"Oh, that's just old Aunt Phoenix," she said. "She doesn't come for herself—she has a little grandson. She makes these trips just as regular as clockwork. She lives away back off the Old Natchez Trace." She bent down. "Well, Aunt Phoenix, why don't you just take a seat? We won't keep you standing after your long trip." She pointed.

The old woman sat down, bolt upright in the chair.

"Now, how is the boy?" asked the nurse.

Old Phoenix did not speak.

"I said, how is the boy?"

But Phoenix only waited and stared straight ahead, her face very solemn and withdrawn into rigidity.

"Is his throat any better?" asked the nurse. "Aunt Phoenix, don't you hear me? Is your grandson's throat any better since the last time you came for the medicine?"

With her hands on her knees, the old woman waited, silent, erect and motionless, just as if she were in armor.

"You mustn't take up our time this way, Aunt Phoenix," the nurse said. "Tell us quickly about your grandson, and get it over. He isn't dead, is he?"

At last there came a flicker and then a flame of comprehension across her face, and she spoke.

"My grandson. It was my memory had left me. There I sat and forgot why I made my long trip."

"Forgot?" The nurse frowned. "After you came so far?"

Then Phoenix was like an old woman begging a dignified forgiveness for waking up frightened in the night. "I never did go to school, I was too old at the Surrender," she said in a soft voice. "I'm an old woman without an education. It was my memory fail me. My little grandson, he is just the same, and I forgot it in the coming."

"Throat never heals, does it?" said the nurse, speaking in a loud, sure voice to old Phoenix. By now she had a card with something written on it, a little list. "Yes. Swallowed lye. When was it?— January—two-three years ago—"

Phoenix spoke unasked now. "No missy, he not dead, he just the same. Every little while his throat begin to close up again, and he not able to swallow. He not get his breath. He not able to help himself. So the time come around, and I go on another trip for the soothing medicine."

"All right. The doctor said as long as you came to get it, you could have it," said the nurse. "But it's an obstinate case."

"My little grandson, he sit up there in the house all wrapped up, waiting by himself," Phoenix went on. "We is the only two left in the world. He suffer and it don't seem to put him back at all. He got a sweet look. He going to last. He wear a little patch quilt and peep out holding his mouth open like a little bird. I remembers so plain now. I not going to forget him again, no, the whole enduring time. I could tell him from all the others in creation."

"All right." The nurse was trying to hush her now. She brought her a bottle of medicine. "Charity," she said, making a check mark in a book.

Old Phoenix held the bottle close to her eyes, and then carefully put it into her pocket.

"I thank you," she said.

"It's Christmas time, Grandma," said the attendant. "Could I give you a few pennies out of my purse?"

"Five pennies is a nickel," said Phoenix stiffly.

"Here's a nickel," said the attendant.

Phoenix rose carefully and held out her hand. She received the nickel and then fished the other nickel out of her pocket and laid it beside the new one. She stared at her palm closely, with her head on one side.

Then she gave a tap with her cane on the floor.

"This is what come to me to do," she said. "I going to the store and buy my child a little windmill they sells, made out of paper. He going to find it hard to believe there such a thing in the world. I'll march myself back where he waiting, holding it straight up in this hand."

She lifted her free hand, gave a little nod, turned around, and walked out of the doctor's office. Then her slow step began on the stairs, going down.

QUESTIONS

"A Worn Path"

1. In this brief story, Eudora Welty gives us a convincing portrait of a very old woman. What are some of the details of physical appearance, gesture, and behavior that help complete this portrait? What details contribute to a realistic picture of an uneducated rural black woman? Which details make her an improbable hero?

2. The title, of course, refers to the fact that Phoenix has walked along this path, gone on one particular quest, many times. Do you think Welty is also trying to suggest that Phoenix's experience is representative of that of many blacks? Support your answer.

3. What is the object of Phoenix Jackson's quest? What are the many ex-

ternal and internal obstacles she faces during this quest, in the form of people, features of the landscape, personal weakness, and fears associated with her age and circumstances?

4. What qualities does Phoenix possess that make it possible for her, despite her great age and physical frailty, to make the long trip to town when necessary? What qualities of character does Phoenix demonstrate at each of the obstacles she encounters during her quest?

5. How is Phoenix treated by the white people she encounters? At whose hands does she receive the worst treatment? The best? How does each of these white people regard her? Can any of them be seen as the helper or guide frequently encountered during the hero's quest?

6. Why does the young man point his gun at Phoenix? Does she understand his action? Why does he say he would offer her money if he had any?

7. From the point of view of some of the characters in this story, Phoenix Jackson is a senile and even comical old woman. Do you share this opinion? Does Welty give us evidence of her shrewdness, too? Explain.

8. Why do we see nothing and hear so little of Phoenix's grandson? What is the symbolic significance of the fact that his condition never improves?

9. Discuss the passage in which Phoenix bends to pick up the dropped nickel. Why does Welty handle this scene as she does?

10. Phoenix arrives in the city where the doctor's office is located at Christmas time. Why does Welty include the scene of the woman laden with presents who stops to lace Phoenix's shoes?

11. Do you think Phoenix Jackson is a charity case, as the nurse in the city says she is? Who has a better understanding of charity, the nurse or Phoenix? Why?

12. Look up the word phoenix in a good dictionary. Why is it an appropriate name for Welty's heroine?

The Open Boat

STEPHEN CRANE

*A Tale Intended to Be after the Fact: Being the Experience of
Four Men from the Sunk Steamer* Commodore

I

None of them knew the color of the sky. Their eyes glanced level, and
were fastened upon the waves that swept toward them. These waves were
of the hue of slate, save for the tops, which were of foaming white, and all
of the men knew the colors of the sea. The horizon narrowed and widened,
and dipped and rose, and at all times its edge was jagged with waves that
seemed thrust up in points like rocks.

Many a man ought to have a bathtub larger than the boat which here
rode upon the sea. These waves were most wrongfully and barbarously
abrupt and tall, and each froth-top was a problem in small-boat navigation.

The cook squatted in the bottom and looked with both eyes at the six
inches of gunwale which separated him from the ocean. His sleeves were
rolled over his fat forearms, and the two flaps of his unbuttoned vest dangled as he bent to bail out the boat. Often he said, "Gawd! that was a
narrow clip." As he remarked it he invariably gazed eastward over the
broken sea.

The oiler, steering with one of the two oars in the boat, sometimes raised
himself suddenly to keep clear of water that swirled in over the stern. It
was a thin little oar, and it seemed often ready to snap.

The correspondent, pulling at the other oar, watched the waves and
wondered why he was there.

The injured captain, lying in the bow, was at this time buried in that
profound dejection and indifference which comes, temporarily at least, to
even the bravest and most enduring when, willy-nilly, the firm fails, the
army loses, the ship goes down. The mind of the master of a vessel is
rooted deep in the timbers of her, though he command for a day or a
decade; and this captain had on him the stern impression of a scene in the

greys of dawn of seven turned faces, and later a stump of a topmast with a white ball on it, that slashed to and fro at the waves, went low and lower, and down. Thereafter there was something strange in his voice. Although steady, it was deep with mourning, and of a quality beyond oration or tears.

"Keep 'er a little more south, Billie," said he.

"A little more south, sir," said the oiler in the stern.

A seat in this boat was not unlike a seat upon a bucking broncho, and by the same token a broncho is not much smaller. The craft pranced and reared and plunged like an animal. As each wave came, and she rose for it, she seemed like a horse making at a fence outrageously high. The manner of her scramble over these walls of water is a mystic thing, and, moreover, at the top of them were ordinarily these problems in white water, the foam racing down from the summit of each wave requiring a new leap, and a leap from the air. Then, after scornfully bumping a crest, she would slide and race and splash down a long incline, and arrive bobbing and nodding in front of the next menace.

A singular disadvantage of the sea lies in the fact that after successfuly surmounting one wave you discover that there is another behind it just as important and just as nervously anxious to do something effective in the way of swamping boats. In a ten-foot dinghy one can get an idea of the resources of the sea in the line of waves that is not probable to the average experience, which is never at sea in a dinghy. As each salty wall of water approached, it shut all else from the view of the men in the boat, and it was not difficult to imagine that this particular wave was the final outburst of the ocean, the last effort of the grim water. There was a terrible grace in the move of the waves, and they came in silence, save for the snarling of the crests.

In the wan light the faces of the men must have been gray. Their eyes must have glinted in strange ways as they gazed steadily astern. Viewed from a balcony, the whole thing would, doubtless, have been weirdly picturesque. But the men in the boat had no time to see it, and if they had had leisure, there were other things to occupy their minds. The sun swung steadily up the sky, and they knew it was broad day because the color of the sea changed from slate to emerald-green streaked with amber lights, and the foam was like tumbling snow. The process of the breaking day was unknown to them. They were aware only of this effect upon the color of the waves that rolled toward them.

In disjointed sentences the cook and the correspondent argued as to the difference between a life-saving station and a house of refuge. The cook had said: "There's a house of refuge just north of the Mosquito Inlet Light, and as soon as they see us they'll come off in their boat and pick us up."

"As soon as who see us?" said the correspondent.

"The crew," said the cook.

"Houses of refuge don't have crews," said the correspondent. "As I understand them, they are only places where clothes and grub are stored for the benefit of shipwrecked people. They don't carry crews."

"Oh, yes, they do," said the cook.

"No, they don't," said the correspondent.

"Well, we're not there yet, anyhow," said the oiler, in the stern.

"Well," said the cook, "perhaps it's not a house of refuge that I'm thinking of as being near Mosquito Inlet Light; perhaps it's a life saving station."

"We're not there yet," said the oiler in the stern.

II

As the boat bounced from the top to each wave the wind tore through the hair of the hatless men, and as the craft plopped her stern down again the spray splashed past them. The crest of each of these waves was a hill, from the top of which the men surveyed for a moment a broad tumultuous expanse, shining and wind-riven. It was probably splendid, it was probably glorious, this play of the free sea, wild with lights of emerald and white and amber.

"Bully good thing it's an on-shore wind," said the cook. "If not, where would we be? Wouldn't have a show."

"That's right," said the correspondent.

The busy oiler nodded his assent.

Then the captain, in the bow, chuckled in a way that expressed humor, contempt, tragedy, all in one. "Do you think we've got much of a show now, boys?" said he.

Whereupon the three were silent, save for a trifle of hemming and hawing. To express any particular optimism at this time they felt to be childish and stupid, but they all doubtless possessed this sense of the situation in their minds. A young man thinks doggedly at such times. On the other hand, the ethics of their condition was decidedly against any open suggestion of hopelessness. So they were silent.

"Oh, well," said the captain, soothing his children, "we'll get ashore all right."

But there was that in his tone which made them think; so the oiler quoth, "Yes! if this wind holds."

The cook was bailing. "Yes! if we don't catch hell in the surf."

Canton-flannel gulls flew near and far. Sometimes they sat down on the sea, near patches of brown seaweed that rolled over the waves with a movement like carpets on a line in a gale. The birds sat comfortably in groups, and they were envied by some in the dinghy, for the wrath of the sea was no more to them than it was to a covey of prairie chickens a thousand miles inland. Often they came very close and stared at the men with black bead-like eyes. At these times they were uncanny and sinister in their unblinking scrutiny, and the men hooted angrily at them, telling them to be gone. One came, and evidently decided to alight on the top of the captain's head. The bird flew parallel to the boat and did not circle, but made short sidelong jumps in the air in chicken fashion. His black eyes were wistfully fixed upon the captain's head. "Ugly brute," said the oiler to the bird. You look as if you were made with a jackknife." The cook and the correspondent swore darkly at the creature. The captain naturally wished to knock it away with the end of the heavy painter, but he did not dare do it, because anything resembling an emphatic gesture would have capsized this freighted boat; and so, with his open hand, the captain gently and carefully waved the gull away. After it had been discouraged from the pursuit the captain breathed easier on account of his hair, and others breathed easier because the bird struck their minds at this time as being somehow gruesome and ominous.

In the meantime the oiler and the correspondent rowed. And also they rowed. They sat together in the same seat, and each rowed an oar. Then the oiler took both oars; then the correspondent took both oars; then the oiler; then the correspondent. They rowed and they rowed. The very ticklish part of the business was when the time came for the reclining one in the stern to take his turn at the oars. By the very last star of truth, it is easier to steal eggs from under a hen then it was to change seats in the dinghy. First the man in the stern slid his hand along the thwart and moved with care, as if he were of Sèvres. Then the man in the rowing-seat slid his hand along the other thwart. It was all done with the most extraordinary care. As the two sidled past each other, the whole party kept watchful eyes on the coming wave, and the captain cried: "Look out, now! Steady, there!"

The brown mats of seaweed that appeared from time to time were like islands, bits of earth. They were travelling, apparently, neither one way nor the other. They were, to all intents, stationary. They informed the men in the boat that it was making progress slowly toward the land.

The captain, rearing cautiously in the bow after the dinghy soared on a great swell, said that he had seen the lighthouse at Mosquito Inlet. Presently the cook remarked that he had seen it. The correspondent was at the oars then, and for some reason he too wished to look at the lighthouse; but his back was toward the far shore, and the waves were important, and for some time he could not seize an opportunity to turn his head. But at last there came a wave more gentle than the others, and when at the crest of it he swiftly scoured the western horizon.

"See it?" said the captain.

"No," said the correspondent, slowly; "I didn't see anything."

"Look again," said the captain. He pointed. "It's exactly in that direction."

At the top of another wave the correspondent did as he was bid, and this time his eyes chanced on a small, still thing on the edge of the swaying horizon. It was precisely like the point of a pin. It took an anxious eye to find a lighthouse so tiny.

"Think we'll make it, Captain?"

"If this wind holds and the boat don't swamp, we can't do much else," said the captain.

The little boat, lifted by each towering sea and splashed viciously by the crests, made progress that in the absence of seaweed was not apparent to those in her. She seemed just a wee thing wallowing, miraculously top up, at the mercy of five oceans. Occasionally a great spread of water, like white flames, swarmed into her.

"Bail her, cook," said the captain, serenely.

"All right, Captain," said the cheerful cook.

III

It would be difficult to describe the subtle brotherhood of men that was here established on the seas. No one said that it was so. No one mentioned it. But it dwelt in the boat, and each man felt it warm him. They were a captain, an oiler, a cook, and a correspondent, and they were friends— friends in a more curiously iron-bound degree than may be common. The hurt captain, lying against the water-jar in the bow, spoke always in a low voice and calmly; but he could never command a more ready and swiftly obedient crew then the motley three of the dinghy. It was more than a mere recognition of what was best for the common safety. There was surely in it a quality that was personal and heart-felt. And after this devotion to the commander of the boat, there was this comradeship, that the correspondent, for instance, who had been taught to be cynical of men, knew even at the time was the best experience of his life. But no one said that it was so. No one mentioned it.

"I wish we had a sail," remarked the captain. "We might try my overcoat on the end of an oar, and give you two boys a chance to rest." So the cook and the correspondent held the mast and spread wide the overcoat; the oiler steered; and the little boat made good way with her new rig. Sometimes the oiler had to scull sharply to keep a sea from breaking into the boat, but otherwise sailing was a success.

Meanwhile the lighthouse had been growing slowly larger. It had now almost assumed color, and appeared like a little gray shadow on the sky. The man at the oars could not be prevented from turning his head rather often to try for a glimpse of this little grey shadow.

At last, from the top of each wave, the men in the tossing boat could see land. Even as the lighthouse was an upright shadow on the sky, this land seemed but a long black shadow on the sea. It certainly was thinner than paper. "We must be about opposite New Smyrna," said the cook, who had coasted this shore often in schooners. "Captain, by the way, I believe they abandoned that life-saving station there about a year ago."

"Did they?" said the captain.

The wind slowly died away. The cook and the correspondent were not now obliged to slave in order to hold high the oar. But the waves continued their old impetuous swooping at the dinghy, and the little craft, no longer under way, struggled woundily over them. The oiler or the correspondent took the oars again.

Shipwrecks are apropos of nothing. If men could only train for them and have them occur when the men had reached pink condition, there would be less drowning at sea. Of the four in the dinghy none had slept any time worth mentioning for two days and two nights previous to embarking in the dinghy, and in the excitement of clambering about the deck of a foundering ship they had also forgotten to eat heartily.

For these reasons, and for others, neither the oiler nor the correspondent was fond of rowing at this time. The correspondent wondered ingenuously how in the name of all that was sane could there be people who thought it amusing to row a boat. It was not an amusement; it was a diabolical punishment, and even a genius of mental aberrations could never conclude that it was anything but a horror to the muscles and a crime against the back. He mentioned to the boat in general how the amusement of rowing struck him, and the weary-faced oiler smiled in full sympathy. Previously to the foundering, by the way, the oiler had worked a double watch in the engine-room of the ship.

"Take her easy now, boys," said the captain. "Don't spend yourselves. If we have to run a surf you'll need all your strength, because we'll sure have to swim for it. Take your time."

Slowly the land arose from the sea. From a black line it became a line of black and a line of white—trees and sand. Finally the captain said that he could make our a house on the shore. "That's the house of refuge, sure," said the cook. "They'll see us before long, and come out after us."

The distant lighthouse reared high. "The keeper ought to be able to make us out now, if he's looking through a glass," said the captain. "He'll notify the life-saving people."

"None of those other boats have got ashore to give word of this wreck," said the oiler, in a low voice, "else the life-boat would be out hunting us."

Slowly and beautifully the land loomed out of the sea. The wind came again. It had veered from the northeast to the southeast. Finally a new sound struck the ears of the men in the boat. It was a low thunder of the surf on the shore. "We'll never be able to make the lighthouse now," said the captain. "Swing her head a little more north, Billie."

"A little more north, sir," said the oiler.

Whereupon the little boat turned her nose once more down the wind, and all but the oarsman watched the shore grow. Under the influence of this expansion doubt and direful apprehension were leaving the minds of the men. The management of the boat was still most absorbing, but it could not prevent a quiet cheerfulness. In an hour, perhaps, they would be ashore.

Their backbones had become thoroughly used to balancing in the boat, and they now rode this wild colt of a dinghy like circus men. The correspondent thought that he had been drenched to the skin, but happening to feel in the top pocket of his coat, he found therein eight cigars. Four of them were soaked with sea-water; four were perfectly scathless. After a search, somebody produced three dry matches; and thereupon the four waifs rode impudently in their little boat and, with an assurance of an impending rescue shining in their eyes, puffed at the big cigars, and judged well and ill of all men. Everybody took a drink of water.

IV

"Cook," remarked the captain, "there don't seem to be any signs of life about your house of refuge."

"No," replied the cook. "Funny they don't see us!"

A broad stretch of lowly coast lay before the eyes of the men. It was of low dunes topped with dark vegetation. The roar of the surf was plain, and sometimes they could see the white lip of a wave as it spun up the beach. A tiny house was blocked out black upon the sky. Southward, the slim lighthouse lifted its little gray length.

Tide, wind, and waves were swinging the dinghy northward. "Funny they don't see us," said the men.

The surf's roar was here dulled, but its tone was nevertheless thunderous and mighty. As the boat swam over the great rollers the men sat listening to this roar. "We'll swamp sure," said everybody.

It is fair to say here that there was not a life-saving station within twenty miles in either direction; but the men did not know this fact, and in consequence they made dark and opprobrious remarks concerning the eyesight of the nation's life-savers. Four scowling men sat in the dinghy and surpassed records in the invention of epithets.

"Funny they don't see us."

The light-heartedness of the former time had completely faded. To their sharpened minds it was easy to conjure pictures of all kinds of incompetency and blindness and, indeed, cowardice. There was the shore of the populous land, and it was bitter and bitter to them that from it came no sign.

"Well," said the captain, ultimately, "I suppose we'll have to make a try for ourselves. If we stay out here too long, we'll none of us have strength left to swim after the boat swamps."

And so the oiler, who was at the oars, turned the boat straight for the shore. There was a sudden tightening of muscles. There was some thinking.

"If we don't all get ashore," said the captain—"if we don't all get ashore, I suppose you fellows know where to send news of my finish?"

They then briefly exchanged some addresses and admonitions. As for the reflections of the men, there was a great deal of rage in them. Perchance they might be formulated thus: "If I am going to be drowned—if I am going to be drowned—if I am going to be drowned, why in the name of the seven mad gods who rule the sea, was I allowed to come thus far and contemplate sand and trees? Was I brought here merely to have my nose dragged away as I was about to nibble the sacred cheese of life? It is preposterous. If this old ninny-woman, Fate, cannot do better than this, she should be deprived of the management of men's fortunes. She is an old hen who knows not her intention. If she has decided to drown me, why did she not do it in the beginning and save me all this trouble? The whole affair is absurd. . . . but no; she cannot mean to drown me. She dare not drown me. She cannot drown me. Not after all this work." Afterward the man might have had an impulse to shake his fist at the clouds. "Just you drown me, now, and then hear what I call you!"

The billows that came at this time were more formidable. They seemed always just about to break and roll over the little boat in a turmoil of foam. There was a preparatory and long growl in the speech of them. No mind unused to the sea would have concluded that the dinghy could ascend these sheer heights in time. The shore was still afar. The oiler was a wily surfman. "Boys," he said swiftly, "she won't live three minutes more, and we're too far out to swim. Shall I take her to sea again, Captain?"

"Yes; go ahead!" said the captain.

This oiler, by a series of quick miracles and fast and steady oarsmanship, turned the boat in the middle of the surf and took her safely to sea again.

There was a considerable silence as the boat bumped over the furrowed sea to deeper water. Then somebody in gloom spoke: "Well, anyhow, they must have seen us from the shore by now."

The gulls went in slanting flight up the wind toward the gray, desolate east. A squall, marked by dingy clouds and clouds brick-red, like smoke from a burning building, appeared from the southeast.

"What do you think of those life-saving people? Ain't they peaches?"

"Funny they haven't seen us."

"Maybe they think we're out here for sport! Maybe they think we're fishin'. Maybe they think we're damned fools."

It was a long afternoon. A changed tide tried to force them southward, but wind and wave said northward. Far ahead, where coast-line, sea, and sky formed their mighty angle, there were little dots which seemed to indicate a city on the shore.

"St. Augustine?"

The captain shook his head. "Too near Mosquito Inlet."

And the oiler rowed, and then the correspondent rowed; then the oiler rowed. It was a weary business. The human back can become the seat of more aches and pains than are registered in books for the composite anatomy of a regiment. It is a limited area, but it can become the theater of innumerable muscular conflicts, tangles, wrenches, knots, and other comforts.

"Did you ever like to row, Billie?" asked the correspondent.

"No," said the oiler; "hang it!"

When one exchanged the rowing-seat for a place in the bottom of the boat, he suffered a bodily depression that caused him to be careless of everything save an obligation to wiggle one finger. There was cold sea-water swashing to and fro in the boat, and he lay in it. His head, pillowed on a thwart, was within an inch of the swirl of a wave-crest, and sometimes a particularly obstreperous sea came inboard and drenched him once more. But these matters did not annoy him. It is almost certain that if the boat had capsized he would have tumbled comfortably out upon the ocean as if he felt sure that it was a great soft mattress.

"Look! There's a man on the shore!"

"Where?"

"There! See 'im? See 'im?"

"Yes, sure! He's walking along."

"Now he's stopped. Look! He's facing us!"

"He's waving at us!"

"So he is! By thunder!"

"Ah, now we're all right! Now we're all right! There'll be a boat out here for us in half an hour."

"He's going on. He's running. He's going up to that house there."

The remote beach seemed lower than the sea, and it required a searching glance to discern the little black figure. The captain saw a floating stick, and they rowed to it. A bath towel was by some weird chance in the boat, and, tying this on the stick, the captain waved it. The oarsman did not dare turn his head, so he was obliged to ask questions.

"What's he doing now?"

"He's standing still again. He's looking, I think. . . . There he goes again—toward the house. . . . Now he's stopped again."

"Is he waving at us?"

"No, not now; he was, though."

"Look! There comes another man!"

"He's running."

"Look at him go, would you!"

"Why, he's on a bicycle. Now he's met the other man. They're both waving at us. Look!"

"There comes something up the beach."

"What the devil is that thing?"

"Why, it looks like a boat."

"Why, certainly, it's a boat."

"No; it's on wheels."

"Yes, so it is. Well, that must be the life-boat. They drag them along shore on a wagon."

"That's the life-boat, sure."

"No, by God, it's—it's an omnibus."

"I tell you it's a life-boat."

"It is not! I can see it plain. See? One of these big hotel omnibuses."

"By thunder, you're right. It's an omnibus, sure as fate. What do you suppose they are doing with an omnibus? Maybe they are going around collecting the life-crew, hey?"

"That's it, likely. Look! There's a fellow waving a little black flag. He's standing on the steps of the omnibus. There come those other two fellows. Now they're all talking together. Look at the fellow with the flag. Maybe he ain't waving it!"

"That ain't a flag, is it? That's his coat. Why, certainly, that's his coat."

"So it is; it's his coat. He's taken it off and is waving it around his head. But would you look at him swing it!"

"Oh, say, there isn't any life-saving station there. That's just a winter-resort hotel omninbus that has brought over some of the boarders to see us drown."

"What's that idiot with the coat mean? What's he signalling, anyhow?"

"It looks as if he was trying to tell us to go north. There must be a life-saving station up there."

"No; he thinks we're fishing. Just giving us a merry hand. See? Ah, there, Willie!"

"Well, I wish I could make something out of those signals. What do you suppose he means?"

"He don't mean anything; he's just playing."

"Well, if he'd just signal us to try the surf again, or to go to sea and wait, or go north, or go south, or go to hell, there would be some reason in it. But look at him! He just stands there and keeps his coat revolving like a wheel! The ass!"

"There come more people."

"Now there's quite a mob. Look! Isn't that a boat?"

"Where? Oh, I see where you mean. No, that's no boat."

"That fellow is still waving his coat."

"He must think we like to see him do that. Why don't he quit it? It don't mean anything."

"I don't know. I think he is trying to make us go north. It must be that there's a life-saving station there somewhere."

"Say, he ain't tired yet. Look at 'im wave!"

"Wonder how long he can keep that up. He's been revolving his coat ever since he caught sight of us. He's an idiot. Why aren't they getting men to bring a boat out? A fishing boat—one of those big yawls—could come out here all right. Why don't he do something?"

"Oh, it's all right now."

"They'll have a boat out here for us in less than no time, now that they've seen us."

A faint yellow tone came into the sky over the low land. The shadows on the sea slowly deepened. The wind bore coldness with it, and the men began to shiver.

"Holy smoke!" said one, allowing his voice to express his impious mood, "if we keep on monkeying out here! If we've got to flounder out here all night!"

"Oh, we'll never have to stay here all night! Don't you worry. They've seen us now, and it won't be long before they'll come chasing out after us."

The shore grew dusky. The man waving a coat blended gradually into this gloom, and it swallowed in the same manner the omnibus and the group of people. The spray, when it dashed uproariously over the side, made the voyagers shrink and swear like men who were being branded.

"I'd like to catch that chump who waved the coat. I feel like socking him one just for luck."

"Why? What did he do?"

"Oh, nothing, but then he seemed so damned cheerful."

In the meantime the oiler rowed, and then the correspondent rowed, and then the oiler rowed. Gray-faced and bowed forward, they mechanically, turn by turn, plied the leaden oars. The form of the lighthouse had vanished from the southern horizon, but finally a pale star appeared, just lifting from the sea. The streaked saffron in the west passed before the all-merging darkness, and the sea to the east was black. The land had vanished, and was expressed only by the low and drear thunder of the surf.

"If I am going to be drowned—if I am going to be drowned—if I am going to be drowned, why, in the name of the seven mad gods who rule the sea, was I allowed to come thus far and contemplate sand and trees? Was I brought here merely to have my nose dragged away as I was about to nibble the sacred cheese of life?"

The patient captain, drooped over the water-jar, was sometimes obliged to speak to the oarsman.

"Keep her head up! Keep her head up!"

"Keep her head up, sir." The voices were weary and low.

This was surely a quiet evening. All save the oarsman lay heavily and listlessly in the boat's bottom. As for him, his eyes were just capable of noting the tall black waves that swept forward in a most sinister silence, save for an occasional subdued growl of a crest.

The cook's head was on a thwart, and he looked without interest at the water under his nose. He was deep in other scenes. Finally he spoke. "Billie," he murmured, dreamfully, "what kind of pie do you like best?"

V

"Pie!" said the oiler and the correspondent, agitatedly. "Don't talk about those things, blast you!"

"Well," said the cook, "I was just thinking about ham sandwiches, and—"

A night on the sea in an open boat is a long night. As darkness settled finally, the shine of the light, lifting from the sea in the south, changed to full gold. On the northern horizon a new light appeared, a small bluish gleam on the edge of the waters. These two lights were the furniture of the world. Otherwise there was nothing but waves.

Two men huddled in the stern, and the distances were so magnificent in the dinghy that the rower was enabled to keep his feet partly warm by thrusting them under his companions. Their legs indeed extended far under the rowing-seat until they touched the feet of the captain forward. Sometimes, despite the efforts of the tired oarsman, a wave came piling into the boat, an icy wave of the night, and the chilling water soaked them anew. They would twist their bodies for a moment and groan, and sleep the dead sleep once more, while the water in the boat gurgled about them as the craft rocked.

The plan of the oiler and the correspondent was for one to row until he lost the ability, and then arouse the other from his sea-water couch in the bottom of the boat.

The oiler plied the oars until his head drooped forward and the overpowering sleep blinded him; and he rowed yet afterward. Then he touched a man in the bottom of the boat, and called his name. "Will you spell me for a little while?" he said, meekly.

"Sure, Billie," said the correspondent, awaking and dragging himself to a sitting position. They exchanged places carefully, and the oiler, cuddling down in the sea-water at the cook's side, seemed to go to sleep instantly.

The particular violence of the sea had ceased. The waves came without snarling. The obligation of the man at the oars was to keep the boat headed so that the tilt of the rollers would not capsize her, and to preserve her from filling when the crests rushed past. The black waves were silent and hard to be seen in the darkness. Often one was almost upon the boat before the oarsman was aware.

In a low voice the correspondent addressed the captain. He was not sure that the captain was awake, although this iron man seemed to be always awake. "Captain, shall I keep her making for that light north, sir?"

The same steady voice answered him. "Yes. Keep it about two points off the port bow."

The cook had tied a life-belt around himself in order to get even the warmth which this clumsy cork contrivance could donate, and he seemed almost stove-like when a rower, whose teeth invariably chattered wildly as soon as he ceased his labor, dropped down to sleep.

The correspondent, as he rowed, looked down at the two men sleeping underfoot. The cook's arm was around the oiler's shoulder, and, with their fragmentary clothing and haggard faces, they were the babes of the sea—a grotesque rendering of the old babes in the wood.

Later he must have grown stupid at his work, for suddenly there was a growling of water, and a crest came with a roar and a swash into the boat, and it was a wonder that it did not set the cook afloat in his life-belt. The cook continued to sleep, but the oiler sat up, blinking his eyes and shaking with the new cold.

"Oh, I'm awful sorry, Billie," said the correspondent, contritely.

"That's all right, old boy," said the oiler, and lay down again and was asleep.

Presently it seemed that even the captain dozed, and the correspondent thought that he was the one man afloat on all the ocean. The wind had a voice as it came over the waves, and it was sadder than the end.

There was a long, loud swishing astern of the boat, and a gleaming trail of phosphorescence, like blue flame, was furrowed on the black waters. It might have been made by a monstrous knife.

Then there came a stillness, while the correspondent breathed with open mouth and looked at the sea.

Suddenly there was another swish and another long flash of bluish light, and this time it was alongside the boat, and might almost have been reached with an oar. The correspondent saw an enormous fin speed like a shadow through the water, hurling the crystalline spray and leaving the long glowing trail.

The correspondent looked over his shoulder at the captain. His face was hidden, and he seemed to be asleep. He looked at the babes of the sea. They certainly were asleep. So, being bereft of sympathy, he leaned a little way to one side and swore softly into the sea.

But the thing did not then leave the vicinity of the boat. Ahead or astern, on one side or the other, at intervals long or short, fled the long sparkling streak, and there was to be heard the *whirroo* of the dark fin. The speed and power of the thing was greatly to be admired. It cut the water like a gigantic and keen projectile.

The presence of this biding thing did not affect the man with the same horror that it would if he had been a picnicker. He simply looked at the sea dully and swore in an undertone.

Nevertheless, it is true that he did not wish to be alone with the thing. He wished one of his companions to be awake by chance and keep him company with it. But the captain hung motionless over the water-jar, and the oiler and the cook in the bottom of the boat were plunged in slumber.

VI

"If I am going to be drowned—if I am going to be drowned—if I am going to be drowned, why, in the name of the seven mad gods who rule the sea, was I allowed to come thus far and contemplate sand and trees?"

During this dismal night, it may be remarked that a man would conclude that it was really the intention of the seven mad gods to drown him, despite the abominable injustice of it. For it was certainly an abominable injustice to drown a man who had worked so hard, so hard. The man felt it would be a crime most unnatural. Other people had drowned at sea since galleys swarmed with painted sails, but still—

When it occurs to a man that nature does not regard him as important, and that she feels she would not maim the universe by disposing of him, he at first wishes to throw bricks at the temple, and he hates deeply the fact that there are no bricks and no temples. Any visible expression of nature would surely be pelleted with his jeers.

Then, if there be no tangible thing to hoot, he feels, perhaps, the desire to confront a personification and indulge in pleas, bowed to one knee, and with hands supplicant, saying, "Yes, but I love myself."

A high cold star on a winter's night is the word he feels that she says to him. Thereafter he knows the pathos of his situation.

The men in the dinghy had not discussed these matters, but each had, no doubt, reflected upon them in silence and according to his mind. There was seldom any expression upon their faces save the general one of complete weariness. Speech was devoted to the business of the boat.

To chime the notes of his emotion, a verse mysteriously entered the correspondent's head. He had even forgotten that he had forgotten this verse, but it suddenly was in his mind.

A soldier of the Legion lay dying in Algiers;
There was lack of woman's nursing, there was dearth of woman's tears;
But a comrade stood beside him, and he took the comrade's hand,
And he said, "I never more shall see my own, my native land."

In his childhood the correspondent had been made acquainted with the fact that a soldier of the Legion lay dying in Algiers, but he had never regarded it as important. Myriads of his school-fellows had informed him of the soldier's plight, but the dinning had naturally ended by making him perfectly indifferent. He had never considered it his affair that a soldier of the Legion lay dying in Algiers, nor had it appeared to him as a matter for sorrow. It was less to him than the breaking of a pencil's point.

Now, however, it quaintly came to him as a human, living thing. It was no longer merely a picture of a few throes in the breast of a poet, meanwhile drinking tea and warming his feet at the grate; it was an actuality—stern, mournful, and fine.

The correspondent plainly saw the soldier. He lay on the sand with his feet out straight and still. While his pale left hand was upon his chest in an attempt to thwart the going of his life, the blood came between his fingers. In the far Algerian distance, a city of low square forms was set against a sky that was faint with the last sunset hues. The correspondent, plying the oars and dreaming of the slow and slower movements of the lips of the soldier, was moved by a profound and perfectly impersonal comprehension. He was sorry for the soldier of the Legion who lay dying in Algiers.

The thing which had followed the boat and waited had evidently grown bored at the delay. There was no longer to be heard the slash of the cutwater, and there was no longer the flame of the long trail. The light in the north still glimmered, but it was apparently no nearer to the boat. Sometimes the boom of the surf rang in the correspondent's ears, and he turned the craft seaward then and rowed harder. Southward, some one had evidently built a watch-fire on the beach. It was too low and too far to be seen, but it made a shimmering roseate reflection upon the bluff in back of it, and this could be discerned from the boat. The wind came stronger, and sometimes a wave suddenly raged out like a mountain cat, and there was to be seen the sheen and sparkle of a broken crest.

The captain, in the bow, moved on his water-jar and sat erect. "Pretty long night," he observed to the correspondent. He looked at the shore. "Those life-saving people take their time."

"Did you see that shark playing around?"

"Yes, I saw him. He was a big fellow, all right."

"Wish I had known you were awake."

Later the correspondent spoke into the bottom of the boat. "Billie!" There was a slow and gradual disentanglement. "Billie, will you spell me?"

"Sure," said the oiler.

As soon as the correspondent touched the cold, comfortable sea-water in the bottom of the boat and had huddled close to the cook's life-belt he was deep in sleep, despite the fact that his teeth played all the popular airs. This sleep was so good to him that it was but a moment before he heard a voice call his name in a tone that demonstrated the last stages of exhaustion. "Will you spell me?"

"Sure, Billie."

The light in the north had mysteriously vanished, but the correspondent took his course from the wide-awake captain.

Later in the night they took the boat farther out to sea, and the captain directed the cook to take one oar at the stern and keep the boat facing the seas. He was to call out if he should hear the thunder of the surf. This plan enabled the oiler and the correspondent to get respite together. "We'll give those boys a chance to get into shape again," said the captain. They curled down and, after a few preliminary chatterings and trembles, slept once more the dead sleep. Neither knew they had bequeathed to the cook the company of another shark, or perhaps the same shark.

As the boat caroused on the waves, spray occasionally bumped over the side and gave them a fresh soaking, but this had no power to break their repose. The ominous slash of the wind and the water affected them as it would have affected mummies.

"Boys," said the cook, with the notes of every reluctance in his voice, "she's drifted in pretty close. I guess one of you had better take her to sea again." The correspondent, aroused, heard the crash of the toppled crests.

As he was rowing, the captain gave him some whiskey-and-water, and this steadied the chills out of him. "If I ever get ashore and anybody shows me even a photograph of an oar—"

At last there was a short conversation.

"Billie! . . . Billie, will you spell me?"

"Sure," said the oiler.

VII

When the correspondent again opened his eyes, the sea and the sky were each of the grey hue of the dawning. Later, carmine and gold was painted upon the waters. The morning appeared finally, in its splendor, with a sky of pure blue, and the sunlight flamed on the tips of the waves.

On the distant dunes were set many little black cottages, and a tall white windmill reared above them. No man, nor dog, nor bicycle appeared on the beach. The cottages might have formed a deserted village.

The voyagers scanned the shore. A conference was held in the boat. "Well," said the captain, "if no help is coming, we might better try a run through the surf right away. If we stay out here much longer we will be too weak to do anything for ourselves at all." The others silently acquiesced in this reasoning. The boat was headed for the beach. The correspondent wondered if none ever ascended the tall wind-tower, and if then they never looked seaward. This tower was a giant, standing with its back to the plight of the ants. It represented in a degree, to the correspondent, the serenity of nature amid the struggles of the individual—nature in the wind, and nature in the vision of men. She did not seem cruel to him then, nor beneficent, nor treacherous, nor wise. But she was indifferent, flatly indifferent. It is, perhaps, plausible that a man in this situation, impressed with the unconcern of the universe, should see the innumerable flaws of his life, and have them taste wickedly in his mind, and wish for another chance. A distinction between right and wrong seems absurdly clear to him, then, in this new ignorance of the grave-edge, and he understands that if he were given another opportunity he would mend his conduct and his words, and be better and brighter during an introduction or at a tea.

"Now, boys," said the captain, "she is going to swamp sure. All we can do is to work her in as far as possible, and then when she swamps, pile out and scramble for the beach. Keep cool now, and don't jump until she swamps sure."

The oiler took the oars. Over his shoulders he scanned the surf. "Captain," he said, "I think I'd better bring her about and keep her head-on to the seas and back her in."

"All right, Billie," said the captain. "Back her in." The oiler swung the boat then, and, seated in the stern, the cook and the correspondent were obliged to look over their shoulders to contemplate the lonely and indifferent shore.

The monstrous inshore rollers heaved the boat high until the men were again enabled to see the white sheets of water scudding up the slanted beach. "We won't get in very close," said the captain. Each time a man could wrest his attention from the rollers, he turned his glance toward the shore, and in the expression of the eyes during his contemplation there was a singular quality. The correspondent, observing the others, knew that they were not afraid, but the full meaning of their glances was shrouded.

As for himself, he was too tired to grapple fundamentally with the fact. He tried to coerce his mind into thinking of it, but the mind was dominated at this time by the muscles, and the muscles said they did not care. It merely occurred to him that if he should drown it would be a shame.

There were no hurried words, no pallor, no plain agitation. The men simply looked at the shore. "Now, remember to get well clear of the boat when you jump," said the captain.

Seaward the crest of a roller suddenly fell with a thunderous crash, and the long white comber came roaring down upon the boat.

"Steady now," said the captain. The men were silent. They turned their eyes from the shore to the comber and waited. The boat slid up the incline, leaped at the furious top, bounced over it, and swung down the long back of the wave. Some water had been shipped, and the cook bailed it out.

But the next crest crashed also. The tumbling, boiling flood of white water caught the boat and whirled it almost perpendicular. Water swarmed in from all sides. The correspondent had his hands on the gunwale at this time, and when the water entered at that place he swiftly withdrew his fingers, as if he objected to wetting them.

The little boat, drunken with this weight of water, reeled and snuggled deeper into the sea.

"Bail her out, cook! Bail her out!" said the captain.

"All right, Captain," said the cook.

"Now, boys, the next one will do for us sure," said the oiler. "Mind to jump clear of the boat."

The third wave moved forward, huge, furious, implacable. It fairly swallowed the dinghy, and almost simultaneously the men tumbled into the sea. A piece of life-belt had lain in the bottom of the boat, and as the correspondent went overboard he held this to his chest with his left hand.

The January water was icy, and he reflected immediately that it was colder than he had expected to find it off the coast of Florida. This appeared to his dazed mind as a fact important enough to be noted at the time. The coldness of the water was sad; it was tragic. This fact was somehow mixed and confused with his opinion of his own situation, so that it seemed almost a proper reason for tears. The water was cold.

When he came to the surface he was conscious of little but the noisy water. Afterward he saw his companions in the sea. The oiler was ahead in the race. He was swimming strongly and rapidly. Off to the correspondent's left, the cook's great white and corked back bulged out of the water; and in the rear the captain was hanging with his good one hand to the keel of the overturned dinghy.

There is a certain immovable quality to a shore, and the correspondent wondered at it amid the confusion of the sea.

It seemed also very attractive; but the correspondent knew that it was a long journey, and he paddled leisurely. The piece of life-preserver lay under him, and sometimes he whirled down the incline of a wave as if he were on a hand-sled.

But finally he arrived at a place in the sea where travel was beset with difficulty. He did not pause swimming to inquire what manner of current had caught him, but there his progress ceased. The shore was set before him like a bit of scenery on a stage, and he looked at it and understood with his eyes each detail of it.

As the cook passed, much farther to the left, the captain was calling to him, "Turn over on your back, cook! Turn over on your back and use the oar."

"All right, sir." The cook turned on his back, and, paddling with an oar, went ahead as if he were a canoe.

Presently the boat also passed to the left of the correspondent, with the captain clinging with one hand to the keel. He would have appeared like a man raising himself to look over a board fence if it were not for the extraordinary gymnastics of the boat. The correspondent marvelled that the captain could still hold to it.

They passed on nearer to shore—the oiler, the cook, the captain—and following them went the water-jar, bouncing gaily over the seas.

The correspondent remained in the grip of this strange new enemy, a current. The shore, with its white slope of sand and its green bluff topped with little silent cottages, was spread like a picture before him. It was very near to him then, but he was impressed as one who, in a gallery, looks at a scene from Brittany or Algiers.

He thought: "I am going to drown? Can it be possible? Can it be possible? Can it be possible?" Perhaps an individual must consider his own death to be the final phenomenon of nature.

But later a wave perhaps whirled him out of this small deadly current, for he found suddenly that he could again make progress toward the shore. Later still he was aware that the captain, clinging with one hand to the keel of the dinghy, had his face turned away from the shore and toward him, and was calling his name. "Come to the boat! Come to the boat!"

In his struggle to reach the captain and the boat, he reflected that when one gets properly wearied drowning must really be a comfortable arrangement—a cessation of hostilities accompanied by a large degree of relief; and he was glad of it, for the main thing in his mind for some moments had been horror of the temporary agony. He did not wish to be hurt.

Presently he saw a man running along the shore. He was undressing with most remarkable speed. Coat, trousers, shirt, everything flew magically off him.

"Come to the boat!" called the captain.

"All right, Captain." As the correspondent paddled, he saw the captain let himself down to bottom and leave the boat. Then the correspondent performed his one little marvel of the voyage. A large wave caught him and flung him with ease and supreme speed completely over the boat and far beyond it. It struck him even then as an event in gymnastics and a true miracle of the sea. An overturned boat in the surf is not a plaything to a swimming man.

The correspondent arrived in water that reached only to his waist, but his condition did not enable him to stand for more than a moment. Each wave knocked him into a heap, and the undertow pulled at him.

Then he saw the man who had been running and undressing, and undressing and running, come bounding into the water. He dragged ashore the cook, and then waded toward the captain; but the captain waved him away and sent him to the correspondent. He was naked—naked as a tree in winter; but a halo was about his head, and he shone like a saint. He gave a strong pull, and a long drag, and a bully heave at the correspondent's hand. The correspondent, schooled in the minor formulae, said, "Thanks, old man." But suddenly the man cried, "What's that?" He pointed a swift finger. The correspondent said, "Go."

In the shallows, face downward, lay the oiler. His forehead touched sand that was periodically, between each wave, clear of the sea.

The correspondent did not know all that transpired afterward. When he achieved safe ground he fell, striking the sand with each particular part of his body. It was as if he had dropped from a roof, but the thud was grateful to him.

It seems that instantly the beach was populated with men with blankets, clothes, and flasks, and women with coffee-pots and all the remedies sacred to their minds. The welcome of the land to the men from the sea was warm and generous; but a still and dripping shape was carried slowly up the beach, and the land's welcome for it could only be the different and sinister hospitality of the grave.

When it came night, the white waves paced to and fro in the moonlight, and the wind brought the sound of the great sea's voice to the men on the shore, and they felt that they could then be interpreters.

QUESTIONS

"The Open Boat"

1. Explain the first line of the story. Why don't any of the men know "the colour of the sky"?

2. From what point of view is "The Open Boat" told? Why do you think Crane chose to narrate the story from this particular angle? Is this perspective maintained uniformly throughout the story, or are there any lapses—places where the author gives us information inconsistent with the prevailing point of view?

3. How would you describe the central conflict in this story? Who or what functions as the antagonist?

4. What is the quest in this story? What ordeals must the four men in the boat undergo to reach their goal; what "road of trials" must they travel?

5. How is the natural world portrayed in this story? Is it malignant, hostile, or merely indifferent? Is it described in largely negative terms, or is there anything beautiful, even sublime, about it?

6. Describe the four men in the boat. How are they typical, rather than highly individualized, characters? What is Crane's purpose in making them typical characters? Why does he refer to them, for the most part, by occupation rather than by name?

7. Discuss the use of irony in this story. Where is it found, and what is its function?

8. Look at the beginning of Section VI. What bitter, infuriating thought keeps running through the correspondent's mind? What does their experience teach the men about their place and importance in the universe—about the "pathos of their situation"? Does anything redeem their situation from utter bleakness? What is it about their ordeal that makes it, for the correspondent, "the best experience of his life"?

9. Look at the passage about "the soldier of the Legion who lay dying in Algiers." What is its significance? Why does the correspondent suddenly recall the little verse?

10. Why does Crane have the oiler, the most powerful man in the boat, drown at the end of the story? What does the last line of the story mean?

11. The following is a short poem by Stephen Crane, from *War Is Kind:*

> A man said to the universe:
> "Sir, I exist!"
> "However," replied the universe,
> "The fact has not created in me
> A sense of obligation."

Do you see any connection between this poem and "The Open Boat"? How are they thematically related?

12. In what way does Crane use the situation in this story—four helpless people trapped in a tiny boat and tossed about by immense, uncontrollable, unknowable forces—as a metaphor for the human condition? In what sense are all of us in a similar situation?

13. Critics Michael Timko and Clinton F. Oliver have written, " 'The Open Boat' takes on an almost mythic quality as Crane makes the 'adventure' of the men seem basically elemental and yet, because of its very lack of complexity, its true simplicity and poignancy, profoundly moving. The narrative takes on a starkness and directness of myth." Discuss this observation. Do you think it is valid?

Idiots First

BERNARD MALAMUD

The thick ticking of the tin clock stopped. Mendel, dozing in the dark, awoke in fright. The pain returned as he listened. He drew on his cold embittered clothing, and wasted minutes sitting at the edge of the bed.

"Isaac," he ultimately sighed.

In the kitchen, Isaac, his astonished mouth open, held six peanuts in his palm. He placed each on the table. "One . . . two . . . nine."

He gathered each peanut and appeared in the doorway. Mendel, in loose hat and long overcoat, still sat on the bed. Isaac watched with small eyes and ears, thick hair graying the sides of his head.

"Schlaf," he nasally said.

"No," muttered Mendel. As if stifling he rose. "Come, Isaac."

He wound his old watch though the sight of the stopped clock nauseated him.

Isaac wanted to hold it to his ear.

"No, it's late." Mendel put the watch carefully away. In the drawer he found the little paper bag of crumpled ones and fives and slipped it into his overcoat pocket. He helped Isaac on with his coat.

Isaac looked at one dark window, then at the other. Mendel stared at both blank windows.

They went slowly down the darkly lit stairs, Mendel first, Isaac watching the moving shadows on the wall. To one long shadow he offered a peanut.

"Hungrig."

In the vestibule the old man gazed through the thin glass. The November night was cold and bleak. Opening the door he cautiously thrust his head out. Though he saw nothing he quickly shut the door.

"Ginzburg, that he came to see me yesterday," he whispered in Isaac's ear.

Isaac sucked air.

"You know who I mean?"

Isaac combed his chin with his fingers.

"That's the one, with the black whiskers. Don't talk to him or go with him if he asks you."

Isaac moaned.

"Young people he don't bother so much," Mendel said in afterthought.

It was suppertime and the street was empty but the store windows dimly lit their way to the corner. They crossed the deserted street and went on. Isaac, with a happy cry, pointed to the three golden balls. Mendel smiled but was exhausted when they got to the pawnshop.

The pawnbroker, a red-bearded man with black horn-rimmed glasses, was eating a whitefish at the rear of the store. He craned his head, saw them, and settled back to sip his tea.

In five minutes he came forward, patting his shapeless lips with a large white handkerchief.

Mendel, breathing heavily, handed him the worn gold watch. The pawnbroker, raising his glasses, screwed in his eyepiece. He turned the watch over once. "Eight dollars."

The dying man wet his cracked lips. "I must have thirty-five."

"So go to Rothschild."

"Cost me myself sixty."

"In 1905." The pawnbroker handed back the watch. It had stopped ticking. Mendel wound it slowly. It ticked hollowly.

"Isaac must go to my uncle that he lives in California."

"It's a free country," said the pawnbroker.

Isaac, watching a banjo, snickered.

"What's the matter with him?" the pawnbroker asked.

"So let be eight dollars," muttered Mendel, "but where will I get the rest till tonight?"

"How much for my hat and coat?" he asked.

"No sale." The pawnbroker went behind the cage and wrote out a ticket. He locked the watch in a small drawer but Mendel still heard it ticking.

In the street he slipped the eight dollars into the paper bag, then searched in his pockets for a scrap of writing. Finding it, he strained to read the address by the light of the street lamp.

As they trudged to the subway, Mendel pointed to the sprinkled sky.

"Isaac, look how many stars are tonight."

"Eggs," said Isaac.

"First we will go to Mr. Fishbein, after we will eat."

They got off the train in upper Manhattan and had to walk several blocks before they located Fishbein's house.

"A regular palace," Mendel murmured, looking forward to a moment's warmth.

Isaac stared uneasily at the heavy door of the house.

Mendel rang. The servant, a man with long sideburns, came to the door and said Mr. and Mrs. Fishbein were dining and could see no one.

"He should eat in peace but we will wait till he finishes."

"Come back tomorrow morning. Tomorrow morning Mr. Fishbein will talk to you. He don't do business or charity at this time of the night."

"Charity I am not interested—"

"Come back tomorrow."

"Tell him it's life or death—"

"Whose life or death?"

"So if not his, then mine."

"Don't be such a big smart aleck."

"Look me in my face," said Mendel, "and tell me if I got time till to-morrow morning?"

The servant stared at him, then at Isaac, and reluctantly let them in.

The foyer was a vast high-ceilinged room with many oil paintings on the walls, voluminous silken draperies, a thick flowered rug at foot, and a marble staircase.

Mr. Fishbein, a paunchy bald-headed man with hairy nostrils and small patent leather feet, ran lightly down the stairs, a large napkin tucked under a tuxedo coat button. He stopped on the fifth step from the bottom and examined his visitors.

"Who comes on Friday night to a man that he has guests, to spoil him his supper?"

"Excuse me that I bother you, Mr. Fishbein," Mendel said. "If I didn't come now I couldn't come tomorrow."

"Without more preliminaries, please state your business. I'm a hungry man."

"Hungrig," wailed Isaac.

Fishbein adjusted his pince-nez. "What's the matter with him?"

"This is my son Isaac. He is like this all his life."

Isaac mewled.

"I am sending him to California."

"Mr. Fishbein don't contribute to personal pleasure trips."

"I am a sick man and he must go tonight on the train to my Uncle Leo."

"I never give to unorganized charity," Fishbein said, "but if you are hungry I will invite you downstairs in my kitchen. We having tonight chicken with stuffed derma."

"All I ask is thirty-five dollars for the train ticket to my uncle in California. I have already the rest."

"Who is your uncle? How old a man?"

"Eighty-one years, a long life to him."

Fishbein burst into laughter. "Eighty-one years and you are sending him this halfwit."

Mendel, flailing both arms, cried, "Please, without names."

Fishbein politely conceded.

"Where is open the door there we go in the house," the sick man said. "If you will kindly give me thirty-five dollars, God will bless you. What is thirty-five dollars to Mr. Fishbein? Nothing. To me, for my boy, is everything."

Fishbein drew himself up to his tallest height.

"Private contributions I don't make—only to institutions. This is my fixed policy."

Mendel sank to his creaking knees on the rug.

"Please, Mr. Fishbein, if not thirty-five, give maybe twenty."

"Levinson!" Fishbein angrily called.

The servant with the long sideburns appeared at the top of the stairs.

"Show this party where is the door—unless he wishes to partake food before leaving the premises."

"For what I got chicken won't cure it," Mendel said.

"This way if you please," said Levinson, descending.

Isaac assisted his father up.

"Take him to an institution," Fishbein advised over the marble balustrade. He ran quickly up the stairs and they were at once outside, buffeted by winds.

The walk to the subway was tedious. The wind blew mournfully. Mendel, breathless, glanced furtively at shadows. Isaac, clutching his peanuts in his frozen fist, clung to his father's side. They entered a small park to rest for a minute on a stone bench under a leafless two-branched tree. The thick right branch was raised, the thin left one hung down. A very pale moon rose slowly. So did a stranger as they approached the bench.

"Gut yuntif," he said hoarsely.

Mendel, drained of blood, waved his wasted arms. Isaac yowled sickly. Then a bell chimed and it was only ten. Mendel let out a piercing anguished cry as the bearded stranger disappeared into the bushes. A policeman came running, and though he beat the bushes with his nightstick, could turn up nothing. Mendel and Isaac hurried out of the little park. When Mendel glanced back the dead tree had its thin arm raised, the thick one down. He moaned.

They boarded a trolley, stopping at the home of a former friend, but he had died years ago. On the same block they went into a cafeteria and ordered two fried eggs for Isaac. The tables were crowded except where a heavy-set man sat eating soup with kasha. After one look at him they left in haste, although Isaac wept.

Mendel had another address on a slip of paper but the house was too far away, in Queens, so they stood in a doorway shivering.

What can I do, he frantically thought, in one short hour?

He remembered the furniture in the house. It was junk but might bring a few dollars. "Come, Isaac." They went once more to the pawnbroker's to talk to him, but the shop was dark and an iron gate—rings and gold watches glinting through it—was drawn tight across his place of business.

They huddled behind a telephone pole, both freezing. Isaac whimpered.

"See the big moon, Isaac. The whole sky is white."

He pointed but Isaac wouldn't look.

Mendel dreamed for a minute of the sky lit up, long sheets of light in all directions. Under the sky, in California, sat Uncle Leo drinking tea with lemon. Mendel felt warm but woke up cold.

Across the street stood an ancient brick synagogue.

He pounded on the huge door but no one appeared. He waited till he had breath and desperately knocked again. At last there were footsteps within, and the synagogue door creaked open on its massive brass hinges.

A darkly dressed sexton, holding a dripping candle, glared at them.

"Who knocks this time of night with so much noise on the synagogue door?"

Mendel told the sexton his troubles. "Please, I would like to speak to the rabbi."

"The rabbi is an old man. He sleeps now. His wife won't let you see him. Go home and come back tomorrow."

"To tomorrow I said goodbye already. I am a dying man."

Though the sexton seemed doubtful he pointed to an old wooden house next door. "In there he lives." He disappeared into the synagogue with his lit candle casting shadows around him.

Mendel, with Isaac clutching his sleeve, went up the wooden steps and rang the bell. After five minutes a big-faced, gray-haired bulky woman came out on the porch with a torn robe thrown over her nightdress. She emphatically said the rabbi was sleeping and could not be waked.

But as she was insisting, the rabbi himself tottered to the door. He listened a minute and said, "Who wants to see me let them come in."

They entered a cluttered room. The rabbi was an old skinny man with bent shoulders and a wisp of white beard. He wore a flannel nightgown and black skullcap; his feet were bare.

"Vey is mir," his wife muttered. "Put on shoes or tomorrow comes sure pneumonia." She was a woman with a big belly, years younger than her husband. Staring at Isaac, she turned away.

Mendel apologetically related his errand. "All I need more is thirty-five dollars."

"Thirty-five?" said the rabbi's wife. "Why not thirty-five thousand? Who has so much money? My husband is a poor rabbi. The doctors take away every penny."

"Dear friend," said the rabbi, "if I had I would give you."

"I got already seventy," Mendel said, heavy-hearted. "All I need more is thirty-five."

"God will give you," said the rabbi.

"In the grave," said Mendel. "I need tonight. Come, Isaac."

"Wait," called the rabbi.

He hurried inside, came out with a fur-lined caftan, and handed it to Mendel.

"Yascha," shrieked his wife, "not your new coat!"

"I got my old one. Who needs two coats for one body?"

"Yascha, I am screaming—"

"Who can go among poor people, tell me, in a new coat?"

"Yascha," she cried, "what can this man do with your coat? He needs tonight the money. The pawnbrokers are asleep."

"So let him wake them up."

"No." She grabbed the coat from Mendel.

He held on to a sleeve, wrestling her for the coat. Her I know, Mendel thought. "Shylock," he muttered. Her eyes glittered.

The rabbi groaned and tottered dizzily. His wife cried out as Mendel
yanked the coat from her hands.

"Run," cried the rabbi.

"Run, Isaac."

They ran out of the house and down the steps.

"Stop, you thief," called the rabbi's wife.

The rabbi pressed both hands to his temples and fell to the floor.

"Help!" his wife wept. "Heart attack! Help!"

But Mendel and Isaac ran through the streets with the rabbi's new fur-
lined caftan. After them noiselessly ran Ginzburg.

It was very late when Mendel bought the train ticket in the only booth
open.

There was no time to stop for a sandwich so Isaac ate his peanuts and
they hurried to the train in the vast deserted station.

"So in the morning," Mendel gasped as they ran, "there comes a man
that he sells sandwiches and coffee. Eat but get change. When reaches
California the train, will be waiting for you on the station Uncle Leo. If
you don't recognize him he will recognize you. Tell him I send best regards."

But when they arrived at the gate to the platform it was shut, the light
out.

Mendel, groaning, beat on the gate with his fists.

"Too late," said the uniformed ticket collector, a bulky, bearded man
with hairy nostrils and a fishy smell.

He pointed to the station clock. "Already past twelve."

"But I see standing there still the train," Mendel said, hopping in his
grief.

"It just left—in one more minute."

"A minute is enough. Just open the gate."

"Too late I told you."

Mendel socked his bony chest with both hands. "With my whole heart I
beg you this little favor."

"Favors you had enough already. For you the train is gone. You shoulda
been dead already at midnight. I told you that yesterday. This is the best
I can do."

"Ginzburg!" Mendel shrank from him.

"Who else?" The voice was metallic, eyes glittered, the expression amused.

"For myself," the old man begged. "I don't ask a thing. But what will
happen to my boy?"

Ginzburg shrugged slightly. "What will happen happens. This isn't my
responsibility. I got enough to think about without worrying about somebody on one cylinder."

"What then is your responsibility?"

"To create conditions. To make happen what happens. I ain't in the an-
thropomorphic business."

"Whatever business you in, where is your pity?"

"This ain't my commodity. The law is the law."

"Which law is this?"

"The cosmic universal law, goddamit, the one I got to follow myself."

"What kind of a law is it?" cried Mendel. "For God's sake, don't you understand what I went through in my life with this poor boy? Look at him. For thirty-nine years, since the day he was born, I wait for him to grow up, but he don't. Do you understand what this means in a father's heart? Why don't you let him go to his uncle?" His voice had risen and he was shouting.

Isaac mewled loudly.

"Better calm down or you'll hurt somebody's feelings," Ginzburg said with a wink toward Isaac.

"All my life," Mendel cried, his body trembling, "what did I have? I was poor. I suffered from my health. When I worked I worked too hard. When I didn't work was worse. My wife died a young woman. But I didn't ask from anybody nothing. Now I ask a small favor. Be so kind, Mr. Ginzburg."

The ticket collector was picking his teeth with a match stick.

"You ain't the only one, my friend, some got it worse than you. That's how it goes in this country."

"You dog you." Mendel lunged at Ginzburg's throat and began to choke. "You bastard, don't you understand what it means human?"

They struggled nose to nose, Ginzburg, though his astonished eyes bulged, began to laugh. "You pipsqueak nothing. I'll freeze you to pieces."

His eyes lit in rage and Mendel felt an unbearable cold like an icy dagger invading his body, all of his parts shriveling.

Now I die without helping Isaac.

A crowd gathered. Isaac yelped in fright.

Clinging to Ginzburg in his last agony, Mendel saw reflected in the ticket collector's eyes the depth of his terror. But he saw that Ginzburg, staring at himself in Mendel's eyes, saw mirrored in them the extent of his own awful wrath. He beheld a shimmering, starry, blinding light that produced darkness.

Ginzburg looked astounded. "Who me?"

His grip on the squirming old man slowly loosened, and Mendel, his heart barely beating, slumped to the ground.

"Go." Ginzburg muttered, "take him to the train."

"Let pass," he commanded a guard.

The crowd parted. Isaac helped his father up and they tottered down the steps to the platform where the train waited, lit and ready to go.

Mendel found Isaac a coach seat and hastily embraced him. "Help Uncle Leo, Isaakil. Also remember your father and mother."

"Be nice to him," he said to the conductor. "Show him where everything is."

He waited on the platform until the train began slowly to move. Isaac sat at the edge of his seat, his face strained in the direction of his journey.

When the train was gone, Mendel ascended the stairs to see what had become of Ginzburg.

QUESTIONS

"Idiots First"

1. In spite of his physical frailty, poverty, and relative insignificance (Ginzburg calls him a "pipsqueak"), Mendel, the main character of this story, emerges as a genuine hero. What makes him and his quest for the pathetically small sum of thirty-five dollars heroic?

2. Though "Idiots First" is set in an ordinary, even shabby, world—a world of tin alarm clocks, seedy pawn shops, and cheap cafeterias—it contains elements of the unreal, the magical, the fabulous. In fact, in many ways, it has the flavor of a folk tale, both in the way it is told and in the things that happen. What are some of the things that give this story its fabulous, folk-tale quality?

3. Who is Ginzburg? Why is Mendel fleeing him?

4. On the basis of this story, how would you characterize Malamud's view of life and human nature? Would you say that it is primarily gloomy or ultimately hopeful? Why?

5. How does Malamud create a sense of tension and suspense in this story? Does Mendel's desperate struggle, his quest to obtain the money he needs, have a thematic function? Is it strictly a narrative device to give momentum to the story and to hold the reader's interest, or does it reveal something important about the human condition? Explain.

6. Why does Ginzburg relent at the end of the story and agree to let Isaac on the train?

7. What is the meaning of the title? To what does it refer?

8. Compare this story to Hawthorne's "My Kinsman, Major Molineux." How do the two stories establish a similar mood or atmosphere? Are there any similarities in the kinds of characters and incidents they contain?

Big Boy Leaves Home

RICHARD WRIGHT

I

Yo mama don wear no drawers . . .

Clearly, the voice rose out of the woods, and died away. Like an echo another voice caught it up:

Ah seena when she pulled em off . . .

Another, shrill, cracking, adolescent:

N she washed 'em in alcohol . . .

Then a quartet of voices, blending in harmony, floated high above the tree tops:

N she hung 'em in the hall . . .

Laughing easily, four black boys came out of the woods into cleared pasture. They walked lollingly in bare feet, beating tangled vines and bushes with long sticks.

"Ah wished Ah knowed som mo lines t tha song."

"Me too."

"Yeah, when yuh gits t where she hangs em out in the hall yuh has t stop."

"Shucks, whut goes wid *hall*?"

"*Call.*"

"*Fall.*"

"Wall."
"Quall."

They threw themselves on the grass, laughing.
"Big Boy?"
"Huh?"
"Yuh know one thing?"
"Whut?"
"Yuh sho is crazy!"
"Crazy?"
"Yeah, yuh crazys a bed-bug!"
"Crazy bout whut?"
"Man, whoever hearda *quall?*"
"Yuh said yuh wanted something to go wid *hall*, didn't yuh?"
"Yeah, but whuts a *quall?*"
"Nigger, a *qualls* a *quall.*"
They laughed easily, catching and pulling long green blades of grass with
their toes.
"Waal, ef a *qualls* a *quall*, whut is a *quall?*"
"Oh, Ah know."
"Whut?"
"Tha ol song goes something like this:

> Yo mama don wear no drawers,
>   Ah seena when she pulled em off,
> N she washed em in alcohol,
>   N she hung em out in the hall,
>   N then she put em back on her QUALL!"

They laughed again. Their shoulders went flat to the earth, their knees
propped up, and their faces square to the sun.
"Big Boy, yuhs CRAZY!"
"Don ax me nothin else."
"Nigger, yuhs CRAZY!"
They fell silent, smiling, drooping the lids of their eyes softly against the
sunlight.
"Man, don the groun feel warm?"
"Jus lika bed."
"Jeeesus, Ah could stay here ferever."
"Me too."
"Ah kin feel that ol sun goin all thu me."
"Feels like mah bones is warm."
In the distance a train whistled mournfully.
"There goes number fo!"
"Hittin on all six!"

"Highballin it down the line!"
"Boun fer up Noth, Lawd, boun fer up Noth!"
They began to chant, pounding bare heels in the grass.

> Dis train boun fo Glory
> Dis train, Oh Hallelujah
> Dis train boun fo Glory
> Dis train, Oh Hallelujah
> Dis train boun fo Glory
> Ef yuh ride no need fer fret er worry
> Dis train, Oh Hallelujah
> Dis train . . .
>
> Dis train don carry no gambler
> Dis train, Oh, Hallelujah
> Dis train don carry no gambler
> Dis train, Oh Hallelujah
> Dis train don carry no gambler
> No fo day creeper er midnight rambler
> Dis train, Oh Hallelujah
> Dis train . . .

When the song ended they burst out laughing, thinking of a train bound
for Glory.
"Gee, thas a good ol song!"
"Huuuuummmmmmmmmman . . ."
"Whut?"
"Geeee whiiiiiiz . . ."
"Whut?"
"Somebody don let win! Das whut!"
Buck, Bobo and Lester jumped up. Big Boy stayed on the ground, feign-
ing sleep.
"Jeeesus, tha sho stinks!"
"Big Boy!"
Big Boy feigned to snore.
"Big Boy!"
Big Boy stirred as though in sleep.
Big Boy!"
"Hunh?"
"Yunh rotten inside!"
"Rotten?"
"Lawd, cant yuh smell it?"
"Smell whut?"
"Nigger, yuh mus gotta bad col!"
"Smell whut?"

"NIGGER, YUH BROKE WIN!"

Big Boy laughed and fell back on the grass, closing his eyes.

"The hen whut cackles is the hen whut laid the egg."

"We ain no hens."

"Yuh cackled, didnt yuh?"

The three moved off with noses turned up.

"C mon!"

"Where yuh-all goin?"

"T the creek fer a swim."

"Yeah, les swim."

"Naw buddy naw!" said Big Boy, slapping the air with a scornful palm.

"Aw, c mon! Don be a heel!"

"N git *lynched?* Hell naw!"

"He ain gonna see us."

"How yuh know?"

"Cause he ain."

"Yuh-all go on. Ahma stay right here," said Big Boy.

"Hell, let im stay! C mon, les go," said Buck.

The three walked off, swishing at grass and bushes with sticks. Big Boy looked lazily at their backs.

"Hey!"

Walking on, they glanced over their shoulders.

"Hey, niggers!"

"C mon!"

Big Boy grunted, picked up his stick, pulled to his feet, and stumbled off.

"Wait!"

"C mon!"

He ran, caught up with them, leaped upon their backs, bearing them to the ground.

"Quit, Big Boy!"

"Gawddam, nigger!"

"Git t hell offa me!"

Big Boy sprawled in the grass beside them, laughing and pounding his heels in the ground.

"Nigger, whut yuh think we is, hosses?"

"How come yuh awways hoppin on us?"

"Lissen, wes gonna double-team on yuh one of these days n beat yo ol ass good."

Big Boy smiled.

"Sho nough?"

"Yeah, don yuh like it?"

"We gonna beat yuh sos yuh cant walk!"

"N dare yuh t do nothing erbout it!"

Big Boy bared his teeth.

"C mon! Try it now!"

The three circled around him.

"Say, Buck, yuh grab his feets!"

"N yuh git his head, Lester!"

"N Bobo, yuh git berhin n grab his arms!"

Keeping more than arm's length, they circled round and round Big Boy.

"C mon!" said Big Boy, feinting at one and then the other.

Round and round they circled, but could not seem to get any closer. Big Boy stopped and braced his hands on his hips.

"Is all three of yuh-all scareda me?"

"Les git im some other time," said Bobo, grinning.

"Yeah, we kin ketch yuh when yuh ain thinkin," said Lester.

"We kin trick yuh," said Buck.

They laughed and walked together.

Big Boy belched.

"Ahm hongry," he said.

"Me too."

"Ah wished Ah hada big hot pota belly-busters!"

"Cooked wid some good ol salty ribs . . ."

"N some good ol egg cornbread . . ."

"N some buttermilk . . ."

"N some hot peach cobbler swimmin in juice . . ."

"Nigger, hush!"

They began to chant, emphasizing the rhythm by cutting at grass with sticks.

> Bye n bye
> Ah wanna piece of pie
> Pies too sweet
> Ah wanna piece of meat
> Meats too red
> Ah wanna piece of bread
> Breads too brown
> Ah wanna go t town
> Towns too far
> Ah wanna ketch a car
> Cars too fas
> Ah fall n break mah ass
> Ahll understan it better bye n bye . . .

They climbed over a barbed-wire fence and entered a stretch of thick woods. Big Boy was whistling softly, his eyes half-closed.

"LES GIT IM!"

Buck, Lester, and Bobo whirled, grabbed Big Boy about the neck, arms, and legs, bearing him to the ground. He grunted and kicked wildly as he went back into weeds.

"Hol im tight!"

"Git his arms! Git his arms!"

"Set on his legs so he cant kick!"

Big Boy puffed heavily, trying to get loose.

"WE GOT YUH NOW, GAWDDAMMIT, WE GOT YUH NOW!"

"Thas a Gawddam lie!" said Big Boy. He kicked, twisted, and clutched for a hold on one and then the other.

"Say, yuh-all hep me hol his arms!" said Bobo.

"Aw, we got this bastard now!" said Lester.

"Thas a Gawddam lie!" said Big Boy again.

"Say, yuh-all hep me hol his arms!" called Bobo.

Big Boy managed to encircle the neck of Bobo with his left arm. He tightened his elbow scissors-like and hissed through his teeth:

"Yuh got me, ain yuh?"

"Hol im!"

"Les beat this bastard's ass!"

"Say, hep me hol his *arms!* Hes got aholda mah *neck!*" cried Bobo.

Big Boy squeezed Bobo's neck and twisted his head to the ground.

"Yuh got me, ain yuh?"

"Quit, Big Boy, yuh choking me; yuh hurtin mah neck!" cried Bobo.

"Turn me loose!" said Big Boy.

"Ah ain got yuh! Its the others whut got yuh!" pleaded Bobo.

"Tell them others t git t hell offa me or ahma break yo neck," said Big Boy.

"Ssssay, yyyuh-all gggit ooooffa Bbig Boy. Hhhes got me," gurgled Bobo.

"Cant yuh hol im?"

"Nnaw, hhes ggot mmah nneck . . ."

Big Boy squeezed tighter.

"N Ahma break it too less yuh tell em t git t hell offa me!"

"Ttturn mmmeee lllloose," panted Bobo, tears gushing.

"Cant yuh hol im, Bobo?" asked Buck.

"Nnaw, yuh-all tturn im lloose, hhhes got mah nnneck . . ."

"Grab his neck, Bobo . . ."

"Ah cant; yugurgur . . ."

To save Bobo, Lester and Buck got up and ran to a safe distance. Big Boy released Bobo, who staggered to his feet, slobbering and trying to stretch a crick out of his neck.

"Shucks, nigger, yuh almos broke mah neck," whimpered Bobo.

"Ahm gonna break yo ass nex time," said Big Boy.

"Ef Bobo coulda hel yuh we woulda had yuh," yelled Lester.

"Ah wuznt gonna let im do that," said Big Boy.

They walked together again, swishing sticks.

"Yuh see," began Big Boy, "when a ganga guys jump on yuh, all yuh gotta do is jus put the heat on one of them n make im tell the others t let up, see?"

"Gee, that a good idee!"

"Yeah, thas a good idee!"

"But yuh almos broke mah neck, man," said Bobo.

"Ahma smart nigger," said Big Boy, thrusting out his chest.

II

They came to the swimming hole.

"Ah ain goin in," said Bobo.

"Done got scared?" asked Big Boy.

"Naw, Ah ain scared . . ."

"How come yuh ain goin in?"

"Yuh know ol man Harvey don erllow no niggers t swim in this hole."

"N jus las year he took a shot at Bob fer swimmin in here," said Lester.

"Shucks, ol man Harvey ain studyin bout us niggers," said Big Boy.

"Hes at home thinkin about his jelly-roll," said Buck.

They laughed.

"Buck, yo mins lowern a snakes belly," said Lester.

"Ol man Harveys too doggone ol t think erbout jelly-roll," said Big Boy.

"Hes dried up; all the saps done lef im," said Bobo.

"C mon, les go!" said Big Boy.

Bobo pointed.

"See tha sign over yonder?"

"Yeah."

"Whut it say?"

"NO TRESPASSIN," read Lester.

"Know whut tha mean?"

"Mean ain no dogs n niggers erllowed," said Buck.

"Waal, wes here now," said Big Boy. "Ef he ketched us even like this thered be trouble, so we just as waal go on in . . ."

"Ahm wid the nex one!"

"Ahll go ef anybody else goes!"

Big Boy looked carefully in all directions. Seeing nobody, he began jerking off his overalls.

"LAS ONE INS A OL DEAD DOG!"

"THAS YO MA!"

"THAS YO PA!"

"THAS BOTH YO MA N YO PA!"

They jerked off their clothes and threw them in a pile under a tree. Thirty seconds later they stood, black and naked, on the edge of the hole under a sloping embankment. Gingerly Big Boy touched the water with his foot.

"Man, this waters col," he said.

"Ahm gonna put mah cloes back on," said Bobo, withdrawing his foot.

Big Boy grabbed him about the waist.

"Like hell yuh is!"

"Git outta the way, nigger!" Bobo yelled.

"Throw im in!" said Lester.

"Duck im!"

Bobo crouched, spread his legs, and braced himself against Big Boy's body. Locked in each other's arms, they tussled on the edge of the hole, neither able to throw the other.

"C mon, les me n yuh push em in."

Laughing, Lester and Buck gave the two locked bodies a running push. Big Boy and Bobo splashed, sending up silver spray in the sunlight. When Big Boy's head came up he yelled:

"Yuh bastard!"

"Tha wuz yo ma yuh pushed!" said Bobo, shaking his head to clear the water from his eyes.

They did a surface dive, came up and struck out across the creek. The muddy water foamed. They swam back, waded into shallow water, breathing heavily and blinking eyes.

"C mon in!"

"Man, the waters fine!"

Lester and Buck hesitated.

"Les wet em," Big Boy whispered to Bobo.

Before Lester and Buck could back away, they were dripping wet from handsful of scooped water.

"Hey, quit!"

"Gawddam, nigger! Tha waters col!"

"C mon in!" called Big Boy.

"We jus as waal go on in now," said Buck.

"Look n see ef anybodys comin."

Kneeling, they squinted among the trees.

"Ain nobody."

"C mon, les go."

They waded in slowly, pausing each few steps to catch their breath. A desperate water battle began. Closing eyes and backing away, they shunted water into one another's faces with the flat palms of hands.

"Hey, cut it out!"

"Yeah, Ahm bout drownin!"

They came together in water up their navels, blowing and blinking. Big Boy ducked, upsetting Bobo.

"Look out, nigger!"

"Don holler so loud!"

"Yeah, they kin hear yo ol big mouth a mile erway."

"This waters too col fer me."

"Thas cause it rained yistiddy."

They swam across and back again.

"Ah wish we hada bigger place t swim in."

"The white folks got plenty swimmin pools n we ain got none."

"Ah useta swim in the ol Missippi when we lived in Vicksburg."

Big Boy put his head under the water and blew his breath. A sound came like that of a hippopotamus.

"C mon, les be hippos."

Each went to a corner of the creek and put his mouth just below the surface and blew like a hippopotamus. Tiring, they came and sat under the embankment.

"Look like Ah gotta chill."

"Me too."

"Les stay here n dry off."

"Jeeesus, Ahm col!"

They kept still in the sun, suppressing shivers. After some of the water had dried off their bodies they began to talk through clattering teeth.

"Whut would yuh do ef ol man Harveyd come erlong right now?"

"Run like hell!"

"Man, Ahd run so fas hed thinka black streaka lightnin shot pass im."

"But spose he hada gun?"

"Aw, nigger, shut up!"

They were silent. They ran their hands over wet, trembling legs, brushing water away. Then their eyes watched the sun sparkling on the restless creek.

Far away a train whistled.

"There goes number seven!"

"Heading fer up Noth!"

"Blazin it down the line!"

"Lawd, Ahm goin Noth some day."

"Me too, man."

"They say colored folks up Noth is got ekual rights."

They grew pensive. A black winged butterfly hovered at the water's edge. A bee droned. From somewhere came the sweet scent of honeysuckles. Dimly they could hear sparrows twittering in the woods. They rolled from side to side, letting sunshine dry their skins and warm their blood. They plucked blades of grass and chewed them.

"Oh!"

They looked up, their lips parting.

"Oh!"

A white woman, poised on the edge of the opposite embankment, stood directly in front of them, her hat in her hand and her hair lit by the sun.

"Its a woman!" whispered Big Boy in an underbreath. "A *white* woman!"

They stared, their hands instinctively covering their groins. Then they scrambled to their feet. The white woman backed slowly out of sight. They stood for a moment, looking at one another.

"Les git outta here!" Big Boy whispered.

"Wait till she goes erway."

"Les run, theyll ketch us here naked like this!"

"Mabbe theres a man wid her."

"C mon, les git our cloes," said Big Boy.

They waited a moment longer, listening.

"Whut t hell! Ahma git mah cloes," said Big Boy.

Grabbing at short tufts of grass, he climbed the embankment.

"Don run out there now!"

"C mon back, fool!"

Bobo hesitated. He looked at Big Boy, and then at Buck and Lester.

"Ahm goin wid Big Boy n git mah cloes," he said.

"Don run out there naked like tha, fool!" said Buck. "Yuh don know whos out there!"

Big Boy was climbing over the edge of the embankment.

"C mon," he whispered.

Bobo climbed after. Twenty-five feet away the woman stood. She had one hand over her mouth. Hanging by fingers, Buck and Lester peeped over the edge.

"C mon back; that womans scared," said Lester.

Big Boy stopped, puzzled. He looked at the woman. He looked at the bundle of clothes. Then he looked at Buck and Lester.

"C mon, les git our cloes!"

He made a step.

"Jim!" the woman screamed.

Big Boy stopped and looked around. His hands hung loosely at his sides. The woman, her eyes wide, her hand over her mouth, backed away to the tree where their clothes lay in a heap.

"Big Boy, come back n wait till shes gone!"

Bobo ran to Big Boy's side.

"Les go home! Theyll ketch us here," he urged.

Big Boy's throat felt tight.

"Lady, we wanna git our cloes," he said.

Buck and Lester climbed the embankment and stood indecisively. Big Boy ran toward the tree.

"Jim!" the woman screamed. "Jim! Jim!"

Black and naked, Big Boy stopped three feet from her.

"We wanna git our cloes," he said again, his words coming mechanically.

He made a motion.

"You go away! You go away! I tell you, you go away!"

Big Boy stopped again, afraid. Bobo ran and snatched the clothes. Buck and Lester tried to grab theirs out of his hands.

"You go away! You go away! You go away!" the woman screamed.

"Les go!" said Bobo, running toward the woods.

CRACK!

Lester grunted, stiffened, and pitched forward. His forehead struck a toe of the woman's shoes.

Bobo stopped, clutching the clothes. Buck whirled. Big Boy stared at Lester, his lips moving.

"Hes gotta gun; hes gotta gun!" yelled Buck, running wildly.

CRACK!

Buck stopped at the edge of the embankment, his head jerked backward, his body arched stiffly to one side; he toppled headlong, sending up a shower of bright spray to the sunlight. The creek bubbled.

Big Boy and Bobo backed away, their eyes fastened fearfully on a white man who was running toward them. He had a rifle and wore an army officer's uniform. He ran to the woman's side and grabbed her hand.

"You hurt, Bertha, you hurt?"

She stared at him and did not answer.

The man turned quickly. His face was red. He raised the rifle and pointed it at Bobo. Bobo ran back, holding the clothes in front of his chest.

"Don shoot me, Mistah, don shoot me . . ."

Big Boy lunged for the rifle, grabbing the barrel.

"You black sonofabitch!"

Big Boy clung desperately.

"Let go, you black bastard!"

The barrel pointed skyward.

CRACK!

The white man, taller and heavier, flung Big Boy to the ground. Bobo dropped the clothes, ran up, and jumped onto the white man's back.

"You black sonofbitches!"

The white man released the rifle, jerked Bobo to the ground, and began to batter the naked boy with his fists. Then Big Boy swung, striking the man in the mouth with the barrel. His teeth caved in and he fell, dazed. Bobo was on his feet.

"C mon, Big Boy, les go!"

Breathing hard, the white man got up and faced Big Boy. His lips were trembling, his neck and chin wet with blood. He spoke quietly.

"Give me that gun, boy!"

Big Boy leveled the rifle and backed away.

The white man advanced.

"Boy, I say give me that gun!"

Bobo had the clothes in his arms.

"Run, Big Boy, run!"

The man came at Big Boy.

"Ahll kill yuh; Ahll kill yuh!" said Big Boy.

His fingers fumbled for the trigger.

The man stopped, blinked, spat blood. His eyes were bewildered. His face whitened. Suddenly, he lunged for the rifle, his hands outstretched.

CRACK!

He fell forward on his face.

"Jim!"

Big Boy and Bobo turned in surprise to look at the woman.

"Jim!" she screamed again, and fell weakly at the foot of the tree.

Big Boy dropped the rifle, his eyes wide. He looked around. Bobo was crying and clutching the clothes.

"Big Boy, Big Boy . . ."

Big Boy looked at the rifle, started to pick up, but didn't. He seemed at
a loss. He looked at Lester, then at the white man; his eyes followed a thin
stream of blood that seeped to the ground.

"Yuh done killed him," mumbled Bobo.

"Les go home!"

Naked, they turned and ran toward the woods. When they reached the
barbed-wire fence they stopped.

"Les git our cloes on," said Big Boy.

They slipped quickly into overalls. Bobo held Lester's and Buck's clothes.

"Whut we gonna do wid these?"

Big Boy stared. His hands twitched.

"Leave em."

They climbed the fence and ran through the woods. Vines and leaves
switched their faces. Once Bobo tripped and fell.

"C mon!" said Big Boy.

Bobo started crying, blood streaming from his scratches.

"Ahm scared!"

"C mon! Don cry! We wanna git home fo they ketches us!"

"Ahm scared!" said Bobo again, his eyes full of tears.

Big Boy grabbed his hand and dragged him along.

"C mon!"

III

They stopped when they got to the end of the woods. They could see the
open road leading home, home to ma and pa. But they hung back, afraid.
The thick shadows cast from the trees were friendly and sheltering. But
the wide glare of sun stretching out over the fields was pitiless. They
crouched behind an old log.

"We gotta git home," said Big Boy.

"They's gonna lynch us," said Bobo, half-questioningly.

Big Boy did not answer.

"Theys gonna lynch us," said Bobo again.

Big Boy shuddered.

"Hush!" he said. He did not want to think of it. He could not think of
it; there was but one thought, and he clung to that one blindly. He had to
get home, home to ma and pa.

Their heads jerked up. Their ears had caught the rhythmic jingle of a
wagon. They fell to the ground and clung flat to the side of a log. Over the
crest of the hill came the top of a hat. A white face. Then shoulders in a
blue shirt. A wagon drawn by two horses pulled into full view.

Big Boy and Bobo held their breath, waiting. Their eyes followed the
wagon till it was lost in dust around a bend in the road.

"We gotta git home," said Big Boy.

"Ahm scared," said Bobo.

"C mon! Les keep t the fields."

They ran till they came to the cornfields. Then they went slower, for last year's corn stubbles bruised their feet.

They came in sight of a brickyard.

"Wait a minute," gasped Big Boy.

They stopped.

"Ahm goin on t mah home n yuh better go on t yos."

Bobo's eyes grew round.

"Ahm scared!"

"Yuh better go on!"

"Lemme go wid yuh; they'll ketch me . . ."

"Ef yuh kin git home mabbe yo folks kin hep yuh t git erway."

Big Boy started off. Bobo grabbed him.

"Lemme go wid yuh!"

Big Boy shook free.

"Ef yuh stay here theys gonna lynch yuh!" he yelled, running.

After he had gone about twenty-five yards he turned and looked; Bobo was flying through the woods like the wind.

Big Boy slowed when he came to the railroad. He wondered if he ought to go through the streets or down the track. He decided on the tracks. He could dodge a train better than a mob.

He trotted along the ties, looking ahead and back. His cheek itched, and he felt it. His hand came away smeared with blood. He wiped it nervously on his overalls.

When he came to his back fence he heaved himself over. He landed among a flock of startled chickens. A bantam rooster tried to spur him. He slipped and fell in front of the kitchen steps, grunting heavily. The ground was slick with greasy dishwater.

Panting, he stumbled through the doorway.

"Lawd, Big Boy, whuts wrong wid yuh?"

His mother stood gaping in the middle of the floor. Big Boy flopped wordlessly onto a stool, almost toppling over. Pots simmered on the stove. The kitchen smelled of food cooking.

"Whuts the matter, Big Boy?"

Mutely, he looked at her. Then he burst into tears. She came and felt the scratches on his face.

"Whut happened t yuh, Big Boy? Somebody been botherin yuh?"

"They after me, Ma! They after me . . ."

"Who!"

"Ah . . . Ah . . . We . . ."

"Big Boy, whuts wrong wid yuh?"

"He killed Lester n Buck," he muttered simply.

"Killed!"

"Yessum."

"Lester n Buck!"

"Yessum, Ma!"

"How killed?"

"He shot em, Ma!"

"Lawd Gawd in Heaven, have mercy on us all! This is mo trouble, mo trouble," she moaned, wringing her hands.

"N Ah killed im, Ma . . ."

She stared, trying to understand.

"Whut happened, Big Boy?"

"We tried t git our cloes from the tree . . ."

"Whut tree?"

"We wuz swimmin, Ma. N the white woman . . ."

"*White* woman? . . ."

"Yessum. She wuz at the swimmin hole . . ."

"Lawd have mercy! Ah knowed yuh boys wuz gonna keep on till yuh got into somethin like this!"

She ran into the hall.

"Lucy!"

"Mam?"

"C mere!"

"Mam?"

"C mere, Ah say!"

"Whutcha wan, Ma? Ahm sewin."

"Chile, will yuh c mere like Ah ast yuh?"

Lucy came to the door holding an unfinished apron in her hands. When she saw Big Boy's face she looked wildly at her mother.

"Whuts the matter?"

"Wheres Pa?"

"Hes out front, Ah reckon."

"Git im, quick!"

"Whuts the matter, Ma?"

"Go git yo Pa, Ah say!"

Lucy ran out. The mother sank into a chair, holding a dish rag. Suddenly, she sat up.

"Big Boy, Ah thought yuh wuz at school?"

Big Boy looked at the floor.

"How come yuh didnt go t school?"

"We went t the woods."

She sighed.

"Ah done done all Ah kin fer yuh, Big Boy. Only Gawd kin hep yuh now."

"Ma, don let em git me; don let em git me . . ."

His father came into the doorway. He stared at Big Boy, then at his wife.

"Whuts Big Boy inter now?" he asked sternly.

"Saul, Big Boys done gone n got inter trouble wid the white folks."

The old man's mouth dropped, and he looked from one to the other.

"Saul, we gotta git im erway from here."

"Open yo mouth n talk! Whut yuh been doin?" The old man gripped Big Boy's shoulders and peered at the scratches on his face.

"Me n Lester n Buck n Bobo wuz out on old man Harveys place swimmin . . ."

"Saul, its a *white* woman!"

Big Boy winced. The old man compressed his lips and stared at his wife. Lucy gaped at her brother as though she had never seen him before.

"Whut happened? Cant yuh-all talk?" the old man thundered with a certain helplessness in his voice.

"We wuz swimmin," Big Boy began, "n then a white woman comes up t the hole. We got up right erway t git our cloes sos we could git erway, n she started screamin. Our cloes wuz right by the tree where she wuz standing, n when we started to git em she just screamed. We tol her we wanted our cloes . . . Yuh see, Pa, she wuz standin right *by* our cloes, n when we went t get em she jus screamed . . . Bobo got the cloes, n then he shot Lester . . ."

"*Who* shot Lester?"

"The white man."

"Whut white man?"

"Ah dunno, Pa. He wuz a soljer, n he had a rifle."

"A *soljer?*"

"Yessuh, Pa. A soljer."

The old man frowned.

"N then whut yuh-all do?"

"Waal, Buck said, 'Hes gotta gun!' N we started runnin. N then he shot Buck, n he fell in the swimmin hole. We didnt see im no mo . . . He wuz close on us then. He looked at the white woman n then he started to shoot Bobo. Ah grabbed the gun, n we started fightin. Bobo jumped on his back. He started beatin Bobo. Then Ah hit im wid the gun. Then he started at me n Ah shot im. Then we run . . ."

"Who seen?"

"Nobody."

"Wheres Bobo?"

"He went home."

"Anybody run after yuh-all?"

"Nawsuh."

"Yuh see anybody?"

"Nawsuh. Nobody but a white man. But he didnt see us."

"How long fo yuh-all lef the swimmin hole?"

"Little while ergo."

The old man nervously brushed his hand across his eyes and walked to the door. His lips moved, but no words came.

"Saul, whut we gonna do?"

"Lucy," began the old man, "go t Brother Sanders n tell im Ah said c mere; n go t Brother Jenkins n tell im Ah said c mere; n go t Elder Peters

n tell im Ah said c mere. N don say nothin t nobody but whut Ah tol yuh.
N when yuh git thu come straight back. Now go!"

Lucy dropped her apron across the back of a chair and ran down the
steps. The mother bent over, crying and praying. The old man walked
slowly over to Big Boy.

"Big Boy?"

Big Boy swallowed.

"Ahm talkin t yuh!"

"Yessuh."

"How come yuh didnt go t school this mawning?"

"We went t the woods."

"Didnt yo ma send yuh t school?"

"Yessuh."

"How come yuh didnt go?"

"We went t the woods."

"Don yuh know thas wrong?"

"Yessuh."

"How come yuh go?"

Big Boy looked at his fingers, knotted them, and squirmed in his seat.

"AHM TALKIN T YUH!"

His wife straightened up and said reprovingly:

"Saul!"

The old man desisted, yanking nervously at the shoulder straps of his
overalls.

"How long wuz the woman there?"

"Not long."

"Wuz she young?"

"Yessuh. Lika gal."

"Did yuh-all say anythin t her?"

"Nawsuh. We just said we wanted our cloes."

"N whut she say?"

"Nothin, Pa. She jus backed erway t the tree n screamed."

The old man stared, his lips trying to form a question.

"Big Boy, did yuh-all bother her?"

"Nawsuh, Pa. We didn *touch* her."

"How long fo the white man come up?"

"Right erway."

"Whut he say?"

"Nothin. He jus cussed us."

Abruptly the old man left the kitchen.

"Ma, cant Ah go fo they ketches me?"

"Sauls doin whut he kin."

"Ma, Ma, Ah don wan em t ketch me . . ."

"Sauls doin whut he kin. Nobody but the good Lawd kin hep us now."

The old man came back with a shotgun and leaned it in a corner. Fasci-
natedly, Big Boy looked at it.

There was a knock at the front door.

"Liza, see whos there."

She went. They were silent, listening. They could hear her talking.

"Whos there?"

"Me."

"Who?"

"Me, Brother Sanders."

"C mon in. Sauls waitin fer yuh."

Sanders paused in the doorway, smiling.

"Yuh sent fer me, Brother Morrison?"

"Brother Sanders, wes in deep trouble here."

Sanders came all the way into the kitchen.

"Yeah?"

"Big Boy done gone n killed a white man."

Sanders stopped short, then came forward, his face thrust out, his mouth open. His lips moved several times before he could speak.

"A *white* man?"

"They gonna kill me; they gonna kill me!" Big Boy cried, running to the old man.

"Saul, cant we git im erway somewhere?"

"Here now, take it easy; take it easy," said Sanders, holding Big Boy's wrists.

"They gonna kill me; they gonna lynch me!"

Big Boy slipped to the floor. They lifted him to a stool. His mother held him closely, pressing his head to her bosom.

"Whut we gonna do?" asked Sanders.

"Ah done sent fer Brother Jenkins n Elder Peters."

Sanders leaned his shoulders against the wall. Then, as the full meaning of it all came to him, he exclaimed:

"Theys gonna git a mob! . . ." His voice broke off and his eyes fell on the shotgun.

Feet came pounding on the steps. They turned toward the door. Lucy ran in crying. Jenkins followed. The old man met him in the middle of the room, taking his hand.

"Wes in bad trouble here, Brother Jenkins. Big Boy's done gone n killed a white man. Yuh-alls gotta hep me . . ."

Jenkins looked hard at Big Boy.

"Elder Peters says hes comin," said Lucy.

"When all this happen?" asked Jenkins.

"Near bout a hour ergo, now," said the old man.

"Whut we gonna do?" asked Jenkins.

"Ah wanna wait till Elder Peters come," said the old man helplessly.

"But we gotta work fas ef we gonna do anythin," said Sanders. "Well git in trouble jus standin here like this."

Big Boy pulled away from his mother.

"Pa, lemme go now. Lemme go now!"

"Be still, Big Boy!"

"Where kin yuh go?"

"Ah could ketch a freight!"

"Thas *sho* death!" said Jenkins. "They'll be watchin em all!"

"Kin yuh-all hep me wid some money?" the old man asked.

They shook their heads.

"Saul, whut kin we do? Big Boy cant stay here."

There was another knock at the door.

The old man backed stealthily to the shotgun.

"Lucy go!"

Lucy looked at him, hesitating.

"Ah better go," said Jenkins.

It was Elder Peters. He came in hurriedly.

"Good evening, everybody!"

"How yuh, Elder?"

"Good evenin."

"How yuh today?"

Peters looked around the crowded kitchen.

"Whuts the matter?"

"Elder, wes in deep trouble," began the old man. "Big Boy n some mo boys . . ."

". . . Lester n Buck n Bobo . . ."

". . . wuz over on ol man Harveys place swimming . . ."

"N he don like us niggers *none*," said Peters emphatically. He widened his legs and put his thumbs in the armholes of his vest.

" . . . n some white woman . . ."

"Yeah?" said Peters, coming closer.

". . . comes erlong n the boys tries t git their cloes where they done lef em under a tree. Waal, she started screamin n all, see? Reckon she thought the boys wuz after her. Then a white man in a soljers suit shoots two of em . . ."

". . . Lester n Buck . . ."

"Huummm," said Peters. "Tha wuz ol man Harveys son."

"Harveys son?"

"Yuh mean the one tha wuz in the Army?"

"Yuh mean Jim?"

"Yeh," said Peters. "The papers said he wuz here fer a vacation from his regiment. N tha woman the boys saw wuz just erbout his wife . . ."

They stared at Peters. Now that they knew what white person had been killed, their fears became definite.

"N what else happened?"

"Big Boy shot the man . . ."

"Harveys *son*?"

"He had t, Elder. He wuz gonna shoot im ef he didnt . . ."

"Lawd!" said Peters. He looked around and put his hat back on.

"How long ergo wuz this?"

"Mighty near an hour, now, Ah reckon."

"Do the white folks know yit?"

"Don know, Elder."

"Yuh-all better git this boy outta here right now," said Peters. "Cause ef yuh don theres gonna be a lynchin . . ."

"Where kin Ah go, Elder?" Big Boy ran up to him.

They crowded around Peters. He stood with his legs wide apart, looking up at the ceiling.

"Mabbe we kin hide im in the church till he kin git erway," said Jenkins.

Peters' lips flexed.

"Naw, Brother, thall never do! Theyll git im there sho. N anyhow, ef they ketch im there itll ruin us all. We gotta git the boy outta town . . ."

Sanders went up to the old man.

"Lissen," he said in a whisper. "Mah son, Will, the one whut drives fer the Magnolia Express Company, is taking a truck o goods t Chicawgo in the mawnin. If we kin hide Big Boy somewhere till then, we kin put im on the truck . . ."

"Pa, please lemme go wid Will when he goes in the mawnin," Big Boy begged.

The old man stared at Sanders.

"Yuh reckon thas safe?"

"Its the only thing yuh *kin* do," said Peters.

"But where we gonna hide im till then?"

"Whut time yo boy leavin out in the mawnin?"

"At six."

They were quiet, thinking. The water kettle on the stove sang.

"Pa, Ah knows where Will passes erlong wid the truck out on Bullards Road. Ah kin hide in one of them ol kilns . . ."

"Where?"

"In one of them kilns we built . . ."

"But theyll git yuh there," wailed the mother.

"But there ain no place else fer im t go."

"Theres some holes big ernough fer me t git in n stay till Will comes erlong," said Big Boy. "Please, Pa, lemme go fo they ketches me . . ."

"Let im go!"

"Please, Pa . . ."

The old man breathed heavily.

"Lucy, git his things!"

"Saul, theyll git im out there!" wailed the mother, grabbing Big Boy.

Peters pulled her away.

"Sister Morrison, ef yuh don let im go n git erway from here hes gonna be caught shos theres a Gawd in Heaven!"

Lucy came running with Big Boy's shoes and pulled them on his feet. The old man thrust a battered hat on his head. The mother went to the stove and dumped the skillet of corn pone into her apron. She wrapped it, and unbuttoning Big Boy's overalls, pushed it into his bosom.

"Heres somethin fer yuh t eat; n pray, Big Boy, cause thas all anybody kin do now . . ."

Big Boy pulled to the door, his mother clinging to him.

"Let im go, Sister Morrison!"

"Run fas, Big Boy!"

Big Boy raced across the yard, scattering the chickens. He paused at the fence and hollered back:

"Tell Bobo where Ahm hidin n tell im t c mon!"

IV

He made for the railroad, running straight toward the sunset. He held his left hand tightly over his heart, holding the hot pone of corn bread there. At times he stumbled over the ties, for his shoes were tight and hurt his feet. His throat burned from thirst; he had had no water since noon.

He veered off the track and trotted over the crest of a hill, following Bullard's Road. His feet slipped and slid in the dust. He kept his eyes straight ahead, fearing every clump of shrubbery, every tree. He wished it were night. If he could only get to the kilns without meeting anyone. Suddenly a thought came to him like a blow. He recalled hearing the old folks tell tales of bloodhounds, and fear made him run slower. None of them had thought of that. Spose blood-houns wuz put on his trail? Lawd! Spose a whole pack of em, foamin n howlin, tore im t pieces? He went limp and his feet dragged. Yeah, thas whut they wuz gonna send after im, blood-houns! N then thered be no way fer im t dodge! Why hadnt Pa let im take tha shotgun? He stopped. He oughta go back n git tha shotgun. And then when the mob came he would take some with him.

In the distance he heard the approach of a train. It jarred him back to a sharp sense of danger. He ran again, his big shoes sopping up and down in the dust. He was tired and his lungs were bursting from running. He wet his lips, wanting water. As he turned from the road across a plowed field he heard the train roaring at his heels. He ran faster, gripped in terror.

He was nearly there now. He could see the black clay on the sloping hillside. Once inside a kiln he would be safe. For a little while, at least. He thought of the shotgun again. If he only had something! Someone to talk to . . . Thas right! Bobo! Bobod be wid im. Hed almost fergot Bobo. Bobod bringa gun; he knowed he would. N tergether they could kill the whole mob. Then in the mawning theyd git inter Will's truck n go far erway, t Chicawgo . . .

He slowed to a walk, looking back and ahead. A light wind skipped over the grass. A beetle lit on his cheek and he brushed it off. Behind the dark pines hung a red sun. Two bats flapped against that sun. He shivered, for he was growing cold; the sweat on his body was drying.

He stopped at the foot of the hill, trying to choose between two patches of black kilns high above him. He went to the left, for there lay the ones he, Bobo, Lester, and Buck had dug only last week. He looked around again; the landscape was bare. He climbed the embankment and stood before a row of black pits sinking four and five feet deep into the earth. He went to the largest and peered in. He stiffened when his ears caught the sound of a whir. He ran back a few steps and poised on his toes. Six foot of snake slid out of the pit and went into coil. Big Boy looked around wildly for a stick. He ran down the slope, peering into the grass. He stumbled over a tree limb. He picked it up and tested it by striking it against the ground.

Warily, he crept back up the slope, his stick poised. When about seven feet from the snake he stopped and waved the stick. The coil grew tighter, the whir sounded louder, and a flat head reared to strike. He went to the right, and the flat head followed him, the blue-black tongue darting forth; he went to the left, and the flat head followed him there too.

He stopped, teeth clenched. He had to kill this snake. Jus had t kill im! This wuz the safest pit on the hillside. He waved the stick again, looking at the snake before, thinking of a mob behind. The flat head reared higher. With stick over shoulder, he jumped in swinging. The stick sang through the air, catching the snake on the side of the head, sweeping him out of coil. There was a brown writhing mass. Then Big Boy was upon him, pounding blows home, one on top of the other. He fought viciously, his eyes red, his teeth bared in a snarl. He beat till the snake lay still, then he stomped it with his heel, grinding its head into the dirt.

He stopped, limp, wet. The corners of his lips were white with spittle. He spat and shuddered.

Cautiously, he went to the hole and peered. He longed for a match. He imagined whole nests of them in there waiting. He put the stick into the hole and waved it around. Stooping, he peered again. It mus be awright. He looked over the hillside, his eyes coming back to the dead snake. Then he got to his knees and backed slowly into the hole.

When inside he felt there must be snakes all about him, ready to strike. It seemed he could see and feel them there, waiting tensely in coil. In the dark he imagined long white fangs ready to sink into his neck, his side, his legs. He wanted to come out, but kept still. Shucks, he told himself, ef there wuz any snakes in here they sho woulda done bit me by now. Some of his fear left, and he relaxed.

With elbows on ground and chin on palms, he settled. The clay was cold to his knees and thighs, but his bosom was kept warm by the hot pone of corn bread. His thirst returned and he longed for a drink. He was hungry, too. But he did not want to eat the corn pone. Naw, not now. Mabbe after erwhile, after Bobo came. Then theyd both eat the corn pone.

The view from his hole was fringed by the long tufts of grass. He could see all the way to Bullard's Road, and even beyond. The wind was blowing, and in the east the first touch of dusk was rising. Every now and then a bird floated past, a spot of wheeling black printed against the sky. Big Boy sighed, shifted his weight, and chewed at a blade of grass. A wasp droned. He heard number nine, far away and mournful.

The train made him remember how they had dug these kilns on long hot summer days, how they had made boilers out of big tin cans, filled them with water, fixed stoppers for steam, cemented them in holes with wet clay, and built fires under them. He recalled how they had danced and yelled when a stopper blew out of a boiler, letting out a big spout of steam and a shrill whistle. There were times when they had the whole hillside blazing and smoking. Yeah, yuh see, Big Boy wuz Casey Jones n wuz speedin it down the gleamin rails of the Southern Paific. Bobo had number two on the Santa Fe. Buck wuz on the Illinoy Central. Lester the Nickel Plate. Lawd, how they shelved the wood in! The boiling water would almost jar the cans loose from the clay. More and more pine-knots and dry leaves would be piled under the cans. Flames would grow so tall they would have to shield their eyes. Sweat would pour off their faces. Then, suddenly, a peg would shoot high into the air, and

Pssseeeezzzzzzzzzzzzzzzzzzzzzz . . .

Big Boy sighed and stretched out his arm, quenching the flames and scattering the smoke. Why didnt Bobo c mon? He looked over the fields; there was nothing but dying sunlight. His mind drifted back to the kilns. He remembered the day when Buck, jealous of his winning, had tried to smash his kiln. Yeah, that ol sonofabitch! Naw, Lawd! He didnt go t say tha! Whut wuz he thinkin erbout? Cussin the dead! Yeah, po ol Buck wuz dead now. N Lester too. Yeah, it wuz awright for Buck t smash his kiln. Sho. N he wished he hadnt socked ol Buck so hard tha day. He wuz sorry fer Buck now. N he sho wished he hadnt cussed po ol Bucks ma, neither. That wuz sinful! Mabbe Gawd would git im fer tha? But he didnt go t do it! Po Buck! Po Lester! Hed never treat anybody like tha ergin, never . . .

Dusk was slowly deepening. Somewhere, he could not tell exactly where, a cricket took up a fitful song. The air was growing soft and heavy. He looked over the fields, longing for Bobo . . .

He shifted his body to ease the cold damp of the ground, and thought back over the day. Yeah, hed been dam right erbout not wantin t go swimmin. N ef hed followed his right min hed neverve gon n got inter all this trouble. At first hed said naw. But shucks, somehow hed just went on wid the res. Yeah, he shoulda went on t school tha mawnin, like Ma told im t do. But, hell, who wouldnt git tireda school? T hell wid school! Tha wuz the big trouble, awways drivin a guy t school! He wouldnt be in all this trouble now ef it wuznt fer that Gawddam school! Impatiently, he took the grass out of his mouth and threw it away, demolishing the little red school house . . .

Yeah, ef they had all kept still n quiet when tha ol white woman showed-up, mabbe shedve went on off. But yuh never kin tell erbout these white folks. Mabbe she wouldntve went. Mabbe tha white man woulda killed all of em! All *fo* of em! Yeah, yuh never kin tell erbout white folks. Then, ergin, mabbe tha white woman woulda went on off n laffed. Yeah, mabbe tha white man woulda said: *Yuh nigger bastards git t hell outta here. Yuh know Gawddam well yuh don berlong here!* N then they woulda grabbed their cloes n run like all hell . . . He blinked the white man away. Where wuz Bobo? Why didnt he hurry up n c mon?

He jerked another blade and chewed. Yeah, ef pa had only let im have tha shotgun! He could stan off a whole mob wid a shotgun. He looked at the ground as he turned a shotgun over in his hands. Then he leveled it at an advancing white man. *Boooom!* The man curled up. Another came. He reloaded quickly, and let him have what the other had got. He too curled up. Then another came. He got the same medicine. Then the whole mob swirled around him, and he blazed away, getting as many as he could. They closed in, but, by Gawd, he had done his part, hadnt he? N the newspapersd say: NIGGER KILLS DOZEN OF MOB BEFO LYNCHED! Er mabbe theyd say: TRAPPED NIGGER SLAYS TWENTY BEFO KILLED! He smiled a little. Tha wouldnt be so bad, would it? Blinking the newspaper away, he looked over the fields. Where wuz Bobo? Why didnt he hurry up n c mon?

He shifted, trying to get a crick out of his legs. Shucks, he wuz gittin tireda this. N it wuz almos dark now. Yeah, there wuz a little bittie star way over ynder in the eas. Mabbe that white man wuznt dead? Mabbe they wuznt even looking fer im? Mabbe he could go back home now? Naw, better wait erwhile. Thad be bes. But, Lawd, ef he only had some water! He could hardly swallow, his throat was so dry. Gawddam them white folks! Thas all they wuz good fer, t run a nigger down lika rabbit! Yeah, they git yuh in a corner n then they let yuh have it. A thousan of em! He shivered, for the cold of the clay was chilling his bones. Lawd, spose they foun im here in this hole? N wid nobody t hep im? . . . But ain no use in thinking erbout tha; wait till trouble come fo yuh start fightin it. But ef tha mob came one by one hed wipe em all out. Clean up the whole bunch. He caught one by the neck and choked him long and hard, choked him till his tongue and eyes popped out. Then he jumped upon his chest and stomped him like he had stomped that snake. When he had finished with one, another came. He choked him too. Choked till he sank slowly to the ground, gasping . . .

"Hoalo!"

Big Boy snatched his fingers from the white man's neck and looked over the fields. He saw nobody. Had someone spied him? He was sure that somebody had hollered. His heart pounded. But, shucks, nobody couldnt see im here in this hole . . . But mabbe theyd seen im when he wuz comin n had laid low n wuz now closin in on im! Praps they wuz signalin fer the othes? Yeah, they wuz creepin up on im! Mabbe he oughta git up n run . . . Oh! Mabbe that wuz Bobo? Yeah, Bobo! He oughta clim out n see ef Bobo wuz lookin fer im . . . He stiffened.

"Hoalo!"

"Hoalo!"

"Wheres yuh?"

"Over here on Bullards Road!"

"C mon over!"

"Awright!"

He heard footsteps. Then voices came again, low and far away this time.

"Seen anybody?"

"Naw. Yuh?"

"Naw."

"Yuh reckon they got erway?"

"Ah dunno. Its hard t tell."

"Gawddam them sonofabitchin niggers!"

"We oughta kill ever black bastard in this country!"

"Waal, Jim got two of em, anyhow."

"But Bertha said there wuz *fo!*"

"Where in hell they hidin?"

"She said one of em wuz named Big Boy, or something like tha."

"We went t his shack lookin fer im."

"Yeah?"

"But we didnt fin im."

"These niggers stick tergether; they don never tell on each other."

"We looked all thu the shack n couldnt fin hide ner hair of im. Then we drove the ol woman n man out n set the shack on fire . . ."

"Jeesus! Ah wished Ah coulda been there!"

"Yuh shoulda heard the ol nigger woman howl . . ."

"Hoalo!"

"C mon over!"

Big Boy eased to the edge and peeped. He saw a white man with a gun slung over his shoulder running down the slope. Wuz they gonna search the hill? Lawd, there wuz no way fer im t git erway now; he wuz caught! He shoulda knowed they'd git im here. N he didnt hava thing, notta thing t fight wid. Yeah, soon as the blood-houns came theyd fin im. Lawd, have mercy! Theyd lynch im right here on the hill . . . Theyd git im n tie im t a stake n burn im erlive! Lawd! Nobody but the good Lawd could hep im now, nobody . . .

He heard more feet running. He nestled deeper. His chest ached. Nobody but the good Lawd could hep now. They wuz crowdin all round im n when they hada big crowd theyd close in on im. Then itd be over . . . The good Lawd would have t hep im, cause nobody could hep im now, nobody . . .

And then he went numb when he remembered Bobo. Spose Bobod come now? Hed be caught sho! Both of em would be caught! They'd make Bobo tell where he wuz! Bobo oughta not try to come now. Somebody oughta tell im . . . But there wuz nobody; there wuz no way . . .

He eased slowly back to the opening. There was a large group of men. More were coming. Many had guns. Some had coils of rope slung over shoulders.

"Ah tell yuh they still here, somewhere . . ."

"But we looked all over!"

"What t hell! Wouldnt do t let em git erway!"

"Naw. Ef they git erway notta woman in this town would be safe."

"Say, whuts tha yuh got?"

"Er pillar."

"Fer whut?"

"Feathers, fool!"

"Chris! Thisll be hot ef we kin ketch them niggers!"

"Ol Anderson said he wuz gonna bringa barrela tar!"

"Ah got some gasoline in mah car ef yuh need it."

Big Boy had no feelings now. He was waiting. He did not wonder if they were coming after him. He just waited. He did not wonder about Bobo. He rested his cheek against the cold clay, waiting.

A dog barked. He stiffened. It barked again. He balled himself into a knot at the bottom of the hole, waiting. Then he heard the patter of dog feet.

"Look!"

"Whuts he got?"

"Its a snake!"

"Yeah, the dogs foun a snake!"

"Gee, its a big one!"

"Shucks, Ah wish he could fin one of them sonofabitchin niggers!"

The voices sank to low murmurs. Then he heard number twelve, its bell tolling and whistle crying as it slid along the rails. He flattened himself against the clay. Someone was singin:

"We'll hang ever nigger t a sour apple tree . . ."

When the song ended there was hard laughter. From the other side of the hill he heard the dog barking furiously. He listened. There was more than one dog now. There were many and they were barking their throats out.

"Hush, Ah hear them dogs!"

"When theys barkin like tha theys foun somethin!"

"Here they come over the hill!"

"WE GOT IM! WE GOT IM!"

There came a roar. Tha must be Bobo; tha must be Bobo . . . In spite of his fear, Big Boy looked. The road, and half of the hillside across the road, were covered with men. A few were on the top of the hill, stenciled against the sky. He could see dark forms moving up the slopes. They were yelling.

"By Gawd, we got im!"

"C mon!"

"Where is he?"

"Theyre bringin im over the hill!"

"Ah got a rope fer im!"

"Say, somebody go n git the others!"

"Where is he? Cant we see im, Mister?"

"They say Berthas comin, too."

"Jack! Jack! Don leave me! Ah wanna see im!"

"Theyre bringin im over the hill, sweetheart!"

"AH WANNA BE THE FIRS T PUT A ROPE ON THAT BLACK BASTARDS NECK!"

"Les start the fire!"

"Heat the tar!"

"Ah got some chains t chain im."

"Bring im over this way!"

"Chris, Ah wished Ah hada drink . . ."

Big Boy saw men moving over the hill. Among them was a long dark spot. Tha mus be Bobo; tha mus be Bobo theys carryin . . . They'll git im here. He oughta git up n run. He clamped his teeth and ran his hand across his forehead, bringing it away wet. He tried to swallow, but could not; his throat was dry.

They had started the song again:

> "We'll hang ever nigger t a sour apple tree . . ."

There were women singing now. Their voices made the song round and full. Song waves rolled over the top of pine trees. The sky sagged low, heavy with clouds. Wind was rising. Sometimes cricket cries cut surprisingly across the mob song. A dog had gone to the utmost top of the hill. At each lull of the song his howl floated full into the night.

Big Boy shrank when he saw the first tall flame light the hillside. Would they see im here? Then he remembered you could not see into the dark if you were standing in the light. As flames leaped higher he saw two men rolling a barrel up the slope.

"Say, gimme a han here, will yuh?"

"Awright, heave!"

"C mon! Straight up! Git t the other end!"

"Ah got the feathers here in this pillar!"

"BRING SOME MO WOOD!"

Big Boy could see the barrel surrounded by flames. The mob fell back, forming a dark circle. Theyd fin im here! He had a wild impulse to climb out and fly across the hills. But his legs would not move. He stared hard, trying to find Bobo. His eyes played over a long dark spot near the fire. Fanned by wind, flames leaped higher. He jumped. That dark spot had moved. Lawd, thas Bobo; thas Bobo . . .

He smelt the scent of tar, faint at first, then stronger. The wind brought it full into his face, then blew it away. His eyes burned and he rubbed them with his knuckles. He sneezed.

"LES GIT SOURVINEERS!"

He saw the mob close in around the fire. Their faces were hard and sharp in the light of the flames. More men and women were coming over the hill. The long dark spot was smudged out.

"Everybody git back!"

"Look! Hes gotta finger!"

"C MON! GIT THE GALS BACK FROM THE FIRE!"

"Hes got one of his ears, see?"

"Whuts the matter!"

"A woman fell out! Fainted, Ah reckon . . ."

The stench of tar permeated the hillside. The sky was black and the wind was blowing hard.

"HURRY UP N BURN THE NIGGER FO IT RAINS!"

Big Boy saw the mob fall back, leaving a small knot of men about the fire. Then, for the first time, he had a full glimpse of Bobo. A black body flashed in the light. Bobo was struggling, twisting; they were binding his arms and legs.

When he saw them tilt the barrel he stiffened. A scream quivered. He knew the tar was on Bobo. The mob fell back. He saw a tar-drenched body glistening and turning.

"THE BASTARDS GOT IT!"

There was a sudden quiet. Then he shrank violently as the wind carried, like a flurry of snow, a widening spiral of white feathers into the night. The flames leaped tall as the tree. The scream came again. Big Boy trembled and looked. The mob was running down the slopes, leaving the fire clear. Then he saw a writhing white mass cradled in yellow flame, and heard screams, one on top of the other, each shriller and shorter than the last. The mob was quiet now, standing still, looking up the slopes at the writhing white mass gradually growing black, growing black in a cradle of yellow flame.

"PO ON MO GAS!"

"Gimme a lif, will yuh!"

Two men were struggling, carrying between them a heavy can. They set it down, tilted it, leaving it so that the gas would trickle down to the hollowed earth around the fire.

Big Boy slid back into the hole, his face buried in clay. He had no feelings now, no fears. He was numb, empty, as though all blood had been drawn from him. Then his muscles flexed taut when he heard a faint patter. A tiny stream of cold water seped to his knees, making him push back to a drier spot. He looked up; rain was beating in the grass.

"Its rainin!"

"C mon, les git t town!"

". . . don worry, when the firegit thu wid im hell be gone . . ."

"Wait, Charles! Don leave me; its slippery here . . ."

"Ahll take some of yuh ladies back in mah ca . . ."

Big Boy heard the dogs barking again, this time closer. Running feet pounded past. Cold water chilled his ankles. He could hear raindrops steadily hissing.

Now a dog was barking at the mouth of the hole, barking furiously, sensing a presence there. He balled himself into a knot and clung to the bottom, his knees and shins buried in water. The bark came louder. He heard paws scraping and felt the hot scent of dog breath on his face. Green eyes glowed and drew nearer as the barking, muffled by the closeness of the hole, beat upon his eardrums. Backing till his shoulders pressed against the clay, he held his breath. He pushed out his hands, his fingers stiff. The dog yawped louder, advancing, his bark rising sharp and thin. Big Boy rose to his knees, his hands before him. Then he flattened out still more against the bottom, breathing lungsful of hot dog scent, breathing it slowly, hard, but evenly. The dog came closer, bringing hotter dog scent. Big Boy could go back no more. His knees were slipping and slopping in the water. He braced himself, ready. Then, he never exactly knew how—he never knew whether he had lunged or the dog had lunged—they were together, rolling in the water. The green eyes were beneath him, beneath him, between his legs. Dognails bit into his arms. His knees slipped backward and he landed full on the dog; the dog's breath left in a heavy gasp. Instinctively, he fumbled for the throat as he felt the dog twisting between his knees. The dog snarled, long and low, as though gathering strength. Big Boy's hands traveled swiftly over the dog's back, groping for the throat. He felt dognails again and saw green eyes, but his fingers had found the throat. He choked, feeling his fingers sink; he choked, throwing back his head and stiffening his arms. He felt the dog's body heave, felt dognails digging into his loins. With strength flowing from fear, he closed his fingers, pushing his full weight on the dog's throat. The dog heaved again, and lay still . . . Big Boy heard the sound of his own breathing filling the hole, and heard shouts and footsteps above him going past.

For a long, long time he held the dog, held it long after the last footstep had died out, long after the rain stopped.

V

Morning found him still on his knees in a puddle of rainwater, staring at the stiff body of a dog. As the air brightened he came to himself slowly. He held still for a long time, as though waking from a dream, as though trying to remember.

The chug of a truck came over the hill. He tried to crawl to the opening. His knees were stiff and a thousand needle-like pains shot from the bottom of his feet to the calves of his legs. Giddiness made his eyes blur. He pulled up and looked. Through brackish light he saw Will's truck standing some twenty-five yards away, the engine running. Will stood on the running board, looking over the slopes of the hill.

Big Boy scuffled out, falling weakly in the wet grass. He tried to call to Will, but his dry throat would make no sound. He tried again.

"Will!"

Will heard, answering:

"Big Boy, c mon!"

He tried to run, and fell. Will came, meeting him in the tall grass.

"C mon," Will said, catching his arm.

They struggled to the truck.

"Hurry up!" said Will, pushing him onto the running board.

Will pushed back a square trapdoor which swung above the back of the driver's seat. Big Boy pulled through, landing with a thud on the bottom. On hands and knees he looked around in the semi-darkness.

"Wheres Bobo?"

Big Boy stared.

"Wheres Bobo?"

"They got im."

"When?"

"Las night."

"The mob?"

Big Boy pointed in the direction of a charred sapling on the slope of the opposite hill. Will looked. The trapdoor fell. The engine purred, the gears whined, and the truck lurched forward over the muddy road, sending Big Boy on his side.

For a while he lay as he had fallen, on his side, too weak to move. As he felt the truck swing around a curve he straightened up and rested his back against a stack of wooden boxes. Slowly, he began to make out objects in the darkness. Through two long cracks fell thin blades of daylight. The floor was of smooth steel, and cold to his thighs. Splinters and bits of saw-dust danced with the rumble of the truck. Each time they swung around a curve he was pulled over the floor; he grabbed at corners of boxes to steady himself. Once he heard the crow of a rooster. It made him think of home, of ma and pa. He thought he remembered hearing somewhere that the house had burned, but could not remember where. . . . It all seemed unreal now.

He was tired. He dozed, swaying with the lurch. Then he jumped awake. The truck was running smoothly, on gravel. Far away he heard two short blasts from the Buckeye Lumber Mill. Unconsciously, the thought sang through his mind: Its six erclock . . .

The trapdoor swung in. Will spoke through a corner of his mouth.

"How yuh coming?"

"Awright."

"How they git Bobo?"

"He wuz coming over the hill."

"Whut they do?"

"They burnt im . . . Will, Ah wan some water; mah throats like fire . . ."

"Well git some when we pass a fillin station."

Big Boy leaned back and dozed. He jerked awake when the truck stopped. He heard Will get out. He wanted to peep through the trapdoor, but was afraid. For a moment, the wild fear he had known in the hole came back. Spose theyd search n fin im? He quieted when he heard Will's footstep on the running board. The trapdoor pushed in. Will's hat came through, dripping.

"Take it, quick!"

Big Boy grabbed, spilling water into his face. The truck lurched. He drank. Hard cold lumps of brick rolled into his hot stomach. A dull pain made him bend over. His intestines seemed to be drawing into a tight knot. After a bit it eased, and he sat up, breathing softly.

The truck swerved. He blinked his eyes. The blades of daylight had turned brightly golden. The sun had risen.

The truck sped over the asphalt miles, sped northward, jolting him, shaking out of his bosom the crumbs of corn bread, making them dance with the splinters and sawdust in the golden blades of sunshine.

He turned on his side and slept.

QUESTIONS

"Big Boy Leaves Home"

1. "Big Boy Leaves Home" is divided into five sections; the first of them consists largely of dialogue and a few songs. What impression do you have of the four adolescent boys as you read this section? What is its prevailing tone? What mood does Wright establish in this section? As you think of the story in retrospect, what incidents or remarks in the first few pages foreshadow what happens later?

2. Several things early in the story distinguish Big Boy from his three friends in the reader's mind. What are these, and what qualities or character traits of his do they express? What do these characteristics have to do with Big Boy's survival on the "road of trials" he must travel in this story?

3. In what respects can Wright's protagonist be said to be a hero?

4. When you imagine a young person's leaving home for the first time, what images do you conjure up? How are Wright's title and indeed his entire story an ironic commentary on the conventional departure from home and family?

5. Look at the early turning point of "Big Boy Leaves Home," the dramatic scene that culminates with the deaths of Buck, Lester, and Jim Harvey. Bertha Harvey is virtually speechless, Jim Harvey is "bewildered," and Big Boy is "puzzled" and "at a loss" over what occurs in this scene. Why are these characters all so surprised and confused?

6. Discuss the pictures of the black family and black community we are given in the third and fifth sections of this story.

7. What is the effect of Wright's giving us only nicknames for two or perhaps even three of the adolescent boys in this narrative, rather than choosing specific full names for these characters?

8. In order for Big Boy to survive, he must go north with Will Sanders. What are the various trials he undergoes in this quest? What events in the story suggest that Big Boy faces a longer and even harder quest in the future? Explain.

9. During the lynching scene, what are the many ways Wright creates a sense of horror in the reader? Discuss the action and attitudes of the white lynchers in this connection. If the hero's quest is usually a journey of discovery, that is, if it involves an expansion of consciousness, what does Big Boy learn about the nature of evil, as he crouches in the kiln?

10. In what respects does this story depict an initiation, the transformation of an adolescent boy into a man? What evidence is there in the first pages of the fourth section that Big Boy is still more boy than man? When does the change come, and how are we made aware that he has changed?

11. Big Boy enters the kiln as a youth; he emerges the next morning a man. Why is the kiln a symbolically appropriate place for this transformation? What other imagery in Section IV suggests that Big Boy is undergoing an initiation on the hillside?

12. Why doesn't Big Boy help his close friend Bobo at the end of the story? What effect does his failure to try to help have on you? Does it deepen your sense of the tragic dimensions of Wright's story? If so, how?

Behind the Blue Curtain

STEVEN MILLHAUSER

On Saturday afternoons in summer my father took me to the movies. All morning long I waited for him to come down from his study, frowning at the bowl of his pipe and slapping the stairs with his slipper-moccasins, as though the glossy dark bowl, the slippers, the waiting itself were a necessary part of my long-drawn-out passage into the realm of dark. I savored every stage: the hot summer sunshine outside the ticket booth, the indoor sunlight of the entranceway with its glass-covered Coming Attractions and its velvet rope, the artificial glow of the red lobby, the mysterious dusk of the theater, the swift decisive darkening—and between the blue folds of the curtain, slowly parting, the sudden shining of the screen. Gravely my father had explained to me that the people on the screen were motionless photographs, passing quickly before my eyes. It was like my black-and-white flip-book from the candy store: a smiling mouse leaped from a diving board toward the water as a frowning shark rose up, opening its jaws wider and wider. And when you did it the other way, see!—the sinking jaws close, the upside-down mouse rises through the air and lands on his feet on the high board. My father was never wrong, but I felt he was trying to shield me from darker knowledge. The beings behind the curtain had nothing to do with childish flip-books or the long strips of gray negatives hanging in the kitchen from silver clips. They led their exalted lives beyond mine, in some other realm entirely, shining, desirable, impenetrable.

One Saturday afternoon when my father had to drive to the university on business, and my mother lay on two pillows in her darkened room, rasping with asthma, and my best friend was spending the day at his cousin Valerie's, it was decided that I could go to the movies alone. I knew that something forbidden was happening, but I greeted it with outward calm. After the second feature I was to go directly to the front of the theater and stand outside under the marquee, where my father would be waiting. I felt that the decision had been arrived at too hastily, that the careful, repeated instructions only revealed the danger in this sudden violation of the usual. I wondered whether I should warn my parents, but I remained silent and watchful. My father dropped me off at the ticket booth, where a short line had formed, and as I watched him drive away I felt an anxious exhilaration, as if in the pride of his knowledge he had failed to reckon with the powers of the dark.

Past the blue velvet rope on its silver post I stepped into the well-lit lobby with its red rug and glass-covered candy counter. The glossy wrappers brilliant under the counter lights, the high popcorn machine with its yellow glass that turned the popcorn butter-yellow, the crimson glow of a nearby exit sign, all these expressed the secret presence of the dark, which here made itself felt by the intensity of the effort to banish it. Behind me, through the open door leading back to the entranceway, I could see sunlight flashing on the glass of a Coming Attraction: in a green-black jungle a man in a pith helmet was taking aim with a rifle at something invisible in the blaze of obscuring light. I turned to the darkening corridor leading away from the candy counter. There the lights grew dim, as if they were candle-flames bending in the wind of the gathering dark, there the world was bathed in a reddish glow. I bought a box of popcorn and made my way along the glowing night of the corridor. The aisle surprised me: it sloped down more sharply than I had remembered. As I passed the arms of seats I felt a slight tugging at my calves, as if I were being pulled forward against my will. Impulsively I chose a row. I slipped past four chair-arms and pulled down a red, sagging seat. I leaned back eagerly, waiting for artificial night to fall, whispers of ushers, the cone of a flashlight beam in the darkened aisle.

Soon the lights went out, on the luminous curtain bright letters danced, the blue folds began to part; and sliding down, far down, I rested my popcorn on my stomach and pressed the back of my head against the fuzzy seat.

And suddenly it was over, the lights came on, people rose to go. Legs pushed past my knees, a coin clinked and someone bent over sharply, slapping at the floor. A foot kicked a popcorn box, a seat came up with a bang. Was it really over? The rolling coin struck something and stopped. A heaviness came over me—I could scarcely drag myself to my feet. Outside my father would be waiting under the marquee: one arm across his stomach, the elbow of the other arm in the palm of the first, the bowl of his pipe supported with thick fingers. I felt that I had let something slip away from me, that I had failed in some way, but my thoughts were sluggish and kept sinking out of sight.

At the top of the aisle I hesitated, looking with disappointment toward the band of sun streaming in through the open door. I went over to the drinking fountain and took a long swallow. At the darkening end of the corridor I noticed a sign that said REST ROOMS, with a red arrow pointing down. Perhaps my father had not arrived yet; the out-streaming crowd was dense, oppressive; I would only be two seconds. Slowly I descended the speckled stone steps, sliding my hand along the dark brass rail. In the men's room a teenager with slicked-back yellow hair and a black leather jacket stood wiping his hands on a soiled roller-towel. I slipped into a stall and listened with relief to the departing footsteps, the banging door. Two people entered without speaking and left one after the other. I felt weary and restless. I didn't know what I wanted. I did not move.

I must have fallen into a stupor or reverie, for I was startled by a clanking sound. I opened the door of the stall and saw an old man in droopy pants standing with his back to me beside a bucket of soapy water. He was slowly pushing a mop whose long gray strings moved first one way, then the other. The mop left glistening patches on the white-and-black tiles. I tiptoed out of the bathroom as if I had been guilty of something and began climbing the stairway, which seemed darker than before. It was very quiet. At the top of the stairs I came to the corridor, now empty and still. At the other end the darkened candy counter was lit by a single bulb. The theater appeared to be deserted. I was nervous and calm, nervous and calm. Nearby I saw the row of closed doors leading to the entranceway; under the doors I could see a disturbing line of sunlight. And clattering around a turn in the spookhouse, suddenly you see a sliver of light at the bottom of the black walls. My father would be striding up and down, up and down, looking at his sunny watch. He would talk to the girl in the ticket booth. All at once a desire erupted in me with such force that I felt as if I had been struck in both temples.

I stepped onto a downward-sloping aisle and plunged into the soothing half-dark, penetrated by the odor of old dark red seat cushions, butter-stained cardboard popcorn boxes, the sticky sweetness of spilled soda. On one seat I saw a fat rubber nose with a broken elastic string. At the end of the aisle I stepped over to the wall and reached up my hand, but the bottom of the great curtain was high above my straining fingers. It was set back, leaving a ledge. The thick dark folds looked heavy as marble. It seemed to me that if only I could touch that curtain, if only I could push it aside and stare for one second at the fearful blankness of the screen, and perhaps graze the magic whiteness with my fingers, then my deep restlessness would be stilled, my heart would grow calm, I could turn away from the theater and hurry back, quickly quickly, to my waiting father, who at any moment was going to burst through the doors or drive away forever. I walked along the wall, desperately searching for something to stand on, say a popcorn box or one of those tall ashtrays with white sand that I had seen near the blue velvet rope. I saw nothing but an empty, carefully folded silver gum-wrapper with its phantom stick of gum. High overhead the curtain stretched away. As I approached the end of the curtain the lower wall curved slightly and I saw a narrow flight of six steps going up. The stairs were cut into the wall. The top stair was half concealed by the final fold of the curtain.

With a glance over my shoulder I climbed swiftly and began to push at the velvety thick folds, which enveloped my arm and barely moved. I had the sense that the curtain was slowly waking, like some great, disturbed animal. Somehow I pushed the final, sluggish fold aside and found myself before a flaking wooden door with dented metal knob. The door opened easily. I stepped into a small room, scarcely larger than a closet. I saw dark brooms, mops in buckets, dustpans, a bulging burlap sack in one corner, an usher's jacket hanging from a nail; in the back wall I made out part of a second door.

Stepping carefully over buckets, cans, and bottles I felt for the knob. The door opened onto a narrow corridor carpeted in red. Glass candle-flames glowed in brass sconces high on the walls. There were no doors. At the end of the passage I came to a flight of red-carpeted stairs going down. I descended to a landing; over the polished wooden rail I saw landings within landings, dropping away. At the bottom of the seventh landing I found myself in another corridor. Through high, open doorways I caught glimpses of festive rooms. I heard footsteps along the corridor and stepped through one of the tall doors.

In the uncanny light of reddish gas lamps, many-branched candelabra, and chandeliers with flaming candles, I saw them taking their ease. They were splendidly costumed, radiantly themselves, expressing their natures through grand and flawless gestures. They lolled against walls, strolled idly about, displayed themselves on great armchairs and couches. I wasn't sur-prised by their massiveness, which suited their extravagant natures, and I looked up at them as if gazing up at the screen from the second row. Even the furniture loomed; my head barely came over the cushions of armchairs.

They seemed to pay no attention to me as I made my way among the great chairs and couches and came to an open place with a high table. Beside it strode a figure with flowing black hair, a great crimson cape, and a glittering sword. He seized a gold goblet and took an immense swallow, while beside him a bearded figure with a leather helmet bearing two sharp silver horns burst into rich laughter, and a lady with high-piled hair and a hoop dress covered with ruffles turned to look over her rapidly fluttering fan. Passing under the table I came to a great couch where a queen with ink-black hair and blue eyelids lay on her side looking coldly before her as she stroked a white cat. Beside her stood a grim figure with a skull and crossbones on his three-cornered hat, a red scarf at his throat, a long-barreled pistol thrust through his belt, and loose pants plunging into thick, cracked boots. I passed the couch and saw on the other side a jungle girl dressed in a leopardskin loincloth and a vineleaf halter, standing with her hands on her hips and her head flung back haughtily as two gray-haired gentlemen in white dinner jackets bent forward to peer through monocles at a jewel in her navel. Farther away I saw a figure in green with a quiver of cloth yard arrows on his back and a stout quarterstaff in one hand, stand-ing beside a tall, mournful ballerina whose shiny dark hair was pulled so tightly back that it looked like painted wood; and far across the room, through high, open doorways, I saw other rooms and other figures, stretching back and back.

Though shy of their glances, I soon realized I had nothing to fear from them. At first I thought they failed to notice me, or, noticing me, shrugged their shoulders and returned to their superior lives. But gradually I rec-ognized that my presence, far from being ignored, inspired them to be more grandly themselves. For weren't they secretly in need of being watched, these lofty creatures, did they not become themselves through the act of being witnessed?

Through a wide doorway I wandered into another room, and then into a third—and always through open doorways I saw other figures, other rooms. The very abundance that drew me proved quickly tiring, and I looked for a quiet place to sit before returning to my father, who perhaps at this very moment was pushing open the glass doors and striding toward the blue velvet rope. He would step into the empty theater and stare at the dark seats, the closed curtain, the red-glowing exit signs. Downstairs in the rest room he would find an old man in droopy pants who would look up with red-rimmed eyes and shake his head slowly: no, no. On the rung of a tall wooden chair I sat down, hooking one arm around the thick leg. Almost at once I became aware of someone pacing up and down before me. She walked close to my chair in a great swirl of petticoats, her ruffled skirts shaking as she walked. She sighed deeply and petulantly, over and over again, and from time to time I caught snatches of muttered monologue: ". . . have to do something . . . impossible . . . unbearable . . ." Suddenly she sat down on a chair opposite; I saw a flowery burst of petticoats settling against white stockings; but she sprang up and continued her odd pantomime, gradually moving away so that I was able to catch a glimpse of her: a tumult of bouncing blond curls shaped like small tubes, a pouting red mouth. and round blue eyes, a neckline that exposed the top third of high, very white breasts, which appeared to be pressed tightly upward. When she walked, all her curls shook like bells, the tops of her breasts shook, her skirts bounced up and down, her eyelids fluttered, her plump cheeks trembled; only her little nose was still. Sometimes she glanced in my direction, but not at me. All at once she stamped her foot, pushed out her bottom lip, and swished away, glancing for a moment over her shoulder. It was clear that she expected to be followed, that she always expected to be followed, and without hesitation I slipped from my rung.

She pushed open a door and I followed her into a red room brilliant with mirrors and the flames of many candles. I saw a high white armchair, a great dressing table with a soaring mirror. Smaller mirrors hung on each wall; the dark red wallpaper was patterned with little pale princesses leaning out of silver towers with their long flaxen hair. She stepped onto a stool before a swivel mirror and clapped her hands sharply twice. An elderly woman in a black dress appeared and began removing her ball gown with its flounced skirts and blue bows. Then she removed another skirt under that, and several petticoats, leaving a billowy, frilled petticoat and a satiny white corset with crisscross laces in back. "Thank you, Maria, now go away, go away, go away now . . ." For a while she stared at herself in the tall mirror, then hopped from the stool and began pacing about, glancing at herself in the swivel mirror, in the mirror over the dressing table, in the mirrors on the walls, in a silver bowl. The room filled with images of her, turning this way and that. As she paced and turned she heaved great sighs, and pushed out her bottom lip, and tossed her curls, and mutterd to herself: "get away with . . . just who does he . . . can't breathe in here . . ."

Though she paid not the slightest attention to me, I felt that my presence permitted her to display her petulance with the richness she required; and as she pranced and pouted she tugged at a fastening at the front of her corset, she kicked off her shoes, she unbound her high-piled hair, which spilled down her flame-lit shoulders and shook as she moved. And as she flickered and shook before me I felt a vague excitement, my skin began to tingle, as if she were brushing against me with her thick, shaking curls, her trembling skin, her white silk stockings. All at once the shaking stopped and I saw her raise the back of a hand to her forehead. Slowly, like a falling leaf, she swooned onto the dark red rug.

I had no thought of calling for help, for the swoon had been executed with such elegance that I felt certain she had intended it to be admired. She lay on the floor between the lion-paw legs of the chair and the red wallpaper. Her heavy yellow ringlets were strewn about her face and shoulders, her lips were partly open, her stomach moved gently up and down, the lines and bands of her corset went in and out, in and out. I stepped over to her and looked down. An unaccountable desire seized me: I wanted to feel the satiny material of her corset, I wanted to place my hand against the fire-lit white breathing cloth. In her white slip my mother had sat at the edge of the bed, drawing on a stocking. Slowly the corset bands went in and out. I bent over, careful not to touch the breathing form in any way; the skin of my palm prickled; I felt tense and anxious, as if I were about to transgress a law. And as I lowered my palm against the forbidden white cloth with its stretching and contracting bands I felt my hands sinking through melting barriers, as when, on a trip to New Hampshire with my parents, one morning I had walked through thick white cottony mist that lay heavy on the grass and parted like air as I passed. So my hand fell through the whiteness of that cloth. My sinking hand struck the velvety hard rug—I felt myself losing my balance—suddenly I was falling through her, plunging through her corset, her breasts, her bones, her blood. For a fearful instant I was inside her. I had a sensation of whiteness or darkness, a white darkness. On the sudden rug I rolled wildly through her, wildly out of her, and sprang up. Blood beat in my temples. She lay there drowsily. My whole body tingled, as if I had dried myself roughly with a towel.

I stared at my hands and shirt and pants as if fearing to see little pieces of cloth and flesh stuck to them, but I saw only myself.

A moment later she sat up, shook her headful of thick, springy curls, and pulled herself lightly to her feet. "Why, I must have . . . fainted or . . . Maria! Oh, where is that woman?" She began pacing up and down, sighing, pouting, flinging back her hair; a corner of her flying petticoat rippled through my hand, which I snatched away; and in the many mirrors her many images appeared and reappeared, thrusting out their bottom lips, darting glances, fluttering their many eyelids.

I didn't know whether I was relieved or bitterly unhappy. Would I have guessed her secret? I knew only that I wanted to go.

In the doorway I stopped and half turned to look at her. Fiercely she paced, exuberantly she sulked, in the full radiance of her being. I was tempted to say something, to shout, to draw attention to myself in some way, but the desire drained swiftly out of me. A shout, a scream, a knife in the throat, a plunge to the death, all were quite useless here.

I stepped through the door and looked for the room I had come from, but found myself in an alien room filled with harsh laughter. I was careful not to touch any of them as I passed. Through a nearby doorway I emerged in a corridor that led to another room, another doorway, another room. I came to an upward-sloping corridor lined with shimmering mirrors; the sudden repetition of my anxious face gave me the sensation that my anxiety had increased in a burst. At the end of the corridor I climbed three steps to a closed door. I opened it and found myself in a dusky room I had never seen before, with many seats and a dark wall-hanging that resembled a curtain; gradually I recognized the theater.

I had entered by another door, beside one of the red-glowing exit signs. I hurried up the sloping aisle, stopped for a moment in the lobby to glance toward the sign that said REST ROOMS, then pushed open one of the metal doors and stepped into the sun-flooded entranceway.

A kneeling usher was sweeping a pile of candy wrappers and cigarette butts into a dustpan. In the white sand of a standing ashtray a slanting white straw cast a rippling shadow across a piece of bright yellow cellophane. The man in the pith helmet was taking aim at a tree concealing an orange tiger upon whose back sat a woman in a black fur loincloth. Through the brilliant glass doors I saw my father frowning at his watch. his look of stern surprise, when he saw me burst through the door into the late-afternoon sun, struck me as wildly funny, and I forgot to chasten my features into repentance as I seized his warm hand.

QUESTIONS

"Behind the Blue Curtain"

1. Approximately how old do you think the narrator of Millhauser's story is? How do you know? Is his age significant in terms of your understanding what happens to him in the movie theater?

2. What is the boy's attitude toward the movies? Why does he find his father's explanation of what a movie is unsatisfactory?

3. Why is there so much emphasis in the story on doorways and corridors?

4. After falling "into a stupor or reverie" in the men's room, the narrator goes back into the theater. Why? What is he searching for?

5. Describe the underground world the boy discovers. What is his relation-

ship to the beings he finds there? Why do you think they are so large? What might they be symbols of?

6. Look at the passage about the woman whom the narrator follows to the red dressing room. Why does he follow her? What kind of fantasy does this scene express? Why is the experience so frightening to the boy, and why does he remember his mother in the midst of it?

7. After the narrator leaves the woman, he finds himself in "an alien room filled with harsh laughter." What is the meaning of this laughter? In the end, rejoining his father, the boy finds "wildly funny" the older man's "look of stern surprise." Why?

8. Early in the story the boy speaks of encountering in the movie theater "the powers of the dark." What are those powers? What is both wonderful and terrifying about the theater? How is what he encounters there different from everyday reality? What does the boy learn from his mysterious journey?

Through the Tunnel

DORIS LESSING

Going to the shore on the first morning of the vacation, the young English boy stopped at a turning of the path and looked down at a wild and rocky bay, and then over to the crowded beach he knew so well from other years. His mother walked on in front of him, carrying a bright striped bag in one hand. Her other arm, swinging loose, was very white in the sun. The boy watched that white naked arm, and turned his eyes, which had a frown behind them, towards the bay and back again to his mother. When she felt he was not with her, she swung around. "Oh, there you are, Jerry!" she said. She looked impatient, then smiled. "Why, darling, would you rather not come with me? Would you rather—" She frowned, conscientiously worrying over what amusements he might secretly be longing for, which she had been too busy or too careless to imagine. He was very familiar with that anxious, apologetic smile. Contrition sent him running after her. And yet, as he ran, he looked back over his shoulder at the wild bay; and all morning, as he played on the safe beach, he was thinking of it.

Next morning, when it was time for the routine of swimming and sunbathing, his mother said, "Are you tired of the usual beach, Jerry? Would you like to go somewhere else?"

"Oh, no!" he said quickly, smiling at her out of that unfailing impulse of contrition—a sort of chivalry. Yet, walking down the path with her, he blurted out, "I'd like to go and have a look at those rocks down there."

She gave the idea for her attention. It was a wild-looking place, and there was no one there; but she said, "Of course, Jerry. When you've had enough, come to the big beach. Or just go straight back to the villa, if you like." She walked away, that bare arm, now slightly reddened from yesterday's sun, swinging. And he almost ran after her again, feeling it unbearable that she should go by herself, but he did not.

She was thinking, Of course he's old enough to be safe without me. Have I been keeping him too close? He mustn't feel he ought to be with me. I must be careful.

He was an only child, eleven years old. She was a widow. She was determined to be neither possessive nor lacking in devotion. She went worrying off to her beach.

As for Jerry, once he saw that his mother had gained her beach, he began the steep descent to the bay. From where he was, high up among red-brown rocks, it was a scoop of moving blueish green fringed with white. As he went lower, he saw that it spread among small promontories and inlets of rough, sharp rock, and the crisping, lapping surface showed stains of purple and darker blue. Finally, as he ran sliding and scraping down the last few yards, he saw an edge of white surf and the shallow, luminous movement of water over white sand, and, beyond that, a solid, heavy blue.

He ran straight into the water and began swimming. He was a good swimmer. He went out fast over the gleaming sand, over a middle region where rocks lay like discoloured monsters under the surface, and then he was in the real sea—a warm sea where irregular cold currents from the deep water shocked his limbs.

When he was so far out that he could look back not only on the little bay but past the promontory that was between it and the big beach, he floated on the buoyant surface and looked for his mother. There she was, a speck of yellow under an umbrella that looked like a slice of orange peel. He swam back to shore, relieved at being sure she was there, but all at once very lonely.

On the edge of a small cape that marked the side of the bay away from the promontory was a loose scatter of rocks. Above them, some boys were stripping off their clothes. They came running, naked, down to the rocks. The English boy swam towards them, but kept his distance at a stone's throw. They were of that coast; all of them were burned smooth dark brown and speaking a language he did not understand. To be with them, of them, was a craving that filled his whole body. He swam a little closer; they turned and watched him with narrowed, alert dark eyes. Then one smiled and waved. It was enough. In a minute, he had swum in and was on the rocks beside them, smiling with a desperate, nervous supplication. They shouted cheerful greetings at him; and then, as he preserved his nervous, uncomprehending smile, they understood that he was a foreigner strayed from his own beach, and they proceeded to forget him. But he was happy. He was with them.

They began diving again and again from a high point into a well of blue sea between rough, pointed rocks. After they had dived and come up, they swam around, hauled themselves up, and waited their turn to dive again. They were big boys—men, to Jerry. He dived, and they watched him; and when he swam around to take his place, they made way for him. He felt he was accepted and he dived again, carefully, proud of himself.

Soon the biggest of the boys poised himself, shot down into the water, and did not come up. The others stood about, watching. Jerry, after waiting for the sleek brown head to appear, let out a yell of warning; they looked at him idly and turned their eyes back towards the water. After a long time, the boy came up on the other side of a big dark rock, letting the air out of his lungs in a sputtering gasp and a shout of triumph. Immediately the rest of them dived in. One moment, the morning seemed full of chattering boys; the next, the air and the surface of the water were empty. But through the heavy blue, dark shapes could be seen moving and groping.

Jerry dived, shot past the school of underwater swimmers, saw a black wall of rock looming at him, touched it, and bobbed up at once to the surface, where the wall was a low barrier he could see across. There was no one visible; under him, in the water, the dim shapes of the swimmers had disappeared. Then one, and then another of the boys came up on the far side of the barrier of rock, and he understood that they had swum through some gap or hole in it. He plunged down again. He could see nothing through the stinging salt water but the blank rock. When he came up the boys were all on the diving rock, preparing to attempt the feat again. And now, in a panic of failure, he yelled up, in English, "Look at me! Look!" and he began splashing and kicking in the water like a foolish dog.

They looked down gravely, frowning. He knew the frown. At moments of failure, when he clowned to claim his mother's attention, it was with just this grave, embarrassed inspection that she rewarded him. Through his hot shame, feeling the pleading grin on his face like a scar that he could never remove, he looked up at the group of big brown boys on the rock and shouted "*Bonjour! Merci! Au revoir! Monsieur, monsieur!*" while he hooked his fingers round his ears and waggled them.

Water surged into his mouth; he choked, sank, came up. The rock, lately weighted with boys, seemed to rear up out of the water as their weight was removed. They were flying down past him now, into the water; the air was full of falling bodies. Then the rock was empty in the hot sunlight. He counted one, two, three . . .

At fifty, he was terrified. They must all be drowning beneath him, in the watery caves of the rock! At a hundred, he stared around him at the empty hillside, wondering if he should yell for help. He counted faster, faster, to hurry them up, to bring them to the surface quickly, to drown them quickly—anything rather than the terror of counting on and on into the blue emptiness of the morning. And then, at a hundred and sixty, the water beyond the rock was full of boys blowing like brown whales. They swam back to the shore without a look at him.

He climbed back to the diving rock and sat down, feeling the hot roughness of it under his thighs. The boys were gathering up their bits of clothing and running off along the shore to another promontory. They were leaving to get away from him. He cried openly, fists in his eyes. There was no one to see him, and he cried himself out.

It seemed to him that a long time had passed, and he swam out to where he could see his mother. Yes, she was still there, a yellow spot under an orange umbrella. He swam back to the big rock, climbed up, and dived into the blue pool among the fanged and angry boulders. Down he went, until he touched the wall of rock again. But the salt was so painful in his eyes that he could not see.

He came to the surface, swam to shore and went back to the villa to wait for his mother. Soon she walked slowly up the path, swinging her striped bag, the flushed, naked arm dangling beside her. "I want some swimming goggles," he panted, defiant and beseeching.

She gave him a patient, inquisitive look as she said casually, "Well, of course, darling."

But now, now, now! He must have them this minute, and no other time. He nagged and pestered until she went with him to a shop. As soon as she had bought the goggles, he grabbed them from her hand as if she were going to claim them for herself, and was off, running down the steep path to the bay.

Jerry swam out to the big barrier rock, adjusted the goggles, and dived. The impact of the water broke the rubber-enclosed vacuum, and the goggles came loose. He understood that he must swim down to the base of the rock from the surface of the water. He fixed the goggles tight and firm, filled his lungs, and floated, face down, on the water. Now he could see. It was as if he had eyes of a different kind—fish eyes that showed everything clear and delicate and wavering in the bright water.

Under him, six or seven feet down, was a floor of perfectly clean, shining white sand, rippled firm and hard by the tides. Two greyish shapes steered there, like long, rounded pieces of wood or slate. They were fish. He saw them nose towards each other, poise motionless, make a dart forward, swerve off, and come around again. It was like a water dance. A few inches above them the water sparkled as if sequins were dropping through it. Fish again—myriads of minute fish, the length of his fingernail—were drifting through the water, and in a moment he could feel the innumerable tiny touches of them against his limbs. It was like swimming in flaked silver. The great rock the big boys had swum through rose sheer out of the white sand—black, tufted lightly with greenish weed. He could see no gap in it. He swam down to its base.

Again and again he rose, took a big chestful of air, and went down. Again and again he groped over the surface of the rock, feeling it, almost hugging it in the desperate need to find the entrance. And then, once, while he was clinging to the black wall, his knees came up and he shot his feet out forward and they met no obstacle. He had found the hole.

He gained the surface, clambered about the stones that littered the barrier rock until he found a big one, and, with this in his arms, let himself down over the side of the rock. He dropped, with the weight, straight to the sandy floor. Clinging tight to the anchor of stone, he lay on his side and looked in under the dark shelf at the place where his feet had gone. He could see the hole. It was an irregular, dark gap; but he could not see deep into it. He let go of his anchor, clung with his hands to the edges of the hole, and tried to push himself in.

He got his head in, found his shoulders jammed, moved them in side-wise, and was inside as far as his waist. He could see nothing ahead. Something soft and clammy touched his mouth; he saw a dark frond moving against the greyish rock, and panic filled him. He thought of octopuses, of clinging weed. He pushed himself out backward and caught a glimpse, as he retreated, of a harmless tentacle of seaweed drifting in the mouth of the tunnel. But it was enough. He reached the sunlight, swam to shore, and lay on the diving rock. He looked down into the blue well of water. He knew he must find his way through that cave, or hole, or tunnel, and out the other side.

First, he thought, he must learn to control his breathing. He let himself down into the water with another big stone in his arms, so that he could lie effortlessly on the bottom of the sea. He counted. One, two, three. He counted steadily. He could hear the movement of blood in his chest. Fifty-one, fifty-two. . . . His chest was hurting. He let go of the rock and went up into the air. He saw that the sun was low. He rushed to the villa and found his mother at her supper. She said only "Did you enjoy yourself?" and he said "Yes."

All night the boy dreamed of the water-filled cave in the rock, and as soon as breakfast was over he went to the bay.

That night, his nose bled badly. For hours he had been underwater, learning to hold his breath, and now he felt weak and dizzy. His mother said, "I shouldn't overdo things, darling, if I were you."

That day and the next, Jerry exercised his lungs as if everything, the whole of his life, all that he would become, depended upon it. Again his nose bled at night, and his mother insisted on his coming with her the next day. It was a torment to him to waste a day of his careful self-training, but he stayed with her on that other beach, which now seemed a place for small children, a place where his mother might lie safe in the sun. It was not his beach.

He did not ask for permission, on the following day, to go to his beach. He went, before his mother could consider the complicated rights and wrongs of the matter. A day's rest, he discovered, had improved his count by ten. The big boys had made the passage while he counted a hundred and sixty. He had been counting fast, in his fright. Probably now, if he tried, he could get through that long tunnel, but he was not going to try yet. A curious, most unchildlike persistence, a controlled impatience, made him wait. In the meantime, he lay underwater on the white sand, littered now by stones he had brought down from the upper air, and studied the entrance to the tunnel. He knew every jut and corner of it, as far as it was possible to see. It was as if he already felt its sharpness about his shoulders.

He sat by the clock in the villa, when his mother was not near, and checked his time. He was incredulous and then proud to find he could hold his breath without strain for two minutes. The words "two minutes," authorised by the clock, brought close the adventure that was so necessary to him.

In another four days, his mother said casually one morning, they must go home. On the day before they left, he would do it. He would do it if it killed him, he said defiantly to himself. But two days before they were to leave—a day of triumph when he increased his count by fifteen—his nose bled so badly that he turned dizzy and had to lie limply over the big rock like a bit of seaweed, watching the thick red blood flow on to the rock and trickle slowly down to the sea. He was frightened. Supposing he turned dizzy in the tunnel? Supposing he died there, trapped? Supposing—his head went around, in the hot sun, and he almost gave up. He thought he would return to the house and lie down, and next summer, perhaps, when he had another year's growth in him—*then* he would go through the hole.

But even after he had made the decision, or thought he had, he found himself sitting up on the rock and looking down into the water; and he knew that now, this moment, when his nose had only just stopped bleeding, when his head was still sore and throbbing—this was the moment when he would try. If he did not do it now, he never would. He was trembling with fear that he would not go; and he was trembling with horror at the long, long tunnel under the rock, under the sea. Even in the open sunlight, the barrier rock seemed very wide and very heavy; tons of rock pressed down on where he would go. If he died there, he would lie until one day—perhaps not before next year—those big boys would swim into it and find it blocked.

He put on his goggles, fitted them tight, tested the vacuum. His hands were shaking. Then he chose the biggest stone he could carry and slipped over the edge of the rock until half of him was in the cool enclosing water and half in the hot sun. He looked up once at the empty sky, filled his lungs once, twice, and then sank fast to the bottom with the stone. He let it go and began to count. He took the edges of the hole in his hands and drew himself into it, wriggling his shoulders in sidewise as he remembered he must, kicking himself along with his feet.

Soon he was clear inside. He was in a small rock-bound hole filled with yellowish-grey water. The water was pushing him up against the roof. The roof was sharp and pained his back. He pulled himself along with his hands— fast, fast—and used his legs as levers. His head knocked against something; a sharp pain dizzied him. Fifty, fifty-one, fifty-two. . . . He was without light, and the water seemed to press upon him with the weight of rock. Seventy-one, seventy-two. . . . There was no strain on his lungs. He felt like an inflated balloon, his lungs were so light and easy, but his head was pulsing.

He was being continually pressed against the sharp roof, which felt slimy as well as sharp. Again he thought of octopuses, and wondered if the tunnel might be filled with weed that could tangle him. He gave himself a panicky, convulsive kick forward, ducked his head, and swam. His feet and hands moved freely, as if in open water. The hole must have widened out. He thought he must be swimming fast, and he was frightened of banging his head if the tunnel narrowed.

A hundred, a hundred and one . . . The water paled. Victory filled him. His lungs were beginning to hurt. A few more strokes and he would be out. He was counting wildly; he said a hundred and fifteen, and then, a long time later, a hundred and fifteen again. The water was a clear jewel-green all around him. Then he saw, above his head, a crack running up through the rock. Sunlight was falling through it, showing the clean, dark rock of the tunnel, a single mussel shell, and darkness ahead.

He was at the end of what he could do. He looked up at the crack as if it were filled with air and not water, as if he could put his mouth to it to draw in air. A hundred and fifteen, he heard himself say inside his head—but he had said that long ago. He must go on into the blackness ahead, or he would drown. His head was swelling, his lungs cracking. A hundred and fifteen, a hundred and fifteen pounded through his head, and he feebly clutched at rocks in the dark, pulling himself forward leaving the brief space of sunlit water behind. He felt he was dying. He was no longer quite conscious. He struggled on in the darkness between lapses into unconsciousness. An immense, swelling pain filled his head, and then the darkness cracked with an explosion of green light. His hands, groping forward, met nothing; and his feet, kicking back, propelled him out into the open sea.

He drifted to the surface, his face turned up to the air. He was gasping like a fish. He felt he would sink now and drown; he could not swim the few feet back to the rock. Then he was clutching it and pulling himself up onto it. He lay face down, gasping. He could see nothing but a red-veined, clotted dark. His eyes must have burst, he thought; they were full of blood. He tore off his goggles and a gout of blood went into the sea. His nose was bleeding, and the blood had filled the goggles.

He scooped up handfuls of water from the cool, salty sea, to splash on his face, and did not know whether it was blood or salt water he tasted. After a time, his heart quieted, his eyes cleared, and he sat up. He could see the local boys diving and playing half a mile away. He did not want them. He wanted nothing but to get back home and lie down.

In a short while, Jerry swam to shore and climbed slowly up the path to the villa. He flung himself on his bed and slept, waking at the sound of feet on the path outside. His mother was coming back. He rushed to the bathroom, thinking she must not see his face with bloodstains, or tears-tains, on it. He came out of the bathroom and met her as she walked into the villa, smiling, her eyes lighting up.

"Have a nice morning?" she asked, laying her hand on his warm brown shoulder a moment.

"Oh, yes, thank you," he said.

"You look a bit pale." And then, sharp and anxious, "How did you bang your head?"

"Oh, just banged it," he told her.

She looked at him closely. He was strained; his eyes were glazed-looking. She was worried. And then she said to herself, Oh, don't fuss! Nothing can happen. He can swim like a fish.

They sat down to lunch together.

"Mummy," he said, "I can stay underwater for two minutes—three minutes, at least." It came bursting out of him.

"Can you, darling?" she said. "Well, I shouldn't overdo it. I don't think you ought to swim any more today."

She was ready for a battle of wills, but he gave in at once. It was no longer of the least importance to go to the bay.

QUESTIONS

"Through the Tunnel"

1. From what narrative point of view is "Through the Tunnel" told?

2. Describe the relationship between Jerry and his mother. How is this relationship important in light of what happens in the story?

3. We are told that Jerry's mother's arms are "very white" and then, after her first day on the beach, sunburned; the local boys are tanned "dark brown." Why are these details important?

4. What are the obstacles Jerry faces in his attempts to swim through the tunnel?

5. What effect do the local boys have on Jerry? Why does he clown in front of them?

6. Why does Jerry want to swim through the tunnel? What will success mean to him? How is he changed by his success?

7. At the end of the story, why doesn't Jerry tell his mother what he has accomplished?

8. All initiations involve metaphorically "dying" to an old existence and being "reborn" in a new one. In what sense is "Through the Tunnel" the story of an initiation? Does the story contain an image of rebirth?

9. Describe Lessing's prose style in "Through the Tunnel." For comparison, you may want to look at the dramatically different style of John Barth's "Night-Sea Journey." Why is Lessing's style here appropriate to her subject?

Night-Sea Journey

JOHN BARTH

"One way or another, no matter which theory of our journey is correct, it's myself I address; to whom I rehearse as to a stranger our history and condition, and will disclose my secret hope though I sink for it.

"Is the journey my invention? Do the night, the sea, exist at all, I ask myself, apart from my experience of them? Do I myself exist, or is this a dream? Sometimes I wonder. And if I am, who am I? The Heritage I supposedly transport? But how can I be both vessel and contents? Such are the questions that beset my intervals of rest.

"My trouble is, I lack conviction. Many accounts of our situation seem plausible to me—where and what we are, why we swim and whither. But implausible ones as well, perhaps especially those, I must admit as possibly correct. Even likely. If at times, in certain humors—stroking in unison, say, with my neighbors and chanting with them 'Onward! Upward!'—I have supposed that we have after all a common Maker, Whose nature and motives we may not know, but Who engendered us in some mysterious wise and launched us forth toward some end known but to Him—if (for a moodslength only) I have been able to entertain such notions, very popular in certain quarters, it is because our night-sea journey partakes of their absurdity. One might even say: I can believe them *because* they are absurd.

"Has that been said before?

"Another paradox: it appears to be these recesses from swimming that sustain me in the swim. Two measures onward and upward, flailing with the rest, then I float exhausted and dispirited, brood upon the night, the sea, the journey, while the flood bears me a measure back and down: slow progress, but I live, I live, and make my way, aye, past many a drownèd comrade in the end, stronger, worthier than I, victims of their unremitting *joie de nager*. I have seen the best swimmers of my generation go under. Numberless the number of the dead! Thousands drown as I think this thought, millions as I rest before returning to the swim. And scores, hundreds of millions have expired since we surged forth, brave in our innocence, upon our dreadful way. 'Love! Love!' we sang then, a quarter-billion strong, and churned the warm sea white with joy of swimming! Now all are gone down—the buoyant, the sodden, leaders and followers, all gone under, while wretched I swim on. Yet these same reflective intervals that keep me afloat have led me into wonder, doubt, despair—strange emotions for a swimmer!—have led me, even, to suspect . . . that our night-sea journey is without meaning.

"Indeed, if I have yet to join the hosts of the suicides, it is because (fatigue apart) I find it no meaningfuller to drown myself than to go on swimming.

"I know that there are those who seem actually to enjoy the night-sea; who claim to love swimming for its own sake, or sincerely believe that 'reaching the Shore,' 'transmitting the Heritage' (*Whose* Heritage, I'd like to know? And to whom?) is worth the staggering cost. I do not. Swimming itself I find at best not actively unpleasant, more often tiresome, not infrequently a torment. Arguments from function and design don't impress me: granted that we can and do swim, that in a manner of speaking our long tails and streamlined heads are 'meant for' swimming; it by no means follows—for me, at least—that we *should* swim, or otherwise endeavor to 'fulfill our destiny.' Which is to say, Someone Else's destiny, since ours, so far as I can see, is merely to perish, one way or another, soon or late. The heartless zeal of our (departed) leaders, like the blind ambition and good cheer of my own youth, appalls me now; for the death of my comrades I am inconsolable. If the night-sea journey has justification, it is not for us swimmers ever to discover it.

"Oh, to be sure, 'Love!' one heard on every side: 'Love it is that drives and sustains us!' I translate: we don't know *what* drives and sustains us, only that we are most miserably driven and, imperfectly, sustained. *Love* is how we call our ignorance of what whips us. 'To reach the Shore,' then: but what if the Shore exists in the fancies of us swimmers merely, who dream it to account for the dreadful fact that we swim, have always and only swum, and continue swimming without respite (myself excepted) until we die? Supposing even that there *were* a Shore—that, as a cynical companion of mine once imagined, we rise from the drowned to discover all those vulgar superstitions and exalted metaphors to be literal truth: the giant Maker of us all, the Shores of Light beyond our night-sea journey!—whatever would a swimmer do there? The fact is, when we imagine the Shore, what comes to mind is just the opposite of our condition: no more night, no more sea, no more journeying. In short, the blissful estate of the drowned.

" 'Ours not to stop and think; ours but to swim and sink. . . .' Because a moment's thought reveals the pointlessness of swimming. 'No matter,' I've heard some say, even as they gulped their last: 'The night-sea journey may be absurd, but here we swim, will-we nill-we, against the flood, onward and upward, toward a Shore that may not exist and couldn't be reached if it did.' The thoughtful swimmer's choices, then, they say, are two: give over thrashing and go under for good, or embrace the absurdity; affirm in and for itself the night-sea journey; swim on with neither motive nor destination, for the sake of swimming, and compassionate moreover with your fellow swimmer, we being all at sea and equally in the dark. I find neither course acceptable. If not even the hypothetical Shore can justify a sea-full of drownèd comrades, to speak of the swim-in-itself as somehow doing so strikes me as obscene. I continue to swim—but only because blind habit, blind instinct, blind fear of drowning are still more strong than the horror of our journey. And if on occasion I have assisted a fellow-thrasher, joined in the cheers and songs, even passed along to others strokes of genius from the drownèd great, it's that I shrink by temperament from making myself conspicuous. To paddle off in one's own direction, assert one's independent right-of-way, overrun one's fellows without compunction, or dedicate oneself entirely to pleasures and diversions without regard for conscience—I can't finally condemn those who journey in this wise; in half my moods I envy them and despise the weak vitality that keeps me from following their example. But in reasonabler moments I remind myself that it's their very freedom and self-responsibility I reject, as more dramatically absurd, in our senseless circumstances, than tailing along in conventional fashion. Suicides, rebels, affirmers of the paradox—nay-sayers and yea-sayers alike to our fatal journey—I finally shake my head at them. And splash sighing past their corpses, one by one, as past a hundred sorts of others: friends, enemies, brothers, fools, sages, brutes—and nobodies, million upon million. I envy them all.

"A poor irony: that I, who find abhorrent and tautological the doctrine of survival of the fittest (*fitness* meaning, in my experience, nothing more than survival-ability, a talent whose only demonstration is the fact of survival, but whose chief ingredients seem to be strength, guile, callousness), may be the sole remaining swimmer! But the doctrine is false as well as repellent: Chance drowns the worthy with the unworthy, bears up the unfit with the fit by whatever definition, and makes the night-sea journey essentially *haphazard* as well as murderous and unjustified.

" 'You only swim once.' Why bother, then?

" 'Except ye drown, ye shall not reach the Shore of Life.' Poppycock.

"One of my late companions—that same cynic with the curious fancy, among the first to drown—entertained us with odd conjectures while we waited to begin our journey. A favorite theory of his was that the Father does exist, and did indeed make us and the sea we swim—but not a-purpose or even consciously; He made us, as it were, despite Himself, as we make waves with every tail-thrash, and may be unaware of our existence. Another was that He knows we're here but doesn't care what happens to us, inasmuch as He creates (voluntarily or not) other seas and swimmers at more or less regular intervals. In bitterer moments, such as just before he drowned, my friend even supposed that our Maker wished us unmade; there was indeed a Shore, he'd argue, which could save at least some of us from drowning and toward which it was our function to struggle—but for reasons unknowable to us He wanted desperately to prevent our reaching that happy place and fulfilling our destiny. Our 'Father,' in short, was our adversary and would-be killer! No less outrageous, and of-

fensive to traditional opinion, were the fellow's speculations on the nature
of our Maker: that He might well be no swimmer Himself at all, but some
sort of monstrosity, perhaps even tailless; that He might be stupid, malicious, insensible, perverse, or asleep and dreaming; that the end for which
He created and launched us forth, and which we flagellate ourselves to
fathom, was perhaps immoral, even obscene. Et cetera, et cetera: there
was no end to the chap's conjectures, or the impoliteness of his fancy; I
have reason to suspect that his early demise, whether planned by 'our Maker'
or not, was expedited by certain fellow-swimmers indignant at his blasphemies.

"In other moods, however (he was given to moods as I), his theorizing
would become half-serious, so it seemed to me, especially upon the subjects of Fate and Immortality, to which our youthful conversations often
turned. Then his harangues, if no less fantastical, grew solemn and obscure, and if he was still baiting us, his passion undid the joke. His objection to popular opinions of the hereafter, he would declare, was their claim
to general validity. Why need believers hold that *all* the drownèd rise to be
judged at journey's end, and non-believers that drowning is final without
exception? In *his* opinion (so he'd vow at least), nearly everyone's fate was
permanent death; indeed he took a sour pleasure in supposing that every
'Maker' made thousands of separate seas in His creative life-time, each
populated like ours with millions of swimmers, and that in almost every
instance both sea and swimmers were utterly annihilated, whether accidentally or by malevolent design. (Nothing if not pluralistic, he imagined
there might be millions and billions of 'Fathers,' perhaps in some 'night-
sea' of their own!) However—and here he turned infidels against him with
the faithful—he professed to believe that in possibly a single night-sea per
thousand, say, one of its quarter-billion swimmers (that is, one swimmer in
two hundred fifty billions) achieved a qualified immortality. In some cases
the rate might be slightly higher; in others it was vastly lower, for just as
there are swimmers of every degree of proficiency, including some who
drown before the journey starts, unable to swim at all, and others created
drowned, as it were, so he imagined what can only be termed impotent
Creators, Makers unable to Make, as well as uncommonly fertile ones and
all grades between. And it pleased him to deny any necessary relation between a Maker's productivity and His other virtues—including, even, the
quality of His creatures.

"I could go on (*he* surely did) with his elaboration of these mad notions—
such as that swimmers in other night-seas needn't be of our kind; that
Makers themselves might belong to different species, so to speak; that our
particular Maker mightn't Himself be immortal, or that we might be not
only His emissaries but His 'immortality,' continuing His life and our own,
transmogrified, beyond our individual deaths. Even this modified immortality (meaningless to me) he conceived as relative and contingent, subject
to accidental or deliberate termination: his pet hypothesis was that Makers
and swimmers *each generate the other*—against all odds, their number being

so great—and that any given 'immortality chain' could terminate after any number of cycles, so that what was 'immortal' (still speaking relatively) was only the cyclic process of incarnation, which itself might have a beginning and an end. Alternatively he liked to imagine cycles within cycles, either finite or infinite: for example, the 'night-sea,' as it were, in which Makers 'swam' and created night-seas and swimmers like ourselves, might be the creation of a larger Maker, Himself one of many, Who in turn et cetera. Time itself he regarded as relative to our experience, like magnitude: who knew but what, with each thrash of our tails, minuscule seas and swimmers, whole eternities, came to pass—as ours, perhaps, and our Maker's Maker's, was elapsing between the strokes of some supertail, in a slower order of time?

"Naturally I hooted with the others at this nonsense. We were young then, and had only the dimmest notion of what lay ahead; in our ignorance we imagined night-sea journeying to be a positively heroic enterprise. Its meaning and value we never questioned; to be sure, some must go down by the way, a pity no doubt, but to win a race requires that others lose, and like all my fellows I took for granted that I would be the winner. We milled and swarmed, impatient to be off, never mind where or why, only to try our youth against the realities of night and sea; if we indulged the skeptic at all, it was as a droll, half-contemptible mascot. When he died in the initial slaughter, no one cared.

"And even now I don't subscribe to all his views—but I no longer scoff. The horror of our history has purged me of opinions, as of vanity, confidence, spirit, charity, hope, vitality, everything—except dull dread and a kind of melancholy, stunned persistence. What leads me to recall his fancies is my growing suspicion that I, of all swimmers, may be the sole survivor of this fell journey, tale-bearer of a generation. This suspicion, together with the recent sea-change, suggests to me now that nothing is impossible, not even my late companion's wildest visions, and brings me to a certain desperate resolve, the point of my chronicling.

"Very likely I have lost my senses. The carnage at our setting out; our decimation by whirlpool, poisoned cataract, sea-convulsion; the panic stampedes, mutinies, slaughters, mass suicides; the mounting evidence that none will survive the journey—add to these anguish and fatigue; it were a miracle if sanity stayed afloat. Thus I admit, with the other possibilities, that the present sweetening and calming of the sea, and what seems to be a kind of vasty presence, song, or summons from the near upstream, may be hallucinations of disordered sensibility. . . .

"Perhaps, even, I am drowned already. Surely I was never meant for the rough-and-tumble of the swim; not impossibly I perished at the outset and have only imagined the night-sea journey from some final deep. In any case, I'm no longer young, and it is we spent old swimmers, disabused of every illusion, who are most vulnerable to dreams.

"Sometimes I think I am my drownèd friend.

"Out with it: I've begun to believe, not only that *She* exists, but that She lies not far ahead, and stills the sea, and draws me Herward! Aghast,

I recollect his maddest notion: that our destination (which existed, mind, in but one night-sea out of hundreds and thousands) was no Shore, as commonly conceived, but a mysterious being, indescribable except by paradox and vaguest figure: wholly different from us swimmers, yet our complement; the death of us, yet our salvation and resurrection; simultaneously our journey's end, mid-point, and commencement; not membered and thrashing like us, but a motionless or hugely gliding sphere of unimaginable dimension; self-contained, yet dependent absolutely, in some wise, upon the chance (always monstrously improbable) that one of us will survive the night-sea journey and reach . . . Her! *Her*, he called it, or *She*, which is to say, Other-than-a-he. I shake my head; the thing is too preposterous; it is myself I talk to, to keep my reason in this awful darkness. There is no She! There is no You! I rave to myself; it's Death alone that hears and summons. To the drowned, all seas are calm. . . .

"Listen: my friend maintained that in every order of creation there are two sorts of creators, contrary yet complementary, one of which gives rise to seas and swimmers, the other to the Night-which-contains-the-sea and to What-waits-at-the-journey's-end: the former, in short, to destiny, the latter to destination (and both profligately, involuntarily, perhaps indifferently or unwittingly). The 'purpose' of the night-sea journey—but not necessarily of the journeyer or of either Maker!—my friend could describe only in abstractions; *consummation, transfiguration, union of contraries, transcension of categories.* When we laughed, he would shrug and admit that he understood the business no better than we, and thought it ridiculous, dreary, possibly obscene. 'But one of you,' he'd add with his wry smile, 'may be the Hero destined to complete the night-sea journey and be one with Her. Chances are, of course, you won't make it.' He himself, he declared, was not even going to try; the whole idea repelled him; if we chose to dismiss it as an ugly fiction, so much the better for us; thrash, splash, and be merry, we were soon enough drowned. But there it was, he could not say how he knew or why he bothered to tell us, any more than he could say what would happen after She and Hero, Shore and Swimmer, 'merged identities' to become something both and neither. He quite agreed with me that if the issue of that magical union had no memory of the night-sea journey, for example, it enjoyed a poor sort of immortality; even poorer if, as he rather imagined, a swimmer-hero plus a She equalled or became merely another Maker of future night-seas and the rest, at such incredible expense of life. This being the case—he was persuaded it was—the merciful thing to do was refuse to participate; the genuine heroes, in his opinion, were the suicides, and the hero of heroes would be the swimmer who, in the very presence of the Other, refused Her proffered 'immortality' and thus put an end to at least one cycle of catastrophes.

"How we mocked him! Our moment came, we hurtled forth, pretending to glory in the adventure, thrashing, singing, cursing, strangling, rationalizing, rescuing, killing, inventing rules and stories and relationships, giving up, struggling on, but dying all, and still in darkness, until only a battered remnant was left to croak 'Onward, upward,' like a bitter echo. Then they too fell silent—victims, I can only presume, of the last frightful wave—and the moment came when I also, utterly desolate and spent, thrashed my last and gave myself over to the current, to sink or float as might be, but swim no more. Whereupon, marvelous to tell, in an instant the sea grew still! Then warmly, gently, the great tide turned, began to bear me, as it does now, onward and upward will-I nill-I, like a flood of joy—and I recalled with dismay my dead friend's teaching.

"I am not deceived. This new emotion is Her doing; the desire that possesses me is Her bewitchment. Lucidity passes from me; in a moment I'll cry 'Love!' bury myself in Her side, and be 'transfigured.' Which is to say, I die already; this fellow transported by passion is not I; *I am he who abjures and rejects the night-sea journey!* I. . . .

"I am all love. 'Come!' She whispers, and I have no will.

"You who I may be about to become, whatever You are: with the last twitch of my real self I beg You to listen. It is *not* love that sustains me! No; though Her magic makes me burn to sing the contrary, and though I drown even now for the blasphemy, I will say truth. What has fetched me across this dreadful sea is a single hope, gift of my poor dead comrade: that You may be stronger-willed than I, and that by sheer force of concentration I may transmit to You, along with Your official Heritage, a private legacy of awful recollection and negative resolve. Mad as it may be, my dream is that some unimaginable embodiment of myself (or myself plus Her if that's how it must be) will come to find itself expressing, in however garbled or radical a translation, some reflection of these reflections. If against all odds this comes to pass, may You to whom, through whom I speak, do what I cannot: terminate this aimless, brutal business! Stop Your hearing against Her song! Hate love!

"Still alive, afloat, afire. Farewell then my penultimate hope: that one may be sunk for direst blasphemy on the very shore of the Shore. Can it be (my old friend would smile) that only utterest nay-sayers survive the night? But even that were Sense, and there is no sense, only senseless love, senseless death. Whoever echoes these reflections: be more courageous than their author! An end to night-sea journeys! Make no more! And forswear me when I shall forswear myself, deny myself, plunge into Her who summons, singing . . .

" 'Love! Love! Love!' "

QUESTIONS

"Night-Sea Journey"

1. It is impossible to fully understand or appreciate this extremely clever story until you have identified the narrator, at which point a number of possi-

bly confusing elements become clear. Who is the narrator? How do you know? Once you have identified him, how does your understanding of the story change? Who is She? The Maker? What is the night-sea? The Heritage?

2. The story's title refers to a widespread mythological motif in which a hero first undergoes a symbolic death or "return to the womb," by descending into a cave, diving into the ocean, or being devoured by a monster, then travels through the "kingdom of the dark," where he or she must survive a number of ordeals, and is finally reborn at the journey's end. (The biblical story of Jonah and the great fish is one well-known version of this myth.) How does Barth use this myth in his story, working clever variations on it? In what ways is the narrators's experience described as a traditional hero's journey? On the other hand, in what ways is the narrator a very nontraditional hero, even an anti-hero? How would you describe him and his character, feelings, and personality?

3. Though "Night-Sea Journey" is extremely ingenious, it is much more than that. Its depth and substance come from the way Barth makes it work on two levels: first, as a fanciful description of a biological process (along with the narrator's philosophical reflections on that process) and, second, as a meditation on the human condition. How does Barth manage this? How do the narrator's situation and the things he says about it relate to humanity in general?

4. This story deals explicitly with the notion of the absurd, the perception of life as an utterly arbitrary, meaningless affair. Where does this theme appear in the story? Why does the narrator regard his journey as absurd? What other stories in this chapter share a similar vision of human life?

5. Although the vision of existence embodied in "Night-Sea Journey" is highly pessimistic, the story is full of comical elements. Point to some of them. How important is the narrator's "elevated" mode of speech in creating a humorous tone? What puns, parodic expressions, and other kinds of wordplay can you find in this story?

6. Point to some of the ironic passages in the story, especially in those parts relating to the speaker's "cynical companion." What is so ironic about the cynic's "mad notions"? Explain what those notions are.

7. At the end of the work, the narrator reveals his purpose in telling his story, his "single hope," his dreams. What is that hope? To whom is it addressed?

8. What happens to the narrator at the end of the story?

CHAPTER FOUR

Helpers and Guides

Because the journey is so difficult, the questers of myth and folklore frequently find themselves at a loss. Faced with an insurmountable obstacle, an insoluble mystery, or an enemy with powers that surpass their own, even the mightiest heroes may need help to reach their goals.

Sometimes, this help comes from very unlikely sources. Fairy-tale and folklore characters are often saved from terrible predicaments by seemingly insignificant creatures that turn out to have exceptional, sometimes indeed magical, abilities. Beasts, birds, or even insects can offer the heroes guidance, wise counsel, and unexpected assistance. For example, when the protagonist of the Grimm Brothers' story "The Queen Bee" must find a thousand pearls scattered beneath a forest floor or be turned into a stone at sunset, he is rescued by an army of friendly ants that rush to his aid and recover every one of the buried gems. Another Grimm Brothers hero, the young prince of "The Three Feathers," is commanded by his father to locate the most beautiful carpet, ring, and woman in the world. He is completely nonplussed until he encounters an enchanted toad that tells him where these treasures can be found. The Irish hero Connad, who is sent on a dangerous quest to bring back three golden apples from a magical kingdom, succeeds only because of the constant advice he receives from his humble pony, a creature that, in spite of its unimpressive appearance, possesses not only superior wisdom but also the power of speech.

Because of its basic implausibility, the figure of the helpful animal is rarely found in the world of serious writers. (An exception is Bernard Malamud's seriocomic fantasy "The Jewbird," in his short story collection *Idiots First*. The story concerns a learned but highly bedraggled bird named Mr. Schwartz, who moves in with a New York family and serves for a while as a tutor to its slow-witted son.) When the protagonists of the stories in this anthology are lost, baffled, discouraged, or deeply uncertain about how to proceed, they may, if they are lucky, be steered through their crises by one of two recurrent characters who, because they are older and more experienced than the heroes, are able to help the younger people on their way. These two figures also have their antecedents in mythology and folklore, where they are known generically as the Good Mother and the Wise Old Man.

The Good Mother may literally be the protagonist's parent, as in Ernest Gaines's story "The Sky Is Gray." On the other hand, she may be childless, even virginal: her role is determined not by biology but by the quality of her assistance, which always has a distinctly maternal character. In ancient mythologies, the Good Mother appears in the form of the earth goddess, who supplies humanity with all of nature's bounties. In the story of "Cinderella," she is the title character's fairy godmother, who comforts the mistreated young girl, magically clothes her in a magnificent gown, and oversees her passage into adulthood. The Good Mother is also a very common character in the popular arts: for example, we find her in *The Wizard of Oz* in the guise of Glinda, Witch of the North, whose kiss acts as a protective talisman, keeping Dorothy from harm on the long and dangerous road to the Emerald City. Frodo, the central character of J. R. R. Tolkien's *The Lord of the Rings*, also receives a talisman from a Good Mother, the elf-queen Galadriel, who presents the quest hero with a phial full of magical light to brighten his way in the darkness as he journeys to the shadowland of Mordor. The gifts the Good Mother bestows, in short, are the kind traditionally identified as motherly: protection, succor, compassion, sustenance, and, in some cases, spiritual nourishment.

Whereas the Good Mother typically gives the hero maternal care and material support—in the form of food, clothing, or a magical amulet to shield the quester from danger—her masculine counterpart, the mythological figure known as the Wise Old Man, tends to offer a different type of assistance. Generally portrayed as a magician, wizard, seer, or sage, he is the possessor of special, often arcane, knowledge, which he passes on to those rare individuals who have shown themselves to be worthy of it. Frequently, the Wise Old Man functions as a surrogate father for quest heroes, taking them under his wing as children, training them in the skills they will need to succeed in their enterprises, and initiating them into the uses and responsibilities of power. A good example can be found in T. H. White's popular retelling of the Camelot legend, *The Once and Future King*, the first part of which, *The Sword in the Stone*, focuses on the figure of the wizard Merlin and his role as tutor to the boy who will grow up to be King Arthur. When his protegés are ready to begin the quest, the Wise Old Man may accompany them on the journey, to warn them of any dangers that lie ahead and point out the path that will lead them to their goals. At other times, he appears only when the hero has arrived at a dead end and is in desperate need of guidance.

For example, when the title character of the Estonian folktale "How an Orphan Boy Unexpectedly Found His Luck" loses his way in the woods and, exhausted, falls into a deep sleep, he awakens to discover an old hermit standing over him, who tells the boy what course he must follow. When Robin, the protagonist of Nathaniel Hawthorne's "My Kinsman, Major Molineux" (see Chapter Three), has reached an impasse in his search and is sitting on the church-door steps, not knowing which way to turn, he meets a middle-aged man who gives him the first friendly advice he has received. When, at the climax of the movie *Star Wars*, Luke Skywalker finds himself unable to hit the enemy target by means of his computerized gunsight, he is suddenly visited by the spirit of his dead mentor, Obi-Wan Kenobi, who reminds the boy of the secret he needs to accomplish his task. In essence, what the Wise Old Man offers his charges—indeed, what he symbolizes in psychological terms—is not only mature knowledge and saving insight but also self-realization. By following his counsel, they are delivered from narrowness and immobility and set on the road that leads ultimately to the release of all their latent powers and capabilities. The Wise Old Man helps them develop into the heroes they have always had the potential to become.

The protagonists of the following stories, most of them either children or young adults, appear along with a variety of older characters whose guidance ranges from the traditional to the highly unconventional. Indeed, some of these fictional helpers fail entirely in their educative roles. For instance, the central irony of Philip Roth's "The Conversion of the Jews" is that the hero's spiritual leader, Rabbi Binder, is a narrow "hidebound" man, as his name suggests. He responds by rote to the thoughtful questions raised by the young protagonist, whose last name, Freedman, is likewise significant. In fact, it is the child who possesses the higher wisdom and ends up teaching his elders and friends an important lesson about God. In Gabriel García Márquez's "Blacamán the Good, Vendor of Miracles," the title character discovers his supernatural powers while being subjected to a kind of initiatory ordeal by his mentor and namesake. But it seems clear that the boy's transformation into a true miracle-worker takes place in spite of—almost in defiance of—the harsh treatment he receives from the old charlatan, on whom the narrator takes a terrible revenge.

Other protagonists in these stories treat their elders badly (though not quite *so* badly). The narrator of Toni Cade Bambara's "The Lesson" behaves with youthful insolence, verging at times on contempt. But a number of these heroes respond to their mentors with the kind of gratitude, devotion, even awe, that a child feels for a beloved parent or grandparent. This is true of Han Fook in Herman Hesse's "The Poet," whose guru, "The Master of the Perfect Word," is the spirit of art personified; of the narrator of Isaac Babel's "Awakening," whose mentor put him in touch for the first time with the physical world of nature and the body; and of the son in Ernest Gaines's "The Sky Is Gray," whose mother guides him on an arduous, though edifying, odyssey through a small Southern town.

Though the woman in Gaines's story functions, to a certain degree, as a traditional Good Mother figure, making sure that her son receives food, shelter, and warmth, as well as relief from the terrible pain he is in, her main concern is one usually associated with masculine helpers: namely, to initiate the boy into manhood. (This is possibly because she has been forced to serve as both father and mother to her children.) Whatever their individual concerns, the helpers in this chapter ultimately teach the same fundamental lesson. By introducing the young protagonists into a larger world than they have previously known and, even more important, by giving them access to the untapped, indeed unsuspected, powers that reside within them, these older and wiser characters show their charges how to lead a fuller life: not simply how to be a man or a woman, a poet or a hunter, but how to be a human being.

The Poet

HERMANN HESSE

The story is told of the Chinese poet Han Fook that from early youth he was animated by an intense desire to learn all about the poet's art and to perfect himself in everything connected with it. In those days he was still living in his home city on the Yellow River and had become engaged—at his own wish and with the aid of his parents, who loved him tenderly—to a girl of good family; the wedding was to be announced shortly for a chosen day of good omen. Han Fook at this time was about twenty years old and a handsome young man, modest and of agreeable manners, instructed in the sciences and, despite his youth, already known among the literary folk of his district for a number of remarkable poems. Without being exactly rich, he had the expectation of comfortable means, which would be increased by the dowry of his bride, and since this bride was also very beautiful and virtuous, nothing whatever seemed lacking to the youth's happiness. Nevertheless, he was not entirely content, for his heart was filled with the ambition to become a perfect poet.

Then one evening when a lantern festival was being celebrated on the river, it happened that Han Fook was wandering alone on the opposite bank. He leaned against the trunk of a tree that hung out over the water, and mirrored in the river he saw a thousand lights floating and trembling, he saw men and women and young girls on the boats and barges, greeting each other and glowing like beautiful flowers in their festive robes, he heard the girl singers, the hum of the zither and the sweet tones of the flute players, and over all this he saw the bluish night arched like the dome of a temple. The youth's heart beat high as he took in all this beauty, a lonely observer in pursuit of his whim. But much as he longed to go across the river and take part in the feast and be in the company of his bride-to-be and his friends, much deeper was his longing to absorb it all as a perceptive observer and to reproduce it in a wholly perfect poem: the blue of the night and the play of the light on the water and the joy of the guests and the yearning of the silent onlooker leaning against the tree trunk on the bank. He realized that at all festivals and with all joys of this earth he would never feel wholly comfortable and serene at heart; even in the midst of life he would remain solitary and be, to a certain extent, a watcher, an alien, and he felt that his soul, unlike most others, was so formed that he must be alone to experience both the beauty of the earth and the secret longings of a stranger. Thereupon he grew sad, and pondered this matter, and the conclusion of his thoughts was this, that true happiness and deep satisfaction could only be his if on occasion he succeeded in mirroring the world so perfectly in his poems that in these mirror images he would possess the essence of the world, purified and made eternal.

Han Fook hardly knew whether he was still awake or had fallen asleep when he heard a slight rustling and saw a stranger standing beside the trunk of the tree, an old man of reverend aspect, wearing a violet robe. Han Fook roused himself and greeted the stranger with the salutation appropriate to the aged and distinguished; the stranger, however, smiled and spoke a few verses in which everything the young man had just felt was expressed so completely and beautifully and so exactly in accord with the rules of the great poets that the youth's heart stood still with amazement.

"Oh, who are you?" he cried, bowing deeply. "You who can see into my soul and who recite more beautiful verses than I have ever heard from any of my teachers!"

The stranger smiled once more with the smile of one made perfect, and said: "If you wish to be a poet, come to me. You will find my hut beside the source of the Great River in the northwestern mountains. I am called Master of the Perfect Word."

Thereupon the aged man stepped into the narrow shadow of the tree and instantly disappeared, and Han Fook, searching for him in vain and finding no trace of him, finally decided that it had all been a dream caused by his fatigue. He hastened across to the boats and joined in the festival, but amid the conversation and the music of the flutes he continued to hear the mysterious voice of the stranger, and his soul seemed to have gone away with the old man, for he sat remote and with dreaming eyes among the merry folk, who teased him for being in love.

A few days later Han Fook's father prepared to summon his friends and relations to decide upon the day of the wedding. The bridegroom demurred and said: "Forgive me if I seem to offend against the duty a son owes his father. But you know how great my longing is to distinguish myself in the art of poetry, and even though some of my friends praise my poems, nevertheless I know very well that I am still a beginner and still on the first stage of the journey. Therefore, I beg you to let me go my way in loneliness for a while and devote myself to my studies, for it seems to me that having a wife and a house to govern will keep me from these things. But now I am still young and without other duties, and I would like to live for a time for my poetry, from which I hope to gain joy and fame."

This speech filled his father with great surprise and he said: "This art must indeed be dearer to you than anything, since you wish to postpone your wedding on account of it. Or has something arisen between you and your bride? If so, tell me so that I can help to reconcile you, or select another girl."

The son swore, however, that his bride-to-be was no less dear to him than she had been yesterday and always, and that no shadow of discord had fallen between them. Then he told his father that on the day of the lantern festival a Master had become known to him in a dream, and that he desired to be his pupil more ardently than all the happiness in the world.

"Very well," his father said, "I will grant you a year. In this time you may pursue your dream, which perhaps was sent to you by a god."

"It may even take two years," Han Fook said hesitantly. "Who can tell?"

So his father let him go, and was troubled; the youth, however, wrote a letter to his bride, said farewell, and departed.

When he had wandered for a very long time, he reached the source of the river, and in complete isolation he found a bamboo hut, and in front of the hut on a woven mat sat the aged man whom he had seen beside the tree on the river bank. He sat playing a lute, and when he saw his guest approach with reverence he did not rise or greet him but simply smiled and let his delicate fingers run over the strings, and a magical music flowed like a silver cloud through the valley, so that the youth stood amazed and in his sweet astonishment forgot everything, until the Master of the Perfect Word laid aside his little lute and stepped into the hut. Then Han Fook followed him reverently and stayed with him as his servant and pupil.

With the passing of a month he had learned to despise all the poems he had hitherto composed, and he blotted them out of his memory. And after more months he blotted out all the songs that he had learned from his teachers at home. The Master rarely spoke to him; in silence he taught him the art of lute playing until the pupil's being was entirely saturated with music. Once Han Fook made a little poem which described the flight of two birds in the autumn sky, and he was pleased with it. He dared not show it to the Master, but one evening he sang it outside the hut, and the Master listened attentively. However, he said no word. He simply played softly on his lute and at once the air grew cool and twilight fell suddenly, a sharp wind arose although it was midsummer, and through the sky which had grown gray flew two herons in majestic migration, and everything was so much more beautiful and perfect than in the pupil's verses that the latter became sad and was silent and felt that he was worthless. And this is what the ancient did each time, and when a year had passed, Han Fook had almost completely mastered the playing of the lute, but the art of poetry seemed to him ever more difficult and sublime.

When two years had passed, the youth felt a devouring homesickness for his family, his native city, and his bride, and he besought the Master to let him leave.

The Master smiled and nodded. "You are free," he said, "and may go where you like. You may return, you may stay away, just as it suits you."

Then the pupil set out on his journey and traveled uninterruptedly until one morning in the half light of dawn he stood on the bank of his native river and looked across the arched bridge to his home city. He stole secretly into his father's garden and listened through the window of the bedchamber to his father's breathing as he slept, and he slipped into the orchard beside his bride's house and climbed a pear tree, and from there he saw his bride standing in her room combing her hair. And while he compared all these things which he was seeing with his eyes to the mental pictures he had painted of them in his homesickness, it became clear to him that he was, after all, destined to be a poet, and he saw that in poets' dreams reside a beauty and enchantment that one seeks in vain in the things of the real world. And he climbed down from the tree and fled out of the garden and over the bridge, away from his native city, and returned to the high mountain valley. There, as before, sat the old Master in front of his hut on his modest mat, striking the lute with his fingers, and instead of a greeting he recited two verses about the blessings of art, and at their depth and harmony the young man's eyes filled with tears.

Once more Han Fook stayed with the Master of the Perfect Word, who, now that his pupil has mastered the lute, instructed him in the zither, and the months melted away like snow before the west wind. Twice more it happened that he was overcome by homesickness. On the one occasion he ran away secretly at night, but before he had reached the last bend in the valley the night wind blew across the zither hanging at the door of the hut, and the notes flew after him and called him back so that he could not resist them. But the next time he dreamed he was planting a young tree in his garden, and his wife and children were assembled there and his children were watering the tree with wine and milk. When he awoke, the moon was shining into his room and he got up, disturbed in mind, and saw in the next room the Master lying asleep with his gray beard trembling gently; then he was overcome by a bitter hatred for this man who, it seemed to him, had destroyed his life and cheated him of his future. He was about to throw himself upon the Master and murder him when the ancient opened his eyes and began to smile with a sad sweetness and gentleness that disarmed his pupil.

"Remember, Han Fook," the aged man said softly, "you are free to do what you like. You may go to your home and plant trees, you may hate me and kill me, it makes very little difference."

"Oh, how could I hate you?" the poet cried, deeply moved. "That would be like hating heaven itself."

And he stayed and learned to play the zither, and after that the flute, and later he began under his Master's guidance to make poems, and he slowly learned the secret art of apparently saying only simple and homely things but thereby stirring the hearer's soul like wind on the surface of the water. He described the coming of the sun, how it hesitates on the mountain's rim, and the noiseless darting of the fishes when they flee like shadows under the water, and the swaying of a young birch tree in the spring wind, and when people listened it was not only the sun and the play of the fish and the whispering of the birch tree, but it seemed as though heaven and earth each time chimed together for an instant in perfect harmony, and each hearer was impelled to think with joy or pain about what he loved or hated, the boy about sport, the youth about his beloved, and the old man about death.

Han Fook no longer knew how many years he had spent with the Master beside the source of the Great River; often it seemed to him as though he had entered this valley only the evening before and been received by the ancient playing on his stringed instrument; often, too, it seemed as though all the ages and epochs of man had vanished behind him and become unreal.

And then one morning he awoke alone in the house, and though he searched everywhere and called, the Master had disappeared. Overnight it seemed suddenly to have become autumn, a raw wind tugged at the old hut, and over the ridge of the mountain great flights of migratory birds were moving, though it was not yet the season for that.

Then Han Fook took the little lute with him and descended to his native province, and when he came among men they greeted him with the salutation appropriate to the aged and distinguished, and when he came to his home city he found that his father and his bride and his relations had died and other people were living in their houses. In the evening, however, the festival of the lanterns was celebrated on the river and the poet Han Fook stood on the far side on the darker bank, leaning against the trunk of an ancient tree. And when he played on the little lute, the women began to sigh and looked into the night, enchanted and overwhelmed, and the young men called for the lute player, whom they could not find anywhere, and they exclaimed that none of them had ever heard such tones from a lute. But Han Fook only smiled. He looked into the river where floated the mirrored images of the thousand lamps; and just as he could no longer distinguish between the reflections and reality, so he found in his soul no difference between this festival and that first one when he had stood there as a youth and heard the words of the strange Master.

QUESTIONS

"The Poet"

1. What is the nature of Han Fook's quest? What is he seeking? What trials or ordeals must he undergo on his way to his goal?

2. How would you define the mood or atmosphere of this story? Does it

seem consistent with what the story is about: a young man's development into a poet? Can you point to any particular lyrical passages?

3. Describe the Wise Old man in this story, the Master of the Perfect Word. How does he communicate his wisdom to Han Fook? What sort of wisdom does he communicate? How does Han Fook feel about the Master? Do his feelings remain consistent throughout the story?

4. Are you sympathetic to Han Fook's decision to abandon his family and his bride to pursue his studies? Do you think he makes the right choice?

5. What makes Han Fook realize that he is "after all, destined to be a poet"?

6. How would you describe the style in which this story is written? (Look, for example, at the very first sentence.) Why do you think Hesse chose to write it in this way? What effect does this style create?

7. While reading this story, did you feel that you came to know either of the main characters as a person, a three-dimensional human being with a distinctive personality? What sort of characters are Han Fook and the Master of the Perfect Word? What do you think Hesse's intention was in creating such characters?

8. In the paragraph beginning "And he stayed and learned to play the zither, ..." why does Hesse describe the poetry Han Fook eventually creates instead of showing us some samples? How does the author give us a sense of Han Fook's art without quoting from it?

The Lesson

TONI CADE BAMBARA

Back in the days when everyone was old and stupid or young and foolish
and me and Sugar were the only ones just right, this lady moved on our
block with nappy hair and proper speech and no makeup. And quite naturally we laughed at her, laughed the way we did at the junk man who went
about his business like he was some big-time president and his sorry-ass
horse his secretary. And we kinda hated her too, hated the way we did the
winos who cluttered up our parks and pissed on our handball walls and
stank up our hallways and stairs so you couldn't halfway play hide-and-seek
without a goddamn gas mask. Miss Moore was her name. The only woman
on the block with no first name. And she was black as hell, cept for her
feet, which were fish-white and spooky. And she was always planning these
boring-ass things for us to 'do, us being my cousin, mostly, who lived on
the block cause we all moved North the same time and to the same apartment then spread out gradual to breathe. And our parents would yank our
heads into some kinda shape and crisp up our clothes so we'd be present-
able for travel with Miss Moore, who always looked like she was going to
church, though she never did. Which is just one of things the grownups
talked about when they talked behind her back like a dog. But when she
came calling with some sachet she'd sewed up or some gingerbread she'd
made or some book, why then they'd all be too embarrassed to turn her
down and we'd get handed out all spruced up. She'd been to college and
said it only right that she should take responsibility for the young ones'
education, and she not even related by marriage or blood. So they'd go for
it. Specially Aunt Gretchen. She was the main gofer in the family. You got
some ole dumb shit foolishness you want somebody to go for, you send for
Aunt Gretchen. She been screwed into the go-along for so long, it's a blood-
deep natural thing with her. Which is how she got saddled with me and
Sugar and Junior in the first place while our mothers were in a la-de-da
apartment up the block having a good ole time.

So this one day Miss Moore rounds us all up at the mailbox and it's
puredee hot and she's knockin herself out about arithmetic. And school
suppose to let up in summer I heard, but she don't never let up. And the
starch in my pinafore scratching the shit outta me and I'm really hating this

nappy-head bitch and her goddamn college degree. I'd much rather go to the pool or to the show where it's cool. So me and Sugar leaning on the mailbox being surly, which is a Miss Moore word. And Flyboy checking out what everybody brought for lunch. And Fat Butt already wasting his peanut-butter-and-jelly sandwich like the pig he is. And Junebug punchin on Q.T.'s arm for potato chips. And Rose Giraffe shifting from one hip to the other waiting for somebody to step on her foot or ask her if she from Georgia so she can kick ass, preferably Mercedes'. And Miss Moore asking us do we know what money is, like we a bunch of retards. I mean real money, she say, like it's only poker chips or monopoly papers we lay on the grocer. So right away I'm tired of this and say so. And would much rather snatch Sugar and go to the Sunset and terrorize the West Indian kids and take their hair ribbons and their money too. And Miss Moore files that remark away for next week's lesson on brotherhood, I can tell. And finally I say we oughta get to the subway cause it's cooler and besides we might meet some cute boys. Sugar done swiped her mama's lipstick, so we ready.

So we heading down the street and she's boring us silly about what things cost and what our parents make and how much goes for rent and how money ain't divided up right in this country. And then she gets to the part about we all poor and live in the slums, which I don't feature. And I'm ready to speak on that, but she steps out in the street and hails two cabs just like that. Then she hustles half the crew in with her and hands me a five-dollar bill and tells me to calculate 10 percent tip for the driver. And we're off. Me and Sugar and Junebug and Flyboy hangin out the window and hollering to everybody, putting lipstick on each other cause Flyboy a faggot anyway, and making farts with our sweaty armpits. But I'm mostly trying to figure how to spend this money. But they all fascinated with the meter ticking and Junebug starts laying bets as to how much it'll read when Flyboy can't hold his breath no more. Then Sugar lays bets as to how much it'll be when we get there. So I'm stuck. Don't nobody want to go for my plan, which is to jump out at the next light and run off to the first bar-b-que we can find. Then the driver tells us to get the hell out cause we are there already. And the meter reads eighty-five cents. And I'm stalling to figure out the tip and Sugar say give him a dime. And I decide he don't need it bad as I do, so later for him. But then he tries to take off with Junebug foot still in the door so we talk about his mama something ferocious. Then we check out that we on Fifth Avenue and everybody dressed up in stockings. One lady in a fur coat, hot as it is. White folks crazy.

"This is the place," Miss Moore say, presenting it to us in the voice she uses at the museum. "Let's look in the windows before we go in."

"Can we steal?" Sugar asks very serious like she's getting the ground rules squared away before she plays. "I beg your pardon," say Miss Moore, and we fall out. So she leads us around the windows of the toy store and me and Sugar screamin, "This is mine, that's mine, I gotta have that, that was made for me, I was born for that," till Big Butt drowns us out.

"Hey, I'm goin to buy that there."

"That there? You don't even know what it is, stupid."

"I do so," he say punchin on Rosie Giraffe. "It's a microscope."

"Whatcha gonna do with a microscope, fool?"

"Look at things."

"Like what, Ronald?" ask Miss Moore. And Big Butt ain't got the first notion. So here go Miss Moore gabbing about the thousands of bacteria in a drop of water and the somethinorother in a speck of blood and the million and one living things in the air around us is invisible to the naked eye. And what she say that for? Junebug go to town on that "naked" and we rolling. Then Miss Moore ask what it cost. So we all jam into the window smudgin it up and the price tag say $300. So then she ask how long'd take for Big Butt and Junebug to save up their allowances. "Too long," I say. "Yeh," adds Sugar, "outgrown it by that time." And Miss Moore say no, you never outgrow learning instruments. "Why, even medical students and interns and," blah, blah, blah. And we ready to choke Big Butt for bringing it up in the first damn place.

"This here costs four hundred eighty dollars," say Rosie Giraffe. So we pile up all over her to see what she pointin out. My eyes tell me it's a chunk of glass cracked with something heavy, and different-color inks dripped into the splits, then the whole thing put into a oven or something. But for $480 it don't make sense.

"That's a paperweight made of semi-precious stones fused together under tremendous pressure," she explains slowly, with her hands doing the mining and all the factory work.

"So what's paperweight?" asks Rosie Giraffe.

"To weight paper with, dumbbell," say Flyboy, the wise man from the East.

"Not exactly," say Miss Moore, which is what she say when you warm or way off too. "It's to weigh paper down so it won't scatter and make your desk untidy." So right away me and Sugar curtsy to each other and then to Mercedes who is more the tidy type.

"We don't keep paper on top of the desk in my class," say Junebug, figuring Miss Moore crazy or lyin one.

"At home, then," she say. "Don't you have a calendar and a pencil case and a blotter and a letter-opener on your desk at home where you do your homework?" And she know damn well what our homes look like cause she nosys around in them every chance she gets.

"I don't even have a desk," say Junebug. "Do we?"

"No. And I don't get no homework neither," says Big Butt.

"And I don't even have a home," say Flyboy like he do at school to keep the white folks off his back and sorry for him. Send this poor kid to camp posters, is his speciality.

"I do," say Mercedes. "I have a box of stationery on my desk and a picture of my cat. My godmother bought the stationery and the desk. There's a big rose on each sheet and the envelopes smell like roses."

"Who wants to know about your smelly-ass stationery," say Rosie Giraffe fore I can get my two cents in.

"It's important to have a work area all your own so that . . ."

"Will you look at this sailboat, please," say Flyboy, cuttin her off and pointin to the thing like it was his. So once again we tumble all over each other to gaze at this magnificent thing in the toy store which is just big enough to maybe sail two kittens across the pond if you strap them to the posts tight. We all start reciting the price tag like we in assembly. "Hand-crafted sailboat of fiberglass at one thousand one hundred ninety-five dollars."

"Unbelievable," I hear myself say and am really stunned. I read it again for myself just in case the group recitation put me in a trance. Same thing. For some reason this pisses me off. We look at Miss Moore and she lookin at us, waiting for I dunno what.

"Who'd pay all that when you can buy a sailboat set for a quarter at Pop's, a tube of glue for a dime, and a ball of string for eight cents? It must have a motor and a whole lot else besides," I say. "My sailboat cost me about fifty cents."

"But will it take water?" say Mercedes with her smart ass.

"Took mine to Alley Pond Park once," say Flyboy. "String broke. Lost it. Pity."

"Sailed mine in Central Park and it keeled over and sank. Had to ask my father for another dollar."

"And you got the strap," laugh Big Butt. "The jerk didn't even have a string on it. My old man wailed on his behind."

Little Q.T. was staring hard at the sailboat and you could see he wanted it bad. But he too little and somebody'd just take it from him. So what the hell. "This boat for kids, Miss Moore?"

"Parents silly to buy something like that just to get all broke up," say Rosie Giraffe.

"That much money it should last forever," I figure.

"My father'd buy it for me if I wanted it."

"Your father, my ass," say Rosie Giraffe getting a chance to finally push Mercedes.

"Must be rich people shop here," say Q.T.

"You are a very bright boy," say Flyboy. "What was your first clue?" And he rap him on the head with the back of his knuckles, since Q.T. the only one he could get away with. Though Q.T. liable to come up behind you years later and get his licks in when you half expect it.

"What I want to know is," I says to Miss Moore though I never talk to her, I wouldn't give the bitch that satisfaction, "is how much a real boat costs? I figure a thousand'd get you a yacht any day."

"Why don't you check that out," she says, "and report back to the group?" Which really pains my ass. If you gonna mess up a perfectly good swim day least you could do is have some answers. "Let's go in," she say like she got something up her sleeve. Only she don't lead the way. So me and

Sugar turn the corner to where the entrance is, but when we get there I kinda hang back. Not that I'm scared, what's there to be afraid of, just a toy store. But I feel funny, shame. But what I got to be shamed about? Got as much right to go in as anybody. But somehow I can't seem to get hold on the door, so I step away for Sugar to lead. But she hangs back too. And I look at her and she looks at me and this is ridiculous. I mean, damn, I have never ever been shy about doing nothing or going nowhere. But then Mercedes steps up and then Rosie Giraffe and Big Butt crowd in behind and shove, and next thing we all stuffed into the doorway with only Mercedes squeezing past us, smoothing out her jumper and walking right down the aisle. Then the rest of us tumble in like a glued-together jigsaw done all wrong. And people lookin at us. And it's like the time me and Sugar crashed into the Catholic church on a dare. But once we got in there and everything so hushed and holy and the candles and the bowin and the handkerchiefs on all the drooping heads, I just couldn't go through with the plan. Which was for me to run up to the altar and do a tap dance while Sugar played the nose flute and messed around in the holy water. And Sugar kept givin me the elbow. Then later teased me so bad I tied her up in the shower and turned it on and locked her in. And she'd be there till this day if Aunt Gretchen hadn't finally figured I was lying about the boarder takin a shower.

Same thing in the store. We all walkin on tiptoe and hardly touchin the games and puzzles and things. And I watched Miss Moore who is steady watchin us like she waitin for a sign. Like Mama Drewery watches the sky and sniffs the air and takes note of just how much slant is in the bird formation. Then me and Sugar bump smack into each other, so busy gazing at the toys, 'specially the sailboat. But we don't laugh and go into our fat-lady bump-stomach routine. We just stare at that price tag. Then Sugar run a finger over the whole boat. And I'm jealous and want to hit her. Maybe not her, but I sure want to punch somebody in the mouth.

"Watcha bring us here for, Miss Moore?"

"You sound angry, Sylvia. Are you mad about something?" Give me one of them grins like she tellin a grown-up joke that never turns out to be funny. And she's lookin very closely at me like maybe she plannin to do my portrait from memory. I'm mad, but I won't give her that satisfaction. So I slouch around the store bein very bored and say, "Let's go."

Me and Sugar at the back of the train watchin' the tracks whizzin by large then small then gettin gobbled up in the dark. I'm thinkin about this tricky toy I saw in the store. A clown that somersaults on a bar then does chin-ups just cause you yank lightly at his leg. Cost $35. I could see me askin my mother for a $35 birthday clown. "You wanna who that costs what?' she'd say, cocking her head to the side to get a better view of the hole in my head. Thirty-five dollars could buy new bunk beds for Junior and Gretchen's boy. Thirty-five dollars and the whole household could go visit Granddaddy Nelson in the country. Thirty-five dollars would pay for the rent and the piano bill too. Who are these people that spend that much for performing clowns and $1,000 for toy sailboats? What kinda work they do and how they live and how come we ain't on it? Where we are is who we are, Miss Moore always pointin out. But it don't necessarily have to be that way, she always adds then waits for somebody to say that poor people have to wake up and demand their share of the pie and don't none of us know what kind of pie she talkin about in the first damn place. But she ain't so smart cause I still got her four dollars from the taxi and she sure ain't getting it. Messin up my day with this shit. Sugar nudges me in my pocket and winks.

Miss Moore lines us up in front of the mailbox where we started from, seem like years ago, and I got a headache for thinkin so hard. And we lean all over each other so we can hold up under the draggy-ass lecture she always finishes us off with at the end before we thank her for borin us to tears. But she just looks at us like she readin tea leaves. Finally she say, "Well, what did you think of F.A.O. Schwartz?"

Rosie Giraffe mumbles, "White folks crazy."

"I'd like to go in there again when I get my birthday money," says Mercedes, and we shove her out the pack so has to lean on the mailbox by herself.

"I'd like a shower. Tiring day," say Flyboy.

Then Sugar surprises me by sayin, "You know, Miss Moore, I don't think all of us here put together eat in a year what that sailboat costs." And Miss Moore lights up like somebody goosed her. "And?" she say, urging Sugar on. Only I'm standin on her foot so she don't continue.

"Imagine for a minute what kind of society it is in which some people can spend on a toy what it would cost to feed a family of six or seven. What do you think?"

"I think," say Sugar pushing me off her feet like she never done before, cause I whip her ass in a minute, "that this is not much of a democracy if you ask me. Equal chance to pursue happiness means an equal crack at the dough, don't it?" Miss Moore is besides herself and I am disgusted with Sugar's treachery. So I stand on her foot one more time to see if she'll shove me. She shuts up, and Miss Moore looks at me, sorrowfully I'm thinkin. And somethin weird is goin on, I can feel it in my chest.

"Anybody else learn anything today?" lookin dead at me. I walk away and Sugar has to run to catch up and don't even seem to notice when I shrug her arm off my shoulder.

"Well, we got four dollars anyway," she says.

"Uh hunh."

"We could go to Hascombs and get half a chocolate layer and then go to the Sunset and still have plenty money for potato chips and ice-cream sodas."

"Uh hunh."

"Race you to Hascombs," she say.

We start down the block and she gets ahead which is O.K. by me cause
I'm goin to the West End and then over to the Drive to think this day
through. She can run if she want to and even run faster. But ain't nobody
gonna beat me at nuthin.

QUESTIONS

"The Lesson"

1. Who is the narrator of this story? Approximately how old is the narrator
when she makes the trip to the toy store? Look at the first lines of "The Lesson": how old is she here? When she is telling the story, does she still feel that
everyone who is old is stupid and only she and her cousin Sugar are "just
right"?

2. Notice that the narrator ceases to speak in the past tense at the end of
the first paragraph and begins to use the present and present continuous ten-
ses. Why? Does the tense change signal the transition from adult narrator to
child narrator, or is that accomplished earlier? If so, where?

3. Two attitudes toward Miss Moore are expressed in "The Lesson." One
attitude is implicit, implied but not directly expressed; the other, Sylvia's as a
child, is explicit. What is young Sylvia's attitude? How different is her attitude
as an adult toward Miss Moore, and how is it implicitly expressed in the story,
through details of plot and characterization?

4. Why does young Sylvia dislike Miss Moore so intensely? What is Miss
Moore's attitude toward Sylvia? Do you think she regards Sylvia as a special
"case"?

5. How realistic a picture of black inner-city youngsters does Bambara give
us? How does she achieve this? What do you think of Sylvia, her cousins, and
her friends?

6. What is the "lesson" Miss Moore attempts to give her "students"? Does
she succeed? Why do they resist her questions and probings? Is she a good
helper and guide?

7. Why do Sylvia and Sugar hesitate to go into the expensive children's
store? Why is it significant that Mercedes is the most composed of all the group
at F.A.O. Schwartz?

8. Do you find "The Lesson" didactic at any point? If so, where?

9. Why does Sylvia become angry when her cousin Sugar responds to Miss
Moore's questions?

10. Look at the last lines of the story. Do they indicate that something has

happened to Sylvia against her will, as a result of Miss Moore's "lesson"? In what sense is the young girl about to embark on a quest?

11. Is the assistance Miss Moore gives her young charges more characteristic of that offered by the Good Mother or by the Wise Old Man?

12. Is "The Lesson" a story of initiation? If so, in what sense?

Cathedral

RAYMOND CARVER

This blind man, an old friend of my wife's, he was on his way to spend the night. His wife had died. So he was visiting the dead wife's relatives in Connecticut. He called my wife from his in-laws'. Arrangements were made. He would come by train, a five-hour trip, and my wife would meet him at the station. She hadn't seen him since she worked for him one summer in Seattle ten years ago. But she and the blind man had kept in touch. They made tapes and mailed them back and forth. I wasn't enthusiastic about his visit. He was no one I knew. And his being blind bothered me. My idea of blindness came from the movies. In movies, the blind moved slowly and never laughed. Sometimes they were led by seeing-eye dogs. A blind man in my house was not something I looked forward to.

That summer in Seattle she had needed a job. She didn't have any money. The man she was going to marry at the end of the summer was in officer's training school. He didn't have any money, either. But she was in love with the guy, and he was in love with her, etc. She'd seen something in the paper: Help Wanted—Reading for Blind Man, and a telephone number. She phoned and went over, was hired on the spot. She'd worked with this blind man all summer. She read stuff to him, case studies, reports, that sort of thing. She helped him organize his little office in the county social service department. They'd become good friends, my wife and the blind man. How do I know these things? She told me. And she told me something else. On her last day in the office, the blind man asked if he could touch her face. She agreed to this. She told me he ran his fingers over every part of her face, her nose—even her neck! She never forgot it. She even tried to write a poem about it. She was always writing a poem. She wrote a poem or two every year, usually after something really important had happened to her.

When we first started going out together, she showed me the poem. In the poem she recalled his fingers and the way they had moved around over her face. In the poem she talked about what she had felt at the time, about what went through her mind as he touched her nose and lips. I can recall I didn't think much of the poem. Of course I didn't tell her that. Maybe I just don't understand poetry. I admit it's not the first thing I reach for when I pick up something to read.

Anyway, this man who'd first enjoyed her favors, the officer-to-be, he'd been her childhood sweetheart. So okay. I'm saying that at the end of the summer she let the blind man run his hands over her face, said good-bye to him, married her childhood etc., who was now a commissioned officer, and she moved away from Seattle. But they'd kept in touch, she and the blind man. She made the first contact after a year or so. She called him up one night from an Air Force base in Alabama. She wanted to talk. They talked. He asked her to send him a tape and tell him about her life. She did this. She sent the tape. On the tape she told the blind man about her husband and about their life together in the military. She told the blind man she loved her husband but she didn't like it where they lived and she didn't like it that he was a part of the military-industrial complex. She told the blind man she'd written a poem and he was in it. She told him that she was writing a poem about what it was like to be an Air Force officer's wife in the Deep South. The poem wasn't finished yet. She was still writing it. The blind man made a tape. He sent her the tape. She made a tape. This went on for years. My wife's officer was posted to one base and then another. She sent tapes from Moody AFB, McGuire, McConnell, and finally Travis, near Sacramento, where one night she got to feeling lonely and cut off from people she kept losing in that moving-around life. She balked, couldn't go it another step. She went in and swallowed all the pills and capsules in the medicine cabinet and washed them down with a bottle of gin. Then she got into a hot bath and passed out.

But instead of dying she got sick. She threw up. Her officer—Why should he have a name? He was the childhood sweetheart, and what more does he want?—came home from a training mission, found her, and called the ambulance. In time, she put it on the tape and sent the tape to the blind man. Over the years she put all kinds of stuff on tapes and sent the tapes off lickety-split. Next to writing a poem every year, I think it was her chief means of recreation. On one tape she told the blind man she'd decided to live away from her officer for a time. On another tape she told him about her divorce. She and I began going out, and of course she told her blind man about this. She told him everything, so it seemed to me. Once she asked me if I'd like to hear the latest tape from the blind man. This was a year ago. I was on the tape, she said. So I said okay, I'd listen to it. I got us drinks and we settled down in the living room. We made ready to listen. First she inserted the tape into the player and adjusted a couple of dials. Then she pushed a lever. The tape squeaked and someone began to talk in this loud voice. She lowered the volume. After a few minutes of harmless chitchat, I heard my own name rasped out by this stranger, this man I didn't even know! And then this: "From all you've said about him, I can only conclude—" But we were interrupted, a knock at the door, some-

thing, and we didn't get back to the tape. Maybe it was just as well. I'd
heard enough, anyway.

Now this same blind stranger was coming to sleep in my house.

"Maybe I could take him bowling," I said to my wife. She was at the
draining board doing scalloped potatoes. She put down the knife she was
using on the onion and turned around.

"If you love me," she said, "you can do this for me. If you don't love
me, okay. But if you had a friend, any friend, and the friend came to visit,
I'd make him feel comfortable." She wiped her hands with the dish towel.

"I don't have any blind friends," I said.

"You don't have *any* friends," she said. "Period. Besides," she said,
"goddamnit, his wife's just died! Don't you understand that? The man's lost
his wife!"

I didn't answer. She'd told me a little about the blind man's wife. The
wife's name was Beulah. Beulah! That's a name for a colored woman.

"Was his wife a Negro?" I asked.

"Are you crazy?" my wife said. "Have you just flipped or something?"
She picked up the onion. I saw it hit the floor, then roll under the stove.
"What's wrong with you?" she said. "Are you drunk?"

"I'm just asking," I said.

Right then my wife filled me in with more detail than I cared to know.
I made a drink and sat at the kitchen table to listen. Pieces of the story
began to fall into place.

Beulah had gone to work for the blind man the summer after my wife
had stopped working for him. Pretty soon Beulah and the blind man had
themselves a church wedding. It was a little wedding—who'd be anxious
to attend such a wedding in the first place?—just the two of them, and the
minister and the minister's wife. But it was a church wedding just the
same. What Beulah had wanted, he'd said. But even then Beulah must
have been carrying cancer in her lymph glands. After they had been inseparable for eight years—my wife's word, *inseparable*—Beulah's health went
into a rapid decline. She died in a Seattle hospital room, the blind man
sitting beside the bed and holding on to her hand. They'd married, lived
and worked together, slept together—had sex, sure—and then the blind
man buried her. All this without his having ever seen what the goddamned
woman looked like. It was beyond my understanding. Hearing this, I felt
sorry for the blind man for a minute. And then I found myself thinking
what a pitiful life this woman must have led. Imagine a woman who could
never see herself reflected in the eyes of her loved one. A woman who
could go on day after day and never receive the smallest compliment from
her beloved. A woman whose husband would never read the expression on
her face, be it misery or something better. Someone who could wear make-
up or not—what difference to him? She could, if she wanted, wear green
eye shadow around one eye, a straight pin in her nostril, yellow slacks and
burgundy pumps, no matter. And then to slip off into death, the blind

man's hand on her hand, his blind eyes streaming tears—I'm imagining now—her last thought maybe this: that her beloved never knew what she looked like, and she on an express to the grave. Robert was left with a small insurance policy and half of a twenty-peso Mexican coin. The other half of the coin went into the box with her. Pathetic.

So when the time rolled around, my wife went to the rail station. With nothing to do but wait—and sure, I blamed him for that—I was having a drink and watching TV when I heard the car pull into the drive. I got up from the sofa with my drink and went to the window to have a look.

I saw my wife laughing as she parked the car. I saw her get out of the car and shut the door. She was still wearing a smile. Just amazing. She went around to the other side of the car to where the blind man was already starting to get out. This blind man, feature this, he was wearing a full beard! A beard on a blind man! Too much, I say. The blind man reached into the back seat and dragged out a suitcase. My wife took his arm, shut the car door, and, talking all the way, moved him down the drive and then up the steps to the front porch. I turned off the TV. I finished my drink, rinsed the glass, dried my hands. Then I went to the door.

My wife said, "I want you to meet Robert. Robert, this is my husband. I've told you all about him." She closed the porch screen. She was beaming. She had this blind man by his coat sleeve.

The blind man let go of his suitcase and up came his hand.

I took it. He squeezed hard, held my hand, and then he let it go.

"I feel like we've already met," he boomed.

"Likewise," I said. I didn't know what else to say. Then I said, "Welcome. I've heard a lot about you." We began to move then, a little group, from the porch into the living room, my wife guiding him by the arm. He carried his suitcase in his other hand. My wife said things like, "To your left here, Robert. That's right. Now watch it, there's a chair. That's it. Sit down right here. This is the sofa. We just bought this sofa two weeks ago."

I started to say something about the old sofa. I'd liked that old sofa. But I didn't say anything. Then I wanted to say something else, small talk, about the scenic Hudson River. How going *to* New York, sit on the right-hand side of the train, and coming *from* New York, the left-hand side.

"Did you have a good train ride?" I said. "Which side of the train did you sit on, by the way?"

"What a question, which side!" my wife said. "What's it matter which side?" she said.

"I just asked," I said.

"Right side," the blind man said. "For the sun. Until this morning," the blind man said, "I hadn't been on a train in nearly forty years. Not since I was a kid. With my folks. That's been a long time. I'd nearly forgotten that sensation. I have winter in my beard now," he said. "So I've been told, anyway. Do I look distinguished, my dear?" he said to my wife.

"You look distinguished, Robert," she said. "Robert," she said. "Robert, it's just so good to see you." My wife finally took her eyes off the blind man and looked at me.

I had the distinct feeling she didn't like what she saw. I shrugged.

I've never met or personally known anyone who was blind. This blind man was late forties, a heavyset, balding man with stooped shoulders, as if he carried a great weight there. He wore brown slacks, brown cordovan shoes, a light brown shirt, a tie, a sports coat. Spiffy. He also had this full beard. But he didn't carry a cane and he didn't wear dark glasses. I'd always thought dark glasses were a must for the blind. Fact was, I wished he had a pair. At first glance, his eyes looked like anyone else's eyes. But if you looked close there was something different about them. Too much white in the iris, for one thing, and the pupils seemed to move around in the sockets without his knowing it or being able to control it. Creepy. As I stared at his face, I saw the left pupil turn in toward his nose, while the other made a futile effort to keep in one place. But it was only an effort, for that eye was on the roam without his knowing it or wanting it to be.

I said, "Let me get you a drink. What's your pleasure? We have a little of everything. It's one of our pastimes."

"Bub, I'm a Scotch man myself," he said fast enough, in this big voice.

"Right," I said. Bub! "Sure you are. I knew it."

He let his fingers touch his suitcase, which was sitting alongside the sofa. He was taking his bearings. I didn't blame him for that.

"I'll move that up to your room," my wife said.

"No, that's fine," he said loudly. "It can go up when I go up."

"A little water with the Scotch?" I said.

"Very little," he said.

"I knew it," I said.

He said, "Just a tad. The Irish actor, Barry Fitzgerald? I'm like that fellow. When I drink water, Fitzgerald said, I drink water. When I drink whiskey, I drink whiskey." My wife laughed. The blind man brought his hand up under his beard. He lifted his beard slowly and let it drop.

I did the drinks, three big glasses of Scotch with a splash of water in each. Then we made ourselves comfortable and talked about Robert's travels. First the long flight from the West Coast to Connecticut, we covered that. Then from Connecticut up here by train. We had another drink concerning that leg of the trip.

I remembered having read somewhere that the blind didn't smoke because, speculation had it, they couldn't see the smoke they exhaled. I thought I knew that much and that much only about blind people. But this blind man smoked his cigarette down to the nubbin and then lit another one. This blind man filled his ashtray and my wife emptied it.

When we sat down to the table for dinner we had another drink. My wife heaped Robert's plate with cube steak, scalloped potatoes, green beans. I buttered him up two slices of bread. I said, "Here's bread and butter for you." I swallowed some of my drink. "Now let us pray," I said, and the blind man lowered his head. My wife looked at me, her mouth agape. "Pray the phone won't ring and the food doesn't get cold," I said.

We dug in. We ate everything there was to eat on the table. We ate like there was no tomorrow. We didn't talk. We ate. We scarfed. We grazed that table. We were into serious eating. The blind man had right away located his foods, he knew just where everything was on his plate. I watched with admiration as he used his knife and fork on the meat. He'd cut two pieces of meat, fork the meat into his mouth, and then go all out for the scalloped potatoes, the beans next, and then he'd tear off a hunk of buttered bread and eat that. He'd follow this up with a big drink of milk. It didn't seem to bother him to use his fingers once in a while, either. He used his bread to scoop beans.

We finished everything, including half of a strawberry pie. For a few moments we sat as if stunned. Sweat beaded on our faces. Finally, we got up from the table and left the dirty plates. We didn't look back. We took ourselves into the living room and sank into our places again. Robert and my wife sat on the sofa. I took the big chair. We had us two or three more drinks while they talked about the major things that had transpired for them in the past ten years. For the most part, I just listened. Now and then I joined in. I didn't want him to think I'd left the room, and I didn't want her to think I was feeling left out. They talked of things that had happened to them—to them!—these past ten years. I waited in vain to hear my name on my wife's sweet lips: "And then my dear husband came into my life"—something like that. But I heard nothing of the sort. More talk of Robert. Robert had done a little of everything, it seemed, a regular blind jack-of-all-trades. But most recently he and his wife had had an Amway distributorship, from which, I gathered, they'd earned their living, such as it was. The blind man was also a ham radio operator. He talked in his loud voice about conversations he'd had with fellow operators in Guam, the Philippines, Alaska, even Tahiti. He said he'd have a lot of friends there if he ever wanted to go visit those places. From time to time he'd turn his blind face toward me, put his hand under his beard, ask me something. How long had I been at my present position? (Three years.) Did I like my work? (I didn't.) Was I going to stay with it? (What were the options?)

Finally, when I thought he was beginning to run down, I got up and turned on the TV.

My wife looked at me with irritation. She was heading toward a boil. Then she looked at the blind man and said, "Robert, do you have a TV?"

The blind man said, "My dear, I have two TVs. I have a color set and a black-and-white thing, an old relic. It's funny, but if I turn the TV on, and I'm always turning it on, I turn the color set on. Always. It's funny."

I didn't know what to say to that. I had absolutely nothing to say about that. No opinion. So I watched the news program and tried to listen to what the announcer was saying.

"This is a color TV," the blind man said. "Don't ask me how, but I can tell."

"We traded up a while ago," I said.

The blind man had another taste of his drink. He lifted his beard, sniffed it, and let it fall. He leaned forward on the sofa. He positioned his ashtray on the coffee table, then put the lighter to his cigarette. He leaned back on the sofa and crossed his legs at the ankles.

My wife covered her mouth, and then she yawned. She stretched. She said, "I think I'll go upstairs and put on my robe. I think I'll change into something else. Robert, you make yourself comfortable," she said.

"I'm comfortable," the blind man said.

"I want you to feel comfortable in this house," she said.

"I am comfortable," the blind man said.

After she'd left the room, he and I listened to the weather report and then to the sports roundup. My wife had been gone so long I didn't know if she was going to come back. I thought she might have gone to bed. I wished she'd come back downstairs. I didn't want to be left alone with a blind man. I asked him if he wanted another drink, and he said sure. Then I asked if he wanted to smoke dope with me. I said I'd just rolled a number. I hadn't, but I planned to do so in about two shakes.

"I'll try some with you," he said.

"Damn right," I said. "That's the stuff."

I got our drinks and sat down on the sofa with him. Then I rolled us two fat numbers. I lit one and passed it. I brought it to his fingers. He took it and inhaled.

"Hold it as long as you can," I said. I could tell he didn't know the first thing.

My wife came back downstairs wearing her robe and pink slippers. "What do I smell?" she said.

"We thought we'd have us some cannabis," I said.

My wife gave me a purely savage look. Then she looked at him and said, "Robert, I didn't know you smoked."

He said, "I do now, my dear. First time for everything," he said. "But I don't feel anything yet."

"This stuff is pretty mellow," I said. "This stuff is mild. It's dope you can reason with. It doesn't mess you up."

"Not much it doesn't, bub," he said, and laughed.

My wife sat on the sofa between the blind man and me. I passed her the number. She took it and inhaled and then passed it back to me. "Which way is this going?" she said. Then she said, "I shouldn't be smoking this. I can hardly keep my eyes open as it is. That dinner did me in. I shouldn't have eaten so much."

"It was the strawberry pie," the blind man said. "That's what did it," he said, and he laughed his big laugh. Then he shook his head.

"There's more strawberry pie," I said.

"Do you want some more, Robert?" my wife asked.

"Maybe in a little while," he said.

We gave our attention to the TV. My wife yawned again. She said, "Your bed is made up when you feel like going to bed, Robert. I know you must have had a long day. When you're ready to go to bed, say so." She pulled his arm. "Robert?"

He came to and said, "I've had a real nice time. This beats tapes, doesn't it?"

I said, "Coming at you," and I put the number between his fingers. He inhaled, held the smoke, and then let it go. It was like he'd been doing it since he was nine years old.

"Thanks, bub," he said. "But I think this is all for me. I think I'm beginning to feel it," he said. He held the burning roach out for my wife.

"Same here," she said. "Ditto. Me too." She took the roach and passed it to me. "I may just sit here for a while between you two guys with my eyes closed. But don't let me bother you, okay? Either one of you. If it bothers you, say so. Otherwise, I may just sit here with my eyes closed until you're ready to go to bed," she said. "Your bed's made up, Robert, when you're ready. It's right next to our room at the top of the stairs. We'll show you up when you're ready. You wake me now, you guys, if I fall asleep." She said that and then she closed her eyes and went to sleep.

The news program ended. I got up and turned the channel. I sat back down on the sofa. I wished my wife hadn't pooped out. Her head lay across the back of the sofa, her mouth open. She'd turned so that her robe had slipped away from her legs, exposing a juicy thigh. I reached to draw her robe over the thigh, and it was then I glanced at the blind man. What the hell! I flipped the robe open again.

"You say when you want some strawberry pie," I said.

"I will," he said.

I said, "Are you tired? Do you want me to take you up to your bed? Are you ready to hit the hay?"

"Not yet," he said. "No, I'll stay up with you, bub. If that's all right. I'll stay up until you're ready to turn in. We haven't had a chance to talk. Know what I mean? I feel like me and her monopolized the evening." He lifted his beard and he let it fall. He picked up his cigarettes and his lighter.

"That's all right," I said. Then I said, "I'm glad for the company." And I guess I was. Every night I smoked dope and stayed up as long as I could before I fell asleep. My wife and I hardly ever went to bed at the same time. When I did go to sleep, I had these dreams. Sometimes I'd wake up from one of them, the heart going crazy.

Something about the Church and the Middle Ages, narrated by an Englishman, was on the TV. Not your run-of-the-mill TV fare. I wanted to watch something else. I turned to the other channels. But there was nothing on them, either. So I turned back to the first channel and apologized.

"Bub, it's all right," he said. "It's fine with me. Whatever you want to watch is okay. I'm always learning something. Learning never ends. It won't hurt me to learn something tonight. I got ears," he said.

We didn't say anything for a time. He was leaning forward with his head turned at me, while his right ear was aimed in the direction of the set. Very disconcerting. Now and then his eyelids drooped and then they snapped open again. Now and then he put his fingers into his beard and tugged, as if thinking about something he was hearing on the television.

On the screen a group of men wearing cowls was being set upon and tormented by men dressed in skeleton costumes and men dressed as devils. The men dressed as devils wore devil masks, horns, and long tails. This pageant was part of a procession. The Englishman said it all took place in Málaga, Spain, once a year. I tried to explain to the blind man what was happening.

"Skeletons," he said. "I know about skeletons," he said, and he nodded.

The TV showed Chartres Cathedral. Then there was a long slow look at Sainte-Chapelle. Finally the picture switched to Notre-Dame, with its flying buttresses, its spires reaching toward clouds. The camera pulled away to show the whole of the cathedral rising above the skyline.

There were times when the Englishman who was telling the thing would shut up, would simply let the camera move around over the cathedrals. Or else the camera would tour the countryside, men in fields walking behind oxen. I waited as long as I could. Then I felt I had to say something. I said, "They're showing the outside of this cathedral now. Gargoyles. Little statues carved to look like monsters. Now I guess they're in Italy. Yeah, they're in Italy. There's fresco paintings on the walls of this one church."

"What's fresco painting, bub?" he asked, and he sipped from his drink.

I reached for my glass. But it was empty. I tried to remember what I could remember about frescoes. "You're asking me what are frescoes?" I said. "That's a good question. I don't know."

The camera moved to a cathedral outside Lisbon, Portugal. The differences in the Portuguese cathedral compared with the French and Italian were not that great. But they were there. Mostly the interior stuff. Then something occurred to me and I said, "Something has occurred to me. Do you have an idea what a cathedral is? What they look like, that is? Do you follow me? If somebody says *cathedral* to you, do you have any notion what they're talking about? Do you know the difference between that and a Baptist church, say? Or that and a mosque, or synagogue?"

He let the smoke issue from his mouth. "I know they took hundreds of workers fifty or a hundred years to build," he said. "I just heard the man say that, of course. I know generations of the same families worked on a cathedral. I heard him say that, too. The men who began their life's work on them, they never lived to see the completion of their work. In that wise, bub, they're no different from the rest of us, right?" He laughed. Then his eyelids drooped again. His head nodded. He seemed to be snoozing. Maybe he was imagining himself in Portugal. The TV was showing another cathedral now. This one was in Germany. The Englishman's voice droned on. "Cathedrals," the blind man said. He sat up and rolled his head back and forth. "If you want the truth, bub, that's about all I know. What I just said. What I heard him say. But maybe you could describe one to me? I wish you'd do it. I'd like that. If you want to know, I really don't have a good idea."

I stared hard at the shot of the cathedral on the TV. It held a minute. Then it was gone, and the view was of the inside with rows of benches and high windows. How could I even begin to describe it? But say my life depended on it. Say my life was being threatened by an insane Turkish bey.

They took the camera outside again. I stared some more at the cathedral before the picture flipped off into the countryside. There was no use. I turned to the blind man and said, "To begin with, they're very tall. Very, very tall." I was looking around the room for clues. I tried again. "They reach way up. Up and up. Toward the sky. They soar. They're like poetry, that's what they're like. They're so big, some of them, they have to have these supports. To help hold them up, so to speak. These supports are called buttresses. They remind me of viaducts for some reason. But maybe you don't know viaducts, either? Sometimes the cathedrals have devils and such carved into the front. Sometimes great lords and ladies. Don't ask me why this is," I said. He was nodding. The whole upper part of his body seemed to be moving back and forth. "I'm not doing so good, am I?" I said.

He stopped nodding and leaned forward on the edge of the sofa. As he listened to me, he was running his fingers through his beard. I wasn't getting through to him though, I could see that. But he waited for me to go on just the same. He nodded, as if trying to encourage me. I tried to think what else I could say. "They're really big. They're massive. They're built of stone. Marble, too, sometimes. In those old days, when they built cathedrals, men aspired to be close to God. In those days God was an important part of everyone's life. This was reflected in their cathedral-building. I'm sorry," I said, "but it looks like that's the best I can do for you. I'm just no good at it."

"That's all right, bub," he said. "Hey, listen. I hope you don't mind my asking you. Can I ask you something? Let me ask you a simple question, yes or no. I'm just curious and there's no offense. You're my host. But let me ask if you are in any way religious? You don't mind my asking?"

I shook my head. He couldn't see that, though. A wink is the same as a nod to a blind man. "I guess I'm agnostic or something. No, the fact is, I don't believe in it. Anything. Sometimes it's hard. You know what I'm saying?"

"Sure, I do," he said.

"Right," I said.

The Englishman was still holding forth. My wife sighed in her sleep. She drew a long breath and continued with her sleep.

"You'll have to forgive me," I said. "But I can't tell you what a cathedral looks like. It just isn't in me to do it. I can't do any more than I've done." The blind man sat very still, his head down, as he listened to me. "The truth is, cathedrals don't mean anything special to me. Nothing. Cathedrals. They're something to look at on late-night TV. That's all they are."

It was then he cleared his throat. He brought something up. He took a handkerchief from his back pocket. In a minute he said, "I get it, bub. It's okay. It happens. Don't worry about it," he said. "Hey, listen to me. Will you do me a favor? I got an idea. Why don't you find us some heavy paper? And a pen. We'll do something. An experiment. Sure, you can do it. You can. We'll draw one together. Get us a pen and some heavy paper. Go on, bub, get the stuff," he said.

So I went upstairs. My legs felt like they didn't have any strength in them. They felt like they did sometimes after I'd run a couple miles. In my wife's room I looked around. I found some ballpoints in a little basket on her table. And then I tried to think where to look for the kind of paper he was talking about.

Downstairs, in the kitchen. I found a shopping bag with onion skins in the bottom of the bag. I emptied the bag and shook it. I brought it into the living room and sat down with it near his legs. I moved some things, smoothed the wrinkles from the bag, spread it out on the coffee table. The blind man got down from the sofa and sat next to me on the carpet.

He ran his fingers over the paper. He went up and down the sides of the paper and the edges, top and bottom. He fingered the corners. "All right," he said. "All right. Let's do her."

He found my hand, the hand with the pen. He closed his hand over my hand. "Go ahead, bub, draw," he said. "Draw. You'll see. I'll follow along with you. It'll be all right. Just begin now, like I'm telling you. You'll see. Draw," he said.

So I began. First I drew a box that resembled a house. It could have been the house I lived in. Then I put a roof on the house. At either end of the roof I drew spires. Crazy.

"Swell," he said. "Terrific. You're doing fine," he said. "Never thought anything like this could happen in your lifetime, did you? Well, it's a strange life, bub, we all know that. Go on now. Keep it up."

I put in windows with arches. I drew flying buttresses. I hung great doors. I couldn't stop. The TV station went off the air. I put down the pen and closed and opened my fingers. The blind man felt around over the paper. He moved the tips of his fingers slowly over the paper, over what I'd drawn, and he nodded. "Doing fine," he said.

I took up the pen, and he found my hand once more. I kept at it. I'm no artist. But I kept drawing just the same.

My wife opened her eyes and gazed at us. She sat up on the sofa, her robe hanging open. She said, "What are you doing? What in the world are you doing?"

I didn't answer her. The blind man said, "We're drawing a cathedral, dear. Me and him are working on something important. Press hard now," he said to me. "That's right. That's good," he said. "Sure. You got it, bub. I can tell. You didn't think you could. But you can, can't you? You're cooking with Crisco now. You'll see. Know what I'm saying? We're going to have us something here in a minute. How's the old arm?" he said. "Put some people in there now. What's a church without people, bub?"

"What's going on?" my wife said. "Robert, what are you doing? What's going on?"

"It's all right," he said to her. "Close your eyes now, bub," he said.

I did that. I closed them just like he said.

"Are they closed?" he said. "Don't fudge."

"They're closed," I said.

"Keep them that way," he said. He said, "Don't stop now." So we kept on with it. His fingers rode my fingers as my hand went over the rough paper. It was like nothing else in my life up to now.

In a minute he said, "I think that's enough. I think you got the idea," he said. "Take a look. What do you think?"

But I had my eyes closed. I thought I'd keep them closed a little longer. I thought it was something I ought not to forget.

"Well?" he said. "Are you looking?"

My eyes were still closed. I was in my house and I knew that. But I didn't feel inside anything.

"It's really something," I said.

QUESTIONS

"Cathedral"

1. What kind of man is the narrator of this story? To help you describe him, look at the things he says, the jokes he makes, and the way he expresses himself. What are his feelings about his job? What kind of marriage has he?

2. What attitude does the narrator have toward Robert, the blind man, before he even meets him? Why does the narrator consistently refer to the visitor as "the blind man" rather than by his name?

3. What attitude does the narrator seem to have toward his wife's relationship with Robert? Characterize that relationship. How is it contrasted with the husband and wife's relationship? Why was Robert's marriage to Beulah incomprehensible to the narrator? What does his incredulity reveal about the narrator?

4. What kind of man is Robert? What things about him surprise the narrator? What does his surprise reveal about him?

5. Over the course of their evening together, the narrator, his wife and

their guest each drink five or six big glasses of scotch—the narrator says drinking is one of married couple's pastimes—and smoke some marijuana, too. The narrator confides "Every night I smoked dope and stayed up as long as I could before I fell asleep." What is Carver suggesting about his characters' lives with these details?

6. What are the narrator's attitudes toward God and religion? What does he say cathedrals mean to him? Reread his attempt to describe cathedrals to Robert. Does his description suggest he feels differently about cathedrals than he says he does?

7. Why does Robert insist that the narrator draw his picture of a cathedral on heavy paper, with a pen? How does the narrator's drawing change as he continues to work on it? How is he enabled to draw even with his eyes closed? What is the nature of the assistance Robert gives to the narrator?

8. At the end of the story, the narrator comments, "I was in my house and I knew that. But I didn't really feel inside anything." What does he mean? What do you think the experience means to him? Do you think he has been changed by it? Discuss.

9. Would you call "Cathedral" a religious story? Why or why not?

10. Characterize Carver's style. What are some of its distinctive features? Is his style appropriate to the theme of his story? Discuss.

Awakening

ISAAC BABEL

All the folk in our circle—brokers, shopkeepers, clerks in banks and steamship offices—used to have their children taught music. Our fathers, seeing no other escape from their lot, had thought up a lottery, building it on the bones of little children. Odessa more than other towns was seized by the craze. And, in fact, in the course of ten years or so our town supplied the concert platforms of the world with infant prodigies. From Odessa came Mischa Elman, Zimbalist, Gabrilowitsch. Odessa witnessed the first steps of Jascha Heifetz.

When a lad was four or five, his mother took the puny creature to Zagursky's. Mr. Zagursky ran a factory of infant prodigies, a factory of Jewish dwarfs in lace collars and patent-leather pumps. He hunted them out in the slums of Moldavanka, in the evil-smelling courtyards of the Old Market. Mr. Zagursky charted the first course, then the children were shipped off to Professor Auer in St. Petersburg. A wonderful harmony dwelt in the souls of those wizened creatures with their swollen blue hands. They became famous virtuosi. My father decided that I should emulate them. Though I had, as a matter of fact, passed the age limit set for infant prodigies, being now in my fourteenth year, my shortness and lack of strength made it possible to pass me off as an eight-year-old. Herein lay father's hope.

I was taken to Zagursky's. Out of respect for my grandfather, Mr. Zagursky agreed to take me on at the cut rate of a rouble a lesson. My grandfather Leivi-ltzkhok was the laughingstock of the town, and its chief adornment. He used to walk about the streets in a top hat and old boots, dissipating doubt in the darkest of cases. He would be asked what a Gobelin was, why the Jacobins betrayed Robespierre, how you made artificial silk, what a Caesarean section was. And my grandfather could answer these questions. Out of respect for his learning and craziness, Mr. Zagursky only charged us a rouble a lesson. And he had the devil of a time with me, fearing my grandfather, for with me there was nothing to be done. The sounds dripped from my fiddle like iron filings, causing even me excruciating agony, but my father wouldn't give in. At home there was no talk about anything save of Mischa Elman, exempted by the Tsar himself from military service. Zimbalist, father would have us know, had been presented to the King of England and had played at Buckingham Palace. The parents of Gabrilowitsch had bought two houses in St. Petersburg. Infant prodigies brought wealth to their parents, but though my father could have reconciled himself to poverty, fame he must have.

"It's not possible," people feeding at his expense would insinuate, "it's just not possible that the grandson of such a grandfather . . ."

But what went on in my head was quite different. Scraping my way through my violin exercises, I would have books by Turgenev or Dumas on my music stand. Page after page I devoured as I deedled away. In the daytime I would relate impossible happenings to the kids next door; at night I would commit them to paper. In our family, composition was a hereditary occupation. Grandfather Leivi-Itzkhok, who went cracked as he grew old, spent his whole life writing a tale entitled "The Headless Man." I took after him.

Three times a week, laden with violin case and music, I made my reluctant way to Zagursky's place on Witte (formerly Dvoryanskaya) Street. There Jewish girls aflame with hysteria sat along the wall awaiting their turn, pressing to their feeble knees violins exceeding in dimensions the exalted persons they were to play to at Buckingham Palace.

The door to the sanctum would open, and from Mr. Zagursky's study there would stagger big-headed, freckled children with necks as thin as flower stalks and an epileptic flush on their cheeks. The door would bang to, swallowing up the next dwarf. Behind the wall, straining his throat, the teacher sang and waved his baton. He had ginger curls and frail legs, and sported a big bow tie. Manager of a monstrous lottery, he populated the Moldavanka and the dark culs-de-sac of the Old Market with the ghosts of pizzicato and cantilena. Afterward old Professor Auer lent these strains a diabolical brilliance.

In this crew I was quite out of place. Though like them in my dwarfishness, in the voice of my forebears I perceived inspiration of another sort.

The first step was difficult. One day I left home laden like a beast of burden with violin case, violin, music, and twelve roubles in cash—payment for a month's tuition. I was going along Nezhin Street; to get to Zagursky's I should have turned into Dvoryanskaya, but instead of that I went up Tiraspolskaya and found myself at the harbor. The allotted time flew past in the part of the port where ships went after quarantine. So began my liberation. Zagursky's saw me no more: affairs of greater moment occupied my thoughts. My pal Nemanov and I got into the habit of slipping aboard the S.S. *Kensington* to see an old salt named Trottyburn. Nemanov was a year younger than I. From the age of eight onward he had been doing the most ingenious business deals you can imagine. He had a wonderful head for that kind of thing, and later on amply fulfilled his youthful promise. Now he is a New York millionaire, director of General Motors, a company no less powerful than Ford. Nemanov took me along with him because I silently obeyed all his orders. He used to buy pipes smuggled in by Mr. Trottyburn. They were made in Lincoln by the old sailor's brother.

"Gen'lemen," Mr. Trottyburn would say to us, "take my word, the pets must be made with your own hands. Smoking a factory-made pipe—might as well shove an enema in your mouth. D'you know who Benvenuto Cellini was? He was a grand lad. My brother in Lincoln could tell you about him. Live and let live is his motto. He's got it into his head that you just has to make the pets with your own hands, and not with no one else's. And who are we to say him no, gen'lemen?"

Nemanov used to sell Trottyburn's pipes to bank-managers, foreign consuls, well-to-do Greeks. He made a hundred percent on them.

The pipes of the Lincolnshire master breathed poetry. In each one of them thought was invested, a drop of eternity. A little yellow eye gleamed in their mouthpieces, and their cases were lined with satin. I tried to picture the life in Old England of Matthew Trottyburn, the last master-pipemaker, who refused to swim with the tide.

"We can't but agree, gen'lemen, that the pets has to be made with your own hands."

The heavy waves by the sea wall swept me further and further away from our house, impregnated with the smell of leeks and Jewish destiny. From the harbor I migrated to the other side of the breakwater. There on a scrap of sandspit dwelt the boys from Primorskaya Street. Trouserless from morn till eve, they dived under wherries, sneaked coconuts for dinner, and awaited the time when boats would arrive from Kherson and Kamenka laden with watermelons, which melons it would be possible to break open against moorings.

To learn to swim was my dream. I was ashamed to confess to those bronzed lads that, born in Odessa, I had not seen the sea till I was ten, and at fourteen didn't know how to swim.

How slow was my acquisition of the things one needs to know! In my childhood, chained to the Gemara, I had led the life of a sage. When I grew up, I started climbing trees.

But swimming proved beyond me. The hydrophobia of my ancestors—Spanish rabbis and Frankfurt money-changers—dragged me to the bottom. The waves refused to support me. I would struggle to the shore pumped full of salt water and feeling as though I had been flayed, and return to where my fiddle and music lay. I was fettered to the instruments of my torture, and dragged them about with me. The struggle of rabbis versus Neptune continued till such time as the local water-god took pity on me. This was Yefim Nikitich Smolich, proofreader of the *Odessa News*. In his athletic breast there dwelt compassion for Jewish children, and he was the god of a rabble of rickety starvelings. He used to collect them from the bug-infested joints on the Moldavanka, take them down to the sea, bury them in the sand, do gym with them, dive with them, teach them songs. Roasting in the perpendicular sunrays, he would tell them tales about fishermen and wild beasts. To grownups Nikitich would explain that he was a natural philosopher. The Jewish kids used to roar with laughter at his tales, squealing and snuggling up to him like so many puppies. The sun would sprinkle them with creeping freckles, freckles that were the same color as lizards.

Silently, out of the corner of his eye, the old man had been watching my duel with the waves. Seeing that the thing was hopeless, that I should simply never learn to swim, he included me among the permanent occupants of his heart. That cheerful heart of his was with us there all the time; it never went careering off anywhere else, never knew covetousness and never grew disturbed. With his sunburned shoulders, his superannuated gladiator's head, his bronzed and slightly bandy legs, he would lie among us on the other side of the mole, lord and master of those melon-sprinkled, paraffin-stained waters. I came to love that man, with the love that only a lad suffering from hysteria and headaches can feel for a real man. I was always at his side, always trying to be of service to him.

He said to me:

"Don't you get all worked up. You just strengthen your nerves. The swimming will come of itself. How d'you mean, the water won't hold you? Why shouldn't it hold you?"

Seeing how drawn I was to him, Nikitich made an exception of me alone of all his disciples. He invited me to visit the clean and spacious attic where he lived in an ambience of straw mats, showed me his dogs, his hedgehog, his tortoise, and his pigeons. In return for this wealth I showed him a tragedy I had written the day before.

"I was sure you did a bit of scribbling," said Nikitich. "You've the look. You're looking in *that* direction all the time; no eyes for anywhere else."

He read my writings, shrugged a shoulder, passed a hand through his stiff gray curls, paced up and down the attic.

"One must suppose," he said slowly, pausing after every word, "one must suppose that there's a spark of the divine fire in you."

We went out into the street. The old man halted, struck the pavement with his stick, and fastened his gaze upon me.

"Now what is it you lack? Youth's no matter—it will pass with the years. What you lack is a feeling for nature."

He pointed with his stick at a tree with a reddish trunk and a low crown.

"What's that tree?"

I didn't know.

"What's growing on that bush?"

I didn't know this either. We walked together across the little square on the Alexandrovsky Prospect. The old man kept poking his stick at trees; he would seize me by the shoulder when a bird flew past, and he made me listen to the various kinds of singing.

"What bird is that singing?"

I knew none of the answers. The names of trees and birds, their division into species, where birds fly away to, on which side the sun rises, when the dew falls thickest—all these things were unknown to me.

"And you dare to write? A man who doesn't live in nature, as a stone does or an animal, will never in all his life write two worthwhile lines.

Your landscapes are like descriptions of stage props. In heaven's name, what have your parents been thinking of for fourteen years?"

What *had* they been thinking of? Of protested bills of exchange, of Mischa Elman's mansions. I didn't say anything to Nikitich about that, but just kept mum.

At home, over dinner, I couldn't touch my food. It just wouldn't go down.

"A feeling for nature," I thought to myself. "Goodness, why did that never enter my head? Where am I to find someone who will tell me about the way birds sing and what trees are called? What do *I* know about such things? I might perhaps recognize lilac, at any rate when it's in bloom. Lilac and acacia—there are acacias along De Ribas and Greek Streets."

At dinner father told a new story about Jascha Heifetz. Just before he got to Robinat's he had met Mendelssohn, Jascha's uncle. It appeared that the lad was getting eight hundred roubles a performance. Just work out how much that comes at fifteen concerts a month!

I did, and the answer was twelve thousand a month. Multiplying and carrying four in my head, I glanced out of the window. Across the cement courtyard, his cloak swaying in the breeze, his ginger curls poking out from under his soft hat, leaning on his cane, Mr. Zagursky, my music teacher, was advancing. It must be admitted he had taken his time in spotting my truancy. More than three months had elapsed since the day when my violin had grounded on the sand by the breakwater.

Mr. Zagursky was approaching the main entrance. I dashed to the back door, but the day before it had been nailed up for fear of burglars. Then I locked myself in the privy. In half an hour the whole family had assembled outside the door. The women were weeping. Aunt Bobka, exploding with sobs, was rubbing her fat shoulder against the door. Father was silent. Finally he started speaking, quietly and distinctly as he had never before spoken in his life.

"I am an officer," said my father. "I own real estate. I go hunting. Peasants pay me rent. I have entered my son in the Cadet Corps. I have no need to worry about my son."

He was silent again. The women were sniffling. Then a terrible blow descended on the privy door. My father was hurling his whole body against it, stepping back and then throwing himself forward.

"I am an officer," he kept wailing. "I go hunting. I'll kill him. This is the end."

The hook sprang from the door, but there was still a bolt hanging onto a single nail. The women were rolling about on the floor, grasping father by the legs. Crazy, he was trying to break loose. Father's mother came over, alerted by the hubbub.

"My child," she said to him in Hebrew, "our grief is great. It has no bounds. Only blood is lacking in our house. I do not wish to see blood in our house."

Father gave a groan. I heard his footsteps retreating. The bolt still hung by its last nail.

I sat it out in my fortress till nightfall. When all had gone to bed, Aunt Bobka took me to grandmother's. We had a long way to go. The moonlight congealed on bushes unknown to me, on trees that had no name. Some anonymous bird emitted a whistle and was extinguished, perhaps by sleep. What bird was it? What was it called? Does dew fall in the evening? Where is the constellation of the Great Bear? On what side does the sun rise?

We were going along Post Office Street. Aunt Bobka held me firmly by the hand so that I shouldn't run away. She was right to. I was thinking of running away.

QUESTIONS

"Awakening"

1. From what point of view is "Awakening" told? Why do you think Babel chose this particular way of telling his story? How would you describe the narrator's tone? Is his language formal? Conversational? What does this language reveal about the speaker's personality?

2. Why do all the families in the narrator's "circle" send their children to music school? What do they hope to accomplish? What is the speaker's attitude toward Mr. Zagursky's "factory of infant prodigies"? Look closely at the language the narrator uses to describe the young musicians. How do you think he feels about them?

3. Why isn't the narrator successful in his musical studies? Why is he "out of place"? Where do his own interests and talents, his "inspiration," lie?

4. Describe the "old salt," Trottyburn. What is his function in the story? What does he represent to the boy? Why does the narrator tell us about his friend Nemanov? How does Nemanov compare to the "infant prodigies" in the first part of the story? Is he similar to them in any way? How is he different?

5. Why is it so important for the narrator to learn how to swim? What sort of change does he detect in himself? Why does he say, "In my childhood . . . I had led the life of a sage. When I grew up I started climbing trees"? Are there any similarities between the section of the story in which the speaker visits the "scrap of sandspit" where the "boys from Primorskaya Street" dwell and Doris Lessing's story "Through the Tunnel" in Chapter Three?

6. How does the narrator feel about Yefim Nikitich Smolich? How does the boy's description of Nikitich convey those feelings? In what way does Nikitich serve as the narrator's mentor and guide? How does he differ from the narra-

tor's other mentor, Mr. Zagursky, the music teacher? What sort of opposition does Babel set up in the contrasting characters of Nikitich and Zagursky? In what sense do these two men represent opposing values, perceptions, and ways of life? How would you characterize that opposition? For example, one might describe it as the contrast between body and mind. What are some other ways of defining it?

7. Why does Nikitich say that "A man who doesn't live in nature, as a stone does or an animal, will never in all his life write two worthwhile lines"? Do you agree with this statement?

8. Although this quest story focuses on the role of the narrator's older helper, who points the hero in the direction of self-fulfillment, it can also be read as a story about the call. Explain.

The Sky Is Gray

ERNEST J. GAINES

1

Go'n be coming in a few minutes. Coming round that bend down there full speed. And I'm go'n get out my handkerchief and wave it down, and we go'n get on it and go.

I keep on looking for it, but Mama don't look that way no more. She's looking down the road where we just come from. It's a long old road, and far's you can see you don't see nothing but gravel. You got dry weeds on both sides, and you got trees on both sides, and fences on both sides, too. And you got cows in the pastures and they standing close together. And when we was coming out here to catch the bus I seen the smoke coming out of the cows's noses.

I look at my mama and I know what she's thinking. I been with Mama so much, just me and her, I know what she's thinking all the time. Right now it's home—Auntie and them. She's thinking if they got enough wood— if she left enough there to keep them warm till we get back. She's thinking if it go'n rain and if any of them go'n have to go out in the rain. She's thinking 'bout the hog—if he go'n get out, and if Ty and Val be able to get him back in. She always worry like that when she leaves the house. She don't worry too much if she leaves me there with the smaller ones, 'cause she know I'm go'n look after them and look after Auntie and everything else. I'm the oldest and she say I'm the man.

I look at my mama and I love my mama. She's wearing that black coat and that black hat and she's looking sad. I love my mama and I want put my arm round her and tell her. But I'm not supposed to do that. She say that's weakness and that's crybaby stuff, and she don't want no crybaby round her. She don't want you to be scared, either. 'Cause Ty's scared of ghosts and she's always whipping him. I'm scared of the dark, too, but I make 'tend I ain't. I make 'tend I ain't 'cause I'm the oldest, and I got to set a good sample for the rest. I can't ever be scared and I can't ever cry. And that's why I never said nothing 'bout my teeth. It's been hurting me and hurting me close to a month now, but I never said it. I didn't say it 'cause I didn't want to act like a crybaby, and 'cause I know we didn't have

enough money to go have it pulled. But, Lord, it been hurting me. And look like it wouldn't start till at night when you was trying to get yourself little sleep. Then soon's you shut your eyes—ummm-ummm, Lord, look like it go right down to your heartstring.

"Hurting, hanh?" Ty'd say.

I'd shake my head, but I wouldn't open my mouth for nothing. You open your mouth and let that wind in, and it almost kill you.

I'd just lay there and listen to them snore. Ty there, right 'side me, and Auntie and Val over by the fireplace. Val younger than me and Ty, and he sleeps with Auntie. Mama sleeps round the other side with Louis and Walker.

I'd just lay there and listen to them, and listen to that wind out there, and listen to that fire in the fireplace. Sometimes it'd stop long enough to let me get little rest. Sometimes it just hurt, hurt, hurt. Lord, have mercy.

2

Auntie knowed it was hurting me. I didn't tell nobody but Ty, 'cause we buddies and he ain't go'n tell nobody. But some kind of way Auntie found out. When she asked me, I told her no, nothing was wrong. But she knowed it all the time. She told me to mash up a piece of aspirin and wrap it in some cotton and jugg it down in that hole. I did it, but it didn't do no good. It stopped for a little while, and started right back again. Auntie wanted to tell Mama, but I told her, "Uh-uh." 'Cause I knowed we didn't have any money, and it just was go'n make her mad again. So Auntie told Monsieur Bayonne, and Monsieur Bayonne came over to the house and told me to kneel down 'side him on the fireplace. He put his finger in his mouth and made the Sign of the Cross on my jaw. The tip of Monsieur Bayonne's finger is some hard, 'cause he's always playing on that guitar. If we sit outside at night we can always hear Monsieur Bayonne playing on his guitar. Sometimes we leave him out there playing on the guitar.

Monsieur Bayonne made the Sign of the Cross over and over on my jaw, but that didn't do no good. Even when he prayed and told me to pray some, too, that tooth still hurt me.

"How you feeling?" he say.

"Same," I say.

He kept on praying and making the Sign of the Cross and I kept on praying, too.

"Still hurting?" he say.

"Yes, sir."

Monsieur Bayonne mashed harder and harder on my jaw. He mashed so hard he almost pushed me over on Ty. But then he stopped.

"What kind of prayers you praying, boy?" he say.

"Baptist," I say.

"Well, I'll be—no wonder that tooth still killing him. I'm going one way and he pulling the other. Boy, don't you know any Catholic prayers?"

"I know 'Hail Mary,' " I say.

"Then you better start saying it."

"Yes, sir."

He started mashing on my jaw again, and I could hear him praying at the same time. And, sure enough, after while it stopped hurting me.

Me and Ty went outside where Monsieur Bayonne's two hounds was and we started playing with them. "Let's go hunting," Ty say. "All right," I say; and we went on back in the pasture. Soon the hounds got on a trail, and me and Ty followed them all 'cross the pasture and then back in the woods, too. And then they cornered this little old rabbit and killed him, and me and Ty made them get back, and we picked up the rabbit and started on back home. But my tooth had started hurting me again. It was hurting me plenty now, but I wouldn't tell Monsieur Bayonne. That night I didn't sleep a bit, and the first thing in the morning Auntie told me to go back and let Monsieur Bayonne pray over me some more. Monsieur Bayonne was in his kitchen making coffee when I got there. Soon's he seen me he knowed what was wrong.

"All right, kneel down there 'side that stove," he say. "And this time make sure you pray Catholic. I don't know nothing 'bout that Baptist, and I don't want to know nothing 'bout him."

3

Last night Mama say, "Tomorrow we going to town."

"It ain't hurting me no more," I say. "I can eat anything on it."

"Tomorrow we going to town," she say.

And after she finished eating, she got up and went to bed. She always go to bed early now. 'Fore Daddy went in the Army, she used to stay up late. All of us sitting out on the gallery or round the fire. But now, look like soon's she finished eating she go to bed.

This morning when I woke up, her and Auntie was standing 'fore the fireplace. She says: "Enough to get there and back. Dollar and a half to have it pulled. Twenty-five for me to go, twenty-five for him. Twenty-five for me to come back, twenty-five for him. Fifty cents left. Guess I get little piece of salt meat with that."

"Sure can use it," Auntie say. "White beans and no salt meat ain't white beans."

"I do the best I can," Mama say.

They was quiet after that, and I made 'tend I was still asleep.

"James, hit the floor," Auntie say.

I still made 'tend I was asleep. I didn't want them to know I was listening.

"All right," Auntie say, shaking me by the shoulder. "Come on. Today's the day."

I pushed the cover down to get out, and Ty grabbed it and pulled it back.

"You, too, Ty," Auntie say.

"I ain't getting no teef pulled," Ty say.

"Don't mean it ain't time to get up," Auntie say. "Hit it, Ty."

Ty got up grumbling.

"James, you hurry up and get in your clothes and eat your food," Auntie says. "What time y'all coming back?" she say to Mama.

"That 'leven o'clock bus," Mama say. "Got to get back in that field this evening."

"Get a move on you, James," Auntie say.

I went in the kitchen and washed my face, then I ate my breakfast. I was having bread and syrup. The bread was warm and hard and tasted good. And I tried to make it last a long time.

Ty came back there grumbling and mad at me.

"Got to get up," he say. "I ain't having no teefes pulled. What I got to be getting up for?"

Ty poured some syrup in his pan and got a piece of bread. He didn't wash his hands, neither his face, and I could see that white stuff in his eyes.

"You the one getting your teef pulled," he say. "What I got to get up for. I bet if I was getting a teef pulled, you wouldn't be getting up. Shucks; syrup again. I'm getting tired of this old syrup. Syrup, syrup, syrup. I'm go'n take with the sugar diabetes. I want me some bacon sometime."

"Go out in the field and work and you can have your bacon," Auntie say. She stood in the middle door looking at Ty. "You better be glad you got syrup. Some people ain't got that—hard's time is."

"Shucks," Ty say. "How can I be strong."

"I don't know too much 'bout your strength," Auntie say; "but I know where you go'n be hot at, you keep that grumbling up. James, get a move on you; your mama waiting."

I ate my last piece of bread and went in the front room. Mama was standing 'fore the fireplace warming her hands. I put on my coat and my cap, and we left the house.

4

I look down there again, but it still ain't coming. I almost say, "It ain't coming yet," but I keep my mouth shut. 'Cause that's something else she don't like. She don't like for you to say something just for nothing. She can see it ain't coming, I can see it ain't coming, so why say it ain't coming. I don't say it, I turn and look at the river that's back of us. It's so cold the smoke's just raising up from the water. I see a bunch of pool-doos not too far out—just on the other side the lilies. I'm wondering if you can eat pool-doos. I ain't too sure, 'cause I ain't never ate none. But I done ate owls and blackbirds, and I done ate redbirds, too. I didn't want to kill the red-birds, but she made me kill them. They had two of them back there. One in my trap, one in Ty's trap. Me and Ty was go'n play with them and let them go, but she made me kill them 'cause we needed the food.

"I can't," I say. "I can't"

"Here," she say. "Take it."

"I can't," I say. "I can't. I can't kill him, Mama, please."

"Here," she say. "Take this fork, James."

"Please, Mama, I can't kill him," I say.

I could tell she was go'n hit me. I jerked back, but I didn't jerk back soon enough.

"Take it," she say.

I took it and reached in for him, but he kept on hopping to the back.

"I can't, Mama," I say. The water just kept on running down my face. "I can't," I say.

"Get him out of there," she say.

I reached in for him and he kept on hopping to the back. Then I reached in farther, and he pecked me on the hand.

"I can't, Mama," I say.

She slapped me again.

I reached in again, but he kept on hopping out my way. Then he hopped to one side and I reached there. The fork got him on the leg and I heard his leg pop. I pulled my hand out 'cause I had hurt him.

"Give it here," she say, and jerked the fork out my hand.

She reached in and got the little bird right in the neck. I heard the fork go in his neck, and I heard it go in the ground. She brought him out and helt him right in front of me.

"That's one," she say. She shook him off and gived me the fork. "Get the other one."

"I can't, Mama," I say. "I'll do anything, but don't make me do that."

She went to the corner of the fence and broke the biggest switch over there she could find. I knelt 'side the trap, crying.

"Get him out of there," she say.

"I can't, Mama."

She started hitting me 'cross the back. I went down on the ground, crying.

"Get him," she say.

"Octavia?" Auntie say.

'Cause she had come out of the house and she was standing by the tree looking at us.

"Get him out of there," Mama say.

"Octavia," Auntie say, "explain to him. Explain to him. Just don't beat him. Explain to him."

But she hit me and hit me and hit me.

I'm still young—I ain't no more than eight; but I know now; I know why

I had to do it. (They was so little, though. They was so little. I 'member how I picked the feathers off them and cleaned them and helt them over the fire. Then we all ate them. Ain't had but a little bitty piece each, but we all had a little bitty piece, and everybody just looked at me 'cause they was so proud.) Suppose she had to go away? That's why I had to do it. Suppose she had to go away like Daddy went away? Then who was go'n look after us? They had to be somebody left to carry on. I didn't know it then, but I know it now. Auntie and Monsieur Bayonne talked to me and made me see.

5

Time I see it I get out my handkerchief and start waving. It's still 'way down there, but I keep waving anyhow. Then it come up and stop and me and Mama get on. Mama tell me go sit in the back while she pay. I do like she say, and the people look at me. When I pass the little sign that say "White" and "Colored," I start looking for a seat. I just see one of them back there, but I don't take it, 'cause I want my mama to sit down herself. She comes in the back and sit down, and I lean on the seat. They got seats in the front, but I know I can't sit there, 'cause I have to sit back of the sign. Anyhow, I don't want sit there if my mama go'n sit back here.

They got a lady sitting 'side my mama and she looks at me and smiles little bit. I smile back, but I don't open my mouth, 'cause the wind'll get in and make that tooth ache. The lady took out a pack of gum and reach me a slice, but I shake my head. The lady just can't understand why a little boy'll turn down gum, and she reach me a slice again. This time I point to my jaw. The lady understands and smiles little bit, and I smile little bit, but I don't open my mouth, though.

They got a girl sitting 'cross from me. She got on a red overcoat and her hair's plaited in one big plait. First, I make 'tend I don't see her over there, but then I start looking at her little bit. She make 'tend she don't see me, either, but I catch her looking that way. She got a cold, and every now and then she h'ist that little handkerchief to her nose. She ought to blow it, but she don't. Must think she's too much a lady or something.

Every time she h'ist that little handkerchief, the lady 'side her say something in her ear. She shakes her head and lays her hands in her lap again. Then I catch her kind of looking where I'm at. I smile at her little bit. But think she'll smile back? Uh-uh. She just turn up her little old nose and turn her head. Well, I show her both of us can turn us head. I turn mine too and look out at the river.

The river is gray. The sky is gray. They have pool-doos on the water. The water is wavy, and the pool-doos go up and down. The bus go round a turn, and you got plenty trees hiding the river. Then the bus go round another turn, and I can see the river again.

I look toward the front where all the white people sitting. Then I look at that little gal again. I don't look right at her, 'cause I don't want all them people to know I love her. I just look at her little bit, like I'm looking out that window over there. But she knows I'm looking that way, and she kind of look at me, too. The lady sitting 'side her catch her this time, and she leans over and says something in her ear.

"I don't love him nothing," that little old gal says out loud.

Everybody back there hear her mouth, and all of them look at us and laugh.

"I don't love you either," I say. "So you don't have to turn up your nose, Miss."

"You the one looking," she say.

"I wasn't looking at you," I say. "I was looking out that window, there."

"Out the window, my foot," she say. "I seen you. Everytime I turned round you was looking at me."

"You must of been looking yourself if you seen me all them times," I say.

"Shucks," she say, "I got me all kind of boyfriends."

"I got girlfriends, too," I say.

"Well, I just don't want you getting your hopes up," she say.

I don't say no more to that little old gal 'cause I don't want have to bust her in the mouth. I lean on the seat where Mama sitting, and I don't even look that way no more. When we get to Bayonne, she jugg her little old tongue out at me. I make 'tend I'm go'n hit her, and she duck down 'side her mama. And all the people laugh at us again.

6

Me and Mama get off and start walking in town. Bayonne is a little bitty town. Baton Rouge is a hundred times bigger than Bayonne. I went to Baton Rouge once—me, Ty, Mama, and Daddy. But that was 'way back yonder, 'fore Daddy went in the Army. I wonder when we go'n see him again. I wonder when. Look like he ain't ever coming back home. . . . Even the pavement all cracked in Bayonne. Got grass shooting right out the sidewalk. Got weeds in the ditch, too; just like they got at home.

It's some cold in Bayonne. Look like it's colder than it is home. The wind blows in my face, and I feel that stuff running down my nose. I sniff. Mama says use that handkerchief. I blow my nose and put it back.

We pass a school and I see them white children playing in the yard. Big old red school, and them children just running and playing. Then we pass a café, and I see a bunch of people in there eating. I wish I was in there 'cause I'm cold. Mama tells me keep my eyes in front where they belong.

We pass stores that's got dummies, and we pass another café, and then we pass a shoe shop, and that bald-head man in there fixing on a shoe. I look at him and I butt into that white lady, and Mama jerks me in front and tells me stay there.

We come up to the courthouse, and I see the flag waving there. This flag ain't like the one we got at school. This one here ain't got but a handful of stars. One at school got a big pile of stars—one for every state. We pass it and we turn and there it is—the dentist office. Me and Mama go in, and they got people sitting everywhere you look. They even got a little boy in there younger than me.

Me and Mama sit on that bench, and a white lady come in there and ask me what my name is. Mama tells her and the white lady goes on back. Then I hear somebody hollering in there. Soon's that little boy hear him hollering, he starts hollering, too. His mama pats him and pats him, trying to make him hush up, but he ain't thinking 'bout his mama.

The man that was hollering in there comes out holding his jaw. He is a big old man and he's wearing overalls and a jumper.

"Got it, hanh?" another man asks him.

The man shakes his head—don't want to open his mouth.

"Man, I thought they was killing you in there," the other man says. "Hollering like a pig under a gate."

The man don't say nothing. He just heads for the door, and the other man follows him.

"John Lee," the white lady says. "John Lee Williams."

The little boy juggs his head down in his mama's lap and holler more now. His mama tells him go with the nurse, but he ain't thinking 'bout his mama. His mama tells him again, but he don't even hear her. His mama picks him up and and takes him in there, and even when the white lady shuts the door I can still hear little old John Lee.

"I often wonder why the Lord let a child like that suffer," a lady says to my mama. The lady's sitting right in front of us on another bench. She's got on a white dress and a black sweater. She must be a nurse or something herself, I reckon.

"Not us to question," a man says.

"Sometimes I don't know if we shouldn't," the lady says.

"I know definitely we shouldn't," the man says. The man look like a preacher. He's big and fat and he's got on a black suit. He's got a gold chain, too.

"Why?" the lady says.

"Why anything?" the preacher says.

"Yes," the lady says. "Why anything?"

"Not us to question," the preacher says.

The lady looks at the preacher a little while and looks at Mama again.

"And look like it's the poor who suffers the most," she says. "I don't understand it."

"Best not to even try," the preacher says. "He works in mysterious ways— wonders to perform."

Right then little John Lee bust out hollering, and everybody turn their head to listen.

"He's not a good dentist," the lady says. "Dr. Robillard is much better. But more expensive. That's why most of the colored people come here. The white people go to Dr. Robillard. Y'all from Bayonne?"

"Down the river," my mama says. And that's all she go'n say, 'cause she don't talk much. But the lady keeps on looking at her, and so she says, "Near Morgan."

"I see," the lady says.

7

"That's the trouble with the black people in this country today," somebody else says. This one here's sitting on the same side me and Mama's sitting, and he is kind of sitting in front of that preacher. He looks like a teacher or somebody that goes to college. He's got on a suit, and he's got a book that he's been reading. "We don't question is exactly our problem," he says. "We should question and question and question—question everything."

The preacher just looks at him a long time. He done put a toothpick or something in his mouth, and he just keeps on turning it and turning it. You can see he don't like that boy with that book.

"Maybe you can explain what you mean," he says.

"I said what I meant," the boy says. "Question everything. Every stripe, every star, every word spoken. Everything."

"It 'pears to me that this young lady and I was talking 'bout God, young man," the preacher says.

"Question Him, too," the boy says.

"Wait," the preacher says. "Wait now."

"You heard me right," the boy says. "His existence as well as everything else. Everything."

The preacher just looks across the room at the boy. You can see he's getting madder and madder. But mad or no mad, the boy ain't thinking 'bout him. He looks at the preacher just's hard's the preacher looks at him.

"Is this what they coming to?" the preacher says. "Is this what we educating them for?"

"You're not educating me," the boy says. "I wash dishes at night so that I can go to school in the day. So even the words you spoke need questioning."

The preacher just looks at him and shakes his head.

"When I come in this room and seen you there with your book, I said to myself, 'There's an intelligent man.' How wrong a person can be."

"Show me one reason to believe in the existence of a God," the boy says.

"My heart tells me," the preacher says.

" 'My heart tells me,' " the boy says. " 'My heart tells me.' Sure, 'My heart tells me.' And as long as you listen to what your heart tells you, you will have only what the white man gives you and nothing more. Me, I don't listen to my heart. The purpose of the heart is to pump blood throughout the body, and nothing else."

"Who's your paw, boy?" the preacher says.

"Why?"

"Who is he?"

"He's dead."

"And your mom?"

"She's in Charity Hospital with pneumonia. Half killed herself, working for nothing."

"And 'cause he's dead and she's sick, you mad at the world?"

"I'm not mad at the world. I'm questioning the world. I'm questioning it with cold logic, sir. What do words like Freedom, Liberty, God, White, Colored mean? I want to know. That's why *you* are sending us to school, to read and to ask questions. And because we ask these questions, you call us mad. No sir, it is not us who are mad."

"You keep saying 'us'?"

" 'Us,' Yes—us. I'm not alone."

The preacher just shakes his head. Then he looks at everybody in the room—everybody. Some of the people look down at the floor, keep from looking at him. I kind of look 'way myself, but soon's I know he done turn his head, I look that way again.

"I'm sorry for you," he says to the boy.

"Why?" the boy says. "Why not be sorry for yourself? Why are you so much better off than I am? Why aren't you sorry for these other people in here? Why not be sorry for the lady who had to drag her child into the dentist office? Why not be sorry for the lady sitting on the bench over there? Be sorry for them. Not for me. Some way or the other I'm going to make it."

"No, I'm sorry for you," the preacher says.

"Of course, of course," the boys says, nodding his head. "You're sorry for me because I rock that pillar you're leaning on."

"You can't ever rock the pillar I'm leaning on, young man. It's stronger than anything man can ever do."

"You believe in God because a man told you to believe in God," the boy says. "A white man told you to believe in God. And why? To keep you ignorant so he can keep his feet on your neck."

"So now we the ignorant?" the preacher says.

"Yes," the boy says. "Yes." And he opens his book again.

The preacher just looks at him sitting there. The boy done forgot all about him. Everybody else make 'tend they done forgot the squabble, too.

Then I see that preacher getting up real slow. Preacher's a great big old man and he got to brace himself to get up. He comes over where the boy is sitting. He just stands there a little while looking down at him, but the boy don't raise his head.

"Get up, boy," preacher says.

The boy looks up at him, then he shuts his book real slow and stands up. Preacher just hauls back and hit him in the face. The boy falls back 'gainst the wall, but he straightens himself up and looks right back at that preacher.

"You forgot the other cheek," he says.

The preacher hauls back and hit him again on the other side. But this time the boy braces himself and don't fall.

"That hasn't changed a thing," he says.

The preacher just looks at the boy. The preacher's breathing real hard like he just run up a big hill. The boy sits down and opens his book again.

"I feel sorry for you," the preacher says. "I never felt so sorry for a man before."

The boys makes 'tend he don't even hear that preacher. He keeps on reading his book. The preacher goes back and gets his hat off the chair.

"Excuse me," he says to us. "I'll come back some other time. Y'all, please excuse me.

And he looks at the boy and goes out the room. The boy h'ist his hand up to his mouth one time to wipe 'way some blood. All the rest of the time he keeps on reading. And nobody else in there say a word.

8

Little John Lee and his mama come out the dentist office, and the nurse calls somebody else in. Then little bit later they come out, and the nurse calls another name. But fast's she calls somebody in there, somebody else comes in the place where we sitting, and the room stays full.

The people coming in now, all of them wearing big coats. One of them says something 'bout sleeting, another one says he hope not. Another one says he think it ain't nothing but rain. 'Cause, he says, rain can get awful cold this time of year.

All round the room they talking. Some of them talking to people right by them, some of them talking to people clear 'cross the room, some of them talking to anybody'll listen. It's a little bitty room, no bigger than us kitchen, and I can see everybody in there. The little old room's full of smoke, 'cause you got two old men smoking pipes over by that side door. I think I feel my tooth thumping me some, and I hold my breath and wait. I wait and wait, but it don't thump me no more. Thank God for that.

I feel like going to sleep, and I lean back 'gainst the wall. But I'm scared to go to sleep. Scared 'cause the nurse might call my name and I won't hear her. And Mama might go to sleep, too, and she'll be mad if neither one of us heard the nurse.

I look up at Mama. I love my mama. And when cotton come I'm go'n get her a new coat. And I ain't go'n get a black one, either. I think I'm go'n get her a red one.

"They got some books over there," I say. "Want read one of them?"

Mama looks at the books, but she don't answer me.

"You got yourself a little man there," the lady says.

Mama don't say nothing to the lady, but she must've smiled, 'cause I seen the lady smiling back. The lady looks at me a little while, like she's feeling sorry for me.

"You sure got that preacher out here in a hurry," she says to that boy.

The boy looks up at her and look in his book again. When I grow up I want be just like him. I want clothes like that and I want keep a book with me, too.

"You really don't believe in God?" the lady says.

"No," he says.

"But why?" the lady says.

"Because the wind is pink," he says.

"What?" the lady says.

The boy don't answer her no more. He just reads in his book.

"Talking 'bout the wind is pink," that old lady says. She's sitting on the same bench with the boy and she's trying to look in his face. The boy makes 'tend the old lady ain't even there. He just keeps on reading. "Wind is pink," she says again. "Eh, Lord, what children go'n be saying next?"

The lady 'cross from us bust out laughing.

"That's a good one," she says. "The wind is pink. Yes sir, that's a good one."

"Don't you believe the wind is pink?" the boy says. He keeps his head down in the book.

"Course I believe it, honey," the lady says. "Course I do." She looks at us and winks her eye. "And what color is grass, honey?"

"Grass? Grass is black."

She bust out laughing again. The boy looks at her.

"Don't you believe grass is black?" he says.

The lady quits her laughing and looks at him. Everybody else looking at him too. The place quiet, quiet.

"Grass is green, honey," the lady says. "It was green yesterday, it's green today, and it's go'n be green tomorrow."

"How do you know it's green?"

"I know because I know."

"You don't know it's green," the boy says. "You believe it's green because someone told you it was green. If someone had told you it was black you'd believe it was black."

"It's green," the lady says. "I know green when I see green."

"Prove it's green," the boy says.

"Sure, now," the lady says. "Don't tell me it's coming to that."

"It's coming to just that," the boy says. "Words mean nothing. One means no more than the other."

"That's what it all coming to?" that old lady says. That old lady got on a turban and she got on two sweaters. She got a green sweater under a black sweater. I can see the green sweater 'cause some of the buttons on the other sweater's missing.

"Yes, ma'am," the boy says. "Words mean nothing. Action is the only thing. Doing. That's the only thing."

"Other words, you want the Lord to come down here and show Hisself to you?" she says.

"Exactly, ma'am," he says.

"You don't mean that, I'm sure?" she says.

"I do, ma'am," he says.

"Done, Jesus," the lady says, shaking her head.

"I didn't go 'long with that preacher at first," the other lady says; "but now—I don't know. When a person says the grass is black, he's either a lunatic or something's wrong."

"Prove to me that it's green," the boy says.

"It's green because the people say it's green."

"Those same people say we're citizens of these United States," the boy says.

"I think I'm a citizen," the lady says.

"Citizens have certain rights," the boy says. "Name me one right that you have. One right, granted by the Constitution, that you can exercise in Bayonne."

The lady don't answer him. She just looks at him like she don't know what he's talking 'bout. I know I don't.

"Things changing," she says.

"Things are changing because some black men have begun to think with their brains and not their hearts," the boy says.

"You trying to say these people don't believe in God?"

"I'm sure some of them do. Maybe most of them do. But they don't believe that God is going to touch these white people's hearts and change things tomorrow. Things change through action. By no other way."

Everybody sit quiet and look at the boy. Nobody says a thing. Then the lady 'cross the room from me and Mama just shakes her head.

"Let's hope that not all your generation feel the same way you do," she says.

"Think what you please, it doesn't matter," the boy says. "But it will be men who listen to their heads and not their hearts who will see that your children have a better chance then you had."

"Let's hope they ain't all like you, though," the old lady says. "Done forgot the heart absolutely."

"Yes ma'am, I hope they aren't all like me," the boy says. "Unfortunately, I was born too late to believe in your God. Let's hope that the ones who come after will have your faith—if not in your God, then in something else, something definitely that they can lean on. I haven't anything. For me, the wind is pink, the grass is black."

9

The nurse comes in the room where we all sitting and waiting and says the doctor won't take no more patients till one o'clock this evening. My mama jumps up off the bench and goes up to the white lady.

"Nurse, I have to go back in the field this evening," she says.

"The doctor is treating his last patient now," the nurse says. "One o'clock this evening."

"Can I at least speak to the doctor?" my mama asks.

"I'm his nurse," the lady says.

"My little boy's sick," my mama says. "Right now his tooth almost killing him."

The nurse looks at me. She's trying to make up her mind if to let me come in. I look at her real pitiful. The tooth ain't hurting me at all, but Mama say it is, so I make 'tend for her sake.

"This evening," the nurse says, and goes on back in the office.

"Don't feel 'jected, honey," the lady says to Mama. "I been round them a long time—they take you when they want to. If you was white, that's something else; but we the wrong color."

Mama don't say nothing to the lady, and me and her go outside and stand 'gainst the wall. It's cold out there. I can feel that wind going through my coat. Some of the other people come out of the room and go up the street. Me and Mama stand there a little while and we start walking. I don't know where we going. When we come to the other street we just stand there.

"You don't have to make water, do you?" Mama says.

"No, ma'am," I say.

We go on up the street. Walking real slow. I can tell Mama don't know where she's going. When we come to a store we stand there and look at the dummies. I look at a little boy wearing a brown overcoat. He's got on brown shoes, too. I look at my old shoes and look at his'n again. You wait till summer, I say.

Me and Mama walk away. We come up to another store and we stop and look at them dummies, too. Then we go on again. We pass a caf where the white people in there eating. Mama tells me keep my eyes in front where they belong, but I can't help from seeing them people eat. My stomach starts to growling, 'cause I'm hungry. When I see people eating, I get hungry; when I see a coat, I get cold.

A man whistles at my mama when we go by a filling station. She makes 'tend she don't even see him. I look back and I feel like hitting him in the mouth. If I was bigger, I say; if I was bigger, you'd see.

We keep on going. I'm getting colder and colder, but I don't say nothing. I feel that stuff running down my nose and I sniff.

"That rag," Mama says.

I get it out and wipe my nose. I'm getting cold all over now—my face, my hands, my feet, everything. We pass another little caf, but this'n for white people, too, and we can't go in there, either. So we just walk. I'm so cold now I'm 'bout ready to say it. If I knowed where we was going I wouldn't be so cold, but I don't know where we going. We go, we go, we go. We walk clean out of Bayonne. Then we cross the street and we come back. Same thing I seen when I got off the bus this morning. Same old trees, same old walk, same old weeds, same old cracked pave—same old everything.

I sniff again.

"That rag," Mama says.

I wipe my nose real fast and jugg that handkerchief back in my pocket 'fore my hand get too cold. I raise my head and I can see David's hardware store. When we come up to it, we go in. I don't know why, but I'm glad.

It's warm in there. It's so warm in here you don't ever want to leave. I look for the heater, and I see it over by them barrels. Three white men standing round the heater talking in Creole. One of them comes over to see what my mama want.

"Got any axe handles?" she says.

Me, Mama and the white man start to the back, but Mama stops me when we come up to the heater. She and the white man go on. I hold my hands over the heater and look at them. They go all the way to the back, and I see the white man pointing to the axe handles 'gainst the wall. Mama takes one of them and shakes it like she's trying to figure how much it weighs. Then she rubs her hand over it from one end to the other end. She turns it over and looks at the other side, then she shakes it again, and shakes her head and puts it back. She gets another one and she does it just like she did the first one, then she shakes her head. Then she gets a brown one and do it that, too. But she don't like this one, either. Then she gets another one, but 'fore she shakes it or anything, she looks at me. Look like she's trying to say something to me, but I don't know what it is. All I know is I done got warm now and I'm feeling right smart better. Mama shakes this axe handle just like she did the others, and shakes her head and says something to the white man. The white man just looks at his pile of axe handles, and when Mama pass him to come to the front, the white man just scratch his head and follows her. She tells me come on and we go on out and start walking again.

We walk and walk, and no time at all I'm cold again. Look like I'm colder now 'cause I can still remember how good it was back there. My stomach growls and I suck it in to keep Mama from hearing it. She's walking right 'side me, and it growls so loud you can hear it a mile. But Mama don't say a word.

10

When we come up to the courthouse, I look at the clock. It's got quarter to twelve. Mean we got another hour and a quarter to be out here in the cold. We go and stand 'side a building. Something hits my cap and I look up at the sky. Sleet's falling.

I look at Mama standing there. I want stand close 'side her, but she don't like that. She say that's crybaby stuff. She say you got to stand for yourself, by yourself.

"Let's go back to that office," she says.

We cross the street. When we get to the dentist office I try to open the door, but I can't. I twist and twist, but I can't. Mama pushes me to the side and she twist the knob, but she can't open the door, either. She turns 'way from the door. I look at her, but I don't move and I don't say nothing. I done seen her like this before and I'm scared of her.

"You hungry?" she says. She says it like she's mad at me, like I'm the cause of everything.

"No, ma'am," I say.

"You want eat and walk back, or you rather don't eat and ride?"

"I ain't hungry," I say.

I ain't just hungry, but I'm cold, too. I'm so hungry and cold I want to cry. And look like I'm getting colder and colder. My feet done got numb. I try to work my toes, but I don't even feel them. Look like I'm go'n die. Look like I'm go'n stand right here and freeze to death. I think 'bout home. I think 'bout Val and Auntie and Ty and Louis and Walker. It's 'bout twelve o'clock and I know they eating dinner now. I can hear Ty making jokes. He done forgot 'bout getting up early this morning and right now he's probably making jokes. Always trying to make somebody laugh. I wish I was right there listening to him. Give anything in the world if I was home round the fire.

"Come on," Mama says.

We start walking again. My feet so numb I can't hardly feel them. We turn the corner and go on back up the street. The clock on the courthouse starts hitting for twelve.

The sleet's coming down plenty now. They hit the pave and bounce like rice. Oh, Lord; oh, Lord, I pray. Don't let me die, don't let me die, Lord.

11

Now I know where we going. We going back to town where the colored people eat. I don't care if I don't eat. I been hungry before. I can stand it. But I can't stand the cold.

I can see we go'n have a long walk. It's 'bout a mile down there. But I don't mind. I know when I get there I'm go'n warm myself. I think I can hold out. My hands numb in my pockets and my feet numb, too, but if I keep moving I can hold out. Just don't stop no more, that's all.

The sky's gray. The sleet keeps on falling. Falling like rain—now plenty, plenty. You can hear it hitting the pave. You can see it bouncing. Sometimes it bounces two times 'fore it settles.

We keep on going. We don't say nothing. We just keep on going, keep on going.

I wonder what Mama's thinking. I hope she ain't mad at me. When summer come I'm go'n pick plenty cotton and get her a coat. I'm go'n get her a red one.

I hope they'd make it summer all the time. I'd be glad if it was summer all the time—but it ain't. We got to have winter, too. Lord, I hate the winter. I guess everybody hate the winter.

I don't sniff this time. I get out my handkerchief and wipe my nose. My hand's so cold I can hardly hold the handkerchief.

I think we getting close, but we ain't there yet. I wonder where everybody is. Can't see a soul but us. Look like we the only two people moving round today. Must be too cold for the rest of the people to move round in.

I can hear my teeth. I hope they don't knock together too hard and make that bad one hurt. Lord, that's all I need, for that bad one to start off.

I hear a church bell somewhere. But today ain't Sunday. They must be ringing for a funeral or something.

I wonder what they doing at home. They must be eating. Monsieur Bayonne might be there with his guitar. One day Ty played with Monsieur Bayonne's guitar and broke one of the strings. Monsieur Bayonne was some mad with Ty. He say Ty wasn't go'n ever 'mount to nothing. Ty can go just like Monsieur Bayonne when he ain't there. Ty can make everybody laugh when he starts to mocking Monsieur Bayonne.

I used to like to be with Mama and Daddy. We used to be happy. But they took him in the Army. Now, nobody happy no more. . . . I be glad when Daddy comes home.

Monsieur Bayonne say it wasn't fair for them to take Daddy and give Mama nothing and give us nothing. Auntie say, "Shhh, Etienne. Don't let them hear you talk like that." Monsieur Bayonne say, "It's God truth. What they giving his children? They have to walk three and a half miles to school hot or cold. That's anything to give for a paw? She's got to work in the field rain or shine just to make ends meet. That's anything to give for a husband?" Auntie say, "Shhh, Etienne, shhh." "Yes, you right," Monsieur Bayonne say. "Best don't say it in front of them now. But one day they go'n find out. One day." "Yes, I suppose so," Auntie say. "Then what, Rose Mary?" Monsieur Bayonne say. "I don't know, Etienne," Auntie say. "All we can do is us job, and leave everything else in His hand . . ."

We getting closer, now. We getting closer. I can even see the railroad tracks.

We cross the tracks, and now I see the café. Just to get in there, I say. Just to get in there. Already I'm starting to feel little better.

12

We go in. Ahh, it's good. I look for the heater; there 'gainst the wall. One of them little brown ones. I just stand there and hold my hands over it. I can't open my hands too wide 'cause they almost froze.

Mam's standing right 'side me. She done unbuttoned her coat. Smoke rises out of the coat, and the coat smells like a wet dog.

I move to the side so Mama can have more room. She opens out her hands and rubs them together. I rub mine together, too, 'cause this keep them from hurting. If you let them warm too fast, they hurt you sure. But if you let them warm just little bit at a time, and you keep rubbing them, they be all right every time.

They got just two more people in the caf. A lady back of the counter, and a man on this side the counter. They been watching us ever since we come in.

Mama gets out the handkerchief and count up the money. Both of us know how much money she's got there. Three dollars. No, she ain't got three dollars, 'cause she had to pay us way up here. She ain't got but two dollars and a half left. Dollar and a half to get my tooth pulled, and fifty cents for us to go back on, and fifty cents worth of salt meat.

She stirs the money around with her finger. Most of the money is change 'cause I can hear it rubbing together. She stirs it and stirs it. Then she looks at the door. It's still sleeting. I can hear it hitting 'gainst the wall like rice.

"I ain't hungry, Mama," I say.

"Got to pay them something for they heat," she says.

She takes a quarter out the handkerchief and ties the handkerchief up again. She looks over her shoulder at the people, but she still don't move. I hope she don't spend the money. I don't want her spending it on me. I'm hungry, I'm almost starving I'm so hungry, but I don't want her spending the money on me.

She flips the quarter over like she's thinking. She's must be thinking 'bout us walking back home. Lord, I sure don't want walk home. If I thought it'd do any good to say something, I'd say it. But Mama makes up her own mind 'bout things.

She turns 'way from the heater right fast, like she better hurry up and spend the quarter 'fore she change her mind. I watch her go toward the counter. The man and the lady look at her, too. She tells the lady something and the lady walks away. The man keeps on looking at her. Her back's turned to the man, and she don't even know he's standing there.

The lady puts some cakes and a glass of milk on the counter. Then she pours a cup of coffee and sets it 'side the other stuff. Mama pays her for the things and comes on back where I'm standing. She tells me sit down at the table 'gainst the wall.

The milk and the cakes's for me; the coffee's for Mama. I eat slow and I look at her. She's looking outside at the sleet. She's looking real sad. I say to myself, I'm go'n make all this up one day. You see, one day, I'm go'n make all this up. I want say it now; I want tell her how I feel right now; but Mama don't like to us to talk like that.

"I can't eat all this," I say.

They ain't got but just three little old cakes there. I'm so hungry right

now, the Lord knows I can eat a hundred times three, but I want my mama
to have one.

Mama don't even look my way. She knows I'm hungry, she knows I want
it. I let it stay there a little while, then I get it and eat it. I eat just on my
front teeth, though, 'cause if cake touch that back tooth I know what'll
happen. Thank God it ain't hurt me at all today.

After I finish eating I see the man go to the juke box. He drops a nickel
in it, then he just stand there a little while looking at the record. Mama
tells me keep my eyes in front where they belong. I turn my head like she
say, but then I hear the man coming toward us.

"Dance, pretty?" he says.

Mama gets up to dance with him. But 'fore you know it, she done grabbed
the little man in the collar and done heaved him 'side the wall. He hit the
wall so hard he stop the juke box from playing.

"Some pimp," the lady back of the counter says. "Some pimp."

The little man jumps up off the floor and starts toward my mama. 'Fore
you know it, Mama done sprung open her knife and she's waiting for him.

"Come on," she says. "Come on. I'll gut you from your neighbo to your
throat. Come on."

I go up to the little man to hit him, but Mama makes me come and stand
'side her. The little man looks at me and Mama and goes on back to the
counter.

"Some pimp," the lady back of the counter says. "Some pimp." She starts
laughing and pointing at the little man. "Yes sir, you a pimp, all right. Yes
sir-ree."

13

"Fasten that coat, let's go," Mama says.

"You don't have to leave," the lady says.

Mama don't answer the lady, and we right out in the cold again. I'm
warm right now—my hands, my ears, my feet—but I know this ain't go'n
last too long. It done sleet so much now you got ice everywhere you look.

We cross the railroad tracks, and soon's we do, I get cold. That wind
goes through this little old coat like it ain't even there. I got on a shirt and
a sweater under the coat, but that wind don't pay them no mind. I look up
and I can see we got a long way to go. I wonder if we go'n make it 'fore I
get too cold.

We cross over to walk on the sidewalk. They got just one sidewalk back
here, and it's over there.

After we go just a little piece, I smell bread cooking. I look, then I see
a baker shop. When we get closer, I can smell it more better, I shut my
eyes and make 'tend I'm eating. But I keep them shut too long and I butt

up 'gainst a telephone post. Mama grabs me and see if I'm hurt. I ain't bleeding or nothing and she turns me loose.

I can feel I'm getting colder and colder, and I look up to see how far we still got to go. Uptown is 'way up yonder. A half mile more, I reckon. I try to think of something. They say think and you won't get cold. I think of that poem, "Annabel Lee." I ain't been to school in so long—this bad weather—I reckon they done passed "Annabel Lee" by now. But passed it or not, I'm sure Miss Walker go'n make me recite it when I get there. That woman don't never forget nothing. I ain't never seen nobody like that in my life.

I'm still getting cold. "Annabel Lee" or no "Annabel Lee," I'm still getting cold. But I can see we getting closer. We getting there gradually.

Soon's we turn the corner, I see a little old white lady up in front of us. She's the only lady on the street. She's all in black and she's got a long black rag over her head.

"Stop," she says.

Me and Mama stop and look at her. She must be crazy to be out in all this bad weather. Ain't got but a few other people out there, and all of them's men.

"Y'all done ate?" she says.

"Just finish," Mama says.

"Y'all must be cold then?" she says.

"We headed for the dentist," Mama says. "We'll warm up when we get there."

"What dentist?" the old lady says. "Mr. Bassett?"

"Yes, ma'am," Mama says.

"Come on in," the old lady says. "I'll telephone him and tell him y'all coming."

Me and Mama follow the old lady in the store. It's a little bitty store, and it don't have much in there. The old lady takes off her head rag and folds it up.

"Helena?" somebody calls from the back.

"Yes, Alnest?" the old lady says.

"Did you see them?"

"They're here. Standing beside me."

"Good. Now you can stay inside."

The old lady looks at Mama. Mama's waiting to hear what she brought us in here for. I'm waiting for that, too.

"I saw y'all each time you went by," she says. "I came out to catch you, but you were gone."

"We went back of town," Mama says.

"Did you eat?"

"Yes, ma'am."

The old lady looks at Mama a long time, like she's thinking Mama might be just saying that. Mama looks right back at her. The old lady looks at me to see what I have to say. I don't say nothing. I sure ain't going 'gainst my mama.

"There's food in the kitchen," she says to Mama. "I've been keeping it warm."

Mama turns right around and starts for the door.

"Just a minute," the old lady says. Mama stops. "The boy'll have to work for it. It isn't free."

"We don't take no handout," Mama says.

"I'm not handing out anything," the old lady says. "I need my garbage moved to the front. Ernest has a bad cold and can't go out there."

"James'll move it for you," Mama says.

"Not unless you eat," the old lady says. "I'm old, but I have my pride, too, you know."

Mama can see she ain't go'n beat this old lady down, so she just shakes her head.

"All right," the old lady says. "Come into the kitchen."

She leads the way with that rag in her hand. The kitchen is a little bitty little old thing, too. The table and the stove just 'bout fill it up. They got a little room to the side. Somebody in there laying 'cross the bed—'cause I can see one of his feet. Must be the person she was talking to: Ernest or Alnest—something like that.

"Sit down," the old lady says to Mama. "Not you," she says to me. "You have to move the cans."

"Helena?" the man says in the other room.

"Yes, Alnest?" the old lady says.

"Are you going out there again?"

"I must show the boy where the garbage is, Alnest," the old lady says.

"Keep that shawl over your head," the old man says.

"You don't have to remind me, Alnest. Come, boy," the old lady says.

We go out in the yard. Little old back yard ain't no bigger than the store or the kitchen. But it can sleet here just like it can sleet in any big back yard. And 'fore you know it, I'm trembling.

"There," the old lady says, pointing to the cans. I pick up one of the cans and set it right back down. The can's so light, I'm go'n see what's inside of it.

"Here," the old lady says. "Leave that can alone."

I look back at her standing there in the door. She's got that black rag wrapped round her shoulders, and she's pointing one of her little old fingers at me.

"Pick it up and carry it to the front," she says. I go by her with the can, and she's looking at me all the time. I'm sure the can's empty. I'm sure she could've carried it herself—maybe both of them at the same time. "Set it on the sidewalk by the door and come back for the other one," she says.

I go and come back, and Mama looks at me when I pass her. I get the other can and take it to the front. It don't feel a bit heavier than that first one. I tell myself I ain't go'n be nobody's fool, and I'm go'n look inside this can to see just what I been hauling. First, I look up the street, then down the street. Nobody coming. Then I look over my shoulder toward the door. That little old lady done slipped up there quite 's mouse, watching me again. Look like she knowed what I was go'n do.

"Ehh, Lord," she says. "Children, children. Come in here, boy, and go wash your hands."

I follow her in the kitchen. She points toward the bathroom, and I go in there and wash up. Little bitty old bathroom, but it's clean, clean. I don't use any of her towels; I wipe my hands on my pants legs.

When I come back in the kitchen, the old lady done dished up the food. Rice, gravy, meat—and she even got some lettuce and tomato in a saucer. She even got a glass of milk and a piece of cake there, too. It looks so good, I almost start eating 'fore I say my blessing.

"Helena?" the old man says.

"Yes, Alnest?"

"Are they eating?"

"Yes," she says.

"Good," he says. "Now you'll stay inside."

The old lady goes in there where he is and I can hear them talking. I look at Mama. She's eating slow like she's thinking. I wonder what's the matter now. I reckon she's thinking 'bout home.

The old lady comes back in the kitchen.

"I talked to Dr. Bassett's nurse," she says. "Dr. Bassett will take you as soon as you get there."

"Thank you, ma'am," Mama says.

"Perfectly all right," the old lady says. "Which one is it?"

Mama nods toward me. The old lady looks at me real sad. I look sad, too.

"You're not afraid, are you?" she says.

"No, ma'am," I say.

"That's a good boy," the old lady says. "Nothing to be afraid of. Dr. Bassett will not hurt you."

"When me and Mama get through eating, we thank the old lady again.

"Helena, are they leaving?" the old man says.

"Yes, Alnest."

"Tell them I say good-bye."

"They can hear you, Alnest."

"Good-bye both mother and son," the old man says. "And may God be with you."

Me and Mama tell the old man good-bye, and we follow the old lady in the front room. Mama opens the door to go out, but she stops and comes back in the store.

"You sell salt meat?" she says.

"Yes."

"Give me two bits worth."

"That isn't very much salt meat," the old lady says.

"That's all I have," Mama says.

The old lady goes back of the counter and cuts a big piece off the chunk. Then she wraps it up and puts it in a paper bag.

"Two bits," she says.

"That looks like awful lot of meat for a quarter," Mama says.

"Two bits," the old lady says. "I've been selling salt meat behind this counter twenty-five years. I think I know what I'm doing."

"You got a scale there," Mama says.

"What?" the old lady says.

"Weigh it," Mama says.

"What?" the old lady says. "Are you telling me how to run my business?"

"Thanks very much for the food," Mama says.

"Just a minute," the old lady says.

"James," Mama says to me. I move toward the door.

"Just one minute, I said," the old lady says.

Me and Mama stop again and look at her. The old lady takes the meat out of the bag and unwraps it and cuts 'bout half of it off. Then she wraps it up again and juggs it back in the bag and gives the bag to Mama. Mama lays the quarter on the counter.

"Your kindness will never be forgotten," she says. "James," she says to me.

We go out, and the old lady comes to the door to look at us. After we go a little piece I look back, and she's still there watching us.

The sleet's coming down heavy, heavy now, and I turn up my coat collar to keep my neck warm. My mama tells me turn it right back down.

"You not a bum," she says. "You a man."

QUESTIONS

"The Sky Is Gray"

1. From what point of view is Gaines's story told? Who is the narrator? What limitations does the choice of narrator impose on Gaines?

2. A substantial proportion of "The Sky Is Gray" consists of the protagonist's traveling or wandering from one place to another with his mother. Why does Gaines devote so much of his story to a description of these activities?

3. What is the object of James's quest? How does his mother serve as a helper and guide? What is she trying to teach and show him throughout the story?

4. Who are the other potential helpers and guides in the story? What guidance do they offer?

5. Describe James's mother, using sections 4, 9, 12, and 13 in particular to arrive at a sense of her character.

6. What is James's relationship with his mother like? She is almost always very stern with him; do we ever see her respond to him differently? What is his attitude toward her? Where is James's father?

7. How clearly and completely does James understand his mother, particularly her responses to his behavior? What are some of her rules of conduct? Do they seem reasonable to you?

8. What is the function of the young man with the book? How is he contrasted with some of the other people in the waiting room, and especially with James's mother?

9. After the preacher hits him once, the student says, "You forgot the other cheek." To what is he alluding? Why is this an effective rebuke?

10. In your opinion, what makes the preacher decide to leave the dentist's waiting room? Why are the people so hostile to the student?

11. Is the young man with the book right in his charges against white people? How does the incident of the elderly white woman in the last section of the story affect your assessment of these charges?

12. How does Gaines, through narrative choices about James's behavior, his language, and the degree and kind of his consciousness, keep us aware that his remarkably mature protagonist is only eight years old?

13. In the scene in the café, James tells us that his mother "gets up to dance" with the man in it. Is James reporting this accurately? Given her reaction to the stranger, are there things she, as an adult, can perceive that her son cannot?

14. Do James and his mother seem poorer than the other people we meet in this story? Would you say that theirs is an impoverished life? How do the story's mood and atmosphere help you answer this question?

15. Why do you think Gaines called his story "The Sky Is Gray"?

Under the Banyan Tree

R. K. NARAYAN

The village Somal, nestling away in the forest tracts of Mempi, had a population of less than three hundred. It was in every way a village to make the heart of a rural reformer sink. Its tank, a small expanse of water, right in the middle of the village, served for drinking, bathing, and washing the cattle, and it bred malaria, typhoid, and heaven knew what else. The cottages sprawled anyhow and the lanes twisted and wriggled up and down and strangled each other. The population used the highway as the refuse ground and in the backyard of every house drain water stagnated in green puddles.

Such was the village. It is likely that the people of the village were insensitive: but it is more likely that they never noticed their surroundings because they lived in a kind of perpetual enchantment. The enchanter was Nambi the story-teller. He was a man of about sixty or seventy. Or was he eighty or one hundred and eighty? Who could say? In a place so much cut off as Somal (the nearest bus-stop was ten miles away), reckoning could hardly be in the familiar measures of time. If anyone asked Nambi what his age was he referred to an ancient famine or an invasion or the building of a bridge and indicated how high he had stood from the ground at the time.

He was illiterate, in the sense that the written word was a mystery to him; but he could make up a story, in his head, at the rate of one a month; each story took nearly ten days to narrate.

His home was the little temple which was at the very end of the village. No one could say how he had come to regard himself as the owner of the temple. The temple was a very small structure with red-striped walls, with a stone image of the Goddess Shakti in the sanctum. The front portion of the temple was Nambi's home. For aught it mattered any place might be his home; for he was without possessions. All that he possessed was a broom with which he swept the temple; and he had also a couple of dhoties and upper cloth. He spent most of the day in the shade of the banyan which spread out its branches in front of the temple. When he felt hungry he walked into any house that caught his fancy and joined the family at dinner. When he needed new clothes they were brought to him by the villagers.

He hardly ever had to go out in search of company; for the banyan shade served as a clubhouse for the village folk. All through the day people came seeking Nambi's company and squatted under the tree. If he was in a mood for it he listened to their talk and entertained them with his own observations and anecdotes. When he was in no mood he looked at the visitors sourly and asked, "What do you think I am? Don't blame me if you get no story at the next moon. Unless I meditate how can the Goddess give me a story? Do you think stories float in the air?" And he moved out to the edge of the forest and squatted there, contemplating the trees.

On Friday evenings the village turned up at the temple for worship, when Nambi lit a score of mud lamps and arranged them around the threshold of the sanctuary. He decorated the image with flowers, which grew wildly in the backyard of the temple. He acted as the priest and offered to the Goddess fruits and flowers brought in by the villagers.

On the nights he had a story to tell he lit a small lamp and placed it in a niche in the trunk of the banyan tree. Villagers as they returned home in the evening saw this, went home, and said to their wives, "Now, now, hurry up with the dinner, the story-teller is calling us." As the moon crept up behind the hillock, men, women, and children gathered under the banyan tree. The story-teller would not appear yet. He would be sitting in the sanctum, before the Goddess, with his eyes shut, in deep meditation. He sat thus as long as he liked and when he came out, with his forehead ablaze with ash and vermilion, he took his seat on a stone platform in front of the temple. He opened the story with a question. Jerking his finger towards a vague, far-away destination, he asked, "A thousand years ago, a stone's throw in that direction, what do you think there was? It was not the weed-covered waste it is now, for donkeys to roll in. It was not the ash-pit it is now. It was the capital of the king. . . ." The king would be Dasaratha, Vikramaditya, Asoka, or anyone that came into the old man's head; the capital was called Kapila, Kridapura, or anything. Opening thus, the old man went on without a pause for three hours. By then brick by brick the palace of the king was raised. The old man described the dazzling durbar hall where sat a hundred vassal kings, ministers, and subjects; in another part of the palace all the musicians in the world assembled and sang; and most of the songs were sung over again by Nambi to his audience; and he described in detail the pictures and trophies that hung on the walls of the palace. . . .

It was story-building on an epic scale. The first day barely conveyed the setting of the tale, and Nambi's audience as yet had no idea who were coming into the story. As the moon slipped behind the trees of Mempi Forest Nambi said, "Now friends, Mother says this will do for the day." He abruptly rose, went in, lay down, and fell asleep long before the babble of the crowd ceased.

The light in the niche would again be seen two or three days later, and again and again throughout the bright half of the month. Kings and heroes, villains and fairy-like women, gods in human form, saints and assassins, jostled each other in that world which was created under the banyan tree. Nambi's voice rose and fell in an exquisite rhythm, and the moonlight and the hour completed the magic. The villagers laughed with Nambi, they wept with him, they adored the heroes, cursed the villains, groaned when the conspirator had his initial success, and they sent up to the gods a heartfelt prayer for a happy ending. . . .

On the day when the story ended, the whole gathering went into the sanctum and prostrated before the Goddess. . . .

By the time the next moon peeped over the hillock Nambi was ready with another story. He never repeated the same kind of story or brought in the same set of persons, and the village folk considered Nambi a sort of miracle, quoted his words of wisdom, and lived on the whole in an exalted plane of their own, though their life in all other respects was hard and drab.

And yet it had gone on for years and years. One moon he lit the lamp in the tree. The audience came. The old man took his seat and began the story. ". . . When King Vikramaditya lived, his minister was . . ." He paused. He could not get beyond it. He made a fresh beginning. "There was the king . . ." he said, repeated it, and then his words trailed off into a vague mumbling. "What has come over me?" he asked pathetically. "Oh, Mother, great Mother, why do I stumble and falter? I know the story. I had the whole of it a moment ago. What was it about? I can't understand what has happened." He faltered and looked so miserable that his audience said, "Take your own time. You are perhaps tired."

"Shut up!" he cried. "Am I tired? Wait a moment; I will tell you the story presently." Following this there was utter silence. Eager faces looked up at him. "Don't look at me!" he flared up. Somebody gave him a tumbler of milk. The audience waited patiently. This was a new experience. Some persons expressed their sympathy aloud. Some persons began to talk among themselves. Those who sat in the outer edge of the crowd silently slipped away. Gradually, as it neared midnight, others followed this example. Nambi sat staring at the ground, his head bowed in thought. For the first time he realized that he was old. He felt he would never more be able to control his thoughts or express them cogently. He looked up. Everyone had gone except his friend Mari the blacksmith. "Mari, why aren't you also gone?"

Mari apologized for the rest: "They didn't want to tire you; so they have gone away."

Nambi got up. "You are right. Tomorrow I will make it up. Age, age. What is my age? It has come on suddenly." He pointed at his head and said, "This says, 'Old fool, don't think I shall be your servant any more. You will be my servant hereafter.' It is disobedient and treacherous."

He lit the lamp in the niche next day. The crowd assembled under the banyan faithfully. Nambi had spent the whole day in meditation. He had been fervently praying to the Goddess not to desert him. He began the story. He went on for an hour without a stop. He felt greatly relieved, so much so that he interrupted his narration to remark, "Oh, friends. The Mother is always kind. I was seized with a foolish fear . . ." and continued the story. In a few minutes he felt dried up. He struggled hard: "And then . . . and then . . . what happened?" He stammered. There followed a pause lasting an hour. The audience rose without a word and went home. The old man sat on the stone brooding till the cock crew. "I can't blame them for it," he muttered to himself. "Can they sit down here and mope all night?" Two days later he gave another installment of the story, and that, too, lasted only a few minutes. The gathering dwindled. Fewer persons began to take notice of the lamp in the niche. Even these came only out of a sense of duty. Nambi realized that there was no use in prolonging the struggle. He brought the story to a speedy and premature end.

He knew what was happening. He was harrowed by the thoughts of his failure. I should have been happier if I had dropped dead years ago, he said to himself. Mother, why have you struck me dumb . . . ? He shut himself up in the sanctum, hardly ate any food, and spent the greater part of the day sitting motionless in mediation.

The next moon peeped over the hillock, Nambi lit the lamp in the niche. The villagers as they returned home saw the lamp, but only a handful turned up at night. "Where are the others?" the old man asked. "Let us wait." He waited. The moon came up. His handful of audience waited patiently. And then the old man said, "I won't tell the story today, nor tomorrow unless the whole village comes here. I insist upon it. It is a mighty story. Everyone must hear it." Next day he went up and down the village street shouting, "I have a most wonderful tale to tell tonight. Come one and all; don't miss it. . . ." This personal appeal had a great effect. At night a large crowd gathered under the banyan. They were happy that the storyteller had regained his powers. Nambi came out of the temple when everyone had settled and said: "It is the Mother who gives the gifts; and it is she who takes away the gifts. Nambi is a dotard. He speaks when the Mother has anything to say. He is struck dumb when she has nothing to say. But what is the use of the jasmine when it has lost its scent? What is the lamp for when all the oil is gone? Goddess be thanked. . . . These are my last words on this earth; and this is my greatest story." He rose and went into the sanctum. His audience hardly understood what he meant. They sat there till they became weary. And then some of them got up and stepped into the sanctum. There the story-teller sat with eyes shut. "Aren't you going to tell us a story?" they asked. He opened his eyes, looked at them, and shook his head. He indicated by gesture that he had spoken his last words.

When he felt hungry he walked into any cottage and silently sat down for food, and walked away the moment he had eaten. Beyond this he had hardly anything to demand of his fellow beings. The rest of his life (he lived for a few more years) was one great consummate silence.

QUESTIONS

"Under the Banyan Tree"

1. Describe Somal, the tiny Indian village of Narayan's story. Why does the writer say it's the sort of place "to make the heart of a rural reformer sink"? What level of material comfort have the villagers achieved? What are the factors, in your opinion, that cut off Somal from the rest of the world?

2. Characterize Nambi as fully as you can. What is his life like? His daily routine? What are his needs? What does he value?

3. An art nearly as old as our species, story-telling flourished in virtually every pre-literate society. Storytellers were honored members of their communities. What human needs does story-telling fulfill? Why do human beings invent stories? Does Narayan's story provide any insight?

4. How does Nambi prepare himself to tell a story? How do his stories transform the villagers' lives? In what sense is he a helper and guide?

5. Four things are connected to Nambi's story-telling: the banyan tree, the lamp, the moon—Nambi tells his stories during the "bright half of the month"—and the temple. What is the symbolic meaning of each of these objects?

6. What happens to Nambi over the course of Narayan's story? Why is it so difficult for the old man to accept?

7. Contrast Nambi's last story with those he has told before. How is it different? Why does he call it the "greatest story" he has ever offered to the villagers? What message is contained in the questions he asks about the jasmine and the lamp? Why don't the villagers understand what he is saying?

8. We are told that, for the remaining years that Nambi lived, the Wise Old Man maintained a "consummate silence." Why?

9. Does Nambi's relationship with the villagers change after his powers fail? Why or why not? How will the silence of the storyteller transform the village?

The Conversion of the Jews

PHILIP ROTH

"You're a real one for opening your mouth in the first place," Itzie said. "What do you open your mouth all the time for?"

"I didn't bring it up, Itz, I didn't," Ozzie said.

"What do you care about Jesus Christ for anyway?"

"I didn't bring up Jesus Christ. He did. I didn't even know what he was talking about. Jesus is historical, he kept saying. Jesus is historical." Ozzie mimicked the monumental voice of Rabbi Binder.

"Jesus was a person that lived like you and me," Ozzie continued. "That's what Binder said—"

"Yeah? . . . So what! What do I give two cents whether he lived or not. And what do you gotta open your mouth!" Itzie Lieberman favored closed-mouthedness, especially when it came to Ozzie Freedman's questions. Mrs. Freedman had to see Rabbi Binder twice before about Ozzie's questions and this Wednesday at four-thirty would be the third time. Itzie preferred to keep *his* mother in the kitchen; he settled for behind-the-back subtleties such as gestures, faces, snarls and other less delicate barnyard noises.

"He was a real person, Jesus, but he wasn't like God, and we don't believe he is God." Slowly, Ozzie was explaining Rabbi Binder's position to Itzie, who had been absent from Hebrew School the previous afternoon.

"The Catholics," Itzie said helpfully, "they believe in Jesus Christ, that he's God." Itzie Lieberman used "the Catholics" in its broadest sense—to include the Protestants.

Ozzie received Itzie's remark with a tiny head bob, as though it were a footnote, and went on. "His mother was Mary, and his father probably was Joseph," Ozzie said. "But the New Testament says his real father was God."

"His *real* father?"

"Yeah," Ozzie said, "that's the big thing, his father's supposed to be God."

"Bull."

"That's what Rabbi Binder says, that it's impossible—"

"Sure it's impossible. That stuff's all bull. To have a baby you gotta get laid," Itzie theologized. "Mary hadda get laid."

"That's what Binder says: 'The only way a woman can have a baby is to have intercourse with a man.' "

"He said *that*, Ozz?" For a moment it appeared that Itzie had put the theological question aside. "He said that, intercourse?" A little curled smile shaped itself in the lower half of Itzie's face like a pink mustache. "What you guys do, Ozz, you laugh or something?"

"I raised my hand."

"Yeah? Whatja say?"

"That's when I asked the question."

Itzie's face lit up. "Whatja ask about—intercourse?"

"No, I asked the question about God, how if He could create the heaven and earth in six days, and make all the animals and the fish and the light in six days—the light especially, that's what always gets me, that He could make the light. Making fish and animals, that's pretty good—"

"That's damn good." Itzie's appreciation was honest but unimaginative: it was as though God had just pitched a one-hitter.

"But making light . . . I mean when you think about it, it's really something," Ozzie said. "Anyway, I asked Binder if He could make all that in six days, and He could *pick* the six days He wanted right out of nowhere, why couldn't He let a woman have a baby without having intercourse."

"You said intercourse, Ozz, to Binder?"

"Yeah."

"Right in class?"

"Yeah."

Itzie smacked the side of his head.

"I mean, no kidding around," Ozzie said, "that'd really be nothing. After all that other stuff, that'd practically be nothing."

Itzie considered a moment. "What'd Binder say?"

"He started all over again explaining how Jesus was historical and how he lived like you and me but he wasn't God. So I said I *understood* that. What I wanted to know was different."

What Ozzie wanted to know was always different. The first time he had wanted to know how Rabbi Binder could call the Jews "The Chosen People" if the Declaration of Independence claimed all men to be created equal. Rabbi Binder tried to distinguish for him between political equality and spiritual legitimacy, but what Ozzie wanted to know, he insisted vehemently, was different. That was the first time his mother had to come.

Then there was the plane crash. Fifty-eight people had been killed in a plane crash at La Guardia. In studying a casualty list in the newspaper his mother had discovered among the list of those dead eight Jewish names (his grandmother had nine but she counted Miller as a Jewish name); because of the eight she said the plane crash was "a tragedy." During free-discussion time on Wednesday Ozzie had brought to Rabbi Binder's attention this matter of "some of his relations" always picking out the Jewish names. Rabbi Binder had begun to explain cultural unity and some other things when Ozzie stood up at his seat and said that what he wanted to know was different. Rabbi Binder insisted that he sit down and it was then that Ozzie shouted that he wished all fifty-eight were Jews. That was the second time his mother came.

"And he kept explaining about Jesus being historical, and so I kept asking him. No kidding, Itz, he was trying to make me look stupid."

"So what he finally do?"

"Finally he starts screaming that I was deliberately simple-minded and a wise guy, and that my mother had to come, and this was the last time. And that I'd never get bar-mitzvahed if he could help it. Then, Itz, then he starts talking in that voice like a statue, real slow and deep, and he says that I better think over what I said about the Lord. He told me to go to his office and think it over." Ozzie leaned his body towards Itzie. "Itz, I thought it over for a solid hour, and now I'm convinced God could do it."

Ozzie had planned to confess his latest transgression to his mother as soon as she came home from work. But it was a Friday night in November and already dark, and when Mrs. Freedman came through the door she tossed off her coat, kissed Ozzie quickly on the face, and went to the kitchen table to light the three yellow candles, two for the Sabbath and one for Ozzie's father.

When his mother lit the candles she would move her two arms slowly towards her, dragging them through the air, as though persuading people whose minds were half made up. And her eyes would get glassy with tears. Even when his father was alive Ozzie remembered that her eyes had gotten glassy, so it didn't have anything to do with his dying. It had something to do with lighting the candles.

As she touched the flaming match to the unlit wick of a Sabbath candle, the phone rang, and Ozzie, standing only a foot from it, plucked it off the receiver and held it muffled to his chest. When his mother lit candles Ozzie felt there should be no noise; even breathing, if you could manage it, should be softened. Ozzie pressed the phone to his breast and watched his mother dragging whatever she was dragging, and he felt his own eyes get glassy. His mother was a round, tired, gray-haired penguin of a woman whose gray skin had begun to feel the tug of gravity and the weight of her own history. Even when she was dressed up she didn't look like a chosen person. But when she lit candles she looked like something better; like a woman who knew momentarily that God could do anything.

After a few mysterious minutes she was finished. Ozzie hung up the phone and walked to the kitchen table where she was beginning to lay the two places for the four-course Sabbath meal. He told her that she would have to see Rabbi Binder next Wednesday at four-thirty, and then he told her why. For the first time in their life together she hit Ozzie across the face with her hand.

All through the chopped liver and chicken soup part of the dinner Ozzie cried; he didn't have any appetite for the rest.

On Wednesday, in the largest of the three basement classrooms of the synagogue, Rabbi Marvin Binder, a tall, handsome, broad-shouldered man of thirty with thick strong-fibered black hair, removed his watch from his pocket and saw that it was four o'clock. At the rear of the room Yakov Blotnik, the seventy-one-year-old custodian, slowly polished the large window, mumbling to himself, unaware that it was four o'clock or six o'clock, Monday or Wednesday. To most of the students Yakov Blotnik's mumbling, along with his brown curly beard, scythe nose, and two heel-trailing black cats, made of him an object of wonder, a foreigner, a relic, towards whom they were alternately fearful and disrespectful. To Ozzie the mumbling had always seemed a monotonous, curious prayer; what made it curious was that old Blotnik had been mumbling so steadily for so many years, Ozzie suspected he had memorized the prayers and forgotten all about God.

"It is now free-discussion time," Rabbi Binder said. "Feel free to talk about any Jewish matter at all—religion, family, politics, sports—"

There was silence. It was a gusty, clouded November afternoon and it did not seem as though there ever was or could be a thing called baseball. So nobody this week said a word about that hero from the past, Hank Greenberg—which limited free discussion considerably.

And the soul-battering Ozzie Freedman had just received from Rabbi Binder had imposed its limitation. When it was Ozzie's turn to read aloud from the Hebrew book the rabbi had asked him petulantly why he didn't read more rapidly. He was showing no progress. Ozzie said he could read faster but that if he did he was sure not to understand what he was reading. Nevertheless, at the rabbi's repeated suggestion Ozzie tried, and showed a great talent, but in the midst of a long passage he stopped short and said he didn't understand a word he was reading, and started in again at a drag-footed pace. Then came the soul-battering.

Consequently when free-discussion time rolled around none of the students felt too free. The rabbi's invitation was answered only by the mumbling of feeble old Blotnik.

"Isn't there anything at all you would like to discuss?" Rabbi Binder asked again, looking at his watch. "No questions or comments?"

There was a small grumble from the third row. The rabbi requested that Ozzie rise and give the rest of the class the advantage of his thought.

Ozzie rose. "I forget it now," he said, and sat down in his place.

Rabbi Binder advanced a seat towards Ozzie and poised himself on the edge of the desk. It was Itzie's desk and the rabbi's frame only a dagger's-length away from his face snapped him to sitting attention.

"Stand up again, Oscar," Rabbi Binder said calmly, "and try to assemble your thoughts."

Ozzie stood up. All his classmates turned in their seats and watched as he gave an unconvincing scratch to his forehead.

"I can't assemble any," he announced, and plunked himself down.

"Stand up!" Rabbi Binder advanced from Itzie's desk to the one directly in front of Ozzie; when the rabbinical back was turned Itzie gave it five-fingers off the tip of his nose, causing a small titter in the room. Rabbi Binder was too absorbed in squelching Ozzie's nonsense once and for all to bother with titters. "Stand up, Oscar. What's your question about?"

Ozzie pulled a word out of the air. It was the handiest word. "Religion."

"Oh, now you remember?"

"Yes."

"What is it?"

Trapped, Ozzie blurted the first thing that came to him. "Why can't He make anything He wants to make!"

As Rabbi Binder prepared an answer, a final answer, Itzie, ten feet behind him, raised one finger on his left hand, gestured it meaningfully towards the rabbi's back, and brought the house down.

Binder twisted quickly to see what had happened and in the midst of the commotion Ozzie shouted into the rabbi's back what he couldn't have shouted to his face. It was a loud, toneless sound that had the timbre of something stored inside for about six days.

"You don't know! You don't know anything about God!"

The rabbi spun back towards Ozzie. "What?"

"You don't know—you don't—"

"Apologize, Oscar, apologize!" It was a threat.

"You don't—"

Rabbi Binder's hand flicked out at Ozzie's cheek. Perhaps it had only been meant to clamp the boy's mouth shut, but Ozzie ducked and the palm caught him squarely on the nose.

The blood came in a short, red spurt on to Ozzie's shirt front.

The next moment was all confusion. Ozzie screamed, "You bastard, you bastard!" and broke for the classroom door. Rabbi Binder lurched a step backwards, as though his own blood had started flowing violently in the opposite direction, then gave a clumsy lurch forward and bolted out the door after Ozzie. The class followed after the rabbi's huge blue-suited back, and before old Blotnik could turn from his window, the room was empty and everyone was headed full speed up the three flights leading to the roof.

If one should compare the light of day to the life of man: sunrise to birth; sunset—the dropping down over the edge—to death; then as Ozzie Freedman wiggled through the trapdoor of the synagogue roof, his feet kicking backwards bronco-style at Rabbi Binder's outstretched arms—at that moment the day was fifty years old. As a rule, fifty or fifty-five reflects accurately the age of late afternoons in November, for it is in that month, during those hours, that one's awareness of light seems no longer a matter of seeing, but of hearing: light begins clicking away. In fact, as Ozzie locked shut the trapdoor in the rabbi's face, the sharp click of the bolt into the lock might momentarily have been mistaken for the sound of the heavier gray that had just throbbed through the sky.

With all his weight Ozzie kneeled on the locked door; any instant he was certain that Rabbi Binder's shoulder would fling it open, splintering the wood into shrapnel and catapulting his body into the sky. But the door did not move and below him he heard only the rumble of feet, first loud then dim, like thunder rolling away.

A question shot through his brain. "Can this be *me?*" For a thirteen-year-old who had just labeled his religious leader a bastard, twice, it was not an improper question. Louder and louder the question came to him— "Is it me? Is it me?"—until he discovered himself no longer kneeling, but racing crazily towards the edge of the roof, his eyes crying, his throat screaming, and his arms flying everywhichway as though not his own.

"Is it me? Is it me ME ME ME ME! It has to be me—but is it!"

It is the question a thief must ask himself the night he jimmies open his first window, and it is said to be the question with which bridegrooms quiz themselves before the altar.

In the few split seconds it took Ozzie's body to propel him to the edge of the roof, his self-examination began to grow fuzzy. Gazing down at the street, he became confused as to the problem beneath the question: was it, is-it-me-who-called-Binder-a-bastard? or, is-it-me-prancing-around-on-the roof? However, the scene below settled all, for there is an instant in any action when whether it is you or somebody else is academic. The thief crams the money in his pockets and scoots out the window. The bride-groom signs the hotel register for two. And the boy on the roof finds a streetful of people gaping at him, necks stretched backwards, faces up, as though he were the ceiling of the Hayden Planetarium. Suddenly you know it's you.

"Oscar! Oscar Freedman!" A voice rose from the center of the crowd, a voice that, could it have been seen, would have looked like the writing on scroll. "Oscar Freedman, get down from there. Immediately!" Rabbi Binder was pointing one arm stiffly up at him; and at the end of that arm, one finger aimed menacingly. It was the attitude of a dictator, but one—the eyes confessed all—whose personal valet had spit neatly in his face.

Ozzie didn't answer. Only for a blink's length did he look towards Rabbi Binder. Instead his eyes began to fit together the world beneath him, to sort out people from places, friends from enemies, participants from spec-tators. In little jagged starlike clusters his friends stood around Rabbi Binder, who was still pointing. The topmost point on a star compounded not of angels but of five adolescent boys was Itzie. What a world it was, with those stars below, Rabbi Binder below . . . Ozzie, who a moment earlier hadn't been able to control his own body, started to feel the meaning of the word control: he felt Peace and he felt Power.

"Oscar Freedman, I'll give you three to come down."

Few dictators give their subjects three to do anything; but, as always, Rabbi Binder only looked dictatorial.

"Are you ready, Oscar?"

Ozzie nodded his head yes, although he had no intention in the world—

the lower one or the celestial one he'd just entered—of coming down even
if Rabbi Binder should give him a million.

"All right then," said Rabbi Binder. He ran a hand through his black
Samson hair as though it were the gesture prescribed for uttering the first
digit. Then, with his other hand cutting a circle out of the small piece of
sky around him, he spoke. "One!"

There was no thunder. On the contrary, at that moment, as though "one"
was the cue for which he had been waiting, the world's least thunderous
person appeared on the synagogue steps. He did not so much come out
the synagogue door as lean out, onto the darkening air. He clutched at the
doorknob with one hand and looked up at the roof.

"Oy!"

Yakov Blotnik's old mind hobbled slowly, as if on crutches, and though
he couldn't decide precisely what the boy was doing on the roof, he knew
it wasn't good—that is, it wasn't-good-for-the-Jews. For Yakov Blotnik life
had fractionated itself simply: things were either good-for-the-Jews or no-
good-for-the-Jews.

He smacked his free hand to his in-sucked cheek, gently. "Oy, Gut!"
And then quickly as he was able, he jacked down his head and surveyed
the street. There was Rabbi Binder (like a man at an auction with only
three dollars in his pocket, he had just delivered a shaky "Two!"); there
were the students, and that was all. So far it-wasn't-so-bad-for-the-Jews.
But the boy had to come down immediately, before anybody saw. The
problem: how to get the boy off the roof?

Anybody who has ever had a cat on the roof knows how to get him down.
You call the fire department. Or first you call the operator and you ask her
for the fire department. And the next thing there is great jamming of brakes
and clanging of bells and shouting of instructions. And then the cat is off
the roof. You do the same thing to get a boy off the roof.

That is, you do the same thing if you are Yakov Blotnik and you once
had a cat on the roof.

When the engines, all four of them, arrived, Rabbi Binder had four times
given Ozzie the count of three. The big hook-and-ladder swung around the
corner and one of the firemen leaped from it, plunging headlong towards
the yellow fire hydrant in front of the synagogue. With a huge wrench he
began to unscrew the top nozzle. Rabbi Binder raced over to him and
pulled at his shoulder.

"There's no fire . . ."

The fireman mumbled back over his shoulder and, heatedly, continued
working at the nozzle.

"But there's no fire, there's no fire . . ." Binder shouted. When the
fireman mumbled again, the rabbi grasped his face with both his hands and
pointed it up at the roof.

To Ozzie it looked as though Rabbi Binder was trying to tug the fire-

man's head out of his body, like a cork from a bottle. He had to giggle
at the picture they made: it was a family portrait—rabbi in black skullcap, fireman in red fire hat, and the little yellow hydrant squatting beside
like a kid brother, bareheaded. From the edge of the roof Ozzie waved
at the portrait, a one-handed, flapping, mocking wave; in doing it his
right foot slipped from under him. Rabbi Binder covered his eyes with his
hands.

Firemen work fast. Before Ozzie had even regained his balance, a big,
round yellowed net was being held on the synagogue lawn. The firemen
who held it looked up at Ozzie with stern, feelingless faces.

One of the firemen turned his head towards Rabbi Binder. "What, is the
kid nuts or something?"

Rabbi Binder unpeeled his hands from his eyes, slowly, painfully, as if
they were tape. Then he checked: nothing on the sidewalk, no dents in
the net.

"Is he gonna jump, or what?" the fireman shouted.

In a voice not at all like a statue, Rabbi Binder finally answered. "Yes,
yes, I think so . . . He's been threatening to . . ."

Threatening to? Why, the reason he was on the roof, Ozzie remembered, was to get away; he hadn't even thought about jumping. He had
just run to get away, and the truth was that he hadn't really headed for the
roof as much as he'd been chased there.

"What's his name, the kid?"

"Freedman," Rabbi Binder answered. "Oscar Freedman."

The fireman looked up at Ozzie. "What is it with you, Oscar? You gonna
jump, or what?"

Ozzie did not answer. Frankly, the question had just arisen.

"Look, Oscar, if you're gonna jump, jump—and if you're not gonna jump,
don't jump. But don't waste our time, willya?"

Ozzie looked at the fireman and then at Rabbi Binder. He wanted to see
Rabbi Binder cover his eyes one more time.

"I'm going to jump."

And then he scampered around the edge of the roof to the corner, where
there was no net below, and he flapped his arms at his sides, swishing the
air and smacking his palms to his trousers on the downbeat. He began
screaming like some kind of engine, "Wheeeee . . . wheeeeee," and leaning way out over the edge with the upper half of his body. The firemen
whipped around to cover the ground with the net. Rabbi Binder mumbled
a few words to Somebody and covered his eyes. Everything happened
quickly, jerkily, as in a silent movie. The crowd, which had arrived with
the fire engines, gave out a long, Fourth-of-July fireworks oooh-aahhh. In
the excitement no one had paid the crowd much heed, except, of course,
Yakov Blotnik, who swung from the door-knob counting heads. "Fier und
tsvansik . . . finf und tsvantsik . . . Oy, Gut!" It wasn't like this with the
cat.

Rabbi Binder peeked through his fingers, checked the sidewalk and net.

Empty. But there was Ozzie racing to the other corner. The firemen raced with him but were unable to keep up. Whenever Ozzie wanted to he might jump and splatter himself upon the sidewalk, and by the time the firemen scooted to the spot all they could do with their net would be to cover the mess.

"Wheeeee . . . wheeeee . . ."

"Hey, Oscar," the winded fireman yelled, "What the hell is this, a game or something?:"

"Wheeeee . . . wheeeee . . ."

"Hey, Oscar—"

But he was off now to the other corner, flapping his wings fiercely. Rabbi Binder couldn't take it any longer—the fire engines from nowhere, the screaming suicidal boy, the net. He fell to his knees, exhausted, and with his hands curled together in front of his chest like a little dome, he pleaded, "Oscar, stop it, Oscar. Don't jump, Oscar. Please come down . . . Please don't jump."

And further back in the crowd a single voice, a single young voice, shouted a lone word to the boy on the roof.

"Jump!"

It was Itzie. Ozzie momentarily stopped flapping.

"Go ahead, Ozz—jump!" Itzie broke off his point of the star and courageously, with the inspiration not of a wise-guy but of a disciple, stood alone. "Jump, Ozz, jump!"

Still on his knees, his hands still curled, Rabbi Binder twisted his body back. He looked at Itzie, then, agonizingly, back to Ozzie.

"OSCAR, DON'T JUMP! PLEASE, DON'T JUMP . . . please please . . ."

"Jump!" This time it wasn't Itzie but another point of the star. By the time Mrs. Freedman arrived to keep her four-thirty appointment with Rabbi Binder, the whole little upside down heaven was shouting and pleading for Ozzie to jump, and Rabbi Binder no longer was pleading with him not to jump, but was crying into the dome of his hands.

Understandably Mrs. Freedman couldn't figure out what her son was doing on the roof. So she asked.

"Ozzie, my Ozzie, what are you doing? My Ozzie, what is it?"

Ozzie stopped wheeeeeing and slowed his arms down to a cruising flap, the kind birds use in soft winds, but he did not answer. He stood against the low, clouded, darkening sky—light clicked down swiftly now, as on a small gear—flapping softly and gazing down at the small bundle of a woman who was his mother.

"What are you doing, Ozzie?" She turned towards the kneeling Rabbi Binder and rushed so close that only a paper-thickness of dusk lay between her stomach and his shoulders.

"What is my baby doing?"

Rabbi Binder gaped up at her but he too was mute. All that moved was the dome of his hands; it shook back and forth like a weak pulse.

"Rabbi, get him down! He'll kill himself. Get him down, my only baby . . ."

"I can't," Rabbi Binder said, "I can't . . ." and he turned his handsome head towards the crowd of boys behind him. "It's them. Listen to them."

And for the first time Mrs. Freedman saw the crowd of boys, and she heard what they were yelling.

"He's doing it for them. He won't listen to me. It's them." Rabbi Binder spoke like one in a trance.

"For them?"

"Yes."

"Why for them?"

"They want him to . . ."

Mrs. Freedman raised her two arms upward as though she were conducting the sky. "For them he's doing it!" And then in a gesture older than pyramids, older than prophets and floods, her arms came slapping down to her sides. "A martyr I have. Look!" She tilted her head to the roof. Ozzie was still flapping softly. "My martyr."

"Oscar, come down, *please*," Rabbi Binder groaned.

In a startlingly even voice Mrs. Freedman called to the boy on the roof. "Ozzie, come down, Ozzie. Don't be a martyr, my baby."

As though it were a litany, Rabbi Binder repeated her words. "Don't be a martyr, my baby. Don't be a martyr."

"Gawhead, Ozz—*be* a Martin!" It was Itzie. "Be a Martin, be a Martin," and all the voices joined in singing for Martindom, whatever *it* was. "Be a Martin, be a Martin . . ."

Somehow when you're on a roof the darker it gets the less you can hear. All Ozzie knew was that two groups wanted two new things: his friends were spirited and musical about what they wanted; his mother and the rabbi were even-toned, chanting, about what they didn't want. The rabbi's voice was without tears now and so was his mother's.

The big net stared up at Ozzie like a sightless eye. The big, clouded sky pushed down. From beneath it looked like a gray corrugated board. Suddenly, looking up into that unsympathetic sky, Ozzie realized all the strangeness of what these people, his friends, were asking: they wanted him to jump, to kill himself; they were singing about it now—it made them that happy. And there was an even greater strangeness: Rabbi Binder was on his knees, trembling. If there was a question to be asked now it was not "Is it me?" but rather "Is it us? . . . Is it us?"

Being on the roof, it turned out, was a serious thing. If he jumped would the singing become dancing? Would it? What would jumping stop? Yearningly, Ozzie wished he could rip open the sky, plunge his hands through, and pull out the sun; and on the sun, like a coin, would be stamped JUMP or DON'T JUMP.

Ozzie's knees rocked and sagged a little under him as though they were setting him for a dive. His arms tightened, stiffened, froze, from shoulders to fingernails. He felt as if each part of his body were going to vote as to whether he should kill himself or not—and each part as though it were independent of *him*.

The light took an unexpected click down and the new darkness, like a gag, hushed the friends singing for this and the mother and rabbi chanting for that.

Ozzie stopped counting votes, and in a curiously high voice, like one who wasn't prepared for speech, he spoke.

"Mamma?"

"Yes, Oscar."

"Mamma, get down on your knees, like Rabbi Binder."

"Oscar—"

"Get down on your knees," he said, "or I'll jump."

Ozzie heard a whimper, then a quick rustling, and when he looked down where his mother had stood he saw the top of a head and beneath that a circle of dress. She was kneeling beside Rabbi Binder.

He spoke again. "Everybody kneel." There was the sound of everybody kneeling.

Ozzie looked around. With one hand he pointed towards the synagogue entrance. "Make *him* kneel."

There was a noise, not of kneeling, but of body-and-cloth stretching. Ozzie could hear Rabbi Binder saying in a gruff whisper, ". . . or he'll *kill* himself," and when next he looked there was Yakov Blotnik off the door-knob and for the first time in his life upon his knees in the Gentile posture of prayer.

As for the firemen—it is not as difficult as one might imagine to hold a net taut while you are kneeling.

Ozzie looked around again; and then he called to Rabbi Binder.

"Rabbi?"

"Yes, Oscar."

"Rabbi Binder, do you believe in God?"

"Yes."

"Do you believe God can do Anything?" Ozzie leaned his head out into the darkness. "Anything?"

"Oscar, I think—"

"Tell me you believe God can do Anything."

There was a second's hesitation. Then: "God can do Anything."

"Tell me you believe God can make a child without intercourse."

"He can."

"Tell me!"

"God," Rabbi Binder admitted, "can make a child without intercourse."

"Mamma, you tell me."

"God can make a child without intercourse," his mother said.

"Make *him* tell me." There was no doubt who *him* was.

In a few moments Ozzie heard an old comical voice say something to the increasing darkness about God.

Next, Ozzie made everybody say it. And then he made them all say they believed in Jesus Christ—first one at a time, then all together.

When the catechizing was through it was the beginning of evening. From the street it sounded as if the boy on the roof might have sighed.

"Ozzie?" A woman's voice dared to speak. "You'll come down now?"

There was no answer, but the woman waited, and when a voice finally did speak it was thin and crying, and exhausted as that of an old man who has just finished pulling the bells.

"Mamma, don't you see—you shouldn't hit me. He shouldn't hit me. You shouldn't hit me about God, Mamma. You should never hit anybody about God—"

"Ozzie, please come down now."

"Promise me, promise me you'll never hit anybody about God."

He had asked only his mother, but for some reason everyone kneeling in the street promised he would never hit anybody about God.

Once again there was silence.

"I can come down now, Mamma," the boy on the roof finally said. He turned his head both ways as though checking the traffic lights. "Now I can come down . . ."

And he did, right into the center of the yellow net that glowed in the evening's edge like an overgrown halo.

QUESTIONS

"The Conversion of the Jews"

1. In the opening scene of this story, we are introduced to two young Jewish boys, Ozzie and Itzie. How are they different from each other? What is Ozzie's reaction to Rabbi Binder's assertion, "The only way a woman can have a baby is to have intercourse with a man"? What is Itzie's reaction when he hears about this comment? What do these two responses reveal about the boys?

2. Why isn't Ozzie satisfied with Rabbi Binder's dismissal of Jesus as "historical"? What bothers him about it?

3. What are the questions that have gotten Ozzie into trouble with Rabbi Binder on two previous occasions? How has the rabbi answered these questions? What does Ozzie mean when he says that "what he wanted to know was different"? What does the boy want to know?

4. Why is Ozzie disturbed when his mother calls the plane crash at La Guardia "a tragedy" because eight of the fifty-eight passengers on board had Jewish names? Why does he say that he "wished all fifty-eight were Jews"?

5. Look at the scene in the Freedman home on Friday night, when Ozzie's

mother performs the Sabbath ritual of lighting the candles. What do we learn about the boy in this scene? When the phone rings during the ceremony, why does he snatch up the receiver and hold it "muffled to his chest"?

6. Describe the custodian of the synagogue, Yakov Blotnik. What is his function in the story?

7. Why does Ozzie accuse the rabbi of not knowing anything about God? Is this accusation justified? Why or why not?

8. How good a spiritual guide is the rabbi? Does he display the traits that are associated with the Wise Old Man? Explain.

9. In what way can Ozzie be seen as a true hero, a protagonist who possesses exceptional courage and integrity? What exactly is he on a quest for?

10. How do the various people on the street—Ozzie's schoolmates, his mother, Rabbi Binder, Yakov Blotnik, the firemen—react when the boy threatens to jump from the roof?

11. Why does Ozzie make the assembled people say they believe in Jesus Christ? What is the significance of the story's title? To what does it refer? What kind of conversion takes place in the story? Do these Jewish people become Christians, or is Roth portraying a different sort of conversion, one that transcends particular theologies?

Blacamán the Good,
Vendor of Miracles

GABRIEL GARCÍA MÁRQUEZ

From the first Sunday I saw him he reminded me of a bullring mule, with his white suspenders that were backstitched with gold thread, his rings with colored stones on every finger, and his braids of jingle bells, standing on a table by the docks of Santa María del Darién in the middle of the flasks of specifics and herbs of consolation that he prepared himself and hawked through the towns along the Caribbean with his wounded shout, except that at that time he wasn't trying to sell any of that Indian mess but was asking them to bring him a real snake so that he could demonstrate on his own flesh an antidote he had invented, the only infallible one, ladies and gentlemen, for the bites of serpents, tarantulas, and centipedes plus all manner of poisonous mammals. Someone who seemed quite impressed by his determination managed to get a bushmaster of the worst kind somewhere (the snake that kills by poisoning the respiration) and brought it to him in a bottle, and he uncorked it with such eagerness that we all thought he was going to eat it, but as soon as the creature felt itself free it jumped out of the bottle and struck him on the neck, leaving him right then and there, without any wind for his oratory and with barely enough time to take the antidote, and the vest-pocket pharmacist tumbled down into the crowd and rolled about on the ground, his huge body wasted away as if he had nothing inside of it, but laughing all the while with all of his gold teeth. The hubbub was so great that a cruiser from the north that had been docked there for twenty years on a goodwill mission declared a quarantine so that the snake poison wouldn't get on board, and the people who were sanctifying Palm Sunday came out of church with their blessed palms, because no one wanted to miss the show of the poisoned man, who had already begun to puff up with the air of death and was twice as fat as he'd been before, giving off a froth of gall through his mouth and panting through his pores, but still laughing with so much life that the jingle bells tinkled all over his body. The swelling snapped the laces of his leggings and the seams of his clothes, his fingers grew purple from the pressure of the rings, he

396

turned the color of venison in brine, and from his rear end came a hint of the last moments of death, so that everyone who had seen a person bitten by a snake knew that he was rotting away before dying and that he would be so crumpled up that they'd have to pick him up with a shovel to put him in a sack, but they also thought that even in his sawdust state he'd keep on laughing. It was so incredible that the marines came up on deck to take colored pictures of him with long-distance lenses, but the women who'd come out of church blocked their intentions by covering the dying man with a blanket and laying blessed palms on top of him, some because they didn't want the soldiers to profane the body with their Adventist instruments, others because they were afraid to continue looking at that idolater who was ready to die dying with laughter, and others because in that way perhaps his soul at least would not be poisoned. Everybody had given him up for dead when he pushed aside the palms with one arm, still half-dazed and not completely recovered from the bad moment he'd had, but he set the table up without anyone's help, climbed on it like a crab once more, and there he was again, shouting that his antidote was nothing but the hand of God in a bottle, as we had all seen with our own eyes, but it only cost two cuartillos because he hadn't invented it as an item for sale but for the good of humanity, and as soon as he said that, ladies and gentlemen, I only ask you not to crowd around, there's enough for everybody.

They crowded around, of course, and they did well to do so, because in the end there wasn't enough for everybody. Even the admiral from the cruiser bought a bottle, convinced by him that it was also good for the poisoned bullets of anarchists, and the sailors weren't satisfied with just taking colored pictures of him up on the table, pictures they had been unable to take of him dead, but they had him signing autographs until his arm was twisted with cramps. It was getting to be night and only the most perplexed of us were left by the docks when with his eyes he searched for someone with the look of an idiot to help him put the bottles away, and naturally he spotted me. It was like the look of destiny, not just mine, but his too, for that was more than a century ago and we both remember it as if it had been last Sunday. What happened was that we were putting his circus drugstore into that trunk with purple straps that looked more like a scholar's casket, when he must have noticed some light inside of me that he hadn't seen in me before, because he asked me in a surly way who are you, and I answered that I was an orphan on both sides whose papa hadn't died, and he gave out with laughter that was louder than what he had given with the poison and then he asked me what do you do for a living, and I answered that I didn't do anything except stay alive, because nothing else was worth the trouble, and still weeping with laughter he asked me what science in the world do you most want to learn, and that was the only time I answered the truth without any fooling, I wanted to be a fortune-teller, and then he didn't laugh again but told me as if thinking out loud that I didn't need much for that because I already had the hardest thing to learn, which was my face of an idiot. That same night he spoke to my father and for one real and two cuartillos and a deck of cards that foretold adultery he bought me forevermore.

That was what Blacamán was like, Blacamán the Bad, because I'm Blacamán the Good. He was capable of convincing an astronomer that the month of February was nothing but a herd of invisible elephants, but when his good luck turned on him he became a heart-deep brute. In his days of glory he had been an embalmer of viceroys, and they say that he gave them faces with such authority that for many years they went on governing better than when they were alive, and that no one dared bury them until he gave them back their dead-man look, but his prestige was ruined by the invention of an endless chess game that drove a chaplain mad and brought on two illustrious suicides, and so he was on the decline, from an interpreter of dreams to a birthday hypnotist, from an extractor of molars by suggestion to a marketplace healer; therefore, at the time we met, people were already looking at him askance, even the freebooters. We drifted along with our trick stand and life was an eternal uncertainty as we tried to sell escape suppositories that turned smugglers transparent, furtive drops that baptized wives threw into the soup to install the fear of God in Dutch husbands, and anything you might want to buy of your own free will, ladies and gentlemen, because this isn't a command, it's advice, and, after all, happiness isn't an obligation either. Nevertheless, as much as we died with laughter at his witticisms, the truth is that it was quite hard for us to manage enough to eat, and his last hope was founded on my vocation as a fortune-teller. He shut me up in the sepulchral trunk disguised as a Japanese and bound with starboard chains so that I could attempt to foretell what I could while he disemboweled the grammar book looking for the best way to convince the world of my new science, and here, ladies and gentlemen, you have this child tormented by Ezequiel's glowworms, and those of you who've been standing there with faces of disbelief, let's see if you dare ask him when you're going to die, but I was never able even to guess what day it was at that time, so he gave up on me as a soothsayer because the drowsiness of digestion disturbs your prediction gland, and after whacking me over the head for good luck, he decided to take me to my father and get his money back. But at that time he happened to find a practical application for the electricity of suffering, and he set about building a sewing machine that ran connected by cupping glasses to the part of the body where there was a pain. Since I spent the night moaning over the whacks he'd given me to conjure away misfortune, he had to keep me on as the one who could test his invention, and so our return was delayed and he was getting back his good humor until the machine worked so well that it not only sewed better than a novice nun but also embroidered birds or astromelias according to the position and intensity of the pain. That was what we were up to, convinced of our triumph over bad luck, when the news reached us that in Philadelphia the commander of the cruiser had tried to repeat the experiment with the antidote and that he'd been changed into a glob of admiral jelly in front of his staff.

He didn't laugh again for a long time. We fled through Indian passes and the more lost we became, the clearer the news reached us that the marines had invaded the country under the pretext of exterminating yellow fever and were going about beheading every inveterate or eventual potter they found in their path, and not only the natives, out of precaution, but also the Chinese, for distraction, the Negroes, from habit, and the Hindus, because they were snake charmers, and then they wiped out the flora and fauna and all the mineral wealth they were able to because their specialists in our affairs had taught them that the people along the Caribbean had the ability to change their nature in order to confuse gringos. I couldn't understand where that fury came from or why we were so frightened until we found ourselves safe and sound in the eternal winds of La Guajira, and only then did he have the courage to confess to me that his antidote was nothing but rhubarb and turpentine and that he'd paid a drifter two cuartillos to bring him that bushmaster with all the poison gone. We stayed in the ruins of a colonial mission, deluded by the hope that some smugglers would pass, because they were men to be trusted and the only ones capable of venturing out under the mercurial sun of those salt flats. At first we ate smoked salamanders and flowers from the ruins and we still had enough spirit to laugh when we tried to eat his boiled leggings, but finally we even ate the water cobwebs from the cisterns and only then did we realize how much we missed the world. Since I didn't know of any recourse against death at that time, I simply lay down to wait for it where it would hurt me the least, while he was delirious remembering a woman who was so tender that she could pass through walls just by sighing, but that contrived recollection was also a trick of his genius to fool death with lovesickness. Still, at the moment we should have died, he came to me more alive than ever and spent the whole night watching over my agony, thinking with such great strength that I still haven't been able to tell whether what was whistling through the ruins was the wind or his thoughts, and before dawn he told me with the same voice and the same determination of past times that now he knew the truth, that I was the one who had twisted up his luck again, so get your pants ready, because the same way as you twisted it up for me, you're going to straighten it out.

That was when I lost the little affection I had for him. He took off the last rags I had on, rolled me up in some barbed wire, rubbed rock salt on the sores, put me in brine from my own waters, and hung me by the ankles for the sun to flay me, and he kept on shouting that all that mortification wasn't enough to pacify his persecutors. Finally he threw me to rot in my own misery inside the penance dungeon where the colonial missionaries regenerated heretics, and with the perfidy of a ventriloquist, which he still had more than enough of, he began to imitate the voices of edible animals, the noise of ripe beets, and the sound of fresh springs so as to torture me with the illusion that I was dying of indigence in the midst of paradise. When the smugglers finally supplied him, he came down to the dungeon to give me something to eat so I wouldn't die, but then he made me pay for that charity by pulling out my nails with pliers and filing my teeth down with a grindstone, and my only consolation was the wish that life would give me time and the good fortune to be quit of so much infamy with even worse martyrdoms. I myself was surprised that I could resist the plague of my own putrefaction and he kept throwing the leftovers of his meals onto me and tossed pieces of rotten lizards and hawks into the corners so that the air of the dungeon would end up poisoning me. I don't know how much time had passed when he brought me the carcass of a rabbit in order to show me that he preferred throwing it away to rot rather than giving it to me to eat, but my patience only went so far and all I had left was rancor, so I grabbed the rabbit by the ears and flung it against the wall with the illusion that it was he and not the animal that was going to explode, and then it happened, as if in a dream. The rabbit not only revived with a squeal of fright, but it came back to my hands, hopping through the air.

That was how my great life began. Since then I've gone through the world drawing the fever out of malaria victims for two pesos, visioning blind men for four-fifty, draining the water from dropsy victims for eighteen, putting cripples back together for twenty pesos if they were that way from birth, for twenty-two if they were that way because of an accident or a brawl, for twenty-five if they were that way because of wars, earthquakes, infantry landings, or any other kind of public calamity, taking care of the common sick at wholesale according to a special arrangement, madmen according to their theme, children at half price, and idiots out of gratitude, and who dares say that I'm not a philanthropist, ladies and gentlemen, and now, yes, sir, commandant of the twentieth fleet, order your boys to take down the barricades and let suffering humanity pass, lepers to the left, epileptics to the right, cripples where they won't get in the way, and there in the back the least urgent cases, only please don't crowd in on me because then I won't be responsible if the sicknesses get all mixed up and people are cured of what they don't have, and keep the music playing until the brass boils, and the rockets firing until the angels burn, and the liquor flowing until ideas are killed, and bring on the wenches and the acrobats, the butchers and the photographers, and all at my expense, ladies and gentlemen, for here ends the evil fame of the Blacamáns and the universal tumult starts. That's how I go along putting them to sleep with the techniques of a congressman in case my judgment fails and some turn out worse than they were before on me. The only thing I don't do is revive the dead, because as soon as they open their eyes they're murderous with rage at the one who disturbed their state, and when it's all done, those who don't commit suicide die again of disillusionment. At first I was pursued by a group of wise men investigating the legality of my industry, and when they were convinced, they threatened me with the hell of Simon Magus and recommended a life of penitence so that I could get to be a saint, but I answered them, with no disrespect for their authority, that it was precisely along those lines that I had started. The truth is that I'd gain nothing by being a saint after being dead, an artist is what I am, and the only thing I want is to be alive so I can keep going along at donkey level in this six-cylinder touring car I bought from the marines' consul, with this Trinida-dian chauffeur who was a baritone in the New Orleans pirates' opera, with my genuine silk shirts, my Oriental lotions, my topaz teeth, my flat straw hat, and my bicolored buttons, sleeping without an alarm clock, dancing with beauty queens, and leaving them hallucinated with my dictionary rhetoric, and with no flutter in my spleen if some Ash Wednesday my faculties wither away, because in order to go on with this life of a minister, all I need is my idiot face, and I have more than enough with the string of shops I own from here beyond the sunset, where the same tourists who used to go around collecting from us through the admiral, now go stumbling after my autographed pictures, almanacs with my love poetry, medals with my profile, bits of my clothing, and all of that without the glorious plague of spending all day and all night sculpted in equestrian marble and shat on by swallows like the fathers of our country.

It's a pity that Blacamán the Bad can't repeat this story so that people will see that there's nothing invented in it. The last time anyone saw him in this world he'd lost even the studs of his former splendor, and his soul was a shambles and his bones in disorder from the rigors of the desert, but he still had enough jingle bells left to reappear that Sunday on the docks of Santa María del Darién with his eternal sepulchral trunk, except that this time he wasn't trying to sell antidotes, but was asking in a voice crack-ing with emotion for the marines to shoot him in a public spectacle so that he could demonstrate on his own flesh the life-restoring properties of this supernatural creature, ladies and gentlemen, and even though you have more than enough right not to believe me after suffering so long from my evil tricks as a deceiver and a falsifier, I swear on the bones of my mother that this proof today is nothing from the other world, merely the humble truth, and in case you have any doubts left, notice that I'm not laughing now the way I used to, but holding back a desire to cry. How convincing he must have been, unbuttoning his shirt, his eyes drowning with tears, and giving himself mule kicks on his heart to indicate the best place for death, and yet the marines didn't dare shoot, out of fear that the Sunday crowd would discover their loss of prestige. Someone who may not have forgotten the blacamanipulations of past times managed, no one knew how, to get and bring him in a can enough *barbasco* roots to bring to the surface all the corvinas in the Caribbean, and he opened it with great desire, as if he were really going to eat them, and, indeed, he did eat them, ladies and gentlemen, but please don't be moved or pray for the repose of my soul, because this death is nothing but a visit. That time he was so honest that he didn't break into operatic death rattles, but got off the table like a crab, looked on the ground for the most worthy place to lie down after some hesitation, and from there he looked at me as he would have at a mother and exhaled his last breath in his own arms, still holding back his manly tears all twisted up by the tetanus of eternity. That was the only time, of course, that my science failed me. I put him in that trunk of premonitory size where there was no room for him laid out. I had a requiem mass sung for him which cost me fifty-four peso doubloons, because the officiant was dressed in gold and there were also three seated bishops. I had the mausoleum of an emperor built for him on a hill exposed to the best seaside weather, with a chapel just for him and an iron plaque on which there was written in Gothic capitals HERE LIES BLACÁMAN THE DEAD, BADLY CALLED THE BAD, DECEIVER OF MARINES AND VICTIM OF SCIENCE, and when those honors were sufficient for me to do justice to his virtues, I began to get my revenge for his infamy, and then I revived him inside the armored tomb and left him there rolling about in horror. That was long before the fire ants devoured Santa María del Darién, but the mausoleum is still intact on the hill in the shadow of the dragons that climb up to sleep in the Atlantic winds, and every time I pass through here I bring him an automobile load of roses and my heart pains with pity for his virtues, but then I put my ear to the plaque to hear him weeping in the ruins of the crumbling trunk, and if by some chance he has died again, I bring him back to life once more, for the beauty of the punishment is that he will keep on living in his tomb as long as I'm alive, that is, forever.

QUESTIONS

"Blacamán the Good, Vendor of Miracles"

1. Though the setting of this story is Caribbean South America, it is obviously not what we would encounter in a travel brochure or documentary film. Describe the world García Márquez conjures up in this story. Why does he portray it this way? What sense of that place do you get from the story?

2. What kind of man is Blacamán the Bad? What are his talents? His faults? What kind of career has he had? Why is he known as "the Bad"?

3. The narration frequently sounds like the patter of a con man or carnival huckster. Point to some examples. Why does the author use this kind of language?

4. Discuss the use of fantasy and magic in this story. How do you account for the incredible things that happen?

5. Why does Blacamán the Bad buy the narrator from the boy's father? What does he see in the boy? What use does he make of his apprentice?

6. In what ways does Blacamán the Bad fulfill the role of the Wise Old Man,

who teaches a young hero about the uses of power or initiates him into some mystery? In what ways does he not conform to that role?

7. A turning point in the story and in the life of the narrator occurs when the boy is imprisoned in a dungeon and tortured by his master. This episode takes the form of an initiation rite: the speaker descends into a dark, tomblike place, undergoes a ritual death, and emerges a new man. How is the narrator changed by the experience?

8. Describe the "great life" the narrator leads after discovering his magical attributes. Why does he have no interest in becoming a saint? How does he dress and entertain himself? Does he match your idea of a true healer and miracle worker?

9. How does Blacamán the Good punish his mentor at the end of the story? Why?

CHAPTER FIVE

The Treasure

The hero's quest, as a persistent narrative pattern underlying literature and mythology, reveals two striking and apparently contradictory features of the human imagination. On the one hand is its *fixedness*, its apparently insatiable appetite for the same essential tale; on the other is its infinite *flexibility*, its power to invent endless variations on a single theme. Throughout history, the story of the quest has provided artists with a vehicle for their original insights and visions. Like the other elements of this pattern we have looked at so far, the ultimate goal of the journey takes innumerable forms. Every version of the quest in myth, fairy tale, and fantasy is built around a particular "boon," often a fabulous treasure: the Golden Fleece, the Holy Grail, the Water of Life, the Plant of Immortality, the Lost Ark of the Covenant, and countless others. In the kind of fiction in this anthology, the prizes that await the hero at the end of the journey are generally less spectacular but no less various. On the surface at least, the protagonists of all fifty stories seem to be searching for different things.

Sometimes, the goal of the quest is a literal treasure: a precious object, hoard of jewels, or hidden fortune. This is the case in Isak Dinesen's "The Blue Jar," in which the protagonist spends a lifetime searching for an ancient china jar of "a particular blue color," and in Ursula K. Le Guin's "Semley's Necklace," in which the title character goes in quest of her priceless birthright, the legendary jewel known as "the Eye of the Sea." In other stories, the prize the hero seeks, though still a tangible object, is comparatively paltry or even worthless (at least in the eyes of the rest of the world). For example, the young narrator of James Joyce's "Araby" makes a futile journey to a tawdry bazaar to buy a trinket for a neighbor girl he adores.

The object of the quest may also be a person, as in Carson Mc-

Culler's "A Tree—A Rock—A Cloud," whose central character is searching for his runaway wife. Ultimately, however, the old man's quest leads him to a momentous discovery: the secret of the "science" of love. This story illustrates an important point, namely, that the treasure is not always a material object. Often, it is something intangible: the acquisition of knowledge, power, spiritual enlightenment, or inner peace. The hero of Ralph Ellison's "Flying Home," for instance, has achieved his life-long goal of becoming a pilot; his larger and still unsatisfied dream, however, is to prove himself in a white man's world, to rise above the demeaning role imposed on him by a bigoted society. And though the protagonist of Hortense Calisher's "The Middle Drawer" possesses the key to a kind of treasure chest—a drawer full of family mementoes—the real treasure is the self-awareness she achieves and her acceptance of her dead mother's shortcomings.

In spite of all the different forms they take, however, the treasures that lie at the end of the quest always share certain characteristics. First, as we have already seen, they are not easily obtained; reaching them requires immense effort of the heroes. Therefore, the goal of the mythological quest is often referred to as "the treasure hard to attain." Indeed, as the stories in this collection show, the main characters commonly fail in their attempts to reach their goals. Charlie Wales, for example, the protagonist of F. Scott Fitzgerald's "Babylon Revisited," in Chapter Three, is defeated in his struggle to regain custody of his daughter by various antagonistic forces, including certain self-destructive tendencies within himself. The title character of Willa Cather's "Paul's Case" (Chapter One) actually manages to reach the destination of his dreams; before very long, however, he is driven back into a reality he no longer finds bearable. In this chapter, the protagonist of James Joyce's "Araby" comes away from his quest empty-handed. At the end of the story, the young hero is left with nothing but the bitter realization of his own delusions. And Todd, the determined flyer of Ralph Ellison's story, suffers a humiliating setback in his quest to prove his manhood—though, in this case, the failure of the quest leads to an unforeseen benefit: the end of Todd's bitter sense of isolation as he comes to feel a growing connection to the black man and boy who come to his aid.

Even when a particular goal has little or no apparent worth, its importance to the quester is incalculable. That the heroes of these stories are willing to risk humiliation, defeat, and possibly death in order to achieve whatever end they are striving for is a sign of its ultimate value. The trifling sum of thirty-five dollars is as precious to Mendel, the dying hero of Malamud's "Idiots First" (Chapter Three), as any hoard of gold. Similarly, the necklace Le Guin's Lady Semley seeks is important to her primarily because of the glory it will restore to her noble but indigent husband. In short, whether the treasure is worth a pittance or "all the money from a whole kingdom," its real value derives from its significance to the hero, from what it represents to him or her.

What exactly does the treasure represent? In story after story, the heroes are willing to undergo every variety of hardship and peril for one fundamental reason: they believe that the things they are looking for will change their lives. For some, the treasure means improvement in their material and economic circumstances. Hawthorne's naïve young hero, Robin, in "My Kinsman, Major Molineux," in Chapter Three, leaves the security of his home in the country and journeys through the city of night because of his uncle's offer to help the boy "rise in the world." As the result of discovering his magical powers, Blacamán the Good, the title character of Gabriel García Márquez's story (Chapter Four) is transformed overnight from a battered, bedraggled servant into a far-famed celebrity, with a six-cylinder touring car, topaz teeth, bicolored buttons, and an endless supply of beauty queens.

For other characters, such as the narrator of James Alan McPherson's "The Story of a Dead Man" and the hero of Ellison's "Flying Home," the treasure represents a change in their position in society. Still others attempt to alter society itself. The hero of Max Apple's "The Oranging of America" is on a life-long quest to re-create the very face of America, by dotting the countryside with the orange-roofed Howard Johnson's rest stops. Finally, some characters try to transform, not the outer world, but their own inner ones—to break free of the fears, weaknesses, and delusions that have trapped them in deeply unhappy lives.

In virtually every instance the treasure stands for the promise of a fresh start. That promise is not always fulfilled. In many stories, the treasure is never found or, as in Willa Cather's "Paul's Case," is possessed only long enough to confirm the protagonist's sense of how sterile his life has become. It is also possible for the treasure to result in changes that are very different from the ones the hero expects. Le Guin's Lady Semley, for example, manages to recover her legendary necklace, but only at a terribly high, wholly unanticipated, personal cost.

Still, to the true hero, the quest for the treasure remains an irresistible challenge. The hero understands that the difficulties involved in attaining the desired object reflect the difficulties of making any significant changes in the world or in one's self. Most people would rather cling to the familiar than face the new, even when the familiar has grown painfully unfulfilling. The desire and the ability to make those changes distinguish the hero from the rest of humankind.

Araby

JAMES JOYCE

North Richmond Street, being blind, was a quiet street except at the hour when the Christian Brothers' School set the boys free. An uninhabited house of two storeys stood at the blind end, detached from its neighbours in a square ground. The other houses of the street, conscious of decent lives within them, gazed at one another with brown imperturbable faces.

The former tenant of our house, a priest, had died in the back drawing room. Air, musty from having long been enclosed, hung in all the rooms, and the waste room behind the kitchen was littered with old useless papers. Among these I found a few paper-covered books, the pages of which were curled and damp: *The Abbot*, by Walter Scott, *The Devout Communicant* and *The Memoirs of Vidocq*. I liked the last best because its leaves were yellow. The wild garden behind the house contained a central apple-tree and a few straggling bushes under one of which I found the late tenant's rusty bicycle-pump. He had been a very charitable priest; in his will he had left all his money to institutions and the furniture of his house to his sister.

When the short days of winter came dusk fell before we had well eaten our dinners. When we met in the street the houses had grown sombre. The space of sky above us was the colour of ever-changing violet and towards it the lamps of the street lifted their feeble lanterns. The cold air stung us and we played till our bodies glowed. Our shouts echoed in the silent street. The career of our play brought us through the dark muddy lanes behind the houses where we ran the gantlet of the rough tribes from the cottages, to the back doors of the dark dripping gardens where odours arose from the ashpits, to the dark odorous stables where a coachman smoothed and combed the horse or shook music from the buckled harness. When we returned to the street light from the kitchen windows had filled the areas. If my uncle was seen turning the corner we hid in the shadow until we had seen him safely housed. Or if Mangan's sister came out on the doorstep to call her brother in to his tea we watched her from our shadow peer up and down the street. We waited to see whether she would remain or go in and, if she remained, we left our shadow and walked up to Mangan's steps resignedly. She was waiting for us, her figure defined by the light from the

half-opened door. Her brother always teased her before he obeyed and I
stood by the railings looking at her. Her dress swung as she moved her
body and the soft rope of her hair tossed from side to side.

Every morning I lay on the floor in the front parlor watching her door.
The blind was pulled down within an inch of the sash so that I could not
be seen. When she came out on the doorstep my heart leaped. I ran to
the hall, seized my books and followed her. I kept her brown figure always
in my eye and, when we came near the point at which our ways diverged,
I quickened my pace and passed her. This happened morning after morning. I had never spoken to her, except for a few casual words, and yet her
name was like a summons to all my foolish blood.

Her image accompanied me even in places the most hostile to romance.
On Saturday evenings when my aunt went marketing I had to go to carry
some of the parcels. We walked through the flaring streets, jostled by
drunken men and bargaining women, amid the curses of labourers, the
shrill litanies of shop-boys who stood on guard by the barrels of pigs' cheeks,
the nasal chanting of street singers, who sang a *come-all-you* about O'Don-
ovan Rossa, or a ballad about the troubles in our native land. These noises
converged in a single sensation of life for me: I imagined that I bore my
chalice safely through the throng of foes. Her name sprang to my lips at
moments in strange prayers and praises which I myself did not understand.
My eyes were often full of tears (I could not tell why) and at times a flood
from my heart seemed to pour itself out into my bosom. I thought little of
the future. I did not know whether I would ever speak to her or not or, if
I spoke to her, how I could tell her of my confused adoration. But my body
was like a harp and her words and gestures were like fingers running upon
the wires.

One evening I went into the back drawing-room in which the priest had
died. It was a dark rainy evening and there was no sound in the house.
Through one of the broken panes I heard the rain impinge upon the earth,
the fine incessant needles of water playing in the sodden beds. Some distant lamp or lighted window gleamed below me. I was thankful that I could
see so little. All my senses seemed to desire to veil themselves and, feeling
that I was about to slip from them, I pressed the palms of my hands together until they trembled, murmuring: *O love! O love!* many times.

At last she spoke to me. When she addressed the first words to me I was
so confused that I did not know what to answer. She asked me was I going
to *Araby*. I forget whether I answered yes or no. It would be a splendid
bazaar, she said; she would love to go.

—And why can't you? I asked.

While she spoke she turned a silver bracelet round and round her wrist.
She could not go, she said, because there would be a retreat that week in
her convent. Her brother and two other boys were fighting for their caps
and I was alone at the railings. She held one of the spikes, bowing her
head towards me. The light from the lamp opposite our door caught the
white curve of her neck, lit up her hair that rested there and, falling, lit

up the hand upon the railing. It fell over one side of her dress and caught the white border of a petticoat, just visible as she stood at ease.

—It's well for you, she said.

—If I go, I said, I will bring you something.

What innumerable follies laid waste my waking and sleeping thoughts after that evening! I wished to annihilate the tedious intervening days. I chafed against the work of school. At night in my bedroom and by day in the classroom her image came between me and the page I strove to read. The syllables of the word *Araby* were called to me through the silence in which my soul luxuriated and cast an Eastern enchantment over me. I asked for leave to go to the bazaar on Saturday night. My aunt was surprised and hoped it was not some Freemason affair. I answered few questions in class. I watched my master's face pass from amiability to sternness; he hoped I was not beginning to idle. I could not call my wandering thoughts together. I had hardly any patience with the serious work of life which, now that it stood between me and my desire, seemed to me child's play, ugly monotonous child's play.

On Saturday morning I reminded my uncle that I wished to go to the bazaar in the evening. He was fussing at the hall-stand, looking for the hatbrush, and answered me curtly:

—Yes, boy, I know.

As he was in the hall I could not go into the front parlour and lie at the window. I left the house in bad humour and walked slowly towards the school. The air was pitilessly raw and already my heart misgave me.

When I came home to dinner my uncle had not yet been home. Still it was early. I sat staring at the clock for some time and, when its ticking began to irritate me, I left the room. I mounted the staircase and gained the upper part of the house. The high cold empty gloomy rooms liberated me and I went from room to room singing. From the front window I saw my companions playing below in the street. Their cries reached me weakened and indistinct and, leaning my forehead against the cool glass, I looked over at the dark house where she lived. I may have stood there for an hour, seeing nothing but the brown-clad figure cast by my imagination, touched discreetly by the lamplight at the curved neck, at the hand upon the railing and at the border below the dress.

When I came downstairs again I found Mrs. Mercer sitting at the fire. She was an old garrulous woman, a pawnbroker's widow, who collected used stamps for some pious purpose. I had to endure the gossip of the tea-table. The meal was prolonged beyond an hour and still my uncle did not come. Mrs. Mercer stood up to go: she was sorry she couldn't wait any longer, but it was after eight o'clock and she did not like to be out late, as the night air was bad for her. When she had gone I began to walk up and down the room, clenching my fists. My aunt said:

—I'm afraid you may put off your bazaar for this night of Our Lord.

At nine o'clock I heard my uncle's latchkey in the halldoor. I heard him talking to himself and heard the hallstand rocking when it had received the weight of his overcoat. I could interpret these signs. When he was midway through his dinner I asked him to give me the money to go to the bazaar. He had forgotten.

—The people are in bed and after their first sleep now, he said.

I did not smile. My aunt said to him energetically:

—Can't you give him the money and let him go? You've kept him late enough as it is.

My uncle said he was very sorry he had forgotten. He said he believed in the old saying: *All work and no play makes Jack a dull boy.* He asked me where I was going and, when I had told him a second time he asked me did I know *The Arab's Farewell to his Steed.* When I left the kitchen he was about to recite the opening lines of the piece to my aunt.

I held a florin tightly in my hand as I strode down Buckingham Street towards the station. The sight of the streets thronged with buyers and glaring with gas recalled to me the purpose of my journey. I took my seat in a third-class carriage of a deserted train. After an intolerable delay the train moved out of the station slowly. It crept onward among ruinous houses and over the twinkling river. At Westland Row Station a crowd of people pressed to the carriage doors; but the porters moved them back, saying that it was a special train for the bazaar. I remained alone in the bare carriage. In a few minutes the train drew up beside an improvised wooden platform. I passed out on to the road and saw by the lighted dial of a clock that it was ten minutes to ten. In front of me was a large building which displayed the magical name.

I could not find any sixpenny entrance and, fearing that the bazaar would be closed, I passed in quickly through a turnstile, handing a shilling to a weary-looking man. I found myself in a big hall girdled at half its height by a gallery. Nearly all the stalls were closed and the greater part of the hall was in darkness. I recognized a silence like that which pervades a church after a service. I walked into the centre of the bazaar timidly. A few people were gathered about the stalls which were still open. Before a curtain, over which the words *Café Chantant* were written in coloured lamps, two men were counting money on a salver. I listened to the fall of the coins.

Remembering with difficulty why I had come I went over to one of the stalls and examined porcelain vases and flowered tea-sets. At the door of the stall a young lady was talking and laughing with two young gentlemen. I remarked their English accents and listened vaguely to their conversation.

—O, I never said such a thing!

—O, but you did!

—O, but I didn't!

—Didn't she say that?

—Yes I heard her

—O, there's a . . . fib!

Observing me the young lady came over and asked me did I wish to buy anything. The tone in her voice was not encouraging; she seemed to have spoken to me out of a sense of duty. I looked humbly at the great jars that stood like eastern guards at either side of the dark entrance to the stall and murmured:

—No, thank you.

The young lady changed the position of one of the vases and went back to the two young men. They began to talk of the same subject. Once or twice the young lady glanced at me over her shoulder.

I lingered before her stall, though I knew my stay was useless, to make my interest in her wares seem the more real. Then I turned away slowly and walked down the middle of the bazaar. I allowed the two pennies to fall against the sixpence in my pocket. I heard a voice call from one end of the gallery that the light was out. The upper part of the hall was now completely dark.

Gazing up into the darkness I saw myself as a creature driven and derided by vanity; and my eyes burned with anguish and anger.

QUESTIONS

"*Araby*"

1. Joyce's opening paragraphs establish the Dublin setting of "Araby." What atmosphere do Joyce's details convey? Why would he twice repeat the word "blind" in the first two sentences? What glimpse of nature do we get in these paragraphs? How can the physical environment of the story and the people who inhabit it be said to be "hostile to romance"? How significant is this last characteristic of his neighborhood to Joyce's protagonist?

2. Who is the narrator? Approximately how old is he when he lives through the events described in "Araby"? Is it possible to tell what the mature narrator's attitude is toward his younger, remembered self? Explain.

3. We see Mangan's sister only a few times in this story: each time she is placed so that she is illuminated by lamplight. Why does Joyce present her in this fashion?

4. Note that there are certain words the narrator uses to express his feelings and perceptions and certain gestures he makes that are associated with the Christian religion. What are these words and gestures? What do they tell you about the protagonists? What do they suggest about his attachment to Mangan's sister?

5. Joyce mentions three books, the abandoned property of the dead priest: Sir Walter Scott's *The Abbot*, a chivalric romance; *The Devout Communicant*, an Easter week devotional book; and *The Memoirs of Vidocq*, the autobiogra-

phy of a notorious reprobate. The boy, we are told, likes the last best "because
its leaves were yellow." Do you find his reason convincing? Why would Joyce
mention these books? What connection have they with his story's theme?

6. What effect does the mere word "Araby" have on the boy? What other
word affects him the same way? Why can't Mangan's sister go to the bazaar?
What difficulties must the narrator overcome to make his quest to Araby? Describe the bazaar in detail. Does it match the boy's expectations? Discuss the
significance of the banal conversation the boy overhears at the bazaar.

7. What role does the boy's uncle play in the story? The poem he refers
to, "The Arab's Farewell to his Steed," was a nineteenth-century work (about
a man who, forced to sell his beloved horse for money, later regrets his act and
flees with the creature) notable only for it sentimentality. What relevance has
this poem to Joyce's story?

8. We are told that the boy's feelings for Mangan's sister and his anticipation of going to Araby make him impatient "with the serious work of life."
What in life is "serious" to the boy throughout most of the story? Can you tell
what is "serious" to the mature narrator?

9. For what is Joyce's protagonist questing? Does he gain the treasure?
What meaning does it have for him? Look at the last line of the story. Why
does the boy feel that he is "a creature driven and derided by vanity"? What
role does Araby itself play in this realization? What role do deeply established
environmental influences play?

10. Is the boy freed of romantic illusion at the end of the story? If so, at
what price?

11. Compare and contrast Joyce's "Araby" with Willa Cather's story "Paul's
Case" (Chapter One) in terms of protagonists and the quests these protagonists
make.

Semley's Necklace

URSULA K. LE GUIN

How can you tell the legend from the fact on these worlds that lie so many years away?—planets without names, called by their people simply The World, planets without history, where the past is the matter of myth, and a returning explorer finds his own doings of a few years back have become the gestures of a god. Unreason darkens that gap of time bridged by our lightspeed ships, and in the darkness uncertainty and disproportion grow like weeds.

In trying to tell the story of a man, an ordinary League scientist, who went to such a nameless half-known world not many years ago, one feels like an archaeologist amid millennial ruins, now struggling through choked tangles of leaf, flower, branch and vine to the sudden bright geometry of a wheel or a polished cornerstone, and now entering some commonplace, sunlit doorway to find inside it the darkness, the impossible flicker of a flame, the glitter of a jewel, the half-glimpsed movement of a woman's arm.

How can you tell fact from legend, truth from truth?

Through Rocannon's story the jewel, the blue glitter seen briefly returns. With it let us begin, here:

Galactic Area 8, No. 62: FOMALHAUT II.
High-Intelligence Life Forms: Species Contacted:

Species I.

A. Gdemiar (singular Gdem): Highly intelligent, fully hominoid nocturnal troglodytes, 120–135 cm. in height, light skin, dark head-hair. When contacted these cave-dwellers possessed a rigidly stratified oligarchic urban society modified by partial colonial telepathy, and a technologically oriented Early Steel culture. Technology enhanced to Industrial, Point C, during League Mission of 252–254. In 254 an Automatic Drive ship (to-from New South Georgia) was presented to oligarchs of the Kiriensea Area community. Status C-Prime.

B. Fiia (singular Fian): Highly intelligent, fully hominoid, diurnal, av. ca. 130 cm. in height, observed individuals generally light in skin and hair. Brief

contacts indicated village and nomadic communal societies, partial colonial telepathy, also some indication of short-range TK. The race appears a-technological and evasive, with minimal and fluid culture-patterns. Currently untaxable. Status E-Query.

Species II.

Liuar (singular Liu): Highly intelligent, fully hominoid, diurnal, av. height above 170 cm., this species possesses a fortress/village, clan-descent society, a blocked technology (Bronze), and feudal-heroic culture. Note horizontal social cleavage into 2 pseudoraces: (a) Olgyior, "midmen," light-skinned and dark-haired; (b) Angyar, "lords," very tall, dark-skinned, yellow-haired—

"That's her," said Rocannon, looking up from the *Abridged Handy Pocket Guide to Intelligent Life-forms* at the very tall, dark-skinned, yellow-haired woman who stood halfway down the long museum hall. She stood still and erect, crowned with bright hair, gazing at something in a display case. Around her fidgeted four uneasy and unattractive dwarves.

"I didn't know Fomalhaut II had all those people besides the trogs," said Ketho, the curator.

"I didn't either. There are even some 'Unconfirmed' species listed here, that they never contacted. Sounds like time for a more thorough survey mission to the place. Well, now at least we know what she is."

"I wish there were some way of knowing *who* she is. . . ."

She was of an ancient family, a descendant of the first kings of the Angyar, and for all her poverty her hair shone with the pure, steadfast gold of her inheritance. The little people, the Fiia, bowed when she passed them, even when she was a barefoot child running in the fields, the light and fiery comet of her hair brightening the troubled winds of Kirien.

She was still very young when Durhal of Hallan saw her, courted her, and carried her away from the ruined towers and windy halls of her childhood to his own high home. In Hallan on the mountainside there was no comfort either, though splendor endured. The windows were unglassed, the stone floors bare; in coldyear one might wake to see the night's snow in long, low drifts beneath each window. Durhal's bride stood with narrow bare feet on the snowy floor, braiding up the fire of her hair and laughing at her young husband in the silver mirror that hung in their room. That mirror, and his mother's bridal-gown sewn with a thousand tiny crystals, were all his wealth. Some of his lesser kinfolk of Hallan still possessed wardrobes of brocaded clothing, furniture of gilded wood, silver harness for their steeds, armor and silver mounted swords, jewels and jewelry—and on these last Durhal's bride looked enviously, glancing back at a gemmed coronet or a golden brooch even when the wearer of the ornament stood aside to let her pass, deferent to her birth and marriage-rank.

Fourth from the High Seat of Hallan Revel sat Durhal and his bride Semley, so close to Hallanlord that the old man often poured wine for Semley with his own hand, and spoke of hunting with his nephew and heir

Durhal, looking on the young pair with a grim, unhopeful love. Hope came hard to the Angyar of Hallan and all the Western lands, since the Starlords had appeared with their houses that leaped about on pillars of fire and their awful weapons that could level hills. They had interfered with all the old ways and wars, and though the sums were small there was terrible shame to the Angyar in having to pay a tax to them, a tribute for the Starlords' war that was to be fought with some strange enemy, somewhere in the hollow places between the stars, at the end of years. "It will be your war too," they said, but for a generation now the Angyar had sat in idle shame in their revel-halls, watching their double swords rust, their sons grow up without ever striking a blow in battle, their daughters marry poor men, even midmen, having no dowry of heroic loot to bring a noble husband. Hallanlord's face was bleak when he watched the fair-haired couple and heard their laughter as they drank bitter wine and joked together in the cold, ruinous, resplendent fortress of their race.

Semley's own face hardened when she looked down the hall and saw, in seats far below hers, even down among the halfbreeds and the midmen, against white skins and black hair, the gleam and flash of precious stones. She herself had brought nothing in dowry to her husband, not even a silver hairpin. The dress of a thousand crystals she had put away in a chest for the wedding-day of her daughter, if daughter it was to be.

It was, and they called her Haldre, and when the fuzz on her little brown skull grew longer it shone with steadfast gold, the inheritance of the lordly generations, the only gold she would ever possess. . . .

Semley did not speak to her husband of her discontent. For all his gentleness to her, Durhal in his pride had only contempt for envy, for vain wishing, and she dreaded his contempt. But she spoke to Durhal's sister Durossa.

"My family had a great treasure once," she said. "It was a necklace all of gold, with the blue jewel set in the center—sapphire?"

Durossa shook her head, smiling, not sure of the name either. It was late in warmyear, as these Northern Angyar called the summer of the eight-hundred-day year, beginning the cycle of months anew at each equinox; to Semley it seemed an outlandish calendar, a midmannish reckoning. Her family was at an end, but it had been older and purer than the race of any of these northwestern marchlanders, who mixed too freely with the Ol-gyior. She sat with Durossa in the sunlight on a stone windowseat high up in the Great Tower, where the older woman's apartment was. Widowed young, childless, Durossa had been given in second marriage to Hallan-lord, who was her father's brother. Since it was a kinmarriage and a second marriage on both sides she had not taken the title of Hallanlady, which Semley would some day bear; but she sat with the old lord in the High Seat and ruled with him his domains. Older than her brother Durhal, she was fond of his young wife, and delighted in the bright-haired baby Haldre.

"It was bought," Semley went on, "with all the money my forebear Ley-nen got when he conquered the Southern Fiefs—all the money from a

whole kingdom, think of it, for one jewel! Oh, it would outshine anything
here in Hallan, surely, even those crystals like koob-eggs your cousin Issar
wears. It was so beautiful they gave it a name of its own; they called it the
Eye of the Sea. My great-grandmother wore it."

"You never saw it?" the older woman asked lazily, gazing down at the
green mountainslopes where long, long summer sent its hot and restless
winds straying among the forests and whirling down white roads to the
seacoast far away.

"It was lost before I was born."

"To the Starlords?"

"No, my father said it was stolen before the Starlords ever came to our
realm. He wouldn't talk of it, but there was an old mid-woman full of tales
who always told me the Fiia would know where it was."

"Ah, the Fiia I should like to see!" said Durossa. "They're in so many
songs and tales; why do they never come to the Western Lands?"

"Too high, too cold in winter, I think. They like the sunlight of the
valleys of the south."

"Are they like the Clayfolk?"

"Those I've never seen; they keep away from us in the south. Aren't
they white like midmen, and misformed? The Fiia are fair; they look like
children, only thinner, and wiser. Oh, I wonder if they know where the
necklace is, who stole it and where he hid it! Think, Durossa—if I could
come into Hallan Revel and sit down by my husband with the wealth of a
kingdom round my neck, and outshine the other women as he outshines
all men!"

Durossa bent her head above the baby, who sat studying her own brown
toes on a fur rug between her mother and aunt. "Semley is foolish," she
murmured to the baby; "Semley who shines like a falling star, Semley whose
husband loves no gold but the gold of her hair . . ."

And Semley, looking out over the green slopes of summer toward the
distant sea, was silent.

But when another coldyear had passed, and the Starlords had come again
to collect their taxes for the war against the world's end—this time using a
couple of dwarfish Clayfolk as interpreters, and so leaving all the Angyar
humiliated to the point of rebellion—and another warmyear too was gone,
and Haldre had grown into a lovely, chattering child, Semley brought her
one morning to Durossa's sunlit room in the tower. Semley wore an old
cloak of blue, and the hood covered her hair.

"Keep Haldre for me these few days, Durossa," she said, quick and calm.
"I'm going south to Kirien."

"To see your father?"

"To find my inheritance. Your cousins of Hagret Fief have been taunting
Durhal. Even that halfbreed Parna can torment him, because Parna's wife
has a satin coverlet for her bed, and a diamond earring, and three gowns,
the dough-faced black-haired trollop! while Durhal's wife must patch her
gown—"

"Is Durhal's pride in his wife, or what she wears?"

But Semley was not to be moved. "The Lords of Hallan are becoming poor men in their own hall. I am going to bring my dowry to my lord, as one of my lineage should."

"Semley! Does Durhal know you're going?"

"My return will be a happy one—that much let him know," said young Semley, breaking for a moment into her joyful laugh; then she bent to kiss her daughter, turned, and before Durossa could speak, was gone like a quick wind over the floors of sunlit stone.

Married women of the Angyar never rode for sport, and Semley had not been from Hallan since her marriage; so now, mounting the high saddle of a windsteed, she felt like a girl again, like the wild maiden she had been, riding half-broken steeds on the north wind over the fields of Kirien. The beast that bore her now down from the hills of Hallan was of finer breed, striped coat fitting sleek over hollow, buoyant bones, green eyes slitted against the wind, light and mighty wings sweeping up and down to either side of Semley, revealing and hiding, revealing and hiding the clouds above her and the hills below.

On the third morning she came to Kirien and stood again in the ruined courts. Her father had been drinking all night, and, just as in the old days, the morning sunlight poking through his fallen ceilings annoyed him, and the sight of his daughter only increased his annoyance. "What are you back for?" he growled, his swollen eyes glancing at her and away. The fiery hair of his youth was quenched, grey strands tangled on his skull. "Did the young Halla not marry you, and you've come sneaking home?"

"I am Durhal's wife. I came to get my dowry, father."

The drunkard growled in disgust; but she laughed at him so gently that he had to look at her again, wincing.

"Is it true, father, that the Fiia stole the necklace Eye of the Sea?"

"How do I know? Old tales. The thing was lost before I was born, I think. I wish I never had been. Ask the Fiia if you want to know. Go to them, go back to your husband. Leave me alone here. There's no room at Kirien for girls and gold and all the rest of the story. The story's over here; this is the fallen place, this is the empty hall. The sons of Leynen all are dead, their treasures are all lost. Go on your way, girl."

Grey and swollen as the web-spinner of ruined houses, he turned and went blundering toward the cellars where he hid from daylight.

Leading the striped windsteed of Hallan, Semley left her old home and walked down the steep hill, past the village of the midmen, who greeted her with sullen respect, on over fields and pastures where the great, wing-clipped, half-wild herilor grazed, to a valley that was green as a painted bowl and full to the brim with sunlight. In the deep of the valley lay the village of the Fiia, and as she descended leading her steed the little, slight people ran up toward her from their huts and gardens, laughing, calling out in faint, thin voices.

"Hail Halla's bride, Kirienlady, Windborne, Semley the Fair!"

They gave her lovely names and she liked to hear them, minding not at all their laughter; for they laughed at all they said. That was her own way, to speak and laugh. She stood tall in her long blue cloak among their swirling welcome.

"Hail Lightfolk, Sundwellers, Fiia friends of men!"

They took her down into the village and brought her into one of their airy houses, the tiny children chasing along behind. There was no telling the age of a Fian once he was grown; it was hard even to tell one from another and be sure, as they moved about quick as moths around a candle, that she spoke always to the same one. But it seemed that one of them talked with her for a while, as the others fed and petted her steed, and brought water for her to drink, and bowls of fruit from their gardens of little trees. "It was never the Fiia that stole the necklace of the Lords of Kirien!" cried the little man. "What would the Fiia do with gold, Lady? For us there is sunlight in warmyear, and in coldyear the remembrance of sunlight; the yellow fruit, the yellow leaves in end-season, the yellow hair of our lady of Kirien; no other gold."

"Then it was some midman stole the thing?"

Laughter rang long and faint about her. "How would a midman dare? O Lady of Kirien, how the great jewel was stolen no mortal knows, not man nor midman nor Fian nor any among the Seven Folk. Only dead minds know how it was lost, long ago when Kireley the Proud whose great-granddaughter is Semley walked alone by the caves of the sea. But it may be found perhaps among the Sunhaters."

"The Clayfolk?"

A louder burst of laughter, nervous.

"Sit with us, Semley, sunhaired, returned to us from the north." She sat with them to eat, and they were as pleased with her graciousness as she with theirs. But when they heard her repeat that she would go to the Clayfolk to find her inheritance, if it was there, they began not to laugh; and little by little there were fewer of them around her. She was alone at last with perhaps the one she had spoken with before the meal. "Do not go among the Clayfolk, Semley," he said, and for a moment her heart failed her. The Fian, drawing his hand down slowly over his eyes, had darkened all the air about them. Fruit lay ash-white on the plate; all the bowls of clear water were empty.

"In the mountains of the far land the Fiia and the Gdemiar parted. Long ago we parted," said the slight, still man of the Fiia. "Longer ago we were one. What we are not, they are. What we are, they are not. Think of the sunlight and the grass and the trees that bear fruit, Semley; think that not all roads that lead down lead up as well."

"Mine leads neither down nor up, kind host, but only straight on to my inheritance. I will go to it where it is, and return with it."

The Fian bowed, laughing a little.

Outside the village she mounted her striped windsteed, and, calling farewell in answer to their calling, rose up into the wind of afternoon and flew southwestward toward the caves down by the rocky shores of Kiriensea.

She feared she might have to walk far into those tunnel-caves to find the people she sought, for it was said the Clayfolk never came out of their caves into the light of the sun, and feared even the Greatstar and the moons. It was a long ride; she landed once to let her steed hunt tree-rats while she ate a little bread from her saddle-bag. The bread was hard and dry by now and tasted of leather, yet kept a faint savor of its making, so that for a moment, eating it alone in a glade of the southern forests, she heard the quiet tone of a voice and saw Durhal's face turned to her in the light of the candles of Hallan. For a while she sat daydreaming of that stern and vivid young face, and of what she would say to him when she came home with a kingdom's ransom around her neck: "I wanted a gift worthy of my husband, Lord. . . ." Then she pressed on, but when she reached the coast the sun had set, with the Greatstar sinking behind it. A mean wind had come up from the west, starting and gusting and veering, and her windsteed was weary fighting it. She let him glide down on the sand. At once he folded his wings and curled his thick, light limbs under him with a thrum of purring. Semley stood holding her cloak close at her throat, stroking the steed's neck so that he flicked his ears and purred again. The warm fur comforted her hand, but all that met her eyes was grey sky full of smears of cloud, grey sea, dark sand. And then running over the sand a low, dark creature—another—a group of them, squatting and running and stopping.

She called aloud to them. Though they had not seemed to see her, now in a moment they were all around her. They kept a distance from her windsteed; he had stopped purring, and his fur rose a little under Semley's hand. She took up the reins, glad of his protection but afraid of the nervous ferocity he might display. The strange folk stood silent staring, their thick bare feet planted in the sand. There was no mistaking them: they were the height of the Fiia and in all else a shadow, a black image of those laughing people. Naked, squat, stiff, with lank hair and grey-white skins, dampish-looking like the skins of grubs; eyes like rocks.

"You are the Clayfolk?"

"Gdemiar are we, people of the Lords of the Realms of Night." The voice was unexpectedly loud and deep, and rang out pompous through the salt, blowing dusk; but, as with the Fiia, Semley was not sure which one had spoken.

"I greet you, Nightlords. I am Semley of Kirien, Durhal's wife of Hallan. I come to you seeking my inheritance, the necklace called Eye of the Sea, lost long ago."

"Why do you seek it here, Angya? Here is only sand and salt and night."

"Because lost things are known of in deep places," said Semley, quite ready for a play of wits, "and gold that came from earth has a way of going

back to the earth. And sometimes the made, they say, returns to the maker."
This last was a guess; it hit the mark.

"It is true the necklace Eye of the Sea is known to us by name. It was
made in our caves long ago, and sold by us to the Angyar. And the blue
stone came from the Clayfields of our kin to the east. But these are very
old tales, Angya."

"May I listen to them in the places where they are told?"

The squat people were silent a while, as if in doubt. The grey wind blew
over the sand, darkening as the Greatstar set; the sound of the sea loud-
ened and lessened. The deep voice spoke again: "Yes, lady of the Angyar.
You may enter the Deep Halls. Come with us now." There was a changed
note in his voice, wheedling. Semley would not hear it. She followed the
Claymen over the sand, leading on a short rein her sharp-taloned steed.

At the cave-mouth, a toothless, yawning mouth from which a stinking
warmth sighed out, one of the Claymen said, "The air-beast cannot come
in."

"Yes," said Semley.

"No," said the squat people.

"Yes. I will not leave him here. He is not mine to leave. He will not
harm you, so long as I hold his reins."

"No," deep voices repeated; but others broke in, "As you will," and after
a moment of hesitation they went on. The cave-mouth seemed to snap shut
behind them, so dark was it under the stone. They went in single file,
Semley last.

The darkness of the tunnel lightened, and they came under a ball of
weak white fire hanging from the roof. Farther on was another, and another; between them long black worms hung in festoons from the rock. As
they went on these fireglobes were set closer, so that all the tunnel was lit
with a bright, cold light.

Semley's guides stopped at a parting of three tunnels, all blocked by
doors that looked to be of iron. "We shall wait, Angya," they said, and
eight of them stayed with her, while three others unlocked one of the doors
and passed through. It fell to behind them with a clash.

Straight and still stood the daughter of the Angyar in the white, blank
light of the lamps; her windsteed crouched beside her, flicking the tip of
his striped tail, his great folded wings stirring again and again with the
checked impulse to fly. In the tunnel behind Semley the eight Claymen
squatted on their hams, muttering to one another in their deep voices, in
their own tongue.

The central door swung clanging open. "Let the Angya enter the Realm
of Night!" cried a new voice, booming and boastful. A Clayman who wore
some clothing on his thick grey body stood in the doorway, beckoning to
her. "Enter and behold the wonders of our lands, the marvels made by
hands, the works of the Nightlords!"

Silent, with a tug at her steed's reins, Semley bowed her head and followed him under the low doorway made for dwarfish folk. Another glaring tunnel stretched ahead, dank walls dazzling in the white light, but, instead of a way to walk upon, its floor carried two bars of polished iron stretching off side by side as far as she could see. On the bars rested some kind of cart with metal wheels. Obeying her new guide's gestures, with no hesitation and no trace of wonder on her face, Semley stepped into the cart and made the windsteed crouch beside her. The Clayman got in and sat down in front of her, moving bars and wheels about. A loud grinding noise arose, and a screaming of metal on metal, and then the walls of the tunnel began to jerk by. Faster and faster the walls slid past, till the fireglobes overhead ran into a blur, and the stale warm air became a foul wind blowing the hood back off her hair.

The cart stopped. Semley followed the guide up basalt steps into a vast anteroom and then a still vaster hall, carved by ancient waters or by the burrowing Clayfolk out of the rock, its darkness that had never known sunlight lit with the uncanny cold brillance of the globes. In grilles cut in the walls huge blades turned and turned, changing the stale air. The great closed space hummed and boomed with noise, the loud voices of the Clayfolk, the grinding and shrill buzzing and vibration of turning blades and wheels, the echoes and re-echoes of all this from the rock. Here all the stumpy figures of the Claymen were clothed in garments imitating those of the Starlords—divided trousers, soft boots, and hooded tunics—though the few women to be seen, hurrying servile dwarves, were naked. Of the males many were soldiers, bearing at their sides weapons shaped like the terrible light-throwers of the Starlords, though even Semley could see these were merely shaped iron clubs. What she saw, she saw without looking. She followed where she was led, turning her head neither to left nor right. When she came before a group of Claymen who wore iron circlets on their black hair her guide halted, bowed, boomed out, "The High Lords of the Gdemiar!"

There were seven of them, and all looked up at her with such arrogance on their lumpy grey faces that she wanted to laugh.

"I come among you seeking the lost treasure of my family, O Lords of the Dark Realm," she said gravely to them. "I seek Leynen's prize, the Eye of the Sea." Her voice was faint in the racket of the huge vault.

"So said our messengers, Lady Semley." This time she could pick out the one who spoke, one even shorter than the others, hardly reaching Semley's breast, with a white, fierce face. "We do not have this thing you seek."

"Once you had it, it is said."

"Much is said, up there where the sun blinks."

"And words are borne off by the winds, where there are winds to blow. I do not ask how the necklace was lost to us and returned to you, its makers of old. Those are old tales, old grudges. I only seek to find it now. You do not have it now; but it may be you know where it is."

"It is not here."

"Then it is elsewhere."

"It is where you cannot come to it. Never, unless we help you."

"Then help me. I ask this as your guest."

"It is said, *The Angyar take; the Fiia give; the Gdemiar give and take.* If we do this for you, what will you give us?"

"My thanks, Nightlord."

She stood tall and bright among them, smiling. They all stared at her with a heavy, grudging wonder, a sullen yearning.

"Listen, Angya, this is a great favor you ask of us. You do not know how great a favor. You cannot understand. You are of a race that will not understand, that cares for nothing but wind-riding and crop-raising and sword-fighting and shouting together. But who made your swords of the bright steel? We, the Gdemiar! Your lords come to us here and in the Clayfields and buy their swords and go away, not looking, not understanding. But you are here now, you will look, you can see a few of our endless marvels, the lights that burn forever, the car that pulls itself, the machines that make our clothes and cook our food and sweeten our air and serve us in all things. Know that all these things are beyond your understanding. And know this: we, the Gdemiar, are the friends of those you call the Starlords! We came with them to Hallan, to Reohan, to Hul-Orren, to all your castles, to help them speak to you. The lords to whom you, the proud Angyar, pay tribute, are our friends. They do us favors as we do them favors! Now, what do your thanks mean to us?"

"That is your question to answer," said Semley, "not mine. I have asked my question. Answer it, Lord."

For a while the seven conferred together, by word and silence. They would glance at her and look away, and mutter and be still. A crowd grew around them, drawn slowly and silently, one after another till Semley was encircled by hundreds of the matted black heads, and all the great booming cavern floor was covered with people, except a little space directly around her. Her windsteed was quivering with fear and irritation too long controlled, and his eyes had gone very wide and pale, like the eyes of a steed forced to fly at night. She stroked the warm fur of his head, whispering, "Quietly now, brave one, bright one, windlord. . . ."

"Angya, we will take you to the place where the treasure lies." The Clayman with the white face and iron crown had turned to her once more. "More than that we cannot do. You must come with us to claim the necklace where it lies, from those who keep it. The air-beast cannot come with you. You must come alone."

"How far a journey, Lord?"

His lips drew back and back. "A very far journey, Lady. Yet it will last only one long night."

"I thank you for your courtesy. Will my steed be well cared for this night? No ill must come to him."

"He will sleep till you return. A greater windsteed you will have ridden, when you see that beast again! Will you not ask where we take you?"

"Can we go soon on this journey? I would not stay long away from my home."

"Yes. Soon." Again the grey lips widened as he stared up into her face.

What was done in those next hours Semley could not have retold; it was all haste, jumble, noise, strangeness. While she held her steed's head a Clayman stuck a long needle into the golden-striped haunch. She nearly cried out at the sight, but her steed merely twitched and then, purring, fell asleep. He was carried off by a group of Clayfolk who clearly had to summon up their courage to touch his warm fur. Later on she had to see a needle driven into her own arm—perhaps to test her courage, she thought, for it did not seem to make her sleep; though she was not quite sure. There were times she had to travel in the rail-carts, passing iron doors and vaulted caverns by the hundred and hundred; once the rail-cart ran through a cavern that stretched off on either hand measureless into the dark, and all that darkness was full of great flocks of herilor. She could hear their cooing, husky calls, and glimpse the flocks in the front-lights of the cart; then she saw some more clearly in the white light, and saw that they were all wingless, and all blind. At that she shut her eyes. But there were more tunnels to go through, and always more caverns, more grey lumpy bodies and fierce faces and booming boasting voices, until at last they led her suddenly out into the open air. It was full night; she raised her eyes joyfully to the stars and the single moon shining, little Heliki brightening in the west. But the Clayfolk were all about her still, making her climb now into some new kind of cart or cave, she did not know which. It was small, full of little blinking lights like rushlights, very narrow and shining after the great dank caverns and the starlit night. Now another needle was stuck in her, and they told her she would have to be tied down in a sort of flat chair, tied down head and hand and foot.

"I will not," said Semley.

But when she saw that the four Claymen who were to be her guides let themselves be tied down first, she submitted. The others left. There was a roaring sound, and a long silence; a great weight that could not be seen pressed upon her. Then there was no weight; no sound; nothing at all.

"Am I dead?" asked Semley.

"Oh, no, Lady," said a voice she did not like.

Opening her eyes, she saw the white face bent over her, the wide lips pulled back, the eyes like little stones. Her bonds had fallen away from her, and she leaped up. She was weightless, bodiless; she felt herself only a gust of terror on the wind.

"We will not hurt you," said the sullen voice or voices. "Only let us touch you, Lady. We would like to touch your hair. Let us touch your hair. . . ."

The round cart they were in trembled a little. Outside its one window lay blank night, or was it mist, or nothing at all? One long night, they had said. Very long. She sat motionless and endured the touch of their heavy grey hands on her hair. Later they would touch her hands and feet and arms, and once her throat: at that she set her teeth and stood up, and they drew back.

"We have not hurt you, Lady," they said. She shook her head.

When they bade her, she lay down again in the chair that bound her down; and when light flashed golden, at the window, she would have wept at the sight, but fainted first.

"Well," said Rocannon, "now at least we know what she is."

"I wish there were some way of knowing *who* she is," the curator mumbled. "She wants something we've got here in the Museum, is that what the trogs say?"

"Now, don't call 'em trogs," Rocannon said conscientiously; as a hilfer, an ethnologist of the High Intelligence Life-forms, he was supposed to resist such words. "They're not pretty, but they're Status C Allies. . . . I wonder why the Commission picked them to develop? Before even contacting all the HILF species? I'll bet the survey was from Centaurus— Centaurans always like nocturnals and cave dwellers. I'd have backed Species II, here, I think."

"The troglodytes seem to be rather in awe of her."

"Aren't you?"

Ketho glanced at the tall woman again, then reddened and laughed. "Well, in a way. I never saw such a beautiful alien type in eighteen years here on New South Georgia. I never saw such a beautiful woman anywhere, in fact. She looks like a goddess." The red now reached the top of his bald head, for Ketho was a shy curator, not given to hyperbole. But Rocannon nodded soberly, agreeing.

"I wish we could talk to her without those tr— Gdemiar as interpreters. But there's no help for it." Rocannon went toward their visitor, and when she turned her splendid face to him he bowed down very deeply, going right down to the floor on one knee, his head bowed and his eyes shut. This was what he called his All-Purpose Intercultural Curtsey, and he performed it with some grace. When he came erect again the beautiful woman smiled and spoke.

"She say, Hail, Lord of Stars," growled one of her squat escorts in Pidgin-Galactic.

"Hail, Lady of the Angyar," Rocannon replied. "In what way can we of the Museum serve the lady?"

Across the troglodytes' growling her voice ran like a brief silver wind.

"She say, Please give her necklace which treasure her blood-kin-forebears long long."

"Which necklace?" he asked, and understanding him, she pointed to the central display of the case before them, a magnificent thing, a chain of yellow gold, massive but very delicate in workmanship, set with one big hot-blue sapphire. Rocannon's eyebrows went up, and Ketho at his shoulder murmured, "She's got good taste. That's the Fomalhaut Necklace— famous bit of work."

She smiled at the two men, and again spoke to them over the heads of the troglodytes.

"She say, O Starlords, Elder and Younger Dwellers in House of Treasures, this treasure her one. Long long time. Thank you."

"How did we get the thing, Ketho?"

"Wait; let me look it up in the catalogue. I've got it here. Here. It came from these trogs—trolls—whatever they are: Gdemiar. They have a bargain-obsession, it says; we had to let 'em buy the ship they came here on, an AD-4. This was part payment. It's their own handiwork."

"And I'll bet they can't do this kind of work anymore, since they've been steered to Industrial."

"But they seem to feel the thing is hers, not theirs or ours. It must be important, Rocannon, or they wouldn't have given up this time-span to her errand. Why, the objective lapse between here and Fomalhaut must be considerable!"

"Several years, no doubt," said the hilfer, who was used to starjumping. "Not very far. Well, neither the *Handbook* nor the *Guide* gives me enough data to base a decent guess on. These species obviously haven't been properly studied at all. The little fellows may be showing her simple courtesy. Or an interspecies war may depend on this damn sapphire. Perhaps her desire rules them, because they consider themselves totally inferior to her. Or despite appearances she may be their prisoner, their decoy. How can we tell? . . . Can you give the thing away, Ketho?"

"Oh, yes. All the Exotica are technically on loan, not our property, since these claims come up now and then. We seldom argue. Peace above all, until the War comes. . . ."

"Then I'd say give it to her."

Ketho smiled. "It's a privilege," he said. Unlocking the case, he lifted out the great golden chain; then, in his shyness, he held it out to Rocannon, saying, "You give it to her."

So the blue jewel first lay, for a moment, in Rocannon's hand.

His mind was not on it; he turned straight to the beautiful, alien woman, with his handful of blue fire and gold. She did not raise her hands to take it, but bent her head, and he slipped the necklace over her hair. It lay like a burning fuse along her golden-brown throat. She looked up from it with such pride, delight, and gratitude in her face that Rocannon stood wordless, and the little curator murmured hurriedly in his own language, "You're welcome, you're very welcome." She bowed her golden head to him and to Rocannon. Then, turning, she nodded to her squat guards—or captors?—and, drawing her worn blue cloak about her, paced down the long hall and was gone. Ketho and Rocannon stood looking after her.

"What I feel . . ." Rocannon began.

"Well?" Ketho inquired hoarsely, after a long pause.

"What I feel sometimes is that I . . . meeting these people from worlds we know so little of, you know, sometimes . . . that I have as it were blundered through the corner of a legend, or a tragic myth, maybe, which I do not understand. . . ."

"Yes," said the curator, clearing his throat. "I wonder . . . I wonder what her name is."

Semley the Fair, Semley the Golden, Semley of the Necklace. The Clayfolk had bent to her will, and so had even the Starlords in that terrible place where the Clayfolk had taken her, the city at the end of the night. They had bowed to her, and given her gladly her treasure from amongst their own.

But she could not yet shake off the feeling of those caverns about her where rock lowered overhead, where you could not tell who spoke or what they did, where voices boomed and grey hands reached out—Enough of that. She had paid for the necklace; very well. Now it was hers. The price was paid, the past was the past.

Her windsteed had crept out of some kind of box, with his eyes filmy and his fur rimed with ice, and at first when they had left the caves of the Gdemiar he would not fly. Now he seemed all right again, riding a smooth south wind through the bright sky toward Hallan. "Go quick, go quick," she told him, beginning to laugh as the wind cleared away her mind's darkness. "I want to see Durhal soon, soon. . . ."

And swiftly they flew, coming to Hallan by dusk of the second day. Now the caves of the Clayfolk seemed no more than last year's nightmare, as the steed swooped with her up the thousand steps of Hallan and across the Chasmbridge where the forests fell away for a thousand feet. In the gold light of evening in the flight-court she dismounted and walked up the last steps between the stiff carven figures of heroes and the two gatewards, who bowed to her, staring at the beautiful, fiery thing around her neck.

In the Forehall she stopped a passing girl, a very pretty girl, by her looks one of Durhal's close kin, though Semley could not call to mind her name. "Do you know me, maiden? I am Semley, Durhal's wife. Will you go tell the Lady Durossa that I have come back?"

For she was afraid to go in and perhaps face Durhal at once, alone; she wanted Durossa's support.

The girl was gazing at her, her face very strange. But she murmured, "Yes, Lady," and darted off toward the Tower.

Semley stood waiting in the gilt, ruinous hall. No one came by; were they all at table in the Revel-hall? The silence was uneasy. After a minute Semley started toward the stairs to the Tower. But an old woman was coming to her across the stone floor, holding her arms out, weeping.

"Oh Semley, Semley!"

She had never seen the grey-haired woman, and shrank back.

"But Lady, who are you?"

"I am Durossa, Semley."

She was quiet and still, all the time that Durossa embraced her and wept, and asked if it were true the Clayfolk had captured her and kept her under a spell all these long years, or had it been the Fiia with their strange arts? Then, drawing back a little, Durossa ceased to weep.

"You're still young, Semley. Young as the day you left here. And you wear round your neck the necklace. . . ."

"I have bought my gift to my husband Durhal. Where is he?"

"Durhal is dead."

Semley stood unmoving.

"Your husband, my brother, Durhal Hallanlord was killed seven years ago in battle. Nine years you had been gone. The Starlords came no more. We fell to warring with the Eastern Halls, with the Angyar of Log and Hul-Orren. Durhal, fighting, was killed by a midman's spear, for he had little armor for his body, and none at all for his spirit. He lies buried in the field above Orren Marsh."

Semley turned away. "I will go to him, then," she said, putting her hand on the gold chain that weighed down her neck. "I will give him my gift."

"Wait, Semley! Durhal's daughter, your daughter, see her now, Haldre the Beautiful!"

It was the girl she had first spoken to and sent to Durossa, a girl of nineteen or so, with eyes like Durhal's eyes, dark blue. She stood beside Durossa, gazing with those steady eyes at this woman Semley who was her mother and was her own age. Their age was the same, and their gold hair, and their beauty. Only Semley was a little taller, and wore the blue stone on her breast.

"Take it, take it. It was for Durhal and Haldre that I brought it from the end of the long night!" Semley cried this aloud, twisting and bowing her head to get the heavy chain off, dropping the necklace so it fell on the stones with a cold, liquid clash. "O take it, Haldre!" she cried again, and then, weeping aloud, turned and ran from Hallan, over the bridge and down the long, broad steps, and darting off eastward into the forest of the mountainside like some wild thing escaping, was gone.

QUESTIONS

"Semley's Necklace"

1. Though Le Guin says at the start of "Semley's Necklace" that the tale she is about to tell is "the story of a man, an ordinary League scientist . . . Rocannon's story," the scientist Rocannon is clearly a subordinate character. Her puzzling identification of him as the protagonist may be explained by the his-

tory of "Semley's Necklace." Originally published in 1964 under the title "Dowry of the Angyar," it was later used by Le Guin as the prologue to her 1966 novel, *Rocannon's World,* in which the scientist is in fact the main character. Though the hero of "Semley's Necklace" is obviously Lady Semley, Rocannon serves an important function. Why does Le Guin begin her story by introducing us to the League scientist and showing us an excerpt from his *Abridged Handy Pocket Guide to Intelligent Life-Forms?* What is the author's purpose in starting this way? How would your response to the story have been different if it had begun with the sentence "She was of an ancient family, a descendent of the first kings, of the Angyar . . ."?

2. In "Semley's Necklace," Le Guin blends two genres of popular literature, which, while interrelated and sometimes overlapping, have distinctive characteristics. The short sections Rocannon appears in are straightforward science fiction; the story of Semley's journey to the realm of the Clayfolk falls into the category of heroic ("sword-and-sorcery") fantasy. How do these two types of fiction differ? What are their respective traits? How, for example, would you compare the language of the *Abridged Handy Pocket Guide to Intelligent Life-Forms* to a passage such as the following: "Fourth from the High Seat of Hallan Revel sat Durhal and his bride Semley, so close to Hallanlord that the old man often poured wine for Semley with his own hand, and spoke of hunting with his nephew and heir Durhal, looking at the young pair with a grim, unhopeful love . . . for a generation now the Angyar had sat in idle shame in their revel-halls, watching their double swords rust, their sons grow up without ever striking a blow in battle, their daughters marry poor men, even midmen, having no dowry of heroic loot to bring a noble husband"? How does Le Guin combine science fiction and heroic fantasy in this story? At what point in the narrative do the two modes overlap? Does the mixture work?

3. By what means does Le Guin create an alien world in "Semley's Necklace"? How successful is she in conjuring up the planet known to Rocannon as Fomalhaut II?

4. What makes Semley, despite her otherworldly qualities, a recognizable, psychologically plausible character? How would you describe her? Were you sympathetic to her quest? What motivates her to undertake it?

5. Describe the different stages of Semley's heroic quest for her treasured necklace. What is the call? What "road of trials" must she travel? What form does her descent into the underworld take? Who are her helpers? Does the figure of the Other appear in the story?

6. Who are the Starlords? How has their arrival affected the way of life on Semley's world? What is the Starlords' relationship to the Gdemiar?

7. How are the Gdemiar and the Fiia compared? Though the two species are described in strictly scientific terms in the *Abridged Handy Pocket Guide* . . . as "highly intelligent, fully hominoid" beings, they seem more like crea-

tures out of a Grimm Brothers' story. What sort of fairy-tale creatures do they remind you of? Does the story contain any other fairy-tale elements?

8. What explanation is given for the ending of "Semley's Necklace"? Why has the rest of the world aged so dramatically during the seemingly short time the hero is away? Are there any clues earlier in the story that prepare you for the outcome? Can "Semley's Necklace" be considered a "surprise-ending" story?

Janus

ANN BEATTIE

The bowl was perfect. Perhaps it was not what you'd select if you faced a shelf of bowls, and not the sort of thing that would inevitably attract a lot of attention at a crafts fair, yet it had real presence. It was as predictably admired as a mutt who has no reason to suspect he might be funny. Just such a dog, in fact, was often brought out (and in) along with the bowl.

Andrea was a real-estate agent, and when she thought that some prospective buyers might be dog lovers, she would drop off her dog at the same time she placed the bowl in the house that was up for sale. She would put a dish of water in the kitchen for Mondo, take his squeaking plastic frog out of her purse and drop it on the floor. He would pounce delightedly, just as he did every day at home, batting around his favorite toy. The bowl usually sat on a coffee table, though recently she had displayed it on top of a pine blanket chest and on a lacquered table. It was once placed on a cherry table beneath a Bonnard still life, where it held its own.

Everyone who has purchased a house or who has wanted to sell a house must be familiar with some of the tricks used to convince a buyer that the house is quite special: a fire in the fireplace in early evening; jonquils in a pitcher on the kitchen counter, where no one ordinarily has space to put flowers; perhaps the slight aroma of spring, made by a single drop of scent vaporizing from a lamp bulb.

The wonderful thing about the bowl, Andrea thought, was that it was both subtle and noticeable—a paradox of a bowl. Its glaze was the color of cream and seemed to glow no matter what light it was placed in. There were a few bits of color in it—tiny geometric flashes—and some of these were tinged with flecks of silver. They were as mysterious as cells seen under a microscope; it was difficult not to study them, because they shimmered, flashing for a split second, and then resumed their shape. Something about the colors and their random placement suggested motion. People who liked country furniture always commented on the bowl, but then it turned out that people who felt comfortable with Biedermeier loved it just as much. But the bowl was not at all ostentatious, or even so noticeable that anyone would suspect that it had been put in place deliberately. They might notice the height of the ceiling on first entering a room, and only

when their eye moved down from that, or away from the refraction of sunlight on a pale wall, would they see the bowl. Then they would go immediately to it and comment. Yet they always faltered when they tried to say
something. Perhaps it was because they were in the house for a serious
reason, not to notice some object.

Once Andrea got a call from a woman who had not put in an offer on a
house she had shown her. That bowl, she said—would it be possible to
find out where the owners had bought that beautiful bowl? Andrea pretended that she did not know what the woman was referring to. A bowl,
somewhere in the house? Oh, on a table under the window. Yes, she would
ask, of course. She let a couple of days pass, then called back to say that
the bowl had been a present and the people did not know where it had
been purchased.

When the bowl was not being taken from house to house, it sat on Andrea's coffee table at home. She didn't keep it carefully wrapped (although
she transported it that way, in a box); she kept it on the table, because she
liked to see it. It was large enough so that it didn't seem fragile or particularly vulnerable if anyone sideswiped the table or Mondo blundered into
it at play. She had asked her husband to please not drop his house key in
it. It was meant to be empty.

When her husband first noticed the bowl, he had peered into it and
smiled briefly. He always urged her to buy things she liked. In recent
years, both of them had acquired many things to make up for all the lean
years when they were graduate students, but now that they had been comfortable for quite a while, the pleasure of new possessions dwindled. Her
husband had pronounced the bowl "pretty," and he had turned away without picking it up to examine it. He had no more interest in the bowl than
she had in his new Leica.

She was sure that the bowl brought her luck. Bids were often put in on
houses where she had displayed the bowl. Sometimes the owners, who
were always asked to be away or to step outside when the house was being
shown, didn't even know that the bowl had been in their house. Once—
she could not imagine how—she left it behind, and then she was so afraid
that something might have happened to it that she rushed back to the
house and sighed with relief when the woman owner opened the door. The
bowl, Andrea explained—she had purchased a bowl and set it on the chest
for safekeeping while she toured the house with the prospective buyers,
and she . . . She felt like rushing past the frowning woman and seizing
her bowl. The owner stepped aside, and it was only when Andrea ran to
the chest that the lady glanced at her a little strangely. In the few seconds
before Andrea picked up the bowl, she realized that the owner must have
just seen that it had been perfectly placed, that the sunlight struck the
bluer part of it. Her pitcher had been moved to the far side of the chest,
and the bowl predominated. All the way home, Andrea wondered how she
could have left the bowl behind. It was like leaving a friend at an outing—
just walking off. Sometimes there were stories in the paper about families

forgetting a child somewhere and driving to the next city. Andrea had only gone a mile down the road before she remembered.

In time, she dreamed of the bowl. Twice, in a waking dream—early in the morning, between sleep and a last nap before rising—she had a clear vision of it. It came into sharp focus and startled her for a moment—the same bowl she looked at every day.

She had a very profitable year selling real estate. Word spread, and she had more clients than she felt comfortable with. She had the foolish thought that if only the bowl were an animate object she could thank it. There were times when she wanted to talk to her husband about the bowl. He was a stockbroker, and sometimes told people that he was fortunate to be married to a woman who had such a fine aesthetic sense and yet could also function in the real world. They were a lot alike, really—they had agreed on that. They were both quiet people—reflective, slow to make value judgments, but almost intractable once they had come to a conclusion. They both liked details, but while ironies attracted her, he was more impatient and dismissive when matters became many-sided or unclear. They both knew this, and it was the kind of thing they could talk about when they were alone in the car together, coming home from a party or after a weekend with friends. But she never talked to him about the bowl. When they were at dinner, exchanging their news of the day, or while they lay in bed at night listening to the stereo and murmuring sleepy disconnections, she was often tempted to come right out and say that she thought that the bowl in the living room, the cream-colored bowl, was responsible for her success. But she didn't say it. She couldn't begin to explain it. Sometimes in the morning, she would look at him and feel guilty that she had such a constant secret.

Could it be that she had some deeper connection with the bowl—a relationship of some kind? She corrected her thinking: how could she imagine such a thing, when she was a human being and it was a bowl? It was ridiculous. Just think of how people lived together and loved each other . . . But was that always so clear, always a relationship? She was confused by these thoughts, but they remained in her mind. There was something within her now, something real, that she never talked about.

The bowl was a mystery, even to her. It was frustrating, because her involvement with the bowl contained a steady sense of unrequited good fortune; it would have been easier to respond if some sort of demand were made in return. But that only happened in fairy tales. The bowl was just a bowl. She did not believe that for one second. What she believed was that it was something she loved.

In the past, she had sometimes talked to her husband about a new property she was about to buy or sell—confiding some clever strategy she had devised to persuade owners who seemed ready to sell. Now she stopped doing that, for all her strategies involved the bowl. She became more deliberate with the bowl, and more possessive. She put it in houses only when no one was there, and removed it when she left the house. Instead of just moving a pitcher or a dish, she would remove all the other objects from a table. She had to force herself to handle them carefully, because she didn't really care about them. She just wanted them out of sight.

She wondered how the situation would end. As with a lover, there was no exact scenario of how matters would come to a close. Anxiety became the operative force. It would be irrelevant if the lover rushed into someone else's arms, or wrote her a note and departed to another city. The horror was the possibility of the disappearance. That was what mattered.

She would get up at night and look at the bowl. It never occurred to her that she might break it. She washed and dried it without anxiety, and she moved it often, from coffee table to mahogany corner table or wherever, without fearing an accident. It was clear that she would not be the one who would do anything to the bowl. The bowl was only handled by her, set safely on one surface or another; it was not very likely that anyone would break it. A bowl was a poor conductor of electricity: it would not be hit by lightning. Yet the idea of damage persisted. She did not think beyond that— to what her life would be without the bowl. She only continued to fear that some accident would happen. Why not, in a world where people set plants where they did not belong, so that visitors touring a house would be fooled into thinking that dark corners got sunlight—a world full of tricks?

She had first seen the bowl several years earlier, at a crafts fair she had visited half in secret, with her lover. He had urged her to buy the bowl. She didn't *need* any more things, she told him. But she had been drawn to the bowl, and they had lingered near it. Then she went on to the next booth, and he came up behind her, tapping the rim against her shoulder as she ran her fingers over a wood carving. "You're still insisting that I buy that?" she said. "No," he said. "I bought it for you." He had bought her other things before this—things she liked more, at first—the child's ebony-and-turquoise ring that fitted her little finger; the wooden box, long and thin, beautifully dovetailed, that she used to hold paper clips; the soft gray sweater with a pouch pocket. It was his idea that when he could not be there to hold her hand she could hold her own—clasp her hands inside the lone pocket that stretched across the front. But in time she became more attached to the bowl than to any of his other presents. She tried to talk herself out of it. She owned other things that were more striking or valuable. It wasn't an object whose beauty jumped out at you; a lot of people must have passed it by before the two of them saw it that day.

Her lover had said that she was always too slow to know what she really loved. Why continue with her life the way it was? Why be two-faced, he asked her. He had made the first move toward her. When she would not decide in his favor, would not change her life and come to him, he asked her what made her think she could have it both ways. And then he made the last move and left. It was a decision meant to break her will, to shatter her intransigent ideas about honoring previous commitments.

Time passed. Alone in the living room at night, she often looked at the bowl sitting on the table, still and safe, unilluminated. In its way, it was perfect: the world cut in half, deep and smoothly empty. Near the rim, even in dim light, the eye moved toward one small flash of blue, a vanishing point on the horizon.

QUESTIONS

"Janus"

1. Characterize Andrea as completely as you can. What do her actions and thoughts reveal about her? What do you learn about her husband's view of her? Her ex-lover's view? Has Andrea an analytical temperament? How much self-knowledge does she possess?

2. What is Andrea's marriage like? Before you learn that she has had at least one lover, are there clues that her marriage is not ideal? Explain.

3. What are the tricks used by Andrea and other real-estate agents to sell houses? What effect are the agents trying to achieve? Do you see any irony in the fact that Andrea does these things? Explain.

4. Discuss Andrea's attitude toward the bowl. What does it mean to her? Why is she so confused by it? At one point she reflects that the bowl brings her nothing but "good fortune," regretting that nothing is asked of her in return. Is she correct in these assumptions?

5. To Andrea, no doubt, the bowl represents a treasure because it helps her sell houses. What is your sense of the bowl's value?

6. Why do you think others (the clients Andrea is selling houses to) respond so powerfully to the bowl?

7. Janus, who gives his name to the first month of the year, was the Roman god of doors and of beginnings. Doors and gates were sacred to this god. The Roman people believed that proper beginnings were crucial to the success of any undertaking, probably because they were the gateway to the future. The god Janus is usually represented pictorially as having two faces that looked, as doors do, in opposite directions. Why does Beattie call her story "Janus"?

8. Andrea instructs her husband not to place his keys in her bowl: she wants it kept empty. In the last paragraph of her story, Beattie comments again on the bowl's emptiness, which to Andrea, apparently, is part of its perfection. Why does she feel this way? What is the symbolic value of the bowl's emptiness?

A Tree · A Rock · A Cloud

CARSON MCCULLERS

It was raining that morning, and still very dark. When the boy reached the streetcar café he had almost finished his route and he went in for a cup of coffee. The place was an all-night café owned by a bitter and stingy man called Leo. After the raw, empty street, the café seemed friendly and bright: along the counter there were a couple of soldiers, three spinners from the cotton mill, and in a corner a man who sat hunched over with his nose and half his face down in a beer mug. The boy wore a helmet such as aviators wear. When he went into the café he unbuckled the chin strap and raised the right flap up over his pink little ear; often as he drank his coffee someone would speak to him in a friendly way. But this morning Leo did not look into his face and none of the men were talking. He paid and was leaving the café when a voice called out to him:

"Son! Hey Son!"

He turned back and the man in the corner was crooking his finger and nodding to him. He had brought his face out of the beer mug and he seemed suddenly very happy. The man was long and pale, with a big nose and faded orange hair.

"Hey Son!"

The boy went toward him. He was an undersized boy of about twelve, with one shoulder drawn higher than the other because of the weight of the paper sack. His face was shallow, freckled, and his eyes were round child eyes.

"Yeah Mister?"

The man laid one hand on the paper boy's shoulders, then grasped the boy's chin and turned his face slowly from one side to the other. The boy shrank back uneasily.

"Say! What's the big idea?"

The boy's voice was shrill; inside the café it was suddenly very quiet.

The man said slowly: "I love you."

All along the counter the men laughed. The boy, who had scowled and sidled away, did not know what to do. He looked over the counter at Leo, and Leo watched him with a weary, brittle jeer. The boy tried to laugh also. But the man was serious and sad.

436

"I did not mean to tease you, Son," he said. "Sit down and have a beer with me. There is something I have to explain."

Cautiously, out of the corner of his eye, the paper boy questioned the men along the counter to see what he should do. But they had gone back to their beer or their breakfast and did not notice him. Leo put a cup of coffee on the counter and a little jug of cream.

"He is a minor," Leo said.

The paper boy slid himself up onto the stool. His ear beneath the upturned flap of the helmet was very small and red. The man was nodding at him soberly. "It is important," he said. Then he reached in his hip pocket and brought out something which he held up in the palm of his hand for the boy to see.

"Look very carefully," he said.

The boy stared, but there was nothing to look at very carefully. The man held in his big, grimy palm a photograph. It was the face of a woman, but blurred, so that only the hat and the dress she was wearing stood out clearly.

"See?" the man asked.

The boy nodded and the man placed another picture in his palm. The woman was standing on a beach in a bathing suit. The suit made her stomach very big, and that was the main thing you noticed.

"Got a good look?" He leaned over closer and finally asked "You ever seen her before?"

The boy sat motionless, staring slantwise at the man. "Not so I know of."

"Very well." The man blew on the photographs and put them back into his pocket. "That was my wife."

"Dead?" the boy asked.

Slowly the man shook his head. He pursed his lips as though about to whistle and answered in a long-drawn way: "Nuuu—" he said. "I will explain."

The beer on the counter before the man was in a large brown mug. He did not pick it up to drink. Instead he bent down and, putting his face over the rim, he rested there for a moment. Then with both hands he tilted the mug and sipped.

"Some night you'll go to sleep with your big nose in a mug and drown," said Leo. "Prominent transient drowns in beer. That would be a cute death."

The paper boy tried to signal to Leo. While the man was not looking he screwed up his face and worked his mouth to question soundlessly: "Drunk?" But Leo only raised his eyebrows and turned away to put some pink strips of bacon on the grill. The man pushed the mug away from him, straightened himself, and folded his loose crooked hands on the counter. His face was sad as he looked at the paper boy. He did not blink, but from time to time the lids closed down with delicate gravity over his pale green eyes. It was nearing dawn and the boy shifted the weight of the paper sack.

"I am talking about love," the man said. "With me it is a science."

The boy half slid down from the stool. But the man raised his forefinger,

and there was something about him that held the boy and would not let
him go away.

"Twelve years ago, I married the woman in the photograph. She was my
wife for one year, nine months, three days, and two nights. I loved her.
Yes . . ." He tightened his blurred, rambling voice and said again: "I loved
her. I thought also that she loved me. I was a railroad engineer. She had
all home comforts and luxuries. It never crept into my brain that she was
not satisfied. But do you know what happened?"

"Mgneeow!" said Leo.

The man did not take his eyes from the boy's face. "She left me. I came
in one night and the house was empty and she was gone. She left me."

"With a fellow?" the boy asked.

Gently the man placed his palm down on the counter. "Why naturally,
Son. A woman does not run off like that alone."

The café was quiet, the soft rain black and endless in the street outside.
Leo pressed down the frying bacon with the prongs of his long fork. "So
you have been chasing the floozie for eleven years. You frazzled old rascal!"

For the first time the man glanced at Leo. "Please don't be vulgar. Besides, I was not speaking to you." He turned back to the boy and said in a
trusting and secretive undertone: "Let's not pay any attention to him, O.K.?"

The paper boy nodded doubtfully.

"It was like this," the man continued. "I am a person who feels many
things. All of my life one thing after another has impressed me. Moonlight.
The leg of a pretty girl. One thing after another. But the point is that when
I had enjoyed anything there was a peculiar sensation as though it was
laying around loose in me. Nothing seemed to finish itself up or fit in with
the other things. Women? I had my portion of them. The same. Afterwards
laying around loose in me. I was a man who had never loved."

Very slowly he closed his eyelids, and the gesture was like a curtain
drawn at the end of a scene in a play. When he spoke again his voice was
excited and the words came first—the lobes of his large, loose ears seemed
to tremble.

"Then I met this woman. I was fifty-one years old and she always said
she was thirty. I met her at a filling station and we were married within
three days. And do you know what it was like? I just can't tell you. All I
had ever felt was gathered together around this woman. Nothing lay around
loose in me any more but was finished up by her."

The man stopped suddenly and stroked his long nose. His voice sank
down to a steady and reproachful undertone: "I'm not explaining this right.
What happened was this. There were these beautiful feelings and loose
little pleasures inside me. And this woman was something like an assembly
line for my soul. I run these little pieces of myself through her and I come
out complete. Now do you follow me?"

"What was her name?" the boy asked.

"Oh," he said. "I called her Dodo. But that is immaterial."

"Did you try to make her come back?"

The man did not seem to hear. "Under the circumstances you can imagine how I felt when she left me."

Leo took the bacon from the grill and folded two strips of it between a bun. He had a gray face, with slitted eyes, and a pinched nose saddled by faint blue shadows. One of the mill workers signaled for more coffee and Leo poured it. He did not give refills on coffee free. The spinner ate breakfast there every morning, but the better Leo knew his customers the stingier he treated them. He nibbled his own bun as though he grudged it to himself.

"And you never got hold of her again?"

The boy did not know what to think of the man, and his child's face was uncertain with mingled curiosity and doubt. He was new on the paper route; it was still strange to him to be out in the town in the black, queer early morning.

"Yes," the man said. "I took a number of steps to get her back. I went around trying to locate her. I went to Tulsa where she had folks. And to Mobile. I went to every town she had ever mentioned to me, and I hunted down every man she had formerly been connected with. Tulsa, Atlanta, Chicago, Cheehaw, Memphis. . . . For the better part of two years I chased around the country trying to lay hold of her."

"But the pair of them had vanished from the face of the earth!" said Leo.

"Don't listen to him," the man said confidentially. "And also just forget those two years. They are not important. What matters is that around the third year a curious thing began to happen to me."

"What?" the boy asked.

The man leaned down and tilted his mug to take a sip of beer. But as he hovered over the mug his nostrils fluttered slightly; he sniffed the staleness of the beer and did not drink. "Love is a curious thing to begin with. At first I thought only of getting her back. It was a kind of mania. But then as time went on I tried to remember her. But do you know what happened?"

"No," the boy said.

"When I laid myself down on a bed and tried to think about her my mind became a blank. I couldn't see her. I would take out her pictures and look. No good. Nothing doing. A blank. Can you imagine it?"

"Say Mac!" Leo called down the counter. "Can you imagine this bozo's mind a blank!"

Slowly, as though fanning away flies, the man waved his hand. His green eyes were concentrated and fixed on the shallow little face of the paper boy.

"But a sudden piece of glass on a sidewalk. Or a nickel tune in a music box. A shadow on a wall at night. And I would remember. It might happen in a street and I would cry or bang my head against a lamppost. You follow me?"

"A piece of glass. . . ." the boy said.

"Anything. I would walk around and I had no power of how and when to remember her. You think you can put up a kind of shield. But remembering don't come to a man face forward—it corners around sideways. I was at the mercy of everything I saw and heard. Suddenly instead of me combing the countryside to find her she begun to chase me around in my very soul. *She* chasing *me*, mind you! And in my soul."

The boy asked finally: "What part of the country were you in then?"

"Ooh," the man groaned. "I was a sick mortal. It was like a smallpox. I confess, Son, that I boozed. I fornicated. I committed any sin that suddenly appealed to me. I am loath to confess it but I will do so. When I recall that period it is all curdled in my mind, it was so terrible."

The man leaned his head down and tapped his forehead on the counter. For a few seconds he stayed bowed over in this position, the back of his stringy neck covered with orange furze, his hands with their long warped fingers held palm to palm in an attitude of prayer. Then the man straightened himself; he was smiling and suddenly his face was bright and tremulous and old.

"It was in the fifth year that it happened," he said. "And with it I started my science."

Leo's mouth jerked with a pale, quick grin. "Well none of we boys are getting any younger," he said. Then with sudden anger he balled up a dishcloth he was holding and threw it down hard on the floor. "You draggle-tailed old Romeo!"

"What happened?" the boy asked.

The old man's voice was high and clear: "Peace," he answered.

"Huh?"

"It is hard to explain scientifically, Son," he said. "I guess the logical explanation is that she and I had fleed around from each other for so long that finally we just got tangled up together and lay down and quit. Peace. A queer and beautiful blankness. It was spring in Portland and the rain came every afternoon. All evening I just stayed there on my bed in the dark. And that is how the science come to me."

The windows in the streetcar were pale blue with light. The two soldiers paid for their beers and opened the door—one of the soldiers combed his hair and wiped off his muddy puttees before they went outside. The three mill workers bent silently over their breakfasts. Leo's clock was ticking on the wall.

"It is this. And listen carefully. I meditated on love and reasoned it out. I realized what is wrong with us. Men fall in love for the first time. And what do they fall in love with?"

The boy's soft mouth was partly open and he did not answer.

"A woman," the old man said. "Without science, with nothing to go by, they undertake the most dangerous and sacred experience in God's earth. They fall in love with a woman. Is that correct, Son?"

"Yeah," the boy said faintly.

"They start at the wrong end of love. They begin at the climax. Can you wonder it is so miserable? Do you know how men should love?"

The old man reached over and grasped the boy by the collar of his leather jacket. He gave him a gentle little shake and his green eyes gazed down unblinking and grave.

"Son, do you know how love should be begun?"

The boy sat small and listening and still. Slowly he shook his head. The old man leaned closer and whispered:

"A tree. A rock. A cloud."

It was still raining outside in the street; a mild, gray, endless rain. The mill whistle blew for the six o'clock shift and the three spinners paid and went away. There was no one in the café but Leo, the old man, and little paper boy.

"The weather was like this in Portland," he said. "At the time my science was begun. I meditated and I started very cautious. I would pick up something from the street and take it home with me. I bought a goldfish and I concentrated on the goldfish and I loved it. I graduated from one thing to another. Day by day I was getting this technique. On the road from Portland to San Diego—"

"Aw shut up!" screamed Leo suddenly. "Shut up! Shut up!"

The old man still held the collar of the boy's jacket; he was trembling and his face was earnest and bright and wild. "For six years now I have gone around by myself and built up my science. And now I am a master. Son, I can love anything. No longer do I have to think about it even. I see a street full of people and a beautiful light comes in me. I watch a bird in the sky. Or I meet a traveler on the road. Everything, Son. And anybody. All strangers and all loved! Do you realize what a science like mine can mean?"

The boy held himself stiffly, his hands curled tight around the counter edge. Finally he asked: "Did you ever really find that lady?"

"What? What say, Son?"

"I mean," the boy asked timidly. "Have you fallen in love with a woman again?"

The old man loosened his grasp on the boy's collar. He turned away and for the first time his green eyes had a vague and scattered look. He lifted the mug from the counter, drank down the yellow beer. His head was shaking slowly from side to side. Then finally he answered: "No, Son. You see that is the last step in my science. I go cautious. And I am not quite ready yet."

"Well!" said Leo. "Well well well!"

The old man stood in the open doorway. "Remember," he said. Framed there in the gray damp light of the early morning he looked shrunken and seedy and frail. But his smile was bright. "Remember I love you," he said with a last nod. And the door closed quietly behind him.

The boy did not speak for a long time. He pulled down the bangs on his forehead and slid his grimy little forefinger around the rim of his empty cup. Then without looking at Leo he finally asked:

"Was he drunk?"

"No," said Leo shortly.

The boy raised his clear voice higher. "Then was he a dope fiend?"
"No."

The boy looked up at Leo and his flat little face was desperate, his voice urgent and shrill. "Was he crazy? Do you think he was a lunatic?" The paper boy's voice dropped suddenly with doubt. "Leo? Or not?"

But Leo would not answer him. Leo had run a night café for fourteen years, and he held himself to be a critic of craziness. There were the town characters and also the transients who roamed in from the night. He knew the manias of all of them. But he did not want to satisfy the questions of the waiting child. He tightened his pale face and was silent.

So the boy pulled down the right flap of his helmet and as he turned to leave he made the only comment that seemed safe to him, the only remark that could not be laughed down and despised:

"He sure has done a lot of traveling."

QUESTIONS

"A Tree • A Rock • A Cloud"

1. Describe the setting of "A Tree • A Rock • A Cloud." How important is the setting? To the paper boy, the café seems "friendly." Is it? Does it seem to you that there is a disjunction between the setting and the ideas expressed by the old man?

2. Although there are a number of people in the café, only three of them—the boy, the old man, and the proprietor—speak. Why? What are the other characters doing? What effect do their activity and their silence have on the story's atmosphere? How do you interpret their silence?

3. What was the orange-haired man's life like before he met the woman who became his wife? How did she transform him?

4. What is the "science of love" the old man invents? Why did he feel compelled to invent it? Are there aspects of the story—details of characterization, bits of dialogue—that make it difficult for the reader to take him or his ideas seriously? Sum up your response to him and to the story he tells. It is possible to see him as a Wise Old Man figure?

5. What is the object of the old man's quest? Does he find the treasure he searches for, or only part of it? How does Leo interpret his failure to fall in love with a woman again? How do you interpret it?

6. The orange-haired man says that his wife "was something like an assembly line for my soul. I run these little pieces of myself through her and I come out complete." What effect does this metaphor have on you? Why do you think McCullers names the wife Dodo?

7. Look at the ways Leo and the old man speak. What does their manner of speaking tell us about them? In general, how is the café's proprietor contrasted with his talkative customer?

8. What is Leo's attitude toward the old man? What effect do Leo's scornful comments have on the reader's attitude toward the orange-haired man? How does Leo appear to value the old man's discovery, the "science of love"? In the exchange between Leo and the boy at the end of the story, is there any indication that Leo, too, thinks the old man has found a treasure? Explain.

9. What is the young boy's attitude toward the man with the orange hair? Does he understand what the man is talking about? Find exchanges of dialogue that support your opinion. Why would the old man choose a young boy for his audience?

10. Why does the young boy sum up the orange-haired man by saying "He sure has done a lot of traveling"? What does the boy mean? How can this line be read metaphorically as well as literally?

The Blue Jar

ISAK DINESEN

There was once an immensely rich old Englishman who had been a courtier and a councillor to the Queen and who now, in his old age, cared for nothing but collecting ancient blue china. To that end he travelled to Persia, Japan, and China, and he was everywhere accompanied by his daughter, the Lady Helena. It happened, as they sailed in the Chinese Sea, that the ship caught fire on a still night, and everybody went into the lifeboats and left her. In the dark and the confusion the old peer was separated from his daughter. Lady Helena got up on deck late, and found the ship quite deserted. In the last moment a young English sailor carried her down into a lifeboat that had been forgotten. To the two fugitives it seemed as if fire was following them from all sides, for the phosphorescence played in the dark sea, and, as they looked up, a falling star ran across the sky, as if it was going to drop into the boat. They sailed for nine days, till they were picked up by a Dutch merchantman, and came home to England.

The old lord had believed his daughter to be dead. He now wept with joy, and at once took her off to a fashionable watering-place so that she might recover from the hardships she had gone through. And as he thought it must be unpleasant to her that a young sailor, who made his bread in the merchant service, should tell the world that he had sailed for nine days alone with a peer's daughter, he paid the boy a fine sum, and made him promise to go shipping in the other hemisphere and never come back. "For what," said the old nobleman, "would be the good of that?"

When Lady Helena recovered, and they gave her the news of the Court and of her family, and in the end also told her how the young sailor had been sent away never to come back, they found that her mind had suffered from her trials, and that she cared for nothing in all the world. She would not go back to her father's castle in its park, nor go to Court, nor travel to any gay town of the continent. The only thing which she now wanted to do was to go, like her father before her, to collect rare blue china. So she began to sail, from one country to the other, and her father went with her.

In her search she told the people, with whom she dealt, that she was looking for a particular blue color, and would pay any price for it. But although she bought many hundred blue jars and bowls, she would always

after a time put them aside and say: "Alas, alas, it is not the right blue." Her father, when they had sailed for many years, suggested to her that perhaps the color which she sought did not exist. "O God, Papa," said she, "how can you speak so wickedly? Surely there must be some of it left from the time when all the world was blue."

Her two old aunts in England implored her to come back, still to make a great match. But she answered them: "Nay, I have got to sail. For you must know, dear aunts, that it is all nonsense when learned people tell you that the seas have got a bottom to them. On the contrary, the water, which is the noblest of the elements, does, of course, go all through the earth, so that our planet really floats in the ether, like a soapbubble. And there, on the other hemisphere, a ship sails, with which I have got to keep pace. We two are like the reflection of one another, in the deep sea, and the ship of which I speak is always exactly beneath my own ship, upon the opposite side of the globe. You have never seen a big fish swimming underneath a boat, following it like a dark-blue shade in the water. But in that way this ship goes, like the shadow of my ship, and I draw it to and fro wherever I go, as the moon draws the tides, all through the bulk of the earth. If I stopped sailing, what would these poor sailors who make their bread in the merchant service do? But I shall tell you a secret," she said. "In the end my ship will go down, to the center of the globe, and at the very same hour the other ship will sink as well—for people call it sinking, although I can assure you that there is no up and down in the sea—and there, in the midst of the world, we two shall meet."

Many years passed, the old lord died and Lady Helena became old and deaf, but she still sailed. Then it happened, after the plunder of the summer palace of the Emperor of China, that a merchant brought her a very old blue jar. The moment she set eyes on it she gave a terrible shriek. "There it is!" she cried. "I have found it at last. This is the true blue. Oh, how light it makes one. Oh, it is as fresh as a breeze, as deep as a deep secret, as full as I say not what." With trembling hands she held the jar to her bosom, and sat for six hours sunk in contemplation of it. Then she said to her doctor and her lady-companion: "Now I can die. And when I am dead you will cut out my heart and lay it in the blue jar. For then everything will be as it was then. All shall be blue round me, and in the midst of the blue world my heart will be innocent and free, and will beat gently, like a wake that sings, like the drops that fall from an oar blade." A little later she asked them: "Is it not a sweet thing to think that, if only you have patience, all that has ever been, will come back to you?" Shortly afterwards the old lady died.

QUESTIONS

"The Blue Jar"

1. Discuss the elements of fiction—plot, character, setting, and so on—that are stressed in Dinesen's story and those that are not. In what ways is this story like a fairy tale?

2. How has Lady Helena been changed by the episode on the lifeboat?

3. Why isn't Dinesen more specific about Lady Helena's nine days aboard the lifeboat? Do you think her experience is connected to her quest? Discuss.

4. Why does Lady Helena's father pay the young sailor who has saved his daughter's life to disappear?

5. Lady Helena is searching for old china of a particular shade of blue, and she speaks longingly of a time "when all the world was blue." What do you think she means by this?

6. What, in your opinion, is the meaning of the ship Lady Helena claims is sailing on the other side of the globe, and with which she must "keep pace"?

7. At last Lady Helena finds her treasure, a jar of the very blue she has been seeking from youth. What does it mean to her? What does it give to her?

8. This brief story is a fictional treatment of something Dinesen called "an anecdote of destiny." What do you think she meant by that, and what does the story tell us about destiny?

The Middle Drawer

HORTENSE CALISHER

The drawer was always kept locked. In a household where the tangled rubbish of existence had collected on surfaces like a scurf, which was forever being cleared away by her mother and the maid, then by her mother, and finally, hardly at all, it had been a permanent cell—rather like, Hester thought wryly, the gene that is carried over from one generation to the other. Now, holding the small, square, indelibly known key in her hand, she shrank before it, reluctant to perform the blasphemy that the living must inevitably perpetrate on the possessions of the dead. There were no revelations to be expected when she opened the drawer, only the painful reiteration of her mother's personality and the power it had held over her own, which would rise—an emanation, a mist, that she herself had long since shredded away, parted, and escaped.

She repeated to herself, like an incantation, "I am married. I have a child of my own, a home of my own five hundred miles away. I have not even lived in this house—my parents' house—for over seven years." Stepping back, she sat on the bed where her mother had died the week before, slowly, from cancer, where Hester had held the large, long-fingered, competent hand for a whole night, watching the asphyxiating action of the fluid mounting in the lungs until it had extinguished the breath. She sat facing the drawer.

It had taken her all her own lifetime to get to know its full contents, starting from the first glimpses, when she was just able to lean her chin on the side and have her hand pushed away from the packets and japanned boxes, to the last weeks, when she had made a careful show of not noticing while she got out the necessary bankbooks and safe-deposit keys. Many times during her childhood, when she had lain blandly ill herself, elevated to the honor of the parental bed while she suffered from the "autointoxication" that must have been 1918's euphemism for plain piggishness, the drawer had been opened. Then she had been allowed to play with the two pairs of pearled opera glasses or the long string of graduated white china beads, each with its oval sides flushed like cheeks. Over these she had sometimes spent the whole afternoon, pencilling two eyes and a pursed mouth on each bead, until she had achieved an incredible string of minute, doll-like heads that made even her mother laugh.

Once while Hester was in college, the drawer had been opened for the replacement of her grandmother's great sunburst pin, which she had never before seen and which had been in pawn, and doggedly reclaimed over a long period by her mother. And for Hester's wedding her mother had taken out the delicate diamond chain—the "lavaliere" of the Gibson-girl era—that had been her father's wedding gift to her mother, and the ugly, expensive bar pin that had been his gift to his wife on the birth of her son. Hester had never before seen either of them, for the fashion of wearing diamonds indiscriminately had never been her mother's, who was contemptuous of other women's display, although she might spend minutes in front of the mirror debating a choice between two relatively gimcrack pieces of costume jewelry. Hester had never known why this was until recently, when the separation of the last few years had relaxed the tension between her mother and herself—not enough to prevent explosions when they met but enough for her to see obscurely, the long motivations of her mother's life. In the European sense, family jewelry was Property, and with all her faultless English and New World poise, her mother had never exorcised her European core.

In the back of the middle drawer, there was a small square of brown-toned photograph that had never escaped into the large, ramshackle portfolio of family pictures kept in the drawer of the old break-front bookcase, open to any hand. Seated on a bench, Hedwig Licht, aged two, brows knitted under ragged hair, stared mournfully into the camera with the huge, heavy-lidded eyes that had continued to brood in her face as a woman, the eyes that she had transmitted to Hester, along with the high cheekbones that she had deplored. Fat, wrinkled stockings were bowed into arcs that almost met at the high-stretched boots, which did not touch the floor; to hold up the stockings, strips of calico matching the dumpy little dress were bound around the knees.

Long ago, Hester, in her teens, staring tenaciously into the drawer under her mother's impatient glance, had found the little square and exclaimed over it, and her mother, snatching it away from her, had muttered, "If that isn't Dutchy!" But she had looked at it long and ruefully before she had pushed it back into a corner. Hester had added the picture to the legend of her mother's childhood built up from the bitter little anecdotes that her mother had let drop casually over the years.

She saw the small Hedwig, as clearly as if it had been herself, haunting the stiff rooms of the house in the townlet of Oberelsbach, motherless since birth and almost immediately stepmothered by a woman who had been unloving, if not unkind, and had soon borne the stern, *Haustyrann* father a son. The small figure she saw had no connection with the all-powerful figure of her mother but, rather, seemed akin to the legion of lonely children who were a constant motif in the literature that had been her own drug—the Sara Crewes and Little Dorrits, all those children who inhabited the familiar terror-struck dark that crouched under the lash of the adult. She saw Hedwig receiving from her dead mother's mother—the Grandmother Rosenberg, warm and loving but, alas, too far away to be of help— the beautiful, satin-incrusted bisque doll, and she saw the bad stepmother taking it away from Hedwig and putting it in the drawing room, because "it is too beautiful for a child to play with." She saw all this as if it had happened to her and she had never forgotten.

Years later, when this woman, Hester's step-grandmother, had come to the United States in the long train of refugees from Hitler, her mother had urged the grown Hester to visit her, and she had refused, knowing her own childishness but feeling the resentment rise in her as if she were six, saying, "I won't go. She wouldn't let you have your doll." Her mother had smiled at her sadly and had shrugged her shoulders resignedly. "You wouldn't say that if you could see her. She's an old woman. She has no teeth." Looking at her mother, Hester had wondered what her feelings were after forty years, but her mother, private as always in her emotions, had given no sign.

There had been no sign for Hester—never an open demonstration of love or an appeal—until the telephone call of a few months before, when she had heard her mother say quietly, over the distance, "I think you'd better come," and she had turned away from the phone saying bitterly, almost in awe, "If she *asks me* to come, she must be dying!"

Turning the key over in her hand, Hester looked back at the composite figure of her mother—that far-off figure of the legendary child, the nearer object of her own dependence, love, and hate—looked at it from behind the safe, dry wall of her own "American" education. We are told, she thought, that people who do not experience love in their earliest years cannot open up; they cannot give it to others; but by the time we have learned this from books or dredged it out of reminiscence, they have long since left upon us their chill, irremediable stain.

If Hester searched in her memory for moments of animal maternal warmth, like those she self-consciously gave her own child (as if her own childhood prodded her from behind), she thought always of the blue-shot twilight of one New York evening, the winter she was eight, when she and her mother were returning from a shopping expedition, gay and united in the shared guilt of being late for supper. In her mind, now, their arrested figures stood like two silhouettes caught in the spotlight of time. They had paused under the brightly agitated bulbs of a movie-theatre marquee, behind them the broad, rose-red sign of a Happiness candy store. Her mother, suddenly leaning down to her, had encircled her with her arm and nuzzled her, saying almost anxiously, "We do have fun together, don't we?" Hester had stared back stolidly, almost suspiciously, into the looming, pleading eyes, but she had rested against the encircling arm, and warmth had trickled through her as from a closed wound reopening.

After this, her mother's part in the years that followed seemed blurred with the recriminations from which Hester had retreated ever farther, al-

ways seeking the remote corners of the household—the sofa-fortressed al-
coves, the store closet, the servants' bathroom—always bearing her amulet,
a book. It seemed to her now, wincing, that the barrier of her mother's
dissatisfaction with her had risen imperceptibly, like a coral cliff built inex-
orably from the slow accretion of carelessly ejaculated criticisms that had
grown into solid being in the heavy fullness of time. Meanwhile, her father's uncritical affection, his open caresses, had been steadiness under her
feet after the shifting waters of her mother's personality, but he had been
away from home on business for long periods, and when at home he, too,
was increasingly a target for her mother's deep-burning rage against life.
Adored member of a large family that was almost tribal in its affections and
unity, he could not cope with this smoldering force and never tried to
understand it, but the shield of his adulthood gave him a protection that
Hester did not have. He stood on equal ground.

Hester's parents had met at Saratoga, at the races. So dissimilar were
their backgrounds that it was improbable that they would ever have met
elsewhere than in the somewhat easy social flux of a spa, although their
brownstone homes in New York were not many blocks apart, his in the
gentility of upper Madison Avenue, hers in the solid, Germanic comfort of
Yorkville. By this time, Hedwig had been in America ten years.

All Hester knew of her mother's coming to America was that she had
arrived when she was sixteen. Now that she knew how old her mother had
been at death, knew the birth date so zealously guarded during a lifetime
of evasion and so quickly exposed by the noncommittal nakedness of funeral routine, she realized that her mother must have arrived in 1900. She
had come to the home of an aunt, a sister of her own dead mother. What
family drama had preceded her coming, whose decision it had been, Hester did not know. Her mother's one reply to a direct question had been a
shrugging "There was nothing for me there."

Hester had a vivid picture of her mother's arrival and first years in New
York, although this was drawn from only two clues. Her great-aunt, re-
marking once on Hester's looks in the dispassionate way of near relations,
had nodded over Hester's head to her mother. "She is dark, like the father,
no? Not like you were." And Hester, with a naïve glance of surprise at her
mother's sedate pompadour, had eagerly interposed, "What was she like,
Tante?"

"*Ach*, when she came off the boat, *war sie hübsch!*" Tante had said,
lapsing into German with unusual warmth, "Such a color! Pink and cream!"

"Yes, a real Bavarian *Mädchen*," said her mother with a trace of contempt. "Too pink for the fashion here. I guess they thought it wasn't real."

Another time, her mother had said, in one of her rare bursts of anecdote,
"When I came, I brought enough linen and underclothing to supply two
brides. At the convent school I was sent, the nuns didn't teach you much
besides embroidery, so I had plenty to bring, plenty. They were nice,
though. Good, simple women. Kind. I remember I brought four dozen

handkerchiefs, beautiful heavy linen that you don't get in America. But they were large, bigger than the size of a man's handkerchief over here, and the first time I unfolded one, everybody laughed, so I threw them away." She had sighed, perhaps for the linen. "And underdrawers! Long red flannel, and I had spent months embroidering them with yards of white eyelet work on the ruffles. I remember Tante's maid came in from the back yard quite angry and refused to hang them on the line any more. She said the other maids, from the houses around, teased her for belonging to a family who would wear things like that."

Until Hester was in her teens, her mother had always employed young German or Czech girls fresh from "the other side"—Teenies and Josies of long braided hair, broad cotton ankles and queer, blunt shoes, who had clacked deferentially to her mother in German and had gone off to marry their waiter's and baker's apprentices at just about the time they learned to wear silk stockings and "just as soon as you've taught them how to serve a dinner," returning regularly to show off their square, acrid babies. "Greenhorns!" her mother had always called them, a veil of something indefinable about her lips. But in the middle drawer there was a long rope of blond hair, sacrificed, like the handkerchiefs, but not wholly discarded.

There was no passport in the drawer. Perhaps it had been destroyed during the years of the first World War, when her mother, long since a citizen by virtue of marriage, had felt the contemporary pressure to excise everything Teutonic. "If that nosy Mrs. Chan asks you when I came over, just say I came over as a child," she had said to Hester. And how easy it had been to nettle her by pretending that one could discern a trace of accent in her speech! Once, when the family had teased her by affecting to hear an echo of "public" in her pronunciation of "public," Hester had come upon her, hours after, standing before a mirror, color and nose high, watching herself say, over and over again, "Public! Public!"

Was it this, thought Hester, her straining toward perfection, that made her so intolerant of me, almost as if she were castigating in her child the imperfections that were her own? "Big feet, big hands, like mine," her mother had grumbled. "Why? Why? When every woman in your father's family wears size one! But their nice, large ears—you must have *those!*" And dressing Hester for Sunday school she would withdraw a few feet to look at the finished product, saying slowly, with dreamy cruelty, "I don't know why I let you wear those white gloves. They make your hands look clumsy, just like a policeman's."

It was over books that the rift between Hester and her mother had become complete. To her mother, marrying into a family whose bookish traditions she had never ceased trying to undermine with the sneer of the practical, it was as if the stigmata of that tradition, appearing upon the girl, had forever made them alien to one another.

"Your eyes don't look like a girl's, they look like an old woman's! Reading! Forever reading!" she had stormed, chasing Hester from room to room, flushing her out of doors, and on one remote, terrible afternoon, whipping the book out of Hester's hand, she had leaned over her, glaring, and had torn the book in two.

Hester shivered now, remembering the cold sense of triumph that had welled up in her as she had faced her mother, rejoicing in the enormity of what her mother had done.

Her mother had faltered before her. "Do you want to be a dreamer all your life?" she had muttered.

Hester had been unable to think of anything to say for a moment. Then she had stuttered, "All you think of in life is money!" and had made her grand exit. But huddling miserably in her room afterward she had known even then that it was not as simple as that, that her mother, too, was whipped and driven by some ungovernable dream she could not express, which had left her, like the book, torn in two.

Was it this, perhaps, that had sent her across an ocean, that had impelled her to perfect her dress and manner, and to reject the humdrum suitors of her aunt's circle for a Virginia bachelor twenty-two years older than herself? Had she, perhaps, married him not only for his money and his seasoned male charm but also for his standards and traditions, against which her railings had been a confession of envy and defeat?

So Hester and her mother had continued to pit their implacable difference against each other in a struggle that was complicated out of all reason by their undeniable likeness—each pursuing in her own orbit the warmth that had been denied. Gauche and surly as Hester was in her mother's presence, away from it she had striven successfully for the very falsities of standard that she despised in her mother, and it was her misery that she was forever impelled to earn her mother's approval at the expense of her own. Always, she knew now, there had been the lurking, buried wish that someday she would find the final barb, the homing shaft, that would maim her mother once and for all, as she felt herself to have been maimed.

A few months before, the barb had been placed in her hand. In answer to the telephone call, she had come to visit the family a short time after her mother's sudden operation for cancer of the breast. She had found her father and brother in an anguish of helplessness, fear, and male distaste at the thought of the illness, and her mother a prima donna of fortitude, moving unbowed, toward the unspoken idea of her death but with the signs on her face of a pitiful tension that went beyond the disease. She had taken to using separate utensils and to sleeping alone, although the medical opinion that cancer was not transferable by contact was well known to her. It was clear that she was suffering from a horror of what had been done to her and from a fear of the revulsion of others. It was clear to Hester, also, that her father and brother had such a revulsion and had not been wholly successful in concealing it.

One night she and her mother had been together in her mother's bedroom. Hester, in her shabby housegown, stretched out on the bed luxuriously, thinking of how there was always a certain equivocal ease, a letting down of pretense, an illusory return to the irresponsibility of childhood, in the house of one's birth. Her mother, back turned, had been standing unnecessarily long at the bureau, fumbling with the articles upon it. She turned slowly.

"They've been giving me X-ray twice a week," she said, not looking at Hester, "to stop any involvement of the glands."

"Oh," said Hester, carefully smoothing down a wrinkle on the bedspread. "It's very wise to have that done."

Suddenly, her mother had put out her hand in a gesture almost of appeal. Half in a whisper, she asked, "Would you like to see it? No one has seen it since I left the hospital."

"Yes," Hester said, keeping her tone cool, even, full only of polite interest. "I'd like very much to see it." Frozen there on the bed, she had reverted to childhood in reality, remembering, as if they had all been crammed into one slot in time, the thousands of incidents when she had been the one to stand before her mother, vulnerable and bare, helplessly awaiting the cruel exactitude of her displeasure. "I know how she feels as if I were standing there myself," thought Hester. "How well she taught me to know."

Slowly her mother undid her housegown and bared her breast. She stood there for a long moment, on her face the looming, pleading look of twenty years before, the look it had once shown under the theatre marquee.

Hester half rose from the bed. There was a hurt in her own breast that she did not recognize. She spoke with difficulty.

"Why . . . it's a beautiful job, Mother," she said, distilling the carefully natural tone of her voice. "Neat as can be. I had no idea . . . I thought it would be ugly." With a step toward her mother, she looked, as if casually, at the dreadful neatness of the cicatrix, at the twisted, foreshortened tendon of the upper arm.

"I can't raise my arm yet," whispered her mother. "They had to cut deep . . . Your father won't look at it."

In an eternity of slowness, Hester stretched out her hand. Trembling, she touched a tentative finger to her mother's chest, where the breast had been. Then, with rising sureness, with infinite delicacy, she drew her fingertips along the length of the scar in a light, affirmative caress, and they stood eye to eye for an immeasurable second, on equal ground at last.

In the cold, darkening room, Hester unclenched herself from remembrance. She was always vulnerable, Hester thought. As we all are. What she bequeathed me unwittingly, ironically, was fortitude—the fortitude of those who have had to live under the blow. But pity—that I found for myself.

She knew now that the tangents of her mother and herself would never have fully met, even if her mother had lived. Holding her mother's hand through the long night as she retreated over the border line of narcosis and coma into death, she had felt the giddy sense of conquering, the heady euphoria of being still alive, which comes to the watcher in the night.

Nevertheless, she had known with sureness, even then, that she would go on all her life trying to "show" her mother, in an unsatisfied effort to earn her approval—and unconditional love.

As a child, she had slapped at her mother once in a frenzy of rebellion, and her mother, in reproof, had told her the tale of the peasant girl who had struck her mother and had later fallen ill and died and been buried in the village cemetery. When the mourners came to tend the mound, they found that the corpse's offending hand had grown out of the grave. They cut it off and reburied it, but when they came again in the morning, the hand had grown again. So, too, thought Hester, even though I might learn— have learned in some ways—to escape my mother's hand, all my life I will have to push it down; all my life my mother's hand will grow again out of the unquiet grave of the past.

It was her own life that was in the middle drawer. She was the person she was not only because of her mother but because, fifty-eight years before, in the little town of Oberelsbach, another woman, whose qualities she would never know, had died too soon. Death, she thought, absolves equally the bungler, the evildoer, the unloving, and the unloved—but never the living. In the end, the cicatrix that she had, in the smallest of ways, helped her mother to bear had eaten its way in and killed. The living carry, she thought, perhaps not one tangible wound but the burden of the innumerable small cicatrices imposed on us by our beginnings; we carry them with us always, and from these, from this agony, we are not absolved.

She turned the key and opened the drawer.

QUESTIONS

"The Middle Drawer"

1. What is the narrative point of view in this story? To whose consciousness do we have access?

2. What kind of relationship with her mother did Hester have as a child? Look particularly at two brief scenes: the one in which Hester and Hedwig are returning home after shopping and the one in which the two of them quarrel over books. What sort of relationship did the young Hester have with her father? How did environment help shape Hester's parents?

3. Discuss Calisher's use of both metaphorical and literal scars and wounds in her story.

4. What kind of cancer does Hedwig have? How does this particular disease begin to unite the two women? How do Hester's father and brother react to the disease?

5. Why does Hedwig want to show her daughter the surgical scar? What is Hester feeling as she looks at and touches it? What does this episode tell us about Hester's character? Why does the narrator say, after the episode, that Hester and her mother stood "on equal ground at last"? Calisher uses the same phrase to refer to Hester's father's ability to protect himself against his wife. Is the same thing meant here? How does the encounter between Hester and her mother affect our understanding of Hester's reflection that there is "a letting down of pretense, an illusory return to the irresponsibility of childhood, in the house of one's birth"?

6. Does Hester bear any permanent scars as a result of her mother's treatment of her? If so, what evidence of them do we see?

7. What has Hester been in quest of, apparently her entire life? At the end of the story, what is her response to her inability to find what she seeks?

8. What sort of thing might we expect the treasure to be, given the title of the story and the opening paragraphs? What in fact does it turn out to be?

Flying Home

RALPH ELLISON

When Todd came to, he saw two faces suspended above him in a sun so hot and blinding that he could not tell if they were black or white. He stirred, feeling a pain that burned as though his whole body had been laid open to the sun which glared into his eyes. For a moment an old fear of being touched by white hands seized him. Then the very sharpness of the pain began slowly to clear his head. Sounds came to him dimly. He done come to. Who are they? he thought. Naw he ain't, I coulda sworn he was white. Then he heard clearly:

"You hurt bad?"

Something within him uncoiled. It was a Negro sound.

"He's still out," he heard.

"Give'im time. . . . Say, son, you hurt bad?"

Was he? There was that awful pain. He lay rigid, hearing their breathing and trying to weave a meaning between them and his being stretched painfully upon the ground. He watched them warily, his mind traveling back over a painful distance. Jagged scenes, swiftly unfolding as in a movie trailer, reeled through his mind, and he saw himself piloting a tailspinning plane and landing and falling from the cockpit and trying to stand. Then, as in a great silence, he remembered the sound of crunching bone, and now, looking up into the anxious faces of an old Negro man and a boy from where he lay in the same field, the memory sickened him and he wanted to remember no more.

"How you feel, son?"

Todd hesitated, as though to answer would be to admit an inacceptable weakness. Then, "It's my ankle," he said.

"Which one?"

"The left."

With a sense of remoteness he watched the old man bend and remove his boot, feeling the pressure ease.

"That any better?"

"A lot. Thank you."

He had the sensation of discussing someone else, that his concern was with some far more important thing, which for some reason escaped him.

"You done broke it bad," the old man said. "We have to get you to a doctor."

He felt that he had been thrown into a tailspin. He looked at his watch; how long had he been here? He knew there was but one important thing in the world, to get the plane back to the field before his officers were displeased.

"Help me up," he said. "Into the ship."

"But it's broke too bad. . . ."

"Give me your arm!"

"But, son . . ."

Clutching the old man's arm he pulled himself up, keeping his left leg clear, thinking, "I'd never make him understand," as the leather-smooth face came parallel with his own.

"Now, let's see."

He pushed the old man back, hearing a bird's insistent shrill. He swayed giddily. Blackness washed over him, like infinity.

"You best sit down."

"No, I'm O.K."

"But, son. You jus' gonna make it worse. . . ."

It was a fact that everything in him cried out to deny, even against the flaming pain in his ankle. He would have to try again.

"You mess with that ankle they have to cut your foot off," he heard.

Holding his breath, he started up again. It pained so badly that he had to bite his lips to keep from crying out and he allowed them to help him down with a pang of despair.

"It's best you take it easy. We gon' git you a doctor."

Of all the luck, he thought. Of all the rotten luck, now I have done it. The fumes of high-octane gasoline clung in the heat, taunting him.

"We kin ride him into town on old Ned," the boy said.

Ned? He turned, seeing the boy point toward an ox team browsing where the buried blade of a plow marked the end of a furrow. Thoughts of himself riding an ox through the town, past streets full of white faces, down the concrete runways of the airfield made swift images of humiliation in his mind. With a pang he remembered his girl's last letter. "Todd," she had written, "I don't need the papers to tell me you had the intelligence to fly. And I have always known you to be as brave as anyone else. The papers annoy me. Don't you be contented to prove over and over again that you're brave or skillful just because you're black, Todd. I think they keep beating that dead horse because they don't want to say why you boys are not yet fighting. I'm really disappointed, Todd. Anyone with brains can learn to fly, but then what? What about using it, and who will you use it for? I wish, dear, you'd write about this. I sometimes think they're playing a trick on us. It's very humiliating. . . ." He wiped cold sweat from his face, thinking, What does she know of humiliation? She's never been down South. Now the humiliation would come. When you must have them judge you, knowing that they never accept your mistakes as your own, but hold it against your whole race—that was humiliation. Yes, and humiliation was when you could never be simply yourself, when you were always a part of this old black ignorant man. Sure, he's all right. Nice and kind and helpful. But he's not you. Well, there's one humiliation I can spare myself.

"No," he said, "I have orders not to leave the ship. . . ."

"Aw," the old man said. Then turning to the boy, "Teddy, then you better hustle down to Mister Graves and get him to come. . . ."

"No, wait!" he protested before he was fully aware. Graves might be white. "Just have him get word to the field, please. They'll take care of the rest."

He saw the boy leave, running.

"How far does he have to go?"

"Might' nigh a mile."

He rested back, looking at the dusty face of his watch. But now they know something has happened, he thought. In the ship there was a perfectly good radio, but it was useless. The old fellow would never operate it. That buzzard knocked me back a hundred years, he thought. Irony danced within him like the gnats circling the old man's head. With all I've learned I'm dependent upon this "peasant's" sense of time and space. His leg throbbed. In the plane, instead of time being measured by the rhythms of pain and a kid's legs, the instruments would have told him at a glance. Twisting upon his elbows he saw where dust had powdered the plane's fuselage, feeling the lump form in his throat that was always there when he thought of flight. It's crouched there, he thought, like the abandoned shell of a locust. I'm naked without it. Not a machine, a suit of clothes you wear. And with a sudden embarrassment and wonder he whispered, "It's the only dignity I have. . . ."

He saw the old man watching, his torn overalls clinging limply to him in the heat. He felt a sharp need to tell the old man what he felt. But that would be meaningless. If I tried to explain why I need to fly back, he'd think I was simply afraid of white officers. But it's more than fear . . . a sense of anguish clung to him like the veil of sweat that hugged his face. He watched the old man, hearing him humming snatches of a tune as he admired the plane. He felt a furtive sense of resentment. Such old men often came to the field to watch the pilots with childish eyes. At first it had made him proud; they had been a meaningful part of a new experience. But soon he realized they did not understand his accomplishments and they came to shame and embarrass him, like the distasteful praise of an idiot. A part of the meaning of flying had gone then, and he had not been able to regain it. If I were a prizefighter I would be more human, he thought. Not a monkey doing tricks, but a man. They were pleased simply that he was a Negro who could fly, and that was not enough. He felt cut off from them by age, by understanding, by sensibility, by technology and by his need to measure himself against the mirror of other men's appreciation. Somehow he felt betrayed, as he had when as a child he grew to discover that his father was dead. Now for him any real appreciation lay with his white officers; and with them he could never be sure. Between ignorant black men and condescending whites, his course of flight seemed mapped by the nature of things away from all needed and natural landmarks. Under some sealed orders, couched in ever more technical and mysterious terms, his path curved swiftly away from both the shame the old man symbolized and the cloudy terrain of white men's regard. Flying blind, he knew but one point of landing and there he would receive his wings. After that the enemy would appreciate his skill and he would assume his deepest meaning, he thought sadly, neither from those who condescended nor from those who praised without understanding, but from the enemy who would recognize his manhood and skill in terms of hate.

He sighed, seeing the oxen making queer, prehistoric shadows against the dry brown earth.

"You just take it easy, son," the old man soothed. "That boy won't take long. Crazy as he is about airplanes."

"I can wait," he said.

"What kinda airplane you call this here'n?"

"An Advanced Trainer," he said, seeing the old man smile. His fingers were like gnarled dark wood against the metal as he touched the low-slung wing.

"Bout how fast can she fly?"

"Over two hundred an hour."

"Lawd! That's so fast I bet it don't seem like you moving!"

Holding himself rigid, Todd opened his flying suit. The shade had gone and he lay in a ball of fire.

You mind if I take a look inside? I was always curious to see. . . ."

"Help yourself. Just don't touch anything."

He heard him climb upon the metal wing, grunting. Now the questions would start, Well, so you don't have to think to answer. . . .

He saw the old man looking over into the cockpit, his eyes bright as a child's.

"You must have to know a lot to work all these here things."

He was silent, seeing him step down and kneel beside him.

"Son, how come you want to fly way up there in the air?"

Because it's the most meaningful act in the world . . . because it makes me less like you, he thought.

But he said: "Because I like it, I guess. It's as good a way to fight and die as I know."

"Yeah? I guess you right," the old man said. "But how long you think before they gonna let you all fight?"

He tensed. This was the question all Negroes asked, put with the same timid hopefulness and longing that always opened a greater void within him than that he had felt beneath the plane the first time he had flown. He felt light-headed. It came to him suddenly that there was something sinister about the conversation, that he was flying unwillingly into unsafe and uncharted regions. If he could only be insulting and tell this old man who was trying to help him to shut up!

"I bet you one thing. . . ."

"Yes?"

"That you was plenty scared coming down."

He did not answer. Like a dog on a trail the old man seemed to smell out his fears, and he felt anger bubble within him.

"You sho' scared me. When I seen you coming down in that thing with it a-rolling' and a-jumpin' like a pitchin' hoss, I thought sho' you was a goner. I almost had me a stroke!"

He saw the old man grinning, "Ever'thin's been happening round here this morning, come to think of it."

"Like what?" he asked.

"Well, first thing I know, here come two white fellers looking for Mister Rudolph, that's Mister Graves's cousin. That got me worked up right away. . . ."

"Why?"

"Why? 'Cause he done broke outta the crazy house, that's why. He liable to kill somebody," he said. "They oughta have him by now though. Then here you come. First I think it's one of them white boys. Then doggone if you don't fall outta there. Lawd, I'd done heard about you boys but I haven't never seen one o' you-all. Cain't tell you how it felt to see somebody what look like me in a airplane!"

The old man talked on, the sound streaming around Todd's thoughts like air flowing over the fuselage of a flying plane. You were a fool, he thought, remembering how before the spin the sun had blazed bright against the billboard signs beyond the town, and how a boy's blue kite had bloomed beneath him, tugging gently in the wind like a strange, odd-shaped flower. He had once flown such kites himself and tried to find the boy at the end of the invisible cord. But he had been flying too high and too fast. He had climbed steeply away in exultation. Too steeply, he thought. And one of the first rules you learn is that if the angle of thrust is too steep the plane goes into a spin. And then, instead of pulling out of it and going into a dive you let a buzzard panic you. A lousy buzzard!

"Son, what made all that blood on the glass?"

"A buzzard," he said, remembering how the blood and feathers had sprayed back against the hatch. It had been as though he had flown into a storm of blood and blackness.

"Well, I declare! They's lots of 'em around here. They after dead things. Don't eat nothing what's alive."

"A little bit more and he would have made a meal out of me," Todd said grimly.

"They bad luck all right. Teddy's got a name for 'em, calls 'em jim-crows," the old man laughed.

"It's a damned good name."

"They the damnedest birds. Once I seen a hoss all stretched out like he was sick, you know. So I hollers, 'Gid up from there, suh!' Just to make sho! An' doggone, son, if I don't see two ole jimcrows come flying right up outa that hoss's insides! Yessuh! The sun was shinin' on 'em and they couldn't a been no greasier if they'd been eating barbecue."

Todd thought he would vomit, his stomach quivered.

"You made that up," he said.

"Nawsuh! Saw him just like I see you."

"Well, I'm glad it was you."

"You see lots a funny things down here, son."

"No, I'll let you see them," he said.

"By the way, the white folks round here don't like to see you boys up there in the sky. They ever bother you?"

"No."

"Well, they'd like to."

"Someone always wants to bother someone else," Todd said. "How do you know?"

"I just know."

"Well," he said defensively, "no one has bothered us."

Blood pounded in his ears as he looked away into space. He tensed, seeing a black spot in the sky, and strained to confirm what he could not clearly see.

"What does that look like to you?" he asked excitedly.

"Just another bad luck, son."

Then he saw the movement of wings with disappointment. It was gliding smoothly down, wings outspread, tail feathers gripping the air, down swiftly— gone behind the green screen of trees. It was like a bird he had imagined there, only the sloping branches of the pines remained, sharp against the pale stretch of sky. He lay barely breathing and stared at the point where it had disappeared, caught in a spell of loathing and admiration. Why did they make them so disgusting and yet teach them to fly so well? It's like when I was up in heaven, he heard, starting.

The old man was chuckling, rubbing his stubbled chin.

"What did you say?"

"Sho', I died and went to heaven . . . maybe by time I tell you about it they be done come after you."

"I hope so," he said wearily.

"You boys ever sit around and swap lies?"

"Not often. Is this going to be one?"

"Well, I ain't so sho', on account of it took place when I was dead."

The old man paused, "That wasn't no lie 'bout the buzzards, though."

"All right," he said.

"Sho' you want to hear 'bout heaven?"

"Please," he answered, resting his head upon his arm.

"Well, I went to heaven and right away started to sproutin' me some wings. Six good ones, they was, Just like them the white angels had. I couldn't hardly believe it. I was so glad that I went off on some clouds by myself and tried 'em out. You know, 'cause I didn't want to make a fool outta myself the first thing. . . ."

It's an old tale, Todd thought. Told me years ago. Had forgotten. But at least it will keep him from talking about buzzards.

He closed his eyes, listening.

". . . First thing I done was to git up on a low cloud and jump off. And doggone, boy, if them wings didn't work! First I tried the right; then I tried the left; then I tried 'em both together. Then Lawd, I started to move on out among the folks. I let 'em see me. . . ."

He saw the old man gesturing flight with his arms, his face full of mock pride as he indicated an imaginary crowd, thinking, It'll be in the newspapers, as he heard, ". . . so I went and found me some colored angels— somehow I didn't believe I was an angel till I seen a real black one, ha, yes! Then I was sho'—but they tole me I better come down 'cause us colored folks had to wear a special kin' a harness when we flew. That was how come they wasn't flyin'. Oh yes, an' you had to be extra strong for a black man even, to fly with one of them harnesses. . . ."

This is a new turn, Todd thought, what's he driving at?

"So I said to myself, I ain't gonna be bothered with no harness! Oh naw! 'Cause if God let you sprout wings you oughta have sense enough not to let nobody make you wear something what gits in the way of flyin'. So I starts to flyin'. Heck, son," he chuckled, his eyes twinkling, "you know I had to let eve'ybody know that old Jefferson could fly good as anybody else. And I could too, fly smooth as a bird! I could even loop-the-loop—only I had to make sho' to keep my long white robe down roun' my ankles. . . ."

Todd felt uneasy. He wanted to laugh at the joke, but his body refused, as of an independent will. He felt as he had as a child when after he had chewed a sugar-coated pill which his mother had given him, she had laughed at his efforts to remove the terrible taste.

". . . Well," he heard, "I was doing all right 'til I got to speeding. Found out I could fan up a right strong breeze, I could fly so fast. I could do all kin'sa stunts too. I started flying up to the stars and divin' down and zooming roun' the moon. Man, I like to scare the devil outa some ole white angels. I was raisin' hell. Not that I meant any harm, son. But I was just feeling good. It was so good to know I was free at last. I accidentally knocked the tips offa some stars and they tell me I caused a storm and a couple lynchings down here in Macon County—though I swear I believe them boys what said that was making up lies on me. . . ."

He's mocking me, Todd thought angrily. He thinks it's a joke. Grinning down at me. . . . His throat was dry. He looked at his watch; why the hell didn't they come? Since they had to, why? One day I was flying down one of them heavenly streets. You got yourself into it, Todd thought. Like Jonah in the whale.

"Justa throwin' feathers in everybody's face. An' ole Saint Peter called me in. Said, 'Jefferson, tell me two things, what you doin' flyin' without a

harness; an' how come you flyin' so fast?' So I tole him I was flyin' without
a harness 'cause it got in my way, but I couldn'ta been flyin' so fast, 'cause
I wasn't usin' but one wing. Saint Peter said, 'You wasn't flyin' with but
one wing?' 'Yessuh,' I says, scared-like. So he says, 'Well, since you got
sucha extra fine pair of wings you can leave off yo' harness awhile. But
from now on one of that there one-wing flyin', 'cause you gittin' up too
damn much speed!' "

And with one mouth full of bad teeth you're making too damned much
talk, thought Todd. Why don't I send him after the boy? His body ached
from the hard ground and seeking to shift his position he twisted his ankle
and hated himself for crying out.

"It gittin' worse?"

"I. . . . I twisted it," he groaned.

"Try not to think about it, son. That's what I do."

He bit his lip, fighting pain with counter-pain as the voice resumed its
rhythmical droning. Jefferson seemed caught in his own creation.

". . . After all that trouble I just floated roun' heaven in slow motion.
But I forgot, like colored folks will do, and got to flyin' with one wing
again. This time I was restin' my old broken arm and got to flyin' fast
enough to shame the devil. I was comin' so fast, Lawd, I got myself called
befo' ole Saint Peter again. He said, 'Jeff, didn't I warn you 'bout that
speedin'?' 'Yessuh,' I says, 'but it was an accident.' He looked at me sadlike
and shook his head and I knowed I was gone. He said, 'Jeff, you and that
speedin' is a danger to the heavenly community. If I was to let you keep
in flyin', heaven wouldn't be nothin' but uproar. Jeff, you got to go!' Son,
I argued and pleaded with that old white man, but it didn't do a bit of
good. They rushed me straight to them pearly gates and gimme a parachute and a map of the state of Alabama. . . .' "

Todd heard him laughing so that he could hardly speak, making a screen
between them upon which his humiliation glowed like fire.

"Maybe you'd better stop awhile," he said, his voice unreal.

"Ain't much more," Jefferson laughed. "When they gimme the parachute
ole Saint Peter ask me if I wanted to say a few words before I went. I felt
so bad I couldn't hardly look at him, specially with all them white angels
standin' around. Then somebody laughed and made me mad. So I tole him,
'Well, you done took my wings. And you puttin' me out. You got charge
of things so's I can't do nothin' about it. But you got to admit just this:
While I was up here I was the flyinest sonofabitch what ever hit heaven!' "

At the burst of laughter Todd felt such an intense humiliation that only
great violence would wash it away. The laughter which shook the old man
like a boiling purge set up vibrations of guilt within him which not even
the intricate machinery of the plane would have been adequate to transform and he heard himself screaming, "Why do you laugh at me this way?"

He hated himself at that moment, but he had lost control. He saw Jefferson's mouth fall open, "What—?"

"Answer me!"

His blood pounded as though it would surely burst his temples and he tried to reach the old man and fell, screaming, "Can I help it because they won't let us actually fly? Maybe we are a bunch of buzzards feeding on a dead horse, but we can hope to be eagles, can't we? Can't we?"

He fell back, exhausted, his ankle pounding. The saliva was like straw in his mouth. If he had the strength he would strangle this old man. This grinning, gray-headed clown who made him feel as he felt when watched by the white officers at the field. And yet this old man had neither power, prestige, rank nor technique. Nothing that could rid him of this terrible feeling. He watched him, seeing his face struggle to express a turmoil of feeling.

"What you mean, son? What you talking 'bout . . . ?"

"Go away. Go tell your tales to the white folks."

"But I didn't mean nothing like that . . . I . . . I wasn't tryin' to hurt your feelings. . . ."

"Please. Get the hell away from me!"

"But I didn't, son. I didn't mean all them things a-tall."

Todd shook as with a chill, searching Jefferson's face for a trace of the mockery he had seen there. But now the face was somber and tired and old. He was confused. He could not be sure that there had ever been laughter there, that Jefferson had ever really laughed in his whole life. He saw Jefferson reach out to touch him and shrank away, wondering if anything except the pain, now causing his vision to waver, was real. Perhaps he had imagined it all.

"Don't let it get you down, son," the voice said pensively.

He heard Jefferson sigh wearily, as though he felt more than he could say. His anger ebbed, leaving only the pain.

"I'm sorry," he mumbled.

"You just wore out with pain, was all. . . ."

He saw him through a blur, smiling. And for a second he felt the embarrassed silence of understanding flutter between them.

"What you was doin' flyin' over this section, son? Wasn't you scared they might shoot you for a cow?"

Todd tensed. Was he being laughed at again? But before he could decide, the pain shook him and a part of him was lying calmly behind the screen of pain that had fallen between them, recalling the first time he had ever seen a plane. It was as though an endless series of hangars had been shaken ajar in the air base of his memory and from each, like a young wasp emerging from its cell, arose the memory of a plane.

The first time I ever saw a plane I was very small and planes were new in the world. I was four-and-a-half and the only plane that I had ever seen was a model suspended from the ceiling of the automobile exhibit at the State Fair. But I did not know that it was only a model. I did not know how large a real plane was, nor how expensive. To me it was a fascinating toy, complete in itself, which my mother said could only be owned by rich little white boys. I stood rigid with admiration, my head straining backwards as I watched the gray little plane describing arcs above the gleaming tops of the automobiles. And I vowed that, rich or poor, someday I would own such a toy. My mother had to drag me out of the exhibit and not even the merry-go-round, the Ferris wheel, or the racing horses could hold my attention for the rest of the Fair. I was too busy imitating the tiny drone of the plane with my lips, and imitating with my hands the motion, swift and circling, that it made in flight.

After that I no longer used the pieces of lumber that lay about our back yard to construct wagons and autos . . . now it was used for airplanes. I built biplanes, using pieces of board for wings, a small box for the fuselage, another piece of wood for the rudder. The trip to the Fair had brought something new into my small world. I asked my mother repeatedly when the Fair would come back again. I'd lie in the grass and watch the sky, and each fighting bird became a soaring plane. I would have been good a year just to have seen a plane again. I became a nuisance to everyone with my questions about airplanes. But planes were new to the old folks, too, and there was little that they could tell me. Only my uncle knew some of the answers. And better still, he could carve propellers from pieces of wood that would whirl rapidly in the wind, wobbling noisily upon oiled nails.

I wanted a plane more than I'd wanted anything; more than I wanted the red wagon with rubber tires, more than the train that ran on a track with its train of cars. I asked my mother over and over again:

"Mamma?"

"What do you want, boy?" she'd say.

"Mamma, will you get mad if I ask you?" I'd say.

"What do you want now? I ain't got time to be answering a lot of fool questions. What you want?"

"Mamma, when you gonna get me one. . . ?" I'd ask.

"Get you one what?" she'd say.

"You know, Mamma; what I been asking you. . . ."

"Boy," she'd say, "if you don't want a spanking you better come on an' tell me what you talking about so I can get on with my work."

"Aw, Mamma, you know. . . ."

"What I just tell you?" she'd say.

"I mean when you gonna buy me a airplane."

"AIRPLANE! Boy, is you crazy? How many times I have to tell you to stop that foolishness. I done told you them things cost too much. I bet I'm gon' wham the living daylight out of you if you don't quit worrying me 'bout them things!!"

But this did not stop me, and a few days later I'd try all over again.

Then one day a strange thing happened. It was spring and for some reason I had been hot and irritable all morning. It was a beautiful spring. I could feel it as I played barefoot in the backyard. Blossoms hung from the thorny black locust trees like clusters of fragrant white grapes. Butterflies flickered in the sunlight above the short new dew-wet grass. I had gone in the house for bread and butter and coming out I heard a steady unfamiliar drone. It was unlike anything I had ever heard before. I tried to place the sound. It was no use. It was a sensation like that I had when searching for my father's watch, heard ticking unseen in a room. It made me feel as though I had forgotten to perform some task that my mother had ordered. . . . then I located it, overhead. In the sky, flying quite low and about a hundred yards off was a plane! It came so slowly that it seemed barely to move. My mouth hung wide; my bread and butter fell into the dirt. I wanted to jump up and down and cheer. And when the idea struck I trembled with excitement: "Some little white boy's plane's done flew away and all I got to do is stretch out my hands and it'll be mine!" It was a little plane like that at the Fair, flying no higher than the eaves of our roof. Seeing it come steadily forward I felt the world grow warm with promise. I opened the screen and climbed over it and clung there, waiting. I would catch the plane as it came over and swing down fast and run into the house before anyone could see me. Then no one could come to claim the plane. It droned nearer. Then when it hung like a silver cross in the blue directly above me I stretched out my hand and grabbed. It was like sticking my finger through a soap bubble. The plane flew on, as though I had simply blown my breath after it. I grabbed again, frantically, trying to catch the tail. My fingers clutched the air and disappointment surged tight and hard in my throat. Giving one last desperate grasp, I strained forward. My fingers ripped from the screen. I was falling. The ground burst hard against me. I drummed the earth with my heels and when my breath returned, I lay there bawling.

My mother rushed through the door.

"What's the matter, chile! What on earth is wrong with you?"

"It's gone! It's gone!"

"What gone?"

"The airplane. . . ."

"Airplane?"

"Yessum, jus' like the one at the Fair. . . . I . . . I tried to stop it an' it kep' right on going. . . ."

"When, boy?"

"Just now," I cried, through my tears.

"Where it go, boy, what way?"

"Yonder, there . . ."

She scanned the sky, her arms akimbo and her checkered apron flapping in the wind as I pointed to the fading plane. Finally she looked down at me, slowly shaking her head.

"It's gone! It's gone!" I cried.

"Boy, is you a fool?" she said. "Don't you see that there's a real airplane 'stead of one of them toy ones?"

"Real . . . ?" I forgot to cry. "Real?"

"Yass, real. Don't you know that thing you reaching for is bigger'n a auto? You here trying to reach for it and I bet it's flying 'bout two hundred miles higher'n this roof." She was disgusted with me. "You come on in this house before somebody else sees what a fool you done turned out to be. You must think these here lil ole arms of you'n is mighty long. . . ."

I was carried into the house and undressed for bed and the doctor was called. I cried bitterly, as much from the disappointment of finding the plane so far beyond my reach as from the pain.

When the doctor came I heard my mother telling him about the plane and asking if anything was wrong with my mind. He explained that I had had a fever for several hours. But I was kept in bed for a week and I constantly saw the plane in my sleep, flying just beyond my fingertips, sailing so slowly that it seemed barely to move. And each time I'd reach out to grab it I'd miss and through each dream I'd hear my grandma warning:

> Young man, young man,
> Yo' arms too short
> To box with God. . . .

"Hey, son!"

At first he did not know where he was and looked at the old man pointing, with blurred eyes.

"Ain't that one of you-all's airplanes coming after you?"

As his vision cleared he saw a small black shape above a distant field, soaring through waves of heat. But he could not be sure and with the pain he feared that somehow a horrible recurring fantasy of being split in twain by the whirling blades of a propeller had come true.

"You think he sees us?" he heard.

"See? I hope so."

"He's coming like a bat outa hell!"

Straining, he heard the faint sound of a motor and hoped it would soon be over.

"How you feeling?"

"Like a nightmare," he said.

"Hey, he's done curved back the other way!"

"Maybe he saw us," he said. "Maybe he's gone to send out the ambulance and ground crew." And, he thought with despair, maybe he didn't even see us.

"Where did you sent the boy?"

"Down to Mister Graves," Jefferson said. "Man what owns this land."

"Do you think he phoned?"

Jefferson looked at him quickly.

"Aw sho'. Dabney Graves is got a bad name on accounta them killings but he'll call though. . . ."

"What killings?"

"Them five fellers . \ . ain't you heard?" he asked with surprise.

"No."

"Everybody knows 'bout Dabney Graves, especially the colored. He done killed enough of us."

Todd had the sensation of being caught in a white neighborhood after dark.

"What did they do?" he asked.

"Thought they was men," Jefferson said. "An' some he owed money, like he do me. . . ."

"But why do you stay here?"

"You black, son."

"I know, but . . ."

"You have to come by the white folks, too."

He turned away from Jefferson's eyes, at once consoled and accused. And I'll have to come by them soon, he thought with despair. Closing his eyes, he heard Jefferson's voice as the sun burned blood-red upon his lips.

"I got nowhere to go," Jefferson said, "an' they'd come after me if I did. But Dabney Graves is a funny fellow. He's all the time making jokes. He can be mean as hell, then he's liable to turn right around and back the colored against the white folks. I seen him do it. But me, I hates him for that more'n anything else. 'Cause just as soon as he gits tired helping a man he don't care what happens to him. He just leaves him stone cold. And then the other white folks is double hard on anybody he done helped. For him it's just a joke. He don't give a hilla beans for nobody—but his-self. . . ."

Todd listened to the thread of detachment in the old man's voice. It was as though he held his words arm's length before him to avoid their destructive meaning.

"He'd just as soon do you a favor and then turn right around and have you strung up. Me, I stays outa his way 'cause down here that's what you gotta do."

If my ankle would only ease for a while, he thought. The closer I spin toward the earth the blacker I become, flashed through his mind. Sweat ran into his eyes and he was sure that he would never see the plane if his head continued whirling. He tried to see Jefferson, what it was that Jefferson held in his hand? It was a little black man, another Jefferson!! A little black Jefferson that shook with fits of belly-laughter while the other Jefferson looked on with detachment. Then Jefferson looked up from the thing in his hand and turned to speak, but Todd was far away, searching the sky for a plane in a hot dry land on a day and age he had long forgotten. He was going mysteriously with his mother through empty streets where black faces peered from behind drawn shades and someone was rapping at a window and he was looking back to see a hand and a frightened face frantically beckoning from a cracked door and his mother was looking down the empty perspective of the street and shaking her head and hurrying him along and at first it was only a flash he saw and a motor was droning as through the sun-glare he saw it gleaming silver as it circled and he was seeing a burst like a puff of white smoke and hearing his mother yell, Come along, boy, I got no time for them fool airplanes, I got no time, and he saw it a second time, the plane flying high, and the burst appeared suddenly and fell slowly, billowing out and sparkling like fireworks and he was watching and being hurried along as the air filled with a flurry of white pinwheeling cards that caught in the wind and scattered over the rooftops and into the gutters and a woman was running and snatching a card and reading it and screaming and he darted into the shower, grabbing as in winter he grabbed for snowflakes and bounding away at his mother's, Come on here, boy! Come on, I say! and he was watching as she took the card away, seeing her face grow puzzled and turning taut as her voice quavered, "Niggers Stay From the Polls," and died to a moan of terror as he saw the eyeless sockets of a white hood staring at him from the card and above he saw the plane spiraling gracefully, agleam in the sun like a fiery sword. And seeing it soar he was caught, transfixed between a terrible horror and a horrible fascination.

The sun was not so high now, and Jefferson was calling and gradually he saw three figures moving across the curving roll of the field.

"Look like some doctors, all dressed in white," said Jefferson.

They're coming at last, Todd thought. And he felt such a release of tension within him that he thought he would faint. But no sooner did he close his eyes than he was seized and he was struggling with three white men who were forcing his arms into some kind of coat. It was too much for him, his arms were pinned to his sides and as the pain blazed in his eyes, he realized that it was a straitjacket. What filthy joke was this?

"That oughta hold him, Mister Graves," he heard.

His total energies seemed focused in his eyes as he searched their faces. That was Graves; the other two wore hospital uniforms. He was poised between two poles of fear and hate as he heard the one called Graves saying, "He looks kinda purty in that there suit, boys. I'm glad you dropped by."

"This boy ain't crazy, Mister Graves," one of the others said. "He needs a doctor, not us. Don't see how you led us way out here anyway. It might be a joke to you, but your cousin Rudolph liable to kill somebody. White folks or niggers, don't make no difference. . . ."

Todd saw the man turn red with anger. Graves looked down upon him, chuckling.

"This nigguh belongs in a straitjacket, too, boys. I knowed that the minit Jeff's kid said something 'bout a nigguh flyer. You all know you cain't let the nigguh git up that high without his going crazy. The nigguh brain ain't built right for high altitudes. . . ."

Todd watched the drawling red face, feeling that all the unnamed horror and obscenities that he had ever imagined stood materialized before him.

"Let's git outta here," one of the attendants said.

Todd saw the other reach toward him, realizing for the first time that he lay upon a stretcher as he yelled.

"Don't put your hands on me!"

They drew back, surprised.

"What's that you say, nigguh?" asked Graves.

He did not answer and thought that Graves's foot was aimed at his head. It landed on his chest and he could hardly breathe. He coughed helplessly, seeing Graves's lips stretch taut over his yellow teeth, and tried to shift his head. It was as though a half-dead fly was dragging slowly across his face and a bomb seemed to burst within him. Blasts of hot, hysterical laughter tore from his chest, causing his eyes to pop and he felt that the veins in his neck would surely burst. And then a part of him stood behind it all, watching the surprise in Graves's red face and his own hysteria. He thought he would never stop, he would laugh himself to death. It rang in his ears like Jefferson's laughter and he looked for him, centering his eyes desperately upon his face, as though somehow he had become his sole salvation in an insane world of outrage and humiliation. It brought a certain relief. He was suddenly aware that although his body was still contorted it was an echo that no longer rang in his ears. He heard Jefferson's voice with gratitude.

"Mister Graves, the Army done tole him not to leave his airplane."

"Nigguh, Army or no, you gittin' off my land! That airplane can stay 'cause it was paid for by taxpayers' money. But you gittin' off. An' dead or alive, it don't make no difference to me."

Todd was beyond it now, lost in a world of anguish.

"Jeff," Graves said, "you and Teddy come and grab holt. I want you to take this here black eagle over to that nigguh airfield and leave him."

Jefferson and the boy approached him silently. He looked away, realizing and doubting at once that only they could release him from his overpowering sense of isolation.

They bent for the stretcher. One of the attendants moved toward Teddy.

"Think you can manage it, boy?"

"I think I can, suh," Teddy said.

"Well, you better go behind then, and let yo' pa go ahead so's to keep that leg elevated."

He saw the white men walking ahead as Jefferson and the boy carried him along in silence. Then they were pausing and he felt a hand wiping his face; then he was moving again. And it was as though he had been lifted out of his isolation, back into the world of men. A new current of communication flowed between the man and boy and himself. They moved him gently. Far away he heard a mockingbird liquidly calling. He raised his eyes, seeing a buzzard poised unmoving in space. For a moment the whole afternoon seemed suspended and he waited for the horror to seize him again. Then like a song within his head he heard the boy's soft humming and saw the dark bird glide into the sun and glow like a bird of flaming gold.

QUESTIONS

"Flying Home"

1. Why is Ellison's story called "Flying Home"?
2. From what point of view is this story told?
3. In what way or ways is Ellison's protagonist "flying blind"?
4. Images of flight and arrested flight are found throughout this story. Locate them and discuss their symbolic significance.
5. Describe Ellison's protagonist, Todd. What do airplanes and flying mean to him? Because Todd is a pilot, can he be said to have gained the treasure he sought? We are told that Todd has a "recurring fantasy" of being split apart by a plane's propeller. In what sense is his fantasy a symbol of his condition?
6. Discuss Todd's attitude toward Jefferson throughout most of "Flying Home." What does the old man symbolize to the young pilot?
7. Look at the long story Jefferson tells about being an angel. What truths does this "tall tale" seem to express to the old man? In what sense is it a parable? Discuss Todd's misinterpretation of those parts of the story that especially disturb him.
8. How does the young Todd's family regard his love of planes and desire to fly? Does their attitude differ from Jefferson's? What does his grandmother's admonition "Young man, young man,/ Yo' arms too short/ To box with God. . . ." suggest? How is her warning related to Jefferson's tall tale?
9. What significance is there in the fact that the Ku Klux Klan's cards are dropped from an airplane?
10. What role do the buzzards play in this story? When Todd hits the buzzard in mid-air, we are told that he has "flown into a storm of blood and blackness." Discuss this metaphor.
11. Why does Todd laugh uncontrollably when Graves kicks him in the chest? How is his deatchment at the point related to his earlier hallucination of Jefferson's holding a miniature replica of himself in his hand? What kind of laughter do Todd and Jefferson share? What gift does Graves's kick ironically bring the downed pilot? How different is this treasure from the one Todd had imagined flying would lead to?
12. Intermittently throughout "Flying Home," the protagonist feels both horror

and dread. How do the objects giving rise to these emotions change over the course of the story? How does the conclusion illustrate Todd's reflection "the closer I spin toward the earth, the blacker I become"? Todd's quest transforms him in a way he never expected and certainly never sought. What is the tone of Ellison's conclusion? What does it suggest about Todd's attitude toward his transformation?

The Oranging of America

MAX APPLE

I

From the outside it looked like any ordinary 1964 Cadillac limousine. In the expensive space between the driver and passengers, where some installed bars or even bathrooms, Mr. Howard Johnson kept a tidy ice-cream freezer in which there were always at least eighteen flavors on hand, though Mr. Johnson ate only vanilla. The freezer's power came from the battery with an independent auxiliary generator as a back-up system. Although now Howard Johnson means primarily motels, Millie, Mr. HJ, and Otis Brighton, the chauffeur, had not forgotten that ice cream was the cornerstone of their empire. Some of the important tasting was still done in the car. Mr. HJ might have reports in his pocket from sales executives and marketing analysts, from home economists and chemists, but not until Mr. Johnson reached over the lowered Plexiglas to spoon a taste or two into the expert waiting mouth of Otis Brighton did he make any final flavor decision. He might go ahead with butterfly shrimp, with candy kisses, and with packaged chocolate-chip cookies on the opinion of the specialists, but in ice cream he trusted only Otis. From the back seat Howard Johnson would keep his eye on the rearview mirror, where the reflection of pleasure or disgust showed itself in the dark eyes of Otis Brighton no matter what the driving conditions. He could be stalled in a commuter rush with the engine overheating and a dripping oil pan, and still a taste of the right kind never went unappreciated.

When Otis finally said, "Mr. Howard, that shore is sumpin, that one is um-hum. That is it, my man, that is it." Then and not until then did Mr. HJ finally decide to go ahead with something like banana-fudge-ripple royale.

Mildred rarely tasted and Mr. HJ was addicted to one scoop of vanilla every afternoon at three, eaten from his aluminum dish with a disposable plastic spoon. The duties of Otis, Millie, and Mr. Johnson were so divided that they rarely infringed upon one another in the car, which was their office. Neither Mr. HJ nor Millie knew how to drive, Millie and Otis understood little of financing and leasing, and Mr. HJ left the compiling of

473

the "Traveling Reports" and "The Howard Johnson Newsletter" strictly to the literary style of his longtime associate, Miss Mildred Bryce. It was an ideal division of labor, which, in one form or another, had been in continuous operation for well over a quarter of a century.

While Otis listened to the radio behind his soundproof Plexiglas, while Millie in her small, neat hand compiled data for the newsletter, Mr. HJ liked to lean back into the spongy leather seat looking through his specially tinted windshield at the fleeting land. Occasionally, lulled by the hum of the freezer, he might doze off, his large pink head lolling toward the shoulder of his blue suit, but there was not too much that Mr. Johnson missed, even in advanced age.

Along with Millie he planned their continuous itinerary as they traveled. Mildred would tape a large green relief map of the United States to the Plexiglas separating them from Otis. The mountains on the map were light brown and seemed to melt toward the valleys like the crust of a fresh apple pie settling into cinnamon surroundings. The existing HJ houses (Millie called the restaurants and motels houses) were marked by orange dots, while projected future sites bore white dots. The deep green map with its brown mountains and colorful dots seemed much more alive than the miles that twinkled past Mr. Johnson's gaze, and nothing gave the ice-cream king greater pleasure than watching Mildred with her fine touch, and using the original crayon, turn an empty white dot into an orange fulfillment.

"It's like a seed grown into a tree, Millie," Mr. HJ liked to say at such moments when he contemplated the map and saw that it was good.

They had started traveling together in 1925: Mildred, then a secretary to Mr. Johnson, a young man with two restaurants and a dream of hospitality, and Otis, a twenty-year-old busboy and former driver of a Louisiana mule. When Mildred graduated from college, her father, a Michigan doctor who kept his money in a blue steel box under the examining table, encouraged her to try the big city. He sent her a monthly allowance. In those early days she always had more than Mr. Johnson, who paid her $16.50 a week and meals. In the first decade they traveled only on weekends, but every year since 1936 they had spent at least six months on the road, and it might have gone on much longer if Mildred's pain and the trouble in New York with Howard Jr. had not come so close together.

They were all stoical at the Los Angeles International Airport. Otis waited at the car for what might be his last job while Miss Bryce and Mr. Johnson traveled toward the New York plane along a silent moving floor. Millie stood beside Howard while they passed a mural of a Mexican landscape and some Christmas drawings by fourth grades from Watts. For forty years they had been together in spite of Sonny and the others, but at this most recent appeal from New York Millie urged him to go back. Sonny had cabled, "My God, Dad, you're sixty-nine years old, haven't you been a gypsy long enough? Board meeting December third with or without you. Policy changes imminent."

Normally, they ignored Sonny's cables, but this time Millie wanted him to go, wanted to be alone with the pain that had recently come to her. She had left Howard holding the new canvas suitcase in which she had packed her three notebooks of regional reports along with his aluminum dish, and in a moment of real despair she had even packed the orange crayon. When Howard boarded Flight 965 he looked old to Millie. His feet dragged in the wing-tipped shoes, the hand she shook was moist, the lip felt dry, and as he passed from her sight down the entry ramp Mildred Bryce felt a fresh new ache that sent her hobbling toward the car. Otis had unplugged the freezer, and the silence caused by the missing hum was as intense to Millie as her abdominal pain.

It had come quite suddenly in Albuquerque, New Mexico, at the grand opening of a 210-unit house. She did not make a fuss. Mildred Bryce had never caused trouble to anyone, except perhaps to Mrs. HJ. Millie's quick precise actions, angular face, and thin body made her seem birdlike, especially next to Mr. HJ, six three with splendid white hair accenting his dark blue gabardine suits. Howard was slow and sure. He could sit in the same position for hours while Millie fidgeted on the seat, wrote memos, and filed reports in the small gray cabinet that sat in front of her and parallel to the ice-cream freezer. Her health had always been good, so at first she tried to ignore the pain. It was gas: it was perhaps the New Mexico water or the cooking oil in the fish dinner. But she could not convince away the pain. It stayed like a match burning around her belly, etching itself into her as the round HJ emblem was so symmetrically embroidered into the bedspread, which she had kicked off in the flush that accompanied the pain. She felt as if her sweat would engulf the foam mattress and crisp percale sheet. Finally, Millie brought up her knees and made a ball of herself as if being as small as possible might make her misery disappear. It worked for everything except the pain. The little circle of hot torment was all that remained of her, and when finally at sometime in the early morning it left, it occurred to her that perhaps she had struggled with a demon and been suddenly relieved by the coming of daylight. She stepped lightly into the bathroom and before a full-length mirror (new in HJ motels exclusively) saw herself whole and unmarked, but sign enough to Mildred was her smell, damp and musty, sign enough that something had begun and that something else would therefore necessarily end.

II

Before she had the report from the doctor, Howard Jr.'s message had given her the excuse she needed. There was no reason why Millie could not tell Howard she was sick, but telling him would be admitting too much to herself. Along with Howard Johnson Millie had grown rich beyond dreams. Her inheritance, the $100,000 from her father's steel box in 1939, went directly to Mr. Johnson, who desperately needed it, and the results of that

investment brought Millie enough capital to employ two people at the Chase
Manhattan with the management of her finances. With money beyond the
hope of use, she had vacationed all over the world and spent some time in
the company of celebrities, but the reality of her life, like his, was in the
back seat of the limousine, waiting for that point at which the needs of the
automobile and the human body met the undeviating purpose of the highway and momentarily conquered it.

Her life was measured in rest stops. She, Howard, and Otis had found
them out before they existed. They knew the places to stop between Buffalo and Albany, Chicago and Milwaukee, Toledo and Columbus, Des Moines
and Minneapolis, they knew through their own bodies, measured in hunger and discomfort in the '30s and '40s when they would stop at remote
places to buy land and borrow money, sensing in themselves the hunger
that would one day be upon the place. People were wary and Howard had
trouble borrowing (her $100,000 had perhaps been the key) but invariably
he was right. Howard knew the land, Mildred thought, the way the Indians
must have known it. There were even spots along the way where the earth
itself seemed to make men stop. Howard had a sixth sense that would
sometimes lead them from the main roads to, say, a dark green field in
Iowa or Kansas. Howard, who might have seemed asleep, would rap with
his knuckles on the Plexiglas, causing the knowing Otis to bring the car to
such a quick stop that Millie almost flew into her filing cabinet. And before
the emergency brake had settled into its final prong, Howard Johnson was
into the field and after the scent. While Millie and Otis waited, he would
walk it out slowly. Sometimes he would sit down, disappearing in a field
of long and tangled weeds, or he might find a large smooth rock to sit on
while he felt some secret vibration from the place. Turning his back to
Millie, he would mark the spot with his urine or break some of the clayey
earth in his strong pink hands, sifting it like flour for a delicate recipe. She
had actually seen him chew the grass, getting down on all fours like an
animal and biting the tops without pulling the entire blade from the soil.
At times he ran in a slow jog as far as his aching legs would carry him.
Whenever he slipped out of sight behind the uneven terrain, Millie felt
him in danger, felt that something alien might be there to resist the civiliz-
ing instinct of Howard Johnson. Once when Howard had been out of sight
for more than an hour and did not respond to their frantic calls, Millie sent
Otis into the field and in desperation flagged a passing car.

"Howard Johnson is lost in that field," she told the surprised driver. "He
went in to look for a new location and we can't find him now."

"The restaurant Howard Johnson?" the man asked.

"Yes. Help us please."

The man drove off, leaving Millie to taste in his exhaust fumes the bar-
barism of an ungrateful public. Otis found Howard asleep in a field of light
blue wild flowers. He had collapsed from the exertion of his run. Millie
brought water to him, and when he felt better, right there in the field, he
ate his scoop of vanilla on the very spot where three years later they opened

the first fully air-conditioned motel in the world. When she stopped to think about it, Millie knew they were more than businessmen, they were pioneers.

And once, while on her own, she had the feeling too. In 1951 when she visited the Holy Land there was an inkling of what Howard must have felt all the time. It happened without any warning on a bus crowded with tourists and resident Arabs on their way to the Dead Sea. Past ancient Sodom the bus creaked and bumped, down, down, toward the lowest point on earth, when suddenly in the midst of the crowd and her stomach queasy with the motion of the bus, Mildred Bryce experienced an overwhelming calm. A light brown patch of earth surrounded by a few pale desert rocks overwhelmed her perception, seemed closer to her than the Arab lady in the black flowered dress pushing her basket against Millie at that very moment. She wanted to stop the bus. Had she been near the door she might have actually jumped, so strong was her sensitivity to that barren spot in the endless desert. Her whole body ached for it as if in unison, bone by bone. Her limbs tingled, her breath came in short gasps, the sky rolled out of the bus window and obliterated her view. The Arab lady spat on the floor and moved a suspicious eye over a squirming Mildred.

When the bus stopped at the Dead Sea, the Arabs and tourists rushed to the soupy brine clutching damaged limbs, while Millie pressed twenty dollars American into the dirty palm of a cab-driver who took her back to the very place where the music of her body began once more as sweetly as the first time. While the incredulous driver waited, Millie walked about the place wishing Howard were there to understand her new understanding of his kind of process. There was nothing there, absolutely nothing but pure bliss. The sun beat her like a wish, the air was hot and stale as a Viennese bathhouse, and yet Mildred felt peace and rest there, and as her cab bill mounted she actually did rest in the miserable barren desert of an altogether unsatisfactory land. When the driver, wiping the sweat from his neck, asked, "Meesez . . . pleeze. Why American woman wants Old Jericho in such kind of heat?" When he said "Jericho," she understood that this was a place where men had always stopped. In dim antiquity Jacob had perhaps watered a flock here, and not far away Lot's wife paused to scan for the last time the city of her youth. Perhaps Mildred now stood where Abraham had been visited by a vision and, making a rock his pillow, had first put the ease into the earth. Whatever it was, Millie knew from her own experience that rest was created here by historical precedent. She tried to buy that piece of land, going as far as King Hussein's secretary of the interior. She imaged a Palestinian HJ with an orange roof angling toward Sodom, a seafood restaurant, and an oasis of fresh fruit. But the land was in dispute between Israel and Jordan, and even King Hussein, who expressed admiration for Howard Johnson, could not sell to Millie the place of her comfort.

That was her single visionary moment, but sharing them with Howard was almost as good. And to end all this, to finally stay in her eighteenth-floor Santa Monica penthouse, where the Pacific dived into California, this seemed to Mildred a paltry conclusion to an adventurous life. Her doctor said it was not so serious, she had a bleeding ulcer and must watch her diet. The prognosis was, in fact, excellent. But Mildred, fifty-six and alone in California, found the doctor less comforting than most of the rest stops she had experienced.

III

California, right after the Second War, was hardly a civilized place for travelers. Millie, HJ, and Otis had a twelve-cylinder '47 Lincoln and snaked along five days between Sacramento and Los Angeles. "Comfort, comfort," said HJ as he surveyed the redwood forest and the bubbly surf while it slipped away from Otis, who had rolled his trousers to chase the ocean away during a stop near San Francisco. Howard Johnson was contemplative in California. They had never been in the West before. Their route, always slightly new, was yet bound by Canada, where a person couldn't get a tax break, and roughly by the Mississippi as a western frontier. Their journeys took them up the eastern seaboard and through New England to the early reaches of the Midwest, stopping at the plains of Wisconsin and the cool crisp edge of Chicago where two HJ lodges twinkled at the lake.

One day in 1947 while on the way from Chicago to Cairo, Illinois, HJ looked long at the green relief maps. While Millie kept busy with her filing, HJ loosened the tape and placed the map across his soft round knees. The map jiggled and sagged, the Mid- and Southwest hanging between his legs. When Mildred finally noticed that look, he had been staring at the map for perhaps fifteen minutes, brooding over it, and Millie knew something was in the air.

HJ looked at that map the way some people looked down from an airplane trying to pick out the familiar from the colorful mass receding beneath them. Howard Johnson's eye flew over the land—over the Tetons, over the Sierra Nevada, over the long thin gouge of the Canyon flew his gaze—charting his course by rest stops the way an antique mariner might have gazed at the stars.

"Millie," he said just north of Carbondale, "Millie . . ." He looked toward her, saw her fingers engaged and her thumbs circling each other in anticipation. He looked at Millie and saw that she saw what he saw. "Millie"— HJ raised his right arm and its shadow spread across the continent like a prophecy—"Millie, what if we turn right at Cairo and go that way?" California, already peeling on the green map, balanced on HJ's left knee like a happy child.

Twenty years later Mildred settled in her eighteenth-floor apartment in the building owned by Lawrence Welk. Howard was in New York, Otis and the car waited in Arizona. The pain did not return as powerfully as it had appeared that night in Albuquerque, but it hurt with dull regularity and an occasional streak of dark blood from her bowels kept her mind on it even on painless days.

Directly beneath her gaze were the organized activities of the golden-age groups, tiny figures playing bridge or shuffleboard or looking out at the water from their benches as she sat on her sofa and looked out at them and the fluffy ocean. Mildred did not regret family life. The HJ houses were her offspring. She had watched them blossom from the rough youngsters of the '40s with steam heat and even occasional kitchenettes into cool mature adults with king-sized beds, color TVs, and room service. Her late years were spent comfortably in the modern houses just as one might enjoy in age the benefits of a child's prosperity. She regretted only that it was probably over.

But she did not give up completely until she received a personal letter one day telling her that she was eligible for burial insurance until age eighty. A $1000 policy would guarantee a complete and dignified service.

Millie crumpled the advertisement, but a few hours later called her Los Angeles lawyer. As she suspected, there were no plans, but as the executor of the estate he would assume full responsibility, subject of course to her approval.

"I'll do it myself," Millie had said, but she could not bring herself to do it. The idea was too alien. In more than forty years Mildred had not gone a day without a shower and change of underclothing. Everything about her suggested order and precision. Her fingernails were shaped so that the soft meat of the tips could stroke a typewriter without damaging the apex of a nail, her arch slid over a 6B shoe like an egg in a shell, and never in her adult life did Mildred recall having vomited. It did not seem right to suddenly let all this sink into the dark earth of Forest Lawn because some organ or other developed a hole as big as a nickel. It was not right and she wouldn't do it. Her first idea was to stay in the apartment, to write it into the lease if necessary. She had the lawyer make an appointment for her with Mr. Welk's management firm, but canceled it the day before. "They will just think I'm crazy," she said aloud to herself, "and they'll bury me anyway."

She thought of cryonics while reading a biography of William Chesebrough, the man who invented petroleum jelly. Howard had known him and often mentioned that his own daily ritual of the scoop of vanilla was like old Chesebrough's two teaspoons of Vaseline every day. Chesebrough lived to be ninety. In the biography it said that after taking the daily dose of Vaseline, he drank three cups of green tea to melt everything down, rested for twelve minutes, and then felt fit as a young man, even in his late eighties. When he died they froze his body and Millie had her idea. The Vaseline people kept him in a secret laboratory somewhere near Cleveland and claimed he was in better condition than Lenin, whom the Russians kept hermetically sealed, but at room temperature.

In the phone book she found the Los Angeles Cryonic Society and asked it to send her information. It all seemed very clean. The cost was $200 a year for maintaining the cold. She sent the pamphlet to her lawyer to be sure that the society was legitimate. It wasn't much money, but, still, if they were charlatans, she didn't want them to take advantage of her even if she would never know about it. They were aboveboard, the lawyer said. "The interest on a ten-thousand-dollar trust fund would pay about five hundred a year," the lawyer said, "and they only charge two hundred dollars. Still, who knows what the cost might be in say two hundred years?" To be extra safe, they put $25,000 in trust for eternal maintenance, to be eternally overseen by Longstreet, Williams, and their eternal heirs. When it was arranged, Mildred felt better than she had in weeks.

IV

Four months to the day after she had left Howard at the Los Angeles International Airport, he returned for Mildred without the slightest warning. She was in her housecoat and had not even washed the night cream from her cheeks when she saw through the viewing space in her door the familiar long pink jowls, even longer in the distorted glass.

"Howard," she gasped, fumbling with the door, and in an instant he was there picking her up as he might a child or an ice-cream cone while her tears fell like dandruff on his blue suit. While Millie sobbed into his soft padded shoulder, HJ told her the good news. "I'm chairman emeritus of the board now. That means no more New York responsibilities. They will have to listen to me because we hold the majority of the stock, but Howard Junior and Keyes will take care of the business. Our main job is new home-owned franchises. And, Millie, guess where we're going first?"

So overcome was Mildred that she could not hold back her sobs even to guess. Howard Johnson put her down, beaming pleasure through his old bright eyes. "Florida," HJ said, then slowly repeated it, "Flor-idda, and guess what we're going to do?"

"Howard," Millie said, swiping at her tears with the filmy lace cuffs of her dressing gown, "I'm so surprised I don't know what to say. You could tell me we're going to the moon and I'd believe you. Just seeing you again has brought back all my hope." They came out of the hallway and sat on the sofa that looked out over the Pacific. HJ, all pink, kept his hands on his knees like paperweights.

"Millie, you're almost right. I can't fool you about anything and never could. We're going down near where they launch the rockets from. I've heard . . ." HJ leaned toward the kitchen as if to check for spies. He looked at the stainless-steel-and-glass table, at the built-in avocado appliances, then leaned his large moist lips toward Mildred's ear. "Walt Disney is planning right this minute a new Disneyland down there. They're trying to keep it a secret, but his brother Roy bought options on thousands of acres. We're going down to buy as much as we can as close in as we can." Howard sparkled. "Millie, don't you see, it's a sure thing."

After her emotional outburst at seeing Howard again, a calmer Millie felt a slight twitch in her upper stomach and in the midst of her joy was reminded of another sure thing.

They would be a few weeks in Los Angeles anyway. Howard wanted to thoroughly scout out the existing Disneyland, so Millie had some time to think it out. She could go, as her heart directed her, with HJ to Florida and points beyond. She could take the future as it happened like a Disneyland ride or she could listen to the dismal eloquence of her ulcer and try to make the best arrangements she could. Howard and Otis would take care of her to the end, there were no doubts about that, and the end would be the end. But if she stayed in this apartment, sure of the arrangements for later, she would miss whatever might still be left before the end. Mildred wished there were some clergyman she could consult, but she had never attended a church and believed in no religious doctrine. Her father had been a firm atheist to the very moment of his office suicide, and she remained a passive nonbeliever. Her theology was the order of her own life. Millie had never deceived herself; in spite of her riches all she truly owned was her life, a pocket of habits in the burning universe. But the habits were careful and clean and they were best represented in the body that was she. Freezing her remains was the closest image she could conjure of eternal life. It might not be eternal and it surely would not be life, but that damp, musty feel, that odor she smelled on herself after the pain, that could be avoided, and who knew what else might be saved from the void for a small initial investment and $200 a year. And if you did not believe in a soul, was there not every reason to preserve a body?

Mrs. Albert of the Cryonic Society welcomed Mildred to a tour of the premises. "See it while you can," she cheerfully told the group (Millie, two men, and a boy with notebook and Polaroid camera). Mrs. Albert, a big woman perhaps in her mid-sixties, carried a face heavy in flesh. Perhaps once the skin had been tight around her long chin and pointed cheekbones, but having lost its spring, the skin merely hung at her neck like a patient animal waiting for the rest of her to join in the decline. From the way she took the concrete stairs down to the vault, it looked as if the wait would be long. "I'm not ready for the freezer yet. I tell every group I take down here, it's gonna be a long time until they get me." Millie believed her. "I may not be the world's smartest cookie"—Mrs. Albert looked directly at Millie—"but a bird in the hand is the only bird I know, huh? That's why when it does come . . . Mrs. A is going to be right here in this facility, and you better believe it. Now, Mr. King on your left"—she pointed to a capsule that looked like a large bullet to Millie—"Mr. King is the gentleman who took me on my first tour, cancer finally but had everything perfectly ready and I would say he was in prime cooling state within seconds and I believe that if they ever cure cancer, and you know they will the way they do most everything nowadays, old Mr. King may be back yet. If anyone got down to low-enough temperature immediately it would be Mr. King." Mildred saw the boy write "Return of the King" in his notebook. "Over here is Mr. and Mizz Winkleman, married sixty years, and went off within a month of each other, a lovely, lovely couple."

While Mrs. Albert continued her necrology and posed for a photo beside the Winklemans, Millie took careful note of the neon-lit room filled with bulletlike capsules. She watched the cool breaths of the group gather like flowers on the steel and vanish without dimming the bright surface. The capsules stood in straight lines with ample walking space between them. To Mrs. Albert they were friends, to Millie it seemed as if she were in a furniture store of the Scandinavian type where elegance is suggested by the absence of material, where straight lines of steel, wood, and glass indicate that relaxation too requires some taste and is not an indifferent sprawl across any soft object that happens to be nearby.

Cemeteries always bothered Millie, but here she felt none of the dread she had expected. She averted her eyes from the cluttered graveyards they always used to pass at the tips of cities in the early days. Fortunately, the superhighways twisted traffic into the city and away from those desolate marking places where used-car lots and the names of famous hotels inscribed on barns often neighbored the dead. Howard had once commented that never in all his experience did he have an intuition of a good location near a cemetery. You could put a lot of things there, you could put up a bowling alley, or maybe even a theater, but never a motel, and Millie knew he was right. He knew where to put his houses but it was Millie who knew how. From that first orange roof angling toward the east, the HJ design and the idea had been Millie's. She had not invented the motel, she had changed it from a place where you had to be to a place where you wanted to be. Perhaps, she thought, the Cryonic Society was trying to do the same for cemeteries.

When she and Howard had started their travels, the old motel courts huddled like so many dark graves around the stone marking of the highway. And what traveler coming into one of those dingy cabins could watch the watery rust dripping from from his faucet without thinking of everything he was missing by being a traveler . . . his two-stall garage, his wife small in the half-empty bed, his children with hair the color of that rust. Under the orange Howard Johnson roof all this changed. For about the same price you were redeemed from the road. Headlights did not dazzle you on the foam mattress and percale sheets, your sanitized glasses and toilet appliances sparkled like the mirror behind them. The room was not just there, it awaited you, courted your pleasure, sat like a young bride outside the walls of the city wanting only to please you, you only you on the smoothly pressed sheets, your friend, your one-night destiny.

As if it were yesterday, Millie recalled right there in the cryonic vault the moment when she had first thought the thought that made Howard Johnson Howard Johnson's. And when she told Howard her decision that evening after cooking a cheese soufflé and risking a taste of wine, it was that memory she invoked for both of them, the memory of a cool autumn day in the '30s when a break in their schedule found Millie with a free afternoon in New Hampshire, an afternoon she had spent at the farm of a man who had once been her teacher and remembered her after ten years. Otis drove her out to Robert Frost's farm, where the poet made for her a lunch of scrambled eggs and 7 Up. Millie and Robert Frost talked mostly about the farm, about the cold winter he was expecting and the autumn apples they picked from the trees. He was not so famous then, his hair was only streaked with gray as Howard's was, and she told the poet about what she and Howard were doing, about what she felt about being on the road in America, and Robert Frost said he hadn't been that much but she sounded like she knew and he believed she might be able to accomplish something. He did not remember the poem she wrote in his class but that didn't matter.

"Do you remember, Howard, how I introduced you to him? Mr. Frost, this is Mr. Johnson. I can still see the two of you shaking hands there beside the car. I've always been proud that I introduced you to one another." Howard Johnson nodded his head at the memory, seemed as nostalgic as Millie while he sat in her apartment learning why she would not go to Florida to help bring Howard Johnson's to the new Disneyland.

"And after we left his farm, Howard, remember? Otis took the car in for servicing and left us with some sandwiches on the top of a hill overlooking a town, I don't even remember which one, maybe we never knew the name of it. And we stayed on that hilltop while the sun began to set in New Hampshire. I felt so full of poetry and"—she looked at Howard—"of love, Howard, only about an hour's drive from Robert Frost's farmhouse. Maybe it was just the way we felt then, but I think the sun set differently that night, filtering through the clouds like a big paintbrush making the top of the town all orange. And suddenly I thought what if the tops of our houses were that kind of orange, what a world it would be, Howard, and my God, that orange stayed until the last drop of light was left in it. I didn't feel the cold up there even though it took Otis so long to get back to us. The feeling we had about that orange, Howard, that was ours and that's what I've tried to bring to every house, the way we felt that night. Oh, it makes me sick to think of Colonel Sanders, and Big Boy, and Holiday Inn, and Best Western . . ."

"It's all right, Millie, it's all right." Howard patted her heaving back. Now that he knew about her ulcer and why she wanted to stay behind, the mind that had conjured butterfly shrimp and twenty-eight flavors set himself a new project. He contemplated Millie sobbing in his lap the way he contemplated prime acreage. There was so little of her, less than one hundred pounds, yet without her Howard Johnson felt himself no match for the wily Disneys gathering near the moonport.

He left her in all her sad resignation that evening, left her thinking she had to give up what remained here to be sure of the proper freezing. But

Howard Johnson had other ideas. He did not cancel the advance reservations made for Mildred Bryce along the route to Florida, nor did he remove her filing cabinet from the limousine. The man who hosted a nation and already kept one freezer in his car merely ordered another, this one designed according to cryonic specifications and presented to Mildred housed in a twelve-foot orange U-Haul trailer connected to the rear bumper of the limousine.

"Everything's here," he told the astonished Millie, who thought Howard had left the week before, "everything is here and you'll never have to be more than seconds away from it. It's exactly like a refrigerated truck." Howard Johnson opened the rear door of the U-Haul as proudly as he had ever dedicated a motel. Millie's steel capsule shone within, surrounded by an array of chemicals stored on heavily padded rubber shelves. The California sun was on her back, but her cold breath hovered visibly within the U-Haul. No tears came to Mildred now; she felt relief much as she had felt it that afternoon near ancient Jericho. On Santa Monica Boulevard, in front of Lawrence Welk's apartment building, Mildred Bryce confronted her immortality, a gift from the ice-cream king, another companion for the remainder of her travels. Howard Johnson had turned away, looking toward the ocean. To his blue back and patriarchal white hairs, Mildred said, "Howard, you can do anything," and closing the doors of the U-Haul, she joined the host of the highways, a man with two portable freezers, ready now for the challenge of Disney World.

QUESTIONS

"The Oranging of America"

1. How does the author turn Howard Johnson into a larger-than-life figure, an American folk hero on the order of Davy Crockett or Johnny Appleseed? Why do you think he chose to construct his fantasy around the person of Howard Johnson? How do you know that the Howard Johnson who appears in this story is a fantasy character?

2. A good deal of the humor of "The Oranging of America" derives from the disparity between the reality of Howard Johnson restaurants and motels— what they are, what they represent—and the tone the author uses in relating the imaginary history of their founder. How would you characterize that tone? What sort of language does Apple use when he describes Mr. HJ and his motels?

3. This story contains a good deal of religious language and imagery. Where does it appear? How does Apple's portrayal of Howard Johnson's career as a

holy quest, a sacred mission, contribute to the story's humor? What is the goal of HJ's quest, the "treasure" he spends his life seeking?

4. In the passage in which Millie muses on Howard's uncanny ability to find ideal spots for his rest stops, what is ironic about the description of HJ's affinity with the land and the analogies Apple draws between Howard and the early inhabitants of the West: the Indians, homesteaders, and pioneers?

5. Look at Millie's memories of her afternoon with the poet Robert Frost and "the moment when she . . . first thought the thought that made Howard Johnson Howard Johnson's." How would you describe the mood of this section? What is amusing about the juxtaposition of Frost and Howard Johnson? How poetic are Howard Johnson motels and restaurants?

6. "The Oranging of America" is filled with references to quintessentially American products, places, and inventions: air-conditioned Cadillac limousines with built-in bars, Vaseline, Howard Johnson motor lodges, Holiday Inns, Disneyworld, cryonics, an apartment building owned by Lawrence Welk. What aspects of American culture is Apple satirizing in this story?

7. Why is Millie horrified at the thought of being buried? Why is cryonics—having her body frozen after death—an appealing alternative to her? What connection does Apple draw between the Cryonic Society and Howard Johnson motels? Is there an implied comment on Howard Johnson motels in this comparison? On American society in general?

8. Why does Apple portray HJ and his companions on a perpetual odyssey across America in a car equipped with an ice-cream freezer? What makes this image so apt? How would the story have been different if Apple had shown the hero of his story working, like Howard Junior, out of an office in New York City?

9. According to the prominent historian of religions Mircea Eliade, "myth narrates a sacred history; it relates an event that took place in . . . the fabled time of the 'beginning.' In other words, myth tells how, through the deeds of Supernatural Beings, a reality came into existence, be it the whole of reality, the Cosmos, or only a fragment of reality—an island, a species of plant, a particular kind of human behavior, an institution. Myth, then, is always an account of a 'creation'; it relates how something was produced, began to be."* With this definition in mind, discuss "The Oranging of America" as a satirical creation myth about the origins of contemporary American culture.

10. The title of this story is a play on Charles Reich's book *The Greening of America*, a bestseller published in 1970 that predicted America's transformation into a new, liberated, nonmaterialistic society, as a result of the "youth revolution" of the sixties. In light of this, why do you think Apple chose to give his story the title he did?

*Mircea Eliade, *Myth and Reality*, trans. Willard R. Trask (New York: Harper & Row/ Harper Torchbooks, 1963), pp. 5–6.

The Revolt of "Mother"

MARY E. WILKINS FREEMAN

"Father!"

"What is it?"

"What are them men diggin' over there in the field for?"

There was a sudden dropping and enlarging of the lower part of the old man's face, as if some heavy weight had settled therein; he shut his mouth tight, and went on harnessing the great bay mare. He hustled the collar on to her neck with a jerk.

"Father!"

The old man slapped the saddle upon the mare's back.

"Look here, father, I want to know what them men are diggin' over in the field for, an' I'm goin' to know."

"I wish you'd go into the house, mother, an' tend to your own affairs," the old man said then. He ran his words together, and his speech was almost as inarticulate as a growl.

But the woman understood; it was her most native tongue. "I ain't goin' into the house till you tell me what them men are doin' over there in the field," said she.

Then she stood waiting. She was a small woman, short and straight-waisted like a child in her brown cotton gown. Her forehead was mild and benevolent between the smooth curves of gray hair; there were meek downward lines about her nose and mouth; but her eyes, fixed upon the old man, looked as if the meekness had been the result of her own will, never of the will of another.

They were in the barn, standing before the wide open doors. The spring air, full of the smell of growing grass and unseen blossoms, came in their faces. The deep yard in front was littered with farm wagons and piles of wood; on the edges, close to the fence and the house, the grass was a vivid green, and there were some dandelions.

The old man glanced doggedly at his wife as he tightened the last buckles on the harness. She looked as immovable to him as one of the rocks in his pasture-land, bound to the earth with generations of blackberry vines. He slapped the reins over the horse, and started forth from the barn.

"*Father!*" said she.

The old man pulled up. "What is it?"

"I want to know what them men are diggin' over there in that field for."

"They're diggin' a cellar, I s'pose, if you've got to know."

"A cellar for what?"

"A barn."

"A barn? You ain't goin' to build a barn over there where we was goin' to have a house, father?"

The old man said not another word. He hurried the horse into the farm wagon, and clattered out of the yard, jouncing as sturdily on his seat as a boy.

The woman stood a moment looking after him, then she went out of the barn across a corner of the yard to the house. The house, standing at right angles with the great barn and a long reach of sheds and out-buildings, was infinitesimal compared with them. It was scarcely as commodious for people as the little boxes under the barn eaves were for doves.

A pretty girl's face, pink and delicate as a flower, was looking out of one of the house windows. She was watching three men who were digging over in the field which bounded the yard near the road line. She turned quietly when the woman entered.

"What are they digging for, mother?" said she. "Did he tell you?"

"They're diggin' for—a cellar for a new barn."

"Oh, mother, he ain't going to build another barn?"

"That's what he says."

A boy stood before the kitchen glass combing his hair. He combed slowly and painstakingly, arranging his brown hair in a smooth hillock over his forehead. He did not seem to pay any attention to the conversation.

"Sammy, did you know father was going to build a new barn?" asked the girl.

The boy combed assiduously.

"Sammy!"

He turned, and showed a face like his father's under his smooth crest of hair. "Yes, I s'pose I did," he said, reluctantly.

"How long have you known it?" asked his mother.

" 'Bout three months, I guess."

"Why didn't you tell of it?"

"Didn't think 'twould do no good."

"I don't see what father wants another barn for," said the girl, in her sweet, slow voice. She turned again to the window, and stared out at the digging men in the field. Her tender, sweet face was full of a gentle distress. Her forehead was as bald and innocent as a baby's, with the light hair strained back from it in a row of curl-papers. She was quite large, but her soft curves did not look as if they covered muscles.

Her mother looked sternly at the boy. "Is he goin' to buy more cows?" said she.

The boy did not reply; he was tying his shoes.

"Sammy, I want you to tell me if he's goin' to buy more cows."

"I s'pose he is."

"How many?"

"Four, I guess."

His mother said nothing more. She went up into the pantry, and there was a clatter of dishes. The boy got his cap from a nail behind the door, took an arithmetic from the shelf, and started for school. He was lightly built, but clumsy. He went out of the yard with a curious spring in the hips, that made his loose homemade jacket tilt up in the rear.

The girl went to the sink, and began to wash the dishes that were piled up there. Her mother came promptly out of the pantry, and shoved her aside. "You wipe 'em," said she; "I'll wash. There's a good many this mornin'."

The mother plunged her hands vigorously into the water, the girl wiped the plates slowly and dreamily. "Mother," said she, "don't you think it's too bad father's going to build that new barn, much as we need a decent house to live in?"

Her mother scrubbed a dish fiercely. "You ain't found out yet we're women-folks, Nanny Penn," said she. "You ain't seen enough of men-folk yet to. One of these days you'll find it out, an' then you'll know that we know only what men-folks think we do, so far as any use of it goes, an' how we'd ought to reckon men-folks in with Providence, an' not complain of what they do any more than we do of the weather."

"I don't care; I don't believe George is anything like that, anyhow," said Nanny. Her delicate face flushed pink, her lips pouted softly, as if she were going to cry.

"You wait an' see. I guess George Eastman ain't no better than other men. You hadn't ought to judge father, though. He can't help it, 'cause he don't look at things jest the way we do. An' we've been pretty comfortable here, after all. The roof don't leak—ain't never but once—that's one thing. Father's kept it shingled right up."

"I do wish we had a parlor."

"I guess it won't hurt George Eastman any to come to see you in a nice clean kitchen. I guess a good many girls don't have as good a place as this. Nobody's ever heard me complain."

"I ain't complained either, mother."

"Well, I don't think you'd better, a good father an' a good home as you've got. S'pose your father made you go out an' work for your livin'? Lots of girls have to that ain't no stronger an' better able to than you be."

Sarah Penn washed the frying-pan with a conclusive air. She scrubbed the outside of it as faithfully as the inside. She was a masterly keeper of her box of a house. Her one living-room never seemed to have in it any of the dust which the friction of life with inanimate matter produces. She swept, and there seemed to be no dirt to go before the broom; she cleaned, and one could see no difference. She was like an artist so perfect that he has apparently no art. To-day she got out a mixing bowl and a board, and rolled some pies, and there was no more flour upon her than upon her daughter who was doing finer work. Nanny was to be married in the fall, and she was sewing on some white cambric and embroidery. She sewed industriously while her mother cooked, her soft milk-white hands and wrists showed whiter than her delicate work.

"We must have the stove moved out in the shed before long," said Mrs. Penn. "Talk about not havin' things, it's been a real blessin' to be able to put a stove up in that shed in hot weather. Father did one good thing when he fixed that stove-pipe out there."

Sarah Penn's face as she rolled her pies had that expression of meek vigor which might have characterized one of the New Testament saints. She was making mince-pies. Her husband, Adoniram Penn, liked them better than any other kind. She baked twice a week. Adoniram often liked a piece of pie between meals. She hurried this morning. It had been later than usual when she began, and she wanted to have a pie baked for dinner. However deep a resentment she might be forced to hold against her husband, she would never fail in sedulous attention to his wants.

Nobility of character manifests itself at loop-holes when it is not provided with large doors. Sarah Penn's showed itself to-day in flaky dishes of pastry. So she made the pies faithfully, while across the table she could see, when she glanced up from her work, the sight that rankled in her patient and steadfast soul—the digging of the cellar of the new barn in the place where Adoniram forty years ago had promised her their new house should stand.

The pies were done for dinner. Adoniram and Sammy were home a few minutes after twelve o'clock. The dinner was eaten with serious haste. There was never much conversation at the table in the Penn family. Adoniram asked a blessing, and they ate promptly, then rose up and went about their work.

Sammy went back to school, taking soft sly lopes out of the yard like a rabbit. He wanted a game of marbles before school, and feared his father would give him some chores to do. Adoniram hastened to the door and called after him, but he was out of sight.

"I don't see what you let him go for, mother," said he. "I wanted him to help me unload that wood."

Adoniram went to work out in the yard unloading wood from the wagon. Sarah put away the dinner dishes, while Nanny took down her curl-papers and changed her dress. She was going down to the store to buy some more embroidery and thread.

When Nanny was gone, Mrs. Penn went to the door. "Father!" she called.

"Well, what is it?"

"I want to see you jest a minute, father."

"I can't leave this wood nohow. I've got to git it unloaded an' go for a load of gravel afore two o'clock. Sammy had ought to helped me. You hadn't ought to let him go to school so early."

"I want to see you jest a minute."

"I tell ye I can't, nohow, mother."

"Father, you come here." Sarah Penn stood in the door like a queen;

she held her head as if it bore a crown; there was the patience which makes authority royal in her voice. Adoniram went.

Mrs. Penn led the way into the kitchen, and pointed to a chair. "Sit down, father," said she; "I've got somethin' I want to say to you."

He sat down heavily; his face was quite stolid, but he looked at her with restive eyes. "Well, what is it, mother?"

"I want to know what you're buildin' that new barn for, father?"

"I ain't got nothin' to say about it."

"It can't be you think you need another barn?"

"I tell ye I ain't got nothin' to say about it, mother; an' I ain't goin' to say nothin'."

"Be you goin' to buy more cows?"

Adoniram did not reply; he shut his mouth tight.

"I know you be, as well as I want to. Now, father, look here"—Sarah Penn had not sat down; she stood before her husband in the humble fashion of a Scripture woman—"I'm goin' to talk real plain to you; I never have sence I married you, but I'm goin' to now. I ain't never complained, an' I ain't goin' to complain now, but I'm goin' to talk plain. You see this room here, father; you look at it well. You see there ain't no carpet on the floor, an' you see the paper is all dirty, an' droppin' off the walls. We ain't had no new paper on it for ten year, an' then I put it on myself, an' it didn't cost but nine-pence a roll. You see this room, father; it's all the one I've had to work in an' eat in an' sit in sence we was married. There ain't another woman in the whole town whose husband ain't got half the means you have but what's got better. It's all the room Nanny's got to have her company in; an' there ain't one of her mates but what's got better, an' their fathers not so able as hers is. It's all the room she'll have to be married in. What would you have thought, father, if we had had our weddin' in a room no better than this? I was married in my mother's parlor, with a carpet on the floor, an' stuffed furniture, an' a mahogany card-table. An' this is all the room my daughter will have to be married in. Look here, father!"

Sarah Penn went across the room as though it were a tragic stage. She flung open a door and disclosed a tiny bedroom, only large enough for a bed and bureau, with a path between. "There, father," said she—"There's all the room I've had to sleep in forty year. All my children were born there—the two that died, an' the two that's livin'. I was sick with a fever there."

She stepped to another door and opened it. It led into the small, ill-lighted pantry. "Here," said she, "is all the buttery I've got—every place I've got for my dishes, to set away my victuals in, an' to keep my milk-pans in. Father, I've been takin' care of the milk of six cows in this place, an' now you're goin' to build a new barn, an' keep more cows, an' give me more to do in it."

She threw open another door. A narrow crooked flight of stairs wound upward from it. "There, father," said she, "I want you to look at the stairs that go up to them two unfinished chambers that are all the places our son an' daughter have had to sleep in all their lives. There ain't a prettier girl in tow.. nor a more ladylike one than Nanny, an't that's the place she has to sleep in. It ain't so good as your horse's stall; it ain't so warm an' tight."

Sarah Penn went back and stood before her husband.

"Now, father," said she, "I want to know if you think you're doin' right an' accordin' to what you profess. Here, when we was married, forty year ago, you promised me faithful that we should have a new house built in that lot over in the field before the year was out. You said you had money enough, an' you wouldn't ask me to live in no such place as this. It is forty year now, an' you've been makin' more money, an' I've been savin' of it for you ever since, an' you ain't built no house yet. You've built sheds an' cow-houses an' one new barn, an' now you're goin' to build another. Father, I want to know if you think it's right. You're lodgin' your dumb beasts better than you are your own flesh an' blood. I want to know if you think it's right."

"I ain't got nothin' to say."

"You can't say nothin' without ownin' it ain't right, father. An' there's another thing—I ain't complained; I've got along forty year, an' I s'pose I should forty more, if it wa'n't for that—if we don't have another house. Nanny she can't live with us after she's married. She'll have to go somewheres else to live away from us, an' it don't seem as if I could have it so, noways, father. She wa'n't ever strong. She's got considerable color, but there wa'n't ever any backbone to her. I've always took the heft of everything off her, an' she ain't fit to keep house an' do everything herself. She'll be all worn out inside of a year. Think of her doin' all the washin' an' ironin' an' bakin' with them soft white hands an' arms, an' sweepin'! I can't have it so noways, father."

Mrs. Penn's face was burning; her mild eyes gleamed. She had pleaded her little cause like a Webster; she had ranged from severity to pathos; but her opponent employed that obstinate silence which makes eloquence futile with mocking echoes. Adoniram arose clumsily.

"Father, ain't you got nothin' to say?" said Mrs. Penn.

"I've got to go off after that load of gravel. I can't stan' here talkin' all day."

"Father, won't you think it over, an' have a house built there instead of a barn?"

"I ain't got nothin' to say."

Adoniram shuffled out. Mrs. Penn went into her bedroom. When she came out, her eyes were red. She had a roll of unbleached cotton cloth. She spread it out on the kitchen table, and began cutting out some shirts for her husband. The men over in the field had a team to help them this afternoon; she could hear their halloos. She had a scanty pattern for the shirts; she had to plan and piece the sleeves.

Nanny came home with her embroidery, and sat down with her needlework. She had taken down her curl-papers, and there was a soft roll of fair hair like an aureole over her forehead; her face was as delicately fine and clear as porcelain. Suddenly she looked up, and the tender red flamed all over her face and neck. "Mother," said she.

"What say?"

"I've been thinking—I don't see how we're goin' to have any—wedding in this room. I'd be ashamed to have his folks come if we didn't have anybody else."

"Mebbe we can have some new paper before then; I can put it on. I guess you won't have no call to be ashamed of your belongin's."

"We might have the wedding in the new barn," said Nanny, with gentle pettishness. "Why, mother, what makes you look so?"

Mrs. Penn had started, and was staring at her with a curious expression. She turned again to her work, and spread out a pattern carefully on the cloth. "Nothin'," said she.

Presently Adoniram clattered out of the yard in his two-wheeled dump cart, standing as proudly upright as a Roman charioteer. Mrs. Penn opened the door and stood there a minute looking out; the halloos of the men sounded louder.

It seemed to her all through the spring months that she heard nothing but the halloos and the noises of the saws and hammers. The new barn grew fast. It was a fine edifice for this little village. Men came on pleasant Sundays, in their meeting suits and clean shirt bosoms, and stood around it admiringly. Mrs. Penn did not speak of it, and Adoniram did not mention it to her, although sometimes, upon a return from inspecting it, he bore himself with injured dignity.

"It's a strange thing how your mother feels about the new barn," he said, confidentially, to Sammy one day.

Sammy only grunted after an odd fashion for a boy; he had learned it from his father.

The barn was all completed ready for use by the third week in July. Adoniram had planned to move his stock in on Wednesday; on Tuesday he received a letter which changed his plans. He came in with it early in the morning. "Sammy's been to the post-office," said he, "an' I've got a letter from Hiram." Hiram was Mrs. Penn's brother, who lived in Vermont.

"Well," said Mrs. Penn, "what does he say about the folks?"

"I guess they're all right. He says he thinks if I come up country right off there's a chance to buy jest the kind of a horse I want." He stared reflectively out of the window at the new barn.

Mrs. Penn was making pies. She went on clapping the rolling-pin into the crust, although she was very pale, and her heart beat loudly.

"I dun' know but what I'd better go," said Adoniram. "I hate to go off jest now, right in the midst of hayin', but the ten-acre lot's cut, an' I guess Rufus an' the others can git along without me three or four days. I can't get a horse round here to suit me, nohow, an' I've got to have another for all that wood-haulin' in the fall. I told Hiram to watch out, an' if he got wind of a good horse to let me know. I guess I'd better go."

"I'll get out your clean shirt an' collar," said Mrs. Penn calmly.

She laid Adoniram's Sunday suit and his clean clothes on the bed in the little bedroom. She got his shaving-water and razor ready. At last she buttoned on his collar and fastened his black cravat.

Adoniram never wore his collar and cravat except on extra occasions. He held his head high, with a rasped dignity. When he was all ready, with his coat and hat brushed, and a lunch of pie and cheese in a paper bag, he hesitated on the threshold of the door. He looked at his wife, and his manner was defiantly apologetic. "If them cows come to-day, Sammy can drive 'em into the new barn," said he; "an' when they bring the hay up, they can pitch it in there."

"Well," replied Mrs. Penn.

Adoniram set his shaved face ahead and started. When he had cleared the door-step, he turned and looked back with a kind of nervous solemnity. "I shall be back by Saturday if nothin' happens," said he.

"Do be careful, father," returned his wife.

She stood in the door with Nanny at her elbow and watched him out of sight. Her eyes had a strange, doubtful expression in them; her peaceful forehead was contracted. She went in, and about her baking again. Nanny sat sewing. Her wedding-day was drawing nearer, and she was getting pale and thin with her steady sewing. Her mother kept glancing at her.

"Have you got that pain in your side this mornin'?" she asked.

"A little."

Mrs. Penn's face, as she worked, changed, her perplexed forehead smoothed, her eyes were steady, her lips firmly set. She formed a maxim for herself, although incoherently with her unlettered thoughts. "Unsolicited opportunities are the guideposts of the Lord to the new roads of life," she repeated in effect, and she made up her mind to her course of action.

"S'posin' I *had* wrote to Hiram," she muttered once, when she was in the pantry—"s'posin' I had wrote, an' asked him if he knew of any horse? But I didn't, an' father's goin' wa'n't none of my doin'. It looks like a providence." Her voice rang out quite loud at the last.

"What you talkin' about, mother?" called Nanny.

"Nothin'."

Mrs. Penn hurried her baking; at eleven o'clock it was all done. The load of hay from the west field came slowly down the cart track, and drew up at the new barn. Mrs. Penn ran out. "Stop!" she screamed—"stop!"

The men stopped and looked; Sammy upreared from the top of the load, and stared at his mother.

"Stop!" she cried out again. "Don't you put the hay in that barn; put it in the old one."

"Why, he said to put it in here," returned one of the hay-makers, wonderingly. He was a young man, a neighbor's son, whom Adoniram hired by the year to help on the farm.

"Don't you put the hay in the new barn; there's room enough in the old one, ain't there?" said Mrs. Penn.

"Room enough," returned the hired man, in his thick, rustic tones. "Didn't need the new barn, nohow, far as room's concerned. Well, I s'pose he changed his mind." He took hold of the horses' bridles.

Mrs. Penn went back to the house. Soon the kitchen windows were darkened, and a fragrance like warm honey came into the room.

Nanny laid down her work. "I thought father wanted them to put the hay into the new barn?" she said, wonderingly.

"It's all right," replied her mother.

Sammy slid down from the load of hay, and came in to see if dinner was ready.

"I ain't goin' to get a regular dinner to-day, as long as father's gone," said his mother. "I've let the fire go out. You can have some bread an' milk an' pie. I thought we could get along." She set out some bowls of milk, some bread, and a pie on the kitchen table. "You'd better eat your dinner now," said she. "You might jest as well get through with it. I want you to help me afterward."

Nanny and Sammy stared at each other. There was something strange in their mother's manner. Mrs. Penn did not eat anything herself. She went into the pantry, and they heard her moving dishes while they ate. Presently she came out with a pile of plates. She got the clothes-basket out of the shed, and packed them in it. Nanny and Sammy watched. She brought out cups and saucers, and put them in with the plates.

"What you goin' to do, mother?" inquired Nanny, in a timid voice. A sense of something unusual made her tremble, as if it were a ghost. Sammy rolled his eyes over his pie.

"You'll see what I'm going to do," replied Mrs. Penn. "If you're through, Nanny, I want you to go up-stairs an' pack up your things; an' I want you, Sammy, to help me take down the bed in the bedroom."

"Oh, mother, what for?" gasped Nanny.

"You'll see."

During the next few hours a feat was performed by this simple, pious New England mother which was equal in its way to Wolfe's storming of the Heights of Abraham. It took no more genius and audacity of bravery for Wolfe to cheer his wondering soldiers up those steep precipices, under the sleeping eyes of the enemy, than for Sarah Penn, at the head of her children, to move all their little household goods into the new barn while her husband was away.

Nanny and Sammy followed their mother's instructions without a murmur; indeed, they were overawed. There is a certain uncanny and superhuman quality about all such purely original undertakings as their mother's was to them. Nanny went back and forth with her light loads, and Sammy tugged with sober energy.

At five o'clock in the afternoon the little house in which the Penns had lived for forty years had emptied itself into the new barn.

Every builder builds somewhat for unknown purposes, and is in a measure a prophet. The architect of Adoniram Penn's barn, while he designed it for the comfort of four-footed animals, had planned better than he knew for the comfort of humans. Sarah Penn saw at a glance its possibilities. Those great box-stalls, with quilts hung before them, would make better bedrooms than the one she had occupied for forty years, and there was a tight carriage-room. The harness room, with its chimney and shelves, would make a kitchen of her dreams. The great middle space would make a parlor, by and by, fit for a palace. Upstairs there was as much room as down. With partitions and windows, what a house would there be! Sarah looked at the row of stanchions before the allotted space for cows, and reflected that she would have her front entry there.

At six o'clock the stove was up in the harness-room, the kettle was boiling, and the table set for tea. It looked almost as home-like as the abandoned house across the yard had ever done. The young hired man milked, and Sarah directed him calmly to bring the milk to the new barn. He came gaping, dropping little blots of foam from the brimming pails on the grass. Before the next morning he had spread the story of Adoniram Penn's wife moving into the new barn all over the little village. Men assembled in the store and talked it over, women with shawls over their heads scuttled into each other's houses before their work was done. Any deviation from the ordinary course of life in this quiet town was enough to stop all progress in it. Everybody paused to look at the staid, independent figure on the side track. There was a difference of opinion with regard to her. Some held her to be insane; some, of a lawless and rebellious spirit.

Friday the minister went to see her. It was in the forenoon, and she was at the barn door shelling pease for dinner. She looked up and returned his salutation with dignity, then she went on with her work. She did not invite him in. The saintly expression of her face remained fixed, but there was an angry flush over it.

The minister stood awkwardly before her, and talked. She handled the pease as if they were bullets. At last she looked up, and her eyes showed the spirit that her meek front had covered for a lifetime.

"There ain't no use talkin', Mr. Hersey," said she. "I've thought it all over an' over, an' I believe I'm doin' what's right. I've made it the subject of prayer, an' it's betwixt me an' the Lord an' Adoniram. There ain't no call for nobody else to worry about it."

"Well, of course, if you have brought it to the Lord in prayer, and feel satisfied that you are doing right, Mrs. Penn," said the minister, helplessly. His thin gray-bearded face was pathetic. He was a sickly man; his youthful confidence had cooled; he had to scourge himself up to some of his pastoral duties as relentlessly as a Catholic ascetic, and then he was prostrated by the smart.

"I think it's right jest as much as I think it was right for our forefathers to come over from the old country 'cause they didn't have what belonged to 'em," said Mrs. Penn. She arose. The barn threshold might have been Plymouth Rock from her bearing. "I don't doubt you mean well, Mr. Hersey," said she, "but there are things people hadn't ought to interfere with. I've been a member of the church for over forty year. I've got my own mind an' my own feet, an' I'm goin' to think my own thoughts an' go my own ways, an' nobody but the Lord is goin' to dictate to me unless I've a mind to have him. Won't you come in an' set down? How is Mis' Hersey?"

"She is well, I thank you," replied the minister. He added some more perplexed apologetic remarks; then he retreated.

He could expound the intricacies of every character study in the Scriptures, he was competent to grasp the Pilgrim Fathers and all historical innovators, but Sarah Penn was beyond him. He could deal with primal cases, but parallel ones worsted him. But, after all, although it was aside from his province, he wondered more how Adoniram Penn would deal with his wife than how the Lord would. Everybody shared the wonder. When Adoniram's four new cows arrived, Sarah ordered three to be put in the old barn, the other in the house shed where the cooking-stove had stood. That added to the excitement. It was whispered that all four cows were domiciled in the house.

Towards sunset on Saturday, when Adoniram was expected home, there was a knot of men in the road near the new barn. The hired man had milked, but he still hung around the premises. Sarah Penn had supper all ready. There was brown-bread and baked beans and a custard pie; it was the supper that Adoniram loved on a Saturday night. She had on a clean calico, and she bore herself imperturbably. Nanny and Sammy kept close at her heels. Their eyes were large, and Nanny was full of nervous tremors. Still there was to them more pleasant excitement than anything else. An inborn confidence in their mother over their father asserted itself.

Sammy looked out of the harness-room window. "There he is," he announced, in an awed whisper. He and Nanny peeped around the casing. Mrs. Penn kept on about her work. The children watched Adoniram leave the new horse standing in the drive while he went to the house door. It was fastened. Then he went around to the shed. That door was seldom locked, even when the family was away. The thought how her father would be confronted by the cow flashed upon Nanny. There was a hysterical sob in her throat. Adoniram emerged from the shed and stood looking about in a dazed fashion. His lips moved; he was saying something, but they could not hear what it was. The hired man was peeping around a corner of the old barn, but nobody saw him.

Adoniram took the new horse by the bridle and led him across the yard to the new barn. Nanny and Sammy slunk close to their mother. The barn doors rolled back, and there stood Adoniram, with the long mild face of the great Canadian farm horse looking over his shoulder.

Nanny kept behind her mother, but Sammy stepped suddenly forward, and stood in front of her.

Adoniram stared at the group. "What on airth you all down here for?" said he. "What's the matter over to the house?"

"We've come here to live, father," said Sammy. His shrill voice quavered out bravely.

"What"—Adoniram sniffed—"what is it smells like cookin'?" said he. He stepped forward and looked in the open door of the harness-room. Then he turned to his wife. His old bristling face was pale and frightened. "What on airth does this mean, mother?" he gasped.

"You come in here, father," said Sarah. She led the way into the harness-room and shut the door. "Now, father," said she, "You needn't be scared. I ain't crazy. There ain't nothin' to be upset over. But we've come here to live, an' we're goin' to live here. We've got jest as good a right here as new horses an' cows. The house wa'n't fit for us to live in any longer, an' I made up my mind I wa'n't goin' to stay there. I've done my duty by you forty year, an' I'm goin' to do it now; but I'm goin' to live here. You've got to put in some windows and partitions; an' you'll have to buy some furniture."

"Why, mother!" the old man gasped.

"You'd better take your coat off an' get washed—there's the wash-basin—an' then we'll have supper."

"Why, mother!"

Sammy went past the window, leading the new horse to the old barn. The old man saw him, and shook his head speechlessly. He tried to take off his coat, but his arms seemed to lack the power. His wife helped him. She poured some water into the tin basin, and put in a piece of soap. She got the comb and brush, and smoothed his thin gray hair after he had washed. Then she put the beans, hot bread, and tea on the table. Sammy came in, and the family drew up. Adoniram sat looking dazedly at his plate, and they waited.

"Ain't you goin' to ask a blessin', father?" said Sarah.

And the old man bent his head and mumbled.

All through the meal he stopped eating at intervals, and stared furtively at his wife; but he ate well. The home food tasted good to him, and his old frame was too sturdily healthy to be affected by his mind. But after supper he went out, and sat down on the step of the smaller door at the right of the barn, through which he had meant his Jerseys to pass in stately file, but which Sarah designed for her front house door, and he leaned his head on his hands.

After the supper dishes were cleared away and the milk-pans washed, Sarah went out to him. The twilight was deepening. There was a clear green glow in the sky. Before them stretched the smooth level of field; in the distance was a cluster of hay-stacks like the huts of a village; the air was very cool and calm and sweet. The landscape might have been an ideal one of peace.

Sarah bent over and touched her husband on one of his thin, sinewy shoulders. "Father!"

The old man's shoulders heaved: he was weeping.

"Why, don't do so, father," said Sarah.

"I'll—put up the—partitions, an'—everything you—want, mother."

Sarah put her apron up to her face; she was overcome by her own triumph.

Adoniram was like a fortress whose walls had no active resistance, and went down the instant the right besieging tools were used. "Why, mother," he said, hoarsely, "I hadn't no idee you was so set on't as all this comes to."

QUESTIONS

"The Revolt of 'Mother' "

1. What is the significance of the description of Sarah Penn near the start of the story, in the paragraph beginning, "Then she stood waiting. She was a small woman, . . ."? How does it reveal as much about Mrs. Penn's character as about her physical appearance? What is paradoxical—and revealing—about the author's observation that "her eyes . . . looked as if the meekness had been the result of her own will, never of the will of another"?

2. How would you describe the relation between the sexes in the world portrayed in this story (i.e., nineteenth-century New England)? What is the position of the men in this world? The women? What is expected of each in regard to work and behavior?

3. Throughout the story, Freeman compares Sarah Penn to figures from the past. Point to these comparisons and explain their significance.

4. How important is Freeman's use of dialect to the success of this story? How does Sarah Penn's manner of speech, unlearned as it is, actually heighten our sense of her "nobility of character"?

5. In what ways does Sarah Penn's heroism display itself throughout this story? How is it evident, not only in the dramatic act at the climax of the story, but in every detail of her day-to-day life?

6. Is there a "call" in this story, an unlooked-for event that sets the heroic deed in motion? Explain.

7. How do the townspeople respond to the news of Mrs. Penn's deed? Why do they respond this way? What does this reaction reveal about the prevailing attitude toward women in that time and place?

8. In one sense, the treasure Mrs. Penn wins is the new house she has lived without for forty years. Is there another, even more significant "treasure" that she attains?

9. What sort of marriage do Sarah and Adoniram seem to have? Do you consider it a good one? What is your impression of Adoniram Penn? Does the ending affect your feelings about him in any way? Why is his wife "overcome by her own triumph"?

CHAPTER SIX

Transformation

To accomplish the quest, to surrender the life you have always known for the treasure that promises a new beginning, is not merely to risk death but, in a sense, to experience it. As we saw in Chapter Three, this fact is symbolized in world mythology by stories in which the quest heroes disappear for a time from the face of the earth. They may be swallowed by a monster, buried alive, lost in a subterranean kingdom, or actually make the journey to the land of the dead. The last of the twelve superhuman labors demanded of the Greek hero Herakles, for example, was to descend into the underworld and capture Cerberus, the monstrous, three-headed hell-hound that guarded the entrance to Hades. The voyage to the netherworld is a common motif in quest literature, found in such works as Homer's *Odyssey*, Dante's *Divine Comedy,* and J.R.R. Tolkien's *Lord of the Rings* (in which the warrior-king Aragorn must travel "the Paths of the Dead").

However, the hero's descent into death, which represents the final casting off of an old and outworn mode of existence, is not the end of the quest, but a prelude to its final stage. Once the treasure has been secured, the hero must still return with it. The fictional characters who successfully complete the journey are never the same people they were when they first started out; the treasure they have sought and found is precisely the transformation of lives that have been too constricted or of selves they have outgrown. For this reason, the last phase of the adventure is not simply a return but a type of resurrection: the heroes die in order to be reborn. The changes that take place within them are profound, affecting their values, perceptions, the very way they experience life. Because of this, everything around them seems transfigured: the world itself wears a new face.

In some quest stories, of course, the world the hero passes into seems worse, at first, than the one she or he was left. This is particularly true of those initiation stories in which the protagonist makes the transition from youthful innocence to mature expeirence. Works like Robert Penn Warren's "Blackberry Winter," Hawthorne's "My Kinsman, Major Molineux," and, in this chapter, Tillie Olsen's "O Yes" portray heroes who, thrust from the paradise of sheltered childhoods, must learn to deal with the harsh demands of adult life. It is common for people, both in and out of fiction, to resist this particular type of transformation. Regarding the past with a piercing nostalgia, they may struggle to hold onto it as long as they can. To let go of the child's world of pleasant irresponsibility is rarely easy; nonetheless, it is necessary. It is just this necessity, along with other difficult and unpleasant facts of life, that the hero must learn to accept or risk remaining a child forever.

Not every hero is able to make this transition. Washington Irving's Rip Van Winkle remains cheerfully childlike even as an old man, having bypassed maturity entirely by skipping straight from his carefree youth to his "second childhood." Other characters, on the other hand, struggle heroically against the forces that work to hold them back, to trap them in perpetual dependency. For example, the protagonist of Jean Stafford's "The Liberation" (see Chapter One) knows that she must make one last desperate effort to break free of her smothering surroundings or remain an infant forever.

Thus, while some characters must reconcile themselves to the changes that occur during their journeys through life, others eagerly quest after transformation or welcome it gratefully if it comes to them by chance. The hunger for rebirth, in fact, is basic to human beings and is manifested in many different ways. In religion, the yearning for rebirth is expressed in such beliefs as reincarnation, the transmigration of souls, and the resurrection of the body after death, as well as in the conversion experience, the conviction that one has been "born again" through the grace of God. Other people long for the kind of rebirth that will affect their *material* rather than spiritual condition; examples are immigrants who come to America looking for a new life. Still others seek to relieve feelings of depletion or stagnation; for example, the city-dweller who hopes to be regenerated by a vacation in the wilderness or the frustrated individual who believes that a change in career, marital status, or geography will make his or her life more fulfilling. Finally, some people struggle toward what is perhaps the most difficult rebirth of all: *psychological* rebirth, the transformation of their own personalities. Depressed by the sense that they have not lived up to their potential or trapped in deeply entrenched patterns of destructive behavior, these people undertake the long and painful process of inner exploration. Their quest is for the self-knowledge that can liberate them from neurosis and put them in touch with their untapped inner resources that can revitalize them.

The transformations in the following stories are brought about by a variety of means. The protagonist of D. H. Lawrence's "The Horse-Dealer's Daughter," Mabel Pervin, whose deadness of feeling is reflected not only in the stonelike impassivity of her face but also in the gray, wintry landscape that surrounds her, is brought back to emotional life by the power of love; her savior, Jack Fergusson, undergoes a similar process of death and rebirth.

The bereaved protagonist of Bharati Mukherjee's "The Management of Grief" makes an odyssey to a Himalyan temple, where the spirit of her dead husband appears with a healing admonition. Similarly, Slepstov, the hero of Vladimir Nabokov's luminous story, "Christmas," is redeemed from despair by a small miracle, a vision of life reborn on the holiday morning. While these stories focus on intense experiences of personal rebirth, Marguerite Yourcenar's "How Wang-Fo Was Saved" deals with metamorphosis of a different order—the power of great art to transfigure our experience of the world itself.

For all their differences, however, the works in this chapter and throughout this anthology attest to the same fundamental feature of the human spirit: not only a perennial hunger for renewal but also an inextinguishable faith in its possibility. Many of the characters in these stories never accomplish their quests; some are defeated before they begin. Like mythology, serious fiction does not minimize the difficulties of the quest. But for every protagonist who fails, another succeeds, and in so doing demonstrates the human potential for meaningful transformation, the ability of people to change their world and themselves for the better.

The Horse-Dealer's Daughter

D. H. LAWRENCE

"Well, Mabel, and what are you going to do with yourself?" asked Joe, with foolish flippancy. He felt quite safe himself. Without listening for an answer, he turned aside, worked a grain of tobacco to the tip of his tongue, and spat it out. He did not care about anything, since he felt safe himself.

The three brothers and the sister sat round the desolate breakfast table, attempting some sort of desultory consultation. The morning's post had given the final tap to the family fortunes, and all was over. The dreary dining-room itself, with its heavy mahogany furniture, looked as it if were waiting to be done away with.

But the consultation amounted to nothing. There was a strange air of ineffectuality about the three men, as they sprawled at table, smoking and reflecting vaguely on their own condition. The girl was alone, a rather short, sullen-looking young woman of twenty-seven. She did not share the same life as her brothers. She would have been good-looking, save for the impassive fixity of her face, "bull-dog," as her brothers called it.

There was a confused tramping of horses' feet outside. The three men all sprawled round in their chairs to watch. Beyond the dark holly-bushes that separated the strip of lawn from the high-road, they could see a cavalcade of shire horses swinging out of their own yard, being taken for exercise. This was the last time. These were the last horses that would go through their hands. The young men watched with critical, callous look. They were all frightened at the collapse of their lives, and the sense of disaster in which they were involved left them no inner freedom.

Yet they were three fine, well-set fellows enough. Joe, the eldest, was a man of thirty-three, broad and handsome in a hot, flushed way. His face was red, he twisted his black moustache over a thick finger, his eyes were shallow and restless. He had a sensual way of uncovering his teeth when he laughed, and his bearing was stupid. Now he watched the horses with a glazed look of helplessness in his eyes, a certain stupor of downfall.

The great draught-horses swung past. They were tied head to tail, four of them, and they heaved along to where a lane branched off from the highroad, planting their great hoofs floutingly in the fine black mud, swinging their great rounded haunches sumptuosly, and trotting a few sudden steps as they were led into the lane, round the corner. Every movement showed a massive, slumbrous strength, and a stupidity which held them in subjection. The groom at the head looked back, jerking the leading rope. And the cavalcade moved out of sight up the lane, the tail of the last horse, bobbed up tight and stiff, held out taut from the swinging great haunches as they rocked behind the hedges in a motionlike sleep.

Joe watched with glazed hopeless eyes. The horses were almost like his own body to him. He felt he was done for now. Luckily, he was engaged to a woman as old as himself, and therefore her father, who was steward of a neighbouring estate, would provide him with a job. He would marry and go into harness. His life was over, he would be a subject animal now.

He turned uneasily aside, the retreating steps of the horses echoing in his ears. Then, with foolish restlessness, he reached for the scraps of bacon-rind from the plates, and making a faint whistling sound, flung them to the terrier that lay against the fender. He watched the dog swallow them, and waited till the creature looked into his eyes. Then a faint grin came on his face, and in a high, foolish voice he said:

"You won't get much more bacon, shall you, you little b———?"

The dog faintly and dismally wagged its tail, then lowered its haunches, circled round, and lay down again.

There was another helpless silence at the table. Joe sprawled uneasily in his seat, not willing to go till the family conclave was dissolved. Fred Henry, the second brother, was erect, clean-limbed, alert. He had watched the passing of the horses with more *sang-froid*. If he was an animal, like Joe, he was an animal which controls, not one which is controlled. He was master of any horse, and he carried himself with a well-tempered air of mastery. But he was not master of the situations of life. He pushed his coarse brown moustache upwards, off his lip, and glanced irritably at his sister, who sat impassive and inscrutable.

"You'll go and stop with Lucy for a bit, shan't you?" he asked. The girl did not answer.

"I don't see what else you can do," persisted Fred Henry.

"Go as a skivvy," Joe interpolated laconically.

The girl did not move a muscle.

"If I was her, I should go in for training for a nurse," said Malcolm, the youngest of them all. He was the baby of the family, a young man of twenty-two, with a fresh, jaunty *museau*.

But Mabel did not take any notice of him. They had talked at her and round her for so many years, that she hardly heard them at all.

The marble clock on the mantel-piece softly chimed the half-hour, the dog rose uneasily from the hearthrug and looked at the party at the break-fast table. But still they sat on in ineffectual conclave.

"Oh, all right," said Joe suddenly, *à propos* of nothing. "I'll get a move on."

He pushed back his chair, straddled his knees with a downward jerk, to get them free, in horsey fashion, and went to the fire. Still he did not go out of the room; he was curious to know what the others would do or say. He began to charge his pipe, looking down at the dog and saying, in a high, affected voice:

"Going wi' me? Going wi' me are ter? Tha'rt goin' further than tha counts on just now, dost hear?"

The dog faintly wagged its tail, the man stuck out his jaw and covered his pipe with his hands, and puffed intently, losing himself in the tobacco, looking down all the while at the dog, with an absent brown eye. The dog looked up at him in mournful distrust. Joe stood with his knees stuck out, in real horsey fashion.

"Have you had a letter from Lucy?" Fred Henry asked of his sister.

"Last week," came the neutral reply.

"And what does she say?"

There was no answer.

"Does she *ask* you to go and stop there?" persisted Fred Henry.

"She says I can if I like."

"Well, then, you'd better. Tell her you'll come on Monday."

This was received in silence.

"That's what you'll do then, is it?" said Fred Henry, in some exasperation.

But she made no answer. There was a silence of futility and irritation in the room. Malcolm grinned fatuously.

"You'll have to make up your mind between now and next Wednesday," said Joe loudly, "or else find yourself lodgings on the kerbstone."

The face of the young woman darkened, but she sat on immutable.

"Here's Jack Fergusson!" exclaimed Malcolm, who was looking aimlessly out of the window.

"Where?" exclaimed Joe, loudly.

"Just gone past."

"Coming in?"

Malcolm craned his neck to see the gate.

"Yes," he said.

There was a silence. Mabel sat on like one condemned, at the head of the table. Then a whistle was heard from the kitchen. The dog got up and barked sharply. Joe opened the door and shouted:

"Come on."

After a moment, a young man entered. He was muffled up in overcoat and a purple woollen scarf, and his tweed cap, which he did not remove, was pulled down on his head. He was of medium height, his face was rather long and pale, his eyes looked tired.

"Hello Jack! Well, Jack!" exclaimed Malcolm and Joe. Fred Henry merely said "Jack!"

"What's doing?" asked the newcomer, evidently addressing Fred Henry.

"Same. We've got to be out by Wednesday.—Got a cold?"

"I have—got it bad, too."

"Why don't you stop in?"

"*Me* stop in? When I can't stand on my legs, perhaps I shall have a chance." The young man spoke huskily. He had a slight Scotch accent.

"It's a knock-out, isn't it," said Joe boisterously, "if a doctor goes round croaking with a cold. Looks bad for the patients, doesn't it?"

The young doctor looked at him slowly.

"Anything the matter with *you*, then?" he asked, sarcastically.

"Not as I know of. Damn your eyes, I hope not. Why?"

"I thought you were very concerned about the patients, wondered if you might be one yourself."

"Damn it, no, I've never been patient to no flaming doctor, and hope I never shall be," returned Joe.

At this point Mabel rose from the table, and they all seemed to become aware of her existence. She began putting the dishes together. The young doctor looked at her, but did not address her. He had not greeted her. She went out of the room with the tray, her face impassive and unchanged.

"When are you off then, all of you?" asked the doctor.

"I'm catching the eleven-forty," replied Malcolm. "Are you goin' down wi' th' trap, Joe?"

"Yes, I've told you I'm going down wi' th' trap, haven't I?"

"We'd better be getting her in then.—So long, Jack, if I don't see you before I go," said Malcolm, shaking hands.

He went out, followed by Joe, who seemed to have his tail between his legs.

"Well, this is the devil's own," exclaimed the doctor, when he was left alone with Fred Henry. "Going before Wednesday, are you?"

"That's the orders," replied the other.

"Where, to Northampton?"

"That's it."

"The devil!" exclaimed Fergusson, with quiet chagrin.

And there was silence between the two.

"All settled up, are you?" asked Fergusson.

"About."

There was another pause.

"Well, I shall miss yer, Freddy boy," said the young doctor.

"And I shall miss thee, Jack," returned the other.

"Miss you like hell," mused the doctor.

Fred Henry turned aside. There was nothing to say. Mabel came in again, to finish clearing the table.

"What are *you* going to do then, Miss Pervin?" asked Fergusson. "Going to your sister's, are you?"

Mabel looked at him with her steady, dangerous eyes, that always made him uncomfortable, unsettling his superficial ease.

"No," she said.

"Well, what in the name of fortune *are* you going to do? Say what you *mean* to do," cried Fred Henry, with futile intensity.

But she only averted her head, and continued her work. She folded the white table-cloth, and put on the chenille cloth.

"The sulkiest bitch that ever trod!" muttered her brother.

But she finished her task with perfectly impassive face, the young doctor watching her interestedly all the while. Then she went out.

Fred Henry stared after her, clenching his lips, his blue eyes fixing in sharp antagonism, as he made a grimace of sour exasperation.

"You could bray her into bits, and that's all you'd get out of her," he said, in a small, narrowed tone.

The doctor smiled faintly.

"What's she *going* to do then?" he asked.

"Strike me if *I* know!" returned the other.

There was a pause. Then the doctor stirred.

"I'll be seeing you to-night, shall I?" he said to his friend.

"Ay—where's it to be? Are we going over to Jessdale?"

"I don't know. I've got such a cold on me. I'll come round to the Moon and Stars, anyway."

"Let Lizzie and May miss their night for once, eh?"

"That's it—if I feel as I do now."

"All's one—"

The two young men went through the passage and down to the back door together. The house was large, but it was servantless now, and desolate. At the back was a small bricked house-yard, and beyond that a big square, gravelled fine and red, and having stables on two sides. Sloping, dank, winter-dark fields stretched away on the open sides.

But the stables were empty. Joseph Pervin, the father of the family, had been a man of no education, who had become a fairly large horse dealer. The stables had been full of horses, there was a great turmoil and come-and-go of horses and of dealers and grooms. Then the kitchen was full of servants. But of late things had declined. The old man had married a second time, to retrieve his fortunes. Now he was dead and everything was gone to the dogs, there was nothing but debt and threatening.

For months, Mabel had been servantless in the big house, keeping the home together in penury for her ineffectual brothers. She had kept house for ten years. But previously, it was with unstinted means. Then, however brutal and coarse everything was, the sense of money had kept her proud, confident. The men might be foul-mouthed, the women in the kitchen might have bad reputations, her brothers might have illegitimate children. But so long as there was money, the girl felt herself established, and brutally proud, reserved.

No company came to the house, save dealers and coarse men. Mabel had no associates of her own sex, after her sister went away. But she did not mind. She went regularly to church, she attended to her father. And she lived in the memory of her mother, who had died when she was fourteen, and whom she had loved. She had loved her father, too, in a different way, depending upon him, and feeling secure in him, until at the age of fifty-four he married again. And then she had set hard against him. Now he had died and left them all hopelessly in debt.

She had suffered badly during the period of poverty. Nothing, however, could shake the curious sullen, animal pride that dominated each member of the family. Now, for Mabel, the end had come. Still she would not cast about her. She would follow her own way just the same. She would always hold the keys of her own situation. Mindless and persistent, she endured from day to day. Why should she think? Why should she answer anybody? It was enough that this was the end, and there was no way out. She need not pass any more darkly along the main street of the small town, avoiding every eye. She need not demean herself any more, going into the shops and buying the cheapest food. This was at an end. She thought of nobody, not even of herself. Mindless and persistent, she seemed in a sort of ecstasy to be coming nearer to her fulfilment, her own glorification, approaching her dead mother, who was glorified.

In the afternoon she took a little bag, with shears and sponge and a small scrubbing brush, and went out. It was a grey, wintry day, with saddened, dark-green fields and an atmosphere blackened by the smoke of foundries not far off. She went quickly, darkly along the causeway, heeding nobody, through the town to the churchyard.

There she always felt secure, as if no one could see her, although as a matter of fact she was exposed to the stare of everyone who passed along under the churchyard wall. Nevertheless, once under the shadow of the great looming church, among the graves, she felt immune from the world, reserved within the thick churchyard wall as in another country.

Carefully she clipped the grass from the grave, and arranged the pinky-white, small chrysanthemums in the tin cross. When this was done, she took an empty jar from a neighbouring grave, brought water, and carefully, most scrupulously sponged the marble headstone and the coping-stone.

It gave her sincere satisfaction to do this. She felt in immediate contact with the world of her mother. She took minute pains, went through the park in a state bordering on pure happiness, as if in performing this task she came into a subtle, intimate connection with her mother. For the life she followed here in the world was far less real than the world of death she inherited from her mother.

The doctor's house was just by the church. Fergusson, being a mere hired assistant, was slave to the countryside. As he hurried now to attend to the outpatients in the surgery, glancing across the graveyard with his quick eye, he saw the girl at her task at the grave. She seemed so intent and remote, it was like looking into another world. Some mystical element was touched in him. He slowed down as he walked, watching her as if spell-bound.

She lifted her eyes, feeling him looking. Their eyes met. And each looked again at once, each feeling, in some way, found out by the other. He lifted his cap and passed on down the road. There remained distinct in his consciousness, like a vision, the memory of her face, lifted from the tombstone in the church-yard, and looking at him with slow, large, portentous eyes. It *was* portentous, her face. It seemed to mesmerise him. There was a heavy power in her eyes which laid hold of his whole being, as if he had drunk some powerful drug. He had been feeling weak and done before. Now the life came back into him, he felt delivered from his own fretted, daily self.

He finished his duties at the surgery as quickly as might be, hastily filling up the bottles of the waiting people with cheap drugs. Then, in perpetual haste, he set off again to visit several cases in another part of his round, before teatime. At all times he preferred to walk, if he could, but particularly when he was not well. He fancied the motion restored him.

The afternoon was falling. It was grey, deadened, and wintry, with a slow, moist, heavy coldness sinking in and deadening all the faculties. But why should he think or notice? He hastily climbed the hill and turned across the dark-green fields, following the black cinder-track. In the distance, across a shallow dip in the country, the small town was clustered like smouldering ash, a tower, a spire, a heap of low, raw, extinct houses. And on the nearest fringe of the town, sloping into the dip, was Oldmeadow, the Pervins' house. He could see the stables and the outbuildings distinctly, as they lay towards him on the slope. Well, he would not go there many more times! Another resource would be lost to him, another place gone: the only company he cared for in the alien, ugly little town he was losing. Nothing but work, drudgery, constant hastening from dwelling to dwelling among the colliers and the iron-workers. It wore him out, but at the same time he had a craving for it. It was a stimulant to him to be in the homes of the working people, moving as it were through the innermost body of their life. His nerves were excited and gratified. He could come so near, into the very lives of the rough, inarticulate, powerfully emotional men and women. He grumbled, he said he hated the hellish hole. But as a matter of fact it excited him, the contact with the rough, strongly-feeling people was a stimulant applied direct to his nerves.

Below Oldmeadow, in the green, shallow, soddened hollow of fields, lay a square, deep pond. Roving across the landscape, the doctor's quick eye detected a figure in black passing through the gate of the field, down towards the pond. He looked again. It would be Mabel Pervin. His mind suddenly became alive and attentive.

Why was she going down there? He pulled up on the path on the slope above, and stood staring. He could just make sure of the small black figure moving in the hollow of the failing day. He seemed to see her in the midst of such obscurity, that he was like a clairvoyant, seeing rather with the mind's eye than with ordinary sight. Yet he could see her positively enough, whilst he kept his eye attentive. He felt, if he looked away from her, in the thick, ugly falling dusk, he would lose her altogether.

He followed her minutely as she moved, direct and intent, like something transmitted rather than stirring in voluntary activity, straight down the field towards the pond. There she stood on the bank for a moment. She never raised her head. Then she waded slowly into the water.

He stood motionless as the small black figure walked slowly and deliberately towards the centre of the pond, very slowly, gradually moving deeper
into the motionless water, and still moving forward as the water got up to
her breast. Then he could see her no more in the dusk of the dead afternoon.

"There!" he exclaimed. "Would you believe it?"

And he hastened straight down, running over the wet, soddened fields,
pushing through the hedges, down into the depression of callous wintry
obscurity. It took him several minutes to come to the pond. He stood on
the bank, breathing heavily. He could see nothing. His eyes seemed to
penetrate the dead water. Yes, perhaps that was the dark shadow of her
black clothing beneath the surface of the water.

He slowly ventured into the pond. The bottom was deep, soft clay, he
sank in, and the water clasped dead cold round his legs. As he stirred he
could smell the cold, rotten clay that fouled up into the water. It was ob-
jectionable in his lungs. Still, repelled and yet not heeding, he moved
deeper into the pond. The cold water rose over his thighs, over his loins,
upon his abdomen. The lower part of his body was all sunk in the hideous
cold element. And the bottom was so deeply soft and uncertain, he was
afraid of pitching with his mouth underneath. He could not swim, and was
afraid.

He crouched a little, spreading his hands under the water and moving
them round, trying to feel for her. The dead cold pond swayed upon his
chest. He moved again, a little deeper, and again, with his hands underneath, he felt all around under the water. And he touched her clothing.
But it evaded his fingers. He made a desperate effort to grasp it.

And so doing he lost his balance and went under, horribly, suffocating
in the foul earthy water, struggling madly for a few moments. At last, after
what seemed an eternity, he got his footing, rose again into the air and
looked around. He gasped, and knew he was in the world. Then he looked
at the water. She had risen near him. He grasped her clothing, and drawing her nearer, turned to take his way to land again.

He went very slowly, carefully, absorbed in the slow progress. He rose
higher, climbing out of the pond. The water was now only about his legs;
he was thankful, full of relief to be out of the clutches of the pond. He
lifted her and staggered on to the bank, out of the horror of wet, grey clay.

He laid her down on the bank. She was quite unconscious and running
with water. He made the water come from her mouth, he worked to restore her. He did not have to work very long before he could feel the
breathing begin again in her; she was breathing naturally. He worked a
little longer. He could feel her live beneath his hands; she was coming
back. He wiped her face, wrapped her in his overcoat, looked round into
the dim, dark-grey world, then lifted her and staggered down the bank and
across the fields.

It seemed an unthinkably long way, and his burden so heavy he felt he
would never get to the house. But at last he was in the stable-yard, and
then in the house-yard. He opened the door and went into the house. In

the kitchen he laid her down on the hearthrug, and called. The house was empty. But the fire was burning in the grate.

Then again he kneeled to attend to her. She was breathing regularly, her eyes were wide open and as if conscious, but there seemed something missing in her look. She was conscious in herself, but unconscious of her surroundings.

He ran upstairs, took blankets from a bed, and put them before the fire to warm. Then he removed her saturated, earthy-smelling clothing, rubbed her dry with a towel, and wrapped her naked in the blankets. Then he went into the dining-room, to look for spirits. There was a little whiskey. He drank a gulp himself, and put some into her mouth.

The effect was instantaneous. She looked full into his face, as if she had been seeing him for some time, and yet had only just become conscious of him.

"Dr. Fergusson?" she said.

"What?" he answered.

He was divesting himself of his coat, intending to find some dry clothing upstairs. He could not bear the smell of the dead, clayey water, and he was mortally afraid for his own health.

"What did I do?" she asked.

"Walked into the pond," he replied. He had begun to shudder like one sick, and could hardly attend to her. Her eyes remained full on him, he seemed to be going dark in his mind, looking back at her helplessly. The shuddering became quieter in him, his life came back in him, dark and unknowing, but strong again.

"Was I out of my mind?" she asked, while her eyes were fixed on him all the time.

"Maybe, for the moment," he replied. He felt quiet, because his strength had come back. The strange fretful strain had left him.

"Am I out of my mind now?" she asked.

"Are you?" he reflected a moment. "No," he answered truthfully, "I don't see that you are." He turned his face aside. He was afraid, now, because he felt dazed, and felt dimly that her power was stronger than his, in this issue. And she continued to look at him fixedly all the time. "Can you tell me where I shall find some dry things to put on?" he asked.

"Did you dive into the pond for me?" she asked.

"No," he answered. "I walked in. But I went in overhead as well."

There was silence for a moment. He hesitated. He very much wanted to go upstairs to get into dry clothing. But there was another desire in him. And she seemed to hold him. His will seemed to have gone to sleep, and left him, standing there slack before her. But he felt warm inside himself. He did not shudder at all, though his clothes were sodden on him.

"Why did you?" she asked.

"Because I didn't want you to do such a foolish thing," he said.

"It wasn't foolish," she said, still gazing at him as she lay on the floor, with a sofa cushion under her head. "It was the right thing to do. *I* knew best, then."

"I'll go and shift these wet things," he said. But still he had not the power to move out of her presence, until she sent him. It was as if she had the life of his body in her hands, and he could not extricate himself. Or perhaps he did not want to.

Suddenly she sat up. Then she became aware of her own immediate condition. She felt the blankets about her, she knew her own limbs. For a moment it seemed as if her reason were going. She looked round, with wild eye, as if seeking something. He stood still with fear. She saw her clothing lying scattered.

"Who undressed me?" she asked, her eyes resting full and inevitable on his face.

"I did," he replied, "to bring you round."

For some moments she sat and gazed at him awfully, her lips parted.

"Do you love me then?" she asked.

He only stood and stared at her, fascinated. His soul seemed to melt.

She shuffled forward on her knees, and put her arms round him, round his legs, as he stood there, pressing her breasts against his knees and thighs, clutching him with strange, convulsive certainty, pressing his thighs against her, drawing him to her face, her throat, as she looked up at him with flaring, humble eyes of transfiguration, triumphant in first possession.

"You love me," she murmured, in strange transport, yearning and triumphant and confident. "You love me. I know you love me, I know."

And she was passionately kissing his knees, through the wet clothing, passionately and indiscriminately kissing his knees, his legs, as if unaware of everything.

He looked down at the tangled wet hair, the wild, bare, animal shoulders. He was amazed, bewildered, and afraid. He had never thought of loving her. He had never wanted to love her. When he rescued her and restored her, he was a doctor, and she was a patient. He had had no single personal thought of her. Nay, this introduction of the personal element was very distasteful to him, a violation of his professional honour. It was horrible to have her there embracing his knees. It was horrible. He revolted from it, violently. And yet—and yet—he had not the power to break away.

She looked at him again, with the same supplication of powerful love, and that same transcendent, frightening light of triumph. In view of the delicate flame which seemed to come from her face like a light, he was powerless. And yet he had never intended to love her. He had never intended. And something stubborn in him could not give way.

"You love me," she repeated, in a murmur of deep, rhapsodic assurance. "You love me."

Her hands were drawing him, drawing him down to her. He was afraid, even a little horrified. For he had, really, no intention of loving her. Yet her hands were drawing him towards her. He put out his hand quickly to steady himself, and grasped her bare shoulder. A flame seemed to burn the hand that grasped her soft shoulder. He had no intention of loving her: his whole will was against his yielding. It was horrible—And yet wonderful was the touch of her shoulder, beautiful the shining of her face. Was she perhaps mad? He had a horror of yielding to her. Yet something in him ached also.

He had been staring away at the door, away from her. But his hand remained on her shoulder. She had gone suddenly very still. He looked down at her. Her eyes were now wide with fear, with doubt, the light was dying from her face, a shadow of terrible greyness was returning. He could not bear the touch of her eyes' question upon him, and the look of death behind the question.

With an inward groan he gave way, and let his heart yield towards her. A sudden gentle smile came on his face. And her eyes, which never left his face, slowly, slowly filled with tears. He watched the strange water rise in her eyes, like some slow fountain coming up. And his heart seemed to burn and melt away in his breast.

He could not bear to look at her any more. He dropped on his knees and caught her head with his arms and pressed her face against his throat. She was very still. His heart, which seemed to have broken, was burning with a kind of agony in his breast. And he felt her slow, hot tears wetting his throat. But he could not move.

He felt the hot tears wet his neck and the hollows of his neck, and he remained motionless, suspended through one of man's eternities. Only now it had become indispensable to him to have her face pressed close to him; he could never let her go again. He could never let her head go away from the close clutch of his arm. He wanted to remain like that for ever, with his heart hurting him in a pain that was also life to him. Without knowing, he was looking down on her damp, soft brown hair.

Then, as it were suddenly, he smelt the horrid stagnant smell of that water. And at the same moment she drew away from him and looked at him. Her eyes were wistful and unfathomable. He was afraid of them, and he fell to kissing her, not knowing what he was doing. He wanted her eyes not to have that terrible, wistful, unfathomable look.

When she turned her face to him again, a faint delicate flush was glowing, and there was again dawning that terrible shining of joy in her eyes, which really terrified him, and yet which he now wanted to see, because he feared the look of doubt still more.

"You love me?" she said, rather faltering.

"Yes." The word cost him a painful effort. Not because it wasn't true. But because it was too newly true, the *saying* seemed to tear open again his newly-torn heart. And he hardly wanted it to be true, even now.

She lifted her face to him, and he bent forward and kissed her on the mouth gently, with the one kiss that is an eternal pledge. And as he kissed her his heart strained again in his breast. He never intended to love her. But now it was over. He had crossed over the gulf to her, and all that he had left behind had shrivelled and become void.

After the kiss, her eyes again slowly filled with tears. She sat still, away from him, with her face drooped aside, and her hands folded in her lap. The tears fell very slowly. There was complete silence. He too sat there motionless and silent on the hearthrug. The strange pain of his heart that was broken seemed to consume him. That he should love her? That this was love! That he should be ripped open in this way!—Him, a doctor!—How they would all jeer if they knew!—It was agony to him to think they might know.

In the curious naked pain of the thought he looked again to her. She was sitting there drooped into a muse. He saw a tear fall, and his heart flared hot. He saw for the first time that one of her shoulders was quite uncovered, one arm bare, he could see one of her small breasts; dimly, because it had become almost dark in the room.

"Why are you crying?" he asked, in an altered voice.

She looked up at him, and behind her tears the consciousness of her situation for the first time brought a dark look of shame to her eyes.

"I'm not crying, really," she said, watching him half frightened.

He reached his hand, and softly closed it on her bare arm.

"I love you! I love you!" he said in a soft, low vibrating voice, unlike himself.

She shrank, and dropped her head. The soft, penetrating grip of his hand on her arm distressed her. She looked up at him.

"I want to go," she said. "I want to go and get you some dry things."

"Why?" he said. "I'm all right."

"But I want to go," she said. "And I want you to change your things."

He released her arm, and she wrapped herself in the blanket, looking at him rather frightened. And still she did not rise.

"Kiss me," she said wistfully.

He kissed her, but briefly, half in anger.

Then, after a second, she rose nervously, all mixed up in the blanket. He watched her in her confusion, as she tried to extricate herself and wrap herself up so that she could walk. He watched her relentlessly, as she knew.

And as she went, the blanket trailing, and as he saw a glimpse of her feet and her white leg, he tried to remember her as she was when he had wrapped her in the blanket. But then he didn't want to remember, because she had been nothing to him then, and his nature revolted from remembering her as she was when she was nothing to him.

A tumbling muffled noise from within the dark house startled him. Then he heard her voice:—"There are clothes." He rose and went to the foot of the stairs, and gathered up the garments she had thrown down. Then he came back to the fire, to rub himself down and dress. He grinned at his own appearance, when he had finished.

The fire was sinking, so he put on coal. The house was now quite dark, save for the light of a street-lamp that shone in faintly from beyond the holly trees. He lit the gas with matches he found on the mantel-piece. Then he emptied the pockets of his own clothes, and threw all his wet things in a heap into the scullery. After which he gathered up her sodden clothes, gently, and put them in a separate heap on the copper-top in the scullery.

It was six o'clock on the clock. His own watch had stopped. He ought to

be back to the surgery. He waited, and still she did not come down. So he
went to the foot of the stairs and called:

"I shall have to go."

Almost immediately he heard her coming down. She had on her best
dress of black voile, and her hair was tidy, but still damp. She looked at
him—and in spite of herself, smiled.

"I don't like you in those clothes," she said.

"Do I look a sight?" he answered.

They were shy of one another.

"I'll make you some tea," she said.

"No, I must go."

"Must you?" And she looked at him again with the wide, strained, doubtful
eyes. And again, from the pain of his breast, he knew how he loved her.
He went and bent to kiss her, gently, passionately, with his heart's painful
kiss.

"And my hair smells so horrible," she murmured in distraction. "And
I'm so awful, I'm so awful! Oh, no, I'm too awful." And she broke into
bitter, heartbroken sobbing. "You can't want to love me, I'm horrible."

"Don't be silly, don't be silly," he said, trying to comfort her, kissing
her, holding her in his arms. "I want you, I want to marry you, we're going
to be married, quickly, quickly—to-morrow if I can."

But she only sobbed terribly, and cried.

"I feel awful. I feel awful. I feel I'm horrible to you."

"No, I want you, I want you," was all he answered, blindly, with that
terrible intonation which frightened her almost more than her horror lest
he should *not* want her.

QUESTIONS

"The Horse-Dealer's Daughter"

1. What is the situation in the Pervin home when the story begins? Why
is the household disbanding?

2. Look at the details Lawrence uses to describe Joe, the eldest of the
Pervin brothers. What quality is emphasized? What parallels does Lawrence
draw between Joe and the "great draught-horses" exercising in the yard? What
do these parallels suggest about Joe? What sort of animal is Fred Henry, the
second brother, compared to?

3. How do the brothers treat their sister, Mabel? In general, what sort of
attitude do the men seem to have toward women? How does Lawrence create
a powerful sense of the Pervin household as a place that is predominantly,

indeed brutally, masculine, a rough "man's world" in which women play a totally subordinate role?

4. How is Mabel described when we first meet her? How is she different from her brothers? What qualities do they possess that she apparently does not? Why does she act the way she does? Why does she look the way she does? What has happened to her as a result of living in the "brutal and coarse" environment of the Pervin home?

5. While Mabel seems totally alienated from her brothers, she, like all the members of her family, has a "sullen, animal pride." How does this trait show itself in her behavior?

6. Why is Mabel so attracted to the "world of her mother"? What exactly is that world? What is Mabel seeking in it? Why does she long so desperately to enter it?

7. "The Horse-Dealer's Daughter" abounds in images of death. Where do they appear? Why has Lawrence filled his story with these images? How do they relate to and reinforce the story's theme?

8. Describe Jack Fergusson. Why is it significant that, when we first see him, he is "muffled up in overcoat and a purple woolen scarf, and his tweed cap . . . [is] pulled down on his head"? How does this bit of physical detail relate to the statement later that his "contact with the rough, strongly-feeling people was a stimulant applied direct to his nerves"? What do these things reveal about him?

9. The episode in which Jack rescues Mabel from her suicide attempt can be seen as a sort of rebirth ritual, a descent into death followed by a resurrection. Discuss the death-rebirth imagery in this scene and in the story as a whole. Why does Lawrence have Mabel attempt to kill herself by drowning in a foul, earthy pond? Of what significance is it that the last part of the story takes place by a fire?

10. What sort of transformation takes place in Mabel when she regains consciousness? How do you account for this change? How do you account for the violence of it? Does it seem believable to you?

11. Look carefully at the description of Jack's reaction to Mabel's sudden metamorphosis, beginning with the sentence, "He looked down at the tangled wet hair, the wild, bare animal shoulders." Why is Mabel's behavior so "distasteful" to Jack? Why is he so frightened by it?

12. What occurs between Jack and Mabel after the first, passionate moment passes and he has declared his love for her? Why does she seem to pull back so abruptly from her own wild expressions of love? Why does she break into "bitter heartbroken sobbing" and call herself "horrible"? Explain the last line of the story.

Twin Beds in Rome

JOHN UPDIKE

The Maples had talked and thought about separation so long it seemed it would never come. For their conversations, increasingly ambivalent and ruthless as accusation, retraction, blow and caress alternated and cancelled, had the final effect of knitting them ever tighter together in a painful, helpless, degrading intimacy. And their love-making, like a perversely healthy child whose growth defies every deficiency of nutrition, continued; when their tongues at last fell silent, their bodies collapsed together as two mute armies might gratefully mingle, released from the absurd hostilities decreed by two mad kings. Bleeding, mangled, reverently laid in its tomb a dozen times, their marriage could not die. Burning to leave one another, they left, out of marital habit, together. They took a trip to Rome.

They arrived at night. The plane was late, the airport grand. They had left hastily, without plans; and yet, as if forewarned of their arrival, nimble Italians, speaking perfect English, parted them deftly from their baggage, reserved a hotel room for them by telephone from the airport, and ushered them into a bus. The bus, surprisingly, plunged into a dark rural landscape. A few windows hung lanternlike in the distance; a river abruptly bared its silver breast beneath them; the silhouettes of olive trees and Italian pines flicked past like shadowy illustrations in an old Latin primer. "I could ride this bus forever," Joan said aloud, and Richard was pained, remembering from the days when they had been content together, how she had once confessed to feeling a sexual stir when the young man at the gas station, wiping the windshield with a vigorous, circular motion, had made the body of the car, containing her, rock slightly. Of all the things she had ever told him, this remained in his mind the most revealing, the deepest glimpse she had ever permitted into the secret woman he could never reach and had at last wearied of trying to reach.

Yet it pleased him to have her happy. This was his weakness. He wished her to be happy, and the certainty that, away from her, he could not know if she were happy or not formed the final, unexpected door barring his way when all others had been opened. So he dried the very tears he had whipped from her eyes, withdrew each protestation of hopelessness at the very point

516

when she seemed willing to give up hope, and their agony continued. "Nothing lasts forever," he said now.

"You can't let me relax a minute, can you?"

"I'm sorry. Do relax."

She stared through the window awhile, then turned and told him, "It doesn't feel as if we're going to Rome at all."

"Where are we going?" He honestly wanted to know, honestly hoped she could tell him.

"Back to the way things were?"

"No. I don't want to go back to that. I feel we've come very far and have only a little way more to go."

She looked out at the quiet landscape a long while before he realized she was crying. He fought the impulse to comfort her, inwardly shouted it down as cowardly and cruel, but his hand, as if robbed of restraint by a force as powerful as lust, crept onto her arm. She rested her head on his shoulder. The shawled woman across the aisle took them for honeymooners and politely glanced away.

The bus slipped from the country. Factories and residential rows narrowed the highway. A sudden monument, a massive white pyramid stricken with light and inscribed with Latin, loomed beside them. Soon they were pressing their faces together to the window to follow the Colosseum itself as, shaped like a shattered wedding cake, it slowly pivoted and silently floated from the harbor of their vision. At the terminal, another lively chain of hands and voices rejoined them to their baggage, settled them in a taxi, and carried them to the hotel. As Richard dropped six hundred-lira pieces into the driver's hand, they seemed the smoothest, roundest, most tactfully weighted coins he had ever given away. The hotel desk was one flight up. The clerk was young and playful. He pronounced their name several times, and wondered why they had not gone to Naples. The halls of the hotel, which had been described to them at the airport as second-class, were nevertheless of rose marble. The marble floor carried into their room. This, and the amplitude of the bathroom, and the imperial purple of the curtains blinded Richard to a serious imperfection until the clerk, his heels clicking in satisfaction with the perhaps miscalculated tip he had received, was far down the hall.

"Twin beds," he said. They had always had a double bed.

Joan asked, "Do you want to call him back?"

"How important is it to you?"

"I don't think it matters. Can you sleep alone?"

"I guess. But—" It was delicate. He felt they had been insulted. Until they finally parted, it seemed impertinent for anything, even a slice of space, to come between them. If this trip were to be kill or cure (and this was, for the tenth time, their slogan), then the attempt at a cure should have a certain technical purity, even though—or, rather, all the more because—in his heart he had already doomed it to fail. And also there was the material question of whether he could sleep without a warm proximate body to give his sleep shape.

"But what?" Joan prompted.

"But it seems sort of sad."

"Richard, don't be sad. You've been sad enough. You're supposed to relax. This isn't a honeymoon or anything, it's just a little rest we're trying to give each other. You can come visit me in my bed if you can't sleep."

"You're such a nice woman," he said. "I can't understand why I'm so miserable with you."

He had said this, or something like it, so often before that she, sickened by simultaneous doses of honey and gall, ignored the entire remark, and unpacked with a deliberate serenity. On her suggestion, they walked into the city, though it was ten o'clock. Their hotel was on a shopping street that at this hour was lined with lowered steel shutters. At the far end, an illuminated fountain played. His feet, which had never given him trouble, began to hurt. In the soft, damp air of the Roman winter, his shoes seemed to have developed hot inward convexities that gnashed his flesh at every stride. He could not imagine why this should be, unless he was sensitive to marble. For the sake of his feet, they found an American bar, entered, and ordered coffee. Off in a corner, a drunken male American voice droned through the grooves of an unintelligible but distinctly female circuit of complaints; the voice, indeed, seemed not so much a man's as a woman's deepened by being played at a slower speed on the phonograph. Hoping to cure the growing dizzy emptiness within him, Richard ordered a "hamburger" that proved to be more tomato sauce than meat. Outside, on the street, he bought a paper cone of hot chestnuts from a sidewalk vender. This man, whose thumbs and fingertips were charred black, agitated his hand until three hundred lire were placed in it. In a way, Richard welcomed being cheated; it gave him a place in the Roman economy. The Maples returned to the hotel, and side by side on their twin beds fell easily into a solid sleep.

That is, Richard assumed, in the cavernous accounting rooms of his subconscious, that Joan also slept well. But when they awoke in the morning, she told him, "You were terribly funny last night. I couldn't go to sleep, and every time I reached over to give you a little pat, to make you think you were in a double bed, you'd say 'Go away' and shake me off."

He laughed in delight. "Did I really? In my sleep?"

"It must have been. Once you shouted 'Leave me alone!' so loud I thought you must be awake, but when I tried to talk to you, you were snoring."

"Isn't that funny? I hope I didn't hurt your feelings."

"No. It was refreshing not to have you contradict yourself."

He brushed his teeth and ate a few of the cold chestnuts left over from the night before. The Maples breakfasted on hard rolls and bitter coffee in the hotel and walked again into Rome. His shoes resumed their inexplicable torture. With its strange, almost mocking attentiveness to their unseen needs, the city thrust a shoe store under their eyes; they entered, and Richard bought, from a gracefully reptilian young salesman, a pair of black alligator loafers. They were too tight, being smartly shaped, but they were dead—they did not pinch with the vital, outraged vehemence of the others. Then the Maples, she carrying the Hachette guidebook and he his American shoes in a box, walked down the Via Nazionale to the Victor Emmanuel Monument, a titanic flight of stairs leading nowhere. "What was so great about him?" Richard asked. "Did he unify Italy? Or was that Cavour?"

"Is he the funny little king in *A Farewell to Arms?*"

"I don't know. But nobody could be *that* great."

"You can see now why the Italians don't have an inferiority complex. Everything is so huge."

They stood looking at the Palazzo Venezia until they imagined Mussolini frowning from a window, climbed the many steps to the Piazza del Campidoglio, and came to the equestrain statue of Marcus Aurelius on the pedestal by Michelangelo. Joan remarked how like a Marino Marini it was, and it was; her intuition had leaped eighteen centuries. She was so intelligent. Perhaps this was what made leaving her, as a gesture, so exquisite in conception and so difficult in execution. They circled the square. The portals and doors all around them seemed closed forever, like the doors in a drawing. They entered, because it was open, the side door of the church of Santa Maria in Aracoeli. They discovered themselves to be walking on sleeping people; life-size tomb-reliefs worn nearly featureless by footsteps. The fingers of the hands folded on the stone breasts had been smoothed to fingershaped shadows. One face, sheltered from wear behind a pillar, seemed a vivid soul trying to rise from the all but erased body. Only the Maples examined these reliefs, cut into a floor that once must have been a glittering lake of mosaic; the other tourists clustered around the chapel preserving, in slippers and vestments, behind glass, the child-sized greenish remains of a pope. They left by the same side door and descended steps and paid admission to the ruins of the Roman Forum. The Renaissance had used it as a quarry; broken columns lay everywhere, loaded with perspective, like a de Chirico. Joan was charmed by the way birds and weeds lived in the crevices of this exploded civic dream. A delicate rain began to fall. At the end of one path, they peeked in glass doors, and a small uniformed man with a broom limped forward and admitted them, as if to a speakeasy, to the abandoned church of Santa Maria Antiqua. The pale vaulted air felt innocent of worship; the seventh-century frescoes seemed recently, nervously executed. As they left, Richard read the question in the broom man's smile and pressed a tactful coin into his hand. The gentle rain continued. Joan took Richard's arm, as if for shelter. His stomach began to hurt—a light, chafing ache at first, scarcely enough to distract him from the pain in his feet. They walked along the Via Sacra, through roofless pagan temples carpeted in grass. The ache in his stomach intensified. Uniformed guards, old men standing this way and that in the rain like hungry gulls, beckoned

them toward further ruins, further churches, but the pain now had blinded
Richard to everything but the extremity of his distance from anything that
might give him support. He refused admittance to the Basilica of Constan-
tine, and asked instead for the *uscita*. He did not feel capable of retracing
his steps. The guard, seeing a source of tips escaping, dourly pointed toward
a small gate in a nearby wire fence. The Maples lifted the latch, stepped
through, and stood on the paved rise overlooking the Colosseum. Richard
walked a little distance and leaned on a low wall.

"Is it so bad?" Joan asked.

"Oddly bad," he said. "I'm sorry. It's funny."

"Do you want to throw up?"

"No. It's not like that." His sentences came jerkily. "It's just a . . . sort
of gripe."

"High or low?"

"In the middle."

"What could have caused it? The chestnuts?"

"No. It's just, I think, being here, so far from anywhere, with you, and
not knowing . . . why."

"Shall we go back to the hotel?"

"Yes. I think if I could lie down."

"Shall we get a taxi?"

"They'll cheat me."

"That doesn't matter."

"I don't know . . . our address."

"We know sort of. It's near that big fountain. I'll look up the Italian for
'fountain.' "

"Rome is . . . full of . . . fountains."

"Richard. You aren't doing this just for my benefit?"

He had to laugh, she was so intelligent. "Not consciously. It has something to do . . . with having to hand out tips . . . all the time. It's really
an ache. It's incredible."

"Can you walk?"

"Sure. Hold my arm."

"Shall I carry your shoebox?"

"No. Don't worry, sweetie. It's just a nervous ache. I used to get them
. . . when I was little. But I was . . . braver then."

They descended steps to a thoroughfare thick with speeding traffic. The
taxis they hailed carried heads in the rear and did not stop. They crossed
the Via dei Fori Imperiali and tried to work their way back, against the
sideways tug of interweaving streets, to the territory containing the fountain, the American Bar, the shoe store, and the hotel. They passed through
a market of bright food. Garlands of sausages hung from striped canopies.
Heaps of lettuce lay in the street. He walked stiffly, as if the pain he carried were precious and fragile; holding one arm across his abdomen seemed
to ease it slightly. The rain and Joan, having been in some way the pressures that had caused it, now b⋅   he pressures that enabled him to

bear it. Joan kept him walking. The rain masked him, made his figure less distinct to passersby, and therefore less distinct to himself, and so dimmed his pain. The blocks seemed cruelly uphill and downhill. They climbed a long slope of narrow pavement beside the Banca d'Italia. The rain lifted. The pain, having expanded into every corner of the chamber beneath his ribs, had armed itself with a knife and now began to slash the walls in hope of escape. They reached the Via Nazionale, blocks below the hotel. The shops were unshuttered, the distant fountain was dry. He felt as if he were leaning backward, and his mind seemed a kind of twig, a twig that had deviated from the trunk and chosen to be this branch instead of that one, and chosen again and again, becoming finer with each choice, until finally there was nothing left for it but to vanish into air. In the hotel room he lay down on his twin bed, settled his overcoat over him, curled up, and fell asleep.

When he awoke an hour later, everything was different. The pain was gone. Joan was lying in her bed reading the Hachette guide. He saw her, as he rolled over, as if freshly, in the kind of cool library light in which he had first seen her; only he knew, calmly, that since then she had come to share his room. "It's gone," he told her.

"You're kidding. I was all set to call up a doctor and have you taken to a hospital."

"No, it wasn't anything like that. I knew it wasn't. It was nervous."

"You were dead white."

"It was too many different things focusing on the same spot. I think the Forum must have depressed me. The past here is so heavy. Also my shoes hurting bothered me."

"Darley, it's Rome. You're supposed to be happy."

"I am now. Come on. You must be starving. Let's get some lunch."

"Really? You feel up to it?"

"Quite. It's gone." And, except for a comfortable reminiscent soreness that the first swallow of Milanese salami healed, it was. The Maples embarked again upon Rome, and, in this city of steps, of sliding, unfolding perspectives, of many-windowed surfaces of sepia and rose ochre, of buildings so vast one seemed to be outdoors in them, the couple parted. Not physically—they rarely left each other's sight. But they had at last been parted. Both knew it. They became with each other, as in the days of courtship, courteous, gay, and quiet. Their marriage let go like an overgrown vine whose half-hidden stem has been slashed in the dawn by an ancient gardener. They walked arm in arm through seemingly solid blocks of buildings that parted, under examination, into widely separated slices of style and time. At one point she turned to him and said, "Darley, I know what was wrong with us. I'm classic, and you're baroque." They shopped, and saw, and slept, and ate. Sitting across from her in the last of the restaurants that like oases of linen and wine had sustained these level elegiac days, Richard saw that Joan was happy. Her face, released from the tension of hope, had grown smooth; her gestures had taken on the flirting irony of the young; she had become ecstatically attentive to everything about her; and her voice, as she bent forward to whisper a remark about a woman and a handsome man at another table, was rapid, as if the very air of her breathing had turned thin and free. She was happy, and, jealous of her happiness, he again grew reluctant to leave her.

QUESTIONS

"Twin Beds in Rome"

1. From what point of view is "Twin Beds in Rome" told? Do we have equal access to the consciousnesses of Joan and Richard?

2. What is the object of the quest that takes the Maples to Rome? Has Richard decided in advance how the quest will end?

3. Discuss the Maples' marriage. Why, according to Richard, is the marriage still intact, despite his and Joan's unhappiness? Do you find the reasons he gives convincing? Note that husband and wife frequently treat each other with kindness and concern. Is this surprising? What does this behavior tell you about the Maples and about their marriage?

4. Why is Richard disturbed that the hotel in Rome has given him a room with twin beds? What does his reaction tell us about him? Who has more trouble adapting to the two beds, Joan or Richard? Why?

5. Do you think there is any connection between Richard's severe stomach pains and his sense, after they vanish, that his marriage has at last come to an end? Explain.

6. What is the importance of the setting to the theme of the story? Is there a connection between the architecture and the geography of Rome—its complex maze of streets and its "sliding, unfolding perspectives"—and the Maples' relationship? Explain.

7. Look at the passage in which the Maples explore the church of Santa Maria in Aracoeli. Does this incident add anything to our knowledge of the couple? Why does Updike linger on this particular Roman sight, and not on any other? Does the description of the floor remind you of a metaphor you encountered earlier in the story?

8. Locate instances of irony in Updike's story. What purpose or purposes does irony serve?

9. Locate several metaphors in this story and discuss their function. How do they reveal character or emphasize the theme of "Twin Beds in Rome"?

10. What is the effect on the Maples' relationship of their realization, at the end of the story, that their marriage has finally "let go"? How are both Richard and Joan transformed by its collapse? What is the effect on Richard of Joan's transformation? Can we be sure, when we finish reading "Twin Beds in Rome," that the marriage has ended? Justify your answer.

The Management of Grief

BHARATI MUKHERJEE

A woman I don't know is boiling tea the Indian way in my kitchen. There are a lot of women I don't know in my kitchen, whispering, and moving tactfully. They open doors, rummage through the pantry, and try not to ask me where things are kept. They remind me of when my sons were small, on Mother's Day or when Vikram and I were tired, and they would make big, sloppy omelets. I would lie in bed pretending I didn't hear them.

Dr. Sharma, the treasurer of the Indo-Canada Society, pulls me into the hallway. He wants to know if I am worried about money. His wife, who has just come up from the basement with a tray of empty cups and glasses, scolds him. "Don't bother Mrs. Bhave with mundane details." She looks so monstrously pregnant her baby must be days overdue. I tell her she shouldn't be carrying heavy things. "Shaila," she says, smiling, "this is the fifth." Then she grabs a teenager by his shirttails. He slips his Walkman off his head. He has to be one of her four children, they have the same doomed and dented foreheads. "What's the official word now?" she demands. The boy slips the headphones back on. "They're acting evasive, Ma. They're saying it could be an accident or a terrorist bomb."

All morning, the boys have been muttering, Sikh Bomb, Sikh Bomb. The men, not using the word, bow their heads in agreement. Mrs. Sharma touches her forehead at such a word. At least they've stopped talking about space debris and Russian lasers.

Two radios are going in the dining room. They are tuned to different stations. Someone must have brought the radios down from my boys' bedrooms. I haven't gone into their rooms since Kusum came running across the front lawn in her bathrobe. She looked so funny, I was laughing when I opened the door.

The big TV in the den is being whizzed through American networks and cable channels.

"Damn!" some man swears bitterly. "How can these preachers carry on like nothing's happened?" I want to tell him we're not that important. You look at the audience, and at the preacher in his blue robe with his beautiful white hair, the potted palm trees under a blue sky, and you know they care about nothing.

The phone rings and rings. Dr. Sharma's taken charge. "We're with her," he keeps saying. "Yes, yes, the doctor has given calming pills. Yes, yes, pills are having necessary effect." I wonder if pills alone explain this calm. Not peace, just a deadening quiet. I was always controlled, but never repressed. Sound can reach me, but my body is tensed, ready to scream. I hear their voices all around me. I hear my boys and Vikram cry, "Mommy, Shaila!" and their screams insulate me, like headphones.

The woman boiling water tells her story again and again. "I got the news first. My cousin called from Halifax before six A.M., can you imagine? He'd gotten up for prayers and his son was studying for medical exams and he heard on a rock channel that something had happened to a plane. They said first it had disappeared from the radar, like a giant eraser just reached out. His father called me, so I said to him, what do you mean, 'something bad'? You mean a hijacking? And he said, *behn*, there is no confirmation of anything yet, but check with your neighbors because a lot of them must be on that plane. So I called poor Kusum straightaway. I knew Kusum's husband and daughter were booked to go yesterday."

Kusum lives across the street from me. She and Satish had moved in less than a month ago. They said they needed a bigger place. All these people, the Sharmas and friends from the Indo-Canada Society had been there for the housewarming. Satish and Kusum made homemade tandoori on their big gas grill and even the white neighbors piled their plates high with that luridly red, charred, juicy chicken. Their younger daughter had danced, and even our boys had broken away from the Stanley Cup telecast to put in a reluctant appearance. Everyone took pictures for their albums and for the community newspapers—another of our families had made it big in Toronto—and now I wonder how many of those happy faces are gone. "Why does God give us so much if all along He intends to take it away?" Kusum asks me.

I nod. We sit on carpeted stairs, holding hands like children. "I never once told him that I loved him," I say. I was too much the well brought up woman. I was so well brought up I never felt comfortable calling my husband by his first name.

"It's all right," Kusum says. "He knew. My husband knew. They felt it. Modern young girls have to say it because what they feel is fake."

Kusum's daughter, Pam, runs in with an overnight case. Pam's in her McDonald's uniform. "Mummy! You have to get dressed!" Panic makes her cranky. "A reporter's on his way here."

"Why?"

"You want to talk to him in your bathrobe?" She starts to brush her mother's long hair. She's the daughter who's always in trouble. She dates Canadian boys and hangs out in the mall, shopping for tight sweaters. The younger one, the goody-goody one according to Pam, the one with a voice so sweet that when she sang *bhajans* for Ethiopian relief even a frugal man like my husband wrote out a hundred dollar check, *she* was on that plane. *She* was going to spend July and August with grandparents because Pam wouldn't go. Pam said she'd rather waitress at McDonald's. "If it's a choice between Bombay and Wonderland, I'm picking Wonderland," she'd said.

"Leave me alone," Kusum yells. "You know what I want to do? If I didn't have to look after you now, I'd hang myself."

Pam's young face goes blotchy with pain. "Thanks," she says, "don't let me stop you."

"Hush," pregnant Mrs. Sharma scolds Pam. "Leave your mother alone. Mr. Sharma will tackle the reporters and fill out the forms. He'll say what has to be said."

Pam stands her ground. "You think I don't know what Mummy's thinking? *Why ever?* that's what. That's sick! Mummy wishes my little sister were alive and I were dead."

Kusum's hand in mine is trembly hot. We continue to sit on the stairs.

She calls before she arrives, wondering if there's anything I need. Her name is Judith Templeton and she's an appointee of the provincial government. "Multiculturalism?" I ask, and she says, "partially," but that her mandate is bigger. "I've been told you knew many of the people on the flight," she says. "Perhaps if you'd agree to help us reach the others . . . ?"

She gives me time at least to put on tea water and pick up the mess in the front room. I have a few *samosas* from Kusum's housewarming that I could fry up, but then I think, why prolong this visit?

Judith Templeton is much younger than she sounded. She wears a blue suit with a white blouse and a polka dot tie. Her blond hair is cut short, her only jewelry is pearl drop earrings. Her briefcase is new and expensive looking, a gleaming cordovan leather. She sits with it across her lap. When she looks out the front windows onto the street, her contact lenses seem to float in front of her light blue eyes.

"What sort of help do you want from me?" I ask. She has refused the tea, out of politeness, but I insist, along with some slightly stale biscuits.

"I have no experience," she admits. "That is, I have an MSW and I've worked in liaison with accident victims, but I mean I have no experience with a tragedy of this scale—"

"Who could?" I ask.

"—and with the complications of culture, language, and customs. Someone mentioned that Mrs. Bhave is a pillar—because you've taken it more calmly."

At this, perhaps, I frown, for she reaches forward, almost to take my hand. "I hope you understand my meaning, Mrs. Bhave. There are hundreds of people in Metro directly affected, like you, and some of them speak no English. There are some widows who've never handled money or gone on a bus, and there are old parents who still haven't eaten or gone outside their bedrooms. Some houses and apartments have been looted. Some wives are still hysterical. Some husbands are in shock and profound depression. We want to help, but our hands are tied in so many ways. We have to distribute money to some people, and there are legal documents—these things can be done. We have interpreters, but we don't always have the human touch, or maybe the right human touch. We don't want to make mistakes, Mrs. Bhave, and that's why we'd like to ask you to help us."

"More mistakes, you mean," I say.

"Police matters are not in my hands," she answers.

"Nothing I can do will make any difference," I say. "We must all grieve in our own way."

"But you are coping very well. All the people said, Mrs. Bhave is the strongest person of all. Perhaps if the others could see you, talk with you, it would help them."

"By the standards of the people you call hysterical, I am behaving very oddly and very badly, Miss Templeton." I want to say to her, *I wish I could scream, starve, walk into Lake Ontario, jump from a bridge.* "They would not see me as a model. I do not see myself as a model."

I am a freak. No one who has ever known me would think of me reacting this way. This terrible calm will not go away.

She asks me if she may call again, after I get back from a long trip that we all must make. "Of course," I say. "Feel free to call, anytime."

Four days later, I find Kusum squatting on a rock overlooking a bay in Ireland. It isn't a big rock, but it juts sharply out over water. This is as close as we'll ever get to them. June breezes balloon out her sari and unpin her knee-length hair. She has the bewildered look of a sea creature whom the tides have stranded.

It's been one hundred hours since Kusum came stumbling and screaming across my lawn. Waiting around the hospital, we've heard many stories. The police, the diplomats, they tell us things thinking that we're strong, that knowledge is helpful to the grieving, and maybe it is. Some, I know, prefer ignorance, or their own versions. The plane broke into two, they say. Unconsciousness was instantaneous. No one suffered. My boys must have just finished their breakfasts. They loved eating on planes, they loved the smallness of plates, knives, and forks. Last year they saved the airline salt and pepper shakers. Half an hour more and they would have made it to Heathrow.

Kusum says that we can't escape our fate. She says that all those people—our husbands, my boys, her girl with the nightingale voice, all those Hindus, Christians, Sikhs, Muslims, Parsis, and atheists on that plane—were fated to die together off this beautiful bay. She learned this from a swami in Toronto.

I have my Valium.

Six of us "relatives"—two widows and four widowers—choose to spend the day today by the waters instead of sitting in a hospital room and scanning photographs of the dead. That's what they call us now: relatives. I've looked through twenty-seven photos in two days. They're very kind to us, the Irish are very understanding. Sometimes understanding means freeing a tourist bus for this trip to the bay, so we can pretend to spy our loved ones through the glassiness of waves or in sunspeckled cloud shapes.

I could die here, too, and be content.

"What is that, out there?" She's standing and flapping her hands and for a moment I see a head shape bobbing in the waves. She's standing in the water, I, on the boulder. The tide is low, and a round, black, head-sized rock has just risen from the waves. She returns, her sari end dripping and ruined and her face is a twisted remnant of hope, the way mine was a hundred hours ago, still laughing but inwardly knowing that nothing but the ultimate tragedy could bring two women together at six o'clock on a Sunday morning. I watch her face sag into blankness.

"That water felt warm, Shaila," she says at length.

"You can't," I say. "We have to wait for our turn to come."

I haven't eaten in four days, haven't brushed my teeth.

"I know," she says. "I tell myself I have no right to grieve. They are in a better place than we are. My swami says I should be thrilled for them. My swami says depression is a sign of our selfishness."

Maybe I'm selfish. Selfishly I break away from Kusum and run, sandals slapping against stones, to the water's edge. What if my boys aren't lying pinned under the debris? What if they aren't stuck a mile below that innocent blue chop? What if, given the strong currents. . . .

Now I've ruined my sari, one of my best. Kusum has joined me, knee-deep in water that feels to me like a swimming pool. I could settle in the water, and my husband would take my hand and the boys would slap water in my face just to see me scream.

"Do you remember what good swimmers my boys were, Kusum?"

"I saw the medals," she says.

One of the widowers, Dr. Ranganathan from Montreal, walks out to us, carrying his shoes in one hand. He's an electrical engineer. Someone at the hotel mentioned his work is famous around the world, something about the place where physics and electricity come together. He has lost a huge family, something indescribable. "With some luck," Dr. Ranganathan suggests to me, "a good swimmer could make it safely to some island. It is quite possible that there may be many, many microscopic islets scattered around."

"You're not just saying that?" I tell Dr. Ranganathan about Vinod, my elder son. Last year he took diving as well.

"It's a parent's duty to hope," he says. "It is foolish to rule out possibilities that have not been tested. I myself have not surrendered hope."

Kusum is sobbing once again. "Dear lady," he says, laying his free hand on her arm, and she calms down.

"Vinod is how old?" he asks me. He's very careful, as we all are. *Is*, not *was*.

"Fourteen. Yesterday he was fourteen. His father and uncle were going to take him down to the Taj and give him a big birthday party. I couldn't go with them because I couldn't get two weeks off from my stupid job in June." I process bills for a travel agent. June is a big travel month.

Dr. Ranganathan whips the pockets of his suit jacket inside out. Squashed roses, in darkening shades of pink, float on the water. He tore the roses off creepers in somebody's garden. He didn't ask anyone if he could pluck the roses, but now there's been an article about it in the local papers. When you see an Indian person, it says, please give him or her flowers.

"A strong youth of fourteen," he says, "can very likely pull to safety a younger one."

My sons, though four years apart, were very close. Vinod wouldn't let Mithun drown. *Electrical engineering,* I think, foolishly perhaps: this man knows important secrets of the universe, things closed to me. Relief spins me lightheaded. No wonder my boys' photographs haven't turned up in the gallery of photos of the recovered dead. "Such pretty roses," I say.

"My wife loved pink roses. Every Friday I had to bring a bunch home. I used to say, why? After twenty odd years of marriage you're still needing proof positive of my love?" He has identified his wife and three of his children. Then others from Montreal, the lucky ones, intact families with no survivors. He chuckles as he wades back to shore. Then he swings around to ask me a question. "Mrs. Bhave, you are wanting to throw in some roses for your loved ones? I have two big ones left."

But I have other things to float: Vinod's pocket calculator; a half-painted model B-52 for my Mithun. They'd want them on their island. And for my husband? For him I let fall into the calm, glassy waters a poem I wrote in the hospital yesterday. Finally he'll know my feelings for him.

"Don't tumble, the rocks are slippery," Dr. Ranganathan cautions. He holds out a hand for me to grab.

Then it's time to get back on the bus, time to rush back to our waiting posts on hospital benches.

Kusum is one of the lucky ones. The lucky ones flew here, identified in multiplicate their loved ones, then will fly to India with the bodies for proper ceremonies. Satish is one of the few males who surfaced. The photos of faces we saw on the walls in an office at Heathrow and here in the hospital are mostly of women. Women have more body fat, a nun said to me matter-of-factly. They float better.

Today I was stopped by a young sailor on the street. He had loaded bodies, he'd gone into the water when—he checks my face for signs of strength—when the sharks were first spotted. I don't blush, and he breaks down. "It's all right," I say. "Thank you." I had heard about the sharks from Dr. Ranganathan. In his orderly mind, science brings understanding, it holds no terror. It is the shark's duty. For every deer there is a hunter, for every fish a fisherman.

The Irish are not shy; they rush to me and give me hugs and some are crying. I cannot imagine reactions like that on the streets of Toronto. Just strangers, and I am touched. Some carry flowers with them and give them to any Indian they see.

After lunch, a policeman I have gotten to know quite well catches hold of me. He says he thinks he has a match for Vinod. I explain what a good swimmer Vinod is.

"You want me with you when you look at photos?" Dr. Ranganathan walks ahead of me into the picture gallery. In these matters, he is a scientist, and I am grateful. It is a new perspective. "They have performed miracles," he says. "We are indebted to them."

The first day or two the policemen showed us relatives only one picture at a time; now they're in a hurry, they're eager to lay out the possibles, and even the probables.

The face on the photo is of a boy much like Vinod; the same intelligent eyes, the same thick brows dipping into a V. But this boy's features, even his cheeks, are puffier, wider, mushier.

"No." My gaze is pulled by other pictures. There are five other boys who look like Vinod.

The nun assigned to console me rubs the first picture with a fingertip. "When they've been in the water for a while, love, they look a little heavier." The bones under the skin are broken, they said on the first day—try to adjust your memories. It's important.

"It's not him. I'm his mother. I'd know."

"I know this one!" Dr. Ranganathan cries out suddenly from the back of the gallery. "And this one!" I think he senses that I don't want to find my boys. "They are the Kutty brothers. They were also from Montreal." I don't mean to be crying. On the contrary, I am ecstatic. My suitcase in the hotel is packed heavy with dry clothes for my boys.

The policeman starts to cry. "I am so sorry, I am so sorry, ma'am. I really thought we had a match."

With the nun ahead of us and the policeman behind, we, the unlucky ones without our children's bodies, file out of the makeshift gallery.

From Ireland most of us go on to India. Kusum and I take the same direct flight to Bombay, so I can help her clear customs quickly. But we have to argue with a man in uniform. He has large boils on his face. The boils swell and glow with sweat as we argue with him. He wants Kusum to wait in line and he refuses to take authority because his boss is on a tea break. But Kusum won't let her coffins out of sight, and I shan't desert her though I know that my parents, elderly and diabetic, must be waiting in a stuffy car in a scorching lot.

"You bastard!" I scream at the man with the popping boils. Other passengers press closer. "You think we're smuggling contraband in those coffins!"

Once upon a time we were well brought up women; we were dutiful wives who kept our heads veiled, our voices shy and sweet.

In India, I become, once again, an only child of rich, ailing parents. Old friends of the family come to pay their respects. Some are Sikh, and inwardly, involuntarily, I cringe. My parents are progressive people; they do not blame communities for a few individuals.

In Canada it is a different story now.

"Stay longer," my mother pleads. "Canada is a cold place. Why would you want to be all by yourself?" I stay.

Three months pass. Then another.

"Vikram wouldn't have wanted you to give up things!" they protest. They call my husband by the name he was born with. In Toronto he'd changed to Vik so the men he worked with at his office would find his name as easy as Rod or Chris. "You know, the dead aren't cut off from us!"

My grandmother, the spoiled daughter of a rich *zamindar*, shaved her head with rusty razor blades when she was widowed at sixteen. My grandfather died of childhood diabetes when he was nineteen, and she saw herself as the harbinger of bad luck. My mother grew up without parents, raised indifferently by an uncle, while her true mother slept in a hut behind the main estate house and took her food with the servants. She grew up a rationalist. My parents abhor mindless mortification.

The zamindar's daughter kept stubborn faith in Vedic rituals; my parents rebelled. I am trapped between two modes of knowledge. At thirty-six, I am too old to start over and too young to give up. Like my husband's spirit, I flutter between worlds.

Courting aphasia, we travel. We travel with our phalanx of servants and poor relatives. To hill stations and to beach resorts. We play contract bridge in dusty gymkhana clubs. We ride stubby ponies up crumbly mountain trails. At tea dances, we let ourselves be twirled twice round the ballroom. We hit the holy spots we hadn't made time for before. In Varanasi, Kalighat, Rishikesh, Hardwar, astrologers and palmists seek me out and for a fee offer me cosmic consolations.

Already the widowers among us are being shown new bride candidates. They cannot resist the call of custom, the authority of their parents and older brothers. They must marry; it is the duty of a man to look after a wife. The new wives will be young widows with children, destitute but of good family. They will make loving wives, but the men will shun them. I've had calls from the men over crackling Indian telephone lines. "Save me," they say, these substantial, educated, successful men of forty. "My parents are arranging a marriage for me." In a month they will have buried one family and returned to Canada with a new bride and partial family.

I am comparatively lucky. No one here thinks of arranging a husband for an unlucky widow.

Then, on the third day of the sixth month into this odyssey, in an abandoned temple in a tiny Himalayan village, as I make my offering of flowers

and sweetmeats to the god of a tribe of animists, my husband descends to
me. He is squatting next to a scrawny *sadhu* in moth-eaten robes. Vikram
wears the vanilla suit he wore the last time I hugged him. The *sadhu* tosses
petals on a butter-fed flame, reciting Sanskrit mantras and sweeps his face
of flies. My husband takes my hands in his.

You're beautiful, he starts. Then, *What are you doing here?*

Shall I stay? I ask. He only smiles, but already the image is fading. *You
must finish alone what we started together.* No seaweed wreathes his mouth.
He speaks too fast just as he used to when we were an envied family in
our pink split-level. He is gone.

In the windowless altar room, smoky with joss sticks and clarified butter
lamps, a sweaty hand gropes for my blouse. I do not shriek. The *sadhu*
arranges his robe. The lamps hiss and sputter out.

When we come out of the temple, my mother says, "Did you feel something weird in there?"

My mother has no patience with ghosts, prophetic dreams, holy men,
and cults.

"No," I lie. "Nothing."

But she knows that she's lost me. She knows that in days I shall be
leaving.

Kusum's put her house up for sale. She wants to live in an ashram in
Hardwar. Moving to Hardwar was her swami's idea. Her swami runs two
ashrams, the one in Hardwar and another here in Toronto.

"Don't run away," I tell her.

"I'm not running away," she says. "I'm pursuing inner peace. You think
you or that Ranganathan fellow are better off?"

Pam's left for California. She wants to do some modelling, she says. She
says when she comes into her share of the insurance money she'll open a
yoga-cum-aerobics studio in Hollywood. She sends me postcards so naughty
I daren't leave them on the coffee table. Her mother has withdrawn from
her and the world.

The rest of us don't lose touch, that's the point. Talk is all we have, says
Dr. Ranganathan, who has also resisted his relatives and returned to Montreal and to his job, alone. He says, whom better to talk with than other
relatives? We've been melted down and recast as a new tribe.

He calls me twice a week from Montreal. Every Wednesday night and
every Saturday afternoon. He is changing jobs, going to Ottawa. But Ottawa is over a hundred miles away, and he is forced to drive two hundred
and twenty miles a day. He can't bring himself to sell his house. The house
is a temple, he says; the king-sized bed in the master bedroom is a shrine.
He sleeps on a folding cot. A devotee.

There are still some hysterical relatives. Judith Templeton's list of those
needing help and those who've "accepted" is in nearly perfect balance.
Acceptance means you speak of your family in the past tense and you make

active plans for moving ahead with your life. There are courses at Seneca and Ryerson we could be taking. Her gleaming leather briefcase is full of college catalogues and lists of cultural societies that need our help. She has done impressive work, I tell her.

"In the textbooks on grief management," she replies—I am her confidante, I realize, one of the few whose grief has not sprung bizarre obsessions—"there are stages to pass through: rejection, depression, acceptance, reconstruction." She has compiled a chart and finds that six months after the tragedy, none of us still reject reality, but only a handful are reconstructing. "Depressed Acceptance" is the plateau we've reached. Remarriage is a major step in reconstruction (though she's a little surprised, even shocked, over *how* quickly some of the men have taken on new families). Selling one's house and changing jobs and cities is healthy.

How do I tell Judith Templeton that my family surrounds me, and that like creatures in epics, they've changed shapes? She sees me as calm and accepting but worries that I have no job, no career. My closest friends are worse off than I. I cannot tell her my days, even my nights, are thrilling.

She asks me to help with families she can't reach at all. An elderly couple in Agincourt whose sons were killed just weeks after they had brought their parents over from a village in Punjab. From their names, I know they are Sikh. Judith Templeton and a translator have visited them twice with offers of money for air fare to Ireland, with bank forms, power-of-attorney forms, but they have refused to sign, or to leave their tiny apartment. Their sons' money is frozen in the bank. Their sons' investment apartments have been trashed by tenants, the furnishings sold off. The parents fear that anything they sign or any money they receive will end the company's or the country's obligations to them. They fear they are selling their sons for two airline tickets to a place they've never seen.

The high-rise apartment is a tower of Indians and West Indians, with a sprinkling of Orientals. The nearest bus stop kiosk is lined with women in saris. Boys practice cricket in the parking lot. Inside the building, even I wince a bit from the ferocity of onion fumes, the distinctive and immediate Indianness of frying *ghee*, but Judith Templeton maintains a steady flow of information. These poor old people are in imminent danger of losing their place and all their services.

I say to her, "They are Sikh. They will not open up to a Hindu woman." And what I want to add is, as much as I try not to, I stiffen now at the sight of beards and turbans. I remember a time when we all trusted each other in this new country, it was only the new country we worried about.

The two rooms are dark and stuffy. The lights are off, and an oil lamp sputters on the coffee table. The bent old lady has let us in, and her husband is wrapping a white turban over his oiled, hip-length hair. She immediately goes to the kitchen, and I hear the most familiar sound of an Indian home, tap water hitting and filling a teapot.

They have not paid their utility bills, out of fear and the inability to write a check. The telephone is gone; electricity and gas and water are soon to follow. They have told Judith their sons will provide. They are good boys, and they have always earned and looked after their parents.

We converse a bit in Hindi. They do not ask about the crash and I wonder if I should bring it up. If they think I am here merely as a translator, then they may feel insulted. There are thousands of Punjabi-speakers, Sikhs, in Toronto to do a better job. And so I say to the old lady, "I too have lost my sons, and my husband, in the crash."

Her eyes immediately fill with tears. The man mutters a few words which sound like a blessing. "God provides and God takes away," he says.

I want to say, but only men destroy and give back nothing. "My boys and my husband are not coming back," I say. "We have to understand that."

Now the old woman responds. "But who is to say? Man alone does not decide these things." To this her husband adds his agreement.

Judith asks about the bank papers, the release forms. With a stroke of the pen, they will have a provincial trustee to pay their bills, invest their money, send them a monthly pension.

"Do you know this woman?" I ask them.

The man raises his hand from the table, turns it over and seems to regard each finger separately before he answers. "This young lady is always coming here, we make tea for her and she leaves papers for us to sign." His eyes scan a pile of papers in the corner of the room. "Soon we will be out of tea, then will she go away?"

The old lady adds, "I have asked my neighbors and no one else gets *angrezi* visitors. What have we done?"

"It's her job," I try to explain. "The government is worried. Soon you will have no place to stay, no lights, no gas, no water."

"Government will get its money. Tell her not to worry, we are honorable people."

I try to explain the government wishes to give money, not take. He raises his hand. "Let them take," he says. "We are accustomed to that. That is no problem."

"We are strong people," says the wife. "Tell her that."

"Who needs all this machinery?" demands the husband. "It is unhealthy, the bright lights, the cold air on a hot day, the cold food, the four gas rings. God will provide, not government."

"When our boys return," the mother says. Her husband sucks his teeth. "Enough talk," he says.

Judith breaks in. "Have you convinced them?" The snaps on her cordovan briefcase go off like firecrackers in that quiet apartment. She lays the sheaf of legal papers on the coffee table. "If they can't write their names, an X will do—I've told them that."

Now the old lady has shuffled to the kitchen and soon emerges with a pot of tea and two cups. "I think my bladder will go first on a job like this," Judith says to me, smiling. "If only there was some way of reaching them. Please thank her for the tea. Tell her she's very kind."

I nod in Judith's direction and tell them in Hindi, "She thanks you for the tea. She thinks you are being very hospitable but she doesn't have the slightest idea what it means."

I want to say, humor her. I want to say, my boys and my husband are with me too, more than ever. I look in the old man's eyes and I can read his stubborn, peasant's message: *I have protected this woman as best I can. She is the only person I have left. Give to me or take from me what you will, but I will not sign for it. I will not pretend that I accept.*

In the car, Judith says, "You see what I'm up against? I'm sure they're lovely people, but their stubbornness and ignorance are driving me crazy. They think signing a paper is signing their sons' death warrants, don't they?"

I am looking out the window. I want to say, *In our culture, it is a parent's duty to hope.*

"Now Shaila, this next woman is a real mess. She cries day and night, and she refuses all medical help. We may have to—"

"—Let me out at the subway," I say.

"I beg your pardon?" I can feel those blue eyes staring at me.

It would not be like her to disobey. She merely disapproves, and slows at a corner to let me out. Her voice is plaintive. "Is there anything I said? Anything I did?"

I could answer her suddenly in a dozen ways, but I choose not to. "Shaila? Let's talk about it," I hear, then slam the door.

A wife and mother begins her new life in a new country, and that life is cut short. Yet her husband tells her: Complete what we have started. We, who stayed out of politics and came halfway around the world to avoid religious and political feuding have been the first in the New World to die from it. I no longer know what we started, nor how to complete it. I write letters to the editors of local papers and to members of Parliament. Now at least they admit it was a bomb. One MP answers back, with sympathy, but with a challenge. You want to make a difference? Work on a campaign. Work on mine. Politicize the Indian voter.

My husband's old lawyer helps me set up a trust. Vikram was a saver and a careful investor. He had saved the boys' boarding school and college fees. I sell the pink house at four times what we paid for it and take a small apartment downtown. I am looking for a charity to support.

We are deep in the Toronto winter, gray skies, icy pavements. I stay indoors, watching television. I have tried to assess my situation, how best to live my life, to complete what we began so many years ago. Kusum has written me from Hardwar that her life is now serene. She has seen Satish and has heard her daughter sing again. Kusum was on a pilgrimage, passing through a village when she heard a young girl's voice, singing one of her daughter's favorite *bhajans*. She followed the music through the squalor of a Himalayan village, to a hut where a young girl, an exact replica of her daughter, was fanning coals under the kitchen fire. When she appeared, the girl cried out, "Ma!" and ran away. What did I think of that?

I think I can only envy her.

Pam didn't make it to California, but writes me from Vancouver. She works in a department store, giving make-up hints to Indian and Oriental girls. Dr. Ranganathan has given up his commute, given up his house and job, and accepted an academic position in Texas where no one knows his story and he has vowed not to tell it. He calls me now once a week.

I wait, I listen, and I pray, but Vikram has not returned to me. The voices and the shapes and the nights filled with visions ended abruptly several weeks ago.

I take it as a sign.

One rare, beautiful, sunny day last week, returning from a small errand on Yonge Street, I was walking through the park from the subway to my apartment. I live equidistant from the Ontario Houses of Parliament and the University of Toronto. The day was not cold, but something in the bare trees caught my attention. I looked up from the gravel, into the branches and the clear blue sky beyond. I thought I heard the rustling of larger forms, and I waited a moment for voices. Nothing.

"What?" I asked.

Then as I stood in the path looking north to Queen's Park and west to the university, I heard the voices of my family one last time. *Your time has come,* they said. *Go, be brave.*

I do not know where this voyage I have begun will end. I do not know which direction I will take. I dropped the package on a park bench and started walking.

QUESTIONS

"The Management of Grief"

1. What things are implied by Mukherjee's title, taken from a speech by a character in the story, the social worker Judith Templeton? What does the phrase reveal about modern Western values? Do the narrator and her Indian friends learn "the management of grief"? Explain.

2. What sort of woman is Shaila Bhave? What is her initial reaction to the disappearance near Ireland of her sons, husband, and friends? How did the narrator's grandmother react, years before, when her husband died? Why does the narrator say that she, Shaila Bhave, is not a model for the other Indians in her community?

3. Why does Judith Templeton approached Shaila Bhave for assistance? What is the narrator's attitude toward the social worker? Why doesn't she explain to Templeton what the Indian community is really thinking and feeling?

4. How are the Irish distinguished from the Canadians in their reaction to the tragedy? How is Pam, Kusum's daughter, different from the other Indians in the story?

5. At one point, while with Judith Templeton, the narrator confesses, "I cannot tell her my days, even my nights, are thrilling." What does she mean? Is there any other character in the story who may be experiencing the same feelings?

6. What is the message Vikram Bhave sends to his wife while she is in the temple in the Himalayan village?

7. Why does the narrator abruptly leave Judith Tempton's care after the visit to the elderly Sikh couple? Why won't that couple accept help from the social worker?

8. At the end of the story, what happens to the narrator? How do you know? Would you say that she has learned to manage her grief? Discuss.

O Yes

TILLIE OLSEN

For Margaret Heaton, who always taught.

1

They are the only white people there, sitting in the dimness of the Negro church that had once been a corner store, and all through the bubbling, swelling, seething of before the services, twelve-year-old Carol clenches tight her mother's hand, the other resting lightly on her friend, Parialee Phillips, for whose baptism she has come.

The white-gloved ushers hurry up and down the aisle, beckoning people to their seats. A jostle of people. To the chairs angled to the left for the youth choir, to the chairs angled to the right for the ladies' choir, even up to the platform, where behind the place for the dignitaries and the mixed choir, the new baptismal tank gleams—and as if pouring into it from the ceiling, the blue-painted River of Jordan, God standing in the waters, embracing a brown man in a leopard skin and pointing to the letters of gold:

REJOICE

I AM THE WAY THE TRUTH THE LIFE

At the clear window, the crucified Christ embroidered on the starched white curtain leaps in the wind of the sudden singing. And the choirs march in. Robes of wine, of blue, of red.

"We stands and sings too," Says Parialee's mother, Alva, to Helen; though already Parialee has pulled Carol up. Singing, little Lucinda Phillips fluffs out her many petticoats; singing, little Bubbie bounces up and down on his heels.

Any day now I'll reach that land of freedom,
                                                Yes, o yes
Any day now, know that promised land

The youth choir claps and taps to accent the swing of it. Beginning to tap, Carol stiffens. "Parry, look. Somebody from school."

"Once more once," says Parialee, in the new way she likes to talk now. "Eddie Garlin's up there. He's in my math."

"Couple cats from Franklin Jr. chirps in the choir. No harm or alarm."

Anxiously Carol scans the faces to see who else she might know, who else might know her, but looks quickly down to Lucinda's wide skirts, for it seems Eddie looks back at her, sullen or troubled, though it is hard to tell, faced as she is into the window of curtained sunblaze.

I know my robe will fit me well
I tried it on at the gates of hell

If it were a record she would play it over and over, Carol thought, to untwine the intertwined voices, to search how the many rhythms rock apart and yet are one glad rhythm.

When I get to heaven gonna sing and shout
Nobody be able to turn me out

"That's Mr. Chairback Evans going to invocate," Lucinda leans across Parry to explain. "He don't invoke good like Momma."

"Shhhh."

"Momma's the only lady in the church that invocates. She made the prayer last week. (Last month, Lucy.) I made the children's 'nouncement last time. (That was way back Thanksgiving.) And Bubbie's 'nounced too. Lots of times."

"Lucy-inda. SIT!"

Bible study announcements and mixed-choir practice announcements and Teen Age Hearts meeting announcements.

If Eddie said something to her about being there, worried Carol, if he talked to her right in front of somebody at school.

Messengers of Faith announcements and Mamboettes announcement and Committee for the Musical Tea.

Parry's arm so warm. Not realizing, starting up the old game from grade

school, drumming a rhythm on the other's arm to see if the song could be
guessed. "Parry, guess."

But Parry is pondering the platform.

The baptismal tank? "Parry, are you scared . . . the baptizing?"

"This cat? No." Shaking her head so slow and scornful, the barrette in
her hair, sun fired, strikes a long rail of light. And still ponders the platform.

New Strangers Baptist Church invites you and Canaan Fair Singers announcements and Battle of Song and Cosmopolites meet. "O Lord, I couldn't
find no ease," a solo. The ladies' choir:

> *O what you say seekers, o what you say seekers,*
> *Will you never turn back no more?*

The mixed choir sings:

> *Ezekiel saw that wheel of time . . .*
> *Every spoke was of humankind*

And the slim worn man in the pin-stripe suit starts his sermon On the
Nature of God. How God is long-suffering. Oh, how long he has suffered.
Calling the roll of the mighty nations, that rose and fell and now are dust
for grinding the face of Man.

O voice of drowsiness and dream to which Carol does not need to listen.
As long ago. Parry warm beside her too, as it used to be, there in the
classroom at Mann Elementary, and the feel of drenched in sun and dimness and dream. Smell and sound of the chalk wearing itself away to nothing, rustle of books, drumming tattoo of fingers of her arm: *Guess.*

And as the preacher's voice spins happy and free, it is the used-to-be
play yard. Tag. Thump of the volley ball. Ecstasy of the jump rope. Parry,
do pepper. Carol, do pepper. Parry's bettern Carol, Carol's bettern
Parry. . . .

Did someone scream?

It seemed someone screamed—but all were sitting as before, though the
sun no longer blared through the windows. She tried to see up where
Eddie was, but the ushers were standing at the head of the aisle now, the
ladies in white dresses like nurses or waitresses wear, the men holding
their white-gloved hands up so one could see their palms.

"And God is Powerful," the preacher was chanting. "Nothing for him to
scoop out the oceans and pat up the mountains. Nothing for him to scoop
up the miry clay and create man. Man, I said, create Man."

The lady in front of her moaned "*O yes*" and others were moaning "*O
yes.*"

"And when the earth mourned the Lord said, Weep not, for all will be returned to you, every dust, every atom. And the tired dust settles back, goes back. Until that Judgment Day. That great day."

"O yes."

The ushers were giving out fans. Carol reached for one and Parry said: "What *you* need one for?" but she took it anyway.

"You think Satchmo can blow; you think Muggsy can blow; you think Dizzy can blow?" He was straining to an imaginary trumpet now, his head far back and his voice coming out like a trumpet.

"Oh Parry, he's so good."

"Well. Jelly jelly."

"Nothing to Gabriel on that great getting-up morning. And the horn wakes up Adam, and Adam runs to wake up Eve, and Eve moans; Just one more minute, let me sleep, and Adam yells, Great Day, woman, don't you know it's the Great Day?"

"*Great Day, Great Day,*" the mixed choir behind the preacher rejoices:

> *When our cares are past*
> *when we're home at last . . .*

"And Eve runs to wake up Cain." Running round the platform, stooping and shaking imaginary sleepers, "and Cain runs to wake up Abel." Looping, scalloping his voice—"Grea-aaa-aat Daaaay." All the choirs thundering:

> *Great Day*
> *When the battle's fought*
> *And the victory's won*

Exultant spirals of sound. And Carol caught into it (Eddie forgotten, the game forgotten) chanting with Lucy and Bubbie: "*Great Day.*"

"Ohhhhhhhhhh," his voice like a trumpet again, "the re-unioning. Ohhhhhhhhh, the rejoicing. After the ages immemorial of longing."

Someone *was* screaming. And an awful thrumming sound with it, like feet and hands thrashing around, like a giant jumping of a rope.

"*Great Day.*" And no one stirred or stared as the ushers brought a little woman out into the aisle, screaming and shaking, just a little shrunk-up woman, not much taller than Carol, the biggest thing about her her swollen hands and the cascades of tears wearing her face.

The shaking inside Carol too. Turning and trembling to ask: "What? . . . that lady?" But Parry still ponders the platform; little Lucy loops the chain of her bracelet round and round; and Bubbie sits placidly, dreamily.

Alva Phillips is up fanning a lady in front of her; two lady ushers are fanning other people Carol cannot see. And her mother, her mother looks in a sleep.

Yes. He raised up the dead from the grave. He made old death behave. *Yes. Yes.* From all over, hushed.

O Yes

He was your mother's rock. Your father's mighty tower. And he gave us a little baby. A little baby to love.

I am so glad

Yes, your friend, when you're friendless. Your father when you're fatherless. Way maker. Door opener.

Yes

When it seems you can't go on any longer, he's there. You can, he says, you can.

Yes

And that burden you been carrying—ohhhhh that burden—not for always will it be. No, not for always.

Stay with me, Lord

I will put my Word in you and it is power. I will put my Truth in you and it is power.

O Yes

Out of your suffering I will make you to stand as a stone. A tried stone. Hewn out of the mountains of ages eternal.

Yes

Ohhhhhhhhhhh. Out of the mire I will lift your feet. Your tired feet from so much wandering. From so much work and wear and hard times.

Yes

From so much journeying—and never the promised land. And I'll wash them in the well your tears made. And I'll shod them in the gospel of peace, and of feeling good. Ohhhhhhhhh.

O Yes.

Behind Carol, a trembling wavering scream. Then the thrashing. Up above, the singing:

They taken my blessed Jesus and flogged him to the woods
And they made him hew out his cross and they dragged him to Calvary
Shout brother, Shout shout shout. He never cried a word.

Powerful throbbing voices. Calling and answering to each other.

They taken my blessed Jesus and whipped him up the hill
With a knotty whip and a raggedy thorn he never cried a word
Shout, sister. Shout shout shout. He never cried a word.

Go tell the people the Saviour has risen
Has risen from the dead and will live forevermore
*   And won't have to die no more.*

Halleloo.

Shout, brother, shout
We won't have to die no more!

A single exultant lunge of shriek. Then the thrashing. All around a clapping. Shouts with it. The piano whipping, whipping air to a froth. Singing now.

I once was lost who now am found
Was blind who now can see

On Carol's fan, a little Jesus walked on wondrously blue waters to where bearded disciples spread nets out of a fishing boat. If she studied the fan—became it—it might make a wall around her. If she could make what was happening (*what* was happening?) into a record small and round to listen to far and far as if into a seashell—the stamp and rills and spirals all tiny (but never any screaming).

wade wade in the water

Jordan's water is chilly and wild
I've got to get home to the other side
God's going to trouble the waters

The music leaps and prowls. Ladders of screamings. Drumming feet of ushers running. And still little Lucy fluffs her skirts, loops the chain on her bracelet; still Bubbie sits and rocks dreamily; and only eyes turn for an instant to the aisle—as if nothing were happening. "Mother, let's go home," Carol begs, but her mother holds her so tight. Alva Phillips, strong Alva, rocking too and chanting, O Yes. No, do not look.

Wade,
Sea of trouble all mingled with fire
Come on my brethren it's time to go higher
Wade wade

The voices in great humming waves, slow, slow (when did it become the humming?), everyone swaying with it too, moving like in slow waves and singing, and up where Eddie is, a new cry, wild and open, "O help me, Jesus," and when Carol opens her eyes she closes them again, quick, but still can see the new known face from school (not Eddie), the thrashing, writhing body struggling against the ushers with the look of grave and loving support on their faces, and hear the torn, tearing cry: "Don't take me away, life everlasting, don't take me away."

And now the rhinestones in Parry's hair glitter wicked; the white hands of the ushers, fanning, foam in the air; the blue-painted waters of Jordan swell and thunder; Christ spirals on his cross in the window, and she is drowned under the sluice of the slow singing and the sway.

So high up and forgotten the waves and the world, so stirless the deep cool green and the wrecks of what had been. Here now Hostess Foods, where Alva Phillips works her nights—but different from that time Alva had taken them through before work, for it is all sunken under water, the creaking loading platform where they had left the night behind; the closet room where Alva's swaddles of sweaters, boots and cap hung, the long hall lined with pickle barrels, the sharp freezer door swinging open.

Bubbles of breath that swell. A gulp of numbing air. She swims into the chill room where the huge wheels of cheese stand, and Alva swims too, deftly oiling each machine: slicers and wedgers and the convey, that at her touch start to roll and grind. The light of day blazes up and Alva is holding a cup, saying: Drink this, baby.

"DRINK IT." Her mother's voice and the numbing air demanding her to pay attention. Up through the waters and into the car.

"That's right, lambie, now lie back." Her mother's lap.

"Mother."

"Shhhhh. You almost fainted, lambie."

Alva's voice. "You gonna be all right, Carol . . . Lucy, I'm telling you for the last time, you and Buford get back into that church. Carol is *fine.*"

"Lucyinda, if I had all your petticoats I could float." Crying. "Why didn't you let me wear my full skirt with the petticoats, Mother."

"Shhhhh, lamb." Smoothing her cheek. "Just breathe, take long deep breaths."

". . . How you doing now, you little ol' consolation prize?" It is Parry, but she does not come in the car or reach to Carol through the open window: "No need to cuss and fuss. You going to be sharp as a tack, Jack."

Answering automatically: "And cool as a fool."

Quick, they look at each other.

"Parry, we have to go home now, don't we, Mother? I almost fainted, didn't I Mother? . . . Parry, I'm sorry I got sick and have to miss your baptism."

"Don't feel sorry. I'll feel better you not there to watch. It was our mommas wanted you to be there, not me."

"Parry!" Three voices.

"Maybe I'll come over to play kickball after. If you feeling better. Maybe. Or bring the pogo." Old shared joys in her voice: "Or any little thing."

In just a whisper: "Or any little thing. Parry. Good-bye, Parry."

And why does Alva have to talk now?

"You all right? You breathin' deep like your momma said? Was it too close'n hot in there? Did something scare you, Carrie?"

Shaking her head to lie, "No."

"I blame myself for not paying attention. You not used to people letting go that way. Lucy and Bubbie, Parialee, they used to it. They been coming since they lap babies."

"Alva, that's all right. Alva, Mrs. Phillips."

"You *was* scared. Carol, it's something to study about. You'll feel better if you understand."

Trying not to listen.

"You not used to hearing what people keeps inside, Carol. You know how music can make you feel things? Glad or sad or like you can't sit still? That was religion music, Carol."

"I have to breathe deep, Mother said."

"Not everybody feels religion the same way. Some it's in their mouth, but some it's like a hope in their blood, their bones. And they singing songs every word that's real to them, Carol, every word out of they own life. And the preaching finding lodgment in their hearts."

The screaming was tuning up in her ears again, high above Alva's patient voice and the waves lapping and fretting.

"Maybe somebody's had a hard week, Carol, and they locked up with it. Maybe a lot of hard weeks bearing down."

"Mother, my head hurts."

"And they're home, Carol, church is home. Maybe the only place they can feel how they feel and maybe let it come out. So they can go on. And it's all right."

"Please, Alva. Mother, tell Alva my head hurts."

"Get Happy, we call it, and most it's good feeling, Carol, when you got all that locked up inside you."

"Tell her we have to go home. It's all right, Alva. Please, Mother. Say good-bye. Good-bye."

When I was carrying Parry and her father left me, and I fifteen years old, one thousand miles away from home, sin-sick and never really believing, as still I don't believe all, scorning, for what have it done to help, waiting there in the clinic and maybe sleeping, a voice called: Alva, Alva. So mournful and so sweet: Alva. Fear not, I have loved you from the foundation of the universe. And a little small child tugged on my dress. He was carrying a parade stick, on the end of it a star that outshined the sun. Follow me, he said. And the real sun went down and he hidden his stick. How dark it was, how dark. I could feel the darkness with my hands. And when I could see, I screamed. Dump trucks run, dumping bodies in hell, and a convey line run, never ceasing with souls, weary ones having to stamp and shove them along, and the air like fire. Oh I never want to hear such screaming. Then the little child jumped on a motorbike making a path no bigger than my little finger. But first he greased my feet with the hands of my momma when I was a knee baby. They shined like the sun was on them. Eyes he placed all around my head, and as I journeyed upward after him, it seemed

I heard a mourning: "Mama Mama you must help carry the world." The rise and fall of nations I saw. And the voice called again Alva Alva, and I flew into a world of light, multitudes singing, Free, free, I am so glad.

2

Helen began to cry, telling her husband about it.

"You and Alva ought to have your heads examined, taking her there cold like that," Len said. "All right, wreck my best handkerchief. Anyway, now that she's had a bath, her Sunday dinner. . . ."

"And been fussed over," seventeen-year-old Jeannie put in.

"She seems good as new. Now *you* forget it, Helen."

"I can't. Something . . . deep happened. If only I or Alva had told her what it would be like. . . . But I didn't realize."

You don't realize a lot of things, Mother, Jeannie said, but not aloud.

"So Alva talked about it after instead of before. Maybe it meant more that way."

"Oh Len, she didn't listen."

"You don't know if she did or not. Or what there was in the experience for her. . . ."

Enough to pull that kid apart two ways even more, Jeannie said, but still not aloud.

"I was so glad she and Parry were going someplace together again. Now that'll be between them too. Len, they really need, miss each other. What happened in a few months? When I think of how close they were, the hours of makebelieve and dressup and playing ball and collecting. . . ."

"Grow up, Mother." Jeannie's voice was harsh. "Parialee's collecting something else now. Like her own crowd. Like jivetalk and rhythmand-blues. Like teachers who treat her like a dummy and white kids who treat her like dirt; boy's who think she's really something and chicks who. . . ."

"Jeannie, I know. It hurts."

"Well, maybe it hurts Parry too. Maybe. At least she's got a crowd. Just don't let it hurt Carol though, 'cause there's nothing she can do about it. That's all through, her and Parialee Phillips, put away with their paper dolls."

"No, Jeannie, no."

"It's like Ginger and me. Remember Ginger, my best friend in Horace Mann. But you hardly noticed when it happened to us, did you . . . because she was white? Yes, Ginger, who's got two kids now, who quit school year before last. Parry's never going to finish either. What's she got to do with Carrie any more? They're going different places. Different places, different crowds, and they're sorting. . . ."

"Now wait, Jeannie. Parry's just as bright, just as capable."

"They're in junior high, Mother. Don't you know about junior high? How they sort? And it's all where you're going. Yes and Parry's colored and Carrie's white. And you have to watch everything, what you wear and how you wear it and who you eat lunch with and how much homework you do and how you act to the teacher and what you laugh at. . . . And run with your crowd."

"It's that final?" asked Len. "Don't you think kids like Carol and Parry can show it doesn't *have* to be that way."

"They can't. They can't. They don't let you."

"No need to shout," he said mildly. "And who do you mean by 'they' and what do you mean by 'sorting'?"

How they sort. A foreboding of comprehension whirled within Helen. What was it Carol had told her of the Welcome Assembly the first day in junior high? The models showing How to Dress and How Not to Dress and half the girls in their loved new clothes watching their counterparts up on the stage—*their* straight hair, their sweater, their earrings, lipstick, hairdo— "How Not to Dress," "a bad reputation for your school." It was nowhere in Carol's description, yet picturing it now, it seemed to Helen that a mute cry of violated dignity hung in the air. Later there had been a story of going to another Low 7 homeroom on an errand and seeing a teacher trying to wipe the forbidden lipstick off a girl who was fighting back and cursing. Helen could hear Carol's frightened, self-righteous tones: ". . . and I hope they expel her; she's the kind that gives Franklin Jr. a bad rep; she doesn't care about anything and always gets into fights." Yet there was nothing in these incidents to touch the heavy comprehension that waited. . . . Homework, the wonderings those times Jeannie and Carol needed help; "What if there's no one at home to give the help, and the teachers with their two hundred and forty kids a day can't or don't or the kids don't ask and they fall hopelessly behind, what then?"—but this too was unrelated. And what had it been that time about Parry? "Mother, Melanie and Sharon won't go if they know Parry's coming." Then of course you'll go with Parry, she's been your friend longer, she had answered, but where was it they were going and what had finally happened? Len, my head hurts, she felt like saying, in Carol's voice in the car, but Len's eyes were grave on Jeannie who was saying passionately:

"If you think it's so goddam important why do we have to live here where it's for real; why don't we move to Ivy like Betsy (yes, I know, money), where it's the deal to be buddies, in school anyway, three colored kids and their father's a doctor or judge or something big wheel and one always gets elected President or head song girl or something to prove oh how we're democratic. . . . What do you want of that poor kid anyway? Make up your mind. Stay friends with Parry—but be one of the kids. Sure. Be a brain—but not a square. Rise on up, college prep, but don't get separated. Yes, stay one of the kids, but. . . ."

"Jeannie. You're not talking about Carol at all, are you, Jeannie? Say it again. I wasn't listening. I was trying to think."

"She will not say it again," Len said firmly, "you look about ready to pull a Carol. One a day's our quota. And you, Jeannie, we'd better cool it. Too much to talk about for one session. . . . Here, come to the window and watch the Carol and Parry you're both all worked up about."

In the wind and the shimmering sunset light, half the children of the block are playing down the street. Leaping, bouncing, hallooing, tugging the kites of spring. In the old synchronized understanding, Carol and Parry kick, catch, kick, catch. And now Parry jumps on her pogo stick (the last time), Carol shadowing her, and Bubbie, arching his body in a semicircle of joy, bounding after them, high, higher, higher.

And the months go by and supposedly it is forgotten, except for the now and then when, self-important, Carol will say: I really truly did nearly faint, didn't I, Mother, that time I went to church with Parry?

And now seldom Parry and Carol walk the hill together. Melanie's mother drives by to pick up Carol, and the several times Helen has suggested Parry, too, Carol is quick to explain: "She's already left" or "She isn't ready; she'll make us late."

And after school? Carol is off to club or skating or library or someone's house, and Parry can stay for kickball only on the rare afternoons when she does not have to hurry home where Lucy, Bubbie, and the cousins wait to be cared for, now Alva works the four to twelve-thirty shift.

No more the bending together over the homework. All semester the teachers have been different, and rarely Parry brings her books home, for where is there space or time and what is the sense? And the phone never rings with: what you going to wear tomorrow, are you bringing your lunch, or come on over, let's design some clothes for the Katy Keane comic-book contest. And Parry never drops by with Alva for Saturday snack to or from grocery shopping.

And the months go by and the sorting goes on and seemingly it is over until that morning when Helen must stay home from work, so swollen and feverish is Carol with mumps.

The afternoon before, Parry had come by, skimming up the stairs, spilling books and binders on the bed: Hey frail, lookahere and wail, your momma askin for homework, what she got against YOU? . . . looking quickly once then not looking again and talking fast. . . . Hey, you bloomed. You gonna be your own pumpkin, hallowe'en? Your momma know yet it's mu-umps? And lumps. Momma says: no distress, she'll be by tomorrow morning see do you need anything while your momma's to work. . . . (Singing: *whole lotta shakin goin on.*) All your 'signments is inside; Miss Rockface says the teachers to write'em cause I mightn't get it right all right.

But do not tell: Does your mother work for Carol's mother? Oh, you're neighbors! Very well, I'll send along a monitor to open Carol's locker but you're only to take these things I'm writing down, nothing else. Now say after me: Miss Campbell is trusting me to be a good responsible girl. And go right to Carol's house. After school. Not stop anywhere on the way. Not lose anything. And only take. What's written on the list.

You really gonna mess with that book stuff? sign on *mine* says do-not-open-until-eX-mas. . . . That Mrs. Fernandez doll she didn't send nothin, she was the only, says feel better and read a book to report if you feel like and I'm the most for takin care for you; she's my most, wish I could get her but she only teaches 'celerated. . . . Flicking the old read books on the shelf but not opening to mock-declaim as once she used to . . . Vicky, Eddie's g.f. in Rockface office, she's on suspended for sure, yellin to Rockface: you bitchkitty don't you give me no more bad shit. That Vicky she can sure sling-ating-ring it. Staring out the window as if the tree not there in which they had hid out and rocked so often. . . . For sure. (Keep mo-o-vin.) Got me a new pink top and lilac skirt. Look sharp with this purple? Cinching in the wide belt as if delighted with what newly swelled above and swelled below. Wear it Saturday night to Sweet's, Modernaires Sounds of Joy, Leroy and Ginny and me goin if Momma'll stay home. IF. (Shake my baby shake.) How come old folks still likes to party? Huh? Asking of Rembrandt's weary old face looking from the wall. How come (softly) you long-gone you. Touching her face to his quickly, lightly. NEXT mumps is your buddybud Melanie's turn to tote your stuff. I'm gettin the hoovus goovus. Hey you so unneat, don't care what you bed with. Removing the boots and binders, ranging them on the dresser one by one, marking lipstick faces—bemused or mocking or amazed—on each paperjacket. Better. Fluffing out smoothing the quilt with exaggerated energy. Any little thing I can get, cause I gotta blow. Tossing up and catching their year-ago, arm-in-arm graduation picture, replacing it deftly, upside down, into its mirror crevice. Joe. Bring you joy juice or fizz water or kickapoo? Adding a frown line to one bookface. Twanging the paper fishkite, the Japanese windbell overhead, setting the mobile they had once made of painted eggshells and decorated straws to twirling and rocking. And is gone.

She talked to the lipstick faces after, in her fever, tried to stand on her head to match the picture, twirled and twanged with the violent overhead.

Sleeping at last after the disordered night. Having surrounded herself with the furnishings of that world of childhood she no sooner learned to live in comfortably, then had to leave.

The dollhouse stands there to arrange and rearrange; the shell and picture card collections to re-sort and remember; the population of dolls given away to little sister, borrowed back, propped all around to dress and undress and caress.

She has thrown off her nightgown because of the fever, and her just budding breast is exposed where she reaches to hold the floppy plush dog that had been her childhood pillow.

Not for anything would Helen have disturbed her. Except that in the unaccustomedness of a morning at home, in the bruised restlessness after the sleepless night, she clicks on the radio—and the storm of singing whirls into the room:

> . . . of trouble all mingled with fire
> Come on my brethren we've got to go higher
> Wade, wade . . .

And Carol runs down the stairs, shrieking and shrieking. "Turn it off, Mother, turn it off." Hurling herself at the dial and wrenching it so it comes off in her hand.

"Ohhhhh," choked and convulsive, while Helen tries to hold her, to quiet.

"Mother, why did they sing and scream like that?"

"At Parry's church?"

"Yes." Rocking and strangling the cries. "I hear it all the time." Clinging and beseeching. ". . . What was it, Mother? Why?"

Emotion, Helen thought of explaining, *a characteristic of the religion of all oppressed peoples, yes your very own great-grandparents*—thought of saying. And discarded.

Aren't you now, haven't you had feelings in yourself so strong they had to come out some way? ("what howls restrained by decorum")—thought of saying. And discarded.

Repeat Alva: *hope . . . every word out of their own life. A place to let go. And church is home.* And discarded.

The special history of the Negro people—history?—just you try living what must be lived every day—thought of saying. And discarded.

And said nothing.

And said nothing.

And soothed and held.

"Mother, a lot of the teachers and kids don't like Parry when they don't even know what she's like. Just because . . ." Rocking again, convulsive and shamed. "And I'm not really her friend any more."

No news. Betrayal and shame. Who betrayed? Whose shame? Brought herself to say aloud: "But may be friends again. As Alva and I are."

The sobbing a whisper. "That girl Vicky who got that way when I fainted, she's in school. She's the one keeps wearing the lipstick and they wipe it off and she's always in trouble and now maybe she's expelled, Mother."

"Yes, lambie."

"She acts so awful outside but I remember how she was in church and whenever I see her now I have to wonder. And hear . . . like I'm her, Mother, like I'm her." Clinging and trembling. "Oh why do I have to feel it happens to me too?

"Mother, I want to forget about it all, and not care,—like Melanie. Why can't I forget? *Oh why is it like it is and why do I have to care?*"

Caressing, quieting.

Thinking: *caring asks doing. It is a long baptism into the seas of human-kind, my daughter. Better immersion than to live untouched. . . . Yet how will you sustain?*

Why is it like it is?

Sheltering her daughter close, mourning the illusion of the embrace.

And why do I have to care?

While in her, her own need leapt and plunged for the place of strength that was not—where one could scream or sorrow while all knew and accepted, and gloved and loving hands waited to support and understand.

QUESTIONS

"O Yes"

1. Why does Olsen begin her story with a description of a religious service? Is it significant that Parialee has gone to the church to be baptized? How are the sentiments expressed by Helen in the last paragraph of the story connected to its opening scene?

2. What is Carol frightened of as she sits in the church with her friend? Occasionally she finds it possible to be at ease there. What helps her to relax? How are Carol's attitudes toward the religious service contrasted with those of the Phillips children?

3. Describe the church service. Analyze Olsen's presentation of it. Do you think you are being given all the details of the service, in the order in which they occur? What effect or effects is Olsen aiming at in her description of the religious service? Is there a connection between the lyrics of the songs sung in the church and the themes of the story?

4. What does Parry say when Carol takes a fan? What is her tone? To what use, later on in the story, does Carol want to put the fan?

5. Why does Alva Phillips attempt to explain the religious service to Carol? What does Alva tell her? Why doesn't Carol listen?

6. Why is Olsen's story called "O Yes"?

7. Like Robert Penn Warren's "Blackberry Winter" and Richard Wright's "Big Boy Leaves Home," "O Yes" depicts a young protagonist's transit from the innocent, uncomplicated world of childhood to the entirely different adult world. Discuss the journey Carol has undertaken. What does she discover? How does she respond to her discoveries?

8. Describe the transformation Carol is undergoing in "O Yes." Is Parialee, too, being transformed? Is either girl likely to be enlarged, to have her life made fuller or richer, by these transformations? Can you find evidence in the story that these transformations are not yet complete?

9. How do Jeannie's comments illuminate the changes her younger sister and Parry are undergoing? Explain what she means when she asks her parents, "If you think it's so goddam important why do we have to live here where it's for real . . . ?" To what does the pronoun "it" refer?

10. Olsen provides some details about Carol and Parialee's junior high school: its pupils, teachers, and student activities. Discuss these details. What is Helen's response to them?

11. What function does Alva Phillips's reminiscence or reverie at the end of the first part of the story have in the story as a whole?

12. In the long passage in which Parialee visits the sick Carol, what do we learn about Parry? What is the effect of this passage? Why does Parry seem to speak in such a rush of words? What is her tone? Are there things left unsaid, feelings left unexpressed? Is the detail of the graduation picture significant? Why don't we hear any of Carol's responses to her old friend?

13. Why does the radio music disturb Carol near the end of the story? What emotions is she feeling as she is held in her mother's arms? Why does she say she is like the girl who has been reprimanded for wearing lipstick in school? Why did this girl's screaming in church particularly upset her?

14. At the end of "O Yes," why doesn't Helen tell her daughter any of the things she thinks of telling her?

The Legend of St. Julian
the Hospitaller

GUSTAVE FLAUBERT

I

Julian's father and mother lived in a castle with a forest round it, on the slope of a hill.

The four towers at its corners had pointed roofs covered with scales of lead, and the walls were planted upon shafts of rock which fell steeply to the bottom of the moat. The pavement of the courtyard was as clean as the flagstones of a church. Long gutter-spouts in the form of leaning dragons spat the rain-water down into the cistern; and on the window ledges of each story, in pots of painted earthenware, a heliotrope or basil flowered.

A second enclosure made with stakes held a fruit-orchard to begin with, and then a flower garden patterned into figures; then a trellis with arbors where you took the air, and an alley for the pages to play mall. On the other side were the kennels, the stables, the bake-house, the presses, and the barns. A green and turfy pasture spread all round this, enclosed in turn by a stout thorn-hedge.

They had lived at peace so long that the portcullis was never lowered now. The moats were full of grass; swallows nested in the cracks of the battlements; and when the sun blazed too strongly the archer who paced all day long the rampart took refuge in his turret and slept like a monk.

Inside there was a sheen of ironwork everywhere; the rooms were hung with tapestries against the cold; the cupboards overflowed with linen; casks of wine were piled up in the cellars, and the oaken coffers creaked with the weight of bags of money. In the armory, between standards and wild beasts' heads, could be seen weapons of every age and every nation, from the slings of the Amalekites and the javelins of the Garamantes to the short swords of the Saracens and Norman coats of mail. The chief spit in the kitchen could roast an ox; the chapel was as splendid as a king's oratory. There was even, in a secluded corner, a Roman vapor-bath; but the good lord abstained from using it, considering it a practice of the heathen.

Wrapped always in a mantle of fox skins, he walked about his castle, administering justice to his vassals and setting the disputes of his neighbors at rest. In winter he watched the snowflakes falling or had stories read to him. With the first fine days he rode out on his mule along the by-ways beside the greening corn, and chatted with the peasants, to whom he gave advice. After many adventures he had taken a lady of high lineage as his wife.

Very white of skin she was, a little proud and serious. The horns of her coif brushed against the door lintel, and the train of her dress trailed three paces behind her. Her household was ordered like the inside of a monastery; every morning she gave out the tasks to the servants, inspected the preserves and unguents, span at her distaff or embroidered altar-cloths. By dint of prayer to God a son was born to her.

Then there were great rejoicings and a banquet which lasted three days and four nights, with the illumination of torches, the sound of harps, and strewing of green branches. They ate of the rarest spices, and fowls as large as sheep; a dwarf came out of a pasty, to amuse the guests; and as the throng was always increasing and the bowls would go round no longer, they were obliged to drink out of horns and helmets.

The lady who had just been made a mother was not present at this cheer. She stayed quietly in her bed. Waking one evening, she saw as it were a shadow moving under a ray of the moon which came through the window. It was an old man in a frieze gown, with a chaplet at his side, a wallet on his shoulder, and all the semblance of a hermit. He came toward her pillow and said to her, without opening his lips:

"Rejoice, O mother, thy son shall be a saint!"

She was just going to cry out, but he glided over the streak of moonlight, rose gently into the air and vanished. The songs of the banqueters broke out louder. She heard angels' voices; and her head fell back on the pillow, over which, framed with garnets, hung a martyr's bone.

Next morning all the servants were questioned and said they had seen no hermit. Whether it were a dream or reality, it must have been a communication from Heaven; but she was careful not to speak of it, fearing she might be taxed with pride.

The guests went off at morning twilight, and Julian's father was outside the postern gate, to which he had just escorted the last to go, when suddenly a beggar rose before him in the mist. He was a gipsy, with a plaited beard and silver rings on his arms, and fiery eyes. With an air of inspiration he stammered these disjointed words:

"Ah, ah! thy son! Blood in plenty! . . . Fame in plenty! . . . Blest always—the family of an emperor!"

And stooping to pick up his alms he was lost in the grass and disappeared.

The good castellan looked right and left, and called with all his might. No one! The wind blew shrill; the mists of morning flew away.

He put down this vision to a weary head, from having slept too little. "If

I speak of it they will make a jest of me," he said to himself. Yet the glories destined to his son dazzled him, although the promise was not clear and he doubted even whether he had heard it.

The husband and wife each kept their secret. But they cherished their child, both of them, with an equal love; and, reverencing him as marked out by God, had an infinite care for his person. His cot was stuffed with the finest down; a lamp shaped like a dove burned continually above it, three nurses rocked him; and well swaddled in his clothes, with his rosy looks and blue eyes, a brocade cloak and a cap set with pearls, he looked a little Jesus. He teethed without crying at any time.

When he was seven his mother taught him to sing. To make him brave his father lifted him on to a big horse. The child smiled with pleasure and before long knew all about chargers.

A learned old monk taught him Holy Writ, the Arabic way of counting, the Latin letters, and how to make dainty pictures on vellum. They worked together high up in a turret away from all noise. The lesson over, they came down into the garden and studied the flowers, pausing at very step.

Sometimes a string of laden beasts was seen passing below in the valley, led by a man on foot dressed in the Eastern way. The castellan, recognizing him for a merchant, would send a servant out to him, and the stranger, taking heart, would turn out of his road. He would be brought into the parlor, where he drew out of his coffers strips of velvet and silk, jewels, perfumes, and curious things of unknown use; after which the worthy man went off, having taken a great profit and suffered no violence. At other times a band of pilgrims would come knocking at the gate. Their draggled garments steamed before the fire; and when they had been well fed they told the story of their travels: wanderings on shipboard over foamy seas, journeyings afoot in burning sands, the furious rage of paynims, the caves of Syria, the Manger and the Sepulchre. Then they would give the young lord scallop-shells from their cloaks.

Often the castellan feasted his old companions-at-arms. While they drank they called to mind their wars and the storming of fortresses, with the crash of warlike engines and the prodigious wounds. Julian listened to them and uttered cries; and his father had no doubt, then, that he would be a conqueror one day. Yet at evening, coming from the Angelus, as he passed between the bending rows of poor, he dipped in his purse with such modesty and so noble a mien that his mother thought surely to see him an archbishop in his time.

His place in chapel was by the side of his parents, and however long the offices might be he stayed kneeling at his stool, with his cap on the floor and his hands clasped in prayer.

One day, while mass was being said, he raised his head and saw a little white mouse coming out of a hole in the wall. It trotted along the first pace of the altar, and after making two or three turns to right and left fled by the way it had come. Next Sunday he was troubled by the thought that he might see it again. It did come back; and then every Sunday he watched for it, was troubled, seized with hatred for it, and determined to get rid of the mouse.

So, having shut the door and sprinkled some cake-crumbs along the altar steps, he took post in front of the hole with a little stick in his hand.

After a very long time a small pink nose appeared, and then the entire mouse. He struck a light blow, and stood lost in amazement at this tiny body which did not stir again. A drop of blood spotted the pavement. Julian wiped it off rapidly with his sleeve, threw the mouse away, and did not say a word to anyone.

There were all kinds of little birds which pecked at the seeds in the garden. Julian had the thought of putting peas into a hollow reed. When he heard the sound of chirruping in a tree he came up softly, lifted his pipe, and blew out his cheeks; and the little creatures rained down in such abundance on his shoulders that he could not help laughing in delight at his trick.

One morning, as he was going back along the curtain wall, he saw a fat pigeon on the top of the rampart, preening itself in the sun. Julian stopped to look at it, and as there was a breach in this part of the wall a fragment of stone lay ready to his hand. He swung his arm, and the stone brought down the bird, which fell like a lump into the moat.

He dashed down after it, tearing himself in the briars and scouring everywhere, nimbler than a young dog. The pigeon, its wings broken, hung quivering in the boughs of a privet. The obstinate life in it annoyed the child. He began to throttle it, and the bird's convulsions made his heart beat, filled him with a savage, passionate delight. When it stiffened for the last time he felt that he would swoon.

At supper in the evening his father declared that it was time for him to learn the art of venery, and he went to look for an old manuscript which contained, in questions and answers, the whole pastime of the chase. A master explained in it to his pupil the craft of breaking-in dogs, taming falcons, and setting snares; how to know the stag by his droppings, the fox by his footmarks, the wolf by his scratchings of the ground; the right way to discern their tracks, the manner of starting them, the usual places of their lairs, the most favorable winds, and a list of all the calls and the rules for the quarry.

When Julian could repeat all this by heart his father gathered a pack of hounds for him.

The first to catch the eye were twenty-four greyhounds from Barbary, swifter than gazelles, but prone to get out of hand; and then seventeen couples of Breton hounds, with red coats and white spots, unshakable in control, deep-chested, loud to bay. To face the wild boar and its dangerous redoublings there were forty boarhounds, as shaggy as bears. Mastiffs from Tartary nearly as tall as asses and flame-colored, with broad backs and straight legs, were assigned to hunt the aurochs. The black coats of the spaniels shone like satin, and the yapping of the talbots matched the chanting of the beagles. In a yard by themselves, tossing their chains and rolling their eyes, growled eight Alain dogs, fearsome animals that fly at the belly of a horseman and have no dread of lions.

All of them ate wheaten bread, drank out of stone troughs, and bore sonorous names.

The falconry, maybe, was choicer even than the pack; for by dint of money the good lord had secured tiercelets of the Caucasus, sakers from Babylonia, gerfalcons of Germany, and peregrines taken on the cliffs at the edge of cold seas in far quarters of the world. They were housed in a big shed roofed with thatch, and fastened to the perching-bar in a row according to their size, with a strip of turf before them where they were placed from time to time to unstiffen their limbs.

Purse-nets, hooks, wolf-traps, and engines of every kind were artfully made.

Often they took out setters into the country, who quickly came to a point. Then huntsmen, advancing step by step, cautiously spread a huge net over their motionless bodies. At a word of command they barked; quails took wing; and the ladies of the neighborhood who had been bidden with their husbands, the children, the handmaids, the whole company darted on the birds and easily caught them. At other times they would beat drums to start the hares; foxes fell into pits, or a trap would spring and take hold of a wolf's paw.

But Julian spurned these handy devices. He preferred to hunt far away from the rest with his horse and his falcon. It was almost always a great Scythian tartaret, white as snow. Its leathern hood was topped with a plume, bells of gold quivered on its blue feet; and it stood firmly in its master's arm while the horse galloped and the plains unrolled below. Julian, freeing the jesses, would suddenly let it go; the daring bird rose straight as an arrow into the sky; and you saw two specks, one larger and one smaller, circle, meet, and then vanish in the high blue spaces. The falcon soon came down, tearing a quarry, and returned to perch on the gauntlet with its wings a-quiver.

In that way Julian flew his falcons at the heron, the kite, the crow, and the vulture.

He loved to blow his horn and follow his hounds as they coursed along the sloping hills, jumped the streams, and climbed to the woods again; and when the stag began groaning under their bites he felled it cleverly, and was delighted by the fury of the mastiffs as they devoured it, hewn in pieces on its reeking hide.

On misty days he went down into a marsh to ambush the geese, otters, and wild duck.

Three squires waited for him from dawn at the foot of the steps, and though the old monk might lean out of his window and make signs to call him back Julian would not turn. He went out in the heat of the sun, under the rain, and amidst storms, drinking water from the springs out of his hand, munching wild apples as he trotted along, and resting under an oak if he were tired; and he came in at midnight covered in blood and mire, with thorns in his hair and the odor of the wild beasts hanging round him. He became as one of them. When his mother kissed him he took her embrace coldly, and seemed to be dreaming of deep things.

He slew bears with strokes of his knife, bulls with the axe, and wild boars with the pike; and once, even, defended himself with nothing but a stick against wolves that were gnawing corpses at the foot of a gibbet.

One winter morning he started in full trim before dawn, with a crossbow on his shoulder and a quiver of arrows at his saddle-bow.

His Danish jennet, followed by two bassets, made the earth ring under its even tread. Drops of rime stuck to his cloak, and a fierce breeze blew. The sky lightened at one side, and in the pale twilight he saw rabbits hopping at the edge of their burrows. The two bassets dashed for them at once, jumping hither and thither as they broke their backs.

Soon after he entered a wood. At the end of a branch a grouse, numbed by the cold, slept with its head under its wing. With a backstroke of his sword Julian cut off its two feet, and without stopping to pick it up went on his way.

Three hours later he found himself on the top of a mountain, which was so high that the sky seemed almost black. A rock like a long wall sloped away in front of him, cresting a precipice; and at the farther end of it two wild goats were looking down into the chasm. Not having his arrows at hand—he had left his horse behind—he thought he would go right down upon the goats; and stooping double, barefoot, he reached the first of them at last and plunged his dagger under its ribs. The other was seized with panic and jumped into the abyss. Julian leaped to strike it, and his right foot slipping, fell across the body of the first, with his face hanging over the gulf and arms flung wide.

He came down into the plain again and followed a line of willows bordering a river. Cranes, flying very low, passed overhead from time to time. Julian brought them down with his whip, not missing one.

Meanwhile the air had grown warmer and melted the rime; there were broad wreaths of vapor floating, and the sun appeared. Far off he saw a still lake glistening like a sheet of lead. In the middle of it was an animal which Julian did not know, a black-headed beaver. In spite of the distance he killed it with an arrow, and was vexed not to be able to carry off its skin.

Then he went on down an avenue of great trees, whose tops made a kind of triumphal arch at the entrance of a forest. A roebuck bounded out of a thicket, a fallow deer showed itself at a crossing, a badger came out of a hole, a peacock spread its tail on the grass; and when he had slain them all more roebuck, deer, badgers, peacocks and blackbirds, jays, polecats, foxes, hedgehogs, lynxes—an endless company of beasts—appeared and grew more numerous at every step. Tremblingly they circled round him, with gentle supplicating looks. But Julian did not tire of killing, by turns bending his cross-bow, unsheathing his long sword, and thrusting with his short, thinking of nothing, with no memory of anything at all. Only the fact of his existence told him that for an indefinite time he had been hunting in some vague country, where all happened with the ease of dreams. An extraordinary sight brought him to a halt. A valley shaped like an arena was filled with stags, who crowded close together warming each other with their breath, which could be seen steaming in the mist.

The prospect of a slaughter like this for a minute or two took Julian's breath away for pleasure. Then he dismounted, rolled up his sleeves, and began to shoot.

At the whistle of the first arrow all the stags turned their heads at once. Hollows opened in the mass, plaintive cries rose, and a great stir shook the herd.

The brim of the valley was too high to climb. They leaped about in this enclosure, trying to escape. Julian aimed and shot, and the arrows fell like rain shafts in a thunderstorm. The maddened stags fought, reared, and climbed on each other's backs; and the bodies and entangled antlers made a broad mound which crumbled and changed.

At last they died, stretched on the sand, their nostrils frothing, entrails bursting, and bellies slowly ceasing to heave. Then all was motionless. Night was close at hand; and behind the woods, in the interspaces of the boughs, the sky was red as a sheet of blood.

Julian leaned back against a tree, and gazed with staring eyes at the enormous massacre; he could not think how it had been done.

Then across the valley, at the edge of the forest, he saw a stag with its hind and its fawn.

The stag was black and hugely tall; it carried sixteen points and a white beard. The hind, pale yellow like a dead leaf, was grazing; and the spotted fawn, without hindering her movements, pulled at her dugs.

Once more the cross-bow sang. The fawn was killed on the spot. Then its mother, looking skywards, bellowed with a deep, heart-breaking, human cry. In exasperation Julian stretched her on the ground with a shot full in the breast.

The great stag had seen it, and made a bound. Julian shot his last arrow at him. It hit the stag in the forehead and stuck fast there.

The great stag did not seem to feel it; striding over the dead bodies, he came on and on, in act to charge and disembowel him; and Julian retreated in unspeakable terror. The monstrous creature stopped, and with flaming eyes, as solemn as a patriarch or judge, said three times, while a bell tinkled in the distance:

"Accurst! accurst! accurst! one day, ferocious heart, thou shalt murder thy father and thy mother!"

The stag's knees bent, his eyes closed gently, and he died.

Julian was thunderstruck, and then suddenly felt crushed with fatigue; disgust and boundless sadness came over him. He buried his face in his hands and wept for a long time.

His horse was lost, his dogs had left him; the solitude which folded round him seemed looming with vague dangers. Seized with alarm, he struck across country, and choosing a path at random found himself almost immediately at the castle-gate.

He could not sleep at night. By the flickering of the hanging lamps he always saw the great black stag. The creature's prophecy besieged him, and he fought against it. "No! no! no! it cannot be that I should kill them!" And then he mused: "Yet if I should wish to kill?" and he was afraid that the Devil might inspire him with the wish.

For three months his mother prayed in anguish by his pillow, and his father walked to and fro along the corridors with groans. He sent for the most famous master physicians, who prescribed quantities of drugs. Julian's malady, they said, was caused by a noxious wind, or by a love-desire. But the young man, in answer to all questions, shook his head.

His strength came back to him, and they took him out to walk in the courtyard, the old monk and the good lord each propping him with an arm.

When he had recovered altogether he obstinately refused to hunt. His father, hoping to cheer him, made him a present of a great Saracen sword. It was in a stand of arms, at the top of a pillar, and a ladder was needed to reach it. Julian went up. The sword was too heavy and slipped from his fingers, and in the fall grazed the worthy lord so close as to cut his mantle; Julian thought he had killed his father, and fainted away.

From that moment he dreaded weapons. The sight of a bare blade made him turn pale. This weakness was a sorrow to his family, and at last the old monk, in the name of God, of honor, and his ancestors, bade him take up the exercises of his gentle birth again.

The squires amused themselves daily at practising with the javelin. Julian very quickly excelled in this; he could throw his javelin into the neck of a bottle, break the teeth of a weather-vane, and hit the nails on a door a hundred paces off.

One summer evening, at the hour when things grow indistinct in the dusk, he was under the trellis in the garden and saw right at the end of it two white wings fluttering by the top of its supports. He made sure it was a stork, and threw his javelin. A piercing cry rang out.

It was his mother, whose bonnet with long flaps stayed pinned to the wall.

Julian fled from the castle and was seen there no more.

II

He took service with a passing troop of adventurers and knew hunger and thirst, fevers and vermin. He grew accustomed to the din of melees and the sight of dying men. The wind tanned his skin. His limbs hardened under the clasp of armor; and as he was very strong, valiant, temperate, and wary he won the command of a company with ease.

When a battle opened he swept on his soldiers with a great flourish of his sword. He scaled the walls of citadels with a knotted rope at night, swinging in the blasts, while sparks of Greek fire stuck to his cuirass and boiling resin and molten lead hissed from the battlements. Often a stone crashed and shivered his buckler. Bridges overladen with men gave way under him. Swinging his battle-axe to and fro, he got rid of fourteen horsemen. In the lists he overcame all challengers. More than a score of times he was left for dead.

Thanks to the favor of Heaven he always came out safely, for he protected clerks, orphans, widows, and, most of all, old men. When he saw one of them walking in front of him he called out to see his face, as though he were afraid of killing him by mistake.

Runaway slaves, peasants in revolt, fortuneless bastards, and venturous men of all sorts flocked under his banner, and he made an army of his own.

It grew, and he became famous. The world sought him out. He succored in turn the Dauphin of France and the King of England, the Templars of Jerusalem, the Surena of the Parthians, the Negus of Abyssinia, and the Emperor of Calicut. He fought against Scandinavians covered with fish-scales, Negroes with bucklers of hippopotamus hide, mounted on red asses, and gold-colored Indians flourishing broadswords brighter than mirrors above their diadems. He subdued the Troglodytes and the Anthropophages. He went through such burning regions that the hair on the head caught fire of itself, like torches, in the sun's heat; through others so freezing that the arms snapped from the body and fell to the ground; and countries where there was so much mist that you walked surrounded by phantoms.

Republics in distress consulted him, and in colloquies with ambassadors he gained unhoped-for terms. If a monarch behaved too badly Julian was quickly on the spot and took him to task. He set free peoples and delivered queens immured in towers. He it was, no other, who slew the viper of Milan and the dragon of Oberbirbach.

Now the Emperor of Occitania, having triumphed over the Spanish Moslems, had taken the sister of the Caliph of Cordova as his concubine, and by her he had a daughter whom he brought up to be a Christian. But the Caliph, feigning a wish to be converted, came to return his visit with a numerous escort, put all his garrison to the sword, and threw him into an underground dungeon, where he used him cruelly to extort his treasure.

Julian hastened to his aid, destroyed the army of the infidels, besieged the town, killed the Caliph, cut off his head, and threw it over the ramparts like a ball. Then he drew the emperor out of prison and set him on his throne again, in the presence of all his court.

To requite this great service the emperor presented him with basketfuls of money; Julian would have none of it. Thinking that he wanted more, he offered him three-quarters of his wealth, and was refused again; then the half of his kingdom; Julian thanked him and declined. The emperor was in tears of distress, seeing no way to show his gratitude, when he tapped his forehead and whispered in a courtier's ear; the curtains of a tapestry lifted and a maiden appeared.

Her large dark eyes gleamed like two gentle lamps; her lips were parted in a winning smile. The ringlets of her hair caught in the jewels of a half-opened robe, and under the transparent tunic the young lines of her body could be guessed. She was slim of figure, all daintiness and softness.

Julian was dazzled with love, the more because he had lived in great chastity till then.

So he took the emperor's daughter in marriage, with a castle that she held from her mother; and when the wedding was over he and his host parted, after a long exchange of courtesies.

It was a palace of white marble, in the Moorish fashion, built on a promontory in a grove of orange-trees. Terraces of flowers sloped to the edge of a bay, where there were pink shells that crackled underfoot. Behind the castle stretched a forest in the shape of a fan. The sky was blue unceasingly, and the trees waved by turns under the sea breeze and the wind from the mountains, which closed the horizon far away.

The rooms were full of shadow, but drew light from their incrusted walls. High columns, slender as reeds, supported their domed vaults, which were embossed in relief to imitate the stalactites in caves. There were fountains in the greater rooms, mosaics in the courts, festooned partitions, delicacies of architecture beyond number, and everywhere so deep a silence that one heard the rustle of a scarf or the echo of a sigh.

Julian made war no longer. He rested with a quiet people round him, and every day a crowd passed before him, making obeisances and kissing hands in the Eastern style.

In his purple dress he would stay leaning in the embrasure of a window, recalling his hunts of former days; and he would have liked to scour the desert after gazelles and ostriches, hide among the bamboos to wait for leopards, traverse forests full of rhinoceroses, climb the most inaccessible mountain-tops to take better aim at eagles, and fight with white bears on icebergs in the sea.

Sometimes, in dreams, he saw himself like our father Adam in the midst of Paradise, among all the beasts. He stretched out his arm against them, and they died; or else, again they defiled before him, two by two according to their size, from the elephants and lions to the ermines and the ducks, as on the day when they entered Noah's ark. From the shadow of a cave he rained darts on them which never missed; other animals appeared; there was no end to them, and he woke with his eyes rolling wildly.

Among his friends there were princes who invited him to hunt. He always refused, thinking that by a penance of this kind he would turn aside his curse, for it seemed to him that the slaughter of animals would decide the fate of his father and mother. But it was a grief to him not to see his parents, and his other secret desire became impossible to bear.

His wife sent for jugglers and dancers to amuse him. She went out with him into the country in an open litter; and at other times they would lie in a boat and watch, over the side, the fish roaming in water as clear as the sky. Often she threw flowers in his face, or crouching at his feet drew music from a three-stringed mandolin; and then, laying her clasped hands on his shoulder, said timidly, "What ails thee then, dear lord?"

He did not answer, or broke into sobs. At last, one day, he confessed his horrible thought.

She fought against it, arguing very well. His father and mother, most likely, were already dead; but if he ever saw them again what chance or purpose could lead him to this abominable deed? His fear was causeless, then, and he should return to the hunt.

Julian smiled as he listened to her, but could not make up his mind to fulfill his desire.

One August evening they were in their chamber, she being just in bed and he kneeling down to pray, when he heard a fox barking, and then some light footfalls under the window. He caught a glimpse, in the dusk, of what seemed to be the shapes of animals. The temptation was too strong, and he took down his quiver.

She showed surprise.

"I do it to obey you," he said; "I shall be back at sunrise." Still, she was afraid of a disastrous venture.

He reassured her and went out, surprised at her inconsistent mood.

Soon afterwards a page came in to say that two strangers, as they could not see the absent lord, were asking instantly to see his lady.

And soon there entered the room an old man and an old woman, bowed and dusty, dressed in rough linen, each leaning on a staff.

Taking courage, they said that they were bringing Julian news of his parents. She leaned out of bed to listen.

But, having first exchanged a look, they asked her if he was still fond of them, and if he spoke of them at times.

"Ah, yes!" she said.

"Well, we are they!" they cried, and, being very weary and spent with fatigue, sat down.

The young wife felt no assurance that her husband was their son, but they proved it by describing some particular marks on his skin.

Then she leaped out of bed, called the page, and a repast was served to them.

They could scarcely eat, though they were very hungry; she observed, aside, how their bony hands trembled as they grasped the cups. They asked countless questions about Julian, and she answered all, but took care not to speak of the ghastly fancy in which they were concerned.

After waiting in vain for his return they had left their castle, and they had been travelling for several years after vague clues, without losing hope. So much money had been swallowed up by river-tolls and inns, the dues of princes and demands of thieves that their purse was emptied to the bottom, and now they begged their way. But what of that, when they would soon embrace their son? They extolled his happiness to have so fair a wife, and could not have enough of watching her and kissing her.

They were much astonished by the richness of the room, and the old man, after examining its walls, asked why the Emperor of Occitania's coat-of-arms was there.

"He is my father," she replied.

At that he started remembering the gipsy's prophecy, while the old woman thought of the hermit's words. Doubtless their son's glory was but the dawn of an eternal splendor; and they both sat open-mouthed under the light of the great candlestick upon the table.

They must have been very handsome in their youth. The mother had kept all her hair, and its fine plaits hung to the bottom of her cheeks like drifts of snow. The father, with his height and his great beard, was like a statue in a church.

Julian's wife persuaded them not to wait for him. With her own hands she placed them in her bed, then shut the window, and they went to sleep. Daybreak was near, and little birds were beginning to sing outside.

Julian had crossed the park and walked through the forest with a springing step, enjoying the soft turf and mild night air. Shadows fell from the trees across the moss. From time to time the moonlight made white patches in the drives and he hesitated to go forward, thinking he saw a pool; or, again, the surface of the still ponds would itself be lost in the color of the grass. There was a deep silence everywhere, and he found no trace of the animals which a few minutes earlier had been straying round his castle.

The wood thickened and grew profoundly dark. Puffs of warm air went by him, with relaxing scents. His feet sank among dead leaves, and he leaned against an oak to breathe a little.

Suddenly, from behind his back, a darker mass leaped out. It was a wild boar. Julian had no time to snatch his bow, and was as vexed as though it was a disaster.

Then, when he had left the wood, he saw a wolf stealing along a hedge. Julian sent an arrow after it. The wolf paused, turned round to look at him, and went on again. It trotted on, always at the same distance, stopping from time to time, and taking flight again as soon as Julian aimed.

In this way Julian went over an endless plain and a tract of sandhills, and came out upon high ground which looked over a great breadth of country. Flat stones lay scattered on it from ruined vaults all round. His feet stumbled on dead bones, and in places there were worm-eaten crosses leaning mournfully askew. But forms stirred in the dim shadow of the tombs; and hyenas rose out of them, scared and panting. Their hoofs clattered on the pave-stones as they came up to Julian, sniffing at him and showing their gums with a yawn. When he drew his sword they went off at once in all directions, with a headlong, limping gallop which lasted till they vanished in the distance under a cloud of dust.

An hour later he met a savage bull in a ravine, lowering its horns and ploughing the sand up with its foot. Julian thrust with his lance at it under the dew-lap. The lance was shivered, as though the animal were made of bronze; he closed his eyes, expecting to be killed. When he reopened them the bull had disappeared.

Then his heart sank for shame. A higher power was bringing his strength to nought, and he went back into the forest to regain his home.

The forest was tangled with creepers; and as he was cutting them with his sword a marten slipped sharply between his legs, a panther made a bound over his shoulder, and a snake wound its way up an ash tree. A huge jackdaw looked down at Julian out of its leaves, and on every side among the branches appeared a multitude of great sparks, as though the firmament had showered all its stars into the forest. They were eyes of animals—wild cats, squirrels, owls, parrots, monkeys.

Julian darted his arrows at them; the feathered shafts settled on the leaves like white butterflies. He threw stones at them, and the stones fell back without touching anything. He cursed, wanted to fight, shouted imprecations, and choked with rage.

And all the animals which he had been hunting appeared again and made a narrow circle round him. Some sat upon their haunches, others stood erect. He was rooted in the middle, frozen with terror, and impotent to move at all. With a supreme effort of will he took a step; the creatures on the branches spread their wings, those on the ground stretched their limbs, and all went on with him.

The hyenas walked in front, the wolf and the boar behind. The bull was on his right, swaying its head, while on his left the serpent wound through the grass and the panther arched its back and advanced with long, velvet-footed strides. He walked as slowly as he could to avoid irritating them; and as he went he saw porcupines, foxes, vipers, jackals, and bears come out of the dense undergrowth.

Julian began to run; they ran too. The serpent hissed, and the stinking creatures slavered. The wild boar's tusks prodded his heels, and the wolf rubbed the palms of his hands with his hairy muzzle. The monkeys pinched him and made faces, and the marten rolled over his feet. A bear swung its paw back and knocked his hat off, and the panther, which had been carrying an arrow in its mouth, let it fall in disdain.

Their sly movements gave peeps of irony. As they watched him out of the corner of their eyes they seemed to be meditating a plan of revenge; while he, deafened by the buzzing insects, lashed by the birds' tails, and smothered by the breath of the animals, walked with arms outstretched and eyes shut like a blind man, without even having strength to cry for mercy.

A cock-crow rang in the air, and others answered. It was day, and he recognized his palace roof beyond the orange-trees.

Then at the edge of a field he saw, three paces off him, some red partridges fluttering in the stubble. He unfastened his cloak and threw it over them as a net. When he uncovered them he found but one, long dead and rotten.

This deception infuriated him more than all the others. His thirst to kill swept over him again, and for want of beasts he would gladly have slain men.

He climbed the three terraces and burst open the door with a blow of his fist; but when he reached the staircase his heart unbent at the thought of his dear wife. She was asleep, doubtless, and he would take her by surprise.

He drew off his sandals, turned the lock gently, and went in.

The pale dawn came dimly through the leaded window-panes. Julian's feet caught in clothes lying on the floor; a little farther, and he knocked against a buffet still laden with plate. "Her supper, doubtless," he said to himself, and went on towards the bed, which he could not see in the darkness at the end of the room. He came close, and to kiss his wife bent down over the pillow where the two heads were lying side by side. Then he felt the touch of a beard against his mouth.

He drew back, thinking he was going mad, but came near the bed again, and as he felt about with his fingers they encountered long tresses of hair. To convince himself that he was wrong he passed his hand again slowly over the pillow. It was really a beard this time, and a man—a man lying with his wife!

In a fit of boundless fury he leaped on them, striking with his dagger; he stamped and foamed, roaring like a wild beast. Then he stopped. The dead folk, pierced to the heart, had not so much as stirred. He listened closely to their dying groans, which almost kept time together; and as they grew feebler another, in the far distance, took them up. Vague at first, this plaintive, long-drawn voice came nearer, swelled, rang cruelly; and he recognized in terror the belling of the great black stag.

And as he turned round he thought he saw his wife's ghost framed in the doorway, with a light in her hand.

The noise of the murder had drawn her there. In one wide glance she grasped it all, and fled in horror, dropping her torch. He picked it up.

His father and mother lay before him, stretched on their backs, with breasts pierced through; and their faces, in a gentle majesty, looked as though they were keeping a secret for ever. Splashes and pools of blood showed on their white skin, over the bed-clothes and the floor, and trickled down an ivory crucifix in the alcove. The scarlet reflection from the window, which the sun was striking, lit up these red patches and cast others, more numerous still, all round the room. Julian walked towards the two dead figures, saying to himself, and struggling to believe, that this thing could not be and that he was deceived by an error—by one of those resemblances which nothing can explain. Finally he bent down a little to look close at the old man, and saw between the unshut eyelids a glazed eye which scorched him like fire. Then he went to the other side of the couch where the other body lay, its white hair hiding part of the face. Julian passed his fingers under the plaits and lifted the head; and holding it at arm's length with one hand, while in the other he held up the torch, he looked at it. Drops of blood were oozing from the mattress and falling one by one upon the floor.

At the end of the day he came into his wife's presence; and in a voice not his own bade her first of all not to answer him, come near him, or even look at him. Under pain of damnation she must follow all his orders, which would not be gainsaid.

The funerals must be carried out according to injunctions which he had left in writing, on a prie-dieu in the chamber of the dead. He ceded to her his palace, his vassals, and all his possessions, not excepting even his clothes or his sandals, which would be found at the head of the stairs.

She had obeyed God's will in making the occasion of his crime, and she must pray for his soul, since from that day he ceased to exist.

The dead were sumptuously buried in an abbey church at three days' journey from the castle. A monk in shrouded hood followed the procession at a distance from the others, and no one dared to speak to him. He remained while the mass lasted, lying flat in the middle of the porch, with his arms making the form of a cross and his forehead in the dust.

After the burial he was seen to take the road leading to the mountains. He turned to look round several times, and finally disappeared.

III

He went onwards, begging his way throughout the world.

He held out his hand to the riders on the high-roads and bent his knee when he approached the reapers. Or he would stand motionless before the gates of courtyards, and his face was so sad that he was never refused alms.

In a spirit of humbleness he would tell his story; and then all fled from him, making the sign of the cross. In the villages which he had passed through before, the people, as soon as they recognized him, shut their doors, shouted abuse at him, threw stones at him. The most charitable of them placed a bowl on their windowsills and then closed the shutters so as not to see him.

Being repulsed everywhere, he shunned mankind, and fed on roots, plants, wayside fruit, and shell-fish which he gathered along the beaches.

Sometimes at the turn of a hillside, he saw a jumble of crowded roofs under his eyes, with stone spires, bridges, towers, and a network of dark streets, from which a ceaseless hum rose up to him. A need to mingle with the life of others would draw him down into the town. But the brutal look in their faces, their noisy crafts and callous words, made his heart freeze. On festal days, when the great cathedral bells tuned the whole populace to joy from daybreak, he watched the folk issuing from their houses, and the dancing in public spaces, the beer fountains at the crossways, the damask hung before the lodgings of princes; and then at evening, through the lower windows, the long family tables where grandparents dandled little children on their knees. Sobs choked him, and he turned away towards the country.

He had thrills of love as he gazed at young horses in the meadows, birds in their nests, and insects on the flowers; all, at his approach, ran farther off, hid in terror, or flew swiftly away.

He sought deserted places. But the wind grated on his ear like the rattle of a death-agony; the dew-drops falling to the ground brought other, heavier drops to mind. Every evening the sun tinged the clouds blood-red, and each night the murder of his parents began again in dreams.

He made himself a hair shirt with iron spikes, and climbed on his knees up every hill which had a chapel at the top. But his pitiless thought dimmed the radiance of the shrines, and stung him even in his acts of mortification. He did not rebel against God for having brought the deed upon him, and yet the idea that he could have done it made him despair.

His own person filled him with such horror that in the hope of release he risked it among dangers. He saved the paralysed from fires and children from the bottom of chasms. The abyss cast him up; the flames spared him.

Time brought no relief to his suffering. It became intolerable, and he resolved to die.

And one day when he was by a spring, leaning over it to judge the water's depth, he saw opposite him on a sudden an emaciated old man, with a white beard and look so dolorous that Julian could not keep back his tears. The other wept also. Without recognizing him exactly, Julian had a confused memory of a face like his. He uttered a cry; it was his father; and he thought no more of killing himself.

So with the burden of his recollections he travelled many lands, and came one day to a river, which, owing to its violence and a great stretch of slime along its banks, was dangerous to cross. No one for a long time had dared to make the passage.

An old boat, whose stern had been embedded, lifted its prow among the reeds. Julian examined it and found a pair of oars; and the thought came to him that he might use his life in the service of others.

He began by making a sort of roadway on the bank to lead down to the channel of the river; and he broke his nails in moving enormous stones, propped them against his waist to carry them, slipped in the mud and sank there, and nearly perished several times. Then he repaired the boat with pieces of wreckage, and made a hut for himself out of clay and tree-trunks.

The ferry came to be heard of and travellers appeared. They waved flags and hailed him from the other side, and Julian at once jumped into his boat. It was very heavy, and they overweighted it with baggage and loads of all kinds, without counting the beasts of burden, who made the crowding worse by kicking in alarm. He asked nothing for his labor; some of the passengers gave him remnants of food out of their wallets or worn-out clothes which they had no more use for. The brutal ones shouted blasphemies. Julian reproved them gently, and they retorted with abuse. He was content to bless them.

A little table, a stool, a bed of dry leaves, and three clay cups—that was the whole of his furniture. Two holes in the wall served for windows. On one side barren plains stretched away out of view, dotted with pale meres here and there; and in front of him the great river rolled its greenish waters. In spring the damp soil breathed an odor of decay. Then came a riotous wind that lifted the dust and whirled it. It found its way everywhere, muddying the water and grating in the mouth. A little later there were clouds of mosquitoes, which pinged and pricked without ceasing day and night. And then came on appalling frosts which turned everything to the hardness of stone and roused a wild craving to eat meat.

Months glided by when Julian did not see a soul. Often he closed his eyes and tried to revive his youth in memory. The courtyard of a castle would rise before him, with greyhounds on a flight of steps, grooms in the armory, and a fair-haired boy under a vine trellis between an old man dressed in furs and a lady wearing a great coif. Suddenly, the two corpses were there. He threw himself face downwards on his bed and kept murmuring with tears:

"Ah, poor father! Poor mother, poor mother!"—and fell into a drowsiness through which the mournful visions still went on.

When he was asleep one night he thought he heard someone calling him. He strained his ears and made out nothing except the roar of the water.

But the same voice cried again: "Julian!"

It came from the other bank, which amazed him, considering the breadth of the river.

A third time he was hailed: "Julian!"

And the loud voice had the tone of a church bell.

Julian lit his lantern and went out of the hovel. A wild hurricane was sweeping through the night. There was an intense darkness, pierced now and then by the whiteness of the leaping waves.

After a moment's hesitation Julian unfastened his moorings. The water instantly became calm, and the boat glided over it to the other bank, where a man stood waiting.

He was wrapped in a tattered cloth and his face was like a plaster mask, with eyes redder than coals. Holding the lantern to him, Julian saw that he was covered with a hideous leprosy; yet there was something of a royal majesty in his posture.

As soon as he entered the boat it sank prodigiously, overwhelmed by his weight. It rose again with a shake, and Julian began to row.

At every stroke the surf tossed the boat by its bows. The water, blacker than ink, ran furiously against the planks on both sides. It hollowed into gulfs and rose into mountains, which the boat leaped over, only to fall back into the depths, where it spun round at the mercy of the wind.

Julian bent low, stretched his arms out, and propping himself against his feet swung back with a twist to get more power. The hail lashed his hands, the rain streamed down his back, he could not breathe in the fierce wind, and stopped. Then the boat drifted and was carried away. But feeling that there was a great matter at stake, an order which might not be disobeyed, he took up the oars again, and the clacking of the thole-pins cut through the stormy clamor.

The little lantern burned in front of him. Birds hid it from time to time as they fluttered by. But he always saw the eyes of the Leper, who stood, motionless as a pillar, at the stern.

It went on long, very long.

When at last they had entered the hovel Julian shut the door; and he saw the Leper sitting on the stool. The kind of shroud which covered him had fallen to his hips; and his shoulders, chest, and wizened arms were hardly to be seen for the scaly pustules which coated them. Immense wrinkles furrowed his brow. He had a hole in place of a nose, like a skeleton, and his bluish lips exhaled a breath as thick as fog, and nauseous.

"I am hungry!" he said.

Julian gave him what he had, an old piece of bacon and the crust of a black loaf. When he had devoured them, the table, the dish, and the handle of the knife bore the same spots that could be seen on his body.

Next he said, "I am thirsty!"

Julian went to get his pitcher, and it gave out an aroma, as he took it, which enlarged his heart and nostrils. It was wine—what happiness! But the Leper put out his arm and emptied the whole pitcher at a draught.

Then he said, "I am cold!"

And Julian, with his candle, set light to a pile of bracken in the middle of the hut.

The Leper came to warm himself, and as he crouched on his heels he trembled in every limb and weakened. His eyes ceased to gleam, his sores ran, and in an almost lifeless voice he murmured:

"Thy bed!"

Julian helped him gently to drag himself there, and even spread the canvas of his boat over him as a covering.

The Leper groaned. His teeth showed at the corners of his mouth, a faster rattle shook his chest, and as each breath was taken his body hollowed to the backbone.

Then he shut his eyes.

"It is like ice in my bones! Come close to me!"

And Julian, lifting the cloth, lay down on the dead leaves side by side with him.

The Leper turned his head.

"Take off thy clothes, that I may have thy body's warmth!"

Julian took off his clothes and lay down on the bed again, naked as when he was born; and he felt the Leper's skin against his thigh, colder than a serpent and rough as a file.

He tried to hearten him, and the other answered in gasps:

"Ah, I am dying! Come closer, warm me! Not with the hands; no, with thy whole body!"

Julian stretched himself completely over him, mouth to mouth and chest on chest.

Then the Leper clasped him, and his eyes suddenly became as bright as stars; his hair drew out like sunbeams; the breath of his nostrils was as sweet as roses; a cloud of incense rose from the hearth, and the waves began to sing. Meanwhile an abundance of delight, a superhuman joy flooded into Julian's soul as he lay swooning; and he who still clasped him in his arms grew taller, ever taller, until his head and feet touched the two walls of the hut. The roof flew off, the firmament unrolled—and Julian rose towards the blue spaces, face to face with Our Lord Jesus, who carried him to heaven.

And that is the story of St. Julian the Hospitaller, more or less as you will find it on a church window in the region where I live.

QUESTIONS

"The Legend of St. Julian the Hospitaller"

1. Saints' legends were brief narratives of the lives of early Christian saints, and Flaubert's title suggests that he is merely retelling one of these legends. What evidence is there, however, that the legend form has been appreciably elaborated, so that Flaubert's work more properly can be called a short story? What elements of legend or myth does it retain?

2. Who is the narrator of Flaubert's story? Why does Flaubert show us so little of the workings of Julian's consciousness, especially in the first two sections of the story? Find those places where we do see Julian anticipating or reflecting on experience. Does Flaubert give us a sense of Julian's psychological motivation, of why he behaves as he does?

3. Analyze the structure of this story. What role does each of its three parts play? Estimate how many years of Julian's life each part describes.

4. Characterize the Julian we meet in the first part of Flaubert's story as fully as you can. How has his environment helped to shape him? What is his relationship to animals and birds? How do hunting and killing animals change him? Why is he such an excessive slaughterer of animals? Where in the story are there other instances of excess? Is there a connection between the narrative exaggerations and the richness and abundance of its sensuous details? What might Flaubert be trying to suggest by these things?

5. Describe the series of events that causes Julian to flee his home. How is the climactic hunt in Part I like a dream?

6. Characterize the Julian of Part II. Has he changed significantly? Explain.

7. What is ironic about Julian's reflections concerning Adam in the garden of Eden and about Noah's ark?

8. Describe the hunt near the end of the second section of the story. What

effect does it have on Julian? What is significant in the fact that he hears, mixed with the death cries of his parents, the "belling of the great black stag"?

9. What does Julian quest for in the final section of the story? Does he find it? Since his fate has been fixed since birth, is he questing toward something even larger, perhaps without knowing it?

10. Characterize the Julian of Part III. Does his quest transform him? Find evidence to support your opinion. How do the people in the various communities through which he journeys perceive him; how do they respond to him? In what sense is his attitude toward them ambivalent? Is Julian able to find peace in nature? Explain.

11. Why does Julian establish his ferry service?

12. Contrast the environment of the miracle at the end of the story with that of the first hunting scene and with the Moorish castle in which Julian lived with his wife. How is the primitive hut at the edge of the river Julian's truest home?

13. Note that the stranger seeking transport in the night calls to Julian three times in a voice that sounds like a "church bell"; similarly, a bell rings as the black stag calls Julian "accurst" three times. Why did Flaubert include these details?

14. In what sense does the leper represent Julian's third test and final fulfillment? Why is it essential to the meaning of the story that the stranger in the boat be so terrifyingly repulsive, so infectious that even the inanimate objects he touches become covered with leprous sores?

15. What is the last transformation Julian undergoes in the story?

Traveler

ELLEN GILCHRIST

It was June in southern Indiana. I was locked in the upstairs bathroom studying the directions on a box of Tampax when the invitation came.

"LeLe," my father called, coming up the stairs with the letter in his hand. "Come out of there. Come hear the news. You're going to the Delta."

It seems my cousin Baby Gwen Barksdale's mother had died of a weak liver, and rather than leave the poor girl alone in a house with a grieving widower the family had invited me to Mississippi to spend the summer as her companion. There was even a suggestion that I might stay and go to school there in the fall.

What luck that the invitation came just as my own mother, giving into a fit of jealous rage, left my father and fled to New Orleans to have a nervous breakdown.

"You'll love it in Clarksville," my father assured me. "Baby Gwen is just your age and just your speed. She'll be so glad to see you." And he pressed several more twenty-dollar bills into my hand and helped me pack my summer clothes.

"You try it for the summer, LeLe," he said. "We'll decide about school later on."

He might need to decide later on, but my mind was made up. I couldn't wait to leave Franklin, Indiana, where the students at Franklin Junior High had made the mistake of failing to elect me cheerleader. I wasn't unpopular or anything like that, just a little on the plump side.

Baby Gwen Barksdale, I whispered to myself as I arranged my things on the Pullman seat. I was sweating heavily in a pink linen suit, and my straw hat was making my head itch, but I sat up straight, trying to look like a lady. I had the latest edition of *Hit Parade Magazine* on my lap, and I was determined to learn every word of the Top Ten on the train ride.

Baby Gwen Barksdale, I said to myself, remembering the stories my father had told me. Baby Gwen, queen of the Delta subdeb dances, daughter of the famous Gwendolyn Montgomery Paine of Shaw, granddaughter of my grandmother's sainted sister, Frances Paine of Natchez. Baby Gwen Barksdale, daughter of Britain Barksdale who played halfback on the Ole Miss Sugar Bowl team.

It was all too good to be true. I marched myself down to the diner and ate several desserts to calm myself down.

By the time the Illinois Central made it all the way to Clarksville, Mississippi, my linen dress was helplessly wrinkled, my third pair of white gloves was damp and stained from the dye of the magazine, and my teeth were worn out from being brushed.

But there on the platform she waited, Baby Gwen Barksdale herself, five feet two inches of sultry dark-skinned, dark-eyed beauty. (The Barksdales have French blood.) She looked exactly like Ida Lupino. She was wearing a navy blue dotted Swiss sun dress and high-heeled shoes and her slip was showing, a thin line of ecru lace. Her dark pink lipstick exactly matched her fingernail polish, and she smelled divinely of Aprodisia perfume.

She was accompanied by a strong boy who smiled a lot and turned out to be the sheriff's son. He had come along to carry the luggage.

"I'm so glad you could come," she said, hugging me for the fourth time. "I can't believe you came all the way on the train by yourself."

"No one in Franklin believed I'd do it either," I said. "I just got elected cheerleader and practically the whole football team came to the station to tell me goodbye. They didn't believe I was leaving. Of course, they all know about Bob Aaron. That's the college boy I love. He's got cancer of the thyroid gland. My parents won't let me go out with him because he's Jewish. He's already had about five operations. He's having one right now in St. Louis. So I might as well be down here."

"Oh, LeLe, that's terrible. It's like my mother. I know just how you feel."

"Well, anyway, I'm here now and we can stick together," I said, taking a deep breath of the Aprodisia. "I love your perfume. It's wonderful."

"It's my signature," she said. "I wear Aprodisia in the summer and Tigress in the winter. There's a bottle in my purse. You can put some on if you want to."

We walked over to the Oldsmobile and Baby Gwen got behind the wheel. She was so short she had to sit on straw pillows to see over the dash, but she turned out to be a superb driver. The sheriff's son climbed into the back seat with my bags, and the three of us drove off down the streets of the town, past the gin and the post office and the Pontiac place, and on down the river road to a white frame house at the end of a street that dead-ended at the levee.

So I arrived in Clarksville, chattering away to a spellbound audience, spraying my neck and arms with Aprodisia perfume, happier than I had ever been in my life.

After her mother's funeral Baby Gwen had moved into the master bedroom as her father was too brokenhearted to ever enter that part of the house again.

I was led up the stairs and into a large sunny room with bay windows and a pale blue chaise lounge. There was a dressing room with a private bath and walk-in closets. Everything was just as Big Gwen had left it.

The closets were filled with unbelievable clothes. Navy blue and green and black silk dresses, gray and beige and brown gabardine suits, pastel evening dresses, house dresses, sun dresses, wool coats, skirts, jackets. There were twenty or thirty pairs of high-heeled shoes and a dozen hatboxes. There were drawers full of handmade underwear. There was a fur stole and several negligees and a real Japanese kimono.

It was all ours.

"You can wear anything you want to," Baby Gwen said. "Most of them are too long for me."

Best of all was the dressing table. It was three feet long with a padded stool and a large mirror surrounded by light bulbs.

On its surface, in a sea of spilled powder, were dozens of bottles and jars. Every product ever manufactured by Charles of the Ritz must have been there. There was foundation cream, astringent, eye shadow, rouge, clarifier, moisturizer, cleanser, refining oil, facial mask, night cream, hand cream, wrinkle cream, eye cream, all pervaded by the unforgettable smell of Revenescence, Charles of the Ritz's secret formula moisturizer.

There were hairpins, hand mirrors, tweezers, eyelash curlers, combs, hair rollers, mascara wands, cuticle sticks, nail polish, emery boards. There were numerous bottles of perfume and cologne and a cut-glass bowl filled with lipsticks.

I had never seen anything like it. I could hardly wait to sit down on the little padded stool and get started.

"You want a Coca-Cola?" Baby Gwen asked, growing bored with my inspection of her riches. "Some boys I know are coming over later this afternoon to meet you."

"Can we smoke?" I asked, pulling my Pall Malls out of my purse.

"We can do anything we want to do," she said, picking a Ronson lighter off the dressing table and handing it to me. She was smiling the famous Barksdale slow smile.

That night we lay awake until two or three in the morning telling each other our life stories. I told her about Bob Aaron's lymph node cancer, and she told me about her cousin Maurice, who taught French and hated Clarksville and was married to an unpleasant woman who sang in the choir. Maurice was secretly in love with Baby Gwen. He couldn't help himself. He had confessed his love at a spring wedding reception. Now they were waiting for Baby Gwen to grow up so they could run away together. In the meantime Baby Gwen was playing the field so no one would suspect.

Finally, exhausted by our passions, we fell asleep in each other's arms, with the night breezes blowing in the windows off the river, in our ironed sheets and our silk pajamas and our night cream, with the radio playing an all-night station from New Orleans. Oh, Bob, Bob, I whispered into Baby

Gwen's soft black hair. Oh, Maurice, Maurice, she sighed into my hair rollers.

In the morning I woke early and wandered downstairs. I went into the kitchen, opened the freezer, found a carton of vanilla ice cream, and began to eat it with my fingers, standing with the freezer door open, letting the cool air blow on my face.

After a while I heard the back door slam and Sirena came in. She was the middle-aged black woman who turned out to be the only person in charge of us in any way. Baby Gwen's father disappeared before dawn to carry the mail and came home in the evenings and sank into his chair with his bourbon and his memories. Occasionally he would put in an appearance at the noon meal and ask us if we wanted anything.

I barely managed to close the freezer door before Sirena caught me. "You want me to make you some breakfast?" she said.

"No, thank you," I said. "I don't eat in the daytime. I'm on a diet."

I have always believed Sirena found my fingerprints in that ice cream. One way or the other I wasn't fooling her, she knew a Yankee when she saw one, even if I was Mr. Leland's daughter.

I wandered into the living room and read a *Coronet* for a while. Then I decided to go back upstairs and see if Baby Gwen was awake.

I found her in the bathroom sitting upright in a tub of soapy water while Sirena knelt beside it slowly and intently bathing her. I had never seen a grown person being bathed before.

Sirena was running her great black hand up and down Baby Gwen's white leg, soaping her with a terry-cloth washrag. The artesian well water was the color of urine and smelled of sulphur and sandalwood soap, and Sirena's dark hand was thick and strong moving along Baby Gwen's flawless skin. I sat down on the toilet and began to make conversation.

"You want to take a sunbath after a while," I said. "I'm afraid I'll lose my tan."

"Sure," she said. "We can do whatever you want to. Someone called a while ago and asked us to play bridge this afternoon. Do you like to play bridge?"

"I love it," I said. "That's practically all we do in Indiana. We play all the time. My mother plays duplicate. She's got about fifty silver ashtrays she won at tournaments."

"I bet you're really good," she said. She was squirming around while Sirena took her time finishing the other leg.

I lit a cigarette, trying not to look at Baby Gwen's black pubic hair. I had never seen anyone's pubic hair but my own, which was red. It had not occurred to me that there were different colors. "Want a drag?" I asked, handing her the cigarette. She nodded, wiped her hand on her terry-cloth turban, took a long luxurious drag, and French inhaled.

The smoke left her mouth in two little rivers, curled deliciously up over the dark hairs above her lips, and into her nostrils. She held it for a long moment, then exhaled slowly through her lips. The smoke mingled with the sunlight, and the steam coming from the bathwater rose in ragged circles and moved toward the open window.

Baby Gwen rose from the water, her flat body festooned with blossoms of sandalwood soap, and Sirena began to dry her with a towel.

So our life together took shape. In the mornings we sunbathed from 11:00 to 12:00. Thirty minutes on one side and thirty minutes on the other. There were two schools of thought concerning sunbathing. One, that it gave you wrinkles. The other, that it was worth it to look good while you were young.

Baby Gwen and I subscribed to the second theory. Still, we were careful to keep our faces oiled so we wouldn't ruin our complexions. There is no way you could believe how serious we were about such matters. The impenetrable mystery of physical beauty held us like a spell.

In the morning we spread our blankets in the backyard where a patch of sunlight shone in through the high branches of the elm trees. We covered the blankets with white sheets and set out our supplies, bottles of baby oil, bottles of iodine, alarm clock, eye pads, sunglasses, magazines. We carefully mixed seven drops of iodine with seven ounces of baby, shook it for three minutes, then rubbed it on the uncovered parts of each other's bodies. How I loved the feel of Baby Gwen's rib cage under my fingers, the smoothness of her shaved legs. How I dreaded it when her fingers touched the baby fat on my own ribs.

When we were covered with oil we would lie back and continue our discussion of our romances. I talked of nothing but the ill-fated Bob Aaron, of the songs I would write and dedicate to his memory, of the trip I would take to his deathbed, of the night he drove me home from a football game and let me wear his gloves, of the child I would have by another man and name for him, Robert or Roberta, Bob or Bobbie.

The other thing that fascinated me was the development of my "reputation." I was intensely interested in what people thought of me, in what was being said about me. I set about to develop a reputation in Clarksville as a "madcap," a "wild child," a girl who would do anything. A summer visitor from Washington, D.C., said in my hearing that I reminded him of a young Zelda Fitzgerald and, although I didn't know exactly who Zelda Fitzgerald was, I knew that she had married a writer and drank like a fish and once danced naked in a fountain in Rome. It sounded like a wonderful thing to have said about myself, and I resolved to try to live up to it.

How wonderful it was to be "home," where people knew "who I was," where people thought I was "hilarious" and "crazy" and "just like Leland." I did everything I could think of to feed my new image, becoming very outspoken, saying *damn* and *hell* at every opportunity, wearing dark glasses all the time, even to church. I must have been the first person of normal vision ever to attend the Clarksville Episcopal Church wearing dark glasses.

Baby Gwen's grandmother called every few days to see how we were getting along and once, in a burst of responsibility, came over bringing a dozen pairs of new cotton underpants she had bought for us at the China-man's store.

We never could figure out where she got the idea that we were in need of cotton underpants, unless Sirena had mentioned it to her. Perhaps Sirena had tired of hand washing the French lingerie we had taken to wearing every day.

The grandmother had outlived both her daughters and existed in a sort of dreamy half-world with her servants and her religion.

Mostly we kept her satisfied by glowing telephone reports of our popularity and by stopping by occasionally to sit on her porch and have a Coca-Cola.

I fell in love nearly every day with one or the other of the seemingly endless supply of boys who came over to call from Drew and Cleveland and Itta Bena and Tutweiler and Rosedale and Leland. Baby Gwen drew boys like honey, and there were always plenty left over to sit around the living room listening to my nonstop conversation.

Boys came by in the evenings, boys called on the telephone, boys invaded our daily bridge games, boys showed up after church, boys took us swimming at the Clarksville Country Club, boys drove us around the cotton fields and down to the river and out to the bootlegger's shack.

The boy I liked best was a good-natured football player named Fielding Reid. Fielding had eyes so blue and hair so blonde and shoulders so wide and teased me so unmercifully about my accent that I completely forgot he was the steady boyfriend of Clarice Fitzhugh, who was off on a trip to Mexico with her family. Fielding had taken to hanging around Baby Gwen and me while he waited for Clarice's return.

He loved to kibitz on our bridge games, eating all the mints and pecans from the little dishes and leaning over my shoulder cheering me on. In the afternoons we played endless polite bridge games, so different from the bitter hard-fought bridge I had played in the forgotten state of Indiana.

Although I was an erratic and unpredictable bidder, I was a sought-after partner for I held good cards and nearly always won.

There was a girl from Drew named Sarah who came over several afternoons a week to play with us. She was Fielding's cousin and she had a wooden arm painted the color of her skin. It was not a particularly well made arm, and the paint was peeling in several places on the hand. She was pleasant enough looking otherwise and had nice clothes with loose sleeves that hid the place where the false arm joined the real one.

I made a great show of being nice to Sarah, lighting her cigarettes, asking her opinion about things, letting her be my bridge partner. She was delighted with the attention I gave her and was always telling someone how "wonderful" I was and how much it meant to her to have me in Clarksville.

The wrist and fingers of Sarah's false arm were hinged and she could move the joints with her good hand and lock them in place. She was in the habit of holding the wooden arm in front of her when she was seated at the bridge table. Then she would place her bridge hand in the wooden fingers and play out of it with her good hand.

Of course, anyone sitting on either side of her could see her cards by the slightest movement of their eyes. It took a lot of pressure off me when she was my partner.

Fielding thought I was "wonderful" too. He went around saying I was his "partner" and took me into his confidence, even telling me his fears that the absent Clarice Fitzhugh was being unfaithful to him in Mexico. That she might be "using" him.

Don't worry, I assured him. Clarice was a great girl. She wouldn't use anyone. He must trust her and not listen to idle gossip. Everything would be fine when she got home, and so forth. Part of my new reputation was that "LeLe never says a bad word about anyone," "LeLe always looks on the bright side," "everyone feels like they've known LeLe all their lives," "you can tell LeLe *anything*."

I was beginning to believe my own publicity, that I was someone very special, that there might be some special destiny in store for me.

Several times that summer I was filled with an elation so powerful and overwhelming that it felt as though my body were leaving the earth. This always happened at night, when I was alone in the yard, caught in the shadow of the Nandina bushes which covered the side of the house like bright dark clouds. I remember standing in the starlight filled with some inexpressible joy. It would become very intense, like music. I was terribly excited by these feelings and could not bring myself to speak of them, even to Baby Gwen.

Often that summer I was given to seizures of abrupt excitement while I was dressing. I would catch a glimpse of myself in a mirror and burst into laughter, or, deciding for a moment that I was pretty, begin to tremble and jump up and go dancing around the room.

I had a recurrent dream that summer. I dreamed that I was walking through our old house in Indiana and I would notice that the dining room opened up into rooms and rooms I had not known existed, strange and oddly shaped rooms full of heavy furniture, expensive dusty dressers with drawers full of treasures, old gowns and sweaters and capes, jewels and letters and old documents, wills and deeds and diaries. These rooms opened onto patios and sun porches and solariums, and I saw that we were wealthy people. I wanted to run back and find my parents and tell them what I had found, but my curiosity drove me forward. I had to keep opening doors until I knew the extent of our riches, so I kept on moving through the strange rooms until I woke.

One morning Fielding came by unexpectedly and asked me to go with him to see about some repairs for his car. We left it with a mechanic at the filling station and walked to the Mayflower Café, a place on the square where farmers and merchants gathered in the mornings for coffee and gossip. I had never been alone in a restaurant with a boy, and I was excited and began talking very fast to cover my excitement. I ordered doughnuts and began turning my turquoise ring around on my finger so the waitress would think it was a wedding band.

"I've been wanting to talk to you alone," Fielding said.

"Sure," I said, choking on a powdered doughnut. It was all too wonderful, sitting in a booth so early in the morning with a really good-looking boy.

"LeLe," he said, smiling at me and reaching across the table to hold my hand. There was his garnet class ring, blazing at me from the tabletop. At any moment it might be mine. I could scarcely breathe. "LeLe," he repeated, "I don't want you to get me wrong when I say this. I don't want to hurt your feelings or anything, but, well, I really want to tell you something." He squeezed my hand tighter. "LeLe, you would be a really beautiful girl if you lost ten pounds, do you know that? Because you have a beautiful face. I'm only saying this because we've gotten to be such good friends and I thought I ought . . ."

I was stunned. But I recovered. "I'm not really this fat," I said. "At home I'm a cheerleader and I'm on the swimming team and I'm very thin. But last year the boy I love got cancer and I've been having a lot of trouble with my thyroid since then. The doctors think there may be something wrong with my thyroid or my metabolism. I may have to have an operation pretty soon."

"Oh, LeLe," he said. "I didn't know it was anything like that. I thought maybe you ate too much or something." He reached out and took my other hand. I was still holding part of a doughnut.

"Don't worry about it, Fielding. How could you know. You didn't hurt my feelings. Besides, I don't mind. The operation may not be so bad. It isn't like having polio or something they can't fix. At least I have something they can fix."

"Oh, LeLe."

"Don't worry about it. And don't tell anyone about it, even Baby Gwen. I don't want people feeling sorry for me. So it's a secret."

"Don't worry, LeLe. I'll never tell anyone. Are you sure it'll be all right? About the operation I mean?"

"Oh, sure. I might not even have to have it. My thyroid might get better all by itself."

After that Fielding and I were closer than ever. I began to halfway believe the part about the thyroid trouble. My mother was always talking about her thyroid and taking some sort of little white pill for it.

Late one afternoon Baby Gwen and I were sitting on the porch swing talking to Fielding. It was one of those days in August when you can smell autumn in the air, a feeling of change coming over the world. I had won at bridge that afternoon. I had made seven hearts doubled and redoubled with Fielding looking over my shoulder, and I was filled with a sense of power.

"Let's all go swimming tomorrow," I said. "They'll be closing the pool soon and I need to practice my strokes."

"Let's go to the lake," Fielding said. "I haven't made my summer swim across the lake. I was waiting for Russell to get home, but I don't guess he'll be back in time so I might as well go on and swim it myself."

"I'll swim it with you," I heard myself saying. "I'm a Junior Red Cross Lifesaver. I can swim forever."

"You couldn't swim this," he said. "It's five miles."

"I can swim a lot further than that," I said. "I practically taught swimming at camp. I never got tired."

"What about your . . . you know . . . your condition?"

"That's all right," I said. "Exercise is good for me. I'm supposed to go swimming all I can. The doctors said it was the best thing I could do."

Baby Gwen looked puzzled. "You can't swim all the way across the lake without a boat," she said. "Girls don't ever swim across the lake."

"I can swim it," I said, "I've been further than that at camp lots of times. What time you want to go, Fielding?"

By the time he came to pick us up the next morning I had calmed Baby Gwen down and convinced her there was nothing to worry about. I really was a good swimmer. Swimming was of no importance to me one way or the other. What mattered to me was that a boy of my own choosing, a first-rate boy, was coming to take me somewhere. Not coming for Baby Gwen and taking me along to be nice, but *coming for me.*

I had been awake since dawn deciding what to wear. I finally settled on my old green Jantzen and a white blouse from Big Gwen's wardrobe. The blouse had little shoulder pads and big chunky buttons and fell across my shoulders and arms in soft pleats. I wasn't worried at all about swimming the lake. The only thing that worried me was whether the blouse was long enough to cover my stomach.

Baby Gwen went with us. As soon as we left the shore she was supposed to drive around to the other side and watch for us. All the way out to the lake she sat beside me looking worried.

"You ought to have a boat going along beside you," she said.

"We don't need a boat," I said. "I'm a Junior Red Cross Lifesaver. I can swim all day if I want."

"It's O.K.," Fielding said. "Russell and I do it every summer."

By the time we got to the lake I felt like I could swim the Atlantic Ocean. The sun was brilliant on the blue water, and as soon as Fielding stopped the car I jumped out and ran down to the shore and looked out across the water to the pine trees on the far shore. It didn't look so far away, only very blue and deep and mysterious. I took off my blouse and shoes and waded out into the water. How clean it felt, how cool. I put my face down and touched my cheek to the water. I felt the water across my legs and stomach. My body felt wonderful and light in the water. I rose up on my toes and my legs felt strong and tall. I pulled in my stomach until my ribs stuck out. I was beautiful. I was perfect. I began to throw handfuls of water up into the air. The water caught in the sunlight and fell back all around me. I threw more into the air and it fell all around me, falling in pieces of steel and glass and diamonds, diamonds falling all around me. I called out, "Come on, Fielding. Either we're swimming across this lake or we aren't."

"Wait," he called back. "Wait up." Then he was beside me in the water and I felt his hands around my waist and the pressure of his knee against my thigh. "Let's go then," he said in a low sweet voice. "Let's do this together."

Then we began to swim out, headed for the stand of pine and oak and cypress on the far shore.

The time passed as if in a dream. My arms moved easily, taking turns pulling the soft yielding water alongside my body. I was counting out the strokes, one, two, three, four, five, six, seven, eight, one, two, three, four, five, six, seven, eight . . . over and over in the good old-fashioned Australian crawl. Every now and then Fielding would touch my arm and we would roll over on our backs and rest for a few minutes, checking our position. Then we would swim for a while on our sides, resting. There were long banks of clouds on the horizon and far overhead a great hawk circling like a black planet. Everytime I looked up he was there.

We swam for what seemed to be a long, long time, but whenever I looked ahead the trees on the shore never seemed to come any closer.

"Are you sure we're going in a straight line," I said, when we turned over to rest for a moment.

"I think so," Fielding said. "The current might be pulling us a little to the left. There's nothing we can do about it now anyway."

"Why," I said. "Why can't we do anything about it?"

"Well, we can't go back," he said. "We're past the point of no return."

The point of no return, I said to myself. Maybe we would die out here and they would change the name of the lake in honor of us. Lake LeLe, Lake Leland Louise Arnold, Lover's Lake. "Don't worry about it then," I said. "Just keep on swimming."

Perhaps an hour went by, perhaps two. The sun was hot on the water, and every now and then a breeze blew up. Once a barge carrying logs to the sawmill passed us without noticing us. We treaded water while it passed and then rocked in the wake for several minutes. They had passed us as though we didn't exist. After the barge went by we began to swim with more determination. I was beginning to feel cold, but it didn't seem to really matter. Nothing mattered but this boy and the sun and the clouds and the great hawk circling and the water touching me everywhere. I put down my head and began to count with renewed vigor, one, two, three, four, five, six, seven, eight, one, two, three, four, . . .

"LeLe," Fielding called out. "LeLe, put your feet down. Put your feet down, LeLe." I looked up and he was standing a few feet away holding his hands up in the air. I let my feet drop and my toes touched the cool flat sand. We were on the sandbar. Then we were laughing and hugging and holding on to each other and moving toward the shore where Baby Gwen stood calling and calling to us. It was wonderful, wonderful, wonderful, wonderful. I was wonderful. I was dazzling. I was LeLe Arnold, the wildest girl in the Mississippi Delta, the girl who swam Lake Jefferson without a boat or a life vest. I was LeLe, the girl who would do anything.

All the way home in the car Fielding kept his arm around me while he drove and Baby Gwen fed me little pieces of the picnic lunch and I was happier than I had ever been in my life and I might have stayed that way forever but when we got home there was a message saying that my parents were on their way to Clarksville to take me home.

My parents. I had forgotten they existed. My father had gotten lonely and driven to New Orleans and talked my mother into coming home.

Later that afternoon they arrived. It seemed strange to see our Buick pulling up in Baby Gwen's driveway. My father got out looking very young and my mother was holding on to his arm. She looked like a stranger, thin and beautiful in a black cotton peasant dress with rows of colored rickrack around the hem and sleeves. Her hair was cut short and curled around her face in ringlets. I was almost afraid to touch her. Then she ran from my father's side and grabbed me in her arms and whirled me around and around and I smelled the delicate perfume on her skin and it made me feel like crying.

When she put me down I turned to my father. "I'm not going home," I said, putting my hands on my hips.

"Oh, yes you are," he said, so I went upstairs and began to pack my clothes.

Baby Gwen followed me up the stairs. "You can have the kimono," she said. "I want you to have it." She folded it carefully and packed it with tissue paper in a box from Nell's and Blum's and put it beside my suitcase.

"Come sit by me, Baby Gwen, and tell me the news," my mother said, and Baby Gwen went over and sat by her on the chaise. My mother put her arms around her and began to talk in a bright voice inviting her to spend Christmas with us in Indiana.

"It will snow for sure," my mother said. "And LeLe can show you the snow."

We left Clarksville early the next morning. Baby Gwen stood in the doorway waving goodbye. She was wearing a pink satin robe stained in places from where she had sweated in it during the hot nights of July, and her little nipples stuck out beneath the soft material.

I kept hoping maybe Fielding had gotten up early to come and tell me goodbye, but he didn't make it.

"I'll fix those hems when she comes to visit," my mother said, "and do something about that perfume."

I was too tired to argue. All the way to Indiana I slumped in the back seat eating potato chips and sneaking smokes in filling-station restrooms when we stopped for gas.

Then it was another morning and I woke up in my old room and put on my shorts and rode my bicycle over to Cynthia Carver's house. She was in the basement doing her Saturday morning ironing. Cynthia hated to iron. How many mornings had I sat on those basement steps watching the forlorn look on her face while she finished her seven blouses.

"So I might as well be dead," I said, taking a bite of a cookie. "So, anyway, I wish I was dead," I repeated, as Cynthia hung a blouse on a hanger and started on a dirndl skirt. "Here I am, practically engaged to this rich plantation owner's son . . . Fielding. Fielding Reid, LeLe Reid . . . so, anyway, my mother and father come and drag me home practically the same day we fell in love. I don't know how they got wind of it unless that damn Sirena called and told them. She was always watching everything I did. Anyway, they drag me home and I bet they won't even let him write to me."

"What's that perfume?" Cynthia said, lifting her eyes from the waistband of the skirt.

"That's my signature," I said. "That's what I wear now. Tigress in the winter and Aprodisia in the summer. That what this writer's wife always wore. She got pneumonia or something from swimming in the winter and died when she was real young. Everyone in Clarksville thinks I'm just like her. She was from Mississippi or something. I think she's sort of my father's cousin."

Cynthia pulled the dirndl off the ironing board and began on a pair of pedal pushers. I leaned back on the stairs, watching the steam from the pedal pushers light up the space over Cynthia Carver's disgruntled Yankee head. I was dreaming of the lake, trying to remember how the water turned into diamonds in my hands.

QUESTIONS

"Traveler"

1. What details are you given about LeLe Arnold's life in Indiana? What are her parents like? Why is she so eager to escape Indiana?

2. How old do you think LeLe is? What clues in the story help you guess her approximate age? How important is her age to the story? Does knowing her age give you insight into her character or help you understand her behavior? Explain.

3. Why does the narrator and protagonist invent so many fictions about herself? What are some of these stories? Do you see any patterns in them? Do they help you understand what her life in Indiana is like?

4. Clearly LeLe is unhappy with her "real" self, her old self. By looking at her behavior in Mississippi and by examining the lies she tells about herself, describe the kind of girl she would like to be.

5. Describe Baby Gwen. Why does her cousin admire her? What is her life like? Her father? Her house? Why does Big Gwen's bedroom appeal to LeLe? How is Baby Gwen's life contrasted to that of Cynthia, LeLe's Indiana friend?

6. What role do adults play in this story? What view of adults does LeLe have? What does Mrs. Arnold's remark about Baby Gwen's hems and perfume tell you about Gwen? How does it suggest a different perspective from LeLe's?

7. Describe LeLe and Baby Gwen's days together in Mississippi. Why would their days appeal to an adolescent?

8. The people LeLe meets in the Delta genuinely like her. Why? What qualities in her new self do they respond to?

9. Recount LeLe's recurrent dream. What do you think it means?

10. What is the significance of the long lake swim LeLe and Fielding take together? Does this episode affect your conception of LeLe? How does she feel at the start of the five-mile swim? At the end?

11. Will LeLe's transformation last—will it survive her return to Indiana? Why or why not?

Rip Van Winkle

WASHINGTON IRVING

Whoever has made a voyage up the Hudson must remember the Kaatskill mountains. They are a dismembered branch of the great Appalachian family, and are seen away to the west of the river, swelling up to a noble height, and lording it over the surrounding country. Every change of season, every change of weather, indeed, every hour of the day, produces some change in the magical hues and shapes of these mountains, and they are regarded by all the good wives, far and near, as perfect barometers. When the weather is fair and settled, they are clothed in blue and purple, and print their bold outlines on the clear evening sky; but, sometimes, when the rest of the landscape is cloudless, they will gather a hood of gray vapors about their summits, which, in the last rays of the setting sun, will glow and light up like a crown of glory.

At the foot of these fairy mountains, the voyager may have descried the light smoke curling up from a village, whose shingle-roofs gleam among the trees, just where the blue tints of the upland melt away into the fresh green of the nearer landscape. It is a little village, of great antiquity, having been founded by some of the Dutch colonists, in the early times of the province, just about the beginning of the government of the good Peter Stuyvesant, (may he rest in peace!) and there were some of the houses of the original settlers standing within a few years, built of small yellow bricks brought from Holland, having latticed windows and gable fronts, surmounted with weather-cocks.

In that same village, and in one of these very houses (which, to tell the precise truth, was sadly time-worn and weather-beaten), there lived many years since, while the country was yet a province of Great Britain, a simple good-natured fellow, of the name of Rip Van Winkle. He was a descendant of the Van Winkles who figured so gallantly in the chivalrous days of Peter Stuyvesant, and accompanied him to the siege of Fort Christina. He inherited, however, but little of the martial character of his ancestors. I have observed that he was a simple good-natured man; he was, moreover, a kind neighbor, and an obedient, hen-pecked husband. Indeed, to the latter circumstance might be owing that meekness of spirit which gained him such

universal popularity; for those men are most apt to be obsequious and con-
ciliating abroad, who are under the discipline of shrews at home. Their
tempers, doubtless, are rendered pliant and malleable in the fiery furnace
of domestic tribulation; and a curtain lecture is worth all the sermons in
the world for teaching the virtues of patience and long-suffering. A termi-
gant wife may, therefore, in some respects, be considered a tolerable blessing; and if so, Rip Van Winkle was thrice blessed.

Certain it is, that he was a great favorite among all the good wives of the
village, who, as usual, with the amiable sex, took his part in all family
squabbles; and never failed, whenever they talked those matters over in
their evening gossipings, to lay all the blame on Dame Van Winkle. The
children of the village, too, would shout with joy whenever he approached.
He assisted at their sports, made their playthings, taught them to fly kites
and shoot marbles, and told them long stories of ghosts, witches, and Indians. Whenever he went dodging about the village, he was surrounded
by a troop of them, hanging on his skirts, clambering on his back, and
playing a thousand tricks on him with impunity; and not a dog would bark
at him throughout the neighborhood.

The great error in Rip's composition was an insuperable aversion to all
kinds of profitable labor. It could not be from the want of assiduity or
perseverance; for he would sit on a wet rock, with a rod as long and heavy
as a Tartar's lance, and fish all day without a murmur, even though he
should not be encouraged by a single nibble. He would carry a fowling-
piece on his shoulder for hours together, trudging through woods and
swamps, and up hill and down dale, to shoot a few squirrels or wild pigeons. He would never refuse to assist a neighbor even in the roughest
toil, and was a foremost man at all country frolics for husking Indian corn,
or building stone-fences; the women of the village, too, used to employ
him to run their errands, and to do such little odd jobs as their less obliging
husbands would not do for them. In a word Rip was ready to attend to
anybody's business but his own; but as to doing family duty, and keeping
his farm in order, he found it impossible.

In fact, he declared it was of no use to work on his farm; it was the most
pestilent little piece of ground in the whole country; everything about it
went wrong, and would go wrong, in spite of him. His fences were continually falling to pieces; his cow would either go astray, or get among the
cabbages; weeds were sure to grow quicker in his fields than anywhere
else; the rain always made a point of setting in just as he had some out-
door work to do; so that though his patrimonial estate had dwindled away
under his management, acre by acre, until there was little more left than
a mere patch of Indian corn and potatoes, yet it was the worst conditioned
farm in the neighborhood.

His children, too, were as ragged and wild as if they belonged to nobody. His son Rip, an urchin begotten in his own likeness, promised to
inherit the habits, with the old clothes of his father. He was generally seen

trooping like a colt at his mother's heels, equipped in a pair of his father's cast-off galligaskins, which he had much ado to hold up with one hand, as a fine lady does her train in bad weather.

Rip Van Winkle, however, was one of those happy mortals, of foolish, well-oiled dispositions, who take the world easy, eat white bread or brown, whichever can be got with least thought or trouble, and would rather starve on a penny than work for a pound. If left to himself, he would have whistled life away in perfect contentment; but his wife kept continually dinning in his ears about his idleness, his carelessness, and the ruin he was bringing on his family. Morning, noon, and night, her tongue was incessantly going, and every thing he said or did was sure to produce a torrent of household eloquence. Rip had but one way of replying to all lectures of the kind, and that, by frequent use, had grown into a habit. He shrugged his shoulders, shook his head, cast up his eyes, but said nothing. This, however, always provoked a fresh volley from his wife; so that he was fain to draw off his forces, and take to the outside of the house—the only side which, in truth, belongs to a hen-pecked husband.

Rip's sole domestic adherent was his dog Wolf, who was as much henpecked as his master; for Dame Van Winkle regarded them as companions in idleness, and even looked upon Wolf with an evil eye, as the cause of his master's going so often astray. True it is, in all points of spirit befitting an honorable dog, he was as courageous an animal as ever scoured the woods—but what courage can withstand the ever-during and all-besetting terrors of a woman's tongue! The moment Wolf entered the house his crest fell, his tail drooped to the ground, or curled between his legs, he sneaked about with a gallows air, casting many a sidelong glance at Dame Van Winkle, and at the least flourish of a broomstick or ladle, he would fly to the door with yelping precipitation.

Times grew worse and worse with Rip Van Winkle as years of matrimony rolled on; a tart temper never mellows with age, and a sharp tongue is the only edged tool that grows keener with constant use. For a long while he used to console himself, when driven from home, by frequenting a kind of perpetual club of the sages, philosophers, and other idle personages of the village; which held its sessions on a bench before a small inn, designated by a rubicund portrait of His Majesty George the Third. Here they used to sit in the shade through a long lazy summer's day, talking listlessly over village gossip, or telling endless sleepy stories about nothing. But it would have been worth any statesman's money to have heard the profound discussions that sometimes took place, when by chance an old newspaper fell into their hands from some passing traveller. How solemnly they would listen to the contents, as drawled out by Derrick Van Bummel, the schoolmaster, a dapper learned little man, who was not to be daunted by the most gigantic word in the dictionary; and how sagely they would deliberate upon public events some months after they had taken place.

The opinions of this junto were completely controlled by Nicholas Vedder, a patriarch of the village, and landlord of the inn, at the door of which he took his seat from morning till night, just moving sufficiently to avoid the sun and keep in the shade of a large tree; so that the neighbors could tell the hour by his movements as accurately as by a sun-dial. It is true he was rarely heard to speak, but smoked his pipe incessantly. His adherents, however (for every great man has his adherents), perfectly understood him, and knew how to gather his opinions. When any thing that was read or related displeased him, he was observed to smoke his pipe vehemently, and to send forth short, frequent and angry puffs; but when pleased, he would inhale the smoke slowly and tranquilly, and emit it in light and placid clouds; and sometimes, taking the pipe from his mouth, and letting the fragrant vapor curl about his nose, would gravely nod his head in token of perfect approbation.

From even this stronghold the unlucky Rip was at length routed by his termagant wife, who would suddenly break in upon the tranquillity of the assemblage and call the members all to naught; nor was that august personage, Nicholas Vedder himself, sacred from the daring tongue of this terrible virago, who charged him outright with encouraging her husband in habits of idleness.

Poor Rip was at last reduced almost to despair; and his only alternative, to escape from the labor of the farm and clamor of his wife, was to take gun in hand and stroll away into the woods. Here he would sometimes seat himself at the foot of a tree, and share the contents of his wallet with Wolf, with whom he sympathized as a fellow-sufferer in persecution. "Poor Wolf," he would say, "thy mistress leads thee a dog's life of it; but never mind, my lad, whilst I live thou shalt never want a friend to stand by thee!" Wolf would wag his tail, look wistfully in his master's face, and if dogs can feel pity I verily believe he reciprocated the sentiment with all his heart.

In a long ramble of the kind on a fine autumnal day, Rip had unconsciously scrambled to one of the highest parts of the Kaatskill mountains. He was after his favorite sport of squirrel shooting, and the still solitudes had echoed and reechoed with the reports of his gun. Panting and fatigued, he threw himself, late in the afternoon, on a green knoll, covered with mountain herbage, that crowned the brow of a precipice. From an opening between the trees he could overlook all the lower country for many a mile of rich woodland. He saw at a distance the lordly Hudson, far, far below him, moving on its silent but majestic course, with the reflection of a purple cloud, or the sail of a lagging bark, here and there sleeping on its glassy bosom, and at last losing itself in the blue highlands.

On the other side he looked down into a deep mountain glen, wild, lonely, and shagged, the bottom filled with fragments from the impending cliffs, and scarcely lighted by the reflected rays of the setting sun. For some time Rip lay musing on this scene; evening was gradually advancing; the mountains began to throw their long blue shadows over the valleys; he saw that it would be dark long before he could reach the village, and he heaved a heavy sigh when he thought of encountering the terrors of Dame Van Winkle.

As he was about to descend, he heard a voice from a distance, hallooing, "Rip Van Winkle! Rip Van Winkle!" He looked round, but could see nothing but a crow winging its solitary flight across the mountain. He thought his fancy must have deceived him, and turned again to descend, when he heard the same cry ring through the still evening air; "Rip Van Winkle! Rip Van Winkle!"—at the same time Wolf bristled up his back, and giving a low growl, skulked to his master's side, looking fearfully down into the glen. Rip now felt a vague apprehension stealing over him; he looked anxiously in the same direction, and perceived a strange figure slowly toiling up the rocks, and bending under the weight of something he carried on his back. He was surprised to see any human being in this lonely and unfrequented place, but supposing it to be some one of the neighborhood in need of his assistance, he hastened down to yield it.

On nearer approach he was still more surprised at the singularity of the stranger's appearance. He was a short, square-built old fellow, with thick bushy hair, and a grizzled beard. His dress was of the antique Dutch fashion—a cloth jerkin strapped round the waist—several pair of breeches, the outer one of ample volume, decorated with rows of buttons down the sides, and bunches at the knees. He bore on his shoulder a stout keg, that seemed full of liquor, and made signs for Rip to approach and assist him with the load. Though rather shy and distrustful of this new acquaintance, Rip complied with his usual alacrity; and mutually relieving one another, they clambered up a narrow gully, apparently the dry bed of a mountain torrent. As they ascended, Rip every now and then heard long rolling peals, like distant thunder, that seemed to issue out of a deep ravine, or rather cleft, between lofty rocks, toward which their rugged path conducted. He paused for an instant, but supposing it to be the muttering of one of those transient thunder-showers which often take place in mountain heights, he proceeded. Passing through the ravine, they came to a hollow, like a small amphitheatre, surrounded by perpendicular precipices, over the brinks of which impending trees shot their branches, so that you only caught glimpses of the azure sky and the bright evening cloud. During the whole time Rip and his companion had labored on in silence; for though the former marvelled greatly what could be the object of carrying a keg of liquor up this wild mountain, yet there was something strange and incomprehensible about the unknown, that inspired awe and checked familiarity.

On entering the amphitheatre, new objects of wonder presented themselves. On a level spot in the centre was a company of odd-looking personages playing at nine-pins. They were dressed in a quaint outlandish fashion; some wore short doublets, others jerkins, with long knives in their belts, and most of them had enormous breeches, of similar style with that of the guide's. Their visages, too, were peculiar: one had a large beard, broad face, and small piggish eyes: the face of another seemed to consist entirely of nose, and was surmounted by a white sugar-loaf hat, set off with a little red cock's tail. They all had beards, of various shapes and colors. There was one who seemed to be the commander. He was a stout old gentleman, with a weather-beaten countenance; he wore a laced doublet, broad belt and hanger, high crowned hat and feather, red stockings, and high-heeled shoes, with roses in them. The whole group reminded Rip of the figures in an old Flemish painting, in the parlor of Dominie Van Shaick, the village parson, and which had been brought over from Holland at the time of the settlement.

What seemed particularly odd to Rip was, that though these folks were evidently amusing themselves, yet they maintained the gravest faces, the most mysterious silence, and were, withal, the most melancholy party of pleasure he had ever witnessed. Nothing interrupted the stillness of the scene but the noise of the balls, which, whenever they were rolled, echoed along the mountains like rumbling peals of thunder.

As Rip and his companion approached them, they suddenly desisted from their play, and stared at him with such fixed statue-like gaze, and such strange, uncouth, lack-lustre countenances, that his heart turned within him, and his knees smote together. His companion now emptied the contents of the keg into large flagons, and made signs to him to wait upon the company. He obeyed with fear and trembling; they quaffed the liquor in profound silence, and then returned to their game.

By degrees Rip's awe and apprehension subsided. He even ventured, when no eye was fixed upon him, to taste the beverage, which he found had much of the flavor of excellent Hollands. He was naturally a thirsty soul, and was soon tempted to repeat the draught. One taste provoked another; and he reiterated his visits to the flagon so often that at length his senses were overpowered, his eyes swam in his head, his head gradually declined, and he fell into a deep sleep.

On waking, he found himself on the green knoll whence he had first seen the old man of the glen. He rubbed his eyes—it was a bright sunny morning. The birds were hopping and twittering among the bushes, and the eagle was wheeling aloft, and breasting the pure mountain breeze. "Surely," thought Rip, "I have not slept here all night." He recalled the occurrences before he fell asleep. The strange man with a keg of liquor— the mountain ravine—the wild retreat among the rocks—the wobegone party at nine-pins—the flagon—"Oh! that flagon! that wicked flagon!" thought Rip—"what excuse shall I make to Dame Van Winkle!"

He looked round for his gun, but in place of the clean well-oiled fowling-piece, he found an old firelock lying by him, the barrel incrusted with rust, the lock falling off, and the stock worm-eaten. He now suspected that the grave roysters of the mountain had put a trick upon him, and, having dosed him with liquor, had robbed him of his gun. Wolf, too, had disappeared, but he might have strayed away after a squirrel or partridge. He whistled after him and shouted his name, but all in vain; the echoes repeated his whistle and shout, but no dog was to be seen.

He determined to revisit the scene of the last evening's gambol, and if he met with any of the party, to demand his dog and gun. As he rose to walk, he found himself stiff in the joints, and wanting in his usual activity.

"These mountain beds do not agree with me," thought Rip, "and if this frolic should lay me up with a fit of the rheumatism, I shall have a blessed time with Dame Van Winkle." With some difficulty he got down into the glen: he found the gully up which he and his companion had ascended the preceding evening; but to his astonishment a mountain stream was now foaming down it, leaping from rock to rock, and filling the glen with babbling murmurs. He, however, made shift to scramble up its sides, working his toilsome way through thickets of birch, sassafras, and witch-hazel, and sometimes tripped up or entangled by the wild grapevines that twisted their coils or tendrils from tree to tree, and spread a kind of network in his path.

At length he reached to where the ravine had opened through the cliffs to the amphitheatre; but no traces of such opening remained. The rocks presented a high impenetrable wall over which the torrent came tumbling in a sheet of feathery foam, and fell into a broad deep basin, black from the shadows of the surrounding forest. Here, then, poor Rip was brought to a stand. He again called and whistled after his dog; he was only answered by the cawing of a flock of idle crows, sporting high in the air about a dry tree that overhung a sunny precipice: and who, secure in their elevation, seemed to look down and scoff at the poor man's perplexities. What was to be done? the morning was passing away, and Rip felt famished for want of his breakfast. He grieved to give up his dog and gun; he dreaded to meet his wife; but it would not do to starve among the mountains. He shook his head, shouldered the rusty firelock, and, with a heart full of trouble and anxiety, turned his steps homeward.

As he approached the village he met a number of people, but none whom he knew, which somewhat surprised him, for he had thought himself acquainted with every one in the country round. Their dress, too, was of a different fashion from that to which he was accustomed. They all stared at him with equal marks of surprise, and whenever they cast their eyes upon him, invariably stroked their chins. The constant recurrence of this gesture induced Rip, involuntarily, to do the same, when, to his astonishment, he found his beard had grown a foot long!

He had now entered the skirts of the village. A troop of strange children ran at his heels, hooting after him, and pointing at his gray beard. The dogs, too, not one of which he recognized for an old acquaintance, barked at him as he passed. The very village was altered; it was larger and more populous. There were rows of houses which he had never seen before, and those which had been his familiar haunts had disappeared. Strange names were over the doors—strange faces at the windows—every thing was strange. His mind now misgave him; he began to doubt whether both he and the world around him were not bewitched. Surely this was his native village, which he had left but the day before. There stood the Kaatskill mountains—there ran the silver Hudson at a distance—there was every hill and dale precisely as it had always been—Rip was sorely perplexed—"That flagon last night," thought he, "has addled my poor head sadly!"

It was with some difficulty that he found the way to his own house, which he approached with silent awe, expecting every moment to hear the shrill voice of Dame Van Winkle. He found the house gone to decay—the roof fallen in, the windows shattered, and the doors off the hinges. A half-starved dog that looked like Wolf was skulking about it. Rip called him by name, but the cur snarled, showed his teeth, and passed on. This was an unkind cut indeed—"My very dog," sighed poor Rip, "has forgotten me!"

He entered the house, which, to tell the truth, Dame Van Winkle had always kept in neat order. It was empty, forlorn, and apparently abandoned. This desolateness overcame all his connubial fears—he called loudly for his wife and children—the lonely chambers rang for a moment with his voice, and then all again was silence.

He now hurried forth, and hastened to his old resort, the village inn— but it too was gone. A large rickety wooden building stood in its place, with great gaping windows, some of them broken and mended with old hats and petticoats, and over the door was painted, "The Union Hotel, by Jonathan Doolittle." Instead of the great tree that used to shelter the quiet little Dutch inn of yore, there now was reared a tall naked pole, with something on the top that looked like a red night-cap, and from it was fluttering a flag, on which was a singular assemblage of stars and stripes—all this was strange and incomprehensible. He recognized on the sign, however, the ruby face of King George, under which he had smoked so many a peaceful pipe; but even this was singularly metamorphosed. The red coat was changed for one of blue and buff, a sword was held in the hand instead of a sceptre, the head was decorated with a cocked hat, and underneath was painted in large characters, GENERAL WASHINGTON.

There was, as usual, a crowd of folk about the door, but none that Rip recollected. The very character of the people seemed changed. There was a busy, bustling disputatious tone about it, instead of the accustomed phlegm and drowsy tranquillity. He looked in vain for the sage Nicholas Vedder, with his broad face, double chin, and fair long pipe, uttering clouds of tobacco-smoke instead of idle speeches; or Van Bummel, the schoolmaster, doling forth the contents of an ancient newspaper. In place of these, a lean, bilious-looking fellow, with his pockets full of handbills, was haranguing vehemently about rights of citizens—elections—members of congress—liberty—Bunker's Hill—heroes of seventy-six—and other words, which were a perfect Babylonish jargon to the bewildered Van Winkle.

The appearance of Rip, with his long grizzled beard, his rusty fowling-piece, his uncouth dress, and an army of women and children at his heels, soon attracted the attention of the tavern politicians. They crowded round him, eyeing him from head to foot with great curiosity. The orator bustled up to him, and, drawing him partly aside, inquired "on which side he voted?" Rip stared in vacant stupidity. Another short but busy little fellow pulled him by the arm, and, rising on tiptoe, inquired in his ear, "Whether he was Federal or Democrat?" Rip was equally at a loss to comprehend the question; when a knowing, self-important old gentleman, in a sharp cocked hat, made his way through the crowd, putting them to the right and left with his elbows as he passed, and planting himself before Van Winkle, with one arm akimbo, the other resting on his cane, his keen eyes and sharp hat penetrating, as it were, into his very soul, demanded in an austere tone, "what brought him to the election with a gun on his shoulder, and a mob at his heels, and whether he meant to breed a riot in the village?"—"Alas! gentlemen," cried Rip, somewhat dismayed, "I am a poor quiet man, a native of the place, and a loyal subject of the king, God bless him!"

Here a general shout burst from the by-standers—"A tory! a tory! a spy! a refugee! hustle him! away with him!" It was with great difficulty that the self-important man in the cocked hat restored order; and, having assumed a tenfold austerity of brow, demanded again of the unknown culprit, what he came there for, and whom he was seeking? The poor man humbly assured him that he meant no harm, but merely came there in search of some of his neighbors, who used to keep about the tavern.

"Well—who are they?—name them."

Rip bethought himself a moment, and inquired, "Where's Nicholas Vedder?"

There was a silence for a little while, when an old man replied, in a thin piping voice, "Nicholas Vedder! why, he is dead and gone these eighteen years! There was a wooden tombstone in the church-yard that used to tell all about him, but that's rotten and gone too."

"Where's Brom Dutcher?"

"Oh, he went off to the army in the beginning of the war; some say he was killed at the storming of Stony Point—others say he was drowned in a squall at the foot of Anthony's Nose. I don't know—he never came back again."

"Where's Van Bummel, the schoolmaster?"

"He went off to the wars too, was a great militia general, and is now in congress."

Rip's heart died away at hearing of these sad changes in his home and friends, and finding himself thus alone in the world. Every answer puzzled him too, by treating of such enormous lapses of time, and of matters which he could not understand: war—congress—Stony Point;—he had no courage to ask after any more friends, but cried out in despair, "Does nobody here know Rip Van Winkle?"

"Oh, Rip Van Winkle!" exclaimed two or three, "Oh, to be sure! that's Rip Van Winkle yonder, leaning against the tree."

Rip looked, and beheld a precise counterpart of himself, as he went up the mountain: apparently as lazy, and certainly as ragged. The poor fellow was now completely confounded. He doubted his own identity, and whether he was himself or another man. In the midst of his bewilderment, the man in the cocked hat demanded who he was, and what was his name?

"God knows," exclaimed he, at his wit's end; "I'm not myself—I'm somebody else—that's me yonder—no—that's somebody else got into my shoes—

I was myself last night, but I fell asleep on the mountain, and they've changed my gun, and every thing's changed, and I'm changed, and I can't tell what's my name, or who I am!"

The by-standers began now to look at each other, nod, wink significantly, and tap their fingers against their foreheads. There was a whisper, also, about securing the gun, and keeping the old fellow from doing mischief, at the very suggestion of which the self-important man in the cocked hat retired with some precipitation. At this critical moment a fresh comely woman pressed through the throng to get a peep at the gray-bearded man. She had a chubby child in her arms, which, frightened at his looks, began to cry. "Hush, Rip," cried she, "hush, you little fool; the old man won't hurt you." The name of the child, the air of the mother, the tone of her voice, all awakened a train of recollections in his mind. "What is your name, my good woman?" asked he.

"Judith Gardenier."

"And your father's name?"

"Ah, poor man, Rip Van Winkle was his name, but it's twenty years since he went away from home with his gun, and never has been heard of since—his dog came home without him; but whether he shot himself, or was carried away by the Indians, nobody can tell. I was then but a little girl."

Rip had but one question more to ask; but he put it with a faltering voice:

"Where's your mother?"

"Oh, she too had died but a short time since; she broke a blood-vessel in a fit of passion at a New-England peddler."

There was a drop of comfort, at least, in this intelligence. The honest man could contain himself no longer. He caught his daughter and her child in his arms. "I am your father!" cried he—"Young Rip Van Winkle once— old Rip Van Winkle now!—Does nobody know poor Rip Van Winkle?"

All stood amazed, until an old woman, tottering out from among the crowd, put her hand to her brow, and peering under it in his face for a moment, exclaimed, "Sure enough! it is Rip Van Winkle—it is himself! Welcome home again, old neighbor—Why, where have you been these twenty long years?"

Rip's story was soon told, for the whole twenty years had been to him but as one night. The neighbors stared when they heard it; some were seen to wink at each other, and put their tongues in their cheeks: and the self-important man in the cocked hat, who, when the alarm was over, had returned to the field, screwed down the corners of his mouth, and shook his head—upon which there was a general shaking of the head throughout the assemblage.

It was determined, however, to take the opinion of old Peter Vanderdonk, who was seen slowly advancing up the road. He was a descendant of the historian of that name, who wrote one of the earliest accounts of the province. Peter was the most ancient inhabitant of the village, and well versed in all the wonderful events and traditions of the neighborhood. He recollected Rip at once, and corroborated his story in the most satisfactory manner. He assured the company that it was a fact, handed down from his ancestor the historian, that the Kaatskill mountains had always been haunted by strange beings. That it was affirmed that the great Hendrick Hudson, the first discoverer of the river and country, kept a kind of vigil there every twenty years, with his crew of the *Half-moon;* being permitted in this way to revisit the scenes of his enterprise, and keep a guardian eye upon the river, and the great city called by his name. That his father had once seen them in their old Dutch dresses playing at nine-pins in a hollow of the mountain; and that he himself had heard, one summer afternoon, the sound of their balls, like distant peals of thunder.

To make a long story short, the company broke up, and returned to the more important concerns of the election. Rip's daughter took him home to live with her; she had a snug, well-furnished house, and a stout cheery farmer for a husband, whom Rip recollected for one of the urchins that used to climb upon his back. As to Rip's son and heir, who was the ditto of himself, seen leaning against the tree, he was employed to work on the farm; but evinced an hereditary disposition to attend to anything else but his business.

Rip now resumed his old walks and habits; he soon found many of his former cronies, though all rather the worse for the wear and tear of time; and preferred making friends among the rising generation, with whom he soon grew into great favor.

Having nothing to do at home, and being arrived at that happy age when a man can be idle with impunity, he took his place once more on the bench at the inn door, and was reverenced as one of the patriarchs of the village, and a chronicle of the old times "before the war." It was some time before he could get into the regular track of gossip, or could be made to comprehend the strange events that had taken place during his torpor. How that there had been a revolutionary war—that the country had thrown off the yoke of old England—and that, instead of being a subject of his Majesty George the Third, he was now a free citizen of the United States. Rip, in fact, was no politician; the changes of states and empires made but little impression on him; but there was one species of despotism under which he had long groaned, and that was—petticoat government. Happily that was at an end; he had got his neck out of the yoke of matrimony, and could go in and out whenever he pleased, without dreading the tyranny of Dame Van Winkle. Whenever her name was mentioned, however, he shook his head, shrugged his shoulders, and cast up his eyes; which might pass either for an expression of resignation to his fate, or joy at his deliverance.

He used to tell his story to every stranger that arrived at Mr. Doolittle's hotel. He was observed, at first, to vary on some points every time he told it, which was, doubtless, owing to his having so recently awaked. It at last settled down precisely to the tale I have related, and not a man, woman, or child in the neighborhood, but knew it by heart. Some always pretended to doubt the reality of it, and insisted that Rip had been out of his head, and that this was one point on which he always remained flighty. The old Dutch inhabitants, however, almost universally gave it full credit. Even to this day they never hear a thunderstorm of a summer afternoon about the Kaatskill, but they say Hendrick Hudson and his crew are at their game of nine-pins; and it is a common wish of all henpecked husbands in the neighborhood, when life hangs heavy on their hands, that they might have a quieting draught out of Rip Van Winkle's flagon.

QUESTIONS

"Rip Van Winkle"

1. How does Irving's opening description of the Catskill mountains contribute to the fairy-tale atmosphere of the story? How would you characterize the *tone* of the story?

2. Describe Rip. What sort of husband, father, and provider is he? Judging strictly by his occupations, pastimes, and pleasures, how old does he seem to you? Does he behave like a grown-up?

3. What kind of woman is Dame Van Winkle? What kind of wife? Describe her relationship to Rip.

4. Can you think of other American heroes, in fiction or film, who leave civilization behind and journey into the wilderness, accompanied only by a faithful companion (in this case, Rip's dog, Wolf)? What do you make of the recurrence of this theme (which one literary critic has called "the myth of the runaway male") in our literature and popular arts? What does it seem to suggest about American society?

5. Describe Rip's meeting with Hendrick Hudson's crew. How are these uncanny figures portrayed? Do you find them—or the episode itself—unsettling in any way? Explain.

6. How has the world changed during Rip's absence? How is his little village different when he returns? What aspects of American society is Irving commenting on in his description of the transformed village?

7. In terms of his physical condition and appearance, Rip undergoes a significant transformation as a result of his experience. But does his personality change as well? Has he learned anything from his experience? Does he undergo any kind of initiation, progressing from childlike innocence to adult knowledge?

8. Discussing the meaning of "Rip Van Winkle," one literary critic has written, "The story has something to do with Time, with both the escape from Time and the victimization by Time. It has something to do with sleep and

with waking, and the ambiguous relation of those two realms of being. It has
something to do with youth and age and attitudes toward growth, including a
refusal to grow up." Discuss the ideas in this quote.

9. Compare this story to Robert Penn Warren's "Blackberry Winter" (Chapter One). How do both works deal with the theme of the "fall"—the passage
from the timeless, golden world of childhood into the realm of history, muta-
bility, aging, and death?

Christmas

VLADIMIR NABOKOV

1

After walking back from the village to his manor across the dimming snows, Sleptsov sat down in a corner, on a plush-covered chair which he never remembered using before. It was the kind of thing that happens after some great calamity. Not your brother but a chance acquaintance, a vague country neighbor to whom you never paid much attention, with whom in normal times you exchange scarcely a word, is the one who comforts you wisely and gently, and hands you your dropped hat after the funeral service is over, and you are reeling from grief, your teeth chattering, your eyes blinded by tears. The same can be said of inanimate objects. Any room, even the coziest and the most absurdly small, in the little used wing of a great country house has an unlived-in corner. And it was such a corner in which Sleptsov sat.

The wing was connected by a wooden gallery, now encumbered with our huge north Russian snowdrifts, to the master house, used only in summer. There was no need to awaken it, to heat it: the master had come from Petersburg for only a couple of days and had settled in the annex, where it was a simple matter to get the stoves of white Dutch tile going.

The master sat in his corner, on that plush chair, as in a doctor's waiting room. The room floated in darkness; the dense blue of early evening filtered through the crystal feathers of frost on the windowpane. Ivan, the quiet, portly valet, who had recently shaved off his mustache and now looked like his late father, the family butler, brought in a kerosene lamp, all trimmed and brimming with light. He set it on a small table, and noiselessly caged it within its pink silk shade. For an instant a tilted mirror reflected his lit ear and cropped gray hair. Then he withdrew and the door gave a subdued creak.

Sleptsov raised his hand from his knee and slowly examined it. A drop of candle wax had stuck and hardened in the thin fold of skin between two fingers. He spread his fingers and the little white scale cracked.

2

The following morning, after a night spent in nonsensical, fragmentary dreams totally unrelated to his grief, as Sleptsov stepped out into the cold veranda, a floorboard emitted a merry pistol crack underfoot, and the reflections of the many-colored panes formed paradisal lozenges on the white-washed cushionless window seats. The outer door resisted at first, then opened with a luscious crunch, and the dazzling frost hit his face. The reddish sand providently sprinkled on the ice coating the porch steps resembled cinnamon, and thick icicles shot with greenish blue hung from the eaves. The snowdrifts reached all the way to the windows of the annex, tightly gripping the snug little wooden structure in their frosty clutches. The creamy white mounds of what were flower beds in summer swelled slightly above the level snow in front of the porch, and further off loomed the radiance of the park, where every black branchlet was rimmed with silver, and the firs seemed to draw in their green paws under their bright plump load.

Wearing high felt boots and a short fur-lined coat with a karakul collar, Sleptsov strode off slowly along a straight path, the only one cleared of snow, into that blinding distant landscape. He was amazed to be still alive, and able to perceive the brilliance of the snow and feel his front teeth ache from the cold. He even noticed that a snow-covered bush resembled a fountain and that a dog had left a series of saffron marks on the slope of a snowdrift, which had burned through its crust. A little further, the supports of a foot bridge stuck out of the snow, and there Sleptsov stopped. Bitterly, angrily, he pushed the thick, fluffy covering off the parapet. He vividly recalled how this bridge looked in summer. There was his son walking along the slippery planks, flecked with aments, and deftly plucking off with his net a butterfly that had settled on the railing. Now the boy sees his father. Forever lost laughter plays on his face, under the turned-down brim of a straw hat burned dark by the sun; his hand toys with the chainlet of the leather purse attached to his belt, his dear, smooth, suntanned legs in their serge shorts and soaked sandals assume their usual cheerful widespread stance. Just recently, in Petersburg, after having babbled in his delirium about school, about his bicycle, about some great Oriental moth, he died, and yesterday Sleptsov had taken the coffin—weighed down, it seemed, with an entire lifetime—to the country, into the family vault near the village church.

It was quiet as it can only be on a bright, frosty day. Sleptsov raised his leg high, stepped off the path, and, leaving blue pits behind him in the snow, made his way among the trunks of amazingly white trees to the spot where the park dropped off toward the river. Far below, ice blocks sparkled near a hole cut in the smooth expanse of white and, on the opposite bank, very straight columns of pink smoke stood above the snowy roofs of log cabins. Sleptsov took off his karakul cap and leaned against a tree trunk. Somewhere far away peasants were chopping wood—every blow bounced resonantly skyward—and beyond the light silver mist of trees, high above the squat izbas, the sun caught the equanimous radiance of the cross on the church.

3

That was where he headed after lunch, in an old sleigh with a high straight back. The cod of the black stallion clacked strongly in the frosty air, the white plumes of low branches glided overhead, and the ruts in front gave off a silvery blue sheen. When he arrived he sat for an hour or so by the grave, resting a heavy, woolen-gloved hand on the iron of the railing that burned his hand through the wool. He came home with a slight sense of disappointment, as if there, in the burial vault, he had been even further removed from his son than here, where the countless summer tracks of his rapid sandals were preserved beneath the snow.

In the evening, overcome by a fit of intense sadness, he had the main house unlocked. When the door swung open with a weighty wail, and a whiff of special, unwintery coolness came from the sonorous iron-barred vestibule, Sleptsov took the lamp with its tin reflector from the watchman's hand and entered the house alone. The parquet floors crackled eerily under his step. Room after room filled with yellow light, and the shrouded furniture seemed unfamiliar; instead of a tinkling chandelier, a soundless bag hung from the ceiling; and Sleptsov's enormous shadow, slowly extending one arm, floated across the wall and over the gray squares of curtained paintings.

He went into the room which had been his son's study in summer, set the lamp on the window ledge and, breaking his fingernails as he did so, opened the folding shutters, even though all was darkness outside. In the blue glass the yellow flame of the slightly smoky lamp appeared, and his large, bearded face showed momentarily.

He sat down at the bare desk and sternly, from under bent brows, examined the pale wallpaper with its garlands of bluish roses; a narrow office-like cabinet, with sliding drawers from top to bottom; the couch and armchairs under slipcovers; and suddenly, dropping his head onto the desk, he started to shake, passionately, noisily, pressing first his lips, then his wet cheek, to the cold, dusty wood and clutching at its far corners.

In the desk he found a notebook, spreading boards, supplies of black pins and an English biscuit tin that contained a large exotic cocoon which had cost three rubles. It was papery to the touch and seemed made of a brown folded leaf. His son had remembered it during his sickness, regretting that he had left it behind, but consoling himself with the thought that the chrysalid inside was probably dead. He also found a torn net: a tarlatan bag on a collapsible hoop (and the muslin still smelled of summer and sun-hot grass).

Then, bending lower and lower and sobbing with his whole body, he began pulling out one by one the glasstopped drawers of the cabinet. In the dim lamplight the even files of specimens shone silklike under the glass. Here, in this room, on that very desk, his son had spread the wings of his captures. He would first pin the carefully killed insect in the cork-bottomed groove of the setting board, between the adjustable strips of wood, and fasten down flat with pinned strips of paper the still fresh, soft wings. They had now dried long ago and been transferred to the cabinet—those spectacular Swallowtails, those dazzling Coppers and Blues, and the various Fritillaries, some mounted in a supine position to display the mother-of-pearl undersides. His son used to pronounce their Latin names with a moan of triumph or in an arch aside of disdain. And the moths, the moths, the first Aspen Hawk of five summers ago!

4

The night was smoke-blue and moonlit; thin clouds were scattered about the sky but did not touch the delicate, icy moon. The trees, masses of gray frost, cast dark shadows on the drifts, which scintillated here and there with metallic sparks. In the plush-upholstered, well-heated room of the annex Ivan had placed a two-foot fir tree in a clay pot on the table, and was just attaching a candle to its cruciform tip when Sleptsov returned from the main house, chilled, red-eyed, with gray dust smears on his cheek, carrying a wooden case under his arm. Seeing the Christmas tree on the table, he asked absently:

"What's that?"

Relieving him of the case, Ivan answered in a low, mellow voice:

"There's a holiday coming up tomorrow."

"No, take it away," said Sleptsov with a frown, while thinking, "Can this be Christmas Eve? How could I have forgotten?"

Ivan gently insisted:

"It's nice and green. Let it stand for a while."

"Please take it away," repeated Sleptsov, and bent over the case he had brought. In it he had gathered his son's belongings—the folding butterfly net, the biscuit tin with the pear-shaped cocoon, the spreading board, the pins in their lacquered box, the blue notebook. Half of the first page had been torn out, and its remaining fragment contained part of a French dictation. There followed daily entries, names of captured butterflies, and other notes:

"Walked across the bog as far as Borovichi, . . ."

"Raining today. Played checkers with Father, then read Goncharov's *Frigate*, a deadly bore."

"Marvelous hot day. Rode my bike in the evening. A midge got in my eye. Deliberately rode by her dacha twice, but didn't see her. . . ."

Sleptsov raised his head, swallowed something hot and huge. Of whom was his son writing?

"Rode my bike as usual," he read on, "Our eyes nearly met. My darling, my love. . . ."

"This is unthinkable," whispered Sleptsov. "I'll never know. . . ."

He bent over again, avidly deciphering the childish handwriting that slanted up then curved down in the margin.

"Saw a fresh specimen of the Camberwell Beauty today. That means autumn is here. Rain in the evening. She has probably left, and we didn't even get acquainted. Farewell, my darling. I feel terribly sad. . . ."

"He never said anything to me. . . ." Sleptsov tried to remember, rubbing his forehead with his palm.

On the last page there was an ink drawing: the hind view of an elephant—two thick pillars, the corners of two ears, and a tiny tail.

Sleptsov got up. He shook his head, restraining yet another onrush of hideous sobs.

"I—can't—bear—it—any—longer," he drawled between groans, repeating even more slowly, "I—can't—bear—it—any—longer. . . ."

"It's Christmas tomorrow," came the abrupt reminder, "and I'm going to die. Of course. It's so simple. This very night. . . ."

He pulled out a handkerchief and dried his eyes, his beard, his cheeks. Dark streaks remained on the handkerchief.

". . . death," Sleptsov said softly, as if concluding a long sentence.

The clock ticked. Frost patterns overlapped on the blue glass of the window. The open notebook shone radiantly on the table; next to it the light went through the muslin of the butterfly net, and glistened on a corner of the open tin. Sleptsov pressed his eyes shut, and had a fleeting sensation that earthly life lay before him, totally bared and comprehensible—and ghastly in its sadness, humiliatingly pointless, sterile, devoid of miracles. . . .

At that instant there was a sudden snap—a thin sound like that of an overstretched rubber band breaking. Sleptsov opened his eyes. The cocoon in the biscuit tin had burst at its tip, and a black, wrinkled creature the size of a mouse was crawling up the wall above the table. It stopped, holding on to the surface with six black furry feet, and started palpitating strangely. It had emerged from the chrysalid because a man overcome with grief had transferred a tin box to his warm room, and the warmth had penetrated its taut leaf-and-silk envelope; it had awaited this moment so long, had collected its strength so tensely, and now, having broken out, it was slowly and miraculously expanding. Gradually the wrinkled tissues, the velvety fringes, unfurled; the fan-pleated veins grew firmer as they filled with air. It became a winged thing imperceptibly, as a maturing face imperceptibly becomes beautiful. And its wings—still feeble, still moist—kept growing and unfolding, and now they were developed to the limit set for them by God, and there, on the wall, instead of a little lump of life, instead of a dark mouse, was a great *Attacus* moth like those that fly, birdlike, around lamps in the Indian dusk.

And then those thick black wings, with a glazy eyespot on each and a purplish bloom dusting their hooked foretips, took a full breath under the impulse of tender, ravishing, almost human happiness.

QUESTIONS

"Christmas"

1. What is the narrative point of view in this story? Why do you think Nabokov chose this point of view instead of, for example, the first person?

2. What is the symbolic significance of the story's taking place during the winter? At Christmas?

3. What in the first paragraph foreshadows an event later in the story?

4. What is Sleptsov in quest of as he walks across his estate, when he goes to church, and when he enters his son's room? Does he find what he is seeking in any of these places? Why don't the church or the vault where his son is buried give him any comfort?

5. Why does Sleptsov insist that Ivan remove the Christmas tree from the annex?

6. What significance do you attach to the fact that Sleptsov had not known of his son's romantic interest in a young girl? What is the father's reaction to this new knowledge?

7. Is there any connection between the story's theme and the son's hobby or between the son's hobby and what the grief-stricken father is attempting to do in the story?

8. What is the primary image of rebirth, of transformation, in "Christmas"? How does it affect your response to and understanding of the rest of the story? What do you think Sleptsov's response will be? Are there other images of transformation in Nabokov's tale?

9. Nabokov remarks near the end of his story that the Attacus moth's wings expanded until "they were developed to the limit set for them by God." How can this remark be seen as a comment on the boy's death and the father's response to that death?

10. Would you call this story, particularly its conclusion, religious? If so, in what sense? What does the story reverence?

How Wang-Fo Was Saved

MARGUERITE YOURCENAR

The old painter Wang-Fo and his disciple Ling were wandering along the roads of the Kingdom of Han.

They made slow progress because Wang-Fo would stop at night to watch the stars and during the day to observe the dragonflies. They carried hardly any luggage, because Wang-Fo loved the image of things and not the things themselves, and no object in the world seemed to him worth buying, except brushes, pots of lacquer and China ink, and rolls of silk and rice paper. They were poor, because Wang-Fo would exchange his paintings for a ration of boiled millet, and paid no attention to pieces of silver. Ling, his disciple, bent beneath the weight of a sack full of sketches, bowed his back with respect as if he were carrying the heavens' vault, because for Ling the sack was full of snow-covered mountains, torrents in spring, and the face of the summer moon.

Ling had not been born to trot down the roads, following an old man who seized the dawn and captured the dusk. His father had been a banker who dealt in gold, his mother the only child of a jade merchant who had left her all his worldly possessions, cursing her for not being a son. Ling had grown up in a house where wealth made him shy: he was afraid of insects, of thunder and the face of the dead. When Ling was fifteen, his father chose a bride for him, a very beautiful one because the thought of the happiness he was giving his son consoled him for having reached the age in which the night is meant for sleep. Ling's wife was as frail as a reed, childish as milk, sweet as saliva, salty as tears. After the wedding, Ling's parents became discreet to the point of dying, and their son was left alone in a house painted vermilion, in the company of his young wife who never stopped smiling and a plum tree that blossomed every spring with pale-pink flowers. Ling loved this woman of a crystal-clear heart as one loves a mirror that will never tarnish, or a talisman that will protect one forever. He visited the tea-houses to follow the dictates of fashion, and only moderately favored acrobats and dancers.

One night, in the tavern, Wang-Fo shared Ling's table. The old man had been drinking in order to better paint a drunkard, and he cocked his head to one side as if trying to measure the distance between his hand and his bowl. The rice wine undid the tongue of the taciturn craftsman, and that night Wang spoke as if silence were a wall and words the colors with which to cover it. Thanks to him, Ling got to know the beauty of the drunkards' faces blurred by the vapors of hot drink, the brown splendor of the roasts unevenly brushed by tongues of fire, and the exquisite blush of wine stains strewn on the tablecloths like withered petals. A gust of wind broke the window: the downpour entered the room. Wang-Fo leaned out to make Ling admire the livid zebra stripes of lightning, and Ling, spell-bound, stopped being afraid of storms.

Ling paid the old painter's bill, and as Wang-Fo was both without money and without lodging, he humbly offered him a resting place. They walked away together. Ling held a lamp whose light projected unexpected fires in the puddles. That evening, Ling discovered with surprise that the walls of his house were not red, as he had always thought, but the color of an almost rotten orange. In the courtyard, Wang-Fo noticed the delicate shape of a bush to which no one had paid any attention until then, and compared it to a young woman letting down her hair to dry. In the passageway, he followed with delight the hesitant trail of an ant along the cracks in the wall, and Ling's horror of these creatures vanished into thin air. Realizing that Wang-Fo had just presented him with the gift of a new soul and a new vision of the world, Ling respectfully offered the old man the room in which his father and mother had died.

For many years now, Wang-Fo had dreamed of painting the portrait of a princess of olden days playing the lute under a willow. No woman was sufficiently unreal to be his model, but Ling would do because he was not a woman. Then Wang-Fo spoke of painting a young prince shooting an arrow at the foot of a large cedar tree. No young man of the present was sufficiently unreal to serve as his model, but Ling got his own wife to pose under the plum tree in the garden. Later on, Wang-Fo painted her in a fairy costume against the clouds of twilight, and the young woman wept because it was an omen of death. As Ling came to prefer the portraits painted by Wang-Fo to the young woman herself, her face began to fade, like a flower exposed to warm winds and summer rains. One morning, they found her hanging from the branches of the pink plum tree: the ends of the scarf that was strangling her floated in the wind, entangled with her hair. She looked even more delicate than usual, and as pure as the beauties celebrated by the poets of days gone by. Wang-Fo painted her one last time, because he loved the green hue that suffuses the face of the dead. His disciple Ling mixed the colors and the task needed such concentration that he forgot to shed tears.

One after the other, Ling sold his slaves, his jades, and the fish in his pond to buy his master pots of purple ink that came from the West. When the house was emptied, they left it, and Ling closed the door of his past behind him. Wang-Fo felt weary of a city where the faces could no longer teach him secrets of ugliness or beauty, and the master and his disciple walked away together down the roads of the Kingdom of Han.

Their reputation preceded them into the villages, to the gateway of fortresses, and into the atrium of temples where restless pilgrims halt at dusk. It was murmured that Wang-Fo had the power to bring his paintings to life by adding a last touch of color to their eyes. Farmers would come and beg him to paint a watchdog, and the lords would ask him for portraits of their best warriors. The priests honored Wang-Fo as a sage; the people feared him as a sorcerer. Wang enjoyed these differences of opinion which gave him the chance to study expressions of gratitude, fear, and veneration.

Ling begged for food, watched over his master's rest, and took advantage of the old man's raptures to massage his feet. With the first rays of the sun, when the old man was still asleep, Ling went in pursuit of timid landscapes hidden behind bunches of reeds. In the evening, when the master, disheartened, threw down his brushes, he would carefully pick them up. When Wang became sad and spoke of his old age, Ling would smile and show him the solid trunk of an old oak; when Wang felt happy and made jokes, Ling would humbly pretend to listen.

One day, at sunset, they reached the outskirts of the Imperial City and Ling sought out and found an inn in which Wang-Fo could spend the night. The old man wrapped himself up in rags, and Ling lay down next to him to keep him warm because spring had only just begun and the floor of beaten earth was still frozen. At dawn, heavy steps echoed in the corridors of the inn; they heard the frightened whispers of the innkeeper and orders shouted in a foreign, barbaric tongue. Ling trembled, remembering that the night before, he had stolen a rice cake for his master's supper. Certain that they would come to take him to prison, he asked himself who would help Wang-Fo ford the next river on the following day.

The soldiers entered carrying lanterns. The flames gleaming through the motley paper cast red and blue lights on their leather helmets. The string of a bow quivered over their shoulders, and the fiercest among them suddenly let out a roar for no reason at all. A heavy hand fell on Wang-Fo's neck, and the painter could not help noticing that the soldiers' sleeves did not match the color of their coats.

Helped by his disciple, Wang-Fo followed the soldiers, stumbling along uneven roads. The passing crowds made fun of these two criminals who were certainly going to be beheaded. The soldiers answered Wang's questions with savage scowls. His bound hands hurt him, and Ling in despair looked smiling at his master, which for him was a gentler way of crying.

They reached the threshold of the Imperial Palace, whose purple walls rose in broad daylight like a sweep of sunset. The soldiers led Wang-Fo through countless square and circular rooms whose shapes symbolized the seasons, the cardinal points, the male and the female, longevity, and the prerogatives of power. The doors swung on their hinges with a musical note, and were placed in such a manner that one followed the entire scale when crossing the palace from east to west. Everything combined to give an impression of superhuman power and subtlety, and one could feel that here the simplest orders were as final and as terrible as the wisdom of the ancients. At last, the air became thin and the silence so deep that not even a man under torture would have dared to scream. A eunuch lifted a tapestry; the soldiers began to tremble like women, and the small troop entered the chamber in which the Son of Heaven sat on a high throne.

It was a room without walls, held up by thick columns of blue stone. A garden spread out on the far side of the marble shafts, and each and every flower blooming in the greenery belonged to a rare species brought here from across the oceans. But none of them had any perfume, so that the Celestial Dragon's meditations would not be troubled by fine smells. Out of respect for the silence in which his thoughts evolved, no bird had been allowed within the enclosure, and even the bees had been driven away. An enormous wall separated the garden from the rest of the world, so that the wind that sweeps over dead dogs and corpses on the battlefield would not dare brush the Emperor's sleeve.

The Celestial Master sat on a throne of jade, and his hands were wrinkled like those of an old man, though he had scarcely reached the age of twenty. His robe was blue to symbolize winter, and green to remind one of spring. His face was beautiful but blank, like a looking glass placed too high, reflecting nothing except the stars and the immutable heavens. To his right stood his Minister of Perfect Pleasures, and to his left his Counselor of Just Torments. Because his courtiers, lined along the base of the columns, always lent a keen ear to the slightest sound from his lips, he had adopted the habit of speaking in a low voice.

"Celestial Dragon," said Wang-Fo, bowing low, "I am old, I am poor, I am weak. You are like summer; I am like winter. You have Ten Thousand Lives; I have but one, and it is near its close. What have I done to you? My hands have been tied, these hands that never harmed you."

"You ask what you have done to me, old Wang-Fo?" said the Emperor.

His voice was so melodious that it made one want to cry. He raised his right hand, to which the reflections from the jade pavement gave a pale sea-green hue like that of an underwater plant, and Wang-Fo marveled at the length of those thin fingers, and hunted among his memories to discover whether he had not at some time painted a mediocre portrait of either the Emperor or one of his ancestors that would now merit a sentence of death. But it seemed unlikely because Wang-Fo had not been an assiduous visitor at the Imperial Court. He preferred the farmers' huts or, in the cities, the courtesans' quarters and the taverns along the harbor where the dockers liked to quarrel.

"You ask me what it is you have done, old Wang-Fo?" repeated the Emperor, inclining his slender neck toward the old man waiting attentively. "I will tell you. But, as another man's poison cannot enter our veins except through our nine openings, in order to show you your offenses I must take you with me down the corridors of my memory and tell you the story of my life. My father had assembled a collection of your work and hidden it in the most secret chamber in the palace, because he judged that the people in your paintings should be concealed from the world since they cannot lower their eyes in the presence of profane viewers. It was in those same rooms that I was brought up, old Wang-Fo, surrounded by solitude. To prevent my innocence from being sullied by other human souls, the restless crowd of my future subjects had been driven away from me, and no one was allowed to pass my threshold, for fear that his or her shadow would stretch out and touch me. The few aged servants that were placed in my service showed themselves as little as possible; the hours turned into circles; the colors of your paintings bloomed in the first hours of the morning and grew pale at dusk. At night, when I was unable to sleep, I gazed at them, and for nearly ten years I gazed at them every night. During the day, sitting on a carpet whose design I knew by heart, I dreamed of the joys the future had in store for me. I imagined the world, with the Kingdom of Han at the center, to be like the flat palm of my hand crossed by the fatal lines of the Five Rivers. Around it lay the sea in which monsters are born, and farther away the mountains that hold up the heavens. And to help me visualize these things I used your paintings. You made me believe that the sea looked like the vast sheet of water spread across your scrolls, so blue that if a stone were to fall into it, it would become a sapphire; that women opened and closed like flowers, like the creatures that come forward, pushed by the wind, along the paths of your painted gardens; and that the young, slim-waisted warriors who mount guard in the fortresses along the frontier were themselves like arrows that could pierce my heart. At sixteen I saw the doors that separated me from the world open once again; I climbed onto the balcony of my palace to look at the clouds, but they were far less beautiful than those in your sunsets. I ordered my litter; bounced along roads on which I had not foreseen either mud or stones, I traveled across the provinces of the Empire without ever finding your gardens full of women like fireflies, or a woman whose body was in itself a garden. The pebbles on the beach spoiled my taste for oceans; the blood of the tortured is less red than the pomegranates in your paintings; the village vermin prevented me from seeing the beauty of the rice fields; the flesh of mortal women disgusted me like the dead meat hanging from the butcher's hook, and the coarse laughter of my soldiers made me sick. You lied, Wang-Fo, you old impostor. The world is nothing but a mass of muddled colors thrown into the void by an insane painter, and smudged by our tears. The Kingdom of Han is not the most beautiful of kingdoms, and I am not the Emperor. The only empire which is worth reigning over is that which you alone can enter, old Wang, by the road of One Thousand Curves and Ten Thousand Colors. You alone reign peacefully over mountains covered in snow that cannot melt, and over fields of daffodils that cannot die. And that is why, Wang-Fo, I have conceived a punishment for you, for you whose enchantment has filled me with disgust at everything I own, and with desire for everything I shall never possess. And in order to lock you up in the only cell from which there is no escape, I have decided to have your eyes burned out, because your eyes, Wang-

Fo, are the two magic gates that open onto your kingdom. And as your hands are the two roads of ten forking paths that lead to the heart of your kingdom, I have decided to have your hands cut off. Have you understood, old Wang-Fo?"

Hearing the sentence, Ling, the disciple, tore from his belt an old knife and leaped toward the Emperor. Two guards immediately seized him. The Son of Heaven smiled and added, with a sigh: "And I also hate you, old Wang-Fo, because you have known how to make yourself beloved. Kill that dog."

Ling jumped to one side so that his blood would not stain his master's robe. One of the soldiers lifted his sword and Ling's head fell from his neck like a cut flower. The servants carried away the remains, and Wang-Fo, in despair, admired the beautiful scarlet stain that his disciple's blood made on the green stone floor.

The Emperor made a sign and two eunuchs wiped Wang's eyes.

"Listen, old Wang-Fo," said the Emperor, "and dry your tears, because this is not the time to weep. Your eyes must be clear so that the little light that is left to them is not clouded by your weeping. Because it is not only the grudge I bear you that makes me desire your death; it is not only the cruelty in my heart that makes me want to see you suffer. I have other plans, old Wang-Fo. I possess among your works a remarkable painting in which the mountains, the river estuary, and the sea reflect each other, on a very small scale certainly, but with a clarity that surpasses the real land-scapes themselves, like objects reflected on the walls of a metal sphere. But that painting is unfinished, Wang-Fo; your masterpiece is but a sketch. No doubt, when you began your work, sitting in a solitary valley, you no-ticed a passing bird, or a child running after the bird. And the bird's beak or the child's cheeks made you forget the blue eyelids of the sea. You never finished the frills of the water's cloak, or the seaweed hair of the rocks. Wang-Fo, I want you to use the few hours of light that are left to you to finish this painting, which will thus contain the final secrets amassed during your long life. I know that your hands, about to fall, will not tremble on the silken cloth, and infinity will enter your work through those unhappy cuts. I know that your eyes, about to be put out, will discover bearings far beyond all human senses. This is my plan, old Wang-Fo, and I can force you to fulfill it. If you refuse, before blinding you, I will have all your paintings burned, and you will be like a father whose children are slaugh-tered and all hopes of posterity extinguished. However, believe, if you wish, that this last order stems from nothing but my kindness, because I know that the silken scroll is the only mistress you ever deigned to touch. And to offer you brushes, paints, and inks to occupy your last hours is like offering the favors of a harlot to a man condemned to death."

Upon a sign from the Emperor's little finger, two eunuchs respectfully brought forward the unfinished scroll on which Wang-Fo had outlined the image of the sea and the sky. Wang-Fo dried his tears and smiled, because that small sketch reminded him of his youth. Everything in it spoke of a fresh new spirit which Wang-Fo could no longer claim as his, and yet something was missing from it, because when Wang had painted it he had not yet looked long enough at the mountains or at the rocks bathing their naked flanks in the sea, and he had not yet penetrated deep enough into the sadness of the evening twilight. Wang-Fo selected one of the brushes which a slave held ready for him and began spreading wide strokes of blue into the unfinished sea. A eunuch crouched by his feet, mixing the colors; he carried out his task with little skill, and more than ever Wang-Fo lamented the loss of his disciple Ling.

Wang began by adding a touch of pink to the tip of the wing of a cloud perched on a mountain. Then he painted onto the surface of the sea a few small lines that deepened the perfect feeling of calm. The jade floor became increasingly damp, but Wang-Fo, absorbed as he was in his painting, did not seem to notice that he was working with his feet in water.

The fragile rowboat grew under the strokes of the painter's brush and now occupied the entire foreground of the silken scroll. The rhythmic sound of the oars rose suddenly in the distance, quick and eager like the beating of wings. The sound came nearer, gently filling the whole room, then ceased, and a few trembling drops appeared on the boatman's oars. The red iron intended for Wang's eyes lay extinguished on the executioner's coals. The courtiers, motionless as etiquette required, stood in water up to their shoulders, trying to lift themselves onto the tips of their toes. The water finally reached the level of the imperial heart. The silence was so deep one could have heard a tear drop.

It was Ling. He wore his everyday robe, and his right sleeve still had a hole that he had not had time to mend that morning before the soldiers' arrival. But around his neck was tied a strange red scarf.

Wang-Fo said to him softly, while he continued painting, "I thought you were dead."

"You being alive," said Ling respectfully, "how could I have died?"

And he helped his master into the boat. The jade ceiling reflected itself in the water, so that Ling seemed to be inside a cave. The pigtails of submerged courtiers rippled up toward the surface like snakes, and the pale head of the Emperor floated like a lotus.

"Look at them," said Wang-Fo sadly. "These wretches will die, if they are not dead already. I never thought there was enough water in the sea to drown an Emperor. What are we to do?"

"Master, have no fear," murmured the disciple. "They will soon be dry again and will not even remember that their sleeves were ever wet. Only the Emperor will keep in his heart a little of the bitterness of the sea. These people are not the kind to lose themselves inside a painting."

And he added: "The sea is calm, the wind high, the seabirds fly to their nests. Let us leave, Master, and sail to the land beyond the waves."

"Let us leave," said the old painter.

Wang-Fo took hold of the helm, and Ling bent over the oars. The sound of rowing filled the room again, strong and steady like the beating of a heart. The level of the water dropped unnoticed around the large vertical rocks that became columns once more. Soon only a few puddles glistened in the hollows of the jade floor. The courtiers' robes were dry, but a few wisps of foam still clung to the hem of the Emperor's cloak.

The painting finished by Wang-Fo was leaning against a tapestry. A rowboat occupied the entire foreground. It drifted away little by little, leaving behind it a thin wake that smoothed out into the quiet sea. One could no longer make out the faces of the two men sitting in the boat, but one could still see Ling's red scarf and Wang-Fo's beard waving in the breeze.

The beating of the oars grew fainter, then ceased, blotted out by the distance. The Emperor, leaning forward, a hand above his eyes, watched Wang's boat sail away till it was nothing but an imperceptible dot in the paleness of the twilight. A golden mist rose and spread over the water. Finally the boat veered around a rock that stood at the gateway to the ocean; the shadow of a cliff fell across it; its wake disappeared from the deserted surface, and the painter Wang-Fo and his disciple Ling vanished forever on the jade-blue sea that Wang-Fo had just created.

QUESTIONS

"How Wang-Fo Was Saved"

1. In the character of the "old painter," Wang-Fo, Yourcenar creates a portrait of the ideal artist whose life is consecrated so completely to the pursuit of beauty that he is utterly oblivious to the material world. How does Yourcenar achieve this depiction? Point to specific details.

2. In addition to the theme of transformation, other mythic motifs appear in this story. Discuss the archetype of the Wise Old Man as it is embodied in the character of Wang-Fo. What similarities do you see between this story and Hermann Hesse's "The Poet" (Chapter Four)?

3. Why does Ling become so devoted to Wang-Fo? What does he learn from Wang-Fo?

4. Why does Ling's wife commit suicide? How does he react to her death? How does Wang-Fo react to it? What do you make of their responses? Is the author commenting here on the nature of the artist? Explain.

5. How does the style of the story suggest the quality of Wang-Fo's art? How would you define that quality?

6. Why does the Celestial Master possess such bitter hatred of Wang-Fo?

What does the Celestial Master speech indicate about the proverbial difference between life and art?

7. What exactly happens at the end of the story? How do you account for this magical denouement? What sort of transformation takes place? What does the story seem to saying about the transfiguring power of great art?

Glossary of Critical Terms

ABSURD: A term used to describe works that are informed by a vision of human life as an ultimately pointless, irrational affair. Such works are often humorous, since artists who share this vision frequently invent comically grotesque situations—a sentient sperm meditating on the meaning of life as he makes his way toward the ovum, for example—to convey their sense of the essential absurdity of life. At the same time, there is a quality of underlying bleakness to absurdist literature, which results from the perception of a universe devoid of order, value, and meaning.

ALLEGORY: A narrative work, in poetry or prose, that is meant to operate on at least two levels. In a successful allegory, the story being told is effective in itself: its characters, incidents, and setting succeed in holding the reader's interest. The reader is also meant to recognize, however, that each of these elements stands for something else: an abstract idea; a state of mind; a social, political, or religious concept; a historical character. In short, the "surface" narrative of the allegory disguises an underlying structure of meaning. For example, John Bunyan's religious allegory *The Pilgrim's Progress* portrays the difficult passage of the Christian soul from a state of sin to one of salvation in the form of a story about a young man named Christian who undertakes a peril-filled quest from the City of Destruction to the Celestial City, passing through such places as Vanity Fair and the Valley of the Shadow of Death along the way.

AMBIGUITY: In literature, ambiguity arises when an author's meanings remain unclear. Sometimes, ambiguity is the result of fuzzy thinking or sloppy writing. Often, however, an artist deliberately creates an ambiguous situation or employs ambiguous language to evoke the complexity of experience, the unreliability of the senses, or the painful contradictions inherent in human nature.

ANTAGONIST: The character or entity that stands in opposition to the protagonist in a work of fiction or drama. Generally, the antagonist is a human rival or adversary. At times, however, it may be a hostile, opposing force: for example, the ocean in Stephen Crane's "The Open Boat." See **Protagonist.**

ANTI-HERO: A peculiarly modern type of fictional protagonist who possesses none of the attributes associated with the traditional hero. Whereas heroes are powerful, enormously competent, and always in command of

614

themselves and their destinies, anti-heroes are the very opposite. They are not evil; they are simply weak, clumsy, easily confused, and ineffectual. See **Hero.**

ATMOSPHERE: The mood or feeling that seems to pervade the particular world created in a literary work. The atmosphere established by Hawthorne in "My Kinsman, Major Molineux," for example, is that of a bad dream—dark, disorienting, and sinister.

CHARACTER: A person in a story or novel. Literary characters fall into different categories. A *flat* or *two-dimensional* character is one who seems to consist of a single personality trait. Two examples from the stories in this collection are the stalwart, uncomplaining oiler in Stephen Crane's "The Open Boat" and the sneering, cynical café owner in Carson McCullers's "A Tree · A Rock · A Cloud." A *stereotype* is a character who has appeared so often in literature and whose traits have been so oversimplified that he or she is immediately recognizable as an exaggerated representative of a particular racial, religious, ethnic, social, or personality type. The "Jewish Mother" is a well-known example. In contrast, a *round* character is a person in a story who seems as complex and individualized as a living human being.
   Characters who remain the same throughout the course of the work are referred to as *static.* If, on the other hand, they undergo a significant change, they are referred to as *dynamic.*

CLIMAX: The incident, realization, or confrontation that occurs at or near the end of a story, which all the previous events have been building up to.

CONFLICT: A central element in all fiction, generated by the protagonist's struggle with an opposing force. There are two main categories of conflict in literary works: *external* and *internal.* In the former, the protagonist struggles against another human being, the natural world, or society. In stories dealing with internal conflict, the protagonist is at odds with herself or himself, torn between contradictory ideas, beliefs, or impulses.

DIALOGUE: The direct conversation among the characters in a literary work: what the characters say to each other.

DICTION: The author's choice of words, the type of vocabulary (formal, colloquial, slang, etc.) he or she uses.

EPISODE: A single, more or less self-contained incident within a story. Narratives consisting of a series of incidents loosely strung together in chronological sequence are said to have an *episodic* structure.

FANTASY: Literature that contains elements of the unreal or portrays a world in which the laws of everyday reality do not apply. Many works of fantasy take place in colorful "otherworlds," e.g., Oz, Narnia, Middle Earth, and similar imaginary lands. Others, such as ghost stories, concern the eruption of the supernatural into the ordinary world. Science fiction, which is often considered a subcategory of the fantastic, is constructed around fanciful premises—the existence of a machine that can travel through time, for example—that are made to seem scientifically plausible.

FIGURATIVE LANGUAGE: Nonliteral language that uses metaphor, simile, or some other figure of speech to produce a striking image, evoke an emotional response in the reader, or create a fresh description through an imaginative analogy. See **Metaphor.**

FORESHADOWING: An incident, a statement by the author, or a bit of dialogue that hints at something (often unfortunate) that will occur later on in the story. This technique is typically used to generate suspense or add an ominous note to what appears to be a benign or hopeful situation. For example, the unhappy ending of Ursula K. Le Guin's "Semley's Necklace" is foreshadowed when, in answer to Semley's simple question about the length of the journey that lies ahead of her, the Lord of the Claymen enigmatically responds, "A very far journey, Lady. Yet it will last only one long night."

GENRE: (French for "kind" or "type") Category of literature characterized by a style, content, form, etc. Traditional genres include tragedy, comedy, epic, and satire. The short story, essay, and novel are more "recent" genres, although these forms can be further subdivided into others—the science fiction novel or the autobiographical essay, for example—each of which is characterized by its own particular conventions.

HERO: Sometimes used interchangeably with *protagonist* to refer to the main character in a story or novel; technically, a protagonist distinguished by particular virtues (strength, nobility, etc.) and a capacity to undertake and accomplish significant action. Heroes, in this stricter sense of the term, are uncommon in works of modern fiction, whose protagonists are typically anti-heroic. See **Anti-hero.**

IMAGERY: The figurative language in a literary work, particularly the metaphors and similes that recur in a play, poem, or piece of fiction, creating a consistent pattern of images that reinforces the underlying theme. The term is also applied to the vivid descriptions authors use to evoke a sensation or conjure up the visual image of a person, place, or thing.

IRONY: There are various forms of irony, but at the heart of each of them is some sort of incongruity, a discrepancy between an appearance or expectation and the underlying reality or eventual result.

In *verbal irony,* we are meant to recognize the disparity between what is said and what is meant. As Hawthorne's story "My Kinsman, Major Molineux" progresses, for example, it becomes clear to the reader that the author's repeated references to Robin as a "shrewd youth" are intended ironically, since the young man has shown himself to be quite naïve, even obtuse.

Sarcasm is a blunt, often crude form of verbal irony.

A piece of literature displays *structural irony* when it is constructed around a particular feature that allows the author to sustain the irony throughout the work. In such cases, the irony is not communicated through an occasional remark; rather, it is "built in" to the very structure of the work. The irony of Jonathan Swift's famous essay "A Modest Proposal," for example, derives from the disparity between the narrator's rational, concerned, humane tone and the insanity of his suggestion that the Irish relieve their poverty by selling their infants and children to English landlords as food.

Dramatic irony arises when the audience possesses important knowledge or information that a character in the play does not have. For example, dramatic irony can be found throughout Sophocles' classic tragedy *Oedipus the King*, in which the hero calls down terrible curses on the head of an unknown criminal, only to discover in the end what the audience has known all along: that he himself is the guilty person.

METAPHOR: An imaginative analogy in which a person, object, emotion, feature of the setting, etc., is described by being compared to something else.

Similes, generally regarded as a subcategory of metaphor, make explicit comparisons introduced by "like" or "as."

In a metaphor proper, the comparison is implied rather than explicit. In Max Apple's "The Oranging of America," for example, the author employs a simile consistent with the subject of his story to describe the map that guides Howard Johnson and his associates, Otis and Millie, on their journeys across America: "The mountains on the map were light brown and seemed to melt toward the valleys like the crust of a fresh apple pie settling into cinnamon surroundings." Later in the story, Apple uses metaphor to describe how Millie feels about the "rest stops" to which she and Howard have devoted so much of their lives: "The HJ houses were her offspring. She had watched them blossom from the rough youngsters of the '40s with steam heat and even occasional kitchenettes into cool mature adults with king-sized beds, color TVs, and room service."

MOTIF: An element, such as an incident, situation, or image, that recurs in folklore, myth, and literature. The "night-sea journey," for example, is a common mythological motif adapted by John Barth for satirical purposes in his story of that title. The term is also applied to repeated images, ideas, phrases, or descriptions within a single work. The motif of blindness and vision, for example, is an important thematic thread in James Joyce's "Araby."

MOTIVATION: The inciting causes for a literary character's actions; the forces, both internal and external, that lie behind his or her behavior; the "reasons" characters do what they do. For a work of fiction or drama to be believable, the author must provide the characters with plausible motivations that permit the reader to understand why they act the way they do. The action in a literary work cannot seem arbitrary; rather, it must appear to proceed from the psychological make-up of the characters, as well as from the circumstances of their lives.

MYTH: One of the most elusive of critical terms. In its strict sense, a myth is an ancient or archaic story about supernatural beings that attempts to explain the origin, nature, and operation of the world or the reasons for a society's customs and beliefs. Largely as the result of the theories of C. G. Jung, a Swiss psychologist who identified what he called "archetypal images"—timeless and universal symbols appearing in dreams, myths, folk tales, and art works of every kind—contemporary "myth critics" often use the term to mean one of the recurrent characters, stories, or images whose persistent appeal suggests that they embody profound meaning for human beings. The hero's quest, the Other, the wise old man, and all the other categories into which this anthology is divided are examples of these mythic archetypes. Other critics apply the term somewhat more loosely to those recurrent themes and motifs that give symbolic expression to the deep, widely shared, often unexamined beliefs and assumptions of a particular society.

NARRATOR: The person or voice that "tells" the story. The work may be narrated by the author, speaking from "outside" the story and referring to its characters in the *third person:* i.e., as "he," "she," "they," and by their names. On the other hand, the work may be narrated by one of the characters within the story itself, in which case it is a *first-person narrative.* See **Point of view.**

PLOT: The arrangement of the events in a work of fiction or drama. Plot is not simply a string of narrative episodes; it is the *organization of the episodes* into a coherent pattern to establish a meaningful, causal relationship among them to achieve a particular effect.

PROTAGONIST: The main character in a work of fiction.

POINT OF VIEW: The vantage point or "angle of narration" from which a story or novel is told. The two main categories of point of view are third person and first person. See **Narrator.**

If an author uses the third person to show us what is going on in the minds of all the characters in a story, revealing not only their thoughts and feelings but even at times their unconscious impulses, wishes, and fantasies, the point of view is *omniscient.* In "The Horse-Dealer's Daughter," for example, D. H. Lawrence takes us into the mind of Mabel as she tends her mother's grave, then shifts freely to the consciousness of Jack as he walks across the fields.

The third-person point of view is *limited* when authors restrict themselves to the perceptions of the protagonist, as in Jean Stafford's "The Liberation" or Vladimir Nabokov's "Christmas."

The first-person point of view, in which the story is told by one of the characters (usually, though not always, the protagonist) is inevitably limited, since such narrators can only offer us their individual perceptions and interpretation of events, which are not always completely reliable or trustworthy.

SETTING: The physical location of the story; the background against which the action takes place. Setting is sometimes used to evoke a particular *mood*. The lengthy description of the school at the start of Poe's "William Wilson," for example, generates a powerfully disquieting atmosphere consistent with the effect of horror the author is attempting to produce. At other times, setting functions *thematically*. The description of the landscape in Lawrence's "The Horse-Dealer's Daughter" reinforces the theme of death and rebirth.

STYLE: An author's characteristic mode of expression. In fiction, the term refers to the way a writer uses prose. Style is the product of various elements, including diction, sentence structure, rhythm, and figurative language. Every truly distinctive style, from Ernest Hemingway's taut, laconic, pared-down prose to the highly charged, overwrought sentences of Poe, is expressive of the author's individual sensibility and artistic vision.

SYMBOL: A concrete object, character, or image that stands for something else or suggests a larger meaning. Unlike an allegorical sign, which stands for something we are intended to recognize from the start, a symbol often resonates with meanings that cannot be put into a few words. For example, unless we understand that the allegorical character Christian personifies the Christian soul, we miss the whole point of Bunyan's *Pilgrim's Progress*. By contrast, as C. G. Jung states, "the true symbol . . . should be understood as the expression of an intuitive idea that cannot be formulated in any other or better way."

THEME: A story's theme is not merely a lesson that can be extracted from it. Serious fiction is not *didactic*: it cannot be reduced to a simple message or moral. Nevertheless, most traditional works of short fiction contain a theme: a central idea, insight, or perception about life embodied in the narrative. The theme or dominating idea of Robert Penn Warren's "Blackberry Winter," for example, is the necessity of accepting certain harsh realities of life: transience, change, death.

TONE: The manner of expression in a literary work, conveying emotion and feeling. Just as, in everyday speech, we use certain tones of voice— angry, sarcastic, loving, sympathetic—to express our feelings either about the thing we are discussing or about the person we are addressing, so writers employ certain tones to convey their attitudes toward both their material and their audience. There are as many possible tones in writing as in speech: ironic, witty, solemn, playful, compassionate, condescending, and so on.

Biographies of the Authors

SHERWOOD ANDERSON (1876–1941) was born in Camden, Ohio, and grew up there and in other small towns around the state. Because his father uprooted the family so frequently, Anderson received a spotty education, which ended when he dropped out of school at fourteen. From that point on, he drifted from job to job—stableboy, housepainter, farmhand, factory worker. In 1898, he joined the army, serving briefly in Cuba during the Spanish-American War. Following his discharge, he worked for a time as an advertising copywriter in Chicago, then returned to Ohio, where he became a paint factory manager. In 1912, he made a dramatic break with the business world, walking out of his job in the middle of dictating a letter. Returning to Chicago, he became friends with some of the leading literary figures of the day and turned his energies to writing. His first book, the autobiographical novel *Windy McPherson's Son*, was published in 1916. A second novel, *Marching Men*, appeared the following year. His undisputed masterpiece, however, is *Winesburg, Ohio* (1919), one of the most influential works of twentieth-century American fiction. An interlocking sequence of twenty-three stories, each focusing on a different character, the book portrays the stultifying effects of Midwestern provincialism on the hearts, souls, and sensibilities of the inhabitants of the titular town (modeled on Clyde, Ohio, where Anderson lived for several years during his late adolescence). In 1927, after publishing several more novels and story collections, Anderson moved to a small town in Virginia, where he edited two newspaper, one Democratic, the other Republican. His novels and essay collections continued to appear throughout the 1930s. In 1941, during a goodwill tour of South America sponsored by the State Department, he accidentally swallowed part of a toothpick and died shortly afterwards of peritonitis. Among his other novels are *Poor White* (1920), *Many Marriages* (1923), and *Dark Laughter* (1925). His story collections include *The Triumph of the Egg* (1921), *Horses and Men* (1923), and *Death in the Woods and Other Stories* (1933).

MAX APPLE (1941–) was born in Grand Rapids, Michigan. In 1970, he received his Ph.D. in English from the University of Michigan and two years later joined the faculty of Rice University, where he teaches creative writing and literature. His first book, *The Oranging of America and Other Stories* (1976), won the Jesse Jones Award from the Texas Institute of Letters and was widely praised by critics for its charm, originality, and stylistic elegance. A gentle satirist with "a fine comic intelligence, a superb ear, and a brilliant way with slapstick" (in the words of critic John Leonard), Apple revels in the rich absurdities of American culture. Often, his fiction playfully combines his own invented characters with historical ones. His first novel, *Zip: A Novel of the Right and Left,* concerns a proverbial "nice Jewish boy" from Detroit who manages a Puerto Rican boxer named Jesus Goldstein and becomes embroiled in a scheme involving Jane Fonda, J. Edgar Hoover, and Howard Cosell. He has also published a second short story collection, *Free Agents* (1984).

ISAAC BABEL (1894–1941), the Russian short story writer, was born in Odessa, where he was raised in a middle-class Jewish household. Influenced by the French writer Guy de Maupassant, he began composing stories in his teens. In 1915, at the age of twenty-one, he moved to St. Petersburg, where he led a bohemnian existence and began publishing stories in a magazine edited by Maxim Gorky, who advised him to "see the world." Over the course of the next seven, turbulent years, he fought in World War I, served with the Cossack First Cavalry Army, and worked at a variety of jobs, including newspaper reporter and printer. In 1925, he published a powerful collection of war stories, *Red Cavalry,* based on his experiences with the Cossack regiment. Another famous collection, *Odessa Tales,* about the legendary Jewish gangster, Benya Krik, and other denizens of the Moldavanka ghetto, appeared in 1931. By then, Babel was widely recognized as a major artist, but by the end of the decade, he had fallen out of favor with Soviet authorities. In 1939, during Stalin's purges, he was arrested and shipped to a concentration camp in Sibera, where he died under mysterious circumstances.

TONI CADE BAMBARA (1939–) was born in New York City and grew up in Harlem and Bedford-Stuyvesant. She began writing stories as a child and, at age sixteen, entered Queens College of the City University of New York, majoring in theater arts and literature. After graduating in 1959, she studied overseas at the University of Florence and the Etienne Decroux School of Mime in Paris before returning to New York, where she received her M.A. from City College in 1964. Actively involved in the

Civil Rights movement of the 1960s, she has continued to work within the black community—lecturing, reading her work at rallies, organizing for community centers. Since 1965, she has also taught English and African-American literature at colleges and universities across the country. After editing two anthologies of African-American writings—*The Black Women* (1970) and *Tales and Short Stories for Black Folks* (1971)—she published a notable collection of her own short stories, *Gorilla, My Love* (1972). A second, equally acclaimed collection, *The Seabirds Are Still Alive*, appeared in 1977. Her first novel, *The Salt Eaters* (1980), won an American Book Award and was widely praised by critics, who saw it (in the words of reviewer John Edgar Wideman) as an eloquent expression of her "abiding concern"—"the necessity for black people to maintain their best traditions, to remain healthy and whole as they struggle for political power."

JOHN BARTH (1930–) has been described as one the masters of contemporary fiction. Born in Cambridge, Maryland, he briefly studied jazz arranging at the Julliard School of Music in New York before entering Johns Hopkins University as a journalism major. He received his B.A. from Hopkins in 1951 and his M.A. degree one year later. From 1953 to 1965 he taught at Pennsylvania State University, then joined the faculty of the State University of New York at Buffalo. In 1973, he left Buffalo for his alma mater, where he is presently Alumni Centennial Professor of English and Creative Writing. Barth's early books were highly praised by reviewers (his first novel, *The Floating Opera*, was a runner-up for the National Book Award in 1956), but it wasn't until the publication of his fourth novel— *Giles Goat-Boy* (1966), a prodigally inventive comic epic—that he attracted a sizable popular, as well as critical, following. Though his highly self-conscious fiction plays with complex philosophical and aesthetic issues, it is redeemed from mere academic cleverness by his exuberant (often bawdy) wit, linguistic virtuosity, and sheer storytelling prowess. Barth's other novels are *The End of the Road* (1958), *The Sot-Weed Factor* (1960), *Letters* (1979), *Sabbatical* (1982), and *Tidewater Tales* (1987). He has also published two collections of short stories, *Lost in the Funhouse* (1968) and *Chimera* (1972).

ANN BEATTIE (1947–) was born in Washington, D.C., and raised in the Maryland suburb of Chevy Chase. After graduating from American University in 1969, she entered graduate school at the University of Connecticut, earning her M.A. degree in 1970. Her first published story appeared in a small literary magazine in 1972. The following year, another of her stories won a prestigious award from *Atlantic Monthly* magazine. Soon afterwards, her fiction began appearing regularly in *The New Yorker*. In 1978, she received a Guggenheim fellowship and since then has been a visiting lecturer at the University of Virginia and Harvard. Written in a plain, almost affectless style (what she herself has described as "flat, simple sentences"), her stories characteristically deal with the emotional and spiritual malaise of her upper middle-class contemporaries—children of the 1960s who find themselves suffering from a profound sense of disillusion and loss after the heady freedoms of that idealistic decade. Her novels to date are *Chilly Scenes of Winter* (1976), *Falling in Place* (1980), *Love Always* (1985), and *Picturing Will* (1989). Her stories have been collected in *Distortions* (1976), *Secrets and Surprises* (1979), *The Burning House* (1984), and *Where You'll Find Me* (1986).

KAY BOYLE (1902–) was born in St. Paul, Minnesota, but lived as an expatriate in France for thirty years. Her European experiences are reflected in her stylistically elegant, semi-autobiographical novels, which include *Plagued by the Nightingale* (1931), *Year Before Last* (1932), and *My Next Bride* (1934). Since her return to America in 1941, she has taught writing at various colleges and universities. A prolific author, Boyle has also published numerous short stories, essays, and poems, many of which have been collected in three volumes: *Fifty Stories* (1980), *Collected Poems* (1962), and *Words that Must Somehow Be Said: Selected Essays of Kay Boyle, 1927–1984* (1985).

HORTENSE CALISHER (1911–) was born and raised in New York City, the setting for much of her fiction. She graduated from Barnard College in 1932, did social work for the Department of Public Welfare in New York, and since 1957 has taught English at various universities, including Columbia, Brandeis, Washington, Brown, and Stanford. Her first short stories appeared in *The New Yorker* magazine during the 1940s. Since then, she has published numerous books, alternating short-story collections with novels and novellas. She has also written a critically acclaimed memoir, *Herself: An Autobiographical Work* (1972). A masterful storyteller whose short fiction has been honored with four O. Henry prizes, Calisher is known for her elegant prose style, her vivid evocation of her Manhattan milieu, and her subtle exploration of character. Her novels include *False Entry* (1961), *The New Yorkers* (1969), *Standard Dreaming* (1972), *On Keeping Women* (1977), and *The Bobby-Soxer* (1986). Her stories have been gathered in *The Collected Stories of Hortense Calisher* (1975).

RAYMOND CARVER (1939–1989) was born in the Oregon logging town of Clatskanie, the son of a sawmill worker and a waitress. Inspired by his father, a gifted storyteller, he first tried his hand at creating fiction as a child. Carver was married at eighteen and soon found himself with two children to support, but, by working evenings, he was able to enroll in Chico State College in California, where he took a creative writing course with novelist John Gardener, who confirmed his determination to write. After graduating from Humboldt State College in 1963, Carver spent a year at the University of Iowa Writer's Workshop, then returned to California, where he worked at a variety of jobs—janitor, waiter, gas station attendant, salesman—while writing in his spare time. In 1967, his story, "Will You Please Be Quiet, Please?" was selected for the anthology, *Best American Short Stories*. Nine years later, it became the title story of his first collection, which was nominated for a National Book Award. Subsequent collections solidified his reputation and helped spark the contemporary short-story renaissance. Rooted in his own experiences, his spare, powerfully moving stories give voice to the inarticulate yearnings of America's working-class poor. In 1983, after a dozen years of teaching at various universities, he received a Mildred and Harold Strauss Living Award, which allowed him to devote himself full time to writing. His 1984 collection, *Cathedral*, was nominated for both a National Book Critics Circle Award and a Pulitzer Prize. Shortly after the publication of his 1988 collection, *Where I'm Calling From*, he was inducted into the American Academy of Arts and Letters. His other short-story collections include *Furious Seasons* (1977) and *What We Talk About When We Talk about Love* (1981).

WILLA CATHER (1873–1947) was born in Virginia but moved to the prairie community of Red Cloud, Nebraska, when she was nine. There, she grew up among immigrant farmers from Scandinavia, Germany, and Central Europe, who became the subject of her best-known writings. After graduating from the University of Nebraska in 1895, she moved to Pittsburgh, where she supported herself first as a journalist, then as a high-school teacher. In the meantime, she was writing and publishing stories and poems. After the appearance of her first novel, *Alexander's Bridge* (1912), she committed herself full time to writing. Over the course of the next five years, Cather produced three major novels inspired by her childhood experiences of frontier life—*O Pioneers!* (1913), *Song of the Lark* (1915), and *My Antonia.* Her later books include *A Lost Lady* (1923), *The Professor's House* (1925), and *Death Comes to the Archbishop* (1927).

KATE CHOPIN (1851–1904) was born in St. Louis, the daughter of an Irish immigrant father and Creole mother. At the age of nineteen, after her marriage to a Louisiana Creole businessman, she moved to New Orleans and, later, to a rural community near a cotton plantation owned by her husband's family. When her husband died in 1884, Chopin returned to St. Louis with her six children and began to write stories based on her experiences in the Deep South. Her tales of Creole and Cajun life, collected in *Bayou Folk* (1894) and *A Night in Arcadie* (1897), won her an admiring audience, but her literary career was effectively ended with the publication of her novel, *The Awakening* (1899), which provoked widespread outrage because of its frank depiction of its heroine's sexual self-realization. The novel was rediscovered in the 1950s and is now generally recognized as an American classic.

JULIO CORTÁZAR (1914–1984) has been described by critics as "one of the world's greatest writers." The son of an Argentine diplomat, he was born in Belgium but raised in Buenos Aires, where he briefly attended the university. After working for several years as a high school teacher and translator, he emigrated permanently to Paris in 1951. His bestselling novel, *Hopscotch* (1966), not only won him widespread acclaim but also helped to create an international audience for contemporary Latin American fiction. Cortázar was a brilliant literary experimentalist, whose best-known works include the novels *62: A Model Kit* (1968) and *A Manual for Manuel* (1973) and the short story collections *End of Game, and Other Stories* (1967) and *Blow-up and Other Stories* (1968).

STEPHEN CRANE (1871–1900) was born in Newark, New Jersey, the youngest of fourteen children of a Methodist minister. After briefly attending Lafayette College and Syracuse University, he moved to New York City in 1891, where he led a hand-to-mouth existence as a freelance journalist. His personal observations of life in the big city slums led to the creation of his first important work, *Maggie: A Girl of the Streets* (1893). This grittily realistic novel about the squalid existence of a Bowery girl who ends up as a streetwalker was strong stuff for its time and failed to find an audience. But Crane's next novel, *The Red Badge of Courage* (1895), brought fame to the young author (who was born six years after the Civil War ended and had never witnessed a battle). For the remainder of his short, adventurous life, Crane travelled widely, covering wars in Cuba and Greece for British and American newspapers. In 1896, his ship sank on the way to Cuba, an experience he transformed into his short story masterpiece, "The Open Boat." Suffering from tuberculosis, he moved to England in 1899 with his common-law wife (the former madam of a Florida brothel called the Hotel de Dream) and spent the last year of his life writing feverishly in an effort to pay off a mountain of debts. He died the following year in a German sanatorium. Crane's stories were collected in *The Open Boat and Other Tales of Adventure* (1898), *The Monster and Other Stories* (1899), and *Wounds in the Rain* (1900).

ISAK DINESEN (1885–1962) was the pseudonym of Baroness Karen Blixen. Born near Elsinore, Denmark, she grew up in her ancestral home, where she received her education from private tutors. A naturally gifted storyteller who thought of herself as a latterday Scheherezade, she published her first works of fiction during her twenties. In 1914, she married her cousin, Baron Bror Blixen. Together, they purchased a six-thousand-acre coffee plantation in British East Africa (now Kenya), where Dinesen lived for the next seventeen years. Seven years after their marriage, the two were divorced, and Dinesen became the sole manager of the plantation, which eventually failed. Following the death of her lover—a dashing English hunter and pilot named Denys Finch Hatton—Dinesen returned to Denmark in 1931. Back at her family estate, she began to write down the tales of wonder and enchantment she had originally invented to beguile Finch Hatton during his visits. When her first collection, *Gothic Tales*, was brought out by the Book-of-the-Month Club in 1934, it became a literary sensation. A second volume of stories, *Winter's Tales* (1942), met with similar critical and commercial success. Between the two story collections, Dinesen published an acclaimed memoir of her African experiences, the 1937 bestseller *Out of Africa* (later made into a popular motion picture). Nominated several times for the Nobel Prize, she went on to produce two more books of short stories, *Last Tales* (1957) and *Anecdotes of Destiny* (1958). Her other books include the essay collection, *Shadows on the Grass* (1961) and the bestselling 1946 thriller, *Angelic Avengers* (written under the pseudonym Pierre Andrezel).

RALPH ELLISON (1914–) has published only a single novel, *Invisible Man* (1952), but such is the power of that masterpiece that it has guaranteed his reputation as one of the great American writers of the post-World War II period. Born in Oklahoma City, Oklahoma, he attended the Tuskegee Institute in Alabama for three years, intending to become a composer. In 1936, he moved to New York, where he worked at odd jobs, played and composed music, experimented with photography and sculpture, and formed friendships with the authors Richard Wright and Langston Hughes, who encouraged him to write. Several years later, his stories and essays began appearing in small, literary periodicals. Beginning in 1942 he edited *The Negro Quarterly* for one year before joining the Merchant Marines. Following his discharge in 1945, he began work on *Invisible Man.* In 1965, Ellison's novel was named in a nationwide poll of literary critics as "the most distinguished work of fiction" published in the United States after World War II. Ellison, who has been at work on a second novel since the 1950s, has also published a notable collection of essays, *Shadow and Act* (1964).

F. SCOTT FITZGERALD (1896–1940) was born in St. Paul, Minnesota. A descendant (and namesake) of the author of "The Star-Spangled Banner," he was educated at an eastern preparatory school and Princeton University, though he dropped out of college to join the U.S. Infantry in 1917. Stationed at Fort Leavenworth, Kansas, he began work on a novel which went through several drafts before it was published in 1920 as *This Side of Paradise*. The book made him an overnight sensation and a spokesman for the young generation of the 1920s—the high-living era Fitzgerald himself named "The Jazz Age." For the rest of the decade, Fitzgerald and his wife, Zelda, pursued the kind of glamorous, extravagant life he had become for famous for chronicling in his fiction. His second novel, *The*

Beautiful and the Damned (1922), received mixed reviews, but it was followed three years later by his masterpiece, *The Great Gatsby* (1925), one of the classic works of modern American literature. During the 1930s, however, Fitzgerald's fortunes declined as precipitously as the nation's economy. His wife suffered a series of mental breakdowns and spent the last seventeen years of her life in sanatoriums. Fitzgerald himself—his literary reputation (and powers) on the wane—succumbed to alcoholism and struggled to stay afloat by turning out Hollywood screenplays. He died of a heart attack at the age of forty-four, leaving his final novel, *The Last Tycoon,* unfinished (it was published posthumously in 1941). Fitzgerald's stories were collected in *Flappers and Philosophers* (1921), *Tales of the Jazz Age* (1922), *All the Sad Young Men* (1926), and *Taps at Reveille* (1935).

GUSTAVE FLAUBERT (1821–1880) was born in Rouen, France, the son of a surgeon. After receiving his baccalaureate from the local *lycée,* he went to Paris to study law but—after suffering a nervous collapse—returned home in 1843 to live with his widowed mother. Three years later, he settled permanently in Croisset, just outside of Rouen. Following a trip to the Levant in 1849–1851, he spent the next five years in the painstaking composition of his first novel, *Madame Bovary* (1857), a masterpiece of literary realism and a milestone in the development of modern fiction. Flaubert's objective treatment of his heroine's adulteries scandalized official sensibilities. He was brought to trial on charges of immorality but acquitted. The rest of his life was outwardly uneventful. Apart from occasional trips to Paris and one to Tunisia in 1860, he remained in Croisset, devoting himself wholly to his art. His other major works are *Salammbô* (1862), *The Sentimental Education* (1869), *Bouvard and Pecuchet* (1881), and *Three Tales* (1877).

MARY E. WILKINS FREEMAN (1852–1930) grew up in Randolph, Massachusetts, a small, economically depressed New England town. As a child, her frail health kept her from leading a normally active life, and she spent much of her time reading. When she was fifteen, her father moved the family to Brattleboro, Vermont, another small town in decline. After graduating from Brattleboro High School in 1870, she attended Mount Holyoke Female Seminary for one year before returning home. In 1881, she sold her first work—a ballad called "The Beggar King"—to a children's magazine for ten dollars. Soon, she switched to the more lucrative area of adult fiction, winning a literary award of fifty dollars from a Boston weekly in 1882 for her piece, "A Shadow Story." By 1883, Freeman was alone, her parents and only sister having died within a few years of each other. Returning to Randolph—where she lived until her marriage at the age of forty-nine—she continued to write and publish adult fiction, which brought her popular success and critical praise both here and abroad. A leading member of the "local color" school of American realism, Freeman often focuses on the inner lives of poor, strong-minded New England women struggling courageously with the harsh conditions of their lives. In 1926, her achievement was officially recognized when she was awarded the William Dean Howells Gold Medal for Fiction by the American Academy of Letters. Later that year, she became (along with Edith Wharton) the first woman to be inducted into the National Institute of Arts and Letters. Among the twelve novels she published are *Jane Field* (1893), *Pembroke* (1894), and *The Portion of Labor* (1901). Her stories—more than two hundred in all—were collected in various volumes, including *A New England Nun and Other Stories* (1891), *Young Lucretia* (1892), and *The Green Door* (1910).

ERNEST GAINES (1933–) was born and raised on a plantation in rural Louisiana. At fifteen, he moved to California, where he attended Vallejo Junior College and San Francisco State. After receiving his B.A. degree in 1957, he won a Wallace Stegner Creative Writing Fellowship at Stanford and did a year of graduate study there. Since 1971, he has been a writer in residence at various universities. Gaines' novels and stories, based on his boyhood memories, are set in an imaginary Louisiana region. Written in a style heavily influenced by Southern storytelling traditions, his fiction (in the words of novelist Alice Walker) "revels in the rich heritage of Southern Black people and their customs," depicting characters who confront the often painful conditions of their lives with dignity and courage. His novels include *Catherine Carmier* (1964), *Of Love and Dust* (1967), *The Autobiography of Miss Jane Pittman* (1971), and *In My Father's House* (1978). He has also published the short-story collection, *Bloodline* (1968).

GABRIEL GARCÍA MÁRQUEZ (1928–) was born in the small Colombian town of Aracata. The oldest of twelve children, he was raised by his maternal grandparents and has traced his love of fantasy to the wondertales he heard from his grandmother. He received his bachelor's degree in 1946 and published his first story the following year. After studying law for three years, he left the university to become a journalist and worked as a foreign correspondent in Rome, Paris, Barcelona, Caracas, and New York. His first novel, *Leaf Storm,* appeared in 1955, followed by *The Evil Hour* (1961), *No One Writes to the Colonel* (1961), and the short story collection, *Big Mama's Funeral* (1962). In 1965, he retreated to his study for a year and a half to work on his best-known book, *One Hundred Years of Solitude* (1967), a comic masterpiece which chronicles the history of a South American family in the mythic town of Macondo. Garcia Marquez's blend of fantasy and social history—a method known as "magical realism"—made the book an enormous international success. Critics praised the book as the greatest work in Spanish since *Don Quixote* and "the first piece of literature since the Book of Genesis that should be required reading for the entire human race." In 1982, Garcia Marquez won the Nobel Prize for literature. His other novels include *The Autumn of the Patriarch* (1976), *Chronicles of a Death Foretold* (1982), and *Love in the Time of Cholera* (1988). His short stories have been gathered in *The Collected Stories of Garbriel Garcia Marquez* (1984).

ELLEN GILCHRIST (1935–) was born and raised in Vicksburg, Mississippi, and received her B. A. from Millsaps College. In 1981, when was forty-six, her first book of short stories, *In the Land of Dreamy Dreams,* was brought out with little fanfare by a small university press. Such was the quality of the collection—fourteen stories set mostly in New Orleans and focusing primarily on the lives of adolescents—that, even without the benefit of advertising or promotion, it quickly attracted a large and enthusiastic audience. Before long, reviewers were hailing Gilchrist as a major new literary talent. Eventually, the book was picked up by a major publishing house, which reissued it in 1985. By then, Gilchrist had published her first novel, *Annunciation* (1983), as well as another, highly acclaimed story collection, *Victory Over Japan* (1984), which won the American Book Award for fiction. A third collection, *Drunk with Love,* appeared in 1986. A resident of Jackson, Mississippi, Gilchrist has also appeared regularly as a storyteller and commentator on National Public Radio.

NATHANIEL HAWTHORNE (1804–1864) was the descendant of a prominent Puritan family, one of whose members had been a judge at the infamous Salem witch trials. After four years at Bowdoin College, he returned to his family home in Salem and entered a prolonged period of relative seclusion during which he read extensively and began writing fiction. *Twice-Told Tales* (1837) was a collection of his earliest stories—dark allegories pervaded by what his friend Herman Melville called a "Puritanic gloom." Another collection, *Mosses from an Old Manse*, appeared in 1846, by which time Hawthorne was married and living in Concord, Massachusetts. His masterpiece, *The Scarlet Letter* (1850), transformed him from "the obscurest man of letters in America" (in his own estimation) into a popular and critically acclaimed author. After publishing two more novels—*The House of the Seven Gables* (1851) and *The Blithedale Romance* (1852)—he was appointed U.S. Consul in Liverpool by the newly elected president, Franklin Pierce, a friend and former college classmate. For the next seven years he lived in Europe, where he wrote his last major novel, *The Marble Faun* (1860). He returned to Concord in 1860 and died four years later during a vacation tour of New Hampshire in the company of his old friend, Franklin Pierce.

HERMAN HESSE (1877–1962) was born in Calw, Germany, the son of parents who had been missionaries in the Orient. After briefly attending the Protestant Theological Seminary at Maulbronn, he went to work in a bookstore and began writing stories, sketches, and poems. In 1904, he left the book trade to devote himself to writing and published his first novel, *Peter Camenzind,* which brought him wide recognition. Repelled by German militarism during World War I, he moved to Switzerland, becoming a citizen in 1923. In the meantime, Hesse's lifelong interest in Eastern mysticism impelled him to undertake a journey to India, an experience reflected in his well-known novel, *Siddhartha* (1922), a book based on the early life of Buddha. In novels like *Demian* (1919) and *Steppenwolf* (1927), Hesse portrays characters questing for spiritual and aesthetic fulfillment within the constraints of bourgeois civilization. He was awarded the Nobel Prize for literature in 1942. Following his death, he became a cult figure to members of the 1960s counterculture, who saw their own fascination with mystical experience reflected in his novels.

WASHINGTON IRVING (1783–1859) was born in New York City, the youngest of eleven children of a prosperous merchant. After being educated at private academies, he joined a law office as a clerk, but soon lost interest in his legal apprenticeship. His first literary success came at nineteen, when, under the pseudonym "Jonathan Oldstyle," he began contributing satirical essays to a New York newspaper edited by his brother. After a two-year tour of Europe, he returned to New York, where he was admitted to the bar in 1806. His commitment to the practice of law, however, remained secondary to his literary interests. In 1807, he joined with his brother and a circle of acquaintances in publishing a satirical magazine, *Salmagundi*. Irving's first book, the burlesque *History of New York*, was an unprecedented success for an American author, bringing him substantial earnings and wide acclaim. For the next ten years, however, he retreated from creative activity. In 1815, he travelled to England to supervise the Liverpool office of the family business. Not until the firm went bankrupt in 1818 did he return to professional writing. Two years later, he published his most enduring work, *The Sketch Book*. This charming collection of essays and tales, including "Rip Van Winkle" and "The Legend of Sleepy Hollow," made him an international celebrity. Irving remained in Europe for seventeen years, serving in several diplomatic posts while continuing to write fiction, travel books, histories, and biographies. Shortly after returning to America in 1832, he undertook an adventurous trip to the Western frontier, then resettled in New York, where he purchased his famous country retreat, Sunnyside. Returning to Europe in 1842, he served as minister to Spain, then spent a year in London on a diplomatic mission. He passed his last years in Sunnyside, universally acknowledged as the dean of American letters.

JAMES JOYCE (1882–1941), by critical consensus the greatest of the literary modernists, was born in Dublin and received a rigorously Catholic education at Clongowes Wood College, Belvedere College, and University College, Dublin. In 1902, he fled the stifling conventionality of Dublin for the larger world of the Continent, though his native city continued to preoccupy his imagination, forming the setting for all his major fiction. Supporting himself by teaching English in Berlitz language schools, he started writing the short stories which were collected in his first important book, *Dubliners* (1914). Naturalistic in style, the book portrayed characters trapped in stultifying lives who experience moments of revelatory insight that Joyce called "epiphanies." His semi-autobiographical novel, *A Portrait of the Artist as a Young Man*, was published serially in 1914 under the sponsorship of Ezra Pound and in book form two years later. When portions of Joyce's next novel, *Ulysses*, began appearing in a New York literary magazine in 1918, they set off a storm of controversy. Highly candid for its time in its treatment of sexual matters, the book (published in its entirety in 1922) was banned as obscene until 1933, when Joyce's artistry was vindicated in a landmark censorship ruling. Since then, the book has achieved universal recognition as one of the masterpieces of English literature, a work whose revolutionary experiments with structure and language had a incalculable impact on the modern novel. Most important of Joyce's innovations was his "stream of consciousness" technique, which evoked the innermost experience of his characters' minds. Joyce carried his bold experimentation to even great heights with *Finnegan's Wake* (1939), the novel he regarded as the culminating achievement of his career.

D. H. LAWRENCE (1885–1930) was born in the English coal mining town of Eastwood, Nottinghamshire, the son of a coal miner and a former schoolteacher. After graduating from Nottingham High School, he worked for a time as a factory clerk and later as a teacher, first in local Eastwood schools, then in South London. His first novel, *The White Peacock*, appeared in 1911, though it was his second, autobiographical novel, *Sons and Lovers* (1913), that established his literary reputation. In 1912, Lawrence eloped with the German wife of an acquaintance. After sojourns in Germany and Italy, they returned to England but were subjected to constant harrassment during World War I. Nevertheless, Lawrence produced two of his finest novels during this period—*The Rainbow* (1915) and *Women in Love* (1920). In 1919, he left England and, for the rest of his life, roamed widely, living for brief periods in Sicily, Ceylon, Australia, Mexico, and the American Southwest. Frail since childhood, he was impelled to wander partly by his need for warmer climates but largely by his quest for "primitive" cultures more closely in touch with the dark, vital energies of myth and instinct than the modern, mechanized civilization he detested. Celebrating intuition over intellect, nature over technology, "blood knowledge" over rationalism, he was a prophet of erotic liberation. The explicit sexual descriptions in his 1928 novel, *Lady Chatterley's Lover*, caused the suppression of that book in England and America for nearly thirty years. In 1925, Lawrence fell seriously ill with tuberculosis. He died five years later in a sanitorium in Southern France. His other books include *Aaron's Rod* (1922), *Kangaroo* (1923), *The Plumed Serpent* (1926), and *The Virgin and the Gypsy* (1930). His stories have been collected in *The Complete Stories* (1961).

URSULA K. LE GUIN (1929–) was born in Berkeley, California, the daughter of writer Theodora Kroeber and the renowned anthropologist, Alfred Louis Kroeber. After receiving her B.A. from Radcliffe College in

1951, she did graduate work at Columbia University, completing her master's thesis in medieval romance literature in 1952. During a year in Paris as a Fulbright scholar, she married historian Charles Le Guin. Though she had been writing fiction since childhood, it wasn't until the 1960s that she began publishing stories, including "Semley's Necklace," which became the opening chapter of her first novel, *Rocannon's World* (1966). Since then, her work has earned her numerous honors, including the Nebula and Hugo Awards (for her 1969 novel, *The Left Hand of Darkness*, which some readers regard her masterpiece) and the National Book Award (for her 1972 fantasy novel, *The Farthest Shore*, the third book in her "Earthsea" series). An elegant stylist who employs the imaginative devices of futuristic literature to explore complex intellectual and psychological themes, Le Guin has come to be recognized (in the words of critic Leslie Fiedler) as "one of the best writers of science fiction in the United States, which is to say one of the best writers of fiction." Among her novels are: *City of Illusions* (1967), *The Dispossessed* (1974), *The Beginning Place* (1980), and *Always Coming Home* (1985). Her story collections include *The Wind's Twelve Quarters* (1975) and *Orsinian Tales* (1976). She has also published several notable volumes of essays, including *The Language of Night* (1976).

DORIS LESSING (1919–) was born in Kermanshah, Persia (now Iran), where her father, an Englishman, worked as a bank manager. In 1924, he moved the family to an isolated farm in South Rhodesia. Her life in Africa, Lessing has written, taught her "the knowledge that man is a small creature, among other creatures, in a large landscape." After five years at the Roman Catholic Convent School in Salisbury, she entered the Girls' High School, but dropped out after only one year, at the age of fourteen. She began writing fiction at eighteen but destroyed the first six novels she composed. Actively involved in Communist politics during her twenties, she eventually became disillusioned and broke with the party. In 1949, after two failed marriages, she left Africa with her young son and moved permanently to London. Her first novel, *The Grass Is Singing* (1950), won high praise from critics, but it was *The Golden Notebook* (1962)—a brilliant study of a writer's struggles to realize herself as an artist and a woman— that established her reputation as one of the major writers of the postwar period. Admired for their "intense social concerns," Lessing's writings have grappled with many of the central issues of our time, from racism to feminism to the moral and psychological fragmentation of modern life. Her many novels and stories are also wide-ranging in form. In recent years, she has experimented with such nonrealistic modes as science fiction and fairy tale. Her six-volume series, *Canopus in Argus: Archives* (1979–1983), is a dense, futuristic allegory set in an alternate universe, while her 1988 novella, *The Fifth Child*, reworks the folklore motif of the changeling into a horrific fable about societal decay. Among her other novels are her tetralogy, *Children of Violence* (1952–1969), *The Golden Notebook* (1962), *Briefing for a Descent into Hell* (1971), and *The Good Terrorist* (1986). Her short story collections include *The Habit of Loving (1960)*, *A Man and Two Women* (1963), *African Stories* (1964), and *The Sun Between Their Feet* (1973).

BERNARD MALAMUD (1914–1986), one of the major American writers of the post-World War II period, was born in Brooklyn, New York, where his immigrant parents owned a small grocery store. He earned his B.A. degree from the City College of New York in 1936 and his M.A. from Columbia University in 1942. After teaching evening classes in high school English for a number of years, he joined the faculty of Oregon State University in 1949. He left Oregon in 1961 for Bennington College in Vermont, where he taught writing until his death, twenty-five years later. Maljamud's first novel, *The Natural* appeared in 1952. Blending realism and myth, baseball lore and Arthurian legend, the book is a powerful fable about the failure of heroism in modernday America. His second novel, *The Assistant* (1957)—which many critics regard as his masterpiece—deals with two of Malamud's dominant themes: Jewishness as a metaphor of the human condition and the redemptive potential of suffering and sacrifice. A master short-story writer whose work reflects the influence both of Jewish storytelling traditions and the moral allegories of American Romantics like Hawthorne and Melville, Malamud won the National Book Award for his first collection, *The Magic Barrel* (1958). He published two more volumes of short stories *Idiot's First* (1963) and *Rembrandt's Hat* (1973). Among his other novels are the Pulitzer Prize-winning *The Fixer* (1966), *The Tenants* (1971), and *Dubin's Lives* (1979).

CARSON MCCULLERS (1917–1967) was born and raised in small-town Georgia, the setting for her best-known fiction. A gifted pianist, she briefly attended the Julliard School of Music in New York City before switching to Columbia University, where she studied creative writing at night while working at various jobs during the day. Her first novel, *The Heart Is a Lonely Hunter*, appeared in 1940, when she was only twenty-three. An immediate popular and critical success, it established her reputation as a literary master in the "Southern gothic" mode. Rife with sensationalistic incidents and populated by freaks, cripples, and grotesques, her novels and stories function as haunting fables about human isolation, portraying desperately lonely characters hungering for compassion and love. Though her second novel, *Reflections in a Golden Eye* (1941) was deemed a disappointment, she followed it with two of her most acclaimed works, "The Ballad of the Sad Cafe" (1943) and *The Member of the Wedding* (1946). In 1950, her stage adaptation of the latter became a hit show on Broadway. The last decade of her life was marked by personal misfortune and failing health. Her final, poorly received novel, *Clock Without Hands*, appeared in 1961, six years before her death at age fifty. Her stories are available in *The Ballad of the Sad Cafe and Other Stories* (1967) and *Collected Stories* (1973).

PATRICK MCGRATH (1950–) was born in London and grew up near Broadmoor Hospital—a lunatic asylum housing some of England's most dangerously deranged criminals—where for many years his father was Medical Superintendent. McGrath's interest in horror and the grotesque was stimulated by the stories he heard from his father, who, at the family dinner table, often related the case histories of his patients—the man who decapitated his mother and baked her head in the oven, the woman who ducked under her bedclothes one night and removed her eyes with a teaspoon. After receiving a B.A. Honors degree from the University of London in 1971, McGrath moved to Canada, where he worked in a maximum security mental hospital. He then spent several years on a remote island in the North Pacific before moving to New York City, his current place of residence, in 1981. Besides his book reviews and essays, which have appeared in various publications, McGrath is the author of three books of Gothic fiction, all widely praised by critics for their elegant prose and imaginative power—*Blood and Water and Other Tales* (1988), *The Grotesque* (1989), and *The Spider* (1990).

JAMES ALAN MCPHERSON (1943–) was born in Savannah, Georgia. His writing career began during his student years at Harvard Law School when one of his short stories won first prize in a major literary contest sponsored by *Atlantic Monthly* magazine. After receiving his law degree, he entered the writing program at the University of Iowa, where he earned an M.F.A. in 1969. His first collection of short stories, *Hue and Cry* (1969), was widely admired by critics, who praised his ability "to look

beneath skin color and cliches of attitude into the hearts of his characters."
His second collection, *Elbow Room* (1977), won the Pulitzer Prize for fiction. In 1981, McPherson was the recipient of one of the prestigious "genius awards" bestowed annually by the MacArthur Foundation.

STEVEN MILLHAUSER (1943–) was born in New York City and grew up in Connecticut. He received his B.A. degree from Columbia University in 1965 and did three years of graduate study at Brown University, beginning in 1968. Millhauser's first novel, *Edwin Mulhouse*—a fictional biography of an eleven-year-old novelist by his twelve-year-old best friend— received critical raves and won France's prestigious Prix de Médicis Etranger in 1975. His second novel, *Portrait of a Romantic* (1977), was praised as a remarkable evocation of male adolescence—"a brilliant, perverse eulogy for American boyhood." Millhauser's stories, which have appeared in various publications—including *The New Yorker, Grand Street, Antaeus,* and *Esquire*—have been collected in two volumes, *In the Penny Arcade* (1985) and *The Barnum Museum* (1990). In 1987, he was given the Award in Literature from the American Academy and Institute of Arts and Letters. Millhauser is currently an associate professor of English at Skidmore College.

ALBERTO MORAVIA (1907–1990) was the pseudonym of Alberto Pincherle. Born in Rome, the son of a prosperous architect and an Austro-Hungarian countess, Moravia contracted a crippling disease at the age of eight which kept him bedridden and solitary for much of the next ten years. Sent to a sanitarium in the Italian Alps when he was sixteen, he began to work on a novel, *Gli Indifferenti (The Time of Indifference),* an attack on the Roman bourgeoisie under Fascism whose publication in 1929 earned him both widespread critical acclaim and the condemnation of government censors. Branded as an anti-Fascist subversive by the Nazis, he fled to the mountains outside Rome in 1943 and remained there until the city was liberated by the Allied forces nine months later. For the next two decades, he produced a steady flow of novels, stories, plays, essays, and magazine articles. A masterful storyteller, Moravia was celebrated for his liberating treatment of sexual themes. Though critics tend to disparage the work of his later years, he is regarded as the preeminent—as well as the most popular—Italian writer of the century. Among his best-known works are: *The*

Woman of Rome (1949), *Two Adolescents* (1950), *The Conformist* (1951), *Conjugal Love* (1951), *Roman Tales* (1957), *Two Women* (1958), and *The Voyeur* (1987).

BHARATI MUKHERJEE (1940–) was born in Calcutta, India. After receiving her B.A. and M.A. degrees from the universities of Calcutta and Boroda respectively, she came to the United States in 1961 to study at the University of Iowa Writers Workshop. For ten years, beginning in 1968, she and her husband, the novelist Clark Blaise, lived in Canada, where she wrote her first two novels, *The Tiger's Daughter* (1972) and *Wife* (1975). Since moving back to the United States in 1980, she has taught at various colleges and universities; been the recipient of grants from the National Endowment for the Humanities and the Guggenheim Foundation; and published a number of critically acclaimed books, including *Days and Nights in Calcutta* (1977)—a journal, written in collaboration with her husband, of a year they spent living in Calcutta—and her short-story collection, *The Middleman*, which won the National Book Critics Circle award for fiction. Rooted in her own experiences, her fiction deals with the conflicts and aspirations of recent Third World immigrants as they struggle to come to redefine themselves as Americans.

VLADIMIR NABOKOV (1899–1977), one of the titans of twentieth-century literature, was born in St. Petersburg, Russia, to noble parents. A child prodigy, he was encouraged to cultivate his boyhood interests in linguistics, mathematical games, chess, sports, and lepidopterology. By the time he reached adolescence, he was proficient in three languages, had become an expert chess and tennis player, and was a recognized authority on butterflies. At fifteen, he also began writing poetry. Forced to leave Russia with his family after the Bolshevik Revolution. Nabokov moved to London, where he received a B.A. with honors from Trinity College, Cambridge, in 1922. Relocating to Berlin, he supported himself by giving boxing and tennis lessons, teaching languages, and constructing crossword puzzles for a Russian newspaper. By night, he worked on his writing, completing nine novels, nine plays, and dozens of short stories during the next fifteen years. Fleeing Nazi Germany in 1938, he moved first to Paris, then to America (becoming a citizen in 1945). After lecturing at Stanford University for a year, he joined the faculty of Wellesley College, where he taught Russian language and literature from 1941 until 1948. During those same years, he was a research fellow in entomology at Harvard, discovering several new species of butterflies. He also continued to produce novels and stories which were admired for their lyrical style, verbal ingenuity, and structural virtuosity. In 1949, he accepted a professorship at Cornell University where he gained a reputation as a brilliant, original lecturer. Nine years later, he published his controversial novel, *Lolita*, which brought him widespread popularity and large enough royalties to make it possible for him to retire from teaching and devote himself completely to his two great passions, writing and butterfly collecting. Returning to Europe, he took up residence in the Montreux-Palace Hotel in Montreux, Switzerland, where he lived until his death. Among his novels are *Laughter in the Dark* (1938), *Pnin* (1957), *Pale Fire* (1982), and *Ada* (1969). His story collections include *Nabokov's Dozen* (1958), *Nabokov's Quartet* (1966), and *Details of a Sunset* (1976).

R. K. NARAYAN (1906–), generally regarded as India's foremost writer in English, was born in Madras into a Brahmin family. When his father, a school headmaster, was relocated to the South Indian town of Mysore, Narayan remained behind with his grandmother, who introduced him to Sanskrit prayers, Vedic poetry, and traditional folk tales and myths. He attended several schools in Madras before joining his father in Mysore, where he studied at Maharaja's High School and Maharaja's College, graduating from the latter in 1930. After working briefly as a teacher, he devoted himself entirely to writing. His first book, *Swami and Friends* (1935), was published at the recommendation of English novelist Graham Greene, who also helped to arrange publication of Narayan's next two works, *The Bachelor of Arts* (1937) and *The Dark Room* (1938). Subsequent novels—particularly *Mr. Sampath* (1949), *The Financial Expert* (1952), and *The Guide* (1958)—brought him international fame. Set in the imaginary village of Malgudi (modeled on his boyhood hometown, Mysore), his novels and stories offer a highly realistic picture of his native land. At the same time, they transcend narrow cultural limits, portraying with serene humor and compassion the universal, abiding realities of human existence. Narayan's other novels include *The English Teacher* (1945), *Waiting for the Mahatma* (1955), *The Man-Eater of Malgudi* (1961), and *The Vendor of Sweets* (1967). Among his story collections are *Malgudi Days* (1941), *Lawley Road* (1956), *Gods, Demons and Others* (1965), and *A Horse and Two Goats and Other Stories* (1970).

FLANNERY O'CONNOR (1925–1964) was born in Savannah, Georgia, and lived there until the age of twelve, when her family moved to the town of Milledgeville. As a student at the Women's College of Georgia, she edited the campus newspaper and literary magazine and won a fellowship to the Writer's Workshop at Iowa University, earning her M.F.A. in 1947. Three years later, while living in New York City, she learned that she was dying of disseminated lupus, the incurable hereditary disease that had killed her father. She returned to the family farm in Milledgeville, where she spent the remainder of her life with her mother, reading, painting, raising peacocks, and writing. Her crippling disease and devout Catholicism are the two most obvious influences on her writing. Full of grotesque, gothic elements, her stories feature tormented characters searching for spiritual grace in a world devoid of faith. During her lifetime, she published two novels—*Wise Blood* (1952) and *The Violent Bear It Away* (1960)— and a collection of short stories, *A Good Man Is Hard to Find* (1955). Her second volume of short stories, *Everything That Rises Must Converge* (1965), was published posthumously.

TILLIE OLSEN (1913–) was born in Omaha, Nebraska, the daughter of working-class Russian immigrants. After leaving school at the end of the eleventh grade, she worked at a variety of jobs in order to help her family through the Depression. At nineteen, she began a novel about the struggles of a poor Midwestern family, the first chapter of which appeared in *The Partisan Review* in 1934. Within a few years, however, Olsen was forced to abandon her novel. Raising four children while working at a variety of clerical jobs, she published nothing during the next two decades. In 1953, when her youngest daughter started school, Olsen enrolled in a fiction class at San Francisco State College. Two years later, she won a Stanford University creative writing fellowship. Four of the stories she produced during this period were collected in her first book, *Tell Me a Riddle*, which established her reputation when they were published in 1961. That year, the title story won the prestigious O. Henry Award for best American short story. In the early seventies, Olsen completed her long-deferred novel, *Yonnondio: From the Thirties*, published to much acclaim in 1974. Though Olsen has produced a comparatively small body of work, it has garnered her many honors, including Guggenheim and Radcliffe Fellowships, a grant from the National Endowment for the Arts, and four honorary doctorates. To contemporary women writers, Olsen is regarded, as novelist Margaret Atwood has observed, with something like reverance, "presumably because women writers, even more than their male counterparts, recognize what a heroic feat it is to have held down a job, raised four children, and still somehow managed to become and to remain a writer."

EDGAR ALLAN POE (1809–1849) was born in Boston, Massachusetts. His parents, travelling actors, died by the time he was three, and Poe was taken into the home of a prosperous merchant, John Allan of Richmond, Virginia, who raised Poe as a son, though without legally adopting him. In 1815, John Allan moved his family to England, where Poe lived for the next five years, attending the school that later served as the model for the opening scenes of "William Wilson." After his return to the United States, Poe entered the University of Virginia, but his drinking and gambling led to a bitter rift with his foster father, who refused to let him return to school at the end of his first year. Running off to Boston, Poe enlisted in the army, where he served honorably for two years. Briefly reconciled with his foster father, Poe entered West Point as a cadet, but engineered his own expulsion after only eight months. Disinherited by Allan, Poe moved to Baltimore to live with his aunt, Maria Clemm, whose thirteen-year-old daughter, Virginia, he married in 1836. The remaining years of Poe's short, tormented life were a mix of personal tragedy, unremitting poverty, and brilliant literary output. A superb editor, Poe worked at a succession of literary magazines, but his personal instability, compounded by his alcoholism, made it difficult for him to hold down a job. After his young wife's death in 1847, Poe struggled to eke out a living through his writing, all the while concocting various publishing schemes, none of which succeeded. In 1849, he became engaged to a wealthy Richmond widow, but during a trip to Philadelphia, he stopped off in Baltimore, where—succumbing to his self-destructive impulses—he apparently indulged in a particularly heavy bout of drinking and was discovered senseless in the street. He died a few days later. One of our country's classic writers, Poe is most famous for his powerfully unsettling horror tales, though he is also renowned as the creator of modern detective fiction. As a poet, he exerted enormous influence on the nineteenth-century French symbolists. He was also an important literary critic, who helped define the short-story form.

PHILIP ROTH (1933–) was born and raised in Newark, New Jersey. He spent one year at the Newark branch of Rutgers University before transferring to Bucknell, where he received his B.A. in 1954. He began publishing fiction during his years of graduate study at the University of Chicago. His short-story collection, *Goodbye, Columbus* (1959), was a spectacular debut for the young writer, earning Roth critical raves and impressive honors, including the National Book Award for fiction. The book—particularly the title novella, a satirical look at the lives of the Jewish upper middle class—also incurred the wrath of many members of the Jewish-American community, establishing a pattern of controversy that has marked Roth's long, prolific career. Though his first two novels met with relatively lukewarm reviews, Roth's fourth book, *Portnoy's Complaint* (1969)—the riotously uncensored confessions of a Jewish analysand—was a critical and commercial sensation, making Roth into a bona-fide celebrity. Roth followed up with a series of wildly inventive novels, including *Our Gang* (1971), a satire of the Nixon administration; *The Breast* (1972), a Kafkaesque parable about a man who metamorphoses into a gigantic breast; and *The Great American Novel* (1973) a "comic extravaganza" about baseball. Since then, Roth has written a series of elegantly crafted, autobiographical novels exploring the complex relationship between a writer's life and fiction. These include: *The Ghost Writer* (1979), *Zuckerman Unbound* (1981), *The Anatomy Lesson* (1983), *The Counterlife* (1987), and *Deception* (1990).

LESLIE MARMON SILKO (1948–) was born in Albuquerque, New Mexico, and grew up on the Laguna Pueblo Reservation, steeped in the storytelling traditions of her tribe. Her earliest memories, she has written, are of her "grandmother telling me stories . . . about incidents from long ago." After receiving her B.A. from the University of New Mexico, she briefly studied law before deciding to pursue a career as a college teacher and author. She has taught English at various schools, including Navajo Community College, the University of Arizona, and her alma mater. Her first novel, *Ceremony* (1977), won her wide acclaim. Her next book, *Storyteller* (1981)—a collection of folk tales, legends, poems, and photographs celebrating her tribal heritage—confirmed her reputation as a major new writer, whose work draws on ancient oral tradition to explore contemporary Native American experience. In 1981, Silko was honored with a MacArthur Foundation "genius award."

ISAAC BASHEVIS SINGER (1904–1991) was born in Radzymin, Poland. The son and grandson of rabbis, Singer, too, studied at a rabbinical seminary but—following the lead of his older brother, the novelist I. J.

Singer—chose instead to become a professional writer. He worked as a journalist in Warsaw for several years, but in 1935, with Nazism on the rise, he emigrated to the United States, where he began to write for the Yiddish-language newspaper, *The Jewish Daily Forward.* Steeped in the supernatural and capturing the spare, vigorous style of traditional folk tales, Singer's marvelous stories of life in the *shtetls* (Jewish villages in Eastern Europe) were, for many years, accessible only to readers of Yiddish. The first English translation of his work appeared in 1950, and since then, he has become universally recognized as a master of modern fiction. The significance of his achievement was confirmed in 1978, when he was awarded the Nobel Prize for literature. Collections of Singer's short stories include *Gimpel the Fool and Other Stories* (1957), *The Spinoza of Market Street and Other Stories* (1961), *A Friend of Kafka and Other Stories* (1970), *A Crown of Feathers and Other Stories* (1973), and *Old Love* (1979). Among his novels are *The Family Moskat* (1950), *Satan in Goray* (1955), *The Magician of Lublin* (1960), *The Manor* (1967), and *Shosha* (1978).

JEAN STAFFORD (1915–1979) was born in Colvina, California, the daughter of novelist John Richard (who wrote Westerns under the pseudonym Jack Wonder). She received her B.A. and M.A. degrees from the University of Colorado, studied for a year at Heidelberg University, and during the 1940s was married to the Pulitzer Prize-winning poet, Robert Lowell. Though she was the author of several well-received novels, she was more highly regarded for her exquisitely crafted stories, known for their sensitive rendering of female psychology. In 1966, she published what some critics consider her masterpiece, *A Mother in History,* a nonfiction portrait of the mother of Lee Harvey Oswald. Her novels include *Boston Adventure* (1944), *The Mountain Lion* (1947), and *The Catharine Wheel* (1952). Her stories can be found in *The Collected Stories of Jean Stafford* (1969).

AMY·TAN (1952–) was born in Oakland, California, the daughter of a Beijing-educated engineer and a mother who left China in 1949—just before the Communist Revolution—and settled in the San Francisco Bay area.

When her father died in 1949, Tan went to live in Switzerland, where she attended high school. Returning to America, she enrolled in a small college in Oregon. After receiving her master's degree in linguistics, she earned her living as a freelance business writer, working for clients like IBM and AT&T. She also began writing autobiographical short stories, one of which appeared in a small literary magazine, where it caught the eye of a literary agent who contacted Tan and urged her to write an outline for a book. After completing the outline, Tan left on a trip to China. She returned to find that the outline had been purchased by a major New York publishing house for a substantial advance. Four months later, Tan completed the first draft of her novel, *The Joy Luck Club* (1989), a series of interlocking vignettes about the conflicts between two generations of Asian women—a foursome of mothers who fled China in the late 1940s and their four, thoroughly Americanized daughters. The book became an instant bestseller and was nominated for a National Book Award. Her second novel, *The Kitchen God's Wife*, was published in 1991.

JOHN UPDIKE (1932–), one of America's most distinguished men of letters, was born and raised in Shillington, a small farming town in southeastern Pennsylvania. By the time he was eight, he had already begun writing stories, though his earliest ambition was to be a cartoonist. After graduating from Harvard—where he wrote for and later edited the *Harvard Lampoon*—he studied art for a year at the Ruskin School of Drawing and Fine Art in Oxford, England, then returned to the United States and went to work for *The New Yorker*, beginning a close association with that magazine which has continued throughout the years. His first novel, *The Poorhouse Fair*, appeared in 1959. Since then, he has published more than thirty books. A writer of enormous technical facility, he is best known as a sensitive chronicler of the powerful hungers—emotional, sexual, spiritual, and material—that define middle- and working-class life in late twentieth-century America. His fiction has achieved both popular and critical success, appearing regularly on bestseller lists and garnering major awards, including the National Book Award and the Pulitzer Prize. He has also published five volumes of poetry and several impressive collections of criticism. Among his novels are: *The Centaur* (1963), *Couples* (1968), *Bech: A Book* (1970), *A Month of Sundays* (1975), *The Coup* (1978), *The Witches of Eastwick* (1984), *Roger's Version* (1986), and his four-volume series about his small-town alter ego, Harry "Rabbit" Angstrom, *Rabbit, Run* (1960), *Rabbit Redux* (1971), *Rabbit Is Rich* (1981) and *Rabbit at Rest* (1990). His story collections include *The Same Door* (1959), *Pigeon Feath-*

ers and Other Stories (1962), *The Music School* (1966), *Museums and Women and Other Stories* (1972), *Too Far to Go* (1979), and *Problems and Other Stories* (1979).

ROBERT PENN WARREN (1905–1989) was one of America's most distinguished men of letters. As an essayist and theoretician, he helped give birth to the so-called "New Criticism," which dominated academic literary study in America for more than twenty years, beginning in the late 1930s. His influential textbooks, *Understanding Poetry* (1938) and *Understanding Fiction* (1943), changed the way an entire generation of students and scholars interpreted serious literature. Warren's bestselling novel, *All the King's Men*, won the 1947 Pulitzer Prize and was later made into an Academy Award-winning motion picture. He won two more Pulitzer Prizes for his poetry and, in 1988, was named the nation's first Poet Laureate. His other books include: *Night Rider* (1939), *Circus in the Attic* (1948), *Brother to Dragons* (1953), *Who Speaks for the Negro?* (1965), and *Incarnations* (1968).

EUDORA WELTY (1909–) has lived most of her life in Jackson, Mississippi, the place of her birth. She attended the Mississippi State College for Women for one year before transferring to the University of Wisconsin. After graduating with a B.A. in 1929, she moved to New York City and enrolled in the Columbia University School of business, where she briefly studied advertising. Returning to Jackson two years later, she did advertising work for local newspapers and radio stations. As a publicity agent for the state office of the Work Progress Administration, she also travelled throughout Mississippi, taking photographs of the rural south (some of which were later exhibited at New York City's Museum of Modern Art). Her first collection of stories, *A Curtain of Green*, appeared in 1941. Since then, she has published a steady flow of popular and critically acclaimed novels and stories dealing with life in Mississippi. Though she is often labeled a "regionalist," her fiction transcends that rather narrow definition, dealing with such universal themes as the transience of life, the indomitable strength of the human spirit, and the redemptive power of love. Her work has won her many honors, including the Pulitzer Prize for her 1972 novel, *The Optimist's Daughter*. Her other novels include *Delta Wedding* (1946), *The Ponder Heart* (1954), and *Losing Battles* (1970). Her stories, published in numerous volumes, have been brought together in *The Collected Stories of Eudora Welty* (1980). Welty is also the author of several collections of critical essays and a best-selling autobiography, *One Writer's Beginnings* (1984).

RICHARD WRIGHT (1908–1960) was born near Natchez, Mississippi, the son of an impoverished sharecropper who deserted his family when Wright was five. After his mother suffered a series of paralytic strokes, Wright was shuffled among relatives and placed for a time in an orphanage. His erratic formal schooling ended when he was fifteen, but he continued to educate himself through his voracious reading, resorting to various strategems to borrow books from the "white only" public libraries of the segregationist South. At the age of nineteen, he migrated to Chicago, where he worked at menial jobs and became involved in radical politics. Five years later, he moved to New York City and served as Harlem correspondent for the Communist newspaper, *The Daily Worker*. His first book, *Uncle Tom's Children* (1938), a collection of four novellas, won a major literary prize. This success was followed two years later by the publication of his masterpiece, *Native Son*, a harrowing and prophetic novel about the brutalizing effects of racism. In 1945, after breaking with the Communist party, he published a powerful autobiography, *Black Boy*. Two years later, he expatriated to Paris where he met Jean-Paul Sarte and became engrossed in existentialist philosophy. His later books include *Black Power* (1954), *The Color Curtain* (1956), *White Man, Listen!* (1957), and *The Long Dream* (1958).

MARGUERITE YOURCENAR (1903–1987), writer and classical scholar, was born in Brussels to a French father, Michel de Crayencour, and a French mother, who died shortly after giving birth. As a child, she travelled widely with her father, who supervised her private education. By the age of eight, she knew Latin and Greek and was reading the work of the seventeenth-century French dramatist, Racine. Her first two books of poetry were published during her adolescence. After her father's death in 1929, Yourcenar—who by then had assumed her permanent pseudonym (an anagram of her family name)—continued to lead a nomadic existence, living for periods in France, Italy, Greece, and other European countries. Her first novel, *Alexis*, was published in Paris in 1929. Ten years later, with the outbreak of the war, she emigrated to the United States, becoming a naturalized citizen in 1947. From 1940 to 1950, she taught comparative literature at Sarah Lawrence College, while continuing to write novels, short stories, poetry and plays. Yourcenar's masterwork, *The Memoirs of Hadrian*—a fictitious but utterly convincing autobiography of the ancient Roman emperor written as a series of letters of his nephew, Marcus Aurelius—appeared in English in 1954 and was universally acclaimed as a classic of twentieth-century fiction, "the finest historical novel of the century." Another historical novel, *The Abyss* (1976), dealing with the life of a fictitious Renaissance doctor, earned similarly high praise. Yourcenar was the recipient of numerous awards. She received her highest honor, however, in 1981, when she became the first woman elected to the Academie Française. Her other books include *Coup de Grace* (1957), *Fires* (1981), *A Coin in Nine Hands* (1982), *The Dark Brain of Piranesi* (1984), *Alexis* (1984), and *Oriental Tales* (1985).

Acknowledgments

Chapter One: The Call

"Blackberry Winter" by Robert Penn Warren
From *The Circus in the Attic and Other Stories*, copyright 1947 by Robert Penn Warren. Reprinted by permission of Harcourt Brace Jovanovich, Inc.

"Paul's Case" by Willa Cather
Reprinted from *Youth and the Bright Medusa*, by Willa Cather, courtesy of Alfred A. Knopf, Inc.

"Astronomer's Wife" by Kay Boyle
From *The White Horses of Vienna and Other Stories*, by Kay Boyle. Copyright 1936, © 1964 by Kay Boyle. Reprinted by permission of A. Watkins, Inc.

"The Island at Noon" by Julio Cortázar
From *All Fires the Fire and Other Stories*, by Julio Cortázar, translated by Suzanne Jill Levine. Copyright © 1973 by Random House, Inc. Reprinted by permission of Pantheon Books, a division of Random House, Inc.

"The Liberation" by Jean Stafford
Reprinted by permission of Farrar, Straus & Giroux, Inc. "The Liberation," from *The Selected Stories of Jean Stafford*. Copyright © 1953, 1956, 1955, 1969 by Jean Stafford. "The Liberation" originally appeared in *The New Yorker*.

"Adventure" by Sherwood Anderson
From *Winesburg, Ohio*. Copyright 1919 by B. W. Huebsch. Copyright renewed 1947 by Eleanor Copenhaven Anderson. Reprinted by permission of Viking Penguin, a division of Penguin Books USA Inc.

Chapter Two: The Other

"The Lost Explorer" by Patrick McGrath
From *Blood and Water and Other Tales*. Copyright 1988 by Patrick McGrath. Reprinted by permission of Poseidon Press, a division of Simon & Schuster, Inc.

"Double Face" by Amy Tan
From *The Joy Luck Club*. Copyright 1989 by Amy Tan. Reprinted by permission of The Putnam Publishing Group.

"Getzel the Monkey" by Isaac Bashevis Singer
Reprinted by permission of Farrar, Straus & Giroux, Inc. "Getzel the Monkey" from *The Seance* by Isaac Bashevis Singer. Copyright © 1964, 1968 by Isaac Bashevis Singer.

"The Story of a Dead Man" by James Alan McPherson
From *Elbow Room* by James Alan McPherson. © 1977 by James Alan McPherson.

By permission of Little, Brown and Company in association with the Atlantic Monthly Press.

"Yellow Woman" by Leslie Marmon Silko
"Yellow Woman" by Leslie Marmon Silko from *The Man to Send Rain Clouds*, edited by Kenneth Rosen. Copyright © 1974 by Kenneth Rosen. Reprinted by permission of Viking Penguin, Inc.

"A Good Man Is Hard to Find" by Flannery O'Connor
Copyright 1953 by Flannery O'Connor. Reprinted from her volume *A Good Man Is Hard to Find and Other Stories* by permission of Harcourt Brace Jovanovich, Inc.

"He and I" by Alberto Moravia
Reprinted by permission of Farrar, Straux & Giroux, Inc. "He and I" from *More Roman Tales* by Alberto Moravia. Copyright © 1963 by Martin Secker & Warburg, Ltd.

Chapter Three: The Journey

"Babylon Revisited" by F. Scott Fitzgerald
F. Scott Fitzgerald, "Babylon Revisited," (copyright 1931 by The Curtis Publishing Comlpany; copyright renewed) in *Taps at Reveille*. Copyright 1935 by Charles Scribner's Sons; copyright renewed. (New York: Charles Scribner's Sons, 1975) Reprinted with the permission of Charles Scribner's Sons.

"A Worn Path" by Eudora Welty
Copyright 1941, 1969 by Eudora Welty. Reprinted from her volume *A Curtain of Green and Other Stories* by permission of Harcourt Brace Jovanovich, Inc.

"Idiots First" by Bernard Malamud
"Idiots First" from *Idiots First* by Bernard Malamud. Copyright © 1961, 1963 by Bernard Malamud.

"Big Boy Leaves Home" by Richard Wright
"Big Boy Leaves Home" from *Uncle Tom's Children* by Richard Wright. Copyright 1936 by Richard Wright; renewed © 1964 by Ellen Wright. Reprinted by permission of Harper & Row, Publishers, Inc.

"Behind the Blue Curtain" by Steven Millhauser
From *The Barnum Museum*. Copyright 1990 by Steven Millhauser. Reprinted by permission of Poseidon Press, a division of Simon & Schuster, Inc.

"Through the Tunnel" by Doris Lessing
"Through the Tunnel" from *The Habit of Loving* by Doris Lessing. Copyright © 1955, 1957 by Doris Lessing. Originally appeared in The New Yorker. Reprinted by permission of Harper & Row, Publishers, Inc.

"Night-Sea Journey" by John Barth
"Night-Sea Journey" from *Lost in the Funhouse* by John Barth. Copyright © 1966 by John Barth. Reprinted by permission of Doubleday & Company, Inc.

Chapter Four: Helpers and Guides

"The Poet" by Hermann Hesse
Reprinted by permission of Farrar, Straus and Giroux, Inc. "The Poet" from *Strange*

News from Another Star by Hermann Hesse, translated by Denver Lindley. Translation copyright © 1972 by Farrar, Straus and Giroux, Inc.

"The Lesson" by Toni Cade Bambara
From *Gorilla, My Love*, by Toni Cade Bambara. Copyright © 1972 by Toni Cade Bambara. Reprinted by permission of Random House, Inc.

"Cathedral" by Raymond Carver
From *Cathedral*. Copyright 1981, 1982, 193 by Raymond Carver. Reprinted by permission of Alfred A. Knopf, Inc.

"Awakening" by Isaac Babel
Reprinted by permission of S. G. Phillips, Inc. from *The Collected Stories of Isaac Babel*. Copyright © 1955 by S. G. Phillips, Inc.

"The Sky Is Gray" by Ernest J. Gaines
© 1963, 64, 68 by Ernest J. Gaines. Reprinted by permission of The Dial Press.

"Under the Banyan Tree" by R. K. Narayan
From *Under the Banyan Tree and Other Stories*. Copyright 1985 by R. K. Narayan. Reprinted by permission of Viking Penguin, a division of Penguin Books USA Inc.

"The Conversion of the Jews" by Philip Roth
From *Goodbye, Columbus* by Philip Roth. Copyright © 1959 by Philip Roth. Reprinted by permission of Houghton Mifflin Company.

"Blacamán the Good, Vendor of Miracles" by Gabriel García Márquez
"Blacamán the Good, Vendor of Miracles" from *Leaf Storm and Other Stories* by Gabriel Garcia Márquez, translated by Gregory Rabassa. English translation copyright © 1972 by Gabriel Garcia Márquez. Reprinted by permission of Harper & Row, Publishers, Inc.

Chapter Five: The Treasure

"Araby" by James Joyce
"Araby" from *Dubliners* by James Joyce. Copyright © 1967 by the Estate of James Joyce. Reprinted by permission of Viking Penguin Inc.

"Semley's Necklace" by Ursula K. Le Guin
Copyright © 1964, 1975 by Ursula K. Le Guin; reprinted by permission of the author and the author's agent, Virginia Kidd.

"Janus" by Ann Beattie
From *Where You'll Find Me*. Copyright 1985 by Ann Beattie. Reprinted by permission of International Creative Management, Inc.

"A Tree · A Rock · A Cloud" by Carson McCullers
From *Collected Short Stories and the Novel, The Ballad of the Sad Cafe* by Carson McCullers. Copyright 1936, 1941, 1942, 1950, 1951, 1955 by Carson McCullers. Reprinted by permission of Houghton Mifflin Company.

"The Blue Jar" by Isak Dinesen
From *Winter's Tales*. Copyright 1942 by Random House, Inc. and renewed 1970 by John Philip Thomas Ingerslev % The Rungstedlund Foundation. Reprinted by permission of Random House Inc.

"The Middle Drawer" by Hortense Calisher
From *The Collected Stories by Hortense Calisher* by Hortense Calisher, copyright

© 1948, 1949, 1950, 1951,k 1952, 1954, 1955, 1956, 1957, 1960, 1962, 1967, 1975 by Hortense Calisher. Reprinted by permission of Arbor House Publishing Company.

"Flying Home" by Ralph Ellison
Reprinted by permission of Wiliam Morris Agency, Inc. on behalf of author. Copyright © 1944 Ralph Ellison

"The Oranging of America" by Max Apple
"The Oranging of America" from *The Oranging of America and Other Stories* by Max Apple. Copyright © 1974, 1975, 1976 by Max Apple. Reprinted by permission of Viking Penguin Inc.

Chapter Six: Transformation

"The Horse-Dealer's Daughter" by D. H. Lawrence
"The Horse-Dealer's Daughter" from *The Complete Short Stories of D. H. Lawrence, Vol. II.* Copyright 1922 by Thomas Seltzer, Inc. copyright renewed 1950 by Frieda Lawrence. Reprinted by permission of Viking Penguin, Inc.

"Twin Beds in Rome" by John Updike
Copyright © 1964 by John Updike. Reprinted from *The Music School: Short Stories,* by John Updike, by permission of Alfred A. Knopf, Inc. First appeared in *The New Yorker.*

"The Management of Grief" by Bharati Mukherjee
From *The Middleman and Other Stories.* Copyright 1988 by Bharati Mukherjee. Reprinted by permission of Grove Weidenfeld, a division of Grove Press, Inc.

"O Yes" by Tillie Olsen
"O Yes" excerpted from the book *Tell Me a Riddle* by Tillie Olsen. Copyright © 1956 by Tillie Olsen. Reprinted by permission of Delacorte Press/Seymour Lawrence.

"The Legend of St. Julian the Hospitaller" by Gustave Flaubert
From *Three Tales,* by Gustave Flaubert, translated by Arthur McDowell. Published 1924 by Alfred A. Knopf, Inc.

"Traveler" by Ellen Gilchrist
From *In the Land of Dreamy Dreams.* Copyright 1981 by Ellen Gilchrist. Reprinted by permission of Don Congdon Associates, Inc.

"Christmas" by Vladimir Nabokov
From *Details of a Sunset and Other Stories,* by Valdimir Nabokov. Reprinted by permission of McGraw-Hill Book Company.

"How Wang-Fo Was Saved" by Marguerite Yourcenar
From *Oriental Tales.* Translation copyright 1983, 1985 by Alberto Manuguel. Reprinted by permission of Farrar, Straus and Giroux, Inc.